CW01433214

LEGENDARY

BOOK TWO

ALLIE SHANTE

A full list of content warnings can be found on the author's website.
Please message the author if any content warnings
need to be added; your mental health matters.
www.authorallieshante.com

Copyright © 2024 Allie Shante

All rights reserved. No part of this book may be reproduced or used in
any manner without the prior written permission of the copyright owner,
except for the use of brief quotations in a book review.

To request permissions, contact the publisher
at allieshanteauthor@gmail.com

First paperback edition March 2024.

Editing: @thefictionfix
Cover design: Halle with AJ Wolf Graphics
Formatting: Halle with AJ Wolf Graphics

Published by: Allie McMillin

*"Love is a meeting of two souls, fully accepting the
dark and the light within each other."*

To anyone who has felt under pressure and like they aren't enough.
You are.
Broken and in pieces, you are enough.

To anyone lost in the dark, find your light…
it's probably been searching for you too.

Living Legend is a series that should be read in order.
Legendary is the 2nd book, so if you have not read Living Legend,
please go back and read that first. You will be missing major pieces of
information and will get spoiled tremendously if you
do not turn back and read the first book.

Enjoy!

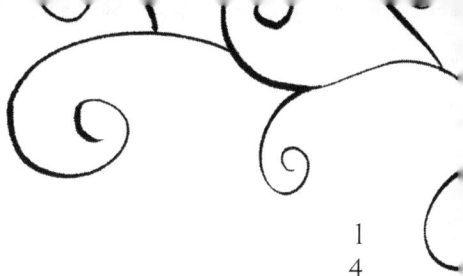

PROLOGUE   1
CHAPTER ONE   4
CHAPTER TWO   17
CHAPTER THREE   27
CHAPTER FOUR   40
CHAPTER FIVE   52
CHAPTER SIX   67
CHAPTER SEVEN   81
CHAPTER EIGHT   95
CHAPTER NINE   108
CHAPTER TEN   125
CHAPTER ELEVEN   146
CHAPTER TWELVE   158
CHAPTER THIRTEEN   172
CHAPTER FOURTEEN   182
CHAPTER FIFTEEN   197
CHAPTER SIXTEEN   210
CHAPTER SEVENTEEN   230
CHAPTER EIGHTEEN   244
CHAPTER NINETEEN   254
CHAPTER TWENTY   265
CHAPTER TWENTY-ONE   278
CHAPTER TWENTY-TWO   291
CHAPTER TWENTY-THREE   302
CHAPTER TWENTY-FOUR   312
CHAPTERTWENTY-FIVE   327
CHAPTER TWENTY-SIX   336
CHAPTER TWENTY-SEVEN   345
CHAPTER TWENTY-EIGHT   358
CHAPTER TWENTY-NINE   369
CHAPTER THIRTY   376
CHAPTER THIRTY-ONE   378
CHAPTER THIRTY-TWO   388
CHAPTER THRITY-THREE   400
CHAPTER THIRTY-FOUR   416
CHAPTER THIRTY-FIVE   419
EPILOGUE   432
ACKNOWLEDGEMENT   437
ABOUT THE AUTHOR   439

PROLOGUE
LILITH

My beautiful girl. My beautiful creation.

So naïve.

Pity, really, to have so much power but be so ungrateful.

She would have torn their world apart and it would have been a glorious sight to behold, but of course things don't always work out the way we hope. I had no time to linger on such thoughts when there was so much to prepare for.

I heard the click of heels on the brick floor, peeking over my shoulder to see my little Enchanter. The Enchanters I've surrounded myself with, the ones forced to be here with me, they are nothing like Isabel. I can taste her rage, her malice, from miles away and it's positively delicious. If only my Soul Seether could be so easily molded, so easily convinced.

"The Oculus wards are stronger than ever. I can't…" She stopped, raising her eyes to the ceiling before continuing. "I can't break through it. I can't tell you their next move."

I gave her a small smile before turning towards her, my red silk dress swishing along the ground, kicking up dust. "It's alright, sweetheart. I'm not angry."

Isabel went from looking at the ceiling to looking at the ground, as she curled a lock of her golden blonde hair around her ear. "I know you aren't, but I want to help. I could try to gain some more power. I could take Natalia, bring her here as bait or something."

I tsked and placed my hand on her cheek; her green eyes looked at me with so much devotion, it was refreshing. "You are a good one, but there is no need for that."

She huffed, her eyes an electric color resembling a rainbow. "Then what are we even doing? I'm not just going to wait here for them to make a move. We did that last time and they made it out alive. I don't doubt you, but you can't just let them waltz in here like nothing happened. Dani has gone rogue, Elise completely disobeyed you and those stupid angels—" Her fingertips flickered with that same rainbow coloring.

"Hmm, yes. Last time, I put too much faith in my Soul Seether. I don't make the same mistakes twice, my dear." I snapped my fingers, and two demon guards came barreling into the room. "If I know her well enough, she'll be ready to rage and fight, right in here, where she belongs."

The guards stood a few feet away from me, awaiting my instructions. I threaded my fingers together in front of me, giving the demons my full attention. "Gather the ones in the holding cells."

"Holding cells? I thought you were done experimenting with those demons. After the ambush, that's what you said." Isabel scrunched up her face in confusion.

I let out a light laugh. "Oh, no, I won't need to *experiment* with them anymore. They are going to do exactly what I know they can do, when I tell them to, as will you when the time comes."

Isabel raised a delicate eyebrow at me as the guards hurried off to bring me my toys. "What are you asking them to do? Kill her?"

I cocked my head to the side, watching her. I'd waited for my Soul Seether for years and when she was in my grasp, I made sure she had all the tools to succeed. Letting her get taken to Heaven's Gate was hard, but it had to be done. Letting an overzealous angel into my plan had been my first mistake; I practically shook my head remembering how he had come to me battered and so very, very angry. I should have known there would be altered plans and outliers, like that boy of hers. Such a handsome boy.

Ah men. They always seemed to get in the way.

No bother, though—they made perfect distractions.

Made us weak.

My lips curved up into a mischievous smile when I answered her. "No. They're going to bring me what's *mine*."

I

NICK

I'd never been the type to pine for something. I've wanted things, of course, but this was different. I hadn't felt the need for something every second I was awake or never constantly thought about that same thing when I went to sleep, but here I was pining. Pining over a girl who clearly wanted nothing to do with me at the moment. I'd tried to distract myself, engaging Daya in conversations about a time when portaling was a regular way of transportation among angels until it was taken away after the war. As much as it pained her, she seemed to adore talking about life before it all, so I leaned into that. My thoughts, like always, never stayed in one place for long and they always landed on the same thing—or rather, the same person.

She had barely looked at me when she'd left my house behind Natalia and Elise. All I had wanted to do was take her hand and tell her I was sorry, that I wanted to understand her more. Knowing Dani, she probably would have just shaken her head and said, 'try again, pretty boy' and walked away. Yes, I probably would have watched her walk away, because I'm starting to feel a bit obsessed. I was chalking it up to the fact that I went from seeing her quite frequently to not seeing her at all for about three months now.

We hadn't heard anything from the girls since they had left months ago, but they *had* left us with a lot to think about. Not only that, but it didn't seem there was any movement on Lilith's side of things either.

I used my back to close my bedroom door and let out a sigh as I relaxed against it. I could hear Reese and my dad walking around in the living room and chatting, and I tried to close my eyes and block them out. I unbuttoned the first few buttons of my dress shirt and slid a hand around the back of my neck.

Ariel had taken care of getting The Skies back in order, with Reese and I trying our best to help, even if being around Ariel was the most mind-numbing experience of my life.

The angels who came back to The Skies were wary of pretty much anything and everything now, although rightfully so since one of the angels they'd trusted betrayed us. Markus had this whole plan and none of us saw it, which made me so fucking angry, I had two distinct fist sized holes in my wall to prove it. Markus had played us so well and he had...he— he killed Jonah.

Jonah.

It took three months for us to get things back in order and for Ariel to achieve his perfect vision for Jonah's ceremony. We'd just returned, it was the longest period Reese had ever kept his mouth closed, so I was thankful for that. Natalia had walked up next to me in a long flowing black dress with gold buttons along the shoulders and waist. She had given me a somber expression, mouthing an "I'm sorry," before she faced forward, clearly holding in her tears.

The man had touched more lives than I had ever known in a way I would never truly understand. I didn't even comprehend how he fit into my life, especially after learning that he fit in a totally different way than I once thought. I pushed away from my door and ripped my black dress jacket off my arms, throwing it onto my perfectly-made bed. I only wore that jacket for special occasions, and Jonah's ceremony was the epitome of a special occasion. I couldn't even remember the last time I wore it, so finding it in my closet when the time came was a surprise.

I had never seen my father so quiet or so tense before. He didn't shed any tears, but I had noticed that his hand would flex around Daya's every so often and she would squeeze back. There were so many angels there, old and young alike. A few would look in my direction and nod or their faces would contort into this look of wariness since, obviously, they were aware

I had been there when he died. He died in my arms and the memory would never leave me.

Angelic death ceremonies were meaningful and beautiful. There was a special area of The Skies for executives who had died so they would remain part of Heaven's Gate. The other executives stood around where Jonah had been laid to rest, expelling pieces of their light towards the ground offering their own magic to him. Where his magic had gone was still a mystery, but that was the least of my worries over these last few months. That was an executive issue, and if I was being honest, executives weren't really high on my list of angels I wanted to speak to.

I moved my jacket further up my bed so I could sit in its previously occupied space. I placed my elbows on my knees, dragging my hands through my hair. I wasn't a crier—I'd never felt the need to cry. Nothing had ever felt like tears were totally necessary. I probably was frustrated enough to cry, but all I wanted to do was talk to the one person who didn't want to talk to me. *Fuck.*

Knuckles rapped on my door.

"Yes?" I answered, knowing my tone was less than friendly.

"You alright?" Reese responded, the concern in his voice apparent. I might have wanted to talk to Dani, but I had a best friend who would always be there when I needed him.

"For the most part."

I heard the knob turn and the door open. Reese poked his head into the room, looking me up and down. His blonde brows turned down as he walked in, closing the door behind him before he crossed his arms over his chest. "You know I hate this touchy feely shit but come on Nick."

I leaned back on my bed. "Come on, what?"

Reese scoffed, rolling up the sleeves of his maroon button down. "The guy died right in front of you, and you're telling me you're fine."

"I never said I was *fine*, alright. I don't know what you want me to say."

"You don't have to talk to me, but just know your dad is a little worried about you," Reese said, placing his hands in his pants pockets. "I want to say something, but I don't know how to say it."

I rubbed my forehead with my fingertips. "He's always worried. That's nothing new." My tone was clipped. "Just say it. I've never known you to be hesitant about anything." I was trying not to spiral more than usual, so thinking about Jonah and how intertwined he was with my life was too much, not to mention that my own father was gatekeeping information like his life depended on it. His death was something I could mourn, but I couldn't let it take over my every thought.

"I might be a little more knowledgeable about the missing souls in the human world than I let on."

"I'm sorry, what?"

He groaned. "It wasn't just me either. A few of us were noticing missing souls, missing bodies, but you know how Ariel can get. We wanted everything to be smooth sailing, so we didn't say anything. None of it really matters anymore, but you've been beating yourself up about not being there for her, and none of us were there for the others."

I ran a hand down my thigh, settling at my knee as I tapped my index finger against it. "I wasn't aware you had such a thick conscience " He shrugged, as if he was waiting for me to forgive his secrecy. "It's good to know I wasn't going completely crazy, and yes, it doesn't do much now, but thanks for telling me."

"And that is called communication, Nicholas. Something you should learn from."

I rolled my eyes at him. "Yet again, I'm fine. I need to learn nothing."

Reese held up his hands, clearly backing off. "Of course, now you claim you're fine. I'm just saying get your thoughts and shit in check before we go through with this awful plan."

I pointed my finger at him. "See another reason why I can't focus on Jonah or whatever right now: the Purgatory crusade."

My best friend rolled his eyes. "The experience from Hell brought to us by the devil incarnate, a literal queen and your hybrid girlfriend."

I let out a small laugh, one that felt foreign given the circumstances. "You agreed to it, remember?"

"Yes, but that doesn't mean I'm happy about it. I won't promise to play nice on this little adventure of ours, either" he stated, rocking back on his heels. He scratched his chin, where he had grown a small amount of stubble. "Did you happen to tell Ariel about this Purgatory trip?"

I raised my brown eyes to his hazel ones. "Um, no."

He scrunched his lips together in confusion. "Do...we need to?"

I opened my mouth to answer, but then closed it—I didn't know. It would have been something to ask the highest executive about, but we didn't have one of those right now. Jonah suddenly dying wasn't something we were prepared for, especially since he didn't leave any offspring to take his place. Ariel couldn't just decide to take his place. It didn't work like that.

"I guess...not?" I said slowly before I blew out a breath. "It's better to ask for forgiveness than permission."

One side of Reese's lips tilted up. "Woah, you sound like me. I'm so proud. Maybe the little halfling changed you for the better. Little rebel."

"It's just Ariel, calm down. A gust of wind could blow the guy over. I'm not scared of him."

Reese tilted his head from left to right, his blonde hair swinging back and forth. "No one is *actually* scared of Ariel, Nick."

We both let out a laugh, as I toed off my shoes and slid them to the side. I heard my door open and watched as my father's face came into view. His mustache was cleanly trimmed, and his hair looked softer than normal which I knew was due to Daya's daughter, Alex, giving him styling product recommendations. He had changed out of his ceremony attire into a pair of black sweatpants and a T-shirt. He looked from me to Reese, who cleared his throat awkwardly.

"I'll let you guys do your thing. I'll just be—," He shoved his thumb over his shoulder towards the direction of the living room before he leaned down and patted my shoulder, giving it a squeeze. "Always have your back, man."

I gave one solid nod before he turned to leave, closing the door on his way out.

My father had the same expression on his face as he did at the ceremony. He looked tense, as if he wanted to say something yet he was holding himself back. I remember Reese tugging on my jacket when everyone had started to disperse after the ceremony, silently telling me it was time to go. Natalia had already left without another word to us, but I had seen the colors of her portal in the distance.

I remember turning around thinking I would find my father and Daya following behind us, but I just saw my father standing in the same spot as Daya kissed his cheek and walked away, giving him his space. I'd watched him for a few minutes, remembering him just looking at the ground and then up to the sky. I recalled seeing his mouth moving as he spoke, but I couldn't make out the words.

I blinked over to my father, realizing he had gotten closer during my small memory. He still cared about Jonah, as messy as their relationship supposedly was. He sat down next to me on my bed, and I moved over a bit to give him more room.

"How are you feeling, son?" he asked, turning his body slightly so he could look at me.

I heaved out a sigh, really hating this kind of questioning nowadays. "Never better." I didn't look at him; if my eyes could have burned a hole in my plain beige wall, they would have done it, right then and there.

"Nick, I've let you do your own thing since you've been here. I didn't bother you much while you were healing, but the ceremony is over, and you have some very big plans. I just want to make sure you're alright." His voice shook a bit as if he didn't exactly know how to phrase his words, but he was trying his best.

I nodded absentmindedly, looking down at my carpet. "I know, Dad. I'm really trying not to overload myself with...everything, but let me tell you, it's really fucking difficult. I just can't...I can't think about the Jonah part of this right now." I cut my eyes to my father, noticing that he was staring at me. "Especially since I'll never have the full story in the first place."

Once the words left my mouth, his eyes closed, and he raised his head towards the ceiling. We'd been dancing around each other for three months, and I was still no closer to understanding anything. It was all half-truths and one-off statements that amounted to me being back to square one with the same amount of information I'd started with. My father had never said he didn't know what Jonah meant but getting him to let up on what he knew was like pulling teeth.

She deserved so much better.

As much as my father tried to cast it aside, no one says that to someone without it meaning something, particularly when you're dying from a sword wound in their lap.

"Nick, I...If you..."

I shook my head and pushed off my bed, heading towards my closet. I unbuttoned and removed my shirt, my pants following straight after it. "Dad, it's whatever. I'll be okay here, and I'll be okay in Purgatory. I really don't need you to be more worried than you already will be."

My back was turned to him as I tugged on a shirt, but I could feel him staring. No matter how old I got, the feeling of his eyes on me still made me tense as if he could read my every thought just by glancing in my vicinity. I heard him let out a breath and swallow loudly in my quiet room.

"It's been awhile since you've all worked together," he pointed out.

I buttoned my pants and turned around, leaning against the door frame of my closet. "I'm sure we'll figure it out. We kind of have to."

"And Dani?"

I narrowed my eyes, but my heart stuttered at mention of her name. "What about Dani?"

"We both know you feel a lot differently about her now as opposed to when this all started."

I cleared my throat. I knew my father well enough, but it still surprised me that he had taken the news that Dani was actually a halfling so well. They all had, actually—Daya and Alex as well. Alex had said it made her even more out of my league than she already was. "What's your point?"

My father ran his index finger over his mustache, letting out a small chuckle. "The point, son, is that you feel bad about what happened between you and that girl. What I wonder is why you never took your ass over to Oculus and did something about it."

"It's called giving her space," I explained. "Besides, she knows I care about her. I mean I may have said some things in between the caring parts that didn't come off so well, but I still said it." I sounded like I was trying to convince myself that the words I was speaking were good enough, even though they really fucking weren't.

I narrowed my eyes at my father as he placed his face in his hands, his shoulders shaking. This man was laughing at me. Fan-fucking-tastic.

He took a few breaths and looked up at me. "You are really lucky Daya isn't here to hear what you just said."

I raised an eyebrow expectedly.

My father gave me a side smile. "Nicholas, you remind me of myself when I was your age, always wanting to do what's right but not looking at it from the angle of anyone else. I have always prided myself on *showing* people how I felt. Words are wonderful, but they are just words. Action needs to be taken to make those words valid, because if not, they just fall flat."

I stuck my tongue out and licked my lower lip, remaining silent.

"Dani, well, she seems like the type who values actions a great deal. She..." he started to say, but he stopped himself.

I walked over to him and returned to my place next to him on my bed. "She what?"

My father reached out his hand and stroked my cheek with his knuckles. "She oddly reminds me a lot of your mother: headstrong and unapologetic." He raised his hands quickly. "I know you don't want to focus on all that, I'm sorry."

I looked down at my hands. "No, it's okay. I think it's nice they have some similarities."

"Don't wait for her to make a move, son. Do it yourself. I've never seen you back down from something you want." He squeezed my shoulder.

What my father didn't know was that I never once planned to back down. No, Dani had three months to decide I wasn't worth her time, potentially making my efforts pointless. I could take rejection, but from her, it might just hurt more than anything. We weren't even in an actual relationship. *Fuck.*

Damnit, he was right.

"Fine, fine. I'll go and, I don't know—put myself out there." I was a whole adult angel who had killed a decent amount of his angelic friends and sustained a pretty hefty wound, yet I was nervous about laying my feelings out to the prettiest girl I'd ever seen.

I walked back over to my closet and yanked a black bomber jacket off a hanger, my father watching as I put it on. "Daya and Alex are coming back over in about an hour, so we'll be here regardless of how it goes."

"You should really just ask her to move in," I mumbled, and I knew he heard me when he grumbled his own noncommittal response. He moved to leave my room, but I caught his arm. "Dad, can you promise me something?"

He tilted his head to the side. "What is it?"

I let my eyes roam his face, taking in all our similarities. I knew this face, the one that I'd looked at for my entire life, the one that held so many secrets. I wondered if they were eating away at him as much as my questions ate away at me. We'd always had a bond, and I didn't want to push so far that our relationship started to crumble because I couldn't just let things lie.

On the other hand, there were things I just needed to know, and he would have to understand.

"When I come back, when we settle this, I want you to tell me *everything*."

His breathing stunted for a moment, and he pressed his lips together. He looked everywhere but at my face, the passing seconds increasing my anticipation for his answer. Finally, he looked at me, genuine fatherly warmth spread over his face. "You make it back like I know you will, and I'll tell you everything you want to know. I promise."

I heaved out a heavy breath, happy to have that settled when my door flung open.

Reese didn't step over the threshold but instead pointed towards the living room. "Sorry to ruin your father-son moment, but we've been summoned." He had changed into more comfortable clothes as well.

My eyebrows pulled down in confusion. "Summoned? By whom?"

Reese gave me a look that told me everything I needed to know.

"Ariel was here?" We'd always gone *to* The Skies and offered our help, but he'd never actually summoned us back.

My best friend snorted. "Fuck no, that man never leaves The Skies unless he literally *has* to. He sent a messenger. He wants us there now, like right now."

I raised my eyes to the ceiling. Dani would have to wait. "Alright." I patted my father's shoulder as I walked past him.

"You could totally come too, Mr. Cassial. After all the stories about how much Ariel can't stand you, I would pay a good chunk of my celestial coins to see you two in a room together, hashing it out," Reese said, looking between us, as if his idea had a chance in Hell of happening.

My father shook his head, chuckling. The lines at the corners of his eyes deepened and made him look dignified as if he earned them. "If you want this meeting with him to go smoothly, it's best I'm not there. As long as he acts accordingly as he has been, we won't have an issue."

"Oh right, sure," Reese laughed. "The guy has been gunning to get his useless ass in Jonah's chair. It's really funny to watch."

My father ruffled Reese's hair as he passed him, heading towards the stairs leading upstairs. "Ariel has a tenacity I admire—one of the only things about him I *do* admire. Now, go on. We all know he'll be upset when you're a half a second late."

I watched him climb the stairs to the second floor as Reese turned back towards the living room. I followed my best friend but stopped short, turning back and jogging towards my room. I opened my top desk drawer and pulled out the portal key Natalia had given me. I had removed it for the ceremony, but other than that, I hadn't taken it off, not once.

I hooked it around my neck, tucking it into my shirt, returning to Reese. Once we were in the backyard, we released our wings and headed towards The Skies. Reese would have opted to use my portal key, but I hadn't used it since everything happened. Personally, I liked the feeling of flying, even though it gave me too much time to think.

I knew where Oculus was from up here, but I had to stop myself from curving completely and heading in the direction I wanted. I had to focus, as impossible as *that* seemed.

I severely hoped she could wait a little bit longer.

Everything looked fairly normal when we landed on the grassy front lawn of The Skies. There were angels in the sky and others strolling in the general area, which to anyone who didn't know what happened here, would look completely run of the mill. Boy, if looks could kill. No one actually looked at me as if I was the issue or as if I had caused all of the wreckage, but they *did* look at me as if I could give them answers to a question they weren't asking. We were ushered inside by two sentries, giving me a small chance to survey everything Ariel had fixed. The windows looked brand new, the stones lining the walls no longer caked in blood. Even the furniture looked like he had sourced only the best of the best.

I couldn't blame him. Natalia could only do so much, and even though she wanted to help, she was still rattled from Jonah's death, just like the rest of us. That, and the fact that Zane made it really fucking clear she needed some time away. We were huddled in the elevator, and I looked around one of the sentries to see what floor we were headed to.

Floor 10

Jonah's floor—or the floor that used to be Jonah's. If I hadn't had a strong hold on my nausea, I would have vomited right then and there. I leaned against the side of the elevator, feeling myself start to sweat. I looked over to where Reese was staring right at me. He narrowed his eyes and mouthed, "You good?"

I closed my eyes and nodded as the elevator lurched to a halt. It was like déjà vu. Everything was exactly as it was. My anger at the entire situation came boiling back and I couldn't even be mad at the person who caused Jonah's death, because he was also dead. It wasn't fair. We walked past what *was* Ariel's office and towards Jonah's. The sentries gave the door one sturdy knock and the familiar wisps of magic and clicking of the lock rang through my ears. The doors creaked as they opened, and the smell of herbs and lavender filled my nostrils.

Ariel was at the bar cart in the corner, his red hair pulled into a sleek top knot, dressed in the teal suit all executives wore. Reese motioned for me to go ahead of him as per usual. I stepped over the threshold, walking further into the room, while eyeing my surroundings. Nothing had really changed—not that Ariel had any right to change anything anyway, but I wouldn't put it past this asshat. Ariel swiped his left hand through the air quickly, closing the office doors.

"Glad you could make it, gentleman," Ariel said, the sound of sloshing ice echoing.

"It's not like we had a choice," Reese muffled under his breath.

I elbowed his arm, and he gave me a look that said, 'we both know it's true.'

Ariel turned around to face us, a martini glass in his hand. "As you can see The Skies is looking brand new and I thought you would like to be a part of what else I have planned."

I watched as he took a sip of his drink. "What else you have planned?"

He tapped his index finger on the glass. "Yes, Nicholas. I want a new and improved Skies. I want better monitoring, better training. Lilith is still out there, so we need to be prepared."

"What do you want *us* to do? We have just as much knowledge on how to beat her as you do, which isn't very much at all," I explained, suddenly thinking his meeting was pointless.

Ariel, who had been swishing his drink around in his glass, cut his eyes over to me. "Jonah would not want us to sit around and do nothing. I am trying to make our people stronger for whatever comes next. I would think you of all people would jump at the chance to be a part of this."

I shoved the sleeves of my jacket up my arms. "That's not what this is about. There are plenty of people who are still scared and put off by what happened. The ones who are here and acting like everything is normal are putting on brave faces. The fact that you can't see that is really not all that surprising." I was pissed.

"Ariel, it's not that we wouldn't love to help you, but you are asking us to help angels protect themselves, which is really fucking great, but half of them just lost friends and family. I mean, I know it's been three months, but damn," Reese added, crossing his arms over his chest.

Ariel shook his head, astonishment in his eyes. "What do you expect us to do in the meantime, hmm? Frolic around and pretend like this is over just because Markus is dead? Please, gentleman, tell me what you think we should do since you know so much." He downed his drink and slammed it on the bar cart. His face was getting redder with each breath he took.

I took a deep breath as I clenched my fists. "No one is trying to tell you what to do. Just maybe have a little compassion for what people are going through, instead of making yourself comfortable in a position that isn't even yours." I let my eyes bore into his and watched his eyes widen to saucers.

Reese let out an awkward cough in the small silence.

Ariel pointed his finger at me. "You may not like how I do things, Mr. Cassial, but I am still your superior. You should be happy I am even including you in anything, what with all the stunts you pulled while Jonah was alive. Sneaking into this office, trips to Oculus, bringing those demons into the Divine Library; it's pure insanity how much you've gotten away with. Jonah was soft on you and let you do as you please, but I will *not*. You have no choice.

"You *will* bring the eager new recruits into The Skies and prepare them more than ever before. As much as people have grieved, Nicholas, they are *angry*. They want to be ready for whatever happens next. You will continue to do your Animus Seeking as before because your duty doesn't just stop because you want it to, or you don't like how things are done." He said it like it was supposed to mean something to me, like it was supposed to hurt me.

"And why us, huh?" Reese asked.

Ariel waved his hand around in nonchalant motion, not looking at me anymore. "Because you lived through what happened. You were unafraid and rallied when needed. Angels need to see that their efforts are worthwhile."

Reese let out a laugh. "Okay, I'm sorry, but I, for one, will admit that I was actually scared shitless when my whole fucking life was on the line." He walked over to one of the chairs facing Jonah's desk and plopped down.

"You both are ridiculous. I want The Skies back in shape and the only way to get there is to try and find some normalcy." Ariel ran a hand down the lapels of his jacket and narrowed his gaze at me. "Of course, since you bring it up, Mr. Cassial, finding a new high executive is one of those matters. Since Jonah left no offspring, where his power went is beyond me, but I'm having archivists help figure that out, along with help from our new friend, the High Priestess."

He said this as if he had befriended Natalia all on his own, as if he found her, fought beside her, and now got to call her a friend. I knew she was doing this only for Jonah, to find the truth about his power and where it was meant to go. Natalia was too regal a person to tell Ariel to eat shit.

"As for your demon friends..."

"Woah, now, let's not use the word friend so easily." Reese held his hands out in front of him.

"What about them?" I inquired, looking towards the large door we had come through.

Ariel shrugged as if what he was about to say didn't mean much to him. "From the story you relayed to me, Lilith wanted the Soul Seether to take Jonah's power into her own to complete her halfling powers. Since Jonah is no longer with us, I highly doubt Lilith will make this mistake again, so the best thing to do is to remove them from the equation. Let her handle them."

"You want to just give them over to her?"

"Yes, it's quite simple, Nicholas."

Reese clucked his tongue. "You could have done that this whole time, but you didn't. I wanted that from the very beginning, but you all said no."

Ariel casually walked back to the bar cart to make himself another drink, and I looked over to Reese, who raised an eyebrow at me in disbelief. Ariel picked up a different glass and dropped two big ice cubes into it. He wrapped his hand around a bottle of amber liquid and poured it over the ice. "Jonah was adamant that she would help us, that they were needed. Of course, Markus had gotten inside his head, gotten me to bring her and that weapon of hers here all under the guise of someone else's plan." He tilted the glass towards us as he turned around. "Now, I'm just giving Lilith her disobedient little problem back to do with as she pleases. Keeping them here does nothing for me or our people so back to Hell they go."

I was raging. I didn't know where Dani and I stood, but I didn't want her to go before I even got to talk to her. Whatever her decision may be, I wanted to at least have the time to change her mind if it didn't include me. "You can't just make decisions for them, Ariel. That's not fair. They helped just as much as we did. They deserve to be treated like everyone else."

Ariel laughed at me as if I was a child. "Naïve. So naïve. No, she didn't rip out Jonah's soul, but I can't take the chance that she'd turn on us. Still, I'm not a monster Nicholas." Ariel looked towards the doors to the office as he took a sip from his drink. I could smell the whiskey from where I stood. "I plan on telling them exactly what is going on. I'll thank them for their service and send them on their way."

I heard the clicking of the door, and the creaking sound was back. A buzz shot through my body as my heart started to create an erratic beat. I didn't have to look up to see why there was a sudden shift in the air.

The overwhelming smell of cinnamon hit me and I almost let out an audible moan; I hadn't smelt that in what felt like forever. I peeked over at Reese, who had his hand over his mouth, staring in the direction of the door. I had told him in so many words my feelings about Dani, but he was never truly concerned with the mushy parts of my complicated relationship with her. I thought about Jonah every day, but I also thought about Dani, more often that I would have liked.

I turned my head slowly towards the door, and my breath caught in my throat. There stood the same curly hair, same brown skin, same petite body that I wanted to pull into mine and tell her I was sorry. I wanted to kiss her. *Fuck,* I wanted to kiss her, but those brown eyes of hers told me she did not feel the same. She had the most calm and collected way about her that I both hated and admired.

I blinked after what felt like a full minute when she spoke. "Long time no see, *Nicholas.*"

2

DANI

I didn't want to be here anymore than Elise did. When Natalia came to us an hour ago, saying that Ariel wanted to speak, I'd rolled my eyes and shrug. I knew our time in this realm was fleeting—it was only a matter of time before they had enough of us. Elise had been much louder about having to go to The Skies, but I blocked her out. I had been blocking her out for three months now—not that she was making an effort in the slightest. Natalia tried to play mediator a few times, but the only thing we *had* agreed on was going to Purgatory. I had wanted to go as quickly as possible, but Natalia told us to wait. Seriously, if this was what having a parental figure was like, I *fucking* hated it.

I hadn't even wanted to invite the boys on our little excursion, but the High Priestess had talked me into it. It wasn't that I didn't think they'd be helpful. It was…well, it wasn't *them*. It was one person, one raven-haired angel who said things that, if I was being honest, hurt me. It took a lot to really get to me like that. When it came to Elise, I wasn't hurt. No, I was severely seething so much, I had to put a lid on it every single day when I saw her stupid fucking face.

Every night that I went to sleep in the room Natalia had offered me, I replayed what felt like my entire existence. I tried to pinpoint the moment I knew something was off, the moment I didn't feel like what everyone told me I was, what Elise and Lilith tried to make me believe. I spent plenty of time trying to get that light to come out, just to maybe have some awkward conversation with it, but then I would get angry and think about all the reasons why I even *have* to have an awkward conversation. Then, I would have to simmer myself down before I covered the entire room in darkness and imploded.

I would manifest my dagger and twirl it in between my fingers as I stared up at the ceiling, letting my thoughts drift. I was frustrated with fucking everyone, and I had forgotten how poorly I handled rage. I could have ripped a soul out at any moment, which had made my dagger send a soothing electric shock through my veins. Bloodshed or sex: those were my two coping mechanisms, and I couldn't do either at the moment.

Fuck. Fuck. Fuck.

Elise and I stood on opposite sides of the elevator as we rode up to the tenth floor, and I watched as she examined her nails, looking as if she hadn't kept a huge secret from me. Her lips were painted a dark red, reminding me of the blood that beaded across her skin when I scratched down her pale face. She looked up at me just as I started to look away, but not before giving me a smirk that had me fuming. I started to take a step toward her, but I stopped when I felt heavy eyes on me. I cut my gaze to Natalia, who had both of her perfectly arched eyebrows raised at me. I slid my tongue over my teeth but remained in place. Natalia had been great to both of us while she'd been reeling with the fact that her ex-girlfriend was a psychotic traitor. I couldn't wait to see her stupid fucking face when we headed...home?

That place wasn't my home. It never was. Then again, neither was this place.

There was a small, microscopic moment when I thought that it could be...

I fingered the end of one of my curls as I tilted my head, looking at the handsome face I hadn't seen in a while. "Long time no see, *Nicholas*."

His mouth gaped open as I watched his eyes move from my face to my black boots, back up to my face. He swallowed as he regained his composure. "Hey."

The look of longing in his eyes thrilled me. He *should* miss me. I was likely the best piece of ass he had ever taken to bed. He had proved that he was with us in this fight, but I didn't entirely trust that he wanted me fully. At least, not in the way I wanted to be wanted.

I wasn't ready to forgive him, but that didn't mean I didn't still find him annoyingly attractive. Three months, and I could still remember what that mouth could do. Those hands. That insanely impressive cock.

Fuck, no. No. I absentmindedly shook my head, looking away from him.

"Did you miss me, Blondie?" Elise asked, wiggling her fingers towards Reese. He grumbled as he tilted his head back in his chair.

"Does anyone ever actually miss you?" Reese said in a flat, monotone voice. She scrunched up her face and blew him a kiss.

Ariel cleared his throat and took a sip from his glass. I smelled whiskey and I almost gagged at the scent. Beer, whiskey, no thank you. Give me a cocktail any day. Hell, I would have taken a shot of tequila right about now. He nodded towards Natalia who walked between me and Elise, letting her long sapphire dress brush my legs.

"Thank you so much for coming. You have been wonderful in helping us through this tough time." Ariel took Natalia's hand which she gave almost as if she knew it was the polite thing to do, when she wanted more than to cringe.

She slid her fingers out of his grasp and wiped her hands along the front of her dress. "Of course. It's my pleasure. I want this in the past for your people just as I do for my own. Alas, we both know this isn't over, Ariel."

Ariel nodded thoughtfully. "Yes, I was just telling the boys that I want to get the new trainees up to par for whatever may come our way. We need to start as soon as possible."

I snorted, which caught the red-haired angel's attention. He let out a huff as if to tell me to speak. "You just buried one of your own." I pointed my finger in his direction, "your highest superior and you just want to get back to the old way of things? You don't even know what you're preparing to fight." I gave him a half smile. "Not that you did much fighting last time."

"It's better to be prepared," he argued, clearly ignoring my last few words.

Elise stalked around them towards the bar cart, barking out a laugh. "Oh yeah, real insightful. You can prepare all you want but training here and hitting each other with pointy sticks isn't going to save your ass." She grabbed a glass and started fumbling with the various bottles of alcohol. It made me miss the bars and parties in Purgatory a little more.

"We never said we were going to help you," Nicholas said, placing his hands in his jean pockets. I could see his biceps flex under his jacket and I remembered how they looked on either side of my head when he was over me in his bed. I ruffled my hair, frustrated with the direction my thoughts had decided to go.

Ariel narrowed his green eyes at the outspoken angel before me. "You want to help your people, do you not? This is how you help. You and I both know you always do what's best for everyone Mr. Cassial."

Nicholas looked at the floor, running a hand through his hair.

Reese slid both his hands down his chair's armrests. "Alright, we get it, but have you actually been out there and talked to some of those parents? The other sentries? Anyone? They are doing whatever you say because I don't think you've given them any other choice." He got up from the chair and walked over to stand beside his best friend.

"Have you appointed yourself their leader now or something?" I asked, curious. Nicholas had told me months ago that he had no idea what happened after Jonah's power left his body.

"Of course not! According to Your Highness over here, he can't do jack shit until they figure out where poor Jonah's powers went," Elise answered, swishing around the amber liquid in her glass, moving the ice cubes around with her finger before sticking it in her mouth. She moved closer to Ariel as he tried to move away discreetly. "Let me guess: you haven't done that, now have you? So that would make you just as useless as you already were."

Ariel was turning red, and Elise simply strutted away, practically chugging her drink.

Natalia put her hand up as her way of telling Ariel she would handle this. "We have yet to figure out where Jonah stowed his power away. Executives like Jonah, they have their own way of doing things, but we'll figure it out." She took a breath and let her eyes linger on Ariel. "Now, why have you summoned us?" She was so elegant and regal with the way she handled herself—I had to admit, I was a bit jealous.

Ariel pulled at the bottom of his teal jacket and straightened his shoulders. "Ah, yes. Well we here in The Skies and Heaven's Gate in general don't want any more problems. So I have made a decision I think we will all be happy with." He looked at each of us as if we were supposed to be bouncing on our toes with anticipation.

The only thing I was anticipating was the minute I would get to leave this room. I couldn't wait to get away from the demon I wanted to strangle and the angel whose eyes I could feel dart over to me every so often as if he thought that if he didn't look at me for a certain amount of time, I would disappear. It was highly annoying.

Ariel drained his glass and placed it on the bar cart, giving me and Elise a determined look. "We are giving you what you want."

I pressed my tongue into my cheek. "And what would that be?"

"You are going home." Ugh that stupid fucking word.

Elise froze with the glass up to her lips and stared daggers at Ariel. "What the fuck did you just say?"

It seemed as if all the air had been sucked out of the room and I could make out every single person's breathing pattern. The overwhelming scent of anxiety emanated from the angels to my right; Nicholas who had stuffed his hands in his jacket pocket, shifting from foot to foot, while Reese looked from Ariel to Elise as if he was waiting for a fight to break out and couldn't figure out whether to intervene or sit back and watch.

Natalia opened her mouth to say something but Ariel cut her off. "I said that we are sending you both home. You should be happy."

"You want us to thank you or something?" I asked, sarcasm lacing my words.

Ariel hummed. "No need. I can't have the people of Heaven's Gate in any more danger, so removing two of the problems will help the healing process." His words held so much faux authority I almost started laughing.

"You can't seriously think that us going back is going to fix your problem, do you? If you do then you are way more of an idiot than I thought." I took a step towards him.

"Lilith is not the only issue. Markus may be dead, but she also has Isabel on her side. You may not have been there, Ariel, but she has much more magic than I thought, much more than she ever let on." Natalia said her ex-girlfriend's name with so much disgust, I could practically taste it from where I stood.

Ariel huffed out a noise of annoyance. "I understand that and I am very sorry she fooled you, that she fooled all of you, but I have to think about what's best. The best thing for *everyone* is to send them back. Lilith is the real villain, Your Highness, and she is their problem, not ours."

Elise drained the last of her drink and started laughing so hard, she hunched over. My eyes widened as I waited for her to calm down. She inhaled a few sharp breaths before she licked her lips. "Yet again, you fucking pricks want us to fix your problems?"

"Correct me if I'm wrong, but Jonah had me bring you here to fix a problem that turns out wouldn't have been an issue if you would have just stayed right where you were. All the issues started with the Soul Seether, so it's simply a case of removing the problem." He looked Elise up and down, nearly turning his nose up at her.

If steam could have come out of Elise's ears, it would have been at that moment. She held her glass so tight, I thought it would shatter in her grip.

Natalia's shoulders jumped a bit when Elise threw her glass past Ariel's head. It shattered against the wall and Ariel looked over his shoulder in horror. Reese let out a choking sound that sounded like he was holding in a laugh, but he stared at the floor. We all knew that if she was looking to hit him, she wouldn't have missed.

Elise stalked towards Ariel, her shoulders tense and I had to blink to make sure I was truly seeing reddish black flames coming from her fingertips. Natalia reached out faster than I knew possible and grabbed her wrist, halting her, Elise didn't let that stop her.

"If you think sending us back is going to save you then I think you all deserve horrible, painful deaths. I just hate that I won't be the one to do it."

Natalia lightly shoved Elise back. "Ariel, you need to think about this. They have been here for quite some time and haven't been an issue. Besides, you have yet to address that the Soul Seether is not exactly what we presumed."

I literally loathed being talked about like I wasn't there, but I didn't really have much to say. I knew what I was—what I was supposed to be—but I didn't feel it. That light, that warmth was one thing, but actually entertaining the idea that it was supposed to be symbiotic with me was proving difficult, especially when the only side I'd ever known was so tempting and so very, very playful.

Ariel turned his back to us and walked towards what I assumed was Jonah's desk, leaning his back against the wooden surface when he faced us again. "How could I forget that thrilling piece of information, hmm?" His green eyes scanned me, as if trying to find any trace of my halfing status. "I am truly sorry for what Lilith did, but that is no concern of mine. You choosing to fight against her instead of doing what she intended was commendable, but the history of what you are doesn't sit well with me. I have no way of helping you, so frankly, we are back to my plan. I shouldn't have let you stay as long as you have. It was a courtesy, really. Natalia can open the portal to send you on your way."

"She saved your ass and you're acting like a dick?" Nicholas shouted, cutting through the tension.

Ariel slowly turned his head as if he was making sure he heard him correctly. "Excuse me?"

Nicholas took a slow, deep breath. "We all worked our asses off to get out of that fight alive, but things would have gone differently if she hadn't made the decision she did. You aren't even giving them a chance."

"Nicholas, I said what she did was commendable. I'm no liar. Would you like me to say thank you before I send them away? Very well then." He spoke to Nicholas like he was a child.

Nicholas looked towards one of the bookshelves on one of the far walls as if trying to keep his cool. "You really are a piece of work you know."

"Nick," Reese mumbled under his breath, leaning his head towards his best friend. He put his hand on his shoulder, but Nicholas just shrugged it off.

"I would watch my tone if I were you, Mr. Cassial." Ariel commanded.

Nicholas clenched his fists as he walked over to Ariel, his long legs getting him in front of the red-headed angel in seconds. "I don't think I have to. Jonah is dead, and right now, I don't answer to you. So, *no* I don't plan to help you. After what happened, I would rather help two demons than have anything to do with your *ideas*." Nicholas pressed his finger into Ariel's chest. "Sending them back to Purgatory will only make *you* happy and from what I remember Heaven's Gate isn't a dictatorship. Have you ever asked the people what they want? You ever think that maybe Dani being both angel and demon could *help* us?"

Ariel glanced over at me and then back to Nicholas, a smirk playing at his lips. He grabbed Nicholas's finger and moved it away from him. "Well said, Mr. Cassial, but the people don't know what they want right now. They need someone to decide for them at the moment." He looked at me again, but this time he did it a little too long which had me throwing up my middle finger. He scoffed and lightly pushed Nicholas back. "Maybe asking you to be a part of this was a mistake, seeing that you seem to be too *close* to the situation. Is that what Markus meant when he said you could use your *charm* to get her to torture that demon?" Ariel gave a feral smile that made me want to shove my fist down his throat.

"Fuck you." Nicholas spat out.

"Oh fuck, pretty boy has claws." Elise snarked. "About time."

The last time I'd seen a feisty Nicholas was at our meeting with Jonah and I had to admit it turned me on…just a little.

Reese got between his best friend and Ariel, his hazel eyes wide and a little thrilled. "As much as I would love to see you two fight, I don't think it would be fair seeing as it would be two on one."

Ariel looked over at Reese in confusion. Reese shrugged, adjusting the collar of his shirt. "You can't really believe I'd not be on Nick's side. As much as I don't really love having them here, you aren't listening to reason. It sounds like you just like hearing yourself talk. *Shocker*."

"Ariel, just listen to us for a moment, I'm sure we can all come up with a plan. In fact…" Natalia started, but Ariel motioned his hand towards her as if he didn't give a flying fuck what she had to say. She closed her mouth and her chest rose and fell with practiced patience.

"I brought you all here as a courtesy. What I'm saying is happening, no matter your thoughts. Jonah always said you had a mind of your own, well I will have none of it." Ariel blinked over to Nicholas with a noncommittal shrug. "You are your father's son, always choosing to make things difficult. Even more like your father to do it over a female."

Reese had to hustle to make it over to Nicholas before he nearly launched himself at Ariel. Reese was using all his weight to keep his friend back, but that didn't stop Nicholas from speaking. "Do not speak about my father!" He was fighting against Reese to get to Ariel, but the red headed angel simply laughed him off.

"I don't have time for this. As I've said, Natalia, you will escort these two back..." Ariel started, but I let out a low whistle, halting his words. I was done with this, and I was done with him.

"This has all been really fucking great, and I'm so honored that you think you have a chance in Hell at telling me what I can and can't do, but there is no need for you to 'send us back', you arrogant dick," I snorted.

"Your meaning?" Ariel asked.

I gave Elise a short-lived side-eye. "We were headed back to Purgatory anyway. I didn't know you had claimed yourself leader or I would have told you. Of course, you are just pretending while you're in this office so, no hard feelings."

Ariel moved around Nicholas to face me. "The sooner you are gone, the faster I can get this place back in line, especially these defiant boys. Do what you must."

"I must say, being a bad boy is fun," Reese said casually to no one in particular, Nicholas still seething behind Ariel. Our eyes locked as I looked around Ariel, and if I wasn't still so upset with him, I would have melted at the way he looked at me.

Elise clucked her tongue. "Well it's a fantastic thing we are taking your defiant boys off your hands, huh?"

"Elise..." Nicholas started, saying her name slowly as if he was proceeding with caution.

Ariel gave her an incredulous look. "What is she talking about? They are remaining here." He looked around as if this was some big joke. His eyes settled on Natalia, and he turned his anger on her. "If you are doing this all because you want some kind of vengeance, I will not have it. I don't care *who* you are." He was practically nose to nose with her, but she just stood there, unbothered and unshaken.

"I would take a few steps back if you wish to say anything more to me, Ariel. Despite what the others in this room say, I *specifically* do not answer to you, therefore, I would move back quickly." Her honey-colored eyes sparkled with a kind of glittering regality that was almost scary, but her voice made you want to straighten your spine on command.

"I would do what she says," I offered with a bratty smile.

Ariel heeded her words, even though he huffed and puffed. She tucked a piece of her dark waves behind her ear, displaying a string of gold ear jewelry. "I didn't make this decision for them, but I back them with my entire heart. This has nothing to do with Isabel, but everything to do with what needs to be done."

"Are you hearing yourself?" Ariel yelled as he shifted to face the boys. "You are going nowhere! You hear me? Mr. Cassial, Mr. Diniel, you are going nowhere with them."

I watched Nicholas look up at the ceiling as he placed his hands on his hips. He took in a few breaths, then looked at Reese who gave a small nod. They had this very weird non-verbal communication that I found oddly cute. Nicholas clapped his hands together before he spoke. "You know Ariel, I think for once you're right." He looked over to me one more time and swallowed, a determined look in his eyes. "I am just like my father. A man who actually thinks this plan is a solid one. This plan that we're following through with whether you like it or not." He motioned between him and Reese.

"If you think we were defiant before...we're defiant as fuck now," Reese chimed in.

I raised one of my eyebrows, blowing a lone curl out of my line of sight. "You're quite outnumbered."

Ariel opened and closed his mouth, almost like a fish. It was comical. I rolled my eyes and turned on my heels to walk out. "And you're welcome, for saving your pathetic ass," I shot back over my shoulder when I stopped by the door.

"Nicholas, you go through with his idiotic plan, and I will not back you. Do not think I will be there when you realize what a colossal mistake you've made aligning yourself with them. Lilith will slaughter you all," Ariel sputtered, his face red and irritated.

"I wouldn't dream of asking you for help—not that you've ever been much help in the first place." Nicholas walked past me, letting his hand brush mine as he went. He yanked on one of the door handles, and it creaked with the movement. I pressed my lips together in a muffled laughter when Reese trailed behind him, turned around swiftly to put up two middle fingers, and then walked out.

"It's always a pleasure Ariel," Natalia said as she walked out. Elise followed, but not before adding, "later, fuckface."

"You will ruin them, you know. You made the choice to defy Lilith when she wasn't around, but what makes you think you'll be able to do the same when she stands right in front of you? The monster in front of its creator," Ariel questioned.

I let out a loud sigh and faced him. "You didn't sound this concerned when you wanted to send us back two seconds ago. Those boys are free to make their own choices, so stop acting like you give a shit."

I could tell that Nicholas had a type of shadow behind his eyes as if now he was doing whatever he wanted, the loyalty he lived by be damned. I admired it, but I also knew that wasn't completely him. Something inside of me hurt at the idea that he was feeling off. Having to kill your own kind can do that to a person, especially having them die in your arms.

"What I wanted was for you to go and deal with your issues without dragging others into your mess, but I suppose you both have already gotten into their heads."

I shook my head, very, very done with this conversation. "Tell me something Ariel: do you think treating your subordinates like shit is the way to get them on your side? From where I stand, you are all alone in your ideals. We asked them to go, and they said yes, no mind tricks involved. We have given them time to back down and say no, and they haven't." I scanned the office, realizing now how big and spacious it really was. "You think I can fix your problem, and maybe I can, but just in case I can't, do you really think those boys are going to fight beside you now? Do you think any of these people, Enchanters included, are going to rally behind you, follow you all because you're telling them what could be coming? Tyranny and fear is one thing, respect is another. Just a thought." I tapped my finger against my chin before smoothly turning around.

"I'd reevaluate how I treat people, especially the monsters that might be your only chance at survival." With that I closed the door and didn't look back.

3

NICK

I could feel my whole body start to ache from the tension I'd built up in a matter of what felt like ten minutes. My muscles ached from the way my shoulders vibrated, and I could feel a headache coming on from the way I was clenching my jaw so tight. I mashed the button for the elevator and started pacing in front of the doors, really, really wanting to go back in that room and punch Ariel right in his stupid fucking face. Everything had been going so well with him, he had been behaving up until now…but now, ugh *now* he wanted to let go of the facade that he was a decent angel. He had always been known to throw some low blows, but fuck, my father and Dani all in one meeting was a new one and I couldn't take it.

I nearly jumped out of my skin when I felt Reese's hand grab my arm. "You alright there killer?" He raised one of his blonde eyebrows at me in question.

I almost let out an exhaustive, ridiculous laugh with how nuts this all was. "I'm fine, just need a minute."

I heard the ding of the elevator and watched as the doors slid open. We both stepped inside right as I heard Elise.

"Quite the show back there, pretty boy. Impressive." She gave me a wide toothed smile as I turned around. Natalia and Dani weren't far behind her, so I held my hand out and kept the doors open for them. They all piled in, making the small elevator space feel more crowded than normal. There were four other people in this elevator but there was only one that I noticed; I could practically read every single one of her movements.

We were on opposite sides of the elevator, but I could make out the rise and fall of her chest as she breathed. I noticed the way she bit her lip as if she was in deep thought as she kept her eyes on the floor. That fucking lip bite would be the death of me. The elevator halted and the doors opened, letting us out of the ground floor.

Once we were all hustled outside, Reese spoke his mind. "Is anyone surprised he didn't send sentries to grab our ass and bring us back?"

"Not really, I mean, it's Ariel, how would it look if you both got thrown over someone's shoulder and reprimanded, hmm?" Elise answered. "I personally would love to see it, but whatever."

Natalia hummed. "She's right. Ariel wouldn't want to cause a scene when he's trying to clearly build a better relationship with everyone here. Wouldn't look great to have you two kicking and screaming now, would it?"

I looked up at the sky, letting out a slow, solid breath. The sun was out, and I had to squint my eyes to be able to appreciate it. The smell of freshly cut grass filled my nostrils and I inhaled deeply. I loved The Skies and I loved Heaven's Gate. This place was my home, but there was something different about it now. Where there used to be light memories and happy moments, now the visions of blood and clashing swords were slowly replacing them. Memories of Jonah's death appeared when I least expected it, and I couldn't get rid of them. Believe me, I fucking tried.

There were other angels that had tried to talk to me, tried to console me. The sentry angels that made it out of that terrible fight alive wanted to know things, to try to understand my feelings. They didn't want the pretty details that covered up all the fucked-up things that we had discovered that led us to that bloody fight. No, they wanted every single minute detail that I didn't want to give. Reese had done most of the talking and given them what they wanted the minute he realized I was living in my own world for a while. I was just trying to keep it together. I still was.

"Still with us?" I heard Dani ask. I blinked over to her, noticing that she had her head tilted to the side as she looked at me. Her brown eyes seemed lighter in the sunlight. "The plan I mean."

"You think I would have done all that, if I wasn't?" I shot back, mirroring her head tilt. She narrowed her eyes at me and pressed her lips together, as if she was testing me, making sure I was still committed to my word.

Natalia brought her hands together in front of her. "Well then I think it's time we really talk about this plan."

"*You* might be ready, but is Blondie over here going to last in Purgatory?" Elise joked, glancing quickly over to Reese.

Reese rolled his eyes. "Oh, how sweet, you almost sound like you care."

Elise laughed. "I don't. Don't get it twisted. I just want to make sure we aren't bringing dead weight with us. I'm not carrying your ass around if you get hurt. Useless angels automatically become demon food." She gave him a smug smile, snapping her teeth together.

"Funny. What makes you think the halfling here won't just feed you to the other demons herself?" Reese countered, nodding over to Dani. "I wouldn't blame her."

I shook my head, realizing that some things were never going to change. I watched as Dani snuck a glance over to Elise and rolled her eyes. Well, they hadn't made up, which told me that Elise was still playing the 'I don't care about Dani or her wellbeing' game.

"We can head to my house." I peeked over to Dani who moved her eyes over to me, that same skepticism in her eyes. "My dad and Daya would be happy to see you, you know, before we go."

Our eyes locked in this way that had me believing we were the only two people in the entire realm. I heard a throat clearing and Elise's voice rang out, "You portaling us, lover boy?"

Everyone else came back into my line of sight and I realized I was being addressed. "What?"

Dani let out a small laugh under her breath. "She asked you if you were portaling us there, *Nicholas*." She pointed to my chest, where my tiger's eye portal key hung around my neck. She had a way of saying my full name as if she was making a point. A clear point, that meant we weren't at that place we had been months ago, and I was afraid that we would never get back there.

"I think it's best if I just take us there," Natalia offered, giving me a soft smile. "I think it's been a minute since you used your portal key, and your emotions might be a little high."

I nodded in agreement. Natalia created that circle of light and magic leading towards my house and knowing I was able to lay back on my couch with a sense of normalcy before I dived into an unknown experience where yet again my life could be on the line sounded like Heaven.

My dad gave Dani one of his hugs he only reserved for people he really cared about, so watching it happen right in front of me had me letting out a smile. She reciprocated it with just as much caring and let him give her a quick once over before sending her over to Daya for the same treatment. Alex was settled on the couch, her dark hair highlighted with neon pink streaks piled high on her head in a messy bun with a pencil stuck in it. She had a sketchpad in her lap and was hunched over it like she could give a fuck who was in the living room. She gave Dani and Elise a nonchalant nod before returning to her work.

Elise hopped up on the kitchen counter, clearly making herself at home since she had grabbed a container of ice cream from my freezer and was already digging into it. Dani fell back into the couch cushions next to Alex, while Reese perched himself on the arm. I leaned against the mantle of the fireplace, taking the drink my father handed me as he made his rounds being a good host. I took a long drink of my beer before getting hit with a memory.

Beer. Living room. Dani.

I pressed the tip of the beer bottle to my temple, but that didn't help the memory fade. It likely only made it stronger. The way she had kissed me and left me a fucking mess unable to sleep at all that night. The way she had pressed me to admit what I wanted.

I looked over my shoulder towards my bedroom and I quickly closed my eyes, but it was too late. Every single fucking moment from that night flashed across my mind. Every position I ever put her in wormed its way into my subconscious.

We really did defile my entire bedroom, *fuck*.

I blinked a few times, trying to simmer down my brain and my dick. I looked back over to where everyone had congregated and knew her eyes were on me. I met her gaze, and she looked as if she knew where my mind had wandered. She let her tongue slip out and lick at her top lip and I couldn't help following that movement. Dani looked away from me when my father caught her attention, causing her to turn and slightly lean over the back of the couch.

I saw a figure move around the window at the front of my house. I couldn't make out much, besides wide shoulders and large biceps. I pointed towards the glass. "Did anyone see that?"

Everyone collectively followed the direction of my finger, and I heard Natalia's lyrical chuckle. "Oh, don't mind Zane. He's been on me like this since the whole catastrophe. I told him he couldn't come to the meeting, but

I did tell him he could meet me here." As if he knew we were talking about him, he turned and peered through the window. Natalia wiggled her fingers in a wave, and he nodded gruffly.

"He got here a little bit before you all did. It was nice to catch up," my father stated, tapping on the window to get Zane's attention, giving him a wave.

Elise let out a snort. "Can someone explain to me why we aren't taking the giant brute of an Enchanter with us to Purgatory? Like isn't that a better option than…" she looked over to my best friend and I, unimpressed, "this."

Alex covered her mouth as a loud laugh left her throat. Daya smacked her daughter lightly on the shoulder, which caused Alex to swat her mother's hands away as if her laugh was completely valid.

"I actually vote for that plan. Let the very large man outside go in my place," Reese offered, his face waiting for us to agree with him.

"We already said we were going. There is no going back now," I reminded him, earning a disgruntled sigh.

Daya took the cup of coffee that my father handed her before speaking, "So, explain to me again what happened?" She perched herself on the arm of the couch next to her daughter.

I started to open my mouth and release the entire contents of what I thought was going to be a task to prove myself to Jonah, but really ended up being a life altering experience I didn't ask for. I didn't get the chance because Dani beat me to it. Without faltering she perfectly explained everything to Daya. Markus losing the women he loved, Isaac Zuriel's self-righteous nature, and how Dani was simply used to complete a plan that had been in dormancy for so long. She made sure to emphasize that Isabel was a raging traitor bitch, getting a collective nod from everyone around her, especially Natalia who despite being upset with her former lovers' actions, had a small hint of sadness in her eyes.

Isabel wasn't innocent by any means, but at least she was alive to pay for her actions. Once we found her, of course. My mind went to that place that I hated, immediately thinking about how Markus wouldn't pay for his. As much shit as Isabel caused with her collected Enchanter powers, Markus was Lilith's initial game master. Lilith pulled the strings, but she gave him enough free reign that he was able to pull the wool over all our eyes.

Markus got Keegan to Purgatory and killed him. *Markus* coaxed Jonah into bringing Dani here. *Markus* helped unleash those demons on us during that meeting. *Markus* sat back and let Isabel invade my fellow angels' minds and let them destroy themselves. *Markus* wanted Jonah dead. And he got his wish. Markus, Markus, fucking *Markus*.

I held the beer bottle so tight that I could almost hear it start to crack.

Reese bumped his shoulder into mine. I rapidly blinked a few times, pulling myself out of my angry thoughts, not even realizing he had gotten up from the couch and stood up next to me. I looked over at him and watched as his eyes bounced from my face down to the bottle currently in a chokehold.

"Are you sure you're okay? Where did you just go?" Reese whispered, inclining his head towards me.

"What are you talking about?"

He looked at me like I had just asked the world's dumbest question. "You just zoned out two minutes ago, Nick. You should be happy I'm the only one that noticed."

"I'm fine. Can you literally stop asking me if I'm okay?" I rolled my shoulders and softened my grip on my beer.

My best friend reached down and snatched the bottle from my hand. I didn't have time to grab it back before he was water-falling the remaining contents into his mouth. "Whatever you want, but I won't have you breaking poor innocent bottles because you won't talk to someone about your shit." He wiped his mouth, giving me a cheeky smile.

Daya's small gasp and choked voice had both of us looking over to where Dani had obviously finished her retelling of the events. My father was at her side immediately, cradling her in his arms. She let him hold her and her shoulders relaxed a bit.

She tucked a piece of her hair behind her ear, swallowing. "A demon, angel baby? You don't mean that Layla..." She stopped talking as she covered her mouth. Alex shot her head up and immediately reached out to grab her mother's hand. "She really was the start to this whole thing. I really didn't want to believe it."

"Whose Layla?" I asked no one in particular.

Dani looked over at me, her lips pressed together tightly. The minute she heard Daya clear her throat she shot her eyes back over to her.

Daya squeezed her daughters' hand and let go, patting the tears away from underneath her eyes and straightened her shoulders. "Layla is my cousin. She was killed in that grand fight that Isaac Zuriel started all those years ago." I could hear Alex tapping the end of her pencil nervously against the sketch pad, as if she was anxious about what was going to be said.

"What does your cousin have to do with any of this?" I pressed.

My father kissed her temple, as if he was telling her it was okay to let it out, whatever it was she seemed to be harboring. Something that clearly by the look on Dani's face, she knew about.

"That baby that Markus spoke about. The halfling child. That was my cousin's baby." She took a breath as if that small amount of information took all her energy out.

"Mom, you don't have to..." Alex started, but Daya shook her head, appearing to be okay with explaining what she could.

Reese rubbed the side of his head with his index and middle finger. "Wait, wait. Your cousin had a baby with a demon, which Lilith killed, therefore starting that entire war. Jonah's father going nuts, Markus losing his girlfriend, all of it?"

Daya nodded.

"And you knew?" I asked this directly to Dani, who cut her gaze to me.

"It's not my story to tell." She shrugged.

"Why would Lilith even do that? It doesn't make sense."

Elise hummed around her spoonful of ice cream. "Of course, it does, you fucking idiot."

I clenched my teeth together as every head in the room swiveled around to look at her.

My father raised his dark eyebrows at her. "Care to explain."

Elise licked her spoon, stuffing it into the now empty pint of ice cream. "Sure. Anything for you, Mr. Cassial." She winked over at him, and I noticed him trying to hold in a chuckle. Daya looked as if she didn't know whether to be protective of my father or just laugh.

Elise sighed heavily before she let her tongue loose and started rambling about how hybrids were super powerful, that they could be lethal if not given proper nurturing and attention. She explained to us that Lilith had told her that creating a hybrid would be better suited than having stolen one.

"I didn't know what she meant by any of it, but I didn't ask much more than that. It honestly fucking baffles me because Lilith never really dirties her own hands like that. I just continued babysitting this ungrateful little shit over here." She nodded over to Dani.

Dani's eyes turned into slits as she seethed on the couch. She swung her head towards Elise. "You really want to have this conversation now? Would you like another fight? Perhaps this time I can actually run this through your fucking face." Dani brought her hand out and manifested her dagger in her hand. The sleek blade looked shiny and untouched. It glinted in the sunlight coming from the window. Each point of the razor slits wafting with darkness, and it nestled around her as if it was happy to be back where it belonged.

Dani was nearly halfway to jumping over the couch when I rushed over to her and grabbed her by the waist, causing her to land on the couch cushion with a soft thud. Her mass of curls settled around her shoulders, while random curls landed in her face. She let out a breath, blowing those curls out of her line of sight. The dagger was lying delicately next to her and she reached for it, letting it disappear once it fit in her grasp.

She rolled her eyes and crossed her arms over her chest, clearly irritated with my meddling. If she wanted to fight like they did in Oculus, they sure as hell wouldn't be doing it in my house. I looked over at my father whose deep brown eyes were narrowed. It was like he wasn't seeing that I just de-escalated a potential natural disaster, it was more like he was seeing me standing over a girl that I tried not to mention because the sound of her name made my chest hurt.

And my dick.

I frustratingly ran a hand through my hair, not really knowing what to say. If I said anything right now it would be a jumbled version of an apology and probably a bunch of variations of how I really, really wanted to kiss her. But I couldn't do that, not until she was looking right at me, ready to listen.

"Are you just going to hover over her or are you going to sit down?" Alex said, still looking at her sketch pad.

I gaped at her as if she really didn't just say that. She looked up from her work and widened her eyes, expectantly. "Well?"

I tilted my chin up and looked at the ceiling, mentally counting to ten. I looked behind me and pushed a few items around on the coffee table, making room for me to sit. I let my eyes drift over to Elise. "So, Dani was the next best plan? Why not just take the baby instead?" I hated talking about this with Daya right here, as if we had no sympathy.

"Because you pretty but stupid man, that baby would be missed. Everyone would have raged to find it but killing it would cause chaos and she loves chaos more than anything else. Lilith loves to make one move and watch everyone else destroy themselves. I can't blame her; it is kind of thrilling when you think about it." She prattled on a bit, before I snapped my fingers bringing her back to the present. She snarled at me. "Ugh, she didn't want something that could be taken back. She found she wanted something of her own. Her own pathetic little hybrid baby who needs cute little weapons to make her feel special, so she knows that she's mommy's favorite." Her words cut deep with spitefulness and an intent to hurt.

I scrubbed a hand down my face as I watched my father step between them. Dani had both hands on the back of the couch and from the looks of it, she was about to rip the stuffing right out of the cushion. Elise was still propped on the counter, swinging her legs back and forth as if she simply said things to get a rise out of Dani.

I needed to get it through my own head that Elise operated on an entirely different wavelength than the rest of us. Our wavelength being sanity and hers being the exact opposite.

Reese sauntered over to the fridge. "I say let the cat fight happen Mr. Cassial."

"You are absolutely no help, Reese."

Dani let her head hang near her shoulders as she slouched, not fully relaxing, but no longer so on edge. "I'm sorry about your cousins' baby, Daya." It almost came out muffled, but the person it was meant for heard it. "I'm sorry about all of it."

Daya let out a small smile, walking over to Dani and turning her around. "Oh honey. It's not your fault. Lilith has ruined things for everyone in this room. You want to go and make her pay for what she's done, then by all means, fight." She cupped Dani's chin with her hand and nodded firmly.

Dani grabbed Daya's wrist and squeezed it. She took a deep breath and turned around catching each of our eyes. "Lilith won't be the only issue we have in Purgatory. From what Markus said before he died, she's been experimenting with removing demons' souls for quite some time now and I hardly think she's stopped."

"She always has a contingency plan," Elise added.

I rubbed my chin. "And you are totally sure that if we dropped down into Purgatory that we won't just be immediately ambushed on sight?"

Both Elise and Dani shrugged.

"It's a possibility, but I feel like coming to her is what she wants. An instant kill isn't what she desires," Dani explained.

Reese hummed, coming to stand next to me again. "Well, yeah, because it seems to me like what she wants is *you*." He pointed at Dani with an accusing finger. She just tilted her head and smirked at him.

"We aren't going to just hand her over," I said, more volume in my voice than I wanted.

Reese rolled his eyes, annoyed. "I didn't say that. I'm just pointing out facts. I want the dark queen dead as much as everyone else in this room. I'm not trying to satisfy her wishes, alright."

Natalia cleared her throat, having been silent throughout our entire back and forth debacle. My father handed her another steaming cup of coffee and she nodded her thanks. She wrapped her ring covered hands around the mug and let the steam waft over her glittering face. "She'll likely have Isabel be her eyes and her scapegoat while you move down there so be mindful."

"Isabel doesn't scare me. *She* should be scared *of* me," Dani said with little puffs of smoke releasing from her fingertips.

Natalia let out a small laugh. "You are quite fearless, which has me putting my utmost faith in you. I will provide a portal for you, but Nicholas—," she placed her mug on the coffee table and motioned her hand for me to come over to her. Once I was in front of her, she held out her hand, palm up. "Your key."

I gave her a skeptical look but dug into my shirt and pulled out my portal key without question. Removing it from around my neck, I dropped it into her waiting hand. Natalia placed her other hand on top, encapsulating the key. A bright orange glowing light peeked out from between her fingers as she concentrated on the task in front of her. The light grew brighter causing me to have to look away.

The light faded until it was snuffed out. Natalia opened up her hand, revealing my key as if she hadn't just done something to alter it. I didn't reach out to grab it immediately. I knew something was different about it, but I just couldn't put my finger on it.

Natalia gave me a wide smile as she placed the key back around my neck. "Don't worry Nicholas, I just made two simple modifications."

I raised one of my eyebrows.

"I'm not coming with you, but I want to make sure that I'm there if you need me, so your key now has a direct link to me. It works exactly like how using a normal portal key works, but instead of thinking about where you want to go, you will only have to think about wanting to speak to me and I'll answer." She chewed on her bottom lip in a nervous way. "It is a little new for me, this kind of manipulation of portals and their keys, so if you do wish to speak to me your physical body in Purgatory will be out of commission. We'll be speaking in a more out of body state, therefore I would choose a good time and a safe place whenever you decide you need me."

She placed her hand on my chest, right over where the key hung. She continued before I could question anything. "Also, I've made it so when you do return you won't have to think about where you want to go. I've made this your primary location. Your home. So, whether you are in a crisis or not, you will be led here no matter what." Her words sent warmth around me. She knew just as much as I did what this home meant to me and if I ever had any choice as to where I felt safest, this would be my first and only option. My eyes cut to my father who gave me a simple nod as if he agreed with my every thought.

The moment was cut short by one of the two people in the room that could ruin this. "Woah! You aren't coming?" Reese exclaimed.

Natalia moved her dark waves over her shoulder. "Sadly no. I would love to, but there are times when Zane is actually right and this is one of those times. My people can't afford for me to be gone for however long this adventure will take."

"We'll be sure to bring Isabel back for you to finish on your own terms." Elise wiped her hands on her thighs and jumped off the counter. "I'll be happy to see one *blonde* get fucking ripped apart." She narrowed her eyes at Reese as she walked past him, ramming her body into his before she made her way to the couch.

"I will be so fucking happy when your ass gets handed to you down there and I can just sit and watch, deciding whether to help you."

Elise blinked innocently at him. "Oh alright. How do you plan to defend yourself down there without your pretty weapons? Heard they got rid of all the weapons left on the lawn after the fight."

Reese opened his mouth to fight back but I placed a hand on his chest, stopping him. "She makes a point."

Elise stuck her tongue out at my best friend who was literally fuming.

"I wouldn't say that just yet," my father chimed in, as he rounded the couch, wagging his finger. He disappeared down the hall and I heard him climbing the stairs. I caught Daya and Alex'sattention.

"Don't look at me," Alex shook her head, letting her eyes travel to her mother. Daya lightly pressed her fingers to her mouth, but a smile peeked out. I turned to the sound of my father entering the room again. He held out his hands to each of us, a weapon dangling from his fingers.

"Oh my fucking god!" Reese shouted, grabbing the sleek wood bow from my father's hand. He ran his hand over its arch, the rich maple wood coloring coming through and let his fingers glide across the silk string. It was pristine and looked brand new. I blinked over to the sword in my father's other hand. He reached out and grabbed my hand, placing the sword in it.

It had weight that I was used to, but I hadn't held a sword in what felt like forever, so the muscle memory was slowly coming back. The steel blade seemed to almost sparkle in the sunlight. The hilt was black leather wrapped tight and strong. I twirled the sword in my hand, missing this feeling so much. "Dad, I don't know what to say."

"A thank you sounds pretty normal to me," Dani offered, watching us as she sat back on the couch cushions.

"Well yeah, thank you." My father shrugged off both of our thanks and placed his hands on his hips. "I just knew the guy to do it, Daya is the one who designed them." Daya clapped her hands in front of her chest.

"Now they've been infused with angelic magic already. Of course, if you want to add your own, by all means," my father suggested.

"Oh, they'll need all the help they can get," Elise added, sarcastically.

I let my eyes glaze over the sword some more, letting my own angelic magic out and felt the hum of the already infused magic mix with my own. It was heady, the feeling of angelic power being heightened through the use of a catalyst. I was still looking at my sword when I said, "so when do we leave?"

"I think bright and early tomorrow will do. Unless you are eager to get started," Natalia answered.

Reese snorted. "Oh yeah, I'm totally excited to go into demon territory with not only Lilith on our asses, but soulless demons and a raging sociopath

Enchanter."

"You could have just said, tomorrow is fine," I said, shaking my head. He pulled his hair into a messy bun and shrugged playfully.

"You follow our lead while we're there and behave, so that I don't have to kill you myself and make a bigger mess than necessary. Got it?" Elise grumbled moving past us as she headed towards the bathroom down the hall.

Placing my sword against the couch, I shuffled around the coffee table to Natalia. I'd had something playing on my mind for quite some time, but seeing as I hadn't had any real time to talk to her for a while. She looked at me expectedly. "Can we talk?"

"Of course, Nicholas," she answered, almost floating as she followed behind me as I guided us to the hallway and right in front of my bedroom door. I leaned against the wall, exhaling. Natalia didn't look impatient as she waited for me to start talking.

I ran my hand over the back of my neck. "I wanted to talk to you about what you said when I was in Oculus, during the whole 'figure out Dani's situation' mission I was on."

She nodded gracefully as if she was sure she knew where I was going with this but wanted me to complete my thought before she interjected.

"You said that there were things missing from my head. That's not something you just forget, but I had to at the time. Now, despite everything happening it's becoming something I'm wondering about, and I didn't know if you'd had any time to look more into it."

Natalia licked her bottom lip before also leaning against the wall, her arm making a soft thud. "Nicholas, I can promise you I have not forgotten and in between my other duties I've tried my best to look into that when I could. I haven't found anything of merit. Nothing I'd want to bring to your attention.

"What I can say is that I would need to see into your mind in greater lengths. Whether I come to you, or you come to Oculus, but without your presence I can only do so much. Whoever did what they did knew exactly what they were doing."

I wasn't necessarily feeling defeated at her words, but having an explanation about something having to do with me would have been great right about now. This trip to Purgatory would be the biggest distraction from my current investigation into my life, then again, focusing on the mission would be just a tiny bit difficult with the *most* attractive distraction I'd ever seen.

I felt Natalia touch my shoulder, causing me to blink back over to her. Her honey-colored eyes were soft and inviting. "I know you've had a hard few months, so I didn't push. Whenever you're ready to proceed, I'm here.

When you come back and this is all finished, we'll start to figure this thing out."

"I like the sound of that. The confidence in us coming back is always nice to hear." I smirked at her, causing her to giggle.

She reached towards my face and held my cheek, letting her thumb slide over my skin. Her hand was warm and comforting. "And maybe while you're there, you can release some of this sadness you're harboring."

My heart stopped and my breathing fell off course. I reared back from her touch as if she'd just shocked me. Sadness? I didn't feel sad, I couldn't. Not when we were about to go right into one of the darkest places I've read about. I needed to be focused and on guard. I had to steel myself for what was to come. I couldn't cry and fall apart right now.

I was fine. Fine, fine, just fucking fine.

I noticed as she brought her hand down to her side as she watched me carefully. I reached for my shirt collar and started fidgeting with it. I had to leave Jonah and my thoughts and feelings about the whole situation here. I couldn't bring them with me.

"Natalia?" A voice tore through my panic. Dani's soft questioning voice. My heart settled and my breathing started to return back to its normal pattern. My anxiety was more aware of itself at this moment when she was around. I liked her being around. I wanted to twirl each of her curls with my fingers, I wanted her to smile at me the way she had after our night in my bed.

Natalia peered over her shoulder at her. "Yes?"

Dani snuck a glance at me, then back at Natalia. "If you guys are done, can I talk to you?"

The High Priestess opened her mouth, but then closed it. She looked at me, unsure if our conversation was over. I ran a hand through my hair roughly and shook my head. "Yeah, we're done. You can use my room if you want."

"Nicholas, I…" Natalia started, but I put my hand up to stop her words, interrupting her with my own. "Go talk, I'm fine. Promise."

I pushed the door open for them as Natalia gave me one last look before entering. Dani kept her head down, not in meekness, but so she didn't have to continually catch my eye. Smart move. When she walked past me into my room, her hand brushed mine and I could almost feel her bristle a bit at the contact, but then I heard her sharp intake of breath, as if that small simple touch had her feeling the same way I felt.

My heart rampaged in my chest as I closed the door behind them.

4

DANI

I took a breath right when I heard the door click behind me. The tingling in my hand from just the small feel of his skin on mine was like an electric shock that I didn't think I would still be feeling after all this time apart. I didn't have time to ponder on that or on *him*, even though my mind wanted to more often than I felt comfortable admitting. Every part of his demeanor had me feeling that he was sorry, but that just wasn't enough. If I were a more forgiving person and probably much, much weaker I would have melted at the way his presence made me feel, but I wasn't that person. I never would be.

Fuck, did I really even know *myself* after everything? I was continuously getting reacquainted with this side of myself that wanted to appear and disappear at the oddest times. I didn't know how to speak to it, and I've never had the best patience…

"Dani." Natalia's voice echoed through my thoughts so easily that I wasn't startled with the fact that she was much closer to me than I had originally thought. I took in her posture and cool attitude, trying to mimic even a fraction of the regality that she had.

I stepped back, collecting my thoughts before I spoke. "What you said in there about using his key to speak to you…is that just for him or any of us?"

Natalia chuckled and walked towards Nicholas's desk near the far wall. "Of course, I am here for any of you. It is his key, but the power is for you all to use if you need it."

"So…you just laid your hand on his key and poof new and improved key?" I tapped my index finger on my chin. "No need for my hair this time," I added sarcastically.

The High Priestess placed a hand over her mouth and actually for the first time since I met her, she looked embarrassed. Her honey-colored eyes were wide with apology and maybe just a tiny bit of humor; humor which I mirrored back to her.

She moved her delicate fingers away from her face. "Dani, my deepest apologies for that. There is really no excuse. Certain pieces of a person can be used for many things, good and bad."

"No excuse, *that* you are right about. I'm not mad though, so you can simmer down with that really strong nervous smell you have radiating from you." I gave her a cheeky smile as I crossed my arms over my chest. "Do you just keep a stash of all of our hair or whatever else somewhere in your humble abode in Oculus?"

She gave me a pointed look to let me know that I was no longer funny, but a small smile peeked out from her lips. "Of course not, actually it was just you. Isabel said…" She trailed off before she could say anymore. That name had my skin burning and made the demonic shadow in me want to lose control, but I heard a small hiccup and stopped. All the raging and anger ceased when I noticed Natalia wiping under her eyes. Even her tears seemed to glisten with beauty, it was truly unfair.

Natalia placed a hand over her chest as if she was steadying her heart rate. "I really am truly, truly sorry for not seeing things sooner. I would tell her everything, she was my confidant and she made it seem like it was a good idea at the time, that even if things went badly, I had a way to get to you if you escaped or went rogue. I didn't know that using it to help Nicholas would also help her, Markus and *Lilith*. She had everything so well planned with the help of all of us putting things right into place. She was right under my nose, Dani." She let her eyes flutter closed as she took in a deep breath that came out shaky when she exhaled. "I should have noticed weird behavior; I should have noticed all the times she was gone for long periods and when she would come back as if she was always there."

She was beating herself up, but at the same time maintaining a solid confident front. She reminded me of a well-muscled angel I knew. "Natalia, stop. It's alright. No one blames you, absolutely *no one*. Honestly, it's all about what you do with the information you have now, and you've been on our side, so just stop. The constant 'I'm sorry's' are just going to piss me off more than anything. So long as you don't have some mysterious stash of our hair follicles somewhere, we are good."

The High Priestess seemed to take my advice as she laughed. She rolled her shoulders and regained her previous cool bravado. "Dani, I'm here for all of you. My knowledge is your knowledge as far as I'm concerned."

I nodded towards my feet as I moved over towards the bed, not sitting on it. That bed had too many memories. When I looked up, she was staring at me, her head tilted and the light that shone from the window made the glitter on her dark skin sparkle even more.

I scrunched my lips up and towards the side of my mouth, trying not to let her words affect me. "Are you worried about Isabel? About us facing her?"

"Are you?"

I shrugged. "No. If I get the chance to get my hands around her throat it's over for her. she and Lilith can burn in the fire of their own making as far as I'm concerned."

"We both know it won't be that easy no matter how much reliance you have in your skills."

"I think you underestimate the power of revenge and fury." I tossed a chunk of my curls over my shoulder. I thought back to the last time I was in this room. The moment those two feelings took up residence in my body. It was heady, that feeling. Nicholas had looked so regretful telling me about Elise, but my feelings about it all wouldn't have changed despite who told me and when. It was the principle. Elise didn't have the balls to truly explain herself that day or any time after that and I'd pushed away the one person I'd considered holding close since my time in Purgatory started; the minute he opened his perfect fucking mouth it was like the spell that we had both been under had broken and I was no longer in some kind of Nicholas Cassial trance. The kind of trance that had me thinking my surroundings could change, but I could still be me. And Nicholas, being who he is, tried to place us under that same spell again by calling me important to him one of the last times we spoke and well, I wasn't quite convinced regardless of how sincere it sounded.

No matter how adorable he looked, giving me puppy dog eyes whenever his brown eyes seemed to find me.

I would make him fight for me. *As he should.*

I hadn't realized that Natalia had moved closer to me, and I took a small step back, needing space. As if my intruding thoughts could somehow be read by her once she was close enough to me. "Dani, let me tell you that I understand the need for revenge, but I wouldn't let it cloud your judgment. I want to see her hurt more than anyone, but my head is always level, I know how to bring myself back from my rage and remember who I am."

I blinked, really taking in her words. She always spoke as if she understood my feelings, my motivations. My time spent in Oculus with her had been enlightening, since I tried to avoid Elise at all costs and Natalia made it easy coming with me as I explored. She tried to talk me down during my moments of pure insanity. She didn't have all the answers, as crazy as that seemed, but she had become a confidant even through all of her own emotions.

"Do you doubt me?" I questioned, looking up at her quizzically.

Natalia shook her head vigorously. "Of course not. I believe in you tremendously. My only quarrel is that you are going into this with less than great relationships."

I propped myself on top of Nicholas's end table next to his bed. "Do tell."

Natalia rubbed her hands together and the spot between her perfectly arched eyebrows wrinkled. "You are clearly fully aware of this disconnect you have with Elise…" I opened my mouth to speak, but she shot her hand up to stop me. "Which I'm sure you can work out on your own, but your angelic companions are a different story entirely."

I tapped my index finger against my bottom lip, rolling my eyes. "Beating around the bush really isn't your style, you know. If you want to ask me about Nicholas, you can."

The High Priestess looked towards where the living room sat beyond the wall she stared at, as if she could see right through it. "A conversation might be in order."

"Then he can talk to me."

It was her turn to roll her eyes and it almost made me laugh to watch her perform such a casual gesture. "You say that as if it's so simple."

"Because it is."

"Put yourself in his shoes, Dani."

I bit down on my tongue so hard I tasted blood. This was ridiculous. "I don't have to. He can say he's sorry and that he cares all he wants, but that's not what I want to hear. I appreciate his words, I do." I placed both my hands on the sides of my head and ran them through my hair, ripping through the small tangles I felt. The pain somehow easing my annoyance. "I won't make things awkward for either of us. He's the one that keeps staring at me all the time, maybe you should have this conversation with him. It won't be my fault if he gets torn to pieces because he couldn't stop watching me." I let out a frustrated groan as if the thought of him getting torn to pieces didn't make my chest constrict.

Natalia nodded slowly and placed a hand on my knee. "I will only say this once and then I'll drop it, alright?"

I got off the end table and rocked back on my heels as I waited for her to say what she needed to say.

"You are fully entitled to how you feel, but when he does talk to you hear him out."

"I already told you if he wants to talk to me, he can talk to me."

Natalia tilted her head in my direction as if silently questioning my words. "But are you prepared to *listen* and perhaps forgive, or will you act like you're listening and then remain in this same state of mind." There was no inflection like she wanted me to answer, but it was like she wanted me to marinate with her words.

If he wanted to talk, I would listen…at least I assumed I would listen. *Fuck*, as much as I liked Natalia, she was annoying as hell.

I glanced down at the ground, digging the toe of my boot into the cream-colored carpet. I let out a huff, shrugging. Without looking at her I let her in on my thoughts. "That all depends on what he says, now doesn't it."

"I suppose it does," she answered, walking past me towards the door. "I am sorry about your hair, again. I promise I'll ask next time."

I spun around following her towards the door. "The answer will be no, so let's just make that clear." I gave her a snarky smile before grabbing the door handle and walking out. I hit a hard body that I was all too familiar with.

I instinctively lifted my hand and placed it on his chest. He was warm and solid. His heartbeat was steady but beating so loud I'm surprised the house didn't vibrate. I counted to three before I looked up at his face and saw that he was looking down at me and that his hands were on my waist. His eyes were a little sad as if he was remembering all the time I spent in his arms and how much we both had enjoyed it.

I'd let him keep those thoughts. I just so happened to enjoy them myself.

I wrapped his shirt in my hand and lightly pushed him away, the warmth from his palms taken away. He blinked rapidly as if he had suddenly brought himself back to reality, realizing that it wasn't just the two of us.

"Sorry, I didn't mean to…" He trailed off, motioning his hand towards the open door to his room. Natalia looked back and forth between us, pressing her lips together, hard.

I cocked my head to the side, waiting to see if he would keep talking. It was extremely funny watching him be flustered by my very presence. Not funny enough to let him kiss me again, but funny, nonetheless.

Nicholas scrubbed a hand down his face, swallowed and then proceeded to start again. "My dad is making food and I was sent to let you know."

"That sounds delightful, Nicholas." Natalia looked over at me with one of her eyebrows raised.

I trailed my eyes from his thick dark hair all the way down his long legs, before biting my bottom lip. His father's cooking was something I had missed, and Maurice Cassial hadn't done anything to push me away so why punish him by not enjoying his food. "Yeah, sounds great, Nicholas." His shoulders tensed and went rigid.

Natalia gave each of us one final look before getting the hell out of this tension-filled hallway we stood in. Nicholas reached up to rub the back of his neck, which caused his shirt to ride up. The small sliver of skin that was revealed right above his waistband instantly caught my attention. I rubbed the heels of my hands into my eyes forcibly telling them that they could not stare at parts of his skin that led to other parts of him that I couldn't help but remember.

Thoroughly remember.

I gave him a tight-lipped smile and started to walk past him, but I stopped. I may have been upset with him, but he had made it clear that he cared a while back, so maybe I could do the same. That didn't mean I was going easy on him though.

I leaned my body inward a little, letting pieces of my hair touch his bicep. "I'm happy you're alright." I knew Natalia would make sure he had everything he needed to heal at home, and I trusted his father to be the best nurse he could be, but I couldn't deny the tiny piece of myself that thought maybe the wounds could have been too much. He could have been fine one day and not the next.

He let out a shaky breath and looked down his shoulder at me. "I'm fine, thanks."

His voice sounded like he was trying to convince *himself* of that fact. Convince himself that he was fine. The silence between us spoke volumes to me. I would never say I knew Nicholas really, really well, but I'd known him long enough to know when he wasn't being completely honest. His eyes searched my face, and his lips moved a bit as if he wanted to say something and I stayed put, waiting.

"Dani, I…"

His words were cut off by an annoyed voice that rattled against my eardrums. My hands balled into fists at my sides, my nails digging into my palms.

"Did you two figure out your lovers quarrel yet or are you going to make us all wait to eat?" Elise asked, her hands on her hips.

Nicholas cleared his throat. "Yeah, we're coming."

She narrowed her eyes at him, but then glanced over at me and licked her front teeth. Her gray eyes pierced into my brown ones as if she was sizing me up. "She sure does know how to hold a grudge, doesn't she." She didn't let me respond as she twirled around and walked back into the living room.

She was a mood killer if I ever met one. I inhaled a deep breath and tried to think of any reason not to yank her outside and rip her to shreds. I felt fingertips graze mine and I looked down to see Nicholas not quite touching me, but almost ghosting the pads of his fingers against mine.

"Come on," he said, walking away from me and taking his electricity inducing fingers with him.

The wind picked up as we all huddled around Natalia in front of the building that had once looked like an abandoned church. The place where we had met with her during one of our trips here. Where there was once broken pews and pounds of dust, now sat a grand building made of red clay stones and the pews were solid oak without a speck of dirt on them. The windows created a kaleidoscope of colors as the sun snuck out from behind some clouds. Everyone looked so antsy around me, as if they were eager to either get this over with or they were silently wishing they didn't have to be here at all. It didn't take a genius to figure which person fit which scenario.

I had watched from a distance as Nicholas and his father shared words outside his house before we left this morning. There were no tears, but it looked meaningful, and their ending hug spoke volumes. Reese had gotten a hug as well, one with just as much love and devotion as Mr. Cassial had given his son. It dawned on me that the blonde angel never really spoke about his parents besides that one time we'd talked and even then, it was hard to get a true grasp on his family situation; not that he would ever tell me the entire story anyway. I had gotten a *look* from Nicholas's father before I'd backed away to walk into Natalia's waiting portal to take us to Oculus.

He had told me to be safe and the typical things I was sure normal people said for stuff like this, but then he gave me a *look*. He had looked over my shoulder at where his son was speaking with Natalia, and I followed his eyes. When I looked back at him, he had slightly raised one of his eyebrows and looked at me with the face of someone who was trying not to meddle but knew there was no way that they couldn't. He had a son and he cared for him. He wanted Nicholas to be happy and thrive. Surprisingly, or maybe unsurprisingly, I wanted that stupid fucking attractive man to be happy and thriving as well.

"Everyone one hundred percent sure this is what we should be doing?" Reese asked, reaching behind his head and fiddling with his new bow that he had strapped across his chest.

Elise scoffed. "If you want to back out now, that's completely fine. Then we can add real muscle to this *team* and bring Sir Muscles over here." She nodded over to where Zane stood next to Natalia. His plain black vest was buttoned, but he wore nothing underneath. His various tattoos were displayed down his arms.

Reese brought his blonde eyebrows together. "I wasn't backing out. I'm just double checking." He pointed his finger at Elise.

"Can you guys just leave whatever this—," Nicholas pointed between them. "Is here and not bring it to Purgatory. I have a bad feeling both of you are going to get us killed because you can't shut the fuck up." He rolled his eyes, taking in a breath before tugging his portal key out of his shirt.

I clucked my tongue, choosing to let him have my attention for a moment. "Someone is a bit feisty today."

He scratched his eyebrow. "I'm not being feisty."

"You're being a little feisty." Reese answered, tilting his hand back and forth. "But fine, I'll behave."

We all looked at Elise whose black hair swished around her earlobes as she stared back at us. "We all know I can never and will never promise you any of that bullshit."

"You really put your trust in them to fix this?" Zane's deep, gravelly voice rang out around us. He didn't seem to mind that we all heard him speculate about us.

Natalia let out a small chuckle that caused her shoulders to bounce. "Yes, Zane. I really do." She winked over at me and started to walk into the middle of our makeshift circle.

"I want to ask you all to please, please be careful. I know you're doing this of your own volition, and I know you have your skills, but be smart about your decisions and your movements going forward." The High Priestess pressed; the colors of the stained-glass windows behind us bouncing off of her glittering shoulders.

I crossed my arms over my chest, tapping my fingers on my biceps. "I think we are aware of what lies in Purgatory."

Natalia hummed. "Well of course, but after everything do you honestly believe that place is exactly the same as when you left it."

"She has a point." Nicholas added, shrugging his shoulders. "We should all be on guard going in."

Elise let out a disgusted sound and stalked over to Natalia. I watched Zane bristle a bit at her proximity to the High Priestess. Natalia simply watched as Elise stopped in front of her. She pushed out her bottom lip in a pout. "I'm so fucking touched by your concern, but lets be honest, there is no *real* fool proof way to keep your wits about yourself in that place. I'm sure every Enchanter down there is now ten times as crazy since we've probably lit a fire under your little girlfriend's asshole."

"For fucks sake, you don't have to be such a raging bitch." I pointed out, watching as she slowly turned her head towards me. "How about you save all that energy for someone deserving of it and spare us the sound of your fucking voice."

Both Zane and Nicholas stepped forward to potentially break up any fight that might occur. I didn't want to fight right now as much as my body would have loved it. The shadows inside of me were practically whining to get some action as of lately. I would do what Natalia wanted though. I would be smart about my movements, but as much as I hated to admit it, Elise had a point. You could have the best laid plans in the world, but Purgatory could swallow you up if you weren't prepared for its mind fuck capabilities.

Elise let out a loud, cackling laugh. "She wants us to be fucking smart. We're bringing two angels into Purgatory, while trying to destroy Lilith of all entities. I wouldn't call us smart. Most people would think we all have death wishes."

"Didn't you agree to this plan of having us come along?" Reese said.

"Lilith and I have the love of chaos in common. I want to see the looks on your angelic baby faces when you finally see that the clusterfuck that's disguising itself as the perfect realm you have here is nothing compared to my home." Elise stretched her arms out above her head.

"We get it, Purgatory and Heaven's Gate are different. That's not new logic." Nicholas informed, readjusting his sword that sat behind his back, his tone just hovering at the level of exasperation.

Elise sighed. "Yes, Nicholas, but Purgatory has never pretended to be something it's not." I noticed Nicholas flex his hands and fingers as he tried to keep his cool.

"Okay, I'm with the Soul Seether on this, I'm tired of hearing your fucking voice so can we please go." Reese took a skinny hair tie from around his wrist and started to put his long hair into a bun.

Natalia cleared her throat. "I can open up a portal to Purgatory but I've never been there so I can't tell you exactly where you'll land..." She was cut off by Elise who walked up next to Nicholas.

"I know where we're going."

I gave her a skeptical look as I approached where they stood. "You do?"

"I told you guys before that I had a place we could stay, but of course, just like before no one fucking listens to me."

"And it's safe?" Nicholas questioned, fingering the portal key around his neck.

Elise scrunched up lips together, thinking. "Don't ask stupid questions. This is the best and only option you have, so deal with it, pretty boy." She reached out her hand towards him, palm up.

Nicholas peered down at her empty hand and then returned to her face. She started to tap her foot impatiently. "What are you waiting for?" I asked her, confused.

"His key," she said smoothly.

"So first you want us to follow you into some place that only you know of and now you want his key? You sure you aren't turning on us already." Reese probed, the distrust in his voice as clear as day.

Elise narrowed her gray eyes at him. "Blondie, I need his key to open up a portal to where I want us to go. Unless you desire the little witch here to drop us into a pool of angry demons. Would you like that?"

Nicholas cut his eyes to Natalia, almost as if he was looking to her for permission to hand his key over to anyone else. Her eyes sparkled with warmth. "It's your personal key, Nicholas. There aren't any restrictions on it, so do what you want." A petite Enchanter cautiously walked up to Natalia tapping her on the shoulder and speaking softly in her ear. The High Priestess nodded with a kind smile, and the Enchanter scurried away.

"I'm afraid my duty calls me away, but I do want to see you off. Remember that I am here to guide you if you so wish." She walked over to where we all stood, Zane right at her heels.

Nicholas hesitantly unclasped the key from around his neck and dropped it into Elise's waiting hand. He pressed his lips together and then let his brown eyes land on Zane. "Take care of my dad, okay." His voice was steady, but I could tell his anxiety was through the roof. I could smell it, along with every other emotion the rest of them were feeling. Nicholas had a way of becoming the thing that went to the forefront of my mind and I really needed to figure out how to stop that shit.

Zane's usually rough glare softened a bit. "Of course, Nicholas." Natalia placed a hand on his massive bicep as she added some comforting words of her own. "We both will."

Elise started lifting the key in the air, but I reached out to grab her wrist. Her shoulders stiffened. "Where are you taking us? We both know it's not to a *friend*." We deserved to know where the fuck she was having us stay.

She ripped her wrist away from me, rolling it. The key dangled from her fingertips. "And we both know I don't do friendships. *Trust*, Dani." She wrinkled her nose at me. "It's what this all boils down to, right."

This bitch really had the *audacity* to expect me to trust her. A growl sat low in my throat as she shrugged away from me. Maybe being in Purgatory would get her talking or at least make her feel at home enough to be honest with me. Natalia wanted me to hear out Nicholas, but did that mean that I also had to be as open to hearing out this sadistic asshole? I shook my head, letting my curls dance around my shoulders and then settle against my chest again.

"One rule when we get there, you psycho. Keep that *fucking* tail to yourself," Reese said each word as if he wanted them to sink in. I observed as each word hit her hard exterior and she smiled.

"No promises," Elise said, looking coyly at him. She lifted her arm back up and started to make a circle to open up the portal.

Zane took Natalia by the shoulder and led her back a few steps. Natalia gazed at me and gave me a friendly nod. We had spoken earlier before we went to Nicholas's house to pick them up. It was more of the same, more of her mother hen type nature, but she continued to implore the same thing to me over and over again. She was worried about me, but I didn't really understand why. I could handle myself. I always had...I was designed to be able to fuck up anyone who thought differently. Natalia didn't know much about Purgatory, but sometimes it caught me off guard how correct she was about certain things. Her words from the prior conversation still haunted me. *Damn* her.

Never forget who you are when you're down there. The darkness is familiar but that doesn't always mean it's the right choice. Always remember who you are.

I knew Purgatory like the back of my hand. It had never felt like home, but it *was* familiar like she claimed. I would never shy away from its darkness, then again, why was I letting her words affect me like this. I was giving them much more thought that I originally assumed I would.

The light from the portal started to blind us. Elise did a giddy little shimmy before tossing the key back to Nicholas. She stepped into the portal and disappeared. Reese followed behind, hesitantly almost looking like he wanted to run in the other direction rather than step foot into this fucking portal. Nicholas clasped the key back around his neck and tucked it back into his shirt.

I tilted my face up to look at him. His profile caught me off guard. He looked so ready for this, yet there was something under the surface. Something I couldn't pinpoint. It was something I wasn't used to seeing when I really focused on him.

It was like he could feel me staring at him because he eventually looked down at me, right as he was about to walk forward. "What?" His voice was deep, and his eyes bore down on me.

I could feel the corner of my lips twitching upwards. Purgatory could be a scary place, but it could also be a place to let go of your inhibitions if you let it. It could even ease the mind of an over-thinker. I licked my lips and blinked up at him. "You plan to be more than just an angelic night light down there?"

He looked over his shoulder at the portal and then back at me, tilting his head to the side. "I planned on it."

I extended my arm and cupped his chin, letting my thumb graze over his jaw. The scar under his eye ticked as he kept my eye contact. His chest rose and fell, pretending like it didn't want to rampage at my closeness. "Good. I look forward to seeing what kind of angelic magic you have in store, Nicholas. I have a feeling you've been withholding. Although I, for one, can't wait to see you handle your *sword* again." I let the innuendo roll off my tongue. I wanted to rile him up, but I, in no way, shape or form was allowing him to get his *sword* anywhere near me until he told me what I wanted to hear.

I tapped my fingers against his cheek as I slid my hand away and sauntered off towards the portal. My angelic light whispered and moved inside of me, but I didn't speak back. I couldn't have it hold me back even if I knew how to *fucking* talk to it. I wasn't choosing one over the other, but there wasn't much of a choice when the scales were unbalanced in my favor anyway. I knew who I was though, I wouldn't forget that. Despite what Natalia thought.

I heard him shuffle around and follow behind me as I stepped through the glowing light of the portal, catching Natalia and Zane in my peripheral vision. Nicholas would have to get used to that now that we were heading into my side of the realms. Whether he did it blindly or with open eyes, he would have to follow me. *Trust*, as Elise so eloquently put it.

And I could guarantee when it came to me, he didn't mind.

5

NICK

The portal seemed to suck us in and then spit us out as if it knew where we were going. I landed right behind Dani nearly running into her with the way that magic portal pushed me out. The moment my feet hit the ground in Purgatory, it was like everything changed. The air was thicker and heady. Wherever we landed smelled like what lingers when a candle is snuffed out. It wasn't dark, but there was no real sunlight anywhere, just flickers of light from the surrounding area. I had no clue if time was the same down here as it was in Heaven's Gate. It looked like it was mid evening but it very well could have been early morning here. There were trees behind us that stayed still as statues, as not even a gust of wind whipped by. I looked forward and saw a bridge. It was wide and curved upwards, made of weathered stone. Water lay beneath it, still and almost peaceful. Candles hung from the columns along the bridge, casting a glowing pathway for us. Their flames were a raging red, overpowering the oranges and yellows of a normal flame.

There was a silence I wasn't used to. It was a bit soothing but in Purgatory

I didn't know if soothing was really all that great.

"This way," Elise ordered, marching ahead of us.

"Are you going to tell us where we're going?" I asked, suspicious.

"You'll know when we get there," she answered, not bothering to look back at me.

Reese walked beside me as we both begrudgingly followed behind her. "I don't like this."

I readjusted my sword that was slung along my back. "Neither do I, but this is all we've got for now."

"Yeah, that makes me more nervous. We are trusting Elise of all people to find a place to keep us *safe*." Reese let out an erratic laugh as if he couldn't believe the words coming out his mouth.

"You two fuckers could have stayed at home with Daddy Cassial alright, so please shut your fucking mouths," Elise yelled from the front of the line.

I heard the crunch of something hard under my feet. I stopped walking to bend down and get a better look. I grazed my hand over what I realized was broken stone. I followed the path and noticed that most of the stones were broken, either completely split or shattered into pieces causing it to resemble gravel. The light from the bridge allowed me to see what should have been grass, but it looked like it had been begging for water for quite some time. The coloring was brown and there were patches that were merely spots of dirt.

"You get too far behind, you'll get lost." I raised my head up to see Dani hovering over me. She had her hands on her hips, tilting her head to the side.

"Is all of Purgatory like this?" I asked, pushing off the ground and towering over her again.

She looked around as if none of this was new to her, but there was something about the way her shoulders seemed a little too tense. "No, some parts are better than others. This isn't even the worst of it actually."

"And you have no idea where she could be taking us?" I questioned, looking back towards the bridge, noticing Reese starting to look back and slow his pace.

Dani began to walk around me and shook her head. "No, Nicholas. I haven't had a full conversation with her in months. Besides, there are a lot of things about Elise I don't know, so this will be a fun discovery for all of us." She turned around and I watched her walk away for a few seconds, taking in the entire shape of her that was illuminated by the candle lights.

I ran a hand through my hair, rallying my thoughts before I jogged over to the others, who just happened to be halfway onto the bridge.

The bridge was sturdy and solid stone. As we walked across it the air seemed to range from incredibly thick like before to normal everyday air. It was as if I had to adjust my breathing every few minutes. The smoke from the flames dissipated in the air and the candle wicks crackled a bit. I wasn't used to being able to hear every little thing, but now that I could it was overwhelming.

"We're on the outskirts, if you must know," Elise offered. She pointed towards the northeast and my gaze followed her extended arm. A large building that looked almost medieval from this distance sat on a tall hill. Everything looked like a dark shadow from here, but I could make out its pointed towers and the ominous way about it. "That is where the enemy lies."

"Lilith is up there?" I shook my shoulders, a chill running down my spine as I stared at the large castle-like structure from this distance.

"Mhmm, why are you scared, pretty boy?" Elise taunted, quickly starting to walk forward again. I cleared my throat as I noticed Dani staring up in that direction as well. Her shoulders were tense, but she simply moved her hair off on her shoulders and kept walking. I really needed to fucking talk to her about everything.

"We aren't scared, you asshole, we just want to know where we will be sleeping tonight since you want to gate-keep information," Reese grumbled, tucking a piece of his blonde hair behind his ear.

Once we were off the bridge the stone ground carried on into what looked like an array of houses or hostels. Most of them were brick while others were pure cement. The roofs were almost clipped in structure, the top peaks seeming to bend in and were black like the sky above them. The blown-out candle smell lingered but now the overwhelming scent of birch and honey filled my nostrils. It was enticing but not enough to make me lose my wits. There were a few lights on in various windows, but I saw no movement. Elise was walking with a purpose to our destination, not worried in the slightest about anything that could occur around us. There was a curve towards the left down the stone road, telling me there was more to this area, but any light that would guide my way looked as if it disappeared beyond what I could see.

"Outskirts?" I asked, remembering Elise's earlier words.

"Not quite the destitute area of our beloved Purgatory, but not the poshest environment either," Elise replied, shrugging before she looked up at one of the larger buildings. "Lilith doesn't quite care about these parts." The building was wider than it was tall, as if it housed multiple rooms, and there was a welcome sign hanging from a nail on the front door. Not something I expected to see down here. Especially since the word 'welcome' was painted in a neon pink.

I heard a door creak open and a head pop out. I looked over my shoulder at the building across from us. A girl with one long braid over her shoulder squinted her eyes at me, as if she was assessing every inch of me. She cocked her head to the side, giving me a small smile. Not a smile that made me feel any better about our situation, but it was a smile, nonetheless.

Movement caught my eye as I noticed someone in the window of the building next to hers. They simply stared, observing quietly. I set my focus back on the girl from before and her small eyes cut to the person next to me which I realized was Dani, she was taking in our surroundings, more than likely scanning the perimeter. I glanced back at the girl in the doorway and her eyes were wide as if she recognized who Dani was, but her look wasn't the nervous kind which I initially assumed. It was one of awe, like if she wanted to, she would have run up and asked for my pretty hybrid's autograph.

No...not *my*—she wasn't mine.

Elise knocked on the door and waited, impatiently, tapping her foot against the ground. After one minute she knocked again. She was about to knock again when the door swung open, stunning me into silence at what greeted us.

"Elise? Oh my god!" A girl with long hot pink hair exclaimed. One side of her head was shaved, leaving her long locks to cascade over one of her shoulders and past her stomach. She was a little taller than Elise and Dani, but not by much. Her skin was a golden brown and freckles surrounded her nose and cheekbones. The girl looked around the already annoyed demon and gawked at all of us behind her. "And you brought friends!"

Elise huffed. "Can we come in or not, Beetee?"

The girl looked flustered as if she was being rude and motioned for us to hustle inside. "Oh duh, come in, come in." Her voice was high-pitched and excited.

I looked behind me and noticed the girl from before was no longer there and neither was the one in the window. *Weird.* The door shut behind me and I immediately took in my surroundings. The entryway was small but not small enough to where we didn't have room to move around freely. I noticed a sitting area to my left with a large hearth fireplace and to my right looked like it led to a kitchen of some sort, but I wasn't sure. My eyes followed the stairs that led to the second floor as I heard footsteps above our heads. The pink haired girl rounded the desk that sat in front of us, her bright blue sundress swishing right above her knees as she walked and leaned over to lightly slap the bell that sat on top of the wood furnishing. The ringing was soft but alarming. She squealed a little and clapped her hands.

"I wondered when you were coming back, I assume you'll want your usual room?" The girl blinked over to Elise, patiently waiting for her reply.

"Usual room? I'm sorry, who the hell are you?" Dani didn't even try to hide her irritation in the slightest. She narrowed her gaze at the female who leaned over the counter she stood behind, her facial expression of pure helpfulness never wavering.

The girl slapped her forehead with the palm of her hand and released a small chuckle. She came around the counter and stood right in front of Dani. She extended her hand out for Dani to take. "I'm all out of sorts tonight. My apologies! I'm Beatrice, but everyone just calls me Beetee, I own this adorable little hostel you are standing in. I call her the Hearth. And it's such an extremely delightful and slightly terrifying pleasure to meet you, Soul Seether."

Dani blinked at Beetee in disbelief or amusement. I couldn't really tell.

Beetee wiggled her fingers as she waited patiently yet again.

"You know Dani?" I asked, curiously.

Beetee placed her hand over her chest. "Oh no, I don't *know* the Soul Seether. But with how much gossip there is going around about you, I feel like I do." She cupped a hand near her mouth, fake whispering towards Dani. "I am hoping you and I can totally be friends when this is over." Dani's mouth ticked up in a small smile.

"Can we get back to the whole how you know Elise thing?" Reese's voice rang out. I looked to my left and noticed he had wandered into the small lounge area, either scanning for issues or just being really fucking nosy.

Elise let out a loud groan, rubbing her temples with her fingertips. "Can we fucking not? This conversation already has me exhausted enough to want to decapitate everyone here, so literally stop."

"Actually, I think we would all love that answer, right about now," I admitted, hearing Elise literally growl in my direction.

Beetee snuck a glance over at Elise and laughed as if she thought the little psycho demon's reaction was hilarious. "Oh, stop it. Don't tell me you brought them here without any context, Ellie."

Elise's eyes widened and she turned to Beetee, her pale cheeks flaming a deep red.

"Me and Ellie have known each other for a long, long time. We were a thing for a while, but it didn't feel right, so we remained friends. I run this little hostel of sorts for demons and magical beings on the outskirts of that big scary castle up there on the hill. I've always had a room here for Ellie.

It can get kind of anxiety inducing there, so I keep my little place open for anyone needing a place. Demons, Enchanters, whoever really. They come and go as they please, it's usually much livelier here as nightfall approaches. Don't let this demon fool you though, she is a total squish." Beetee reached out and pinched Elise's cheek and tapped her nose with all the confidence in the world.

Reese choked with laughter as he came back to stand next to me, obviously done exploring for the time being. He held his stomach as he doubled over, taking deep breaths as he regained his composure. "I'm sorry, can we just rewind please. *Ellie*?"

"I would tread very carefully if I were you, Blondie. You are here because I brought you here. Don't think that I won't remove you from my presence just as fast," Elise threatened through clenched teeth.

Reese couldn't help himself though. "And you used to date?" His eyes bounced between the two of them, his eyebrows scrunching inward. "Wait, you actually enjoyed this one's company enough to *date* her?" I placed my foot on top of his own, hard, to cease his line of questioning.

Dani hummed as she adjusted the collar of the black leather jacket that she wore. "It's quite fascinating Reese. Nicknames are usually reserved for people who are really close," Dani tapped her chin, pressing her lips together as if she was in contemplation. "Like a *friend*. But we both know you don't do friends, isn't that right, *Ellie*?"

Elise stuck her tongue in her cheek but remained quiet as she looked over at her. Beetee cast a look of confusion in Dani's direction. "Doesn't *do* friends? Okay, I mean Ellie is a hard sell when it comes to friendship but believe me, she doesn't give half a mind towards people she doesn't consider a friend and you, Soul Seether was all she talked...ow!" Elise roughly tugged on the demon's long pink hair.

"I came here—we came here—for a place to stay, Beetee. Can you provide that or not?"

Beetee gave a bright smile full of white teeth. "Oh my god! Of course! It's been a bit slow with patrons as of lately. I'm not surprised though seeing as you've turned the realm upside down Soul Seether." She winked over at Dani as she placed her hands on her hips, her nails were each painted a different color.

I grabbed the strap pressed against my chest with both my hands, bringing my sword closer towards my neck as it slung across my back. The cold metal cooling my heating skin at the slightly awkward encounter in front of us. "You're aware of everything going on?"

"Everyone is. Pretty juicy gossip even if some of the details are likely muddled."

"So, you know why we're here? Were you *expecting* us?" I leaned forward a bit, prepared to listen to her answer carefully. Elise hadn't made it seem like wherever we were going was prepared for what we were doing. The dark-haired demon just looked annoyed at our entire conversation if I was being honest.

Beetee stuck her tongue out, licking her lips. "I wasn't expecting you of course. Ellie usually comes alone or with some wayward demons that need assistance. I don't really think twice when she's at my doorstep asking for help." Her eyes seemed to slide to the window behind me, as if she was momentarily caught in a quick memory. "The ones that you find in this side of Purgatory aren't fond of Lilith, not to say that her little followers aren't around. You might not believe it, but there are some Enchanters who regret siding with her in your little war a while ago."

"*Our little war?* Wait, you know what we are?" I pointed towards myself and then to Reese.

Beetee snorted, wrinkling her freckled nose, as if what I said was ridiculous. "Oh please, if you didn't smell like angels, your whole demeanor would give you away. It's adorable that you both think you can move around here unnoticed...as if you haven't already been noticed anyway."

"Hmm, alright, so you don't mind us being here, despite what that would mean with Lilith." She opened her mouth to answer but was quickly cut off by a sound to my left.

Reese huffed, ripping his bow and quiver over his head, holding them tight in his grip. "Fucking great! This place already gives me the creeps to begin with. I knew this was a bad fucking idea." He lifted his head towards the ceiling, shaking his head.

Dani chuckled, having moved over to the wooden counter. She slid her index finger over the top as if she was inspecting for dust. "Calm yourself with your whiny dramatics. What Beetee is trying to explain is that we are fine here, everyone here wants the same thing as us, so they won't get in our way, angel or not. Not everyone is as immediately discriminating as you, you know." She raised her eyebrows at Reese, who leveled his hazel eyes at her, but said nothing. "Besides, they should know not to get in my way." Translucent shadows emanated from her fingertips as she spoke.

Beetee cleared her throat. "To answer your question, you curious angelic thing, I don't mind at all. I don't mind a leader being in charge, but Lilith treats her reign like tyranny and throws out the demons that don't suit her. There are plenty of places like my little hostel riddled throughout Purgatory. She doesn't come around here because she simply doesn't care for what doesn't get in her way. I love bloodshed as much as the next demon, but sometimes there is a stopping point, you know?" She turned her head at footsteps coming down the stairs.

A large male demon with scars over his face and down one of his arms towards his wrists, steered her attention away from us. His other arm had scales of varying shades of gray overlapping that overtook his shoulder all the way to his fingertips. He glanced over to us, settling on Reese and me for a long moment before looking away. His eyes were curious and aware but not threatening. I could nearly feel the tension radiating off of my best friend as he kept his eyes trained on the demon before us. Beetee and the man exchanged words in low voices, and she patted his shoulder when they looked like they were done. He nodded and snuck a look over her shoulder at Dani. His eyes widened just like the girl across the street. He dipped his head down and let out a muffled, "*Soul Seether*" before retreating back up the stairs.

She really was like royalty in this place.

"Fuck, hope your head doesn't get too big while we're here," Elise taunted, tilting her head to the side.

"I came here for a reason and getting gawked over isn't one of them." Dani tapped her foot against the wood floor. She turned towards Beetee. "So, rooms?"

"Shouldn't we make some sort of legit plan now that we're here? We have an end goal but the path to get there is not even somewhat formed," I questioned, feeling anxiety start to settle into my bones. "Besides we left Oculus at like ten in the morning, you can't really be wanting us to go to sleep right now."

Dani leaned against the counter. The leggings she wore hugged her hips and thighs just right and I tried my hardest to keep my eyes from wandering anywhere they weren't supposed to. "If you must know it's like mid-day right now and I admire you wanting to just jump right in and believe me, I want to do the same, but you both need to settle into Purgatory for a night, release some of that angelic bravado in a probably mediocre night's sleep or a nap. Fuck, I would settle for some food right about now. Then we can set this path you want. You are in my world, so we play by my rules." She ruffled her hand through her hair, the curls bouncing around as they settled wherever they wanted. "You can do that, can't you *Nicholas*?" She caught her tongue between her teeth as she stared at me. Her brown eyes danced with amusement.

For the love of all that was ethereal she was the hottest thing I had ever laid my eyes on; she knew that I wanted her. I respected and admired her, but

I couldn't help admitting that I wanted her in the most disrespectful way, and I thought about that often, all the ways I wanted to have her. All to myself. If she just said the word, I would have my face between her legs before she even had time to blink. That wasn't enough for her, though.

And I understood that. Genuinely, I did.

Beetee looked from me to Dani and then back again. "Is this your guys' version of a weird staring contest or is there something I should know?"

Elise snickered. "You'll get used to it."

Beetee plastered on her sunshine smile again and gave me a meaningful look. "Well, Nicholas...I can call you Nicholas, right? You are safe to get some sleep here, I promise. Feel free to call me Beatrice if you like, but don't get offended if I don't immediately answer, I've just gotten so used to Beetee. You must know that Lilith already knows you've stepped foot in Purgatory so it's better that you get your bearings. You leave and come back covered in someone else's blood and I got you! I'm your girl!" Despite her words, she had this purposeful look on her face. She wanted me to heed her words and wholeheartedly trust her. Her eyes were a lilac purple, throwing me off guard, yet I felt like I wanted to trust her.

This was *about trust, wasn't it?*

I nodded, rubbing my hands down the front of my jacket and dipping them into my pants pockets. "Fine, we'll settle. Then tomorrow we make a solid plan or a form of one." I gave our host what I hoped was a charming smile. "Nick is fine and that's Reese." Reese gave a short wave.

"I prefer winging it, but whatever you fuckers want to do." Elise waved her hand in my direction, clearly annoyed.

"So, one room for girls, one room for boys? Then maybe some food and a small, but safe tour when you're all settled," Beetee offered looking around at us. Her purple eyes twinkled with delight.

Dani shook her head fiercely. "No. Fuck no. No, thank you. She can keep her room and I'll have one of my own if that's okay."

Beetee pushed her bottom lip out and shot a tentative glance over to Elise. "Ellie, what did you do?"

For a small, minuscule moment Elise's face morphed into something of regret, but she rallied and quickly scrubbed a hand down her face, turning on her heels away from us. Her black combat boots echoed along the floor as she started up the stairs. Beetee simply rolled her eyes and faced Dani again. "Okay, so a room for everyone?"

"We aren't quite as difficult so we can share," Reese answered, waving his hand towards Elise's retreating form.

The pink haired demon gave him a small smile and clapped her hands together. "Alrighty! Follow me!" She twirled around, making the ends of her dress propel upwards with her movement. We all trailed behind her as she led us up the stairs.

The hallway upstairs was wide enough so that Reese and I could walk side by side, making it so that we both almost completely shadowed Dani's small body in front of us. There were copper lanterns that hung from the wall on both sides, illuminating our pathway. I kept assuming every door we passed was ours, but Beetee kept walking. I noticed the intense hold that Reese had on his bow as he walked next to me. He'd have to wrangle that energy in and let it out only when necessary.

I ran right into Dani causing me to realize that we'd stopped walking. I looked to my left and noticed Elise leaning against one of the doors that lined the walls. Beetee smiled her shining white teeth over at Elise. "Don't worry, Ellie, your room is the same as always."

Elise gave her a tight-lipped smile that almost looked painful.

"Wow, your friend does all these nice things for you and your companions, and you can't even say fucking thank you. Although, I'm not surprised since you are the world's biggest bitch," Dani said, shaking her head at the floor.

"As much as I would love to see it, this hallway is much too small for a catfight. And my mind is far too overstimulated with our new surroundings for me to properly pay attention, if said catfight were to occur," Reese explained, earning an eye roll from each one of us.

Beetee's high-pitched voice broke the overwhelming tension. "It's totally fine! Ellie and I don't have the most conventional relationship and I don't take her stoic attitude to heart. You really can't take much to heart down here." She cocked her head towards Dani, a smile ticking at the corners of her mouth. "But! My heart is so full knowing that the Soul Seether is staying under *my* roof, despite the reasons for you being here. I mean what Lilith did to you was awful and you deserve revenge. I mean who knows maybe those other powers you've been harboring will..."

Dani's brown eyes shot straight into Beetee's lilac ones. I saw the way her jaw clenched as if she was grinding her teeth. "*Excuse me?*"

Beetee opened her mouth and then closed it, finally landing on the words she wanted. "The other powers you have, you know. Like the angelic...ow!" The pink-haired demon swung her head to where Elise was next to her and stomped on her foot.

"Beetee, shut the fuck up!"

"Woah, wait, you know?" I asked, stunned.

Beetee opened her mouth, but glanced over at Elise and quickly closed it. She awkwardly adjusted the strap of her sundress even though it looked perfectly fine. She was fidgeting and I could see her cheeks growing a hue of red under her brown skin. Elise let out a low chuckle as she stared at the ceiling. "Here we go."

"You fucking told her?!" Dani yelled, banging her fist into the wall. "And you just decided to leave me to just assume whatever about myself. You decide to tell your little secret friend and not, *I don't know*, the person it was happening to?"

Elise pushed her bottom lip out in a pout. "Ah and what exactly would you have done if I'd told you, huh? Put yourself in a corner and cried thinking about *what could have been*. Don't worry I'm sure the pretty angel boy over here has filtered through all the what ifs for you." Elise peeked over at me smirking.

Why was she making this so fucking difficult?

Dani's eyes became slits filled with rage and I instantly felt the need to ease that feeling for her, yet there was a part of me that knew I would just make it worse if I did. Her eyes connected with mine for just a moment before she looked back at Elise. "You really have no fucking remorse, do you? Even if I couldn't change it, that information was mine to know, and you went and opened your fucking mouth telling everyone else *but* me."

Beetee let out a sigh. "Dani, I can assure you that Ellie only wanted the…"

Dani held her hand up, silencing her. "I don't want to fucking hear it." She stalked over to Elise who crossed her arms over chest. She waited patiently as Dani almost came nose to nose with her. "I severely hope that Lilith decides to tear you apart before I finally end her, because from where I'm standing if you don't start feeling anything soon you might as well trudge your lying ass up to her castle and go stand by her side and beg for her forgiveness."

Elise smirked. "I really hope Lilith tears me apart as well, try as she will, just so I don't have to hear your incessant whining anymore."

"Fuck, you are always so fucking upfront and honest when it suits you, but when I ask you right to your face you can't do the simplest thing!"

"I told you in Oculus and if you weren't fucking listening then that's on you!"

A door swung over behind us and a woman in a black tank top stuck her head out. Small horns poked out from each of her shoulders. "Can you keep it down, some of us are trying to fucking nap."

"Stay out of it!" Both demons said to the woman, who reared back, surprised. Beetee gave her an apologetic look. The woman shook her head but retreated back into her room.

"Dani, I think we should all—" I started, but Dani gave me a look that had me closing my mouth instantly. She sucked her top lip into her mouth using her front teeth as if she was contemplating Elise's earlier words. Elise *had* said some things to her that would make her story make sense. She *had* said key points and from where I stood told Dani the factual truth.

Elise said that truth with about as much anger as I assumed was normal for her, but that particular emotion didn't make sense with the words she had said.

"You said Lilith was going to kill me if I didn't fall in line, so you did as she said. You also said you should have let her kill me. You sound more like Lilith's pet than I do."

Elise's eyes blazed as red sparks came from her fingertips. "Watch yourself."

"Which is it, Elise? Have an emotion other than perpetual bitch for once. Why didn't you just let her kill me and move on? Why did you come with me to Heaven's Gate if Lilith wasn't continuously buzzing in your ear? You could have said no."

I saw Elise's chest rise and fall. I didn't know if she was even considering Dani's words.

Beetee let out the world's most awkward cough trying to break the stressful transaction of words in front of us. "I think it would be best if we all just got settled and then met up in the lounging area for that little tour I mentioned, okay?"

"You seem to thrive on honesty until it doesn't suit you anymore, huh."

"I was honest with you, you insufferable piece of shit." Elise clenched and unclenched her fists at her sides.

Dani manifested her dagger in her hands and pointed it straight at Elise, who didn't move an inch. Beetee sucked in a breath and Reese mumbled *here we fucking go* under his breath. I just watched her, knowing she wouldn't actually strike right now, but the amount of control she had in herself was enthralling, but it was hard to watch any of this when I knew all the things Elise refused to say. Elise *never* actually admitted to caring about Dani, but she and I both knew that I was right. I had hoped that somewhere along the way she would be exhausted from harboring her friendly affection towards Dani, but maybe I was asking for too much in that regard.

I was so hung up on this team aspect, I had never really taken the time to realize how hard it would be to achieve even a sliver of what I envisioned. Not to say that my mind wasn't occupied with other things though, but those things, mainly Jonah and my lack of grieving emotion, weren't important right now. It couldn't be.

"You could have let her kill me and never thought twice about it. She would have just found another for you to train and make into a feared monster, yet you put all your effort into *me*. You followed *me* and put your life on the line with Lilith. *Why?*" Dani was trying to pull at a thread that had been dangling for a while, but Elise refused to ever let her take hold of it. She always yanked it out of her grasp.

"Ellie, I really think you should just…" Again, Beetee was cut off and Elise let out a loud annoyed sigh, clearly unmoved by Dani's words. She grabbed Dani's wrist and twisted it, bringing it down as Dani let the dagger disappear into thin air.

"So desperate for answers. Desperation is so unattractive." She leaned towards her left and stuck her hand out, palm up, towards the pink-haired demon. "Key to my room."

Beetee fumbled digging into the pockets of her sundress and pulled out a small bracelet with a tiny key on it. She placed the key into Elise's waiting palm, quickly pulling her hand away as Elise's fingers curled around it. Elise turned around letting her hair graze Dani lightly in the face. We all watched as she unlocked the door to her room and started to walk inside.

Dani's light laugh surrounded us. It was a laugh that if I didn't know any better was one that would have brought a smile to my face, but when I looked over at her, she had a finger to her forehead as if she was rubbing out a headache. "No wonder you kept trying to push me away. You don't fucking deserve friends."

Elise's shoulders tensed as she stood in her doorway, but she didn't turn around. Her shoulders relaxed a little and almost looked as if she was tired, as if the entire weight of her holding in all the feelings she had about Dani were maybe becoming too much. I had no idea why she kept adding to what had to be years of cider blocks of withholding from her so-called *friend*. She eventually slammed the door behind her, and the motion rattled the walls, making the lanterns move left to right quickly.

Dani turned to face Beetee and pointed to the room in front of her. "Is this mine?"

Beetee nodded.

"Great. Key, please."

The pink-haired demon sighed and dug in her pocket for the key. This key was a different shape and size all together than Elise's. She handed it to Dani, who nodded thankfully in her direction before putting it in the keyhole.

"The door will automatically lock when you leave, so if you happen to leave your key inside just come find me and I can let you back in." She chewed on her bottom lip as she explained. She choked at the start of her next sentence and that caught Dani's attention. "I know you are upset with her and I can understand why, but—"

Dani pushed open her door lightly and placed her hand on Beetee's shoulder. "I get that she's your friend as fucked up as that is, but right now I'm done caring. I'll be out in a few for that little tour." Before she fully went inside, she looked at me as curls laid over one of her eyes and her bottom lip pushed out in an involuntary pout. I wanted to kiss her; I really fucking did. Not because I knew it would feel amazing and not because I wanted anything sexual out of it. I wanted to kiss her because she looked a little defeated and unwanted by the one person she always had at her side. She closed her door behind her, leaving the two of us and Beetee alone in the hallway.

Beetee twirled her fingers together in front of her as she nervously chewed her bottom lip again. "I really messed that up by opening my mouth, didn't I?"

"Uh, no," I said at the same time as Reese said, "yeah you did."

I shoved him lightly and he shrugged.

"Sometimes I just speak without thinking. I would say it's one of my biggest flaws. I told Ellie not to tell me secrets, but she insisted that I would be the only person she would tell, that she just needed to get it off her chest." She played with the ends of her long hair. Another nervous habit I assumed.

"And you haven't told anyone ever since she confided in you?" I questioned.

"No, I guess I didn't. It was pretty idiotic of me to think it was something that wouldn't harbor consequences, especially for Ellie. She was so adamant about just removing the information from her conscience and I was happy to be there, but I didn't mean for all this to happen. I really hope this doesn't ruin your plans."

I shook my head giving her a small smile. "Believe me, you aren't the issue. They just have to work things out on their own, hopefully sooner rather than later. I just can't believe she told you."

Beetee hummed but said nothing. It was as if she wanted to say more, but it wasn't the right time. I couldn't blame her, so much had happened in the last two minutes that I needed a moment to breathe.

"I personally can't believe you guys even get along. I mean she's like a rainy cloud and you're like a big ball of sunshine," Reese said, scratching his chin with his index finger.

Beetee giggled. "Well thank you." She nodded her head towards the rest of the hallway and turned around so we could follow her.

"You make me want to like demons just a fraction more than I did before," he continued.

I rolled my eyes. "Baby steps I presume."

"Exactly." He patted me on the back.

Beetee looked over her shoulder at us to make sure we were following. I noticed a tattoo on her back peeking out from under her sundress. From what I could see it looked like the tail of a snake, but I wasn't quite sure, and the rest of it was covered by her clothes.

"So Beetee, let me ask you…you don't happen to have a tail, do you?" Reese asked, curiosity and a little bit of nervousness in his tone.

Beetee stopped in front of a door and let out a loud belly laugh as she dug in her pocket to dig out the key. She unlocked the door and pushed it open. She ducked her head inside and tossed the key onto a desk, or it looked like a desk from what I could see. The sunshine demon rapped her knuckles on the door's threshold and gave us a bright smile, her freckles wildly displayed on her face. She walked past us back down the hallway, ignoring Reese's question all together.

6

DANI

I landed on the bed with a solid thud, letting all the exhaustion I felt leave my body slowly. It was an odd feeling being back here, in this place I knew all too well. I heard Nick and Reese walk away from the door and at that moment I could let the much needed very long sigh leave my lips. Weakness in Purgatory was hardly tolerated, especially when you were brought up at the hand of Lilith. I didn't bother scooting back and getting more comfortable, even if the mattress underneath me felt incredible.

How in the fuck did Beetee swing for top tier sheets?

The pink-haired demon seemed sweet. Way too sweet to be so close to the lying heathen across the hall from me. I could sense something different about her though, nothing that alarmed me and made me question her helpfulness, but just something that told me her undying sweet demeanor could be morphed into something terrifying. She was good at letting it sit right under the surface of the face she put on for all her patrons. I let out a small chuckle thinking about her wreaking havoc, and it made my blood pump harder thinking about being a complete menace.

I opened my palm out in front of me and dark shadows and wisps formed allowing my dagger to manifest and appear before me. It settled into my hand, the familiar weight somehow easing but also increasing the blood boiling inside of me. I had been in Purgatory less than an hour and I was already feeling the effects. The dagger spoke to me in a way I couldn't really explain. There were no words, but it had a language all on its own. I had already gathered that it was very happy to be home.

Home. Fuck that *fucking* word.

I flipped the dagger over and over again in my palm. My name glinted off the silver from the small lamp that created light throughout the room. I gripped the hilt in my hand, hard, so hard that I felt my fingers becoming numb. I threw my weapon across the room, not looking at where it went, but I heard when it connected with the wall. While it was out of my hands, I took a moment to inspect the room I was in.

It was larger than I expected, although I didn't expect much when we had ended up on this side of the portal. When Elise had offered a place she knew, I would have bet my left tit that she was having us stay in some rat-infested shack. This was— surprising. The bed was queen- sized with a black cotton headboard and matching black comforter and sheets. There was a daybed in the far-left corner, an antique dresser facing the bed and a simple desk near the door. I noticed the makings of a linoleum floor behind a door near the corner of the room, telling me there was a bathroom hidden there. The walls were a simple beige, but they were lined with artwork. Each framed piece was splatters of different colors meshed together to make some unknown color that I'm sure didn't have a name. There were no windows, but that didn't really matter, seeing as Purgatory never really saw real sunlight.

That was one thing I severely missed about Heaven's Gate. The natural sunlight. It was much harder to tell the time here than it was in Nicholas's precious home. I slid off the bed and walked over to one of the pieces of art on the wall. I ran my index finger over the parts where the paint splatters were dense and heavy. A small knock had me looking towards the door. I waited for a moment, hoping that whoever it was would just go away.

Knock, knock.

"Hmm, yes?" I answered, hesitantly.

"It's just me." Beetee's voice was small and had so much hesitation that I could practically taste it.

I ran my tongue along my front teeth. "Come in."

She turned the knob and tentatively peeked her head into the room. Her lilac eyes looked a little stunned to see me so close to the door, but her expression quickly changed to apologetic. "Um, I just wanted to say I am so sorry again. I didn't want any of this to get out of hand."

I kept my face neutral, letting her speak.

"I haven't seen Ellie in so long and I just sometimes let my mouth run and my brain just can't keep up." She chewed the side of her lip as she stood in the doorway. She was holding something close to her chest.

I cocked my head to the side, leaning against the desk. "I'm not upset with you, Beetee."

Her face instantly relaxed. "Oh good. I was worried I had made an enemy of you, Soul Seether."

"Just call me Dani. That kind of formality in this place makes me want to barf." I rolled my shoulders.

She nodded vigorously. "I should have asked! I'll make sure everyone who's here knows to just address you as Dani or just not speak. Or do you prefer one over the other?" She blinked her cute little doe eyes at me.

I narrowed my eyes at this demon and then my shoulders were shaking from laughing. "Beetee, I don't know. I just got here. Why don't you just let me decide what I want myself, no need to announce it. I'm not royalty alright."

She tapped her multicolored fingernails against the items in her hands that were still held close to her chest. "You are here to end this whole fucked up mess, right? I think that makes you pretty special in my eyes. You won't find many that disagree. Royalty or not, you are something special."

I scoffed, "So I keep getting told." Beetee hummed a bit before looking at my face and realizing I was staring at her. She seemed a bit startled at my blatant eye contact, but I waited for her to say anything else. I nodded towards the items in her hand. "Are those for me?"

She looked down and snorted. Her wide smile claimed her whole face. "Oh my god! Of course! A change of clothes. I mean unless you love the clothes you have on now. I just assumed you would want some choices." She handed me the neatly folded clothes and I took them, feeling the soft material against my fingers.

"You really don't have to do this, you know." I fingered the clothes', noticing underwear was tucked between two tops. I inwardly laughed as I placed them on the table in front of me.

"Any friend of Ellie's is..." she trailed off, catching her misspoken words. Or maybe she heard my growl I let out.

Beetee leaned her body so she could see around me. I followed her eyes and caught the smoke coming from my dagger that was still impaled into the wall. I let my rage start to simmer, noticing the way the dark shadows started to disperse and disappear altogether. When I caught our gracious host's lilac eyes again, her lips were pressed tightly together.

I pointed at my dagger. "Sorry about that."

She swung her hand back and forth in a *don't worry about it* motion. "It's just a wall, Dani. Just please watch out for the paintings when you are aiming that thing, pretty please." Her voice was slightly hesitant as if trying to ask me to do anything was like having a death wish.

I chuckled a genuine laugh. I heard a groan from the wall behind me and lifted up my hand, catching my dagger in midair. "As you wish." I let the dagger turn into nothing but a translucent shadow.

She rocked back on her heels and ran her palms down the front of her dress. She was slightly less nervous in my presence, but anyone with eyes could see how she was constantly trying to choose her words carefully around me. I had no need to hurt her, nor did I have any desire to cause her distress. She just had the most interesting choice in friendships. If she got all of Elise's honesty, then so be it.

That didn't mean that it didn't hurt the feelings I didn't even know I had.

Her voice brought me back to the here and now. "I'll let you get back to your rest. I need to make my way to Ellie's room and your cute angelic companions."

I nodded, shrugging out of my jacket and hanging it over the desk chair in front of me. My hair tickled my shoulders as it made contact with my skin.

Beetee put her hand over her mouth, stifling a small laugh. I cocked my head to the side, confused. She ran her index and middle along the shaved side of her head.

"Care to share what's so funny?" I asked, dragging my tongue over my front teeth.

She gave me a small shrug, her pink hair swinging a bit. "I just didn't see the infamous Soul Seether with an angel for a boyfriend."

My insides practically shut down from her words. She'd known us for all of less than an hour and she already could sense that angel's complete obsession for me. And knowing Nicholas, he would say obsession was an exaggerated explanation, but anyone with fucking eyes could see. I wasn't going to play stupid and pretend like I didn't know he looked at me anytime I was around.

Did I thrive on this fact? Yes.

His cock was like a compass, and I was true north.

"He isn't my boyfriend."

She squinted and opened her mouth to speak, but then closed her mouth again. She was choosing her words carefully again. "Not your boyfriend?"

I shook my head. "He wishes."

Beetee placed her thumb in her mouth, biting her nail. Her eyes looked off to the side as if she was contemplating. "And you don't...," she slowed her words, "wish for that?"

It was my turn to almost speak and then halt. I didn't want to lie, but in reality, I didn't actually know *how* to answer her question. I responded with the only answer I had.

"That's a long story that I don't want to get into right now."

She nodded thoughtfully as if she understood what I was saying, but she didn't press for answers. "I'm a good listener if you do want to explain it. I've been told it's what makes me a good host."

I really wanted to ask her more about this place. How she started all this. I got that she wanted a place for demons and Enchanters to be at peace and out from under Lilith's thumb. No one could ever truly be out of the dark queen's grasp, but Lilith didn't really give much thought towards those that didn't suit or benefit her. That very idea put me on edge, now this place didn't have such a peaceful demeanor since I was standing here right now. I benefited Lilith. I suited her.

I didn't want innocents to be caught in this crossfire that was coming.

"I'll leave you to your thoughts. Don't be a stranger downstairs, okay. There are a lot of people here that would love to tell you how much you inspire them." Beetee gave me a small wave before she stepped out of the room, closing the door behind her.

Inspire? Inspiration and Soul Seether didn't really go hand in hand, so that declaration shocked me to my core. People used to cower at the very thought of me and now it sounded like they couldn't wait to get my autograph. There was a small part of me that couldn't wait to meet all these supposed supporters of mine.

I hadn't seen many, if any, people downstairs in that lounge area or even in the kitchen I had glanced at, but the day was just winding down here in Purgatory. People would likely hustle in to get ready to go out, or even probably come here to book rooms ahead of time for however the evening might end. Heaven's Gate was a lively place when the sun was out, shining from above. The beaming sun came with judgements though. Purgatory was its polar opposite. The goodness of Purgatory was embodied in the temptation and the pleasure of the darkness. Most knew it was a life without expectations.

I had lived my entire existence with one expectation and that was to be the best at what I did, never forgetting who I was. Now I was something different than what I assumed.

People here expected me to save them, knowing full well they all but feared me months ago. I would do what I had to do here, but that didn't make me a good person.

That didn't make me a hero.

I had opted to change clothes once we came back from the tour that Beetee was so fucking eager to lead. She was cute when she bounced on her toes and pointed towards one area and then glided over to another. I had taken the stairs to the bottom floor two at a time, halting when I saw Elise and Beetee whispering near the front desk. Elise had a look of pure exhaustion and annoyance written on her face, while Beetee pointed her index finger at her as she spoke. It looked like Beetee was letting her have it, like she was scolding her.

Elise had rolled her eyes and then stiffened as she caught my eye as I made it to the bottom step. We broke eye contact as I looked to my right and noticed the boys were already seated on the large L-shaped couch, weapons in tow as per usual. Beetee had put on an enthusiastic face when she waved them over and started explaining each room more in depth and continuously telling us how safe this place was. I got the sense that the reassurance was more for our angelic companions. We had made it past the kitchen, which was always stocked with food, the pantry, a room she called the recovery room—due to the fact that many demons came to this place not always in the best shape, and the few extra bathrooms she had down here when she had us circling back to the front door.

"I can show you some of the grounds if you'd like?" Beetee offered, placing her hand delicately on the doorknob.

I caught the look that Nicholas and Reese gave each other as they silently had a conversation amongst the two of them. Nicholas nodded. "It would probably be good to see the surroundings."

"And what are you gonna do, pretty boy? Fly up with your big white angel wings and get a bird's eye view of the place?" Elise taunted, shoving past all of us.

"Ellie, stop being a heathen alright." Beetee shook her head and opened the door, leading us outside and into the warm air. It wasn't humid, but there was no breeze. There were no changing seasons here, there was no need to worry about descending temperatures at some point or sweltering heat. It was always this. I would never admit it out loud, but my bones seemed to relax as I took a true deep breath, right into my lungs as I closed my eyes.

"Are you good?" I heard a familiar deep voice ask. I peeked to see Nicholas looking down at me, placing his hands in his pockets. His forehead crinkled with a look of concern.

I shrugged and started walking past him. "I'm perfectly fine." He worried too much. Especially about me.

"...and you remember you came from the Abyss Bridge, that bridge is the number one landmark of knowing you are close to my hostel. Lilith's very large, very ominous castle looms over us as you can see, but I'm sure you've seen that already. There is forest all around us, but I wouldn't go deep into it on foot, not that I think you will, but just be cautious. Umm, the surrounding buildings are people's homes, demons and Enchanters alike. They start right at the bridge and end right towards there." She pointed to where the gravelly trail went around a corner that seemed to be shrouded in darkness. "That's the trail you would follow if you wanted to get to other parts of this area, there are a bit of woods, but it's honestly not as bad as—"

"Why would we want to go through some dark ass woods? To leisurely explore, yeah no thank you." Reese said, looking up and around as if at any moment something would come from the sky and grab him.

"We can't stay in the hostel forever. I mean *you* can, but I have a feeling you would feel left out." I taunted, pushing out my bottom lip.

Reese narrowed his eyes at me, but looked away, not wanting to admit how right I was. "How would we even see if we *did* plan to head that way? It's dark as fuck."

Beetee motioned for us to follow her as I checked out the houses that we passed. There were lights on here and there and I caught a few glances out of the windows, but nothing seemed out of the ordinary. I would have loved living in this area, I would have loved not having a manipulating queen breathing down my back and lying to me either, but the past was the past.

The moment we got to the last houses where the trail led into a row of trees and a stone pathway, we discovered that Reese was correct. It was dark, but once Beetee stepped on one of the stones a red light illuminated from one of the trees. It was dim and not so vibrant, but it was something. She continued to step even further as more red lights from the various trees lit up. Each light was singular, but with each one the path got easier and easier to see. I followed behind her as I watched Nicholas look pretty amazed at the sight in front of him.

"You could have just said this would happen," Reese grumbled. If I knew anything about him, he was just trying to play off how cool he found this. As we all followed behind our host, I started to get a sense of déjà vu as we got further away from the hostel. I could hardly make out the area we were headed to, but I could see the smallest hues of pulsing lights or hear the whispers of drunken laughter. Wherever we were headed, I had been there before and then something in me clicked. I stopped walking just to feel Elise run into my back.

"Fuck, warn someone when you want to just be in their way."

I ignored her as Beetee stopped as well, turning to face me. She tilted her head in confusion as she waited for me to collect myself. I nodded over to the area behind her. "Is that where—" I was cut off by a branch breaking. Then another.

And another.

The laughter I heard before was gone. I zeroed in on whatever had caught my attention. The tiny light from the trees didn't help much in the extensive forest area. No more breaking branches, just the sound of breathing was all my ears could make out.

"Don't worry about it, it's probably just a hellhound. They are pretty harmless, or they at least try to be. Just don't provoke them," Beetee attempted to reassure.

Nicholas and Reese both answered at the same time. "Hellhound!?"

I was about to believe her and then explain the concept of hellhounds to the now overly nervous, but feigning confidence angels at my side, when a whispering voice invaded my ears.

Dani.

Soul Seether.

The voice was sharp, it felt like a literal gust of wind. So sharp it could have cut my skin. I shut my eyes for a moment, feeling as it sliced into my mind.

Dani.

I felt the urge to slaughter something, whatever it was. I stretched my fingers out and felt my dagger manifest in my hand.

"What are you doing?" I heard Elise ask next to me, slight hesitation in her voice. She wasn't unnerved by me, but she also didn't know how to react.

Before I realized what was happening, I was moving. I headed towards the woods, into the darkness. I had never liked true darkness, the kind that encapsulated you, blinded you. I preferred the darkness when I knew I could leave, when I knew I could open my eyes and see things clearly. I overlooked the suffocated forestry and focused on the familiarity of what I was being pulled towards.

Soul Seether.

My shadows caressed me as they snaked up my legs and around my arms. An armor I didn't know I needed. I stopped walking and looking around, just waiting. I heard the sound of crunching leaves and twigs as the others came up behind me.

"Dani, what's going on?" Nicholas asked, but I didn't look at him. I didn't have an answer for him. I did hear him slowly slide his sword out from behind his back. He may have been concerned about me, but he wasn't an idiot. It was so fucking dark I couldn't see—

A hand was around my throat, squeezing hard, before I could reassess. I was lifted off the ground and thrown to the side. My body slammed against a tree which shook violently, causing some of its leaves to drop down on my head.

"Woah, what the fuck!" I heard Reese yell as the sound of arrows now entered my ears. I couldn't make anyone out and I didn't even know who we were fighting. I used the tree to steady myself and felt a hand on my arm, twisting it. The pain was bad, but not bad enough for me to get distracted by it.

I grabbed whatever had me and felt a familiar demonic energy. We were fighting demons. Beetee had said this area was safe, yet she did say Lilith followers could make an appearance. I maneuvered my body so that I had them pinned to the tree and quickly slid my hands up to their neck, easily twisting until they stopped squirming. I was suddenly being pulled back by more hands, slamming me down on the ground and dragging me across the forest floor by my hair.

I heard grunts of fighting around me, telling me that I wasn't alone in my endeavors. I begrudgingly turned to my side and grabbed the demon's ankle, snaking dark shadows around it. The darkness took hold of its other ankle as well. They let go of my hair as my magic pulled them to the ground. I let my shadows tell me where they were in this darkness, and I let my dagger establish itself in my palm as I brought it down into the chest of my assailant. I looked up to see light moving back and forth. I squinted my eyes to see better, focusing.

It was his sword. Maurice had told Nicholas that he had made sure that both their weapons were already infused with angelic magic. This was one way to prove he wasn't lying. Not that I ever doubted Maurice Cassial. His sword was glowing, pulsing with the kind of light that I knew was somewhere inside of me, but I just couldn't reach it. I watched as Nicholas swung and jumped back from the demons. He slashed down one and twirled his sword in his hand, spinning around and facing yet another. I caught glimpses of what he was fighting.

They looked just like the demons from the briefing room. The ambush. This was Lilith's doing.

Nicholas seemed to give his all to this fight, as he did every fight I assumed, and he plunged his glowing sword into the demon. The creature writhed and as he removed his weapon, swiftly taking a few steps back. The demon disintegrated into dust, too weak to withstand angelic magic, just like all of Lilith's experiments.

Three arrows, glowing just like Nicholas's sword shot out, one of them headed straight for me. But it didn't. It was aimed behind me.

I got up from where I was kneeling over the dead demon and heard a thud. Two more thuds followed, but they were closer now. I kicked my foot out feeling a limp body, right before it was nothing but dust on my boot.

Dani.

Soul Seether.

What the fuck? My head was reeling with the noise.

I felt something scratching at my side, hard. The sound of skin tearing had me screaming, but I rallied. I used my dagger to ram the silver metal into the arm of whatever was clawing at me, damn near stabbing myself in the process.

"Fuck this!" I heard Elise shout. I blinked once and then saw a bolt of flaming red fire being tossed into the air and towards the trees. The ball of flame raged once it hit the foliage. The area around us was stricken into light. All the demons came into view as did Beetee who had two by the throat in each of her hands, practically shaking them.

Elise had let her tail out and was whipping them around as best she could. She released her red tinted smoke in waves as more demons approached. Elise shot out her wings and ascended towards the sky, likely hoping to get the advantage of higher ground. I may have severely hated her right now, but she had a good idea.

I was about to head towards the sky myself as I released my wings, but I was yanked back down by my shoulder. I was pushed forward and rammed into the ground, my face skidding against the small rocks embedded in the dirt. I placed my hands flat on both sides of my head, flipping over. My eyes widened and then immediately became tiny slits of rage when I came face to face with the one person I severely hoped Lilith would see was pointless to keep around.

"Oh, where do you think you're going, huh," Isabel said in a voice that was so smooth, but full of venom. "Did you miss me, Soul Seether?"

Her shoes crunched on the ground as she stepped closer to me. I quickly looked around me and saw that everyone else was occupied. It was like they were oblivious to her even being here. It was just me and her. She looked the same as before. Same blonde hair, same blue eyes, but the fire light made her look less innocent and gave away her true colors.

I felt my need to ravage and seethe deep in my belly. Just looking at her made me see red. Blood red. The kind of red that blinds you. The shadows filtered around my hands as I prepared to lasso it around her neck and squeeze so tight her eyes would bulge out of her pretty fucking face. I lashed out and she grabbed my black shadow rope in one of her hands. As fast as I could blink Isabel let out a rainbow color of magic down my shadow and it felt like it went into my veins, like my insides were burning. My darkness was screaming, and the wisps of shadows were rippling inside of me as I tried to cast out the foreign sensation.

She yanked me over to her with my own magical rope in one movement and shoved me onto my back as she straddled me. "Does that hurt? Do you feel pain?" She leaned down near my face, lifting up her hand that was covered in white gauze. "That little High Priestess bitch of yours did this to me! That's no matter though, I can take out my anger on you can't I!" She pulsed that volt of magic into me again, the pain nearly increasing. She pressed her good hand to the side of my face, and I had to bite my own tongue to try to not pass out from the burning sensation I felt.

I groaned loudly as I flexed my hand out, feeling my dagger reform into my grip. I would end her fucking life. Natalia would have to find some other way of retribution because this one was mine.

"Lilith wanted to welcome you home properly. Of course, you don't appreciate it." I tried to buck her off of me, but she wouldn't budge. "You heard her in your head, didn't you? Strong enough to kill poor Cullen and Markus, but you aren't strong enough to wean yourself out from under mommy's thumb." She cackled with laughter at her own words. I used that as my way to strike her across the face with my dagger, the lingering effects of her magic making my head pound. She sucked in a breath, but not before I pushed out from underneath her just enough for me to kick her in the stomach, sending her flying back on her ass a few feet away from me. I bolted over to her, grabbing her shoulders and slammed her body into the ground once more.

"She doesn't own me." The words were coming out through my teeth. I felt the sweet hum of pain and no mercy fill my system. It gave a delicious burn to my soul. Being in Heaven's Gate, I didn't want to let it out if it wasn't needed. I didn't need to give them more of a reason to see me as an enemy.

Isabel merely laughed at my remark. "Oh, you stupid, stupid girl. Stupid demon, with your stupid friends. She owns you whether you like it or not.

This place *owns* you."

The second the words left her lips; I felt an odd familiar strength fill me. I could do what I needed to do in Heaven's Gate, of course, no question about it. In Purgatory, *fuck*, in Purgatory I could pull from so much to find more darkness, more shadows, more magic. I felt the weight of my dagger in my hand as I grabbed the hilt so tightly my fingers started cramping.

Isabel's eyes widened in interest as she took in what I knew was a dark cloud of magic surrounding me, my eyes had likely divulged into pools of inky black. A demon tried to ram into me from the side, but I sunk my blade into its stomach before it even had a chance to touch me. I summoned heavy, thick black ribbons from the ground to clamp around her throat and chest.

"Do your worst, Soul Seether. You will always be hers no matter how much you try to push her out. You are just as strong as she wanted you to be, maybe even more. Pity how you don't see how it's your downfall."

I pressed my dagger to her chest, clearly hearing her heartbeat. It was steady, no stutters, not a single beat off rhythm. "I'm not her pet. You are. It's pathetic." I pulled my dagger from her chest, turning my body slightly to stab her already wounded hand again. I twisted the blade into her skin, continuing until I knew it was pushed all the way through. She cried out in agony, and I could have squawked with laughter at the sound. Blood oozed from her hand, but I wanted more, I needed more.

You are so strong, my Soul Seether.

My head throbbed and felt my face twitch at the voice in my head again.

"You should be so happy I can't kill you, you fucking bitch!" Isabel screamed as I twisted my dagger in more.

"Isabel, what the hell?" I heard Elise's angry voice through my haze, but I was still lost in my own enraged temperament.

I wondered what an Enchanter's soul looked like. Would it have a color? Would it be wispy like a cloud or thick like gel? I wanted to find out.

Do it. Do what you're meant to do.

My face was hot, and my limbs were on autopilot, but I was somehow still in total control. I wanted this. I needed this.

"Dani!" I blinked. Then I blinked again. There was a tug at my chest at the deep voice, but this tug wasn't dark, it wasn't lusting for chaos. No, this tug was like a much-needed stroke of comfort and affection...

Never forget who you are when you're down there. The darkness is familiar but that doesn't always mean it's the right choice. Always remember who you are.

Natalia's words wrapped around me in a chokehold.

This tug was lighter, and it distorted my vision, making things clearer. I looked up and to my right and saw Nicholas looking at me as if he wanted to help, but he halted, likely seeing how into my demonic side I'd gone. It was slithering away though. He looked down to where Isabel was writhing in pain as if seeing her for the first time, as if the veil that blinded him was gone. His eyes went back to mine and locked on in this way that had my breathing coming out in a more normal pace. He seemed to be taking steps towards me again as if the madness around him didn't matter. The detour in my thoughts left an opening for Isabel to yank my dagger out of her hand and shoot me back with her heavy hitting magic.

Isabel shot a stream of magic at Elise, who was still up in the air, causing her to fall downward at a quickened pace. Isabel used some more magic, her fingertips glowing white and nearly sparkling to push Elise towards Reese and Nicholas. The blonde Enchanters' eyes were flooded with colors of the rainbow as she used her magic. I wasn't concerned about Elise running into the angels until I noticed her tail was out. She failed to get balance once she skidded to the ground and her tail whipped out and struck Nicholas in the stomach and again in the face. He groaned a loud, almost deafening cry, stumbling backwards towards a bundle of tree trunks before collapsing. Reese sprinted over to him dodging Elise's tail in the process.

"Maybe I should just kill you and deal with the consequences," Isabel threatened, the blood from her wounded hand slipping down her fingers.

I stood up from the ground and was prepared to continue to fight now that I had my senses back when I heard a hiss. Not the soft hiss of a garden snake simply minding its business, but the hiss of a rattlesnake that was preparing to make you its next meal. Isabel's shoulders stiffened as we both looked over to where the biggest snake I'd ever seen sat a few feet in front of us.

Its eyes were a bright yellow with diamond pupils. Its scales were black but had iridescent sparkles along the edges. The tail shook and rattled the trees, creating a faux wind all by itself. It lashed out its tail at every demon that came in its direction, sending them flying. It brought its head down and gobbled up a few in its mouth. Reese was huddled over an unconscious Nicholas as Elise just stared at the large reptile in front of us, as if she had seen this before. She almost looked comfortable around it.

"What in the fuck is that?!" Reese shouted as he tried to use his body to protect his best friend.

Isabel sensibly shrank back as the snake locked its yellow eyes on her. The blonde Enchanters mouth gaped open as she looked from me to the snake and back again. She had the angriest expression on her face. "She is always watching you, Soul Seether. You are bonded." She looked back at the snake, who slithered closer to us, its eyes set on Isabel.

"I may be her pet, but you are her *monster*," Isabel said, letting a portal take her away before I could say anything else.

The fire from the trees was blazing, practically circling around us. The giant snake blinked over to me as I stood there speechless. I had never fought a reptile before, or really any giant non-human-like creature so this was new.

Something stopped me though. The snake stuck out its tongue, almost in a friendly gesture. Its tongue was pink. Hot pink.

Well fuck.

Dark, wispy smoke surrounded the reptile as it shrunk back away from me. Its body got smaller and less terrifying. I started to move closer to get a better look, my curiosity peaked. The smoke started to dissipate, revealing a very naked Beetee. She stood in all her glory as she smiled brightly at me. Her long hair covered only one of her breasts. She was no longer that beastly, but impressive creature. She was herself again. Those neon yellow eyes were gone and replaced with her pretty lilac ones.

I tentatively walked over to her, shrugging off my jacket and helping her put her arms through it, not before noticing the snake tattoo on her back, the rattlesnake tail meeting right at the middle of her shoulder blades, the head of the snake curling halfway up. Elise stepped to her other side, still scanning the perimeter. "We'll be safe here, huh?" She raised one of her dark eyebrows, the firelight playing along her gray eyes.

Beetee blew out a breath and shook her head. She shushed Elise before tugging the jacket closer to her chest. Beetee leaned around me, looking over my shoulder. "Tour is cut short; we should get him back to the hostel. Make use of the recovery room." She nodded her head to both of us as if she was in charge and strutted over to the boys—sans pants. If this whole mess wasn't so mind altering, I would have laughed. Reese was going to have a field day with this. Laughing is the last thing I wanted to do though, I really didn't deserve to.

I may be her pet, but you are her monster.

It was more accurate than the hero.

7

NICK

My face hurt. My stomach also hurt. *Fuck.*

I mentally counted to ten before I made any attempt to move or even just open my eyes.

"You are all a bunch of fucking babies; he's going to be fine." Elise's snarky voice rang out clear as day.

Next, I heard Reese's frustration fueled tone. "He's unconscious. He would be fucking awake if it wasn't for you and your flailing appendage."

"Me! I didn't start that fight! Lilith and her little blonde bitch did."

Their arguing sounded like someone was continuously punching me in the side of the head. Fuck, Elise's venom really did hurt like a bitch, and I hated imagining someone getting tortured with it for hours on end. I hadn't felt it immediately when it sliced through my stomach, but when the pain did hit, it was brutal. The hit to my face was what stung me the worst. The paralyzing feeling of it, but then the burning, *fuck*, the burning had me tripping over my own feet and then everything went black.

"Maybe you guys should lower your voices just a smidge. Unconscious people can probably still hear you." I could tell Beetee was trying to mediate between them. I would have easily told her that was a lost cause.

"Well maybe Nicholas should be aware of how much of a whiny little shithead his friend is," Elise fired back.

"Shithead?!"

I decided that now was the best time to release a groan and let everyone know I was okay and could hear them perfectly. There were a few sharp intakes of breath as I slowly started to open my eyes and realized I was lying on my back, looking up at the ceiling. It took a moment for me to get the room to stop spinning. I turned my head to the side with pain that had me clenching my teeth together noticing three sets of eyes staring at me.

Beetee clapped her hands, letting her palms close softly together, which I assumed was to try not to startle me with supremely loud noises. She was overly considerate, compared to the two jackasses next to her. She took a few steps toward me.

"Hey, sleepy head. How do you feel?" Her nose wrinkled with concern.

I took a short breath in and blew it out, licking my extremely dry lips. "I'm good, just, uh...I feel like shit."

Elise snorted. "You look like shit."

"Ellie!" Beetee scolded, swinging her head around to look at her friend.

Reese shoved Elise out of the way, while Beetee stepped to the side to let him by. "Do you want to sit up?" His blonde hair was tied in a bun, but was flopping over to the side a bit, as if he did it in a hurry.

I nodded as best I could and let him gingerly wrap one hand around my right shoulder and then reach towards my left as he helped me up. I tried to not twitch with pain at each minuscule movement. He reached down and carefully swung my legs around so that I was sitting up with my legs swinging over the bed. Reese placed both hands on my biceps, tilting his head down so he could look me in the eyes, his own hazel ones searching my face.

"Are you good to sit up on your own?" he asked, keeping a strong hold on me.

"Yeah, I'm good." I looked down at the tattered parts of my shirt. The inky black stains on the ripped ends. Forever remnants of Elise's tail venom.

Reese let go of me and I wobbled but maintained my balance. I placed both my hands on either side of my legs, taking three long breaths in and out before lifting my head and looking at them. They were all staring at me expectantly, probably wondering if I would start asking a million and one questions or just pass out on the floor. Either was an option at this point, although I only had one question on my mind. One simple question the second the blackness peeled back from my mind, and I could think at least a fraction clearly.

"Where's Dani?"

I remembered the fight for the most part. I remembered Isabel appearing, causing us issues once again. And I remembered Dani's face. The same lost look in her eyes. Eyes that were as black as midnight and she had this almost suffocating tension around her that should have pushed me away, but it didn't. It never did. Not when she was torturing Cullen and not during that fight. I wasn't scared of her, but that darkness she harbored worried me. She had so much more of it compared to the angelic part of her.

Reese scoffed. "Seriously? You just woke up from being bitch slapped by a tail and that's your first question?"

I bit my lower lip and simply nodded. I peeked over at Beetee whose smile was so wide it looked like it hurt. Elise looked over at her and rolled her eyes. "What are you smiling for?"

Beetee shrugged, hiding her smile as best she could. "Oh nothing, nothing at all. I called for one of the Enchanters who stays here to mix you up something. It won't be as fast acting or probably as great as the tonics you have in Oculus, but we do our best."

I gave her a grateful smile, but then looked back over to the others. "Is someone going to answer my question?" I didn't like to think of myself as an impatient kind of person, but this was an answer I really wanted to know.

"I'm right here." All eyes were on her when her voice broke through the small silence. Dani leaned against the door frame casually as if what had transpired in the last two hours hadn't happened. She had changed into leggings and a slouchy black crop top that slid off of one of her shoulders. Her hair was draped over her shoulders, each curl more defined than the one next to it. I found myself letting out an audible breath of relief when she appeared.

"See look, she is fine," Elise pointed out.

Dani stepped further into the room, making sure she had space between her and Elise. "Isabel made sure to let me know that Lilith said *welcome home*."

"She does know that a simple flower arrangement is a good welcome home present as well, right?" Reese joked, rubbing his forehead.

"If she sent flowers, I guarantee they would be poisonous," Elise mumbled, crossing her arms over her chest. "My question is where the fuck did Isabel even come from? One minute she's not there and the next she is. Honestly, for a minute it looked like you were just fighting air." She cocked her head towards Dani, who narrowed her eyes at her former friend.

Beetee cleared her throat. "I'm pretty sure she glamoured herself so that only Dani could see and hear her, but—"

"But, when you stabbed her hand, it was like that severe pain caused her to let go of her glamour. That's when we all saw her," I cut in, leaning back on my hands.

"Makes perfect sense to me," Dani said, leaning against the wall.

"Let's not make it a habit though alright, you know, you running into the woods." Elise didn't wait for a response when she was finished speaking. I heard her grumble, *glad you're fine* under her breath as she passed Dani when she stomped out of the room. If Dani had heard it as well, she didn't show any indication that she cared.

A soft knock came at the door. A man with cropped short blonde hair cautiously looked into the room. Beetee rushed over to him as he handed her a clear jar of translucent liquid. From where I was sitting there was a slight sparkle to the contents. "Thanks, Blake. I'll be out in a minute." The man nodded and quickly scurried out of sight.

"Hmm, I thought you said they were all so happy to see us fighting for them and they were all against Lilith and what not? That guy didn't even want to step into the room with us," Reese questioned, furrowing his blonde brows.

"Well, I don't like being rude, so I'll put it plainly, I guess. You two are angels, the beings that stormed in and practically destroyed his home." Beetee looked apologetic as if her words were offensive and cruel.

"Hey." She looked over at me when I spoke to her, "It's fine and understandable."

Reese groaned. "Oh yeah, it's totally fine that he is so comfortable with the demon princess over there, but not us." He hooked his thumb over his shoulder and pointed at Dani.

"Or maybe he doesn't like the stench of your arrogance. It's literally filling up the whole room. I'm fucking suffocating over here," she retorted, examining her nails without a care in the world. "You can't expect them to just fucking trust you."

Reese barked out a laugh. "Trust? You are one to talk with all your fucking trust issues."

Dani pushed off the wall and right when I thought I would have to muster all my strength and stop her from pummeling him, she walked right past him and took the jar from Beetee's hands. "Is this for his wounds?"

The pink-haired demon nodded, shifting from one foot to the other. She had a different dress on than before. This one was bright yellow and strapless with pockets in the front. She pointed to the jar and then to Reese. "I was going to let him do it…"

Dani looked over her shoulder and up at Reese, shrugging. "No, I got it, thanks. You can all leave."

"Excuse me, he's my friend," Reese argued, "I'll do it." He tried to grab the jar from her, but she whirled around and shoved him back.

"Okay okay, stop. Reese, it's alright." I gave him a look that caused him to let out a huff of defeat. He really was the world's best guard dog. I blinked over to Dani who was starting to unscrew the top off the jar and headed towards the countertop that took over an entire corner of the room. "I'll talk to you when I'm done."

Reese raised his head towards the ceiling. "Whatever, fine." Beetee started to follow him out of the room, but not before I heard him ask, "so did you turn into a fucking snake earlier?" Beetee's high pitched giggle echoed in the hall as the door closed behind them.

A snake? How long had I been out?

The oxygen in the room seemed to be pulled when it was just me and her. There was silence and it was fucking awkward, but comfortable for us. I reached up to touch the side of my face that got hit and hissed once the pads of my fingers touched the raised cuts.

"You shouldn't be touching it, who knows if there are remnants of her venom still on it," she warned. Dani placed a bowl of water, washcloths, and the jar of translucent substance on a steel tray and walked over to me. She placed the tray next to me and suddenly grabbed my face, turning my head to the side.

"She got you good."

"It was an accident."

She raised an eyebrow at me. "Are you defending her?"

"No, I just know it was none of our faults and Isabel is the cause of me being in this very uncomfortable state."

Dani hummed, letting go of my face and snatching a cloth. "Lilith is the reason, Nicholas. Isabel is just a pet. She does her bidding, just like everyone else we've come across that has anything to do with her." She dipped the cloth in the water and brought it to my face. The water was warm as it hit my cheek, but I flinched and started to rear back as she pressed it into my wound. Dani let up and started patting around the tender flesh.

"You big baby."

"It fucking stings."

"I could sedate you. Knock you out and then clean it. Would you like that?" she asked sarcastically, pressing her tongue into her cheek.

I rolled my eyes and let her continue, biting my tongue. There wasn't as much pain after a minute once I started to focus on something other than the stinging. Her scent started to wrap itself around me and I had to fight my instincts not to touch her, not to try and bring her closer to me. She was close, so close that I could make out every single one of her eyelashes, but she still wasn't close enough. I wanted her wrapped around me, breathing me in as if she felt all the same things I did.

"Stop," she said, putting the cloth down and picking up the jar, sticking her finger inside and scooping out some of the contents. I noticed it had a wet consistency as some of it dripped off her finger and onto the tray.

"What?"

"Stop looking at me like that."

"Dani, I'm not doing anything."

She looked at me like I was stupid. "Yes, you are. You can't look at me like that. You can't look at me like…"

I grabbed her wrist before she could spread the wet liquid onto my face. "Like what?"

She looked from her captured wrist to my face and something in her eyes told me that I shouldn't play with fire, that I would get severe burns if I did.

I liked her fire though.

I felt something curl around my wrist, it tickled but I knew it was nothing to laugh about. Dark shadows took hold of me and squeezed, the bones in my wrist were screaming as her shadows pressed their weight into me, threatening to snap my wrist like a twig.

"Alright, shit." I released her, then noticed a small smirk play at her lips as she swiped the translucent substance against my wound. It was cool and refreshing, there was no smell to it, but slowly my face felt a little less swollen.

"Your father wasn't lying when he said your weapons had angelic magic infused, huh."

I started to reach up and touch my cheek, but she swatted my hand away. Her stern brown eyes silently warned me to stop touching my wounds. "We could always pump our own magic into it, like Reese did with his old bow when you and Elise had your fight, but you can get it pre-fueled."

Dani wiped her finger on a clean cloth and nodded. "Why don't you use your own magic with your sword?"

I bit the inside of my cheek. "I've never needed it. Life was pretty fucking simple before everything happened. And as for right now, well, the magic that's already in the sword does its job. There is such a thing as a magic overload. And angelic magic that's too stacked can be a problem, just like anything else."

"Too much of a good thing." She licked her lips. "Too much goodness just explodes into a heaping pile of brightly colored bullshit."

I chuckled. "That's one way to put it, I guess."

She reached up and ruffled her hair a bit, lost in her own thoughts.

"Dani, did you hear something before you rushed into the woods?" There was a fifty-fifty chance that I was going to get an actual answer from her.

"Take off your shirt."

My eyes widened. I stuttered as I got the only word I could out. "W-what?"

"You did get hit in the stomach, didn't you? Take off your shirt." She blinked, taking a small step back.

I delicately reached back behind me and yanked my shirt over my head, balling it up and tossing it next to me. Without the fabric in the way, I got a good look at where Elise's tail had gotten me. Two long slice marks adorned my skin. They were raised and red, with black charred pieces littering the top. I looked up at Dani to find her staring at the marks as well.

Then I realized that her mind was starting to betray her when her eyes started to wander. They landed on my abs and then searched my chest, my neck and then made it to my face where I had one of my eyebrows raised waiting for her to meet my gaze.

She clucked her tongue and took a step back over to me, reaching for the same cloth as before. She dipped it in the water, conveniently not looking at me anymore.

"You didn't answer my question," I said.

"Take that as a hint."

She repeated her movements from before, pressing the warm cloth to my stomach. "Dani, we both know I'm probably going to keep asking. It's who I am."

She huffed out a breath. "And is the reason you'll keep asking the same reason you keep looking at me like you do?" She said the words to my stomach as she patted, but the warm water from the cloth might as well have been cold as ice. She was way more intuitive than I ever gave her credit for.

I watched as she balled up the cloth and tossed it aside, making a move towards the jar of clear healing liquid. "I do care about you."

"I know you do, but that's beside the point." She started to spread the cool liquid onto my skin and I watched as some of the black charring pieces disintegrated, the redness starting to lessen. Her fingers danced over my skin in a way that showed that she was being cautious of how much pressure she was applying. Her skin felt good on mine and it took a lot for me not to get turned on by the proximity of her hand to the waistband of my pants.

She was quiet for a moment before she spoke again, "I heard something, yes."

"Heard something like....?"

"Nicholas, I don't know. I just got really riled up hearing it. And then shit happened and Isabel basically told me Lilith is in my head fucking with me. Isabel apparently isn't allowed to hurt me or at least she made it seem that way. She would have gone for my head if she wasn't on such a tight leash. Now is that enough information for you not to spiral." Dani wiped her fingers against the cloth one last time before giving me her full attention.

When I looked at her face, I wanted to kiss her. Immediately. I was patient, though. Well, I was patient *enough*. "For now. Lilith wants you alive and well, that part doesn't surprise me. What happened to you out there, was that because of Lilith too?"

"Nothing happened that you haven't seen before," she said, planting her hands on my legs. Her thumbs shifted back and forth along the inside of my thighs. Her voice was so stoic as if she wanted this part of the conversation to end.

I placed my hands on top of hers. "The last time you looked like that was with Cullen and you went to a dark place. I just want to make sure—"

"I have it under control, Nicholas. Just because you're all hot and shirtless doesn't mean I need you to come and save me." She brought her finger up to my sternum and slid it down right to my belt. She was insanely good at distracting me from trying to be concerned. "You need to make sure that you are strong enough to save *yourself* if it comes down to it. Jonah wouldn't want you to sit back on the sidelines."

Another rush of cold, freezing ice ran through my veins. Every time someone brought him up, it was like I wanted to vomit. I saw him dying in my arms and then there was a flash of every single angel I had to take down, their blood on my hands. I saw the way I imagined their families looked when they got told what happened. I didn't regret my actions, it had to be done, but that didn't make it hurt any less. That didn't make me feel like I could have done so much more to see the things I didn't and stop what had happened. My head was starting to spin with the raging memories and Jonah's last words to me. Elise's venom wounds were no longer an issue. I was clearly causing pain to myself.

"Hey, what's wrong?" I felt her hands on my biceps, shaking me slightly. I took a few short breaths and ran a hand through my hair. My vertigo was subsiding, and my stomach settled back into its dormant state. Dani had a look of concern in her eyes and slight confusion. "Where did you go just now?"

"I didn't go anywhere, I'm right here." I knew what she meant, but I couldn't tell her anything. I couldn't say how I felt, because if I did, it would become a whole thing and that thing wasn't the priority. It wasn't high on my list of matters to deal with as much as my father, Reese and fucking everyone else would like me too. "I think I just haven't eaten, so I'm hungry. It's been a long day."

Dani gave me a skeptical look, one that said *you're lying but whatever you say.* "Sure."

"You look like you care about me." I decided I was going to try to push my luck. I wanted to see if trying with Dani was worth it, but at the end of the day even if it seemed like a lost cause I was always going to try.

She grabbed the tray from beside me and walked it over to the counter, putting it down. She knocked her knuckles against the granite top and let out a long sigh, her eyes finally connected with mine. "Maybe I do, but I do remember telling you that if you came to Purgatory, I wouldn't treat you any different. I wouldn't see you differently, despite what people may say. That Enchanter out there is afraid of you because you're an angel, yet I still see you just the same."

"I remember that," I acknowledged, "Dani, I've told you I'm sorry. If I haven't said that enough, then I'm sorry again."

She shook her head, clearly not impressed. "I know Nicholas. And those apologies are great, and I accept them. You're just a guy who wants the best for the people he cares about, but then you're also the guy who cares about what people think." She stalked over to me and wedged herself between my legs, leaning into me. I instinctually leaned forward, that cinnamon scent of hers wrapping itself around my whole body. "I'm sure by now you've realized that caring what people think is exhausting. Caring what people think costs you the things you *want*." She carried that last word with purpose.

"I don't care what people think, Dani." At least I didn't anymore. I shouldn't have in the first place.

"Then tell me what I want to hear."

I opened my mouth to speak but then stopped, unsure of my response. I couldn't put my finger on what she wanted from me. If she wanted me to define how I felt about her, I couldn't do that since I had no fucking idea. I wasn't going to tell her some made up falsehood about my feelings just so she would let me hold her again. I was eager but I wasn't an idiot. "I thought what you wanted *was* an I'm sorry. I thought coming here and continuing to stand by you would prove that to you. I'm not a mind reader, Dani. I honestly don't know what else..."

She let out a low, small chuckle, cutting me off. It was laced with exhaustion. "You want me?" She tilted her head to the side.

There was a small fire in her mischievous eyes, one that I could have been mesmerized by for hours. I reached up and used my fingers to tuck one of her curls behind her ear. Her hair was soft and even the shitty lighting in the room made her brown skin glow. I felt my cock twitch in my pants. The answer was obvious. "Yes."

She didn't recoil at the gesture, but she did squeeze my thighs with her hands, applying more pressure than I assumed her body weight would allow her. It took everything in me not to grab her and place her in my lap, letting her wrap her legs around my waist. "Ah well, I'm sorry comes in many different flavors. Use that big brain of yours and figure out which one I'm craving."

"Dani…"

She pulled away from me and moved her hair over her shoulder and towards her back. "Get some rest, Nicholas." Giving me a small shrug of her exposed shoulder, she sauntered out of the room.

Reese sat down next to me on the bed that I'd chosen in our room. I'd been back in our room for less than ten minutes and he'd already asked me if I wanted a glass of water three times. I'd shaken my head each and every time but appreciated the way he was doting on me. He had even gotten me a new shirt to put on, seeing as my other one was in the garbage now. We were both a little surprised when Beetee brought us fresh clothes earlier today when we settled in, asking us to make sure everything fit and not hesitate to ask for anything. I had a big feeling that he was all over me only because he didn't need me to die here and leave him alone with the demons in *their* territory. I looked around the room and noticed that my sword was casually leaning against the wall near my end table. Its angelic magic hummed and I could hear it plain as day, but I was too tired to answer its call and hold it again.

"At least your face looks better," he noted, pointing at my cheek.

I smiled a little. "Thanks. I still feel like ass."

"Yeah, Beetee did say that if you aren't a demon or you haven't gotten hit with her venom before it can linger for longer. Not the paralytics but you know, the pain," Reese explained, rubbing his hands on his pants. "You scared the shit out of me, man."

I peeked over at him and noticed his posture was a bit off and he didn't have the same cocky swagger about himself. "It's not like I meant to get knocked unconscious."

Reese waved me off, taking his hair out of the bun at the top of his head. His blonde locks fell over his shoulders in slight waves. "I know, but still, it freaked me out. I'd rather us both be knocked unconscious, fighting for our lives together and all that."

"That's.... sweet I guess." I chuckled. "No one I'd rather be fighting impending death with than you I suppose." I reached up and punched his shoulder, playfully.

Reese stroked his chin with his index finger. "So why was she so adamant about taking care of you?"

"Huh?"

He rolled his eyes, getting up from the bed. "Dani."

I licked my lips, thinking of how I wanted to answer his question. "I don't know, but keep your shit together, she really did just clean me up and make sure I was fine."

"But why?"

"Fuck, Reese, I don't know. Because she's a decent person."

My best friend narrowed his eyes at me and scrunched his mouth up to the side. "She didn't try to use her feminine wiles on you, did she? Her demonic compulsion and shit."

I let out a loud groan, placing my face in my hands, careful of my healing cheek and gave him a muffled answer. "Nope, no feminine wiles." Not like I would have minded if she did. She really didn't have to do much for me to be completely beguiled by her. "And no demon compulsion."

"Good, because we don't need to be set back by your one-night stand. We are in demon town right now and its fucking with my head."

His head?

My own head throbbed at the fact that Reese knew nothing about what I actually felt. Not to mention the fact that I personally couldn't put how I felt into a cohesive sentence, but that was beside the point. I had skipped the entire training room sex and told him a summed-up version of that very, very long night in my bedroom. He seemed to be satisfied that it was only the one time and I had moved on. And I had made it out like I had moved on as well, when all I had really done was tuck my feelings away with everything else that I didn't want to talk about.

I wanted to tell him a great deal of things, if not *everything*, but Reese was always a hot head and he tended to jump to conclusions unnecessarily most times. I hated risking setting his mood off. He was fine with Dani for the most part but telling him that *one night stand* might not be the best word for what Dani was. That wasn't something I was ready to face.

"Right. Can we just go to bed?"

Reese nodded, reaching down to pat me on the shoulder. "Oh yeah, sure. Beetee said we can all reconvene in the morning. She has an idea for our next move. Just get some rest, let me know if you need anything."

I started to unbutton my pants, way too eager to just be in my underwear and passed out underneath the surprisingly soft sheets when I remembered something. "Hey, Reese, can I ask you something?" I shoved off my pants and scooted back gingerly, so I could get under the covers.

He pulled the sheets down from the top of his bed and turned to me. "Sure."

"When you and Beetee left the room earlier you mentioned her, uh, being a snake."

Reese turned around so quickly, covering his mouth with one of his hands. He hustled over to my bed with wide hazel eyes. "Oh, my fucking god. Shit was wild!"

I adjusted the sheets around my lap, reaching behind me to fix my pillows. I was missing the number of pillows I slept with at home. "So... she is a snake?"

Reese put both his hands into his hair and yanked at his golden locks. "Fucking wild! I ran over to you to make sure you were fine and then the next time I turn around there was this huge ass fucking snake near me. Nearly shit my pants."

"So not only does she have a tail, but she's a whole reptile." It wasn't a question, but I was just in shock.

"I guess when she gets super upset or riled up, she just morphs into this huge snake, it was unreal. She said she's always been able to do it, the tattoo on her back keeps it in check. It definitely made the list of the top ten things I'll never forget in my life." His eyes were amazed and full of awe. He sounded like he was a little out of breath even though all he'd been doing was reiterating a story and sitting on my bed.

"You sound like you're impressed by a demon," I said skeptically.

Reese waved his hand in my direction, as if dismissing my words. "She's too cheery to be a demon. Also, I've seen her naked and demon or not, I ain't mad at her."

I blinked a few times, reaching for my stomach as a small sting of pain startled me when I repositioned myself. "You saw her naked? What the fuck, how long was I out?"

Reese shook his head, laughing. "No, Nick, not like that. When she stopped being a snake, she went back to her normal form, but that form didn't include clothes." He wiggled his eyebrows before getting up from my bed and walking back over to his. "Don't worry the only person in this room who has fucked a demon is still you."

I sunk back into my pillows and let out a heavy groan. "Alright, I think that's enough information for me tonight."

He jumped into his bed and reached over, cutting off his lamp that sat on his end table. "Night. You need anything, just say the word. If you ever feel the need to just leave here in the middle of the night and whisk us back home, then perfect." I heard him start to get comfortable and eventually I heard nothing at all. Since his lamp was the only thing that flooded the room with light, I was now looking into pure darkness. There were no windows in our room and the silence around me should have been soothing, but it wasn't. Silence left me with my own thoughts, which was never a good thing nowadays. I closed my eyes and wished for a night of nothing at all.

My thoughts had turned into a scary place and having them as the only thing to occupy me had me staying awake for longer than I wanted. Every time I closed my eyes, I kept seeing the same thing. Every. Single. Time.

Jonah and the way he fought beside me, hoping for a different ending. All those angels who weren't in their right mind and had only violence and murder as their end goals. I saw so much blood, so much pain. I felt the wave of my choices wash over me and land on my chest like a weight I wasn't strong enough to lift off. My throat felt dry and filled with dust as I woke up. I tried taking in deep breaths, but it ended up shallow and useless. The weight in my chest was thick and I needed to get out of here. I needed to move, leave, remove myself from my own thoughts. I heard chatter coming from outside our room, but it was muffled and the thudding in my head overpowered it.

I blinked into the darkness as I shoved the covers off of myself, feeling too hot and overwhelmed. Jonah's face appeared and then was gone, causing my vertigo to rage. His face was distorted at times and then I would blink and he was perfectly clear.

The bodies of those angels, the way my sword sliced through them played like a never-ending memory in my brain, I had no way to pause it or just delete it. I got up from my bed with wobbly legs to guide me, breathing heavy and deep, that concrete weight still creating so much pressure on my lungs. I tried my best to tiptoe to the bathroom while also trying to keep my footing. Everything in me wanted to just double over and crash to the ground. Once I'd pushed the door open and cut the light on, I closed the door behind me reaching for the sink.

I looked at myself in the mirror and I could have sworn I saw Jonah's face looking back at me. I saw Ollie and all those others, their lives I'd ended because someone else had used them as pawns in a game I didn't want to play. A game that we were all *still* playing. My cheek looked much better than before, but my eyes were bloodshot. I felt myself starting to heave over the sink, my stomach boiling. I was hyperventilating and I felt everything start to rise to the surface. I leaned over the sink hoping that if I could throw up then I could just pass out from pure and utter exhaustion, but nothing came out. My fingers dug into the side of the sink as my frustration grew, then I looked at myself in the mirror once again.

Jonah's face.

I turned one of the knobs on the sink to get the water to flow out and splashed some onto my face. The liquid felt heavy and thick. It felt like blood. Not my own but someone else's. Everyone else's. I quickly cut the water off and had to stop myself from nearly slapping my own cheek to pull myself together. I closed my eyes so tight I was sure I popped a blood vessel as I pushed off the sink and backed up against the door. I let out one breath after another, over, and over, and over. I felt the wood hit my sweaty back and the coolness of it calmed me just a bit. I slid down the door until my butt hit the linoleum floor. The pain from my wounds didn't matter at this point, right now nothing really mattered. My mind was on repeat from Jonah and his secrets, my father and his secrets, keeping it together with Reese and finding some kind of path back into Dani's circle of trust. I could do it. I could handle it all, I just needed to breathe.

Why was I breathing so *fucking* hard. The last time this happened my father had almost caught me, but I ended up playing it off like I didn't feel well. Maurice Cassial wasn't stupid, but it had been so early in my recovery from the fight that he didn't push.

Jonah wouldn't want you on the sidelines. Dani had caught me off guard with that.

She deserved so much better. Jonah had left me with so many questions. He was a good man who only wanted to help me, but I had doubted him.

I tilted my head back and let it knock against the door with a small thud. I closed my eyes, bringing my knees up to my chest. I felt myself shaking. I was literally vibrating as if I was cold. I willed sleep to take me, anything to get me out of my own head. Everything started to go numb as I drifted off to an unsettling sleep, but there was always something in the back of my mind pulling at me. Always pulling.

Jonah in my arms. Dying. Not letting me save him.

I could have. He wouldn't let me. He died in my arms.

They died by my hand.

What kind of hero did that make me?

8

DANI

The water from the shower hit my back like singular tiny punches, the searing heat of the water burning my skin. I let out a sigh of relief because it felt good. I had simply changed clothes minus the shower when we got back from our short-lived tour. It was extremely late but what better time to take a long, hot shower than when everyone was dead asleep and couldn't bother you. I placed my forehead on the porcelain wall and took a few breaths in. I was at a loss for words on what had happened to me, so how the fuck did Nicholas expect me to explain it. I had the willpower to withstand Lilith and her supposed hold on me. I wasn't a meek little thing. She sent me a fight as a welcome present. If I wasn't so fucking pissed, I'd be flattered. Demons used to offer me fucking limbs just to get a front row seat to watch me pull a soul. I was livid at the fact that she sent her enchantress pet to me, rather than herself. Was I not worth showing her face for?

Isabel wouldn't be so enthralled to help Lilith if she knew that her beloved mistress tried to push me to end her life. Lilith didn't speak in a demanding tone either, it was almost soothing, like a loving caress. In reality, I really didn't need the push at all, but with the power the darkness gave me, the *bond* I guess I had with Lilith made me feel stronger, it made me feel invincible. I liked power. Fuck that…I *loved* power. In Heaven's Gate, I had it, but it was diluted, it was mild. *Here*, it was felt in full force and there was more I could gather, so much more. The thing I didn't like was anyone having power over me. Physically or emotionally. It was all the same. I was Lilith's creation, but she didn't own me. She wouldn't tell me who I was or what I could do. She. Didn't. Own. Me.

Lilith hated a mess, but she did love a good show. So, did that make me her main event? She could always come and snatch me up at any minute, but no, she wanted to watch me. She wanted me to feel Purgatory's pull on what she knew would be my resistance. It's extremely delicious pull because, *fuck,* was it pulling.

I punched the wall of the shower so hard my whole hand vibrated. I tilted my head back letting the water run down my face, running a hand through my wet hair. It was heavy when it was wet and there were way more tangles than I would like to admit. Tangles that I would likely spend the rest of the night trying to get out. I turned around and ducked my head further under the water and ran my hand down my face, feeling the water fall down my body, hitting the shower floor beneath my feet.

I needed to think about something completely off topic before I went into full rage mode and created a mess in this bathroom, and I didn't think Beetee would appreciate having to clean up the results of my tantrum. My thoughts bounced around as I searched. Elise popped into my head and oh fuck, no. My shadows and darkness bubbled up, willing me to boil over. I shook my head, pieces of my hair slapping me in the face. Beetee and her weird snake shifting ability was something, but I would much rather talk to her about that in person than ponder on it. I turned around so my back was against the shower wall and continued to think. I could have tried to create more of a plan, channel my inner Nicholas Cassial and try to be a *leader of the pack* type, but so much had happened today that I wasn't in the right headspace for strategy, but—

Nicholas Cassial. I didn't have to *like* him at the moment to think about him.

There was something off about him lately that I couldn't put my finger on, but thinking about him right now had me aching to put my finger somewhere else. I wasn't giving into his charm or that pretty face by letting him invade my thoughts. He wasn't a mind reader, I was well aware, but he didn't need to search the ten circles of Hell to figure out what I wanted to hear. I wasn't going to give him all the answers though. He'd admitted he wanted me, so he could deduce what the answer to getting me back into his good graces was.

Even so, I loved watching him pine.

He was still insanely attractive, even though he was fucking dense. I had to stop myself from staring too hard when he pulled off his shirt. Venom wounds and all, he was incredibly built, and I knew what that body looked like with no clothes on at all, and it was the best thing to empty my mind too. I bit my lip as I slid my hand down between my breasts and over my stomach. My thighs shook slightly at the anticipation as my fingers lightly teased my clit. I tilted my head back at that small touch and closed my eyes. I could want my distance from him now, but in my head his hands were all over me. Those very, very skilled hands. I imagined his lips kissing my neck and those long fingers of his exploring between my legs and playing with me. I dipped my fingers lower, pressing one inside of me. I used my other hand to massage my breast, toying with my nipple while I let out a moan at the feeling.

I remembered his hands were rougher than mine, yet he was still gentle. I tweaked and played with my nipples as I fucked myself with my own hand, adding another finger alongside the previous one. "Fuck, oh, fuck." My fingers were no match for the size of him though. They didn't fill and stretch me the same way he did, and it was a fucking shame. I felt myself growing wetter at the thought of him thrusting inside of me relentlessly, wrapping his large hand around my neck. I moved my hand faster and more urgently, using my memories of him and the way we were that night to push me along.

I removed my hand from my breast and traced it down my slick, wet skin to my clit. I needed to mimic that sensation of his fingers and tongue. I could never do it properly, but I could fucking try. I massaged the sensitive area and hissed through my teeth. I could admit I wanted his tongue. If he ever lost his skillful ability with a sword, then he could just be the master of eating out. I curled my body over as I worked my fingers inside myself and rubbed my clit in a harmonious rhythm. Flashes of everything that we'd done, every position he'd put me in, every single time I came played across my closed eyes and I used it. I used those vivid pictures to push myself closer and closer to that edge I longed for.

I rubbed my clit harder and faster, somehow remembering how his breath felt on my neck, his voice in my ear and how good he felt holding my hips as he pounded into me from behind. That praise that he gave me for coming all over his cock. *Good girl.* "Shit, shit, fuck." I pumped my fingers into my pussy so hard as the tingling sensation of my orgasm shot through me. I let his name tumble past my lips in a desperate kind of plea as I circled my clit, over and over.

I let my shoulders relax and tried to push myself off the wall and stand on my shaky legs. I'd pleasured myself many, many times before but that was different. My vision was slightly blurry from closing my eyes so tight, but it also could have been from the steam that the hot water had been creating all this time. My chest rose and fell with my steadying breaths. I felt a little lightheaded, but better than I did before so I felt accomplished at least.

I turned off the shower and reached for the towel I'd hung up. I stepped carefully out of the shower and padded over to the mirror. I wiped my hand down the fogged glass and looked at myself, my mass of wet curls plastered to my back. What looked back at me was an incredibly sated halfling.

Even if we weren't on the best of terms, Nicholas should be happy that he could still satisfy me.

I felt better in the morning, much more relaxed than I was last night. I changed my clothes and trotted downstairs, taking them two at a time. I smelt coffee before I'd made it to the last step, and I'd never been so eager for a beverage in all of my existence. The reddish-orange glow from the window told me it was mid-morning and it also made me miss the glowing sunshine that Heaven's Gate provided. There was light outside, but it wasn't as bright, and it didn't bring with it potential for *fun* adventures. I heard chatter coming from the lounge area and turned my head to see two females sitting together on the couch. They looked identical with long black hair and dark skin. One of them looked over their shoulder at me in a way that told me that she was sizing me up. Her face seemed to morph into something of respect in the same moment as if she was just starting to realize who I was. She nudged the female next to her, who looked over her shoulder in awe and smiled at me.

A few of her teeth were shaved down to points telling me that they were definitely demons, not that I wouldn't have been able to sniff them out, and that this side of Purgatory was not where they originally resided. I shifted out of the way when a few people came down the stairs and rushed out the door. The Hearth wasn't crowded, but there were a shit ton more people here right now, which meant more eyes on me. I didn't mind it, but that didn't mean I wanted attention when I didn't ask for it. I walked past the kitchen, noticing an older woman and a younger man sitting at the breakfast bar and before I could casually walk into the dining area, a shot of yellow magic flew past my face.

"What the fuck," I yelled, shooting my own dark shadows at the direction the magic came from.

I heard a groan and the sound of a body hitting a wall. A few faces turned to me, some full of nerves and others looked impressed. A boy rubbed the back of his head as he got up from the floor on the other side of the room. His magic gave off that he was an Enchanter. He looked up at me and narrowed his eyes as if he was prepared to start some type of fight. It would be a fight he wouldn't win. He had sandy blonde hair that fell just above his ears. Ears that were burning red at the tips from what I assumed was embarrassment. I stood my ground as he started to stalk over to me when another guy who was seated got up and grabbed him shaking his head and whispered something in his ear. I caught two words.

Soul Seether.

The blonde boys' eyes widened and his whole big and tough demeanor began to dissolve. "I was just messing around Soul Seether, I'm sorry."

Beetee came rushing in, wiping her hands on a rag as she looked up and noticed the tension in the room. "What is happening?"

I walked over to the Enchanter and manifested my dagger in my hands, causing a few of the people around us to scoot their chairs back and I heard a few intakes of breath. I took my dagger and lifted his chin up with it. "Oh nothing. Careful next time, yes?"

He rapidly nodded, maintaining my eye contact like a champ. I let my dagger disappear as I looked over to Beetee whose face was a small shade of pink. "All good. Can we talk?"

She wiped her hands down her floral orange dress and nodded, tilting her head towards the small kitchen. I winked at the kid in front of me and turned around on the tips of my toes, letting the ponytail I had placed my massive curls in swing behind me.

"We're happy you're here." I heard someone behind me say. I turned around to find out who it was, but no one spoke up. Every face I looked at was still rattled with nerves, but they all seemed to show some kind of overwhelming approval of the statement.

"Even if you are slightly terrifying." I twirled back around to see one of the females from earlier eyeing me with a smirk at her lips.

Beetee stood next to me and slightly took my arm, leading me towards the kitchen. "See I told you."

"You said I was an inspiration to them. An inspiration of what? Being someone's bitch pawn for years. Oh yeah, definitely something to aspire to." I rolled my eyes and jumped up on one of the stools at the bar. The women and man from before were gone, leaving just me and her.

She grabbed a mug and filled it with the dark caffeinated liquid I was craving. "No, Dani. Some people may take some time to actually admit it to you, but while you are terrifying, you know who to unleash your voracious violence on. Everyone here has been hurt in some way by Lilith, so really if you just spoke to them, you would see the common enemy." She placed the mug in front of me, the orange of her dress making her golden-brown skin stand out more than usual. She had a sparkly clip in her hair, pulling her bang out of her face. "Fun fact…the enemy isn't you."

I stuck my tongue out at her which she returned with a cheeky smile. I wrapped my hands around the mug, bringing the coffee to my lips and taking a long drink. "I'm going to guess that you don't turn into a snake often?"

Beetee pressed her lips together, her face turning that shade of pink again. The answer to my question solidified. "Um, well…"

"I'm impressed. You even scared me for a moment and that's saying something."

The pink in her face subsided a bit and she started to stand a little taller at my praise.

"When I first realized I could do it, I got really bad headaches when I would change back, but now not so much. I can get a little scared of *myself* sometimes."

I tilted my head to the side. "I've only seen a few demons with an anchoring tattoo." I reached behind myself and pointed towards my back. She absentmindedly reached towards her own back as well. Anchoring tattoos weren't really rare, but I personally hadn't seen many demons with them. You were usually born with something like that. I remember asking Elise if her switchblades tattoo was an anchor, but she just shook her head and explained how her tattoo was done at a club one night because she was bored, but instead of the normal ingredients of crushed up brimstone particles and demon blood, she'd opted to use her venom instead of blood. It explained why the tattoo pulsed and moved along with her whenever her power was boiling to the surface.

It was odd, since most demons with anchoring tattoos were closely associated with Lilith. If I was the queen of darkness, I would want all the heavy hitters I could get. Beetee made it seem like she'd never associated with Lilith, so it was just odd for now.

"Oh, you saw that."

"Well, you were butt ass naked, Beetee."

She slapped her hand over her eyes in embarrassment. "Another reason why I hate doing it."

"You recovered well, don't worry. I'm pretty sure Reese saw enough to satisfy him for days." We both laughed and took a few breaths before continuing. "It seems like you have it under control, though."

She smiled at me. "Took forever. My parents had to reign me in a few times."

A woman and two young boys hustled outside the door of the hostel, one of the boys pointing his index finger at the other's backside, sending a spark of blue magic from his fingertip. The other one squealed as they started fighting playfully. I fixed my eyes back on Beetee, noticing she now also had a cup of coffee in front of her.

"I thought Enchanters gave their powers to Isabel so that she could take on Natalia and damn near destroy us all?" I side-eyed the guy from earlier who was now nowhere to be found.

"I don't think she needed every single Enchanter to make it happen, but most of the ones here fled from Lilith's reign. I don't ask many questions when they come here. I just provide what I can." Beetee shrugged as if what she said was obvious and simple.

"And they get along in this close proximity? Enchanters and demons?" I would see how Enchanters had more of an issue with demons, but still, it was a valid question.

Beetee giggled. The high-pitched sound caught some attention around us. "There have been a few fights, but nothing major. Sometimes anger gets the better of us, but anyone here would rather step outside and take a few breaths or meditate before they accidentally tore this place apart all because… I don't know, someone didn't say excuse me when they bumped into them."

I took another sip of my coffee and hummed, letting the steam hit my face. Another question dawned on me. "It was quiet last night. That's surprising seeing as I assume people like to come here after nights out."

Beetee turned around reaching into a cabinet above her head, pulling out a muffin. The top was covered in sugar. "Marissa encased the Hearth in noise magic." She pointed to a brunette girl who was seated at the table in the dining room.

"Noise magic?"

She placed the muffin on a plate and slid it over to me. "After a certain time of night, the hostel will cancel out the noise. You'll hear small sounds here and there, but nothing too loud or alarming. I wanted my patrons to be able to get a good night's sleep, but I also want my late-night patrons to not feel like they have to walk on eggshells."

I picked at the muffin, feeling her lilac eyes watching me. "And what about if something happens? An attack? Or hell, I don't know anything bad."

"I'm not worried. There are plenty of regular creatures that come here who never really sleep. Too much trauma or dark memories from Lilith and even Lucifer. They are the alarms and patrol I didn't ask for, but they're here."

I popped a sugary piece of the pastry in my mouth, swallowing before I spoke again. "What about you? No encounter with Lilith to speak about?" My curiosity was peaking this morning.

She picked off a piece of my muffin and popped it into her mouth. "Nope. I've lived a Lilith free life. I just deal with the consequences of her actions from my patrons. That's enough for me." She gave me a sympathetic smile.

I heard a door close and the sound of a highly familiar deep voice, along with another male voice. Beetee and I both craned our necks around the corner of the dining room to see Nicholas and the Enchanter from yesterday, Blake. They were walking side by side and the male Enchanter let out a small laugh as Nicholas lightly punched his shoulder in a friendly gesture. It was an immediate change from the way he looked yesterday. Some of the others around the dining table gave them both nods and small waves as if they were now best buddies or legitimately cordial on purpose. They both came into the kitchen, noticing us.

"Will he live, Blake?" Beetee asked.

He gave Nicholas a once over and nodded. "Yeah, everything is healing nicely."

I took the chance to look at my raven-haired angel whose cheek was nearly fully healed, the small remnants of a scar left in place of the open gash that was there, complimenting the scar under his eye. The sleeves of the t-shirt he wore wrapped around his biceps in this perfect way that was truly unfair. His hair was tousled, which told me he hadn't done much to it, but maybe took one pass of his hand.

"You guys seem close now." I pointed out, tucking one of the stray pieces of hair that didn't make it into my ponytail behind my ear.

Nicholas looked from Blake to me and shrugged. "I thought we got off on the wrong foot yesterday. I'd rather be on good terms and the same page." A demon walked past him and gave him a nod as if they were friends.

What the hell was going on.

"Making yourself at home in Purgatory, huh. New friends and all." I let my eyes follow the demon he was friendly towards and lifted my leg up, placing my foot on the stool next to me. My shorts started to ride up my thigh a little more and his eyes immediately went to the exposed skin before he collected himself.

"Let's not get ahead of ourselves, I got up a little early and just started having conversations, it's amazing how much people just want to talk. It's not much, but I'm *trying*." He flicked his eyes to mine as if he was trying to tell me something else entirely. He was trying to show me he could be an angel and be just the way he was with these creatures around us. He wasn't showing prejudice against them; he accepted them. I was impressed that he was getting comfortable here. I had honestly thought he would squirm more and it would take days to get him to loosen up. Beetee's little piece of Purgatory wasn't the real thing though and he would find that out soon enough.

"I can see that," I answered, giving him the amount of eye contact that usually made people look away. All he did was blink and try to dig those brown eyes further into my soul.

"He is quite adorable." A female voice rang out next to me. I looked to my left to see one of the demon females who had been sitting on the couch, now leaning over the breakfast bar. Her breasts were practically spilling out of her top. It was a classic move, and I would have laughed in an amicable type of way if she had been directing her sexual energy at anyone else.

The female smiled, sharp teeth on display. She had high cheekbones and a mole right at the top of her lip. A tattoo of cascading stars lined the left side of her face. I peeked over at Nicholas who was looking at her, but not in a way that showed any interest, but like he didn't want to be rude and not give her any attention whatsoever. I would rather him be fucking rude. "I'm Rae and this is Eva." She pointed to her friend who was getting up from the couch.

"You must be very, very brave to be working with the Soul Seether." The other demon, Eva, walked up next to her friend, her voice letting off that same sexual energy. Eva was slightly shorter, but she had more legs than torso and they went on for miles. The orange tinted light from outside made her hooped eyebrow piercing twinkle. Neither one of them seemed scared of me, which told me they either had nothing to lose or they were just as dumb as they looked.

"Brave, sure. She is a difficult one to keep up with. I guess you can say it's an honor and I like a challenge," he said with the kind of confidence that made my lips quirk up into a small smile.

The females both looked at each other and then back at him. The Enchanter, Blake, let out a small cough as he turned to leave and Beetee turned around, making herself busy doing whatever she could find to steal her attention away. Rae giggled and responded, "We can always teach you how to keep up with a demon, if you ever find yourself in need of some help." I watched her eyes travel up and down his body as if he was the tastiest snack. I *had* tasted him, and I could tell her honestly, he *was*.

I felt my shadows start to seam together. I felt the darkness as it started to rise inside of myself. Nicholas could be flirted with; he was attractive enough to warrant the attention. And if any of them knew what he was like in bed, *fuck*, he would have demons fighting over him in an instant. I didn't pin myself as the jealous type, I'd never really cared about anyone I'd slept with, but things were different now. My shadows wanted to claim ownership of him and that was odd. Very odd.

If he was interested, he could come to her but for now she could get the *fuck* out of my peripheral vision. I never had to say much to other demons to get my points across and if they happened to wake up with my dagger in their throats, well sucks to suck. Lessons are taught the hard way down here.

Nicholas cleared his throat and licked his lips, furrowing his brow. "Thanks, but I think there is only one demon I want to focus on."

Both demons pouted and I laughed under my breath at his obvious show of loyalty, but not before catching Beetee's eye as she leaned against the counter opposite the bar. I felt that warmth of light creep into my subconscious and it nearly shot up my spine. I couldn't help liking the way he spoke about me, if only he could figure out the words I wanted to hear, but of course he wanted to go about this the hard way.

Stomping came from the stairs as both Reese and Elise were nearly shoving each other as they came down.

"Fuck, you can either go in front of me or not," Reese shouted, letting out a heavy sigh.

"If you wanted me to go in front of *you*, why are you trying to go in front of me? I will legit shove you down these stairs, I swear to fuck," Elise shouted back, pushing past him and stopping when she saw all of us.

I noticed the female demons twirling their shiny black hair with their fingers as they eyed Reese as well. "Oh, another one."

They moved on quickly.

Reese craned his head back, taking in the entire scene in front of him. He opened his mouth a little and then closed it. His blonde hair was tied up into a low bun and he had his bow held tightly in his hand. Reese craned his neck around to look at his best friend on the other side of the room, who was still eyeing me like if I gave him the okay, he would close the distance between us and kiss me. "Why do I feel like I have clothes on, but they are just picturing me naked?"

"We wouldn't mind that," Eva said, giggling, her sharp teeth on display. I saw Reese inwardly cringe, likely at the idea of having his dick anywhere near that. I appreciated the forwardness, especially since it was no longer directed towards a certain angel.

"It stinks of desperation in here. Don't make me vomit." Elise snuck around Beetee and grabbed a muffin for herself. "And he'd rather kill either of you than fuck you, so please get lost." Her eyes glowed with a fiery red color as she stared them both down until they looked away with snarky glares.

"Fine." Rae said, adjusting her short skirt. "But you should come see us at the club one night. Have some fun." She winked over at Nicholas, who pressed his lips together and showed no interest in the slightest. I could have strangled her.

"Club?" Nicholas and Reese both asked at the same time.

"Oh yes, the club. You should come. You would be the *sweetest* treat." Eva batted her eyelashes and snapped her teeth at him, grabbing her friend's hand as they made their way out of the hostel.

I had a feeling I knew exactly what club they were referring to. They would most definitely be the sweetest treats in that place. Not that I would ever think of taking them there…maybe.

"Wow, Nicholas, you just can't stop yourself from attracting demons." Elise stuck her tongue out at him. He ran a hand through his hair trying his best not to make eye contact with her.

Reese placed his bow on the breakfast bar and pointed to the door. "What the hell was that about?"

"It was someone showing interest in you. I know it must be a shock, since that never happens, right?" Elise licked her fingers, cleaning off the remaining remnants of the muffin she scarfed down.

Reese gave her both his middle fingers. "If you don't have anything nice to say, then shut the fuck up."

"You know I hope you get lost here one night and those girls find you and bite your dick off."

"Oh my god! Ellie!" Beetee exclaimed, pressing her hand over her mouth.

I couldn't help but chuckle. Elise was laughing too and when we both noticed we were laughing at the same time, we stopped. Her gray eyes narrowed at me before she looked away. That joke was something we would have both laughed about for hours if circumstances were different.

"Fuck you, alright," Reese replied, rolling his eyes. He focused on Nicholas next, who was massaging the back of his neck with his hand. "You alright? I found you sleeping on the bathroom floor last night when I had to take a leak. Had to get your ass back into bed, even though you were a little out of it."

I pinched my eyebrows together in confusion. The bathroom floor?

Nicholas stopped messing with his neck as if he was frozen in place. "I didn't...umm...feel good, so you know..." He shrugged as if that was enough of an answer.

Reese scratched the side of his chin where small bits of stubble were starting to appear. "So, you decided to sleep on the bathroom floor? Why didn't you come get me?"

I could literally taste how uncomfortable Nicholas was. The instant his mood went from nonchalant to instant anxiety. "I didn't want to bother you. I mean it came and went and I don't know, I must have just passed out from exhaustion. I don't really remember. I got back to bed, that's all that matters." He started staring at the floor as if it was the most interesting thing in the room. Something was going on with him that I couldn't help but want to figure out. He reached up and started to massage his neck again.

"You were literally covered in sweat, Nick. Maybe we should just sit out on whatever we are doing today and let you rest..."

"No. I'm fine. Blake said I was good. Just leave it alright." It looked like Reese wanted to say more, but the look that Nicholas was giving him told him to just do what his best friend was asking. Reese scrubbed a hand down his face and sighed. "So, what's on the agenda for today, reptile queen."

Beetee snorted. "That's a terrible name for starters. But Soul Seether— ugh, Dani— you asked about Enchanters which brings me to our travels today."

"Beetee, please don't tell me we're going to..." Elise started, taking a long inhale through her nose.

"Shush, just behave and you'll be fine," Beetee said, clearly understanding Elise's apprehension while the rest of us were in the dark. "We are going to see some friends of mine. The path there is a little bit hidden. They used to be pretty close with Lilith and well, I'll let them tell their own story. Finding demons willing to spill their Lilith secrets is easy, Enchanters not so much, especially the ones that turned against her."

"Like Elise *friends* or legit friends?" I asked.

Elise snarled. "What the fuck is that supposed to mean?"

"Oh, you know, just like friends we can trust. Actual *friends*. But forgive me if you don't know what that means." I gave her a noncommittal shrug as if there was nothing more for her to say.

Reese clapped his hands together. "Well, I am up for anything that makes the little sour psycho demon over there uncomfortable. When do we leave?"

Beetee laughed that high pitch laugh of hers and began to answer him, but I was more interested in someone else at the moment. I got up from my stool and walked over to Nicholas who was still rubbing the pads of his fingers into his neck.

He was so tall, I had to look up at him from where I stood, my head at his bicep. We were toe to toe, the tips of our high-top sneakers touching. I reached up and yanked his arm away from his neck. "The bathroom floor isn't comfortable I presume?"

Nicholas gave me an awkward chuckle. "I guess not."

"You want to explain to me why you were really on the bathroom floor in the middle of the night?"

"I already said why."

"We all know that was a lie."

He sighed. "It wasn't." His words said one thing, but his eyes said something different. They were almost a little sad—sad and tired. What the hell happened between the time I left him to right now? He and I were on the same wavelength, wanting the other to figure something out that we weren't willing to say up front. At least when it came to me, it would be as simple as him just not being so logical and overthinking everything. What I wanted didn't require thought and Nicholas could outthink the best of them. He was the one keeping his emotions close to his chest on this one.

I hummed as I settled with letting him keep whatever was going on to himself for now. "Fine, fine I'll leave it." We both knew I would find a way to bring it up later. I looked at his neck again, remembering the way he was really trying to dig his fingers into his neck muscles. "Seems like you could use a neck massage."

"Are you offering?" he asked, smirking.

Oh, there he was. Confident little shit. The sadness in his eyes was still there, but they shined a little with his not-so-subtle flirting.

"Mmm...no. You haven't earned that. But when you figure out what I want then maybe I'll massage more than just your neck. Deal?" I traced my finger along his chin and turned on my heels away from him.

I was an action kind of girl and Nicholas coming here with me, fighting next to me, made my stomach flip but what I really wanted was for him to tell me I was *enough*. That I was accepted and that his prior words were stupid, and he took them all back. I wanted him to tell me that I could be whatever kind of hybrid, halfling, whatever the fuck and he would still see me just the same. A simple I'm sorry was way too broad. I wanted him to tell me *those* words.

And if that meant I had to bring him to his knees for him to say it, so be it.

9

NICK

Beetee made sure we were all fed before we headed out to wherever her friends were located. I readjusted my sword behind my back as we all waited for the pink-haired demon to come back to the lounge area. Most of the patrons I saw earlier in the day had left or had headed back to their rooms. I'd been told that the hostel was pretty quiet around this time and not much happened unless it was early morning or late at night. I didn't let it be known that I hadn't heard anything last night since I had another episode that nearly took me out...again. And I'd had to save face with everyone when Reese decided to word-vomit unnecessary details about what happened.

I recovered as best I could, but I knew Dani was starting to get suspicious of my mood so I would have to fix that. I wanted to take her into another room and explain everything to her, just let someone else in on my thoughts and how dark my mind could really get, but I couldn't do it. After the fight, after I saw that familiar look on her face, I couldn't bring her down with my own baggage.

Beetee skipped towards us, her ankle boot covered feet making small thuds on the wood floor. "Are we ready?"

We all started to head towards the front door, but she shook her head. She looked over her shoulder. "Follow me, please." She motioned for us to follow her as she turned around and started heading in the other direction. She led us towards the back of the hostel as we passed rooms we had seen before, but eventually I saw a door that had a small window near the top. The odd lighting from the sky outside shined through.

Beetee placed her hand on the door and pushed it open, the humid air immediately hitting my skin. Purgatory in the daytime, if you could even call it that, was much different than whatever time we had gotten here yesterday. It wasn't the kind of humidity that was suffocating, but there was no breeze to help it out as I stepped outside. The sky was actually kind of beautiful once you really looked at it. There were reds and oranges that ran together in a blended haze.

It had been so dark when we got here that I couldn't get a good look at anything. The trees were tall, but the branches were bent and every few moments it sounded like one was cracking and falling to the ground. The leaves weren't as lush and vibrantly green as they were in Heaven's Gate. They were a dark brown or dark yellow color, almost as if this place was in a perpetual state of autumn. The forest we were looking at wasn't quite as ominous as it was before the fight, but there was something that crawled up my spine when I looked at it straight on. It wasn't scary really, just that there was more than what you were initially looking at.

"You want us to trek through the woods? That didn't bode well last time." Reese pointed out, tilting his head left and right to try and get a view into the depths of the woods.

"You don't have to come, Blondie. You can just stay here and wait for the two sharp teeth twins to come back." Elise smirked.

"No, I'm just saying we could just fly," Reese said as if that was the obvious answer.

Beetee giggled. "Oh of course, two angels flying high in the sky. I thought you didn't like all the demon attention." She put her hands on her hips. "I already have—"

Reese pinched the bridge of his nose and cut her off. "Fine, another idea. How about they fly and carry us, you know payback for when we had to do it."

I immediately gave him my answer to that. "I don't like the idea of being cradled in the sky by them, or by anyone, so no." Reese raised both his hands up in disgruntled defeat. I ran a finger over my healed cheek and watched as

Dani seemed to be distracted. She was looking around as if something had caught her eye, or she'd heard something that alarmed her. "What's wrong?"

She ignored me and started going around to the side of the hostel. I looked over at Reese who had his eyebrows raised as he waited. Dani returned a moment later empty handed and shrugged. "I thought I heard something, but I guess not." She still looked skeptical as if there was no way she could have been wrong.

"What did you think you heard?" I asked.

"Panting."

"Panting?" Elise mimicked, her voice sounding as if that was the weirdest answer she'd ever heard.

I was about to say something when Reese cut me off. "Well, that's fucking weird—" A rustle from nearby caught his attention. "The fuck." He turned around looking towards where the sound had come from.

There was rustling again and all of sudden in a matter of seconds, something small and black was barreling towards him. It was fast, whatever it was, and it jumped up pushing against Reese's chest. My best friend fell to the ground, while dust collected around us from the impact.

"Reese, are you okay?" I said, starting to hurry over to him.

"I knew I heard something." Dani confirmed, stepping up behind me to see what it was.

Beetee giggled as she casually walked up to the semi-circle we had created around Reese. "This is not the way I wanted you guys to meet."

Reese wasn't hurt or trying to fight whatever had attacked him. Well, he *was* fighting it, but he was fighting to get it to stop licking him. It was a dog. A small black dog. Its body shape was long and narrow, with floppy ears and onyx-colored eyes. Its little pink tongue darted out and licked up the side of Reese's face, leaving a long stripe of saliva on his skin. It was a tiny thing, but it knocked him down like it was nothing at all. The paws on it were huge compared to its body, but not so much that it looked deformed. It actually looked harmless.

"Can somebody get this thing off of me!" Reese was trying to block his face while the small dog kept nuzzling its little black nose closer, fighting him back.

"I actually really like this," Elise said, holding her stomach as she bent over laughing. I tried to fight my own laugh, but it ended up coming out anyway. Eventually we all started laughing as Beetee bent down to grab the dog from Reese's chest.

"You guys' fucking suck, you know that." Reese scrambled to get up as he started to brush the dirt covering his shirt.

Beetee held the dog in her arms as it panted and squirmed.

"You want to explain?" I asked her, thinking that the dog *was* kind of cute.

The pink-haired demon was rocking the dog in her arms as she answered me. The animal burrowed its head into her neck. "The path there can be a little rocky, so this guy is going to be your ride."

"Excuse me?" Dani piped up, a small laugh leaving her lips.

"Are you joking?" I looked at Beetee who wasn't looking at any of us. She was looking at Elise.

Elise was staring back at her with her tongue pressed to the inside of her cheek. "He's a hellhound."

My eyes widened as I looked from the dog to her. "That tiny thing is a hellhound?" I was shell shocked.

Dani hummed. "It's not too hard to believe. Vicious things do come in tiny packages." She tilted her head and looked at me. She was vicious that was for sure, but instead of her attitude pushing me away, it made me want to do viciously wicked things *to* her in return.

"Axel might be tiny, but he's a fucking menace." Elise explained.

At the sound of his name, he poked his head out from Beetee's neck and focused his black eyes on Elise. His tail started wagging—no, not wagging— vibrating. Beetee couldn't hold him any longer as he ripped himself out of her grasp, nearly clawing at her skin. The hellhound bounded over to Elise who easily picked him up. To everyone's surprise she didn't shy away from his kisses.

"Aw, he missed you." Beetee placed her hand over her heart.

"Woah, woah. I'm sorry but are you...his owner?" Reese questioned; a disbelieving look in his hazel eyes.

"Let's just add this to the never-ending list of things you've kept from me," Dani mumbled.

Elise groaned as Axel panted against her face. "Can we please just fucking go."

"You *actually* own another living thing? And it *actually* likes you?" Reese kept going with his questions.

"He was a gift a long time ago, you annoying dick and...ugh, Axel stop." He continuously kept licking her face as if he hadn't seen her in decades. The dog ceased licking her, tilting its head back to stare at each of us. His eyes landed on Dani and its tail began to vibrate again. Elise followed his gaze and rolled her eyes. She turned the dog around and held it up to look at her, his tongue hanging out the side of his mouth. "Be fucking scary you little fucker."

She dropped the dog on the ground and for a moment, nothing happened.

Then a rumbling sound filled my ears. I looked around and the ground was still intact and there was no swaying in the trees. The rumbling sounded again. I looked down to see that it was coming from Axel. His whole body was vibrating now as he planted his massive paws towards the ground.

"What is happening?" Reese whispered.

Elise just gave a small kind of creepy smile before focusing her gray eyes on her dog. A dog that was now baring its teeth and thrashing back and forth in quick motions. His paws started to grow bigger, and his body somehow started to pulse as if it was about to explode at any moment. I heard shuffling as Reese began to back up and I followed suit. Beetee had her hands clapped together in front of her as if she was so eager to see the result of whatever was happening. It was hard to tell but Elise almost looked a little proud of her...pet.

Axel started to become a blur as his fur started to fall off his body, piles of hair scattered around him. He started to growl, drool descending as his mouth grew larger and his head followed suit. His floppy ears started to shrink to upward points and if his eyes could have grown any darker, they would have. I started to back up more as his body grew and grew, becoming muscular and stocky. His shadow extended on the ground and if there had been a sun above us, he would have been blocking it. I looked down at his paws that were now bigger than my head and his nails dug into the dirt. His front canines hung out of his mouth and smoke blew out of his snout.

Silence fell over all of us when he was done...transforming.

"I've never seen a hellhound this size before," Dani said, looking up at Axel. He loomed over her and made her small stature even *more* apparent. She didn't shy away from him though. She stood her ground and just inspected him with her arms crossed.

"There are hellhounds bigger than this?" I asked.

Dani shook her head. "No, actually. Smaller."

"Then how in the hell did you end up with this monster?" Reese created a wide berth as he circled around Axel who had his now forked tongue hanging out the side of his mouth. Despite his size and scary exterior, he looked dopey.

Elise stepped up to her hellhound and tilted his head down, a puff of smoke hitting her face. "He was a gift like I already fucking said. Now, Axel down, let's go."

Her pet immediately went to lay down on the floor, patiently waiting.

"We're riding him?" I questioned.

"I mean if you would like to walk, pretty boy, that is fine by me. I'm sure that face of yours will help you out if you get caught up," Elise snarked, jumping up and sitting astride Axel's back.

"Yeah, no thanks." Reese said, sarcastically. "You are fucking crazy though, if you think I'm sitting behind you."

Dani shoved past him and started to jump up to get on Axel's back, but she stumbled a bit and started to fall back. I ran up behind her and caught her waist. My heart was thundering in my chest at the contact. My fingers squeezed as she fell back against me. Her hair tickled my cheek as she leaned into me, trying to regain her balance. I felt her tense up as she side-eyed me.

"You good?" I inquired, pushing her forward and up a bit.

"Mhmm," she said quickly, grabbing onto the thick wrinkles of Axel's skin and hooked her leg around to the other side.

I jumped on after and Reese followed, leaving Beetee leaning in front of Axel's very large head, whispering something in his ear. She giggled a little and then I felt Axel start to rise underneath me. I felt so high up, to the point where I had to duck a little from varying tree branches. "He knows where to go, and he'll bring you back so don't worry."

"Wait, you aren't coming?" I raised one of my eyebrows down at her.

"I need to stay here, and you don't need me there. Just knock on the door and tell them I sent you." Beetee gave a solid nod and started to walk away, but quickly turned on her heels and looked directly at Elise. "Behave, Ellie."

Ellie grunted up at the front, letting out a muffled *whatever* before patting Axel on the side of his head. He huffed out more smoke from his nostrils and raised his paws to start walking into the woods. His tail slapped the ground as he took one long stride after another.

Axel had been trotting along for what felt like an hour, but I still didn't understand how time worked here in Purgatory. The further we got into the woods, the less I saw the red-orange sky. The tops of the trees huddled together to create an overcast that made any chance of seeing what was ahead extremely difficult. There were small sounds around us that sounded like something other than normal woodsy sounds. And I could have sworn I saw shadows snaking around the trees, whispering to us. Smaller versions of Axel bounded around the surrounding area, but the big beast paid them no mind. Dani took the time to at least explain to us that those were what normal hellhounds looked like. Axel still had only two eyes, whereas some of these creatures had three or they had split tails.

I was starting to settle into this ride, but I was finding it hard to figure out what to do with my hands. I could hold onto Axel's thick, coarse, back rolls or I could hold onto something that pleased me much, much more.

There had been numerous times in the past hour that I instinctively wanted to grab her waist and yank her closer to me. I did have to hold onto her a few times when Axel jumped over fallen tree trunks, but I wanted more. She would readjust herself each time, almost like she was conflicted having to decide whether to shift closer to Elise or move back towards me. She had her hair in a ponytail, and I had to force my eyes away from her neck. I wanted my mouth on her skin, on that tender part of her neck that made her shiver and claw at my back.

I felt the back of my neck starting to sweat, but I didn't feel hot. It was weird. There was something about this place that made me a little unfocused. Dani was a tempting individual, but down here she had me wanting to focus solely on her, to be in pure tunnel vision. Something I was highly against when it came to training and fights but focusing on Lilith and the plan had me thinking about Dani at the same time, so nothing truly fucking helped. The other night I felt like something was clawing at my mind, yanking at my nightmares and thoughts, but I was strong, and I was able to handle it... for now. Natalia and the girls did say that Purgatory had a way of digging its teeth into you. I would have to continue to keep my wits about myself if I was going to make it out of here with at least half of my mental state intact.

"Are we almost fucking there?" Reese complained, letting out a loud sigh.

"I will have him buck you off, if you don't shut up," Elise threatened.

There was a rock formation coming up and it was massive, with moss growing on the rocks and mud splattered along the perimeter. We had stopped moving, I noticed, so I looked around wondering when we would start again. Elise slid off Axel, landing on the ground with easy agility. She scratched behind Axel's ear as he eased himself down to the dirt. We all remained on top of him as we looked at her suspiciously.

"Well get the fuck off." She rolled her eyes, the impatience heavy in her tone.

"It's a fucking rock." Reese pointed ahead of us as he swung his legs over and jumped off the large beast.

I jumped off after him and instinctively turned around, reaching up to help Dani. Surprisingly, she let me, but the contact didn't last long before she was out of my hold and walking behind Elise towards the giant rocks.

I patted Axel on the head as I walked by and he huffed out more smoke from his snout. Fallen leaves danced around as his nostril smoke breezed past them. Reese sidled up next to me. "I'm not crazy right, that's a fucking rock."

I reached over and ruffled his hair. "I'm pretty sure we should start thinking that everything is not as it seems."

He looked over his shoulder at the hellhound. "Ain't that the truth."

Elise had walked around the rock formation, letting her fingers drag along the rock's exterior. We were so far away from where we had started that if anything were to happen, I wouldn't know which way was the right direction. I didn't exactly feel nervous about wherever we were, but I was getting antsy. Dani broke the short silence.

"Are you going to explain anything right now?"

"And what would you like for me to explain? Beetee wanted you to talk to her friends so here we are," Elise grumbled.

"You fucking know that's not what I mean."

I sighed not wanting to intervene, but if they started fighting again, we could all be fucked. "Can you both just not, please."

Elise flicked her eyes to me and narrowed them. "Aw, your little boyfriend thinks he has a say in any of this."

"He's not my boyfriend." Dani bared her teeth. I could admit how much that stung just a tiny bit. I wasn't upset by her statement, but still…

Elise tapped her finger against her pursed lips. "Oh right, he's *your* boyfriend." She pointed at Reese before twirling around and moving along the rock again.

Reese stood there with his mouth open and anger in his eyes.

"Over here!" Elise shouted and we all hustled over to her.

As we wrapped around the rock, I didn't notice anything different until my eyes caught on a smaller rock attached to the larger formation. It was red and rounded out almost like a knob, but there was no indication of a door. Elise rapped her knuckles along the area where the knob sat, then waited. I looked back behind me, still seeing Axel fully awake, but nestled on his stomach. I heard Elise knock again, then she let out a loud groan. "Beetee sent us to talk, so letting us in would be greatly appreciated." The nice tone in her voice sounded so fake I almost laughed.

There was a straining noise as if something heavy was placed on top of something that couldn't bear its weight. The red rock glittered and long cracks started to show in the rock, making the shape of a jagged edged door. The door slid to the left as if it was transparent to the rest of the rock. A woman poked her head out, her hair in two braids running down the sides of her head. I couldn't make out her face well enough yet, but she focused her attention on Elise who didn't seem phased by any of this.

"Beetee sent *you?*" She was practically whispering, but from what I could tell her words were sharp.

Elise clucked her tongue. "Beetee sent all of us." She motioned towards us in a nonchalant fashion.

The woman turned her head and gave us each a quick look. She motioned for us to follow her inside, but Reese and I hesitated. Elise followed her easily and Dani took one more look around before she stepped through the doorway as well. She peeked back out when I assumed she noticed we weren't right behind her. She had her hand on the door and let her head tilt to the side, her hair swinging aimlessly. "You are welcome to stay out here by yourselves. I wouldn't suggest it though since I won't be out here to protect you." She smirked at both of us then disappeared.

Reese and I both looked at each other before we made a mutual decision to head inside. I placed my hand on the side of the rock as I let my head peek inside before I let the rest of my body enter. It smelled like citrus the minute I inhaled, citrus and a hint of something that smelled like home. Not a scent that made me think of my father or my village, but the kind of scent that made your shoulders relax and eased your anxiety. Once we were both inside, the door slid closed behind us, any indication that it was ever an actual door now gone. It took me a minute to gauge what I was looking at. The interior had no rocks whatsoever. The walls were wood and the short hallway that was in front of me was adorned with sconces on the wall, casting the area in dim but welcoming light.

The woman from before caught my attention and nodded her head towards the open area to her right. Reese's head was swiveling from left to right, his stunned expression speaking volumes. The room was small, but homey. There was a simple rug and two tall lamps with stands that looked like they had been made from tree bark. A singular window sat on the far wall, and I could see Axel in all his sleepy glory. The ceiling was high and there were small shelves and just tiny touches around the room that let you know that people lived here. Enchanters were a resilient bunch. Dani was already leaning up against the wall to my left and Elise had made herself comfortable on the couch that sat in the middle of the room. Reese and I hovered in the doorway as the woman who let us in watched Elise carefully.

She gave us her attention and her eyes seemed to widen for a moment before they settled back to their normal state. Her features were dark, her eyes a deep brown, her hair was the same, but her skin was a light honey color. She had different earrings, varying between gold and silver, cascading down from the top of her ears all the way to her earlobes. She wore a tank top that showed off all the decorated markings on one of her arms, but there were raised scars there as well.

"I'm Leah and you are..." she waited patiently for our answers.

She reached my shoulder, but when I looked down, I saw that she wore heeled boots that gave her the illusion of being taller. She gave off this casual air of confidence that I'd only ever gotten from one person. My eyes floated to Dani, but then back to Leah as I answered.

"I'm Nicholas and this is Reese." I nodded my head towards my best friend who lifted his arm and gave a quick wave before continuing to not so subtly gawk at his surroundings. I pointed over to Dani to continue my introductions when Leah brought her hand up to stop me.

"I am well aware of who the Soul Seether is, Nicholas. Just like I'm very aware that you are both angels."

Reese wrinkled his nose. "Can you smell it on us too?"

Leah shook her head. "No, you just look—angelic. Like you'll fight for someone's honor immediately."

"Oh, well she has you pegged pretty well, Nicholas," Elise chuckled.

Leah side-eyed Elise before turning around to settle down on the couch opposite her. "If you would have asked me years ago if I wanted the Soul Seether in my house, I would have said Hell no, but that was then, back when I thought you were quite the mindless puppet."

I watched as Dani's mouth flew open, but she thought better of it for the moment and stopped. She paused and looked as if she was trying to choose her words wisely. "Well thanks for changing your mind, I suppose."

Leah settled back on the couch and waved her hand over to us. "Hmm, well come on over, you two just standing there is making me anxious."

We both walked over, as Reese leaned in and whispered in my ear, "So like am I wrong for saying I find her super attractive?"

"Umm, no," I whispered back.

"Good, good, because I do."

We placed our weapons against the wall and plopped down on the couch beside her, while Reese wormed his way to the spot closest to her. Dani sauntered over to the other couch, sitting as far away from Elise as possible. Leah took notice of their distance. "Ah, still making friends so easily, are we?" Her question was directed towards Elise, who gave her a forced fake smile.

Leah morphed her face into a serious one. "Alright now, what brings you here of all places?"

"Beetee sent us here because *she* thought you would be able to help us," I answered.

Leah placed her hands in her lap. "That I am aware of. I'm just unsure of how I'm meant to help you."

Elise rolled her eyes. "Well, you *and* Garrett obviously."

Reese cleared his throat. "Is Garrett your boyfriend?"

Dani snorted. "Wow, you're subtle."

Leah looked over at Reese, eyeing him up and down before pressing her lips together trying not to laugh. "Husband, actually." He wasn't wrong, she was beautiful, but I had a feeling Reese was starting to have a thing for unavailable women. I, on the other hand, seemed to only have eyes for one person in particular.

I ran a hand through my hair, knowing that I needed to be the one to get this back on track. "So, you're Enchanters who live in a rock? A glamoured rock, clearly." I really didn't know how else to start.

Leah laughed a little but nodded. "Yes, Garrett and I made this place a safe haven after we fled from Lilith. We settled at Beetee's hostel for a good while, but then needed a place of our own. I'm skilled in glamour magic, thanks to Moira."

"So, you were well acquainted with Natalia's mom?" Dani inquired.

"We weren't best friends, but I could talk to her about most things and her daughter was the sweetest thing. That war ruined everything for a lot of people."

"But you left Oculus willingly. You went with Lilith on your own accord." Dani pointed out.

Leah sighed. "Yes, yes, I know. Isaac was attacking and Lilith was so tempting. I was younger then and that's no excuse, but an Enchanter's powers are everything to them and he wanted to remove them from us all because of something that we had nothing to do with. If you had been there, you would have seen so much blood from people I knew and spent time with and Lilith…she said things in such a way that made you forget who she was. We had seen demons come and go for so long, maybe she had changed. It sounds so stupid now."

"I guess I can understand doing what felt right in the moment," I said, absentmindedly placing my hand on her knee.

"I do hope that Moira forgave me in her last moments, well, forgave all of us really." Her eyes were a little glassy, like she was trying her hardest to keep it together.

"How do you know that Moira passed?" I asked.

Leah smiled at me thoughtfully. "Enchanters know when their High Priestess passes over and a new one comes into power. That sweet girl must be a powerful thing now isn't she?"

"You fucking bet," Reese said, whistling.

Leah quickly wiped her eyes and rolled her shoulders as she sat up straighter. "I'm sorry to turn this into such a somber moment. Now what do you want to know?"

"We saw plenty of Enchanters at the hostel, none of which went through the trouble of doing all this, so I don't understand. Why go to these lengths?" I asked, leaning in so I could focus on her response.

"Lilith doesn't go searching much for things and people she doesn't need. The forest will take you if you aren't careful, or the hellhounds will from what I've heard. This place can smell fear in great detail and misguided confidence does not get you far. Many demons left because they were infuriated by her anti-aging curse which she then topped with her cease in procreation curse as well. Any demon who showed any resistance to her was eliminated and well, that lit a fire under some, but others were terrified of her and had no means of fighting back. Garrett and I fled from her castle on the hill and never looked back. Once Lilith started preparing for Isabel's power ascension, Garrett wanted us to leave since he knew I would be one of the unlucky ones to have to give my powers to her. That and uh, after.... everything..."

"Everything?" Reese raised a blonde eyebrow.

Leah looked down at the ground and the room was quiet for a moment. "We have quite a history with Lilith which I assume is the reason why Beetee sent you here. Most Enchanters that have encountered Lilith had been with her for small periods of time and then saw her for what she was, especially with her favoritism towards Isabel. I mean frankly, she only really wanted them for their magic in the end and some were so desperate to get out of this place that they offered it up willingly. Garrett and I, we...she had different plans for us. We thought we had to stay for survival's sake especially after—" She flicked one of her braids over her shoulder and took in a deep breath.

"After I killed you."

All of our eyes went to Elise who sat back on the couch, unapologetically.

Leah licked her lips. "Yes, after you killed me."

"Woah, what the fuck, shouldn't you be dead then?" Dani asked.

"I'm sorry, you killed her?" Reese nearly stuttered.

Elise rolled her eyes. "Not on purpose, well, okay on purpose, but like it was an order. Do with that what you will."

The tension now made sense between Elise and Leah.

"Lilith ordered you to kill her?" Dani's eyes widened.

"Oh please, don't act like you haven't gotten your hands dirty, Soul Seether." Elise grumbled, clearly annoyed.

They were both silent as they stared at each other from either side of the couch.

"Are we not going to get more elaboration on this or what?" Reese looked from Elise to Leah as if waiting for one of them to speak up.

A cracking sound came from around the corner telling me that the glamoured door was being opened. No one spoke as we waited, listening to feet shuffling and the door closing shut.

"We're in here, Garrett," Leah said, getting up from the couch and turning towards the opening of the room.

A male voice answered back. "We? What are you talking about, we?" He got to the threshold when he stopped, taking us all in. It only took him a moment to zero in on Elise. His eyes became narrow as he balled his hands into fists. "What the hell is *she* doing here?"

Leah walked around the back of the couch and over to Garrett, wrapping as much of her hand around his bicep and using her other hand to turn his face towards hers. "It's okay. Beetee asked them to come."

He seemed to visibly relax, at least it looked like he was. He scrubbed a hand down his face, collecting himself. "Apologies. I'm Garrett." We all introduced ourselves, Elise remaining as quiet as can be. Garrett had dark skin with a few tattoos peeking out from his shoulder beneath his t-shirt sleeve. His hair was done in a multitude of long braids, which were wrapped in a thin ribbon and ended at his lower back. He had a thick silver bar pierced in the shell of his ear and a stud in his ear lobe. His eyes were a golden color and they threw me off being such a contrast to the dark color of his skin. His thick eyebrows drew together as he scanned both Reese and I after our introductions.

I moved to the arm of the couch so that he could sit next to Leah.

"Where are the littles?" Leah asked him.

"Outside with the big beast."

Reese coughed. "Wait, you have kids? And you let them play with that thing outside?"

"He's not a thing, he's a hellhound. Get it right, Blondie. Don't and I'll make sure he eats you," Elise threatened.

Garrett pointed at the window. "Axel is actually really great with kids. Believe me I was quite nervous at first, but our two little warriors weren't afraid of him at all."

I craned my neck to see two children jumping on top of Axel and giggling. "It's safe for them to just be out there like that?"

Garrett nodded. "He's only a menace and a monster when he's threatened or is in protective mode. He'll keep them safe."

"Well, we definitely know he didn't get his soft side from his mother,"

Reese pointed his index finger at Elise. "But, how about we circle back to you killing Leah, shall we?"

We all could feel the instant tension in the room from Garrett alone. Leah placed her hand on his knee, and I watched as her fingers flexed, squeezing.

"Lilith wanted to test his powers and she needed Leah dead to do it. It was motivation for lack of a better word." Elise shrugged.

"Motivation?" Garrett leaned forward, his breathing getting a little more intense.

"What does that have to do with you killing her and her now being alive? How does he come in?" I questioned.

Dani tilted her head to the side. "Resurrection?" It was more a question for Garrett and no one else.

The Enchanter flicked his eyes to Dani as if he was surprised she even knew what that word meant. After a minute he condescended, nodding. Reese placed both his hands on either side of his head and pulled his hair in both directions. "Resurrection as in necromancy? As in one of the few powers that have been legitimately outlawed, like it's written on paper outlawed."

"That's the one," Leah confirmed. "There were very few before Jonah's father and the fight and now Garrett is one of the last remaining ones."

"I guess there isn't a need to ask why Lilith would see that as important." I ran my fingers along my chin, thinking.

"Exactly. Resurrection is tough on the body and the mind; it takes a lot to focus. You are quite literally reconstructing someone's soul back together, their entire being. And I refused to do it, I would rather her kill me than have me use it for her own bidding. She had the upper hand though; she knew what it would take just to see me use it once." Garrett wrapped his arm around Leah's shoulders, pulling her close.

"Damn, Elise. Just fucking up people's lives left and right, aren't you." Reese snickered.

"Lilith has made us all do some shitty things okay, whether we knew we were doing it or not, so let's just move the fuck on." Elise seemed agitated, more than usual. It was hard to tell if she was actually remorseful in her own way, deep, deep down somewhere in her subconscious. I knew she cared about Dani, and I knew she had her reasons for lying to her, so maybe this was something she had actual emotions about as well. It was fucked up, but Lilith had had a hold on her, so maybe giving her the benefit wasn't a bad idea.

"I'm sure Lilith searched for you guys like a mad woman," Reese said.

"Oh, I'm sure she did, but I assume I wasn't the priority since she had her Soul Seether and her plan was in motion."

Dani drummed her fingers on her knees. "What do you know about the demons Lilith has been experimenting on?" She meant the soulless demons we'd been fighting for some time now.

Leah and Garrett both looked at each other, a silent conversation happening between them. Garrett spoke first. "It was years later; the dark queen was all out of sorts until one day she just wasn't anymore. It was like the idea about you sparked something in her. She didn't start doing it until about halfway into her search for you. I saw a few of the unlucky bastards that got their angelic choice taken from them and they never lasted more than a week. She had most of us housed in her castle so you could hear the screams and pleas easily. She summoned me to resurrect the victims of her chosen ones, so they would have to keep going, falling harder into their darkness, but they never panned out.

"I overheard her speaking about wanting to use a new tactic with you when you arrived, so it seemed that she resorted to other means to keep you in line. I guess she needed someone who already embodied darkness just fine." He narrowed his eyes towards Elise who narrowed hers right back at him.

"She sometimes kept me close to her; I was almost like her necromancy bodyguard just in case one of her own went rogue against her. Leah and I fled a few months into your arrival, Soul Seether. You had been working with Elise and I noticed demons going to her chambers more often, but I never saw them again. At night I would hear chaotic screams and it was agonizing, I learned from some others that she was keeping those soulless creatures locked up until who knows. They were bloodthirsty, but they weren't strong enough to be manageable. But they could kill for her, so she let them live for the moment.

"She would have her minions fight them and when the shadow demons won out, I would resurrect her fallen. I was always at her beck and call even when she tried to get me to resurrect her soulless demons from nothing. It's not impossible but I didn't have the willpower to perform with that much energy for her, I would have gone into a coma from doing something like that. That got me beat and tortured for denying her, but I took it for Leah's sake. I was cautious weeks later when I questioned her, but she did tell me that she was never a one idea kind of woman. That she had a good contingency plan if her *monster* ever failed her. She said nothing more, nothing less."

"So, she was prepared for if you didn't play your role in her plan the first time." I said to Dani, who gave me eye contact for a small moment then looked away. Urging Dani to take Jonahs's power, rip open the portal and let Lilith out didn't work, so what was next?

"I'm still confused, why wouldn't she just use plain old demons to do whatever she wanted, instead of going through all this? You know, instead of yanking out souls." Reese asked, stretching his arm across the back of the couch.

Leah's voice piped up. "As malicious as she is, Lilith has her reasons for everything. Soulless demons to her *seemed* moldable since they were still *her* demons. Demons with their souls intact will always have their own thoughts, their own feelings and they could defy her if they ever wanted to. She likely wanted to remove that aspect altogether. They did what she said.... yes, but when she said kill, that was *all* they wanted to do. They were useful in a way, but still unstable and as much as she loves to create chaos, she likes clean chaos in her own house."

"She was experimenting for her own sake and no one else's. She'll keep doing it until she has what she wants. I'm pretty sure she has plenty of them still locked up and ready to let loose," Garrett added.

"Oh yeah, we met them already," I said, recounting the fight in the woods the day before.

Garrett let out a loud exhale. "She was grooming Isabel over the years before we left. I had been summoned by her and caught a glimpse of Isabel working her magic on someone. It looked painful. The demons' eyes were black, they thrashed back and forth in this aimless way with shadows enveloping them and that told me that they no longer had their soul. Lilith seemed to be trying everything to gain control of them even when they were out of her sight, but I guess that didn't pan out either."

"They are definitely strong, but they aren't unbeatable. One hit and they are pretty much done for," Elise said examining her nail beds. "It's like she's just using them to taunt us now."

"We also know all about Isabel's fucking magic," Reese huffed, giving me a look like he was also remembering having to fight our own kind. Kill them. Remove the problems. My stomach curdled at the thought, and I had to take in a few short inhales to stop myself from ending up on Leah and Garrett's floor in the fetal position.

"How is an Enchanter supposed to help with a voided demon?" Dani asked, her brown eyes locked in confusion.

Leah furrowed her arched eyebrows. "I actually don't know. Isabel's magic was only getting stronger by then so I can see how Lilith would want to use it, but I honestly don't know how it would affect them. The High Priestess should know something on the matter, but I'm sure she didn't come with you on this little excursion to Purgatory."

"She did not, but we have a way to speak to her," I said, placing my hand on my chest and feeling my portal key. I looked up to see Leah looking at me in a way that told me she had something to say that had more to do with me than the situation.

She opened her mouth to speak when a loud growl echoed through the room. The walls vibrated and the couch shook, nearly knocking me off. Another growl came through and then a scream. It was high pitched but didn't sound like an adult. It sounded like a child. My head swung towards the window, but Garrett was already running towards the glass.

All I saw were Axel's eyes that were not black anymore, they were red. A bright, neon red. His teeth were on full display, and drool was oozing down the side of his mouth. Leah screamed for her husband, but Garrett was already past us and headed towards the door. The last thing I saw, before Reese and I quickly grabbed our weapons, were those two children hiding behind one of Axel's large front legs as he snarled and growled at whatever was endangering them.

We ran outside prepared to fight right alongside a hellhound.

IO

DANI

I could feel them before I could see them. They were hellhounds and they were angry. Axel growled at the creature that was inching its way towards him, Leah and Garrett's children huddled behind one of his large front legs. This beast in front of me had a scar down the middle of its face and a tail split in half. Its claws were wide and dug into the ground with every step it took. I could smell the fear on Leah and the ferocity on Garrett at wanting to save his children. Hellhounds weren't the greatest creatures, but they were usually harmless unless provoked—or if they were vicious beasts, it was likely due to grooming from their owner. Axel's size gave me the feeling that they wouldn't usually mess with him unless given some false bravado by a higher power.

"Yuri! Jasmine!" Leah yelled. Both children looked at her, pure terror in their eyes. They looked like both of their parents in different ways. Leah was motioning for them to come over to her, but they shook their heads as another hellhound stepped out from behind the trees to our left, removing any chance they had of getting to their mother unharmed. This one had one black eye and one red. Its teeth were rows of sharp points, and its tail was full of scales.

I heard the sound of Reese notching his arrow and a deep low growl from Elise. I saw magic surge past me as Leah let a stream of yellow light leave her hands as she headed straight for the creature terrorizing her children. The beast got knocked down by the hit, but it wasn't enough to deter it. It was just focused on Leah now. It started moving towards us when I felt somebody run past me as magic spewed from their hands towards the hellhound. Garrett managed to directly hit the beast, sending it flying backwards past the rock structure and out of our view. The beast to our left was eyeing them as if they were a tasty meal, but before I could move, I saw Nicholas twirl his sword in his hand, in hopes of getting its attention. The hellhound focused his eyes on the angel in front of me, sniffing the air and probably smelling something much more satisfying. Nicholas moved away from the group, keeping his sword close to his body, but in a position where if he needed to strike it would be easy to fight.

The kids were clinging to Axel's leg, more than likely frozen with unbridled fear, but my eyes widened when I saw what was creeping up behind them. It was a hellhound, a little bigger than the others, but it was moving meticulously behind Axel. Garrett was paying attention to his children, not seeming to notice. Its eyes were a simple deep black, but there were red dots in the middle. It had two bottom teeth that hooked upward and were about as large as my entire arm. It beat its tail against the ground and all of a sudden started charging, running much faster than I had anticipated. I didn't think, I just moved forward, feeling that shadow of darkness overtake me. Before the beast could get even an inch towards Garrett and the children, I rammed into it with all the strength I had.

The hellhound jumped back a bit from what I had done, but it rallied. It showed me its teeth, trying to scare me, intimidate me. I could have almost laughed. This beast had no idea that I had teeth as well and I would rip it to shreds and spit out the pieces. The hellhound started scraping its front paw against the dirt and right when I thought it was about to lunge, it let out the deepest growl I'd ever heard. The ground shook and I nearly lost my balance.

"What the fuck was that?" I heard Reese ask behind me. I wanted to ask the exact same thing, but I heard a huff and grunt when I realized the hellhound was charging right at me. I was taken off guard for a second, but before I could blink, I was being yanked to the side and out of harm's way. I looked over to Axel whose eyes were still red and lethal, but despite his looks, I knew he was protecting me. I nodded toward him, letting him know in my own way I was fine, and untangled myself from the way his tail was trying to collapse my lung with how tight he was holding me.

I summoned my dagger into my grip and made a move towards the beast. It lunged forward, snapping its teeth at me and I swung down and to the side, nearly slicing its shoulder. The hellhound Nicholas had decided to fight was fast, practically becoming invisible with how fast it was moving. Nicholas didn't seem to mind, since he was just as fast. He swung left and right, jumping out of the way when the beast whipped its tail around to trip him. The hellhound from before bounded around the rock formation, opening its mouth wide when Reese sent a glowing arrow right into its open mouth. The arrow made a clean exit out the back of the beast's head. The large creature hit the ground at Reese's feet and the look on his face was one of pure enjoyment.

Nicholas swung right, hoping to get a direct cut into his hellhound's neck, but the creature moved out of his reach and swiped at his leg, causing him to hit the ground hard. The large beast pounced on him, huffing out smoke in his face. Nicholas tried to reach for his sword that was a few inches away, but the hellhound slammed a paw on his arm, keeping him in place. I pounded my fist into the head of the creature in front of me, moving it from my line of sight, but before I could blink, an arrow and a bolt of reddish-black flame barreled towards the creature on top of him. It stilled while its body caught fire and it backed off of Nicholas, whining and finally killing over.

I felt rough pads and claws hit my face as I flew backwards, hitting Axel's body. Garrett and his children were still there, caught in the middle. I reached up and touched my cheek, placing my hand in front of my face and seeing blood. I looked directly at the children. "Go now, go to your mother," I told them. There was only one hellhound now, they could be safe.

Garrett nodded at me, gratitude in his eyes as he huddled around his children as best he could and started heading towards Leah who was kneeling down with her hands outstretched waiting. They were halfway to their mother when I heard a low growl. And then another.

And another. And another.

The hellhound wasn't simply asserting dominance before. He was calling on his pack.

Rustling sounds came from every direction and every single one of us was staring at a different part of the woods, trying to gauge where the first hound would come from. A deranged sound came from behind me as a black creature came out of nowhere and landed right on Axel, digging its claws into the side of Elise's pet. Axel let out a loud cry and started bucking the creature off of him, snapping his teeth in all directions.

Axel successfully got the creature off of him and turned his head, opening his mouth and letting fire erupt out. I shielded my face from the heat and smoke of it. The fire burnt the tail of the other hellhound which only made it more aggressive. It pounced onto Axel once again, who blew out more fire and swatted at the creature with his tail, slamming it to the ground.

More rustling grew as the black eyed, stocky, claw footed creatures gained numbers. I heard movement in front of me as the hellhound stalked over to me, tilting its head. I had no power to talk to animals, but there was something about this one. I almost felt frozen in place by it as if it was something else I was looking at when I stared directly into its eyes. Not something, but someone. I felt its hot breath against my skin as I tried to back up and get away from its menacing stare.

"NO!" I heard Leah shout. I flicked my eyes over the beast's shoulder to see a creature grab Garrett by the shirt and fling him towards a row of trees. The children scrambled and tried to get their footing. Leah shot out her own stream of magic and she hit her target, but it wasn't enough. The hellhounds growled and created so much bad energy that I felt a surge of strength. I wanted it, but I didn't.

I watched as Axel ran over to the hellhound heading for the children and snatched the creature into his mouth, bearing down and a loud crunch surrounded us. It was enough of a distraction to bring me out of my own head. I lifted my leg back up, kicking the beast in front of me in its chest. The hellhound skidded across the ground but regained its footing, shaking its whole body before it charged for me again.

I heard the zip of an arrow threw the air and looked up to see Reese, basically saying *fuck it* and extend his wings out. A hellhound got hit by three of his arrows and rolled over onto its side unmoving. His arrows pulsed with a glowing light and then snuffed out. A rattling growl filled my ears as one of the new hellhounds moved its shoulders in an unnatural way and wings began to form. Wings that looked broken and mangled but they worked enough for it to ascend from the ground.

"Oh fuck," Reese exclaimed, flapping his wings and giving space between him and the creature that was circling him.

I blocked hit after hit from the hellhound I'd been fighting from the start. It had me wrapped up in its tail, but I manifested my dagger in my hand and sliced down its tail. When I got out of its grip, I whirled around and stabbed it in the chest with my weapon, hooking the tip into its skin. I pulled the dagger out and plunged it back in. Again, again and again. It felt good. The breaking of skin, the look like the end was coming…it felt really good.

I ripped my dagger out one more time and I could feel myself getting pulled under, pulled to that place that used to keep me warm at night. Shadows pooled at my feet and shaped themselves around my arms. I looked up from the dead hellhound and watched like a bystander as Nicholas dodged two hellhounds, jumping behind a tree when a large paw tried to rip at his skin. He twirled the sword in his hand as it started to glow and jumped out from behind the tree trunk. He took a quick step to the right, the fire that the hellhound dispersed from its mouth missing him. Nicholas sliced the creature deep into its neck, jumped over its falling body, and ducked under the second one, creating a smooth line down the other's stomach. Both beasts were down for the count, and I couldn't have found him any more attractive.

Arrows flew through the air, and I saw a hellhound go flying across the trees as Axel threw one of them and then Elise sent a flaming black smoke ball in its direction, setting it on fire. I pushed myself off of the hellhound underneath me and caught sight of another one coming on my right. I created a lasso of black shadow ribbon and circled it around its neck before it could even try to fight me. I tightened the ribbon hard while the hellhound choked and tried to get free.

Colorful magic was shooting out now and I knew it had to be coming from Leah, who had been trying to get her children inside, but there was a hellhound standing near the pathway back to their home. Another one sprung up and jumped on top of the large rock formation looking down on us.

"Leave them alone!" I heard Garrett yell as he staggered over to his family. There was blood coming from the side of his head and he looked like he was limping, but that didn't stop him. He pushed out as much of his magic as he could, but the creatures just kept getting closer as if they wanted to bring terror just as much as they wanted to bring death. The children were sobbing, clasping their mother's leg with all the strength they had.

Axel grabbed one of the hellhounds and chucked them up in the air before letting it fall to the ground with a rough thud and then incinerating it. Elise ran straight for the one near their magic front door and grabbed it by its jaw, throwing it off guard. She let her venom seep into its skin and the most ear-piercing cry came from the creature's mouth. Reese shot his arrows down towards the tortured beast, putting it out of its misery. There was a part of me that wanted the painful cries. My hand was vibrating with that darkness that was within me. I wanted to hear those screams again, I wanted to see the pain as much as I wanted to feel it.

It only took a minute for the hellhound on the rock to jump down swatting Elise with its tail, and she landed against the rock with a disgruntled huff. It jumped high enough to scratch down the side of Axel's face which caused him to howl and blow out fire straight at Leah and her children. They jumped out of the way which was what the creature wanted when it grabbed one of Leah's children by their arm and started dragging them away.

"Yuri!" Leah screamed right alongside her son. The hellhound jumped and dodged Garrett's attack as he tried to retrieve his child. Hellhounds thought they were the scariest things around in these woods, but that was a mistake on their part, even ones with this much bloodlust. I placed my hand on the ground and watched as a stream of my dark magic slithered with great speed toward the hellhound. The hound didn't make it far before the magic enveloped it and knocked both it and Yuri into a nearby tree. Reese descended from the sky and started running with Nicholas at his heels. I quickly made my way over, watching as the hellhound's chest rose and fell as if it were in shock. I hooked my leg over its large body and grabbed it by the mouth. I lifted its face up to me, not even feeling its weight as I maneuvered the beast. I heard Garrett run past me to check on Yuri, but my concern was with what I currently held. I held my hand out and my dagger returned to me. I placed my dagger at the hellhound's throat, looking into its eyes.

I could feel the flesh ripping even before my weapon touched it. I could taste it. I could…

Soul Seether.

That voice again. It wrapped itself around my head, my body.

Soul Seether.

Dani.

The shadows pulled and raged. They were trying to redirect me somehow. I sliced down the hellhound's throat feeling a shiver go through my body from the pure enjoyment of it. I dropped the creature to the ground as if it was garbage.

Soul Seether.

More.

More.

I heard a heartbeat. It was thundering, but it was small. That blood that rushed through their veins gave me a sense of excitement.

Do it, Soul Seether.

I turned my head, looking over my shoulder at the small child that was huddled underneath his father's body. The hellhound wasn't enough. No, no not enough. I wanted more.

Do it. The voice was smooth but demanding. Like the tone of an overly confident mother.

I fingered my dagger as I whirled around and tilted my head. I saw Garrett look up at me not understanding.

"Dani." I heard a deep familiar voice, one that pulled at my chest, but it was cast out by the sobbing of the child in front of me. I liked the sobbing. This part of me loved it.

You crave it. So do it.

I stalked over to Yuri while Garrett started to rise and get in my way. "What are you doing? You stop right—" I didn't give him a chance to finish when I wrapped my hand around his throat and squeezed hard, chucking him to the side. Feet started moving behind me, readying to stop me, but they were halted. My shadow magic claimed their ankles and yanked them to the ground, slithering up their bodies and wrapping around their arms. A bigger shadow began enveloping all around us. Yuri's eyes widened as he took in what I had let take over me, what I seemed to welcome. Black eyes, smoky exterior, the need for ruin and torture oozing out of me at every turn. His fear was so sweet, it was truly delectable. I reached my hand out and gripped his little body with my magic, lifting him up, but keeping him flat against the tree trunk.

I pressed my dagger to the tip of his nose. "You want your daddy?"

Yuri gave me a nod before blubbering out another cry.

"He can't save you. No one can," I whispered, giving him a mischievous grin that made him cry out for his father and mother even more. I heard more footsteps, but I cloaked us further in the shadows. I dragged my dagger down his body and landed on his chest. I let the sharp hooked tip of my weapon tear at his shirt, missing the skin. "I promise this is going to hurt so much."

Do it, Soul Seether.

Before I could dig my blade into his skin, I felt a bolt of reddish black hit my back, dispersing around me and I turned my head to see a very baffled and annoyed Elise. "Put him down, Dani."

Remove the soul. Kill.

I shook my head, remnants of her shadows still lost in my hair. "I want this." I said through my teeth. There was a small, small part of me I could feel that didn't want this though, but *that* part didn't matter. That part didn't have a voice. It had no tether; it had no leg to stand on.

It felt right.

It felt *wrong*.

But it felt so damn good.

"Well, that's too fucking bad," Elise said, angrily as she shot out her stream of inky black venom in my direction which I evaded, but not before Axel's tail hit me right in the stomach. The fog started to disappear, after the hit, and I knew I was losing my upper hand. I saw some of my shadows start to retreat. As I was knocked back, I threw my dagger out aiming for Yuri, still pushed up against the tree.

My body forcefully hit the ground when I heard, "God, you *fucking* bitch." I smiled as I pulled myself off the ground and saw Elise with my dagger in her shoulder, standing in front of a struggling Yuri. Her breathing was heavy and if I could just get back over to her and create more holes in her body, it would be a beautiful sight to see. Axel seemed to look at me with discontent in his red eyes as if he didn't know if he should charge me or stand down. I honestly didn't fucking care.

I started fast walking over to Elise, beginning to summon my dagger back towards me when a body got in my way. Large hands wrapped around my arms and halted me. I would kill whoever thought they could simply stop me with this sort of maneuver. "Dani. Stop."

There was that voice again. It reminded me of that voice inside of me that I didn't understand. My head started to throb from the mental whiplash I was involved in. I looked up at Nicholas who gave my body one hard shake as he said my name again, trying to jolt me back to whatever his reality may be. "Let me go!" I yelled.

"I'm not going to let you go, Dani. Just stop! Come back." He shook me again, but this time his hands started to glow just a little bit. It was odd the feeling it gave me.

I used all the force I had to push him away. I heard Reese notch his bow, but that didn't matter to me. They didn't scare me. I made a quick move to get around him, but he was nearly just as fast, stopping me before I could get to Elise. My shadows were angry, my magic was furious, and I wanted to shove every dark shadow down his throat. "Remember who you are, Dani." He gripped my arms and whirled me around, but the light in his hands wasn't just for show now. That light shot through my body as if I was being electrocuted and my darkness fled, trying to hold on but seeking shelter in the place it dwelled when I wasn't in need of it.

The feeling was sharp and quick. It felt warm but had a slight burn that I didn't understand. My shadows hissed and I heard a thud from behind me as Yuri fell from his position against the tree. My vision wasn't as hazy as I blinked up at him, knowing my eyes were no longer black orbs. I took a few breaths in, but then everything was shaky, and the vertigo was starting to make an appearance. "Dani, woah. Are you okay?"

He let me go but I lost my footing, and I felt his arms catch me and pull me close to his chest. I blinked and looked up at the sky that always looked like it was on fire this time of day. A face came into my view when I blinked again, but I was too out of it to do anything. It was a face that I knew was only meant for me to see and no one else.

"So easily manipulated by her maker. Poor Soul Seether, what is it gonna take for you to understand that you don't *save* people. You corrupt them," Isabel's blonde hair swished around her face as she sized me up. She blew me a kiss and backed away, surveying the damage I knew she had caused. "Lilith sends her love and to tell you that your necromancer is safe for now. She knows you'll make the right decision soon enough. All good monsters do." She let out a laugh before she disappeared from my vision.

I heard Yuri crying and Leah scurrying over to him, picking him up in her arms. I watched them through my foggy vision as Jasmine was cuddled with Axel, blood still dripping down the side of his face. Reese hovered over me with his arms crossed. His expression was hard to read, but I was too tired to try. I felt sorry. I *was* sorry. I felt a solid, powerful warmth as I was pulled towards a broad chest. Everything became clouded and I passed out thinking one thing.

Monster. Monster. Monster.

I woke up to a very, very dark room. I felt around my body and was met with the soft feeling of a plush comforter. It felt like my bed at the hostel if I wasn't mistaken. I was surprised that I was in my room and not in the recovery room we had taken Nicholas to. I wondered what time it was and how long I'd been out. I remembered the few minutes before my mind went numb and then nothing. I knew whatever had happened wasn't good and I didn't know how much damage control I would have to do. I reached up and scrubbed a hand down my face.

It took me a moment to realize I wasn't simply put on the bed and left to make myself comfortable, but I was tucked under the covers. My body was snuggled well enough that I probably could have passed out again. I was about to do that very thing when I heard soft breathing from across the room. I ceased my own breathing for a moment so I could try to make out whoever it was. The room was so dark I couldn't make out a silhouette, but when I racked my brain for choices on who it could be, only one came to mind. I reached behind me and grabbed one of the pillows that was keeping me propped up. A small snort came from across the room, but then the soft, meticulous breathing started again. I listened hard and then when I felt like it was the perfect time, I launched the pillow across the room.

The desk chair got shoved back and the sound of a body hitting the wooden floor echoed around the room. "What the fuck." Nicholas's voice whispered, confused. His tone wasn't angry, but it was sleepy which made me laugh.

I reached over and cut on the lamp at my bedside. The room was flooded in dim light, but it was all I needed to see Nicholas still sitting on his ass by the desk with the chair a few feet next to him. He used his index finger to rub at both his eyes, probably trying to adjust to the new lighting. I sat up and scooted back so that I was parallel to the headboard. He let out a yawn before he spoke again. "How long have you been awake?"

"Just now."

He pushed up from the ground, taking the chair and tucking it back under the desk. He reached down and picked the pillow up off the floor, spinning it between his hands. "And your first thought when you realize someone is sleeping in the room with you is to throw a pillow at them?"

I shrugged. "Kind of feels like deja vu. Us, in a dark room, while you complain about pillows..." I trailed off wanting that mental image to create a home inside his mind.

He let out a shaky breath as he practically hovered over me. He stood at the side of the bed, staring down at the pillow in his hands. It was as if he was trying to erase the memory of my face shoved into one of those while he pounded into me from behind. He shook his head and tossed the pillow on the bed.

"What are you doing here anyway?" I asked, reaching forward, and grabbing the pillow to hug it to my chest.

"What do you mean?"

"You, sleeping in the chair?"

He looked over his shoulder and then back at me, rubbing the back of his neck. A nervous habit I'd come to notice. He looked so young and boyish with his still slightly sleepy expression. "I wanted to make sure you were alright."

I played with the tiny, frayed pieces of the pillowcase. "Were you planning on sleeping there all night?"

"If I needed to, yes."

I nodded more to myself than to him. I chewed on my bottom lip, curious as to how much he would tell me. "What happened?"

He moved towards the end of the bed and sat down. "You don't remember?"

"Well, I wouldn't be asking if I did," I said, slightly annoyed.

He rubbed his chin, looking like he was carefully choosing his words. "Honestly, I don't even know what happened. One minute we're talking with Leah and Garrett, the next we're fighting hellhounds and you're..."

"Leah and Garrett." I looked towards the door, a million questions jolting through my mind.

"They're fine. And so are Yuri and Jasmine. We all came back here and settled down. Axel, Reese, Elise, we're all fine. I brought you to your room while Beetee went and tended to them." Flashes of what happened started barreling into my mind, one after the other. None of it seemed to be in order, but I saw Yuri up against a tree and Axel getting his face mangled. Every memory raged and clawed against my head.

"Dani, hey, hey, woah. They're shaken up, but that's to be expected. We all were a little out of it." He placed his hand on my leg, rubbing small circles with his thumb. A jolt went through me, nothing painful or alarming, but something warm and comforting. It was soothing and I didn't want to stop it. It settled my mind. It didn't surprise me one bit since I remembered his touch always being this way. Small flashes of light ran through my memory. Light came from his hands, not in an obvious way, but in a way that made me focus. There was no light coming from his hands now, but I still felt that jolt.

"You said we were fighting hellhounds and I what? What did I do?"

His lingering thumb stopped abruptly as if he was frozen in place for a minute. I knew what he was going to say wasn't good, but I needed to hear it. I was never one to hide from my mistakes, even when I didn't know I had made one in the first place.

He cleared his throat and hesitantly said, "A hellhound had gotten a hold of Yuri and we all thought you were saving him, which I guess you did, but then you just shifted. Your focus was on him, but like *really* on him. You tried to kill him."

My eyes widened and I bunched the pillow up on either side with my fists. "I tried to kill their son and you tell me they're *just* shaken up."

"Of course, they were angry and upset, but they didn't try to rampage against you the minute we got back here if that's what you're thinking. Beetee didn't want so much attention on everything so that's why you're here and not the recovery room."

I threw the pillow down next to me and leaned my head back against the headboard. Everything inside of me was quiet right now. I tilted my head down to find him staring at me. "You look like you want to ask me something."

"I'll ask you the same question you asked me. What happened?"

"I can't answer that if I don't know. That was the whole point of me asking you."

"Oh, no, you know. We aren't in your head, Dani. I can only go off what I see, but I don't know what *you* see. Even if you don't have all the details, you know enough to give me something. Anything."

I reached down for my thighs, squeezing them, needing to put pressure on something. "I don't remember much okay; it's all really fucking choppy. I mean I do…"

Blonde hair. Traitorous face. *All good monsters do.*

"Isabel." I looked down at the comforter, trying to picture her face more clearly. She was like a mirage, like something meant to always be antagonizing me as a placeholder for Lilith. She really was a fucking pet.

"Isabel? Isabel wasn't there, Dani."

"She was, just not to you. Just like before, she wanted to be only visible to me. Taunt me like the fucking trash that she is. She's just pissed she can't kill me. Mommy's orders."

I flashed back to that look the hellhound gave me, like it knew me so well. Like we were so familiar with each other. Lilith always had her methods. She had never been the biggest fan of hellhounds, she never liked cleaning up after them, but she knew they had their uses.

"Another one of Lilith's calling cards. Isabel is just her eyes on the ground, while she occasionally tries to fuck with my head."

"I figured that might be the case. Pretty sure you might have even scared Elise, just a tiny bit. If that makes you feel better."

I laughed and got up, tucking my legs beneath my thighs. "And what about you? Do I scare you?"

He held my gaze for a minute and his eyes went from skeptical to honest and heartfelt. They melted into this kind of adoration that I knew he couldn't help but exude whenever he looked at me. He made that very apparent. Nicholas shook his head. "No, Dani. You *did* scare me today, but not in the way you think." I could feel his need for me like a creature starving for water after centuries of not having it. He maintained his self-control well, but a storm was brewing inside of him, and I was eager to see it. I couldn't help but want him to figure it out, but I was a demon who was fine with playing the long game if that's what it took. I did love instant gratification and we would both be happy if I kissed him and let him use my body in all the ways I knew he could, but what would that really mean?

He started to reach for my hand, but I moved out of the way and off the bed. Nicholas didn't have to shout to the entire world how he felt; that I was simply enough for him, but I needed him to fucking say it to *me*. Preferably on his knees. Then I'd consider getting on mine and making him regret all the time he'd spent away from me. He seemed caught off guard, but he regained his composure, eyeing me as if he was trying to figure out my next move.

"Are they still here?"

"Uh, yeah. I know Beetee told them they could stay here as long as they needed, so they might have gone to their room, or they might still be downstairs with her and Elise. I know Reese already passed out for the night."

I started making my way to the door when I stopped and turned on my heels. "I'm not a parent by any means, but what parent in their right mind wouldn't be livid about someone trying to murder their child."

Nicholas let out a choked laugh. "Oh, they were livid, believe me, but umm, they understand the whole weird connection you have with Lilith. They obviously don't love it, but they know you didn't do it on purpose. They know you aren't some kind of monster, Dani."

I flinched at that word. It was used way too often for my liking. I was happy to be a monster, but on my own accord, not someone else's. It made me curious though. "What do you mean, they understand?"

He leaned back on the bed, his hands resting behind him on the comforter. "We all tried to explain it, but in the end, only one person *really* could." He had one of his eyes closed and the other open as if he was cautiously using his words as I waited for him to continue. "Elise."

I didn't say anything when I left the room, especially since the memory of my dagger in Elise's shoulder appeared in my mind so vividly, it was like I was there all over again. Out of all the memories of course that one was the most colorful. My dagger started to manifest in my hand, but I put it away. I didn't want to play right now, I actually wanted to talk.

I walked down the stairs, hearing an array of voices. There were a few I recognized, like Beetee's but then there were others that were unfamiliar. When I got to the last step, I noticed that the reddish orange coloring of the sky was now black. It was a comforting kind of dark that I looked out at, but it also made me realize that I had been out longer than I thought. The lounge area had a few occupants that gave me wide-eyed looks, but I paid them no mind. The door opened and two very drunk demons stumbled in and one of them laughed as they passed me, nudging my shoulder. The amount of annoyance I had to push down was lethal.

"Dani." I heard Beetee call my name. I turned my head and watched as she tentatively walked towards me, stopping at the threshold between the dining area and the small kitchen. I rolled my shoulders and made my way over to her. I reached up behind me and ripped the tie from my hair, letting my ponytail lose. My head felt lighter as my curls fell down my back and I ruffled them out. Beetee gave a small very cute smile, but I knew it was a smile that was holding back something. She didn't know how to approach this situation.

As I got closer, I saw Leah and Garrett seated on one side of the long table. Elise sat on the other, her feet up on the table as she leaned back in her chair. I kept my face neutral when I was finally in front of all of them. I had never been so fidgety and—regretful—in all of my existence. *Regretful.*

"How was your beauty sleep, princess?" Elise asked, inspecting her nails.

I rolled my eyes, ignoring her.

"What she means to ask is, how are you feeling?" Beetee gingerly touched my arm.

"I'm good. Everything is coming back in pieces," I admitted. I couldn't look Leah and Garrett in the eyes, not just yet. I could feel the tension coming from them. It wasn't a tension filled with hate, but it was the cautious kind, which I understood.

"How about I relay everything to you really quickly, huh. We got attacked by hellhounds, Yuri got yanked away by one, and you tried to play hero and almost killed him. Luckily you came to your fucking senses," Elise explained, counting each thing off on her fingers.

Beetee nearly growled under her breath before swiftly turning around and stalking over to Elise. Before I could even blink, she swatted her on the back of the head and grabbed her legs, ripping them off the table. "I told you to be nice, Ellie. So be *nice*! And how many times do I have to tell you to get your feet off my table."

I held my breath waiting for Elise to pounce on her, but she just arranged her face in a look of disgusted agitation and groaned. Beetee turned back to me, just for Elise to give her a middle finger to her back. "Have a seat, I mean if you want."

"I'm okay standing." I leaned against the doorframe. I cleared my throat, finally looking over to Leah and Garrett. "I'm sorry."

Leah let out a soft sigh. "We know you are, it's just a lot, Soul Seether. That's our child."

"How is he?"

Garrett tapped on the table. "He was shaken up, along with Jasmine. Leah tried to glamour their memories as best she could, but some things can be so frightening that it's hard to fix. They're asleep upstairs now."

I flicked my brown eyes to his golden ones. "Glamour their memories?"

"Not everyone can do it. The majority of Enchanters can glamour, but memories are a bit harder. It's easier if you're close, like family. And it's even easier if the party is a willing participant. It's not permanent, but they're so young, I hope that it does stick in their memory."

I nodded in understanding. "I would never do that on purpose, I hope

you know that. I just...I'm unsure what even happened. This place is just..."
I couldn't find the words that would help me out and I actually didn't feel like trying to justify my behavior.

Leah waved her hand out in front of her. "Please, it's alright. You don't have to explain. Beetee told us what happened to you, and Elise told us all about Lilith's hold on you."

I cut my eyes over to Elise, but she was looking down, practically burning a hole through the table.

"As long as you want to bring Lilith down and that's your one goal then we can move forward. I'm not leaving you alone with my children anytime soon, but I can give you the benefit of the doubt," Leah continued.

"I don't think Axel will let you anywhere near them, right now. He made sure he was cuddled right with them when we tucked them into bed," Garrett added. I imagined the large hellhound in his little dog form snuggled up with the kids upstairs. It almost made me laugh, but then I remembered I was going to have to gain the trust of a hellhound as well. A hellhound that belonged to...

"Elise," I said, walking further into the room. The sound of feet running down the stairs and the hostel door opening and closing echoed behind me. Drunken laughter from the other side of the room was drowned out by how hard I was staring at her.

"What?" she answered, narrowing her eyes at me as she gave me her attention.

"Can we talk?"

She looked around the room, at the three other people near us. "Are we not talking right now?"

"Alone."

Before she could respond, Beetee answered for her, "Of course, yes, you can." She motioned for Leah and Garrett to follow her out. The two Enchanters nodded in understanding and got up from their chairs.

"We should probably head to bed as well," Leah said as she awkwardly looked from Elise to me. She took a step forward, but then stopped, placing her hands on the table and leaning forward toward Elise. "You saved my child. There will be no more discussion of our past, alright."

Elise licked her lips and tilted her head. "We're even. Perfect."

Garrett lightly grabbed Leah's arm and pulled her towards the exit. He let out a deep breath as he passed me, saying in a low voice, "I know how manipulative Lilith can be. We will fight with you, but if you ever try to hurt my child again, I will end you."

I gave him my full attention and simply nodded. I wasn't shocked by his words. They were warranted. I was impressed he'd said it to my face, but then again, the man had worked closely enough with Lilith, so I hardly doubted he was afraid of much these days. I wanted to tell him about what Isabel had said to me, about how he was safe from Lilith for now, but that would have to wait until tomorrow.

Beetee followed after them, wiggling her eyebrows, her lilac eyes glowing with mischief. "She vouched for you hard. Like it was weird, even for her." She looked over her shoulder. "Nice, Ellie. Fucking nice. I don't curse often, but I swear…"

Elise placed her elbows on the table and placed her chin in her upturned palms. "Yes, I got it, you annoying reptile."

Beetee shook her head and raised her eyes to the ceiling as she left us alone. Despite all the noise around us, it felt silent with just the two of us in this one area. She had her eyes closed and seemed to have no intention of acknowledging me. She blew out a breath. "Are you just going to stand there like a freak, or are you going to sit?"

I walked over to one of the chairs, pulling it out and sitting down. The minute my butt hit the chair, Elise pushed away from the table and got up. I cocked my head back in confusion. "You basically ask me to sit down and now you're just gonna leave?"

She quickly looked over to me as she kept moving. "Just sit pretty for two seconds, alright?"

I watched as she disappeared from the room into the small kitchen. I heard fumbling around and then she was back, with a large bottle of clear liquid and two glass cups. "Beetee thinks she can hide the good stuff from me, but clearly she cannot."

A man lumbered into the dining area, saying some words, but they were slurred and jumbled together. Yeah, this was definitely not the time for all of this nonsense to start. Elise hissed over at him, "If you want to be able to use your dick tomorrow, I highly suggest you get out of this room and out of my face." Her eyes blazed with flames and the man quickly turned around, almost running into the wall behind him and made his way out of our presence.

"A bit harsh," I noted, watching as she unscrewed the top off the bottle and started pouring it into the cups.

"I was being nice."

She pushed the cup over to me, some of the contents sloshing out. I lifted it to my nose and, yup, that's vodka.

"Speak," she practically commanded. Elise tilted her cup back and drank half of what was in it. I needed to match her energy, so I did the same.

140

I licked my lips, the burn of the alcohol sliding down my throat. I liked the burn. "You are really fucking confusing you know that?"

She chuckled, pouring another large amount into her cup. "This should be good."

"No, really. You come with me to Heaven's Gate, you give me every indication that we are friends, but then you can't even say sorry about lying to me and basically call me a pathetic bitch. Then in the same sentence admit that you kept me alive for what? The sake of keeping me alive. And let's not forget the part where you have a way too good for you *friend*, a pet hellhound, you save a child's life and then you make sure my ass is covered, so I don't look like a total bad guy. Fucking confusing."

She circled the rim of her glass with her fingertip, pressing her tongue into her cheek. "Is there some sort of response you wanted?"

I downed the rest of my glass and reached for the bottle. "I want a fucking answer. Something with merit. Not some half-assed reply that doesn't help at all. You don't put a good word in for *anyone*, Elise. Yet, you did with me."

"The whole point of being here is so you can fight the big bad lady, right? What would be the point if Garrett got all his little Enchanter friends to raid this place and attempt to rip you limb from limb, all because Lilith has some unhealthy obsession with you. It would be pointless since I highly doubt your little boyfriend would let that happen, but still."

"And?"

"And what, Dani. *Fuck.* What more do you want from me?" She looked tired and irritated, maybe a bit tortured.

I nearly slammed my glass down on the table. "Do you literally not fucking listen when I speak? I want the truth. Why keep this halfling thing a secret, huh? No one is going to come here and tear you apart because you admit you, I don't know, give a flying fuck." I noticed that she had both hands on her glass and was staring into the vodka like she wished she could dive right into it and get away from this conversation. I didn't stop though; this was my chance. "Why. Didn't. You. Let. Lilith. Kill. Me?"

The sound of glass shattering caused me to blink as I looked down and saw shards of glass scattered around the table. She no longer had her cup in her hands, but the skin above her wrist was now wet with vodka. Her hands had small cuts on them, but she hardly noticed. I didn't know whether she planned to pick up a large piece of glass and stab me or open her mouth and speak. "Fuck! Dani, you were so pathetic when I first met you. You asked too many stupid questions and complained a lot. I could only tell you so much, but I had to keep you focused and eventually you figured it out. You started to need my help with weapons, magic and torture less and less. You never asked me to do things for you or even when Lilith showed you attention, you never acted like you were better than anyone else." She shot up from her chair and disappeared from the room again, coming back with a rag and another glass.

She pushed the pieces of glass to the side, creating a small pile. Elise poured herself another glass and sat down, letting out a sigh. "You just wanted to hang out with me, which was fucking weird. I had nothing better to do, so I invited you out and ugh, you just wouldn't leave me alone. You kept wanting to be around me and you weren't completely and totally lame, so I allowed it, over and over again so much that I guess you felt the need to start confiding in me with information, like things beyond who you took to bed and how thrilling your last kill was."

I didn't want to interrupt her, but when she didn't just continue, I realized I would have to push. "What does that have to do with anything, Elise?"

She rubbed her eyes before taking another long drink. "I have only called two people a friend in this fucking place and one of them got on Lilith's bad side. Our dark queen thought she was distracting me from my training when I first came to her, so she took it upon herself to get rid of her. Slashed her pretty throat while I watched. She told me I needed to focus on what was coming. Lilith has made me do a lot of fucked up things and Hell, I've done so many fucked up things on my own accord, but maybe that one thing hardened me, I don't fucking know, but after that, I didn't see the point in getting close until you and your annoying ass demeanor bounded into my life." She made a disgruntled sound as she tipped her glass against her lips. When she put it down, she motioned for me to give her my empty glass, so she could refill it. "When Lilith told me about you, I wasn't going to have your blood on my hands because, I don't know, you didn't deserve to fucking die all because your angelic light couldn't shut the fuck up."

Elise had been with Lilith for a long time, I knew that, but she was never forthcoming with how her time had been before I got there. I didn't know if Elise was ever a happy, go-lucky type of demon—which I highly doubted—or if she had always been the way she was. She had feelings, despite how deep down they were, and someone had broken her walls down enough to be her friend. Lilith snatched that from her, just like Lilith had snatched that from me. We were similar in so many ways, yet different. She hadn't completely cut off that little piece of herself that showed she cared, she just wasn't a fan of putting it on display for it to get trampled over and ripped away. I had no desire to ask about this previous friend of hers, to feel her loss. Elise never spoke of any family, so having Lilith as some sort of parental figure must have been a fucking mess.

It had to be lonely. Despite the clubs and the continuous bedmates she had, lonely would still be the word I'd use.

"So, you do have a moral compass," I inquired.

"Lilith wanted you perfect, so I made sure you remained perfect." There was something else that she wasn't saying.

"So, what if I wanted to get close to you, so what if we hung out? You could have done that with the next one, Elise. What makes me so special, so different, so…"

She ran a hand through her hair, pushing her bangs back just for them to fall back in front of her forehead. "Because maybe a small, small, very minuscule part of me gives a fuck about you."

There it was.

"You went to Heaven's Gate with me, you fought beside me, you lied to me to keep me alive, and you told Garrett and Leah things to help me because you give a fuck about me," I said, leaning in while I took a swig of vodka.

She poured herself another glass, nearly filling up her cup, and started chugging it down. "Sure."

"And what? You couldn't call me your friend because it would hurt… losing me?" I was pushing hard, but better now than never.

"Ugh, I would smash your face into this table if I thought Beetee wouldn't get mad about all the blood." She pointed at me as she poured herself another glass yet again. I finished mine and stole the bottle away from her to refill my own.

"I'll take that threat as a yes," I shrugged. "You ran to tell Beetee about my little issue, so I assume she's your second friend."

"She says friend, I say unlikely acquaintance." She and I both knew she was lying.

I shook my head. "I don't know that many unlikely acquaintances that share as much as you two do. She seems to know a lot about you, Elise."

She picked up one of the shards of glass, flipping it between her fingers. "She isn't attached to Lilith in any way. I met her at a club one night and we hit it off. The sex was good, but she's the relationship type, so we just kept it friendly, which…"

"Turned into you telling her everything about yourself and her hostel becoming one of your safe spaces. You don't say it out loud, but that girl is your friend. Got it."

Elise didn't say anything, she just flicked the glass shard back onto the table in silence. She was silently agreeing with me, and we both knew it.

"Are you going to say sorry for it? For not telling me?"

Elise's gray eyes bore into my brown ones, wanting to keep my attention. "No."

"No?"

"If I would've told you the truth, you would've acted just like your angelic boyfriend and tried to fix it, tried to be what you were meant to be, and she would have killed you. Thrown you away like you didn't fucking matter and moved on to the next. So no, I'm not sorry. I would do it again if given the opportunity."

That answer didn't make me angry, and it didn't boil my blood. That answer actually made me happy. To know that she would go to such lengths to keep me right where I was nearly brought a smile to my face. Elise didn't show emotion like everybody else. She was never going to look me in the eye and tell me she cared, but she would do whatever it took to keep me alive even if that meant lying to my face and keeping me at a distance that I didn't know was such an incredible amount. There were things I didn't know about her, but little by little I would and maybe there were some things I would never know.

"Oh fuck, don't think that this means I'm going to hug you or some shit. I already had that kid wanting to hug me, thanking me for saving him. Disgusting," she scoffed.

I drank the rest of my drink and nodded, holding in my chuckle. I knew she didn't regret stepping in front of my dagger and taking the hit. That kind of pain was probably a turn on for her. "I'm at least sorry for saying you didn't deserve friends."

She raised one of her brows. "You're probably right, though, so it is what it is. Not many people can tolerate my attitude as Beetee likes to say, so hey maybe you are right. Friendship is exhausting and like I've always said, a distraction."

"Hmm, but it can also provide you with a place to stay if you ever need it and a confidant or two." I pointed to myself, hoping she would catch the hint. "We could have had this conversation months ago; do you plan to always be this stubborn?"

"Depends on my mood."

I reached for the bottle, but she kept it out of my reach as she poured some more into her cup. "Are you gonna tell me about Axel?"

"What about Axel?"

"Not many demons have hellhounds of his caliber, Elise. Did Lilith give him to you?"

She licked the side of her glass where some of the vodka had spilled over. "Nope."

I gave her an incredulous look, stopping before I poured the rest of what was in the vodka bottle into my glass. She started drinking and looked as if she was planning on keeping that information to herself.

"But he was a gift?"

"Yup."

"Lilith knows about him."

She nodded.

"And she hasn't tried to keep him for herself. He's quite a sight."

Elise laughed a little under her breath. "I'm sure she would love him, but she has no intention of taking him from me. I let Beetee watch him when I'm not around, he…keeps her safe." She said those last words like a whisper as if she wanted the realms to swallow them up for no one else to hear.

I clucked my tongue, curious. "Does Beetee know who gifted him?"

Elise let out a groan. "Yes, she does." She got up from her chair, grasping the neck of the empty bottle and stepping out of the room. I waited as she came back in with another bottle of vodka, already unscrewing the top. "I'm really not interested in talking about Axel's origin story, but if you want to still sit here with me and talk then let's talk about how I'm pretty sure your angelic lover boy comes in his pants every time you enter a room." She started pouring more liquid into our glasses.

"So…we're friends now?"

Elise sucked in a sharp breath and pursed her lips. "I don't want to see you dead, alright."

I narrowed my eyes, taking a sip of my drink, the vodka getting to my head a small bit. "You did try to kill me in Oculus that day with your tail, so I don't follow."

Elise's face melted into a laugh and then she hiccupped. A sign that the vodka was getting to her as well. "Dani, I was never going to actually kill you. I will fuck you up, but I would never kill you." Her face was serious now and I understood what she was saying. "I was never going to let you come to Heaven's Gate by yourself, dipshit," she added, as if she knew it might be something I'd want to hear.

"Because we're friends?"

Elise rolled her eyes, smirking as she tilted her glass up to her lips, swallowing some more vodka before setting it down with a small thud. "Yeah, that."

II

NICK

I'd been able to get to sleep just fine last night, give or take the few times I'd woken up in a cold sweat. I'd remained in my bed and hadn't slept on the bathroom floor, even though I felt suffocated in this room. Reese had been snoring and never stirred each time I sat up, brought my knees to my chest and took several deep breaths. He stepped out of the shower, shirtless with just his underwear on and his hair dripping wet. I sat back on my hands as I watched him shake his hair out and tie it up in an unruly knot.

He hadn't really questioned me when I'd said I wanted to stay with Dani while she was unconscious last night, and he hadn't mentioned it at all this morning. He had simply given me a look of confusion and had continued to give me that same look of confusion when I had closed Dani's door behind me as I stepped inside her room, but he had just let it be. It wasn't like I could have talked to him about it, since he had passed out by the time I went to bed. Despite the chair not being the most comfortable sleeping arrangement, I didn't have one fit, or nightmare during the time I'd spent in her room. Something about it didn't surprise me. Reese sauntered over to the dresser, pulling out a pair of pants and stepping into them. I brought my hands around to rest on my thighs, feeling them start to get sweaty as I rubbed them against my pants.

"Are you still with me, Nick?" Reese asked, chucking a pillow at my face. The pillow landed at my feet as I ran a hand down my face, bringing him back into my view. I didn't know when I had zoned out, but apparently, I had.

"Yeah, yeah, I'm here."

Reese picked up a shirt off the bed, which I guess I hadn't realized he'd taken out and put it on, pulling it down his torso. "You sure? You are zoning out a lot lately."

"I told you I'm fine. Are you done?" I was getting frustrated with his need to ask me if I was alright. I appreciated it, but fuck, I was *fucking* fine.

He narrowed his hazel eyes at me in a way that told me he actually wasn't done. I knew that look and it brought me back to our early stages of friendship. That look never changed and it was just as annoying then as it was now. He crossed his arms over his chest and sucked his teeth, telling me he could stand like this all day and wait for me to open my mouth and speak words other than *I'm fine.*

I let out a groan. "What do you want me to say, huh?"

He shrugged his broad shoulders. "I don't know, Nick. How about you start by explaining why we're here?"

"The fuck does that mean. You *know* why we're here."

He took a few steps back and leaned against the wall. "I mean I thought so, but from where I'm standing, I feel like you have other reasons. Reasons that seem to be taking precedence in your mind."

I licked my lips and shook my head. "I'm confused. What are you getting at?"

Reese let out a short laugh. "You carried her to her room and slept in there to watch over her, Nick."

"She passed out, Reese. I was being nice, I wanted to make sure she was okay. I didn't know that was a bad thing." I got up from the bed and squared my shoulders.

He slid his index finger over his chin in thought as if my words were actually making him think. He rolled his eyes. "Right. Let us add the fact that any time you're in a room with her, you can hardly focus on anything else. Listen I don't know if you think I'm fucking stupid, but I can assure you I'm not."

I didn't need this. I didn't need a lecture from the one person who has only ever taken a handful of things seriously in his entire life. "No one's calling you stupid, Reese, but this whole thing is really uncalled for. I'm one hundred percent in this. Lilith is the end goal. Helping our people and all the people we've met here is the end goal. So, I really don't understand—"

"So, this has nothing to do with Dani."

I felt my hands begin to ball into fists at my side. "No."

"Not even a little?"

I could hear my teeth grinding together. "I've already said no."

He pulled his hair out of the knot at the top of his head and when he looked at me, it was the most serious I'd ever seen him. "Fuck, Nick, you have been off even before we left, and I don't know what that's about. I'm not gonna push you with all your Jonah stuff and whatever's going on with your fucking dad, but one thing you aren't going to hide from me is this. I let you do your thing because you said it happened once, but it's not worth explaining, so I let it go. But I'm not going to let you downplay something that could likely have a major impact on all of us."

I ran my hands through my hair, my frustration starting to boil to the surface. "All this because I showed a little compassion for her?"

Reese pointed a finger at me. "No, Nick. That's not it. You're doing the one thing you always told me never to do. You have tunnel vision."

"No, I—" But he cut me off.

"You have tunnel vision for a demon, hybrid, whatever the fuck she is and you think that no one sees it. You want to pretend like this is all for the sake of Heaven's Gate and everything else, but come on, *come on,* I saw the way you clung to her after she tried to kill that kid. The way you cradled her fucking head when you took her to her room. Like fuck, you immediately asked about her after you woke up from your fucking coma!"

I chewed on the inside of my cheek because he was right. Well, he wasn't *completely* right, but he wasn't completely wrong either. I wanted Lilith to answer for what she'd done, what she'd made all of us do without us even realizing it. All the demons and Enchanters I'd spoken to yesterday had told me as much of their stories as they felt comfortable and I wanted to do it for them as well, not to mention I wanted to see the look on stupid Ariel's face when we came back victorious. There was a constant lingering thought in the back of my head, and it wanted me to come out of this with a beautiful, petite girl by my side. I was trying to prioritize my time with this mission while also figuring out how to get her to want to kiss me again. It sounded pretty pathetic, and I knew I should invest more of my time into one over the other, but Dani *was* important. Maybe not to Reese, but she was to me.

"I'm focused, Reese, I am. Nothing has changed. I went into this knowing the end goal and I haven't faltered from that. I can divide my time just fine. Whatever is going on with the Dani side of things is on me and it's my business."

Reese clucked his tongue, his blonde brows coming together. "I was with you against all that shit with Markus and I, yet again, pursued another mission with you. That was *my* choice, and I don't regret it at all because it's what you and I do for each other. I didn't sign up for you to divide your time between fighting Lilith and your one-night stand. Lilith is a much different beast than Markus ever was. He was a snake, but she is a literal monster, with so many weapons at her disposal, but you want to try to give even a fraction of your time to a hook up. Especially when said hook up literally went rogue yesterday!"

"I know what I'm doing! I've been right here. I have fought every single time right next to you since we've gotten here. Me and Dani, that…" I took in a breath, swallowing. "It shouldn't matter to you."

"It matters! If this is going to work, if we are going to make it out of this at all, you need to focus on what's important. You want to stop Lilith, perfect. Me too. I can get behind that. What I won't do is blindly follow you thinking you're hyper focused on one thing, but really find out you're just chasing after a piece of ass. I mean I'm pretty sure I've read that demons are tempting as fuck, but her pussy must have been fucking phenomenal if you're even considering splitting your time."

I didn't think, I just acted. It was like my body wasn't my own when I charged over to him and threw him against the wall. He let out a loud groan as we landed against the wood. My hands were fisted in his shirt and my body weight was pressed against him. My chest was heaving and all I felt was white hot anger. I didn't like the idea of her being reduced to something that could be so easily thrown away. I especially didn't like it coming from someone I trusted more than most.

I felt my best friend's heart thundering under my fists. "It's fucking insulting that you think that I would put my life and yours at risk like that. I know why I'm here, Reese, I haven't forgotten that. Every day I wake up and we aren't in Heaven's Gate I fucking remember why we're here." He shoved at me, my stance faltering, but I rallied and pushed back against him. He huffed out a breath when he connected with the wall again. "Not everything is so black and white like you think it is. I didn't tell you much about Dani and me because a lot had fucking happened. Reese, people died, people we knew and *Jonah*—" I heard my voice crack a bit, so I stopped, closed my eyes for a second, then started again. "You had just started to accept her into this fucked up team we've made, and I wasn't going to risk that by telling you details that you wouldn't have accepted in the first place." I brought my face closer to his so he could see my eyes and hear my words so very clearly. "You're here because you trust me, so just trust that when it comes down to it that I will fight with you until my last dying breath. But also trust me when I tell you to watch your *fucking* mouth when you talk about her."

His hazel eyes widened into saucers when I finished. He opened his mouth to speak, but then closed it as if he was carefully collecting all the words he wanted to say and exactly how to phrase them. He didn't try to fight me back anymore. It actually felt like his muscles were relaxing and his eyes started to narrow as they scanned my face. I didn't have to be the smartest guy in the room to know that my last sentence gave a lot away. Reese leaned his head back, letting it knock against the wall as he looked at the ceiling. He raised his arms in a surrendering move, and I removed my grip from his shirt, backing off.

We'd had our moments growing up where situations led to physical violence, but this felt different. I didn't want to cause him harm in any way, because I knew he was just worried about us being here and making sure everything went as smoothly as possible, even if villainous hellhounds got in the way. Dani wasn't even mine, but I *felt* like I had to defend her like she was.

He let out an exasperated laugh, not like something was funny, but like something was finally dawning on him. "Nick, tell me something, would you?"

"Sure." I said, hesitantly.

"She wasn't just a one-night stand, was she?" His question was so stark and upfront. It was almost like he knew the answer but wanted me to speak it into existence.

I just stared at him, wondering if I should shape my words a certain way, if I should try to dress them up to make the answer more appealing to him. Reese looked at me as if he was just waiting for me to say something stupid and dig myself an even deeper hole. I placed both my hands on the back of my neck and brought my elbows together, leaning my head back. "No." The amount of tension that I didn't even know I had immediately lifted once the word left my mouth.

Reese tapped his front teeth together, processing my answer. He started pacing in front of me. To the left, to the right, stop, left, right, stop. I had to close my eyes to stop watching him. He finally ceased his movements and dropped his shoulders in a defeated way. "Well, fuck."

"That's one way to put it."

"Nick. So, ugh, you're telling me that the time you spent with her in your bedroom wasn't the first time?"

I pressed my lips together. I hadn't considered that I would have to explain the training room to anyone. "No."

"Well…okay." He blew out a breath, opening his mouth and then blowing out another breath. "When?"

I raised one of my eyebrows, suspiciously. "You really want to know all the details regarding that?"

Reese shrugged. "I'm genuinely wondering *when* you would have had time to even have sex with her. Predictable, rule-follower Nick has spontaneous sex with a demon, like you skipped the starter and went straight for the whole meal."

I quickly looked down at the floor, rubbing the tip of my shoe against the wood. "You'd be surprised."

Reese waved his hands in front of him. "You know what, whatever. I knew shit was off when I initially found out you guys fucked. You've only done a one-night stand twice and both times I had to talk you out of trying to take them out on dates the next time you saw them. You just aren't the type which I respect but come on Nick. A demon?"

"It's not like I wanted this to happen, okay. I'm in unknown territory with her and with that I'm very, very fucking confused."

"She's got your overthinking ass working overtime," he joked, stepping forward so that he was a few steps in front of me. "So…you like her?" He squinted as if what I said next would mold his words afterwards.

I rubbed the space over my eyebrow, feeling like a headache could appear at any moment. I knew my answer though. That was easy. "Yes."

"Even though she tried to kill a child, she might end up *actually* killing all of us," he added.

I rolled my eyes. "You can't say shit like that. As much as you aren't her biggest fan, you and I both know she didn't want to kill Yuri and she would never intentionally try to hurt us. Natalia told all of us to try to keep our wits and she's trying to do the same, but it's probably a lot harder for her."

Reese made a small gagging noise. "Oh, shit. You really, *really* like her."

"Shut up."

"I do mean it though Nick, Lilith first, your weird situation with Dani later or I promise you, I will keep my promise and call you Nick the Dick at your funeral. There are a lot of people depending on us to be focused. You and I both know we can't leave them in the hands of Ariel for long." It was meant to be a joke, but in all honesty he was right. Even though I hadn't asked her, I knew Natalia was doing her best to be the leader for Oculus but also keep an eye on The Skies while also accompanying Zane to check on my family. Reese had a point in making it known that I didn't lose focus for that reason alone. "I want you to be happy, but you know, I also don't want to die. Not yet anyway."

"I know. I'm pretty good at multitasking. One of the many things I'm better at than you."

He lightly punched me in the shoulder. "The whole you being super off lately… is that because of her?"

I knew by 'off' he meant my sleeping on the bathroom floor, constantly zoning out, and particularly cagey behavior. You didn't have to be the smartest person in the room to figure that one out. He had just found out that Dani was a lot more to me than just a teammate and as much as I wanted to confide in my best friend, I couldn't. He was already worried I wasn't focused enough; I didn't need him to be more concerned.

I shook my head. "No, that's just me trying to figure my shit out. I'm not leaving anything to chance so stop worrying. Like I said the other day, I didn't feel too hot that night, so I passed out in the bathroom." I took both his shoulders in my hands. "Dani isn't the problem."

I was the problem, but that was for me to figure out. Not him.

He let out a sigh, nodding. "I'm sorry for what I said. She's not just a piece of ass, got it, that was a bad comment."

"Thanks. Happy you understand—"

"On the other hand, you went back for more, so I would *assume* her pussy is phenomenal, I mean…"

"*Watch it*," I said, hearing a sharpness to my tone that had him shutting his mouth quicker than I anticipated.

Instead of being pushed away by my words, he let out a sly smile. "Okay, tough guy, if you're all growly about her then why did she make it seem like you guys weren't much of a thing when she came to talk to me after her and Elise's fight in Oculus?"

"I wasn't aware she told you that, but I mean we aren't. We aren't anything, Reese. It's complicated."

"Clearly." He patted my cheek. "So, you put your foot in your mouth. Classic Nick."

I pulled back, a bit insulted. "You can't just assume that."

"I can and I did. What I can say is you are one of the best when it comes to forming a plan, so I'm sure you'll figure it out. And maybe when you do, I'll have come to terms with my best friend lusting after a demon. Right now, I'm on the fence."

I let myself fall backwards onto the bed behind me, my back hitting the cold sheets. "Sorry I got angry."

"I don't think I would have believed you liked her if you didn't. And we both know that if we had an actual fight, I would win, or did you forget how you got that scar?" I absentmindedly reached up and touched the scar under my eye. I remember trying so hard not to cry when it happened, especially since I was eleven and I wanted to give off this persona like nothing hurt me, like prioritizing my pain wasn't worth anything.

I guess I was still doing that. And the end result would be the same. I would heal over time and there would be a scar in place of the pain. I could see it every day, but it wouldn't hurt as much. At least I hoped it would be like that.

I pushed myself up and onto my elbows, realizing that I had an entirely different plan for today. Reese came and sat down next to me, leaning back on his hands. "Can we put the Dani talk away for a minute?" He nodded.

"I want to talk to Natalia."

Reese and I bounded down the steps and met Beetee at the front desk. She was hunched over some papers with a coffee at her side. The lounge area was empty, and she didn't seem to notice us when we approached. Reese rapped his knuckles on the counter and greeted her.

"Good morning, reptile queen."

Beetee shot her head up, reaching her arm across the counter, and covering his mouth. She pressed her index finger to her lips and nodded over towards the dining area. We looked past the few patrons that were in the kitchen, who were being oddly quiet, and that's when I noticed them. Two bodies, in opposite chairs, asleep at the table.

"What the hell?" I said as I looked from Beetee to the dining area.

She let out a small giggle. "I'll discuss with Ellie later about asking before ruthlessly ripping off the lock on the liquor cabinet, but I guess they decided to talk."

"This I have got to see." Reese started walking in their direction and I followed suit. The others started watching us as we made our way over to our two companions. They seemed to think it was quite assuming that we were even attempting to startle the women in front of us. Dani had her arm under her head and her curls were splayed out around the table. She looked like she was in a deep sleep and fuck, she was cute. Her small breaths made tiny pieces of her hair flail around before they settled back towards her face again. I looked to my left to see Elise slumped in her chair. Her head was down, and her shoulders were hunched. Her body was swaying every few seconds as if she could lose her balance and fall off the chair at any moment. I leaned down so I was near Dani's face and took hold of her shoulder, shaking it gently. She didn't wake up immediately, so I shook her again, adding a little bit more force this time. Her eyes fluttered open, squinting just a bit to adjust. She blinked a few times before her eyes told me she was really taking me in.

"Nicholas?"

"Yeah, it's me." I reached around her head and plucked the half empty glass from the table. I brought it to my nose and sniffed, before placing it back down. "Vodka. Solid choice."

She groaned but winced when she heard the chair across from her rattling along the floor. She moved her head up, resting her chin on the table. Reese had the back of Elise's chair in his hands as he moved it from side to side, erratically. Elise held onto the table with a look on her face that gave me no indication that she was exhausted from last night at all.

Reese was having way too much fun to realize that Elise had released her tail and slithered it around the back of the chair. She placed her tail in a perfectly horizontal position and sliced right along both of Reese's hands.

"Fuck, fuck, fuck!" he yelled, dropping the chair and holding his hands out. I knew the feeling of that venom and it wasn't pleasant. "That shit burns."

"Your hands will be just as useless as you for a few moments," Elise pointed out before running her hands over her eyes.

I watched as Reese tried to shake one of his hands and nothing happened. I choked back a laugh and looked down at Dani who had now fully sat up. She placed her elbows on the table and ran a hand into her hair. After a second, she spoke. "I know you're staring at me and I'm fine. Straight vodka has never really been my drink of choice."

I turned the empty bottle that was in the middle of the table around, tilting it to read the label. "Seems like you enjoyed it."

"Are we back to being friends? Or do I still have to be weird with you two?" Beetee asked curiously. She looked from Elise to Dani, but honestly, I knew all her focus wanted to remain on Elise since *she* was the reason Dani was so furious in the first place.

Elise hooked her arm around the back of her chair and glanced over at Dani, who was looking back at her just the same. They both gave each other small smiles of mutual respect and nodded. "Sure, Beetee. That's a word for it."

Beetee rolled her eyes and carried two drinks of thick brown liquid into the room. She sat it down in front of both women and then took a step back.

Reese leaned over Elise's chair, inspecting the contents. He was starting to move one finger at a time by now. "The fuck is that?"

Elise leaned down to sniff it and made a face like she was about to vomit. "I would rather lick my own asshole than drink that, thanks." It seemed to bubble on its own and I could attest that it smelled like ass.

The hot pink haired demon didn't shy away from the chaotically blunt demon. "Drink it." Her lilac eyes shifted a bit, just for a moment, so I could see diamond pupils. Oh right, she was part snake or something like that. Elise scoffed, but both she and Dani grabbed the cups and downed them in one movement.

Dani coughed a few times, sticking out her tongue as if she couldn't get rid of the taste as fast as she wanted to. "That's disgusting."

"There are better ways to cure mild hangovers than this weird shit," Elise pointed out, wiping a hand down her mouth. Beetee explained to us that while coffee and denial were Elise's hangover cures, this brown liquid was an Enchanter's concoction and she had seen it be the most effective.

I cleared my throat so I could have everyone's attention. I really didn't understand why I was so nervous; we all knew that we would have to do this at some point. "I think it's time we spoke with Natalia."

"Natalia?" Elise raised one of her eyebrows.

"Yeah, I think now is as good as any to bring her into the loop. We all want to know what Lilith is keeping Isabel for, besides obviously fucking up portals and dropping in to cause issues. Plus, we should check in if anything else."

Dani stood up from her seat on slightly wobbly legs. "If that's what you want to do, then we'll do it."

Beetee started to clean the glass that I guess the girls had broken on the table last night. "How do you plan to speak with your High Priestess?"

I broke down how exactly we would be able to communicate with Natalia, which she seemed intrigued to hear. Her full attention was on me the entire time I spoke. She was a solid listener, it made sense given the level of hospitality she'd shown us and everyone else here. At least half of the creatures I spoke to all had something wonderful to say about her, the other half weren't as interested in talking to me, but I understood that as well.

"Alright ladies, single file line up the stairs," Reese ordered, pointing towards the stairs in the other room.

Elise shoved her chair back, causing it to land right into his chest before she strutted out of the room. Dani gave me a look before she followed after Elise, brushing her hand against mine as she passed me. It was subtle and likely unintentional, but I felt a small jolt of electricity run through my fingertips, so I took it as a good sign. Before we could make it towards the stairs, the sound of large and small footsteps were heard descending them.

Leah and Garrett caught my eye and waved. Their children were closely behind them, nearly on their heels. There was a mild shift in the air when I looked from Dani to the young Enchanters who were staring up at her. Yuri barely reached his father's back, but he hid behind him as best he could. His sister, Jasmine, did the same, but Yuri made a point to not remove his eyes from her. Dani didn't speak but she also didn't move. I knew she meant well, and I knew that what happened and how she had behaved was eating away at her.

After a moment, she spoke. "I think it's for the best if you all stay here."

Leah and Garrett looked at each other with confusion.

"Lilith knows where you are, or at least where you were. I don't think she'll come for you, but I'm thinking about your—" she peeked down at Yuri and Jasmine again but didn't say anything else.

Beetee clasped her hands together in front of her chest, stepping into our awkward circle. "You can stay as long as you'd like. You know it's never an issue."

I heard padding down the stairs, and I expected to see another child, but what I actually saw didn't have two feet, but four paws.

"Oh, fuck me," Reese complained, right before Axel ran across the floor and lunged at him. Luckily this time Reese was a bit more prepared and held his arms out to catch him. "Why do you fucking like me?" Axel licked his face and wagged his tail incessantly. I scratched his head which he thoroughly enjoyed. Little spaces of hair were missing from around his eye, where he had gotten attacked by another hellhound, but other than that, he was perfectly fine.

"I'm wondering that as well," Elise muttered, patting her pet on the head and pulling him out of Reese's grasp. Axel swiveled and squirmed in her grip, but his black eyes locked onto Dani's brown ones, and he started to growl. He didn't make a move towards her, but he just growled in a more protective nature.

Dani stood there with her eyebrows furrowed but her feet were planted firmly on the ground like she was willing to take whatever grilling came her way, from either Yuri's parents or the hellhound in front of her.

"Ugh, Axel. Stop," Elise scolded, tilting her head towards the hound's floppy ear and speaking into it. Her words were hushed, but once she was done, his barking ceased. He wiggled out of her arms and propelled himself into Dani's unsuspecting ones. He licked a long stripe up her face, then jumped out of her arms and headed towards the kids, who were more than happy to be occupied by him.

"What did you say to him?" I asked Elise, who was already starting to walk past us and up the stairs. She shrugged as she sat her foot on the bottom step.

"Nothing of importance, Nicholas."

Garrett turned to Beetee. "We'll stay here, thank you for the warning." He nodded over to Dani but turned around to focus his attention on his children. Dani trailed after Elise and Reese followed after them. I was about to head that way myself, but Leah caught my arm. Her two braids from before were now out of their confinement and her hair was now in long glossy waves that framed her face. Her eyes scanned my face as if she was trying to find the right words for whatever she was preparing to say to me.

"I was going to say it back at the house, but I never got the chance." Her eyes dug into mine so deeply that I almost admitted how uncomfortable I started to feel. "You look so much like someone I used to know."

I'd heard that before. Not in those words exactly, but I'd heard a form of them by the very person I was getting ready to speak to. I really didn't know what she wanted me to say back. "I assume you're speaking about my mother."

"Perhaps. I can see a resemblance even in the smallest form, like your eyes. I remember Moira and her were inseparable. She was in Oculus probably more than any angel I'd ever seen. There was a man that used to visit and speak with Moira as well and he would follow your mom around like a puppy dog sometimes." She tilted her head to the side, seeming to try to get a better angle of my face. "Come to think of it, you kind of look like him too. You actually *really* look like him."

"Yeah, probably my dad."

She nodded thoughtfully and then started laughing. It wasn't a loud, boisterous laugh, but a laugh more to herself. "If I remember things correctly, she was the headstrong type, so I can tell where you get it from. I know it may not be much coming from me, but your parents must be so proud of what you're trying to accomplish here, if not a bit scared out of their minds."

I didn't try to correct her by saying that *parents* should be corrected to *parent*. I knew that she was speaking with a mother's heart, and I appreciated it more than she would understand. I had just my father for so long that I hadn't realized how different those words could sound coming from her. She reached for my arm, giving it a gentle squeeze.

"I'll keep that in mind," I said, placing my hand over hers. She looked over her shoulder as Jasmine called for her mother. She gave me a small smile which I reciprocated before she turned away from me.

12

NICK

I closed the door to my shared bedroom with Reese and took in a breath. I knew we needed to do this, but that didn't mean I was any less anxious about it. I could feel sweat developing at the back of my neck. It really was not that big of a deal, but a small piece of me kind of wanted someone else to talk to Natalia through my portal key. I could have and it wouldn't have been an issue, but I wanted to be the one to do it so here we were back to square one in my ever present spiraling mindset.

"So how is this working?" Dani asked, sitting down on my bed while Reese leaned against the headboard of his own. Elise placed her back against the wall, eyeing me.

"I'll lay on the bed, and I guess use this to try to communicate with her. I need to be watched since my physical body will be vulnerable." I plucked my portal key from within my shirt, feeling the texture of it around my fingers.

"And you know what you're doing?" Elise asked, knowing full well I didn't. I didn't give her any type of response.

"We'll all be here waiting for you to wake up, alright?" Reese assured me. I stepped over to my bed and laid my head on the pillow, feeling incredibly awkward just lying there. Dani moved around so that she was looking down at me. She grabbed the portal key in one hand and my mildly sweaty hand in the other. She wrapped my shaky hand around the tiger's eye key and smirked. "Remember what she said, you idiot. Close your eyes and think about wanting to talk to her. The magic should do the rest."

"Let us hope she doesn't decide to just ignore you. I know I fucking would," Elise said, chuckling under her breath.

Reese sat down on the side of his bed that was closest to me and I noticed the moment Dani let go of my hand. She placed both her hands in her lap and patiently watched me. I blinked once, twice, then closed my eyes for good. I let my mind wander to the High Priestess who seemed to know so much, but I knew there were things that she was still very much in the dark about. She couldn't always be an encyclopedia of knowledge but for this, I knew she had to know something of the sort. Most of the Enchanters here knew things, but they were limited. Leah had the pleasure of learning things alongside a High Priestess herself, but others were not granted that kind of luxury.

Isabel had ended up just pulling from willing and unwilling participants when Lilith had Enchanters bestow their magic onto her. Some she had completely drained of their powers while others had just enough left to get by. Their magic was a part of them and trying to coax any type of story from them was daunting enough, especially when you saw the haunted looks on their faces when you realized their eyes had glazed over and they were right back in that moment of no return. There were some that made it out completely unscathed- not *completely* unscathed- their magic was intact, like Garrett and Leah, but they still had nightmares. They still couldn't be completely themselves here, even though they had sided with Lilith's intoxicating words of freedom and the idea of no consequences.

I willed myself to focus on Natalia, on wherever she was right now, and how much I needed to talk to her. I was unsure how I would know when it was working, but I tried to relax. I tried to numb my mind. I tried to focus. Focus, focus, focus. I felt numb suddenly. I couldn't feel my fingers around my portal key, and I couldn't feel the bed underneath me. This reminded me of when I found out that Dani was a hybrid, but this time I wasn't going into the past, I was moving in real time. I heard the crunch of leaves and the grinding of gravel underneath my shoes as I looked down at where my mind had taken me. I looked around, seeing the trees that looked so familiar to Oculus and the precise way the wind moved, making the leaves at my feet dance around.

The sky looked like the sun was starting to rise and the light was causing my shadow to extend further and further. I didn't know what else to do now,

I felt like I was here in the right place, but what now?

"Ah, Nicholas, I was wondering when I would see your face again." I whirled around to see Natalia walking around a few trees. Her musically light voice echoed around me. Her dark purple dress shined and glittered as she walked towards me, moving with her at every step. Her long dark hair was decorated in a multitude of knots on the top of her head, each one tied off with a golden ribbon to secure it in place. Tendrils of her hair framed her face, the sparkles on her cheeks on full display, her dark skin flawless.

The bangles on her wrists jingled as she smoothed out her dress. Her face turned serious. "I do have to ask, your friends are watching over you, yes?"

I nodded. "Yeah, don't worry."

Her shoulders seemed to relax. It was sweet how much she cared about my well-being.

"Are we in Oculus right now?" I asked, taking another look around.

She hummed thoughtfully. "Yes and no. When I heard your call, the way I answered was by creating the setting to speak to you in. We are in Oculus, yes, but it's cloaked, so we are in our own bubble here. I will tell you though, Zane wasn't a fan of me whisking myself away to speak with you, but I made a promise to be here so he will have to pretend like he has any say over what I do later."

I chuckled, thinking about the hulking man who clearly always had her best interest at heart, even if it was a bit overbearing. "Hopefully this won't take long, and you can get back to whatever you were doing. We are just a little lost on something at the moment."

She nodded and started walking past me, then turned around to face me again. "Okay, well start from the beginning. I'll help as best I can."

I inhaled deeply. I told her everything I could remember from the very beginning of our arrival in Purgatory, to the fight with Lilith's shadow demons, and the meeting with Leah and Garrett. I tried to be as detailed as I could be when it came to my reiteration of Leah and Garrett's story. There were obvious pieces I didn't understand generally and then there were parts that I knew I didn't understand due to what I was. I was an angel who considered loyalty as one of the pillars of my entire existence. It was something I never quite understood about their story or really when it came to any of the Enchanters. Even though Jonah had kept things from me, Markus was a snake and Ariel was just a power hunger dick, I still wanted to be loyal to where I was from. I couldn't comprehend leaving someplace that gave you nothing but the best for a temporary solution. I didn't know Natalia's mother, but I had a feeling she was altogether a gracious and kind individual. Enchanters had traded that for Lilith and her tempting words.

I couldn't help but judge, yet I knew it wouldn't do me any good now. The Enchanters that resided in Purgatory regretted their choices immensely and all they really wanted to do was be back in their home, following Natalia.

I peeked up at the High Priestess when I was finished speaking and she looked at me so intensely, those honey-colored eyes soft but commanding. "Are you finished?" she asked politely. I nodded.

She raised her head towards the sky. "Isabel has been quite busy hasn't she." It wasn't meant to be a question; I knew that much. "There is a small part of me that wants to help her, pull her over to the better side of things. Then there is the part of me that wants her to burn for what she's done." Her voice sounded far away, like she was deep in her own thoughts.

"I know hearing I'm sorry is probably pointless right now and coming from me it likely doesn't mean much, but still, I'm sorry nonetheless."

"Oh, Nicholas. Don't worry, I've shed my tears and moved on as best I can. I really can't let someone like her get in the way of what I have to do here. That gives her too much power over me and that's not fair to me nor my people, hmm?" She was right as per usual.

She shook herself off and gave me her attention as if her thoughts about Isabel were so easily thrown away. "Back to what you were saying. You want to understand why Lilith would need Isabel to help with the shadow demons?"

"Yeah, I mean what exactly could Enchanter magic even do for her in that situation?"

"Well, Isabel's magic is more enhanced than any normal Enchanter. And from what you've told me Lilith can't seem to fully control those soulless demons as she would like to. If I were Lilith, I would be using Isabel to focus them, help them gain more structure, but some things are too far gone to give any structure too. With no foundation it's hard to understand where to start."

I put my hand over my mouth, sliding my fingers across my lips as I started to think. Natalia continued. "I'm thinking that Isabel anchored them enough to have them travel to The Skies during that fight at the meeting, so they didn't go off and just kill anyone and everyone, but that is it. It was quiet over at The Skies after that because she had Isabel dispose of them. I don't know any of this for sure, but that's my best guess. It's one or the other with this sort of experimentation she's doing. You either have creatures like Dani and Elise who have souls and a conscience, or you have creatures without souls and nothing to ground them, that's not even something Isabel is able to fix."

"Is it because she isn't powerful enough?" I questioned.

Natalia shook her head. "Oh no. It's because those demons she's choosing aren't strong enough to withstand soul pulling. You can't just rip it out and put it back in, that's just not how that works. Lilith seems to be trying to get Isabel to manipulate what's left of the demon, to be more submissive and willing to follow her while in that dark of a state. You can't just do that to something that was never prepared to bear that kind of weight."

"What about the help of a necromancer *and* Isabel? Could both of them change that?"

Natalia furrowed her delicate brows and then realization dawned on her face. "Ah, you did say Garrett had the power of resurrection. It is nerve wracking to know she had one of those in such close quarters, resurrection in the hands of Lilith could be a dangerous feat. It is quite interesting though since that power is nearly extinct now. Only a few ever really had it. I can't do it myself, even being a High Priestess. Funny isn't it."

My eyebrows raised, but I remained quiet. "To answer your question though, no that still wouldn't help. Resurrection might bring them back, I mean there are always no guarantees when you are working with that kind of magic, but normally they would return with their soul intact and nothing would have changed. Unless Isabel could figure out a way to manipulate the soul into not returning to its host then that would be the only way, but Lilith would ultimately be back to square one."

"Then this doesn't make any sense. She has plenty of demons to do her bidding, what's even the point of any of these so-called experiments."

"It does in a way." Natalia brought her lower lip into her mouth using her teeth. "Those soulless demons, as fickle as they may be, are getting the job done. Distracting you while she doesn't have to waste her other demons on you. The hellhounds are no different, with the obvious help of Isabel to manipulate them, just like she did with the angels at The Skies. Her reasons for keeping Isabel around are vast, she'll need that kind of magic if she has any intention of trying to claim Heaven's Gate again, if that's even her plan at all." I almost flinched when she mentioned that fight. I closed my eyes tightly to try to stop every single moment from erupting into my mind. "Those voided demons have no loyalties, no sense of right or wrong, no moment of clarity that what they may be doing could be seen as malevolent, if they go, they go. She likely has a million of them by now, waiting to slow you down, mess with you."

"But for what?"

"Lilith moves in a different way than you do. You all are so direct and willing to be on the front lines. She isn't. Lilith has made the mistake of trusting Markus to get her plans ahead and that didn't pan out so she's taking a different route, while still maintaining her way of doing things, meticulously and moving all the pieces around at different times, having them make moves when it benefits her." Maybe we were all pawns in Lilith's game, just not understanding what part we played and how much importance we had when it was game over. The High Priestess looked over her shoulder as if her home with all the people who loved her was just beyond the trees. "These shadow demons aren't the main issue; they are likely another moving piece meant to distract you from what's really going on. Lilith always means to use them, but they aren't what she's after. As much as she loves watching the chaos, she loves stability, loves when everything falls into place with minimal effort on her side, when others are to blame for her actions."

Those demons had no stability, nothing to *ground* them as she said. Then why would Lilith waste her time with them? Unless Natalia was right, and those soulless demons were just a means to an end. Based on what I knew about Lilith, that wouldn't surprise me one bit.

"If you are trying to tell me she wants Dani, then that's old news. We know she wants her back."

Natalia pressed her lips together as if she was trying not to laugh. "That's not what I'm saying. I'm saying that she got Dani back in Purgatory, step one, now what's next? She has the means to snatch Dani up, get her to have a conversation. She could very well just end her life and all of yours, but she isn't. She's letting you move along like everything's fine. It's actually kind of frightening if you think about it."

"Isabel's mentioned having to keep Dani alive, which would give your theory some merit."

Natalia laughed, the sound almost musical. "I don't say things unless they have merit, Nicholas. I can promise you that." She gave me a knowing look. "Do you want to know what I think you should do as of right now?"

I was desperate at this point. "Yes. Very much so."

"I think you should try talking to a demon that was close to Lilith. Not an Elise type, but one that would have been more in the loop than others."

"We are staying at a hostel full of both demons and Enchanters, believe me, there are demons that were close to Lilith. They don't love talking about their experiences."

Natalia shook her head. The tendrils of hair in front of her face, swaying back and forth. "No, I mean a demon who may still have Lilith as an ally in some way. I would of course be cautious with whom you speak to, but you are never going to get the full story or even a sliver of it from someone who is going to filter themselves." She tapped on her chin. "You need someone with an Elise type mouth, but without the loyalty to Dani."

I looked at her in surprise. She laughed and it sounded like power, but every note was feathery and in tune. "Oh, please. I may have much on my mind these days, but I'm not blind. Elise talks a big game, but she has great respect for your Soul Seether."

I tilted my head left and right, realizing how much weight her words carried and how right she was. "Well, now that they're back to being whatever they are to each other, finding this mysterious, potentially helpful demon might be a little easier."

"And the fact that you have some kind of—what was it…shape-shifting demon on your side?"

It was my turn to laugh. "Yeah, Beetee. She's one of the good guys if you can call a demon that, I guess."

Natalia adjusted one of the skinny straps of her dress. "I don't think it matters much anymore what you are when determining good guys and bad guys, don't you think?" Her face was serious as if she was trying to get me to understand that what I'd said went back on everything that had happened to us in the past months.

"Right." I swiped a hand across the back of my neck nervously. "How's my dad? Daya?"

Natalia smiled warmly. "They're good. Worried about you, but that's to be expected."

"And Ariel?" She stuck her tongue in her cheek before she answered me.

"Um, he's quite honestly the same. He is making it seem like you all aren't coming back or won't make it back. Whichever is the case, he has already started his training of sentries and seems to want to continue with his plan of action. The place is still intact though, so don't worry."

She hadn't mentioned Jonah's missing power, so that had to mean that he either hadn't figured out where it went, or he had just given up on it altogether. I would bet all my celestial coins; it was the former. Ariel would never just dismiss that kind of power being up for grabs.

When I looked back at the High Priestess, she was smiling at me. The smile was small and light, but it was there. "And how is Dani?"

"Dani's fine. Adjusting to being back in her home of sorts, but she's fine."

"Have you spoken?"

I gave her a look of confusion. "Spoken? I do have to speak to her to get shit done Natalia, of course I've spoken to her."

Natalia tucked one of her tendrils of hair behind her ear, the earrings she had on had various colored gemstones in them. "You and I both know that's not what I mean."

I let out a breath, a little annoyed that she seemed more intuitive about whatever this was between me and Dani than I did. "No, not really. I mean there's been a lot going on and I just don't want to say something wrong that's going to make it worse. I don't want to have the same conversation with her if I can just get the right thing out the first time."

"Hmm...well if you want my advice, I think it's okay to be nervous. When you do say what it is you want to say, do it with confidence so there won't be a need to repeat yourself. There will be no skepticism." She nodded as if that was an order. "Also, maybe, if you really want insight, you should speak with the one person who knows her better than all of you."

I let my eyes close at the idea of having to express my thoughts and whatever feelings I had to the person she was talking about. I felt Natalia grab my face and my eyes popped open. "Are you keeping your wits down there?"

"Trying." And I *was* trying. Honestly, I was. It was hard when there was nothing but deep, haunted energy. The kind of energy that fed off of whatever I kept feeling, all the things I didn't want to talk about. Purgatory just made the attacks I'd been having more suffocating than when I had them at home. The visuals were vibrant and the way I couldn't breathe was even thicker and heavier against my chest.

She looked into my eyes, moving from one to the other. Back and forth as if she would be able to see everything I'd felt. "That's all we can do, I presume. Make sure she's doing the same. Having Lilith's voice in my head wouldn't do me any favors if I was her. Try to be a better voice for her to hear."

"I'll see what I can do." I knew I would do anything I could for her.

Natalia wrinkled her nose up and smiled. Before I could say anything else, a deafening cry rang out, practically vibrating the scene around me. It was so loud and shrill it felt like my ears were bleeding. I pressed my hands to the sides of my head and started to back away from the High Priestess. Her voice was faint when she cried out for me.

"Nicholas, are you alright? Nicholas."

I couldn't answer her. This felt just like all those other times before. My chest started to get heavy, my palms were sweaty. The shrill sound came again and nearly brought me to my knees, but I caught myself when I placed my hands on my thighs. This felt like before but different, like something was trying to dig inside my brain, scratching and pulling. It burned with how much it wanted inside my head. It pulled up Jonah's face and flashes of my sword moving left and right, slicing through the bodies of all those people I knew. I wanted to scream from the harrowing pain that I was enduring but I bit down on my tongue, willing it to stop, just *please* stop.

I was usually asleep when this started to happen, but now I was fully awake. Well, I was awake in a way. I wasn't trying to numb the pain with sleep or push away any thoughts right now. I came here for a reason, and I was focused on just that. I didn't know where this was coming from, why I felt this overwhelming darkness flood into my veins as if it liked what I was seeing in my darkest moments. I finally fell to the ground and clenched my teeth together as the dark feeling compressed on my chest.

I felt a hand on my shoulder and saw Natalia kneel down. She grabbed my face in her hand and jerked my head to look at her. "Nicholas, look at me." I didn't realize I had my eyes closed, until I went to do the very thing she was asking. "Look at me."

"Fuck, make it stop." I pressed one of my hands to my head, pulling at my hair.

"I don't know what's doing this, but you need to leave. You need to wake up."

"Ugh, fuck, I don't know how," I grunted out through clenched teeth.

Natalia squeezed my face, giving me a stern look. She wasn't afraid to be near me, yet I could see she was a little out of her realm. "Think about where you need to go back to. Focus or whatever it is will tear you apart."

I gave her a helpless nod as I closed my eyes again. I dragged a shaky hand up my chest and wrapped my fingers around my portal key. I thought about where I needed to be, who I needed to be *with*. And that was all it took. One tiny thought of her face, one burning need to be back with her and get through this assault on my very being and everything was quieted. I felt a small whoosh, as if I was being transported somewhere, but my head and chest felt lighter. I felt someone shaking me and my prior headache started to creep back.

"Nick! Nick!" I blinked up to a very nervous, very frantic Reese above me. His blonde hair fell around his face as he looked down at me. He gripped my shoulders so tight, I felt like his fingertips would leave an imprint.

"What! I'm back," I assured him, reaching up and prying his hands off me. I looked around for a second to make sure my words rang true. Elise was perched on the end of the bed and Dani had her legs bent underneath her as she sat next to me on my right. She had her bottom lip pulled into her mouth in a nervous way, as if she was concerned.

"The fuck happened?" I asked, rubbing my forehead.

"Well, you were fine and then you weren't," Elise explained, vaguely.

Reese rolled his eyes. "You were good and then you just started flinching a bit, then that became some type of convulsing. We couldn't wake you up."

It seemed like they got a lesser version of what I got in my dream-like state with Natalia. "Yeah, I don't know what happened."

"Your hands started glowing," Dani said, almost in a whisper.

I instantly brought my hands up to my face, but they looked like they also had.

"It stopped when you woke up. I thought you were about to light up this whole place for a minute. That's probably the most aggressive I've seen your angelic light man," Reese described, sitting at the edge of the bed next to my legs.

"Yeah, sorry," I apologized, still staring at my hands. Everything felt so real and so close during my time with Natalia. That attack felt so personal, as if it only wanted me, was feeding off of me.

"What happened to you in there?" Reese questioned, the concern for me laced in his tone.

I opened my mouth but closed it. I didn't know how to explain it to any of them. Maybe Purgatory didn't like me using its space as a means for communication, or maybe it was something else entirely. I gave the only honest answer I had.

"I don't know actually. But it's over."

Elise clucked her tongue and shrugged. "Alright, well we are oh, so happy you made it out unscathed pretty boy. Now tell us what the witch said."

I had, in great detail, explained to the best of my ability everything that Natalia had told me. They all sat around patiently as I finished my retelling, well, as patient as Elise could get. She paced the room for half of it. When I had mentioned Natalia's idea about talking to a demon to get more insight, Dani and Elise had both looked at each other. They silently spoke, in a world of their own before breaking eye contact. A few mumbled words about Isabel not being shit tumbled from Elise's mouth as she walked out of the room, after we'd planned to reconvene later that night. Reese flopped back onto his bed but kept his eyes on me and Dani as she swung her legs around and pushed herself off of the bed.

I had to physically pull my eyes away from watching her walk away from me, even though I actually kind of enjoyed it. It was one of my most favorite views. She stopped and turned to face us; her eyes narrowed. "If you both want to leave, I wouldn't blame you."

167

"Leave?" We both said in unison. She nodded, waiting.

"Dani, we aren't going to leave," I stated, a little insulted by her words.

"I'm just saying. We won't think less of you if you want to."

Reese laughed. "Oh, right, cause little psycho demon back there won't call us complete assholes if we just removed ourselves from the situation. As much as I don't like this, we come as a package deal. So, if he wants to stay, then so am I."

I smiled to myself. We may fight, but the end result was always undying loyalty. "We're staying."

"Good." That was all she said before she turned around on the balls of her feet and strolled out of the room. Reese followed her with his eyes as she closed the door behind her. He looked back at me and whistled. He settled back in his bed, throwing his hands behind his head. "Are you sure you're good?"

I nodded.

"And you want to stay here and continue to do this? Play Lilith's little game, fight her distractions as Natalia put it." He wasn't trying to get me to change my mind, but he was trying to get me to tell him point blank what I was thinking.

"Yeah, I do," I answered, but then quickly added. "And it's not for Dani's sake, well not completely."

Reese chuckled. "I gotcha. As long as you're sure… about *everything*." He made sure his last word was drawn out, like he was insinuating something other than the mission in front of us. He was making sure that I was sure about a certain hybrid that just left the room. I looked over at him and saw that he was looking right back at me. His hazel eyes were friendly, but they gave off a mischievous tone. He rolled his eyes, before closing them.

I heard Reese softly snoring next to me as I stared at the ceiling. I felt better than I had before, but Natalia's words kept replaying in my head over and over again. I couldn't really continue to ponder on how to fix this Lilith ordeal, at least not without everyone present, so I just focused on the one thing I could control. There was one person I needed to talk to, and I was dreading doing it the whole time it kept circling back to the forefront of my mind.

"Fuck it," I told myself as I jumped off my bed and made my way to the door. I opened it quickly, stepping out into the hallway and walking towards the stairs. I severely hoped that Elise was downstairs, or I would likely find some excuse to go back to my room, forgetting about this whole thing.

I took the stairs cautiously, peeking my head around the corner to see into the lounge area. I saw the top of her black hair as she sat on one of the couches with Beetee. I hurried down the rest of the stairs, catching Beetee's eye.

"Nicholas, I'm surprised to see you down here." Beetee smiled at me and moved further onto the couch.

Elise turned her head enough to bring me into her view. "Ah, I thought you and Blondie would be snuggled up taking a nap together." I walked around the couch towards one of the smaller couches. I noticed Axel laying at Elise's feet, his eyes were closed, and his little head was burrowed underneath one of his paws.

"Ha, very funny."

"I was just filling Beetee in on everything so far," Elise offered.

Beetee brought her legs up and cradled them to her chest. "Anything on your mind?"

I licked my lips, not quite sure how to say what I wanted to say. "Umm, yeah, well—"

"You want to know how to get back into Dani's panties?"

I cut my eyes to Elise, who blinked back at me as if she hadn't said one of the bluntest statements I had ever heard. "What?"

"I don't believe I stuttered, Nicholas."

"Ellie, you really are a terror, aren't you?" Beetee shook her head, kicking her foot out and connecting it with Elise's arm.

This was a bad idea. I ran a hand through my hair and let out an exasperated sigh. "I'll just head back upstairs now." I was halfway off the couch when Elise spoke. "Sit down, Nicholas."

I hovered for a moment but did as she said. I noticed that the kitchen and even beyond towards the dining room was littered with Enchanters and demons. Not too many to fill the rooms, but enough to have me wonder where she puts them all.

"I hope you aren't expecting me to give you some profound love advice because if that's the case then you can take your demon obsessed ass right upstairs," she challenged.

I looked towards the hearth of the fireplace. There was no real light from outside to give the room some natural illumination, so the sconces on the walls and the firelight had to do the trick. "I'm not. I'm just expecting honesty. I know you've had your issues with that, but not anymore, right." I leaned forward, resting my elbows on my knees, raising an eyebrow at her.

Elise laughed a little, ruffling her bangs. "No, not anymore."

Beetee leaned her head onto the back of the couch, making herself comfortable. "Can I ask why you two aren't already, umm...together?" Her golden skin blushed a red color as if she just asked the most scandalizing question.

"Because dear sweet Nicholas here put his foot in his stupid mouth. That's all you need to know." She looked at me, one of her eyebrows raised. "The real issue now is what to say to make it all better. Dani is stubborn, but she isn't unshakeable and for some reason your *acceptance* is something she wants."

I started to lean in, waiting for her to give me the answers.

Elise placed her hand on her forehead as if she was utterly annoyed. "Oh fuck, you dumb handsome creature. You really don't know what to say to her do you?"

"That's kind of why I'm down here. I thought we already established that."

"Well, yeah, but I thought you already had some kind of speech in place, I don't know— *something*. I wasn't aware you were completely lost."

Beetee giggled next to her. It was like they were on the same wavelength. I fell back into the couch cushions, already a little more than exhausted with this conversation and it hadn't even gone anywhere. The pink haired demon hummed. "Have you said you're sorry?"

"Of course I have."

Elise scooted closer to the edge of the couch, causing Axel to wake up and readjust himself. "Listen, I don't love this whole relationship bullshit, so I'm not an expert on how any of this gross nonsense works but I'm sor—." She nearly choked on the word. "Ugh, apologizing is fucking great I guess, but regardless of what Dani is or isn't you need to tell her the opposite of how you've made her feel." She rolled her eyes and shook her head as if I should be getting it by now.

I rubbed my index and thumb along my temple in thought. *Opposite of how I made her feel.* When we had that fight in my bedroom, she thought I wanted to change her. I never *saw* her any differently after I discovered what she was supposed to be, what she really was. Maybe I hadn't expressed that enough. I was so fixated on wanting her to accept both sides of herself that I had fumbled my words and maybe I hadn't heard her side of things well enough. Ever since that day she had thought that I couldn't be with her due to my own ideals and that wasn't the case. My loyalties were all over the place, but now they were planted in place and weren't going anywhere. I was already completely lost in her before I went to visit Natalia that day. I thought she was perfect. I still did.

My eyes widened when it dawned on me. Fuck, fuck, fuck.

"Has the idiot seen the proverbial light?" Elise quipped, finding humor at my expense.

I looked towards the stairs, and I felt my body get up and start to head upstairs. My feet were moving on their own and I let them.

"Never hurts to throw in another I'm sorry as well," Beetee offered, giggling again. I really did wonder how she and Elise got on so well. They were total opposites but maybe that was the whole point.

"And Nicholas," Elise called, causing me to turn around as my foot hit the first step. "Everything sounds so much better when you're on your knees."

13

DANI

I flipped my dagger over in my hands, trying to understand what Nicholas had said. I had come here knowing that Lilith wouldn't just remove me from the equation all at once. I knew she was much more calculated than that and all this taunting behavior was getting tiring. I started thinking back to when we had that massive fight in the briefing room and that shadow demon had looked at me as if it knew me, as if it wanted me. I hadn't told anyone about that feeling I got, like it was trying to connect with me while also trying to kill me.

Or maybe killing me wasn't what it was supposed to do. They were strong enough to fight, but they weren't strong enough to hold their own. And Lilith needed something strong enough, she wanted something to match her energy while also doing her bidding.

Out of all the things Natalia had to offer, she wanted us to speak to a demon who likely had ties to Lilith. I oddly didn't want to put any of them in unnecessary danger, but then again, the odds that things would get out of hand again were astronomical. I knew Elise and I had the same thought; the same name came to mind when it came to a demon of interest. It would be something to discuss and I knew someone who wouldn't like it at all.

Knock, knock.

I shadowed my dagger away and walked over to the door, my shoeless feet feeling the cold of the wood floor. I inched it open to see a very anxious angel. He looked down at me as soon as the door opened and gave me a small, shy smile. I looked around him and then back at his face, curious as to what he wanted.

"Can I help you?" I asked.

He bit his lower lip. "Yeah…can I come in?"

"Why?"

"To talk."

I still held onto the doorknob, so I leaned against the open door. "About?"

"Dani."

"Yes?"

He reached his arm out and rested it on the door frame. He leaned in casually and furrowed his brows. He didn't speak, he just stood there, acknowledging me like I should know the answer. I rolled my eyes and pulled the door open more. I swung my arm out in front of me, ushering him inside. He tentatively stepped over the threshold, walking past me and further into the room.

I closed the door behind me and leaned against it, putting as much space between us as I could. I didn't want to fully admit it, but even this amount of proximity was suffocating. The amount of tension he could gather into the room was insane. I wasn't angry at it, but it wasn't fair that he made me extremely hot and bothered whenever we were alone together.

"You wanted to talk, so talk."

He looked down at the floor, then around the room and then right at me. "I did want to start off by saying I'm sorry, again. I'm sorry for making you feel like I wanted one side of you or that your demon side was unneeded or unwarranted."

I crossed my arms over my chest, taking a few steps towards him. "I hear you and I already said that's fine, Nicholas. You don't have to keep apologizing when I've told you that's not…" He cut me off.

"I know, I know. *Fuck*, I know. I honestly didn't know what you wanted from me. I thought you wanted actions, so I gave that to you but maybe you wanted words, so…"

"So, you decided to leave me alone for three months, while you wallowed in your thoughts about me and what I wanted?" I said, tilting my head to the side.

He shrugged. "I didn't think you wanted to talk to me. I was giving you space."

"That's understandable, but you didn't even try, Nicholas. Going there would have been an action and then you would have given me words. You don't have to give me one without the other, you're allowed to provide both." I gave him an incredulous look like what I was saying should have been an obvious statement.

He let out a loud sigh and his shoulders dropped. "I get it. I'm not going to go back into the past and try to fix anything because that's done. All I can do is give you what you want right now. I'm here, Dani, this is my action."

I ruffled my curls, taking a large section and moving it to the other side of my head. "I'm impressed you're in Purgatory, but that's not…"

"Let me finish." His eyes bore into mine and just the act of that small assertiveness was enough to impress me just a little. I closed my mouth and nodded towards him to continue.

"I know just me being here isn't enough and I just…I've been thinking so much about how I could fix this, that I never really thought about what you said in my room that day. I heard you, but maybe I didn't listen hard enough or maybe I didn't read between the lines."

"Nicholas, it really doesn't matter…"

"Fuck, Dani, it does." He walked over to me but stopped when he felt like he was close enough. "You matter, alright. You want actions *and* words, so that's what I'll give you."

I blinked over at him, not really understanding. My eyes went wide as I watched him slowly but confidently get down on his knees in front of me. It was a sight to see and not because most stubborn men wouldn't even consider doing this, but because he was being vulnerable with me. Even in this state he was tall, meeting me now just an inch above my stomach. He looked up at me, sliding a hand across the back of his neck. I waited patiently, watching as his chest rose and fell, his cheeks were a little red, but his eyes were as sure as I'd ever seen them.

"Dani, I'm sorry for making you feel like you weren't enough…because you are. You're so much more than just an angel or just a demon, okay. None of that matters to me and I should have made that clearer. You're confident, a little scary and sexy as hell and I should have never told you that you could be better or that you *should* be better. I should have just told you what the truth really was and that's that you're fucking perfect. You can choose to be whatever you want, whoever you want, and I'll be there, so long as you'll let me. I need you to trust me again, please, with whatever you're willing to give me. I'm literally begging you to believe me. I'm on my knees here."

I forced my expression to remain neutral when all I wanted to do was break out into a face splitting grin. He was pleading and honest and would probably be on his knees for hours if I asked him too. I didn't truly know how I would react whenever he finally said what I wanted. Everything was moving in slow motion now. We stood like that staring at each other for what felt like hours and hours when I knew it was only a few seconds.

I held his gaze a little longer and watched as he swallowed in a nervous way as if he was waiting for me to turn him down and walk away from him. I couldn't even get myself to consider doing anything like that. My heart thundered in my chest, so loud I was surprised he couldn't hear it. "Are you finished?"

"Yeah," he answered in a small voice, almost like a whisper.

I couldn't hold the smile in anymore and I let it blossom on my face as I stepped closer to him, reaching my hand out and letting my fingers fiddle with his hair. I guided my fingers down the side of his face and under his chin, letting my thumb graze back and forth over his skin. "Took you long enough."

His shoulders immediately relaxed as his eyebrows rose slightly. He looked relieved. "I'm aware."

I let my thumb pull his bottom lip down and his tongue snuck out a small bit and licked at the tip of my finger. I bit my lower lip as I let his lip go and patted his shoulder. "You're very sexy on your knees, Nicholas, and as much as I love having you at my mercy like this, please get up."

I helped him up and didn't try to move back when he was at his full height and looming over me. Placing my hands on his shirt, I squeezed the material in my fist. The sound of our mutual breathing and the pure smell of his need for me was overwhelming my senses. I was on a high from his words and I had to admit to myself that trusting him again had me turned on in a way that I knew only he could understand. I noticed his hand reach out and tuck a piece of my hair behind my ear and I shivered slightly. He'd obviously done that move before but after his little speech this time was different.

He let out a slow breath and started to caress my cheek. "Can I *please* kiss you?"

I giggled and nodded. "Yes."

He leaned his head down instantly, while I got on the tips of my toes to reach his lips. It felt like the room was all of a sudden too hot when I felt his lips touch mine. He was slow about it and tentative as if he was treating me like I was timid. We both knew I wasn't in the slightest. He kept one hand on my cheek and placed the other on my waist. His lips were soft and skillful, just like I remembered them. *Fuck*, I missed his mouth. I moved mine against his and I heard the very small groan that came from his throat. He gave me one small kiss when he pulled away. When I looked up into his eyes, he looked genuinely happy. As he should be.

I leaned towards him and pecked him on the lips again, lingering for a minute. "Now, *please* kiss me like you *want* too?"

His mouth opened as if he was looking to challenge me. This man hadn't kissed me in months, he couldn't really expect me to believe *that* was the kiss he wanted. One corner of my mouth lifted up as he pressed his forehead to mine and found my lips again. This time though his mouth was more urgent and needy. I had to regain my composure when he bent down to place his hands behind my thighs and lifted me up, causing me to wrap my legs around his waist. We were moving and I felt a wall behind my back as he pressed me up against the cool wood. His lips never left mine as he explored my mouth with his tongue. This kiss was so much more aggressive and impatient, filled with longing and desire. I let my own tongue play with his as he pressed more of his weight against me. A soft moan escaped my lips at the feel of his hardening cock between my legs.

He broke the kiss to slide his lips down to my neck, nipping and sucking at my skin as if he couldn't get enough. He kissed that place on my neck that had me pushing against him, rubbing myself where he was rigid and stiff. He gripped my ass with his hands, holding me up with ease. I felt his body let out an audible shudder as he kissed my skin. I heard him breathe me in as if my scent alone was comforting, as if he could just do this, be this with me in a little bubble of our own. He dug his lower body into me, and I reciprocated the movement as he nuzzled his nose into my hair. "Fuck, Dani, I..." He let his words dissipate as he pressed his forehead to mine. The look he gave me told me there were a million things he wanted to say, but none of them wanted to be spoken.

I didn't know what I wanted to say at that moment either, so I said the only thing that was on my mind. "I missed you too, you handsome idiot." He chuckled and I felt him squeezed my ass harder, pulling me into him as he found my mouth again.

I pulled his bottom lip into my mouth quickly before letting it go. I felt his breath on my face, and I remembered the last time he had me up against a wall in this same position. Except that time there were no clothes between us, and I had just started to realize how much I had underestimated Nicholas Cassial's stamina.

He burrowed his face in my neck, running his nose along my skin and kissing my jaw. "I want to taste you."

"You *want* to?" I asked, teasing him.

He pressed more of his weight into me and shifted so he was holding me up with one arm, while he wrapped his other hand around my throat, and I let out a moan. "I *need* to taste you. Is that better?"

"Much better." He gave my throat a tiny squeeze, a teaser telling me that he missed my bratty attitude, and he would do something about it soon. I reached for his shirt and tugged him closer. "I suggest you get your face between my legs if you *need* to taste me so badly, Nicholas."

He yanked me from the wall and turned to walk us to the bed, his lips nearly glued on mine as we kissed. He lightly tossed me on the bed and was over me in seconds, kissing me again with the kind of savage need that had wetness starting to pool between my legs. I leaned up on my elbows to get closer, but his kisses started to descend heading down my neck and my chest. He was so eager but his hands were steady as they lifted my shirt so he could lick between my breasts and down my stomach. I watched him as he didn't hesitate for a second to pull my leggings down and throw them behind him.

He ran his hands over my legs, letting his fingertips tickle my skin. Nicholas slid his hands down my thighs and my legs twitched. He gave the inside of my ankle a gentle kiss. "Spread your legs."

I did as he said, looking into those intoxicating brown eyes of his. He tilted his head to the side and licked his lips as he stared between my legs. He placed his fingers right to the center of my panties and rubbed. I knew he felt the wetness building. "Slide them over and let me see you."

I slid my hand down my stomach, looking right at him, when I grabbed my panties and moved them to the side. Nicholas let out a shaky breath as he squeezed my thighs harder. He yanked me to the end of the bed, got down on his knees and let his fingers glide over my pussy. He spread me open, and the sexiest smile of admiration graced his face. "Mm, you have the prettiest pussy."

I didn't get a chance to answer him when his tongue took a long lick right up my center. My thighs tightened at the sensation and my eyes shot to where his head moved back and forth as he explored. He swirled his tongue around my clit, and I had to stop myself from mildly convulsing because *fuck* I missed his tongue. He fluttered it over my clit at a speed that had me fighting to keep my legs open. Nicholas stuck his tongue inside of me and used his fingers to rub my clit in a rhythm that was just right.

I threw my head back and my mouth opened in a loud, very long moan. "Fuck, that's so good."

He forced my legs open more as he devoured me. Licking and sucking like he was the happiest angel in any realm. He flicked his eyes up my body and focused on my face as he slid two of his long fingers inside of me. The area around his mouth was wet from me and he had never looked so fucking hot. I bit my lip hard, I'm pretty sure I tasted blood.

"I forgot how fucking good you taste," he said against me as he pumped and curled his fingers inside while running the tip of his tongue against my aching clit. I wanted to keep watching him, but my eyes closed as he kept pushing me further and further to the climax I could feel wanting to explode.

"Let's hope you never have to forget again," I said as I caught my breath. He groaned against me as he buried his face between my legs, his tongue working overtime to follow the rhythm of his fingers.

"God, Nick, don't stop," I pleaded as he pushed off of the floor and pressed his arm to the back of my thighs, pressing them further into me so I was practically folded in half. He kept pushing his fingers in, his tongue lapping and licking over, and over, and over again.

"You taste so fucking sweet," he said, in-between swipes of his tongue.

I was ripping at the comforter and ran my hand through my curls, teetering at the edge. My brain was malfunctioning, and I was so overheated. His fingers were so rough and nearly brutal. My own fingers were nothing compared to this. I was lost trying to figure out how I thought I could compare. "Oh fuck, yes, yes, right there."

He ripped his mouth away from me and pumped his fingers in faster as he watched my skin flush red and small whimpers leave my lips. He pressed one of his knees into the mattress so he could hover over me and watch as his fingers fucked me. His face broke out into a lust filled kind of smirk, like he knew what he was doing felt good, that despite all my distance from him, I couldn't fake my feelings about *this*. He leaned down towards my ear, curling his fingers again and bringing his thumb up to press against my clit. "Be a good girl and come for me."

Ugh those words. I closed my eyes so tight as I felt my orgasm push through. It was so strong, and I felt like all the air had been sucked out of my lungs. He slowed his hand and just started to caress his fingers inside of me. "That's my girl." He kissed my cheek, nuzzling his nose against it. I turned my head so that I could kiss him and he happily greeted me with his own kiss back. He got up from his position and settled himself between my legs, gripping my hips and pushing me further up the bed so he had more room.

My chest rose and fell heavily and my pussy was still tingling from the sensation of his fingers and mouth. He wiped a hand down his mouth as he got to work unbuttoning his pants. He reached for his zipper, sliding it down and started to shimmy his pants over his hips and down his legs, kicking them off with his shoes. His cock jutted out and shit, I missed everything about him it seemed. He was so big that I almost let out an audible whimper. My pussy pulsed with how much I wanted it inside of me, filling me in that way I remembered.

I wasn't going to submit so quickly though. As much as I wanted him to fuck me, I liked my fair share of teasing. Why should I give him the luxury of tasting me and fucking me all in one night? I quickly slid backwards and steadied myself as I propped myself up on my knees. Nicholas gave me a confused expression as I grabbed his shirt and pulled him completely onto the bed, turning him and making him lay on his back. I straddled him, making sure my pussy was right near his aching cock. His hands went to my hips as I started rocking back and forth over him. He was so hard and it took everything I had, not to simply lift up and sink down onto him.

"You enjoy teasing me, don't you?" He asked, squeezing my hips, and rocking upward so that his cock slid harder over my clit.

"I do what I can." I stifled a moan. "You didn't think I'd just stop being myself, did you?"

He let out a low laugh as he started to help move my hips more and more, seeming to be perfectly fine with the way things were going. He squeezed my ass hard, eyeing the way he slid back and forth so easily against me from how wet I was. That was no fun for me. I reached down and grabbed his hands from my body and placed them on the pillows so that they rested next to his head. He made a hissing sound as I let my shadows out, wrapping themselves around his wrists.

I pulled away and smirked. He tried to jerk upward but couldn't. He craned his neck to see better. Shadowy, dark ribbons enveloped his wrists and they bit at his skin every time he tried to move. He huffed out a breath after his fourth attempt to escape the restraints and looked at me. I stared back at him innocently.

"Dani." His voice was stern, like he wasn't amused by my antics. That made one of us.

"Oh, what's wrong, Nicholas. You don't like when you can't touch me," I taunted, bending down to kiss his chest and up to his collarbone. I rocked my hips again, sliding over him and he jerked against my restraints.

"Fuck, you're such a brat. This is really unfair."

I pushed my bottom lip out in a pout as I crawled forward a bit to reach his mouth. "If the wing fits, Nicholas." I didn't kiss him; I just hovered over his waiting lips. His eyes were hooded and pleading. He had made me wait for his words, so he would wait for my body. "You want to be inside of me so bad. You want to be inside my tight little pussy, don't you?"

His hands turned into fists as he let the shadows cinch and dig into his skin. He pulled against them, and I tapped his lips with my index finger. Leaning down near his ear, I licked his ear lobe, nipping. "Such a shame I didn't get to scream your name last time, huh? When you were so fucking deep."

"*Fuck*, come on," he whined. I giggled at his pleas. I slid down his body, past his stomach and settled my face near his pelvis, right between his legs. I grabbed his cock in my hand and licked up the side of it, swirling my tongue around the tip. I repeated the motion, keeping my eyes up and directed at him. I flicked my tongue over the tip, over and over again. I felt his thighs tighten and noticed his stomach contract.

Without a bit of warning, I took him into my mouth, flattening my tongue to the underside of his cock. I was about halfway down his shaft before he hit the back of my throat, a choked noise escaping him. "Fuck, Dani." His mouth dropped open, but no more words came out.

I released him from my mouth just to dip back and suck him down again. I used my hand to work the parts of him my mouth couldn't reach. I bobbed up and down, making sure to move my hair out of the way so that he could see everything. I wanted him to witness me swallowing him, how he was too big for my mouth to take in completely.

He tried to lift his hips, tried to fuck my mouth and I let him for a minute. I gagged and his body shuddered at the sound. I tore my mouth away from him, using my hand to stroke him from base to tip in a quick rhythm, twisting my wrist every so often. I licked a circle around the head of his cock and smiled at him while he just looked at me with this antagonized lustful expression. I reached down between my legs, swiping my fingers over my pussy that was very, very wet and shimmied up his body. I never let go of his cock, but I placed my fingers on his lips, letting him taste me again.

"I can be nice sometimes, see." He licked his lips. His face told me he wanted more of it, more of my taste. "Tell me, Nicholas. Am I enough?"

He let out a heavy breath as I pumped my fist around his cock. It was wet from my mouth and my hand slid over it with ease. "Yes, yes, fuck, you're enough." I remembered most of the signs that pointed out when he was about to come, and by the way his brows were turned inward I knew he would be done for any moment now.

"Happy you learned your lesson and let's hope you don't forget it." He started to lift his hips, fucking into my hand, but then I stopped. I maneuvered over to the other side of the bed and readjusted my panties.

I heard Nick start speaking and then stop, utterly baffled. "What are you doing?"

I padded over to where my leggings were in a pile on the floor and started to put them back on. "I'm going downstairs."

"I...I...what?"

"You said you wanted to taste me, and you did. All is forgiven, you handsome ethereal creature." I spun around and scanned my eyes to where his wrists were still bound, down to where his cock was still hard and pointed towards the ceiling. "Now I guess just marinate with that." I walked over to him and bent down, kissing his lips. I turned around, leaving him with his thoughts.

"Dani, you don't actually plan to leave me like this right?"

I looked over my shoulder, giving him a cheeky smile. "Well, not forever."

"Dani, do not leave me like this. I swear...Dani. Fuck. Dani!"

I blew him a kiss, reaching for the doorknob and quickly walked out. I placed a hand over my mouth to stop myself from laughing, but I couldn't. I could hear him still yelling for me, but it just made me laugh harder. He would be alright, probably a little pouty later, but fine, nonetheless. He was a big boy; he could handle a bit of teasing. I heard a door open down the hall and Reese walked out, his blonde hair in a tousled mess.

He walked over to me and scrunched up his mouth in confusion. "Have you seen Nick?"

I pressed my lips together trying so hard not to smile. "Umm...he's in my room."

Reese raised his eyebrows and nodded as if that wasn't surprising at all.

"He actually, uh, wanted to talk to you," I pressed my tongue behind my front teeth to keep my facial expression neutral. I grabbed my tiny wristlet where my key dangled and held it out for him.

He looked down at it and then up at me, his curiosity clearly peaked. I let it dangle between us, waiting for him to take it. "What's this for?"

"You should go see your friend, Reese. He *really* wants to talk to you." I nodded over my shoulder to the door behind me. "Bring me back the key when you're done." I started to walk away from the door as he stepped around me. I moved slowly, not wanting to miss a thing.

I heard the door open and...

"Woah, what the fuck! Nick, what the fuck!"

"Uh, what the hell! Just stop looking!"

"I literally can't not look, what the fuck did she do to you!" Reese's shouting laughter echoed as I slapped both my hands over my mouth and scurried away, down the stairs. I let the shadows know they could release Nicholas from the restraints, hoping he wasn't *too* mad at me.

Actually, I didn't care. I would make it up to him later...maybe.

14

NICK

I didn't come out of my room for a few hours, refusing to give her the satisfaction of seeing my face. I'd grabbed a pillow and slammed it over my face the minute we were back in our room, really hoping it would just suffocate me. Reese hadn't stopped laughing about it, especially when the shadowed restraints had disappeared from my wrists the minute he walked into the room. He was still making fun of me when we walked down the stairs and rounded the corner. I wasn't mad, since we were in a good place again, but that didn't mean I was happy about how things had ended. I only felt that way because I was edged to the point of no return, and she expected me to just bounce back like nothing happened.

Fuck, she was such a brat and all I could think about was how much I liked that.

Dani and the others were huddled in the dining room, each in their own respective chairs.

"Good of you guys to finally join us," Elise greeted, sarcastically.

Axel darted across the room towards Reese, who caught him up in his arms, seeming to have a growing soft spot for the hellhound. He scratched him behind the ears as he pulled out a chair and sat down. I took a seat across from Dani, who casually took a sip of her water, giving me a simple glance. Her tongue darted out and she licked her lips, before refocusing her attention. My cock twitched at the last thing I remembered that mouth doing. She had looked at me the entire time she swallowed my cock, trying to take it all in her mouth. If I had known she was just doing it to eventually end up leaving me without letting me finish, then I wouldn't have given in to her so easily.

Beetee practically skipped over, placing a glass of water in front of me. I took it happily, drinking down half the contents. It still wasn't enough to get the taste of her out of my mouth. Not that I was trying that hard, she tasted like a fucking dream. I would happily stay between her legs and give her as many orgasms as she could handle if that's what she wanted. I prided myself on being the kind of guy that paid attention in bed and tried to give my partner the best experience. I was gathering that she liked certain words, certain phrases, but I'd have to test it out another time.

"So, we've been talking about what Natalia said," Dani said, pushing her water to the side.

"And we've settled on someone to talk to," Elise continued, narrowing her eyes at her pet, who was passing out in Reese's arms. "For someone who has a chip on his shoulder about demons, you sure do look loved up with a hellhound."

Reese rolled his eyes, giving her a middle finger as best he could. "He keeps coming up to me, alright. It's not my fault that I'm naturally irresistible."

Elise snorted as she laughed in disbelief.

"I can't say I'm the happiest about the decision you've come to," Beetee said, leaning against the wall.

"Your two cents have been heard Beetee, don't worry. We aren't going to listen but understand that we did hear you, so be happy for that." Elise batted her eyelashes at her friend.

Beetee rolled her eyes, shaking her head.

"You guys are completely sure about this demon you've chosen?" I asked, looking from Elise to Dani.

"Completely sure isn't the right way to put it. It's kind of the only way to go," Dani explained, chewing on her bottom lip.

I thought this over. "Okay, well, this is your area of expertise so there isn't much we can say about it. When do we leave?"

Dani's eyebrows raised as she flicked her eyes over to Elise who snorted. Elise scratched her temple. "Yeah, you aren't coming."

"Not coming?" Reese said before I could.

Elise gave him a one-shoulder shrug. "You aren't needed. Pretty boy said it best, this is our area of expertise, so you two can hang out here and keep Beetee company."

I ran a hand through my hair, frustrated. "You can't just tell us we aren't coming. That's not your decision to make."

"Telling me I can't do something, just makes me want to do it more. As much as I don't like the idea of seeking a demon's help, I don't like you telling me no way more," Reese shot back.

Dani laughed. "You don't like the idea of seeking a demon's help, but you followed one into Purgatory."

Reese sighed. "I followed *him*, not you two." He pointed at me, while Axel jumped up on the table and trotted around before curling up and making himself a centerpiece.

Elise gave me a look like she couldn't care less how I felt. "You don't have to like it to accept it, Nicholas."

"I don't accept it. We're coming along. We've fought fucking hellhounds. I think we can handle a conversation with a demon." This could be a huge step in the right direction, and I wasn't going to miss it.

"I told you they would want to come," Dani stated, swinging her index finger between the two of us.

Elise tapped her fingers against the wood of the dining table. I noticed demons and Enchanters passing by, poking their heads in, but quickly choosing not to interfere. Some of them made their way through the room in passing to head out the back doorway, but they didn't pay us much mind. It was hard to believe that this much of a relaxed environment existed in the likes of Purgatory at all.

"They'll never last in there," Elise snarked, rolling her gray eyes.

"We'll never last where? What are you guys even talking about?" I asked, looking from Dani to Elise.

Elise leaned over and rested her elbow on the table, placing her hand on her cheek, letting her palm gently hit her skin. A small devilish smile played on her lips. "A club, Nicholas. A place where people dance and drink."

I mimicked her movements and leaned against the table myself. I was overly annoyed with the idea that they wanted to leave us behind. "I know what a club is, Elise. We can handle dancing and drinking."

She hummed. "And of course, the occasional fucking." She said it as if it was obvious, as if that sort of thing happened all the time.

"The occasional..." I started, swallowing hard and looked over at Dani. She was watching me with her head tilted slightly as if knowing that any mention of sex had me searching for her, thinking about her.

Elise cackled, her laugh almost losing sound. "Oh boy, you aren't ready for Leviathan."

"Leviathan?" Reese and I said in unison along with one other voice. I hadn't realized Garrett had come downstairs until he was currently standing in the doorway.

"Don't tell me *you've* been there?" Elise asked, her curiosity on high alert.

Garrett shook his head vigorously. He had braided his multitude of braids into one thick one down his back, tied off by a thick ribbon. "Oh no, I just remember when we used to stay here, I would hear talk about that place. Quite the wild establishment."

"It is a sight I can tell you that much," Beetee mumbled.

"A sight which two angels would get completely throttled by. I'm not fucking babysitting you both while we're there." Elise leaned back in her chair, as if her word was final.

"No one is asking you to. We're grown-ups, I think we can compose ourselves in a demon club." I swung my arm over the back of my chair.

Elise narrowed her eyes at me playfully. "That's the concern. You want to be composed in a demon club. If you plan to come along, you are going to have to take that stick out of your ass before a demon yanks it out themselves and spanks you with it."

Dani leaned her head back and laughed along with Elise. She collected herself, sitting back in her chair. "If you want to come, that's fine. You don't have to do any of the talking. Maybe it will be good for you to see another part of Purgatory." She winked over at me.

"I've heard Leviathan was run by some creatures of Hell, they wanted a spot to congregate here in Purgatory, so they created the club. It was passed down to one of the original owner's sons, I think. Any merit to that story?" Garrett inquired, walking over, and standing by Beetee.

Dani nodded. "Yeah, there are still dealings with Hell and Purgatory within its bowels, but it's become much more about the club than its original use. I knew I felt a sense of deja vu when we were walking down that pathway when we first got here. I'd been there before. Believe me, the new owner turned it into every demon's wet dream. The smell of debauchery and sex so thick you can taste it."

"Unfortunately, there is no fighting allowed in the club, so you'll have to leave your weapons here if you want to come," Elise informed, seeming to wait for us to back down.

I hesitated for a minute, but then answered her. "Fine. We can do that." I looked over at Reese who had an even more skeptical look on his face, but he shrugged accepting whatever came next. His eyes glanced over at Dani and then at me, his face morphing into what looked like another fit of laughter, but he stopped himself. He would honestly never let me live that moment in my life down ever again. I had a feeling he liked Dani just a little more now, not that he'd openly admit it just yet.

"I'd keep your head on straight while you're in that part of the area. The club is one thing but it's open season for those bewitching type demons," Garrett warned.

Beetee walked over and patted him on the shoulder. "Don't scare them, Garrett. It's not terrible and I know you're strong and capable angels, but I would stick close to these two if you don't want to get whisked away somewhere and end up in someone's sex dungeon."

"Some sex dungeons aren't even that bad," Reese said to no one in particular.

I gave him a bewildered expression. I knew a lot about my best friend, but I didn't know everything. He tended to overshare, but there were some things that he didn't, and when those things slipped out it always left me a little shell shocked.

Elise leaned over the table and picked up Axel. "Maybe you aren't half bad, Blondie. Now I really do hope someone does whisk you away to their sex dungeon and denies you many orgasms."

"I can have Leah make you a glamouring tonic that makes you not appear so…angelic," Garrett offered.

"I'm sure we can blend in," Reese said confidently.

"It's not about that," Dani said to him. "You both smell like Heaven's Gate and angelic magic. You have an aura about you that just oozes white wings and rules."

I looked up at Garrett, catching his golden eyes. "And she'll be able to mask it?"

"She'll be able to minimize it, so that you aren't completely bombarded while you're there. You are entering Leviathan at your own risk, so we can only do so much."

"We appreciate whatever help you'll give us," I said, gratefully.

"I'll go let her know. Just came down here for some glasses of water for Yuri and Jasmine," he gave Dani a small nod, which she reciprocated. It was like an odd, tension filled understanding between them. He waved to the rest of us before heading into the kitchen.

Reese leaned back in his chair, letting the front two legs lift off the ground. "You coming too, reptile queen?"

Beetee giggled, shaking her head. "No, I'll be sitting this one out."

"Again?" I asked.

She opened her mouth to explain, but Elise beat her to it. "It's not that she wants to sit it out, she *has* to." She pushed away from the table, her hellhound in her arms. "She isn't allowed back there after she nearly tore the place apart."

Reese slammed his chair back onto the ground. "I'm sorry, please explain."

"You're exaggerating, Ellie, ugh, it was not that dramatic."

Elise gave her a knowing look. "Oh, right because every establishment just enjoys a huge snake in their building."

Beetee raised her lilac eyes to the ceiling. "Not my proudest moment."

Dani pushed away from the table as well, placing both her hands on the edge of the wood. "Are we going to get any elaborate details?"

Beetee waved her hands. "Nope. Not today."

"Just know that the first time I met her, she was naked, shaking and getting reprimanded about club rules. There aren't many, but not letting your anchoring tattoo loose is one of them." Elise stuck her tongue out at the pink haired demon and started to walk out of the room. "Oh, yeah, we leave tonight, so I'd say get your shit together before we leave."

The rest of us followed after her, but Dani caught my arm before I could make it to the stairs.

"You really want to come?" she asked, some of her smaller curls falling into her face. She casually brushed them back before I had the instinct to do so myself.

"Yes, Dani, is that so hard to believe?"

One corner of her mouth lifted in a half-smile. "Not at all." She reached out and grazed her index finger along the front of my shirt. "You are going to change though. I prefer something black and tight. Those biceps of yours deserve some recognition."

I caught her hand, letting my fingers intertwine with hers for a moment. "There's a dress code?"

She didn't yank her hand away from me, but she did move her hand up my arm, stepping closer to me. "Not a dress code, but it's kind of like an unspoken rule to dress a certain way, but no one is going to stop you otherwise."

I looked down at her mouth, then back up at her eyes. Her brown irises were beautiful in this way that had me wanting to stare at her for longer than she'd likely allowed for. "And what are you planning on wearing?" I questioned, trying to sound like I would be fine with not knowing, when inside I was more than eager.

She gave me a mischievously cheeky smile. "Oh, nothing special."

"I highly doubt that's true."

Dani let out a small laugh. "Don't worry, it will still give off bad girl vibes."

I stepped closer to her, so that she had to tilt her head up more than normal to look at me. Her scent wrapped around me as I brought my hand to her chin and let my thumb skate over her skin. Skin that was flushed an hour and a half ago from the orgasm I pulled out of her with my mouth and fingers. "And here I thought you liked being a good girl."

Her sharp intake of breath wasn't missed and the way she blinked away, the quick way her eyes started to glaze over, had me smirking in victory. She pulled her bottom lip into her mouth and stood on the tips of her toes. "I like to think that's just for you." She raised one of her dark eyebrows, before she ghosted her lips over mine and lightly shoved me back. I watched her walk towards the stairs as I caught my breath for a moment before I walked up the stairs as well.

———†———

Reese readjusted his black denim jacket for the sixth time as we stood in the lounge area waiting on the girls. I slapped his hand away, getting up from the couch and crossing my arms over my chest. Beetee had given us some clothes to change into that she thought we'd be comfortable in while at Leviathan. She'd given me exactly what Dani had suggested: a black shirt that was tight around my arms, but I did have to admit that it was flattering. She paired it with gray pants and Reese's outfit was identical except she'd given him a denim jacket which he'd uncuffed the sleeves and rolled them up to his elbows.

"Where are they?" He asked, for the third time.

"Like I told you last time. I don't know. Still getting ready."

He leaned back onto the couch, resting his head against it and closed his eyes. "You are going to be able to focus tonight, correct?"

"I thought we already had this discussion about my priorities," I said in a warning tone, really not in the mood to have this conversation again.

Reese popped one of his eyes open. "That's not what I meant."

"Okay, well then what *do* you mean?"

"Oh, I don't know, maybe the fact that we are going to a demon club with the girl who has you so severely whipped you can hardly see it."

I propped my arm up against the wall. "I'm not whipped."

Reese let out a belly laugh. "Yeah, keep telling yourself that, Nick the Dick. See how far that shit gets you. Just don't go all feral if some guy tries to hit on her, keep your shit together."

"Whatever. You keep *your* shit together. I'm surprised you're this calm about going to a demon club in the first place."

My best friend ran his fingers through his blonde locks. "Believe me, I don't like it in the slightest, but I don't need the little psycho to hold that against me. I'll have the composure of a saint."

I opened my mouth to say something back when I heard feet coming down the stairs. We both looked at the same time and watched as Elise came into view and walked over to us. She had on the tightest black pants I'd ever seen and a crop top that was so short, we could see right underneath her breasts. Her lips were painted a deep red and her eyeliner was heavy, like she had taken extra effort in the way she looked tonight. She tapped her black combat boots on the ground, ignoring us.

"Where is the rest of your top?" Reese asked as he tried to hide his eyes.

Elise snorted. "Oh please, Blondie. We both know you like what you see, it's okay, you can admit it."

Reese made a gagging sound. "Don't make me vomit. I'm just trying to make sure that I won't look over and see one of your tits just out on display."

"Well, you would get an eyeful wouldn't you. Probably one of the few breasts you'll see in your lifetime," Elise joked, sticking her tongue out at him.

"Can we put the back and forth aside until we get back?" I asked them, nearly pleading. I pointed at Reese. "You don't want me to be unfocused and I don't want that for you either, so just fucking stop."

Elise pushed out her bottom lip. "There you go again, trying to tell me what to do like I'll listen. It's cute when you get all authoritative, I can see why the ladies must line up to suck your dick."

I scrubbed a hand down my face. "Um, okay. Where's Dani?"

Elise started to speak but swiveled her head around when the click of heels sounded on the stairs. I cut my eyes to Dani, who settled at the last step, her hand on the railing. My mouth automatically opened as I took her in, piece by piece. She wore heels that weren't too tall but gave her some height. I dragged my eyes up her exposed legs, every inch of glowing brown skin on display. When my eyes had finally had enough of her legs, I took in the rest of her and fuck...

That. Fucking. Dress.

The black dress was some type of silk material that met just at the middle of her thighs. It glided over her body and curves like it was made just for her and I wanted to run my fingers over it. There was a small tie around the waist of the dress that added to its subtleness. Lace detailing covered the part that encapsulated her chest, pushing her breasts up. The design was intricate and pretty; the bust met long flare sleeves that matched the silk texture of the rest of the dress with delicate black shoulder straps adorned along her collarbones. The hem of the dress was so short I wanted to slide my hands up her legs and see if she had anything on underneath. I could feel myself getting hard way too quickly and shifted my stance.

I rolled my shoulders and tried to seem like none of what I just committed to memory would be a problem for me.

"Everything okay, Nicholas," Dani asked. It almost came out like a purr.

I blinked up to her face and nearly forgot how to breathe. She had simple eye makeup on, and her lips were pink, much pinker than normal. Her hair was down and cascaded over her shoulders, the mass of curls were defined, forming tight ringlets and less tight spirals. They framed her face in this perfect way that I couldn't describe. Actually, I didn't forget how to breathe; she just took my breath away. And she could keep it for as long as she wanted.

"Uh, yeah. I-I'm good. You?" I stuttered, clearing my throat. She giggled and took a few steps towards us.

"Perfect." She tucked a piece of her hair behind her ear, taking in everyone else around us.

Reese looked from Dani to me and got up from the couch, patting me on the shoulder. "You are so fucked," he whispered, walking around the couch to the front door.

I let out a sigh, not noticing that Dani wasn't following the others, but she was only a few feet in front of me. She made a move to shuffle forward a bit, closing the distance between us even more. She reached her fingers out and trailed them along my arm, tugging at my shirt sleeve. "Told you the black shirt would be a good choice."

I couldn't keep my eyes from scanning her face and down her body. Again.

She hummed. "How do I look, Nicholas?" She peeked up at me from under her lashes that looked longer than they normally did.

"Dani, you know how you look."

She stuck her tongue between her teeth, playfully. "I know, but I want you to tell me."

"Fishing for compliments?"

She shrugged. "I think we both know what you're thinking about and what you want to say are two very different things." Her expression screamed, *tell me I'm wrong.* It was like she knew that it was my instinct to tell her something controlled, but really all I was thinking about was how much I wanted to have her bent over this couch, mumbling unintelligible sounds and screaming while I fucked her from behind. I didn't say that though, as much as she would have thrilled at it.

"You look beautiful," I said, playing with the material of her sleeve. "You always look beautiful," I added, feeling the back of my neck heating up.

She looked down, away from my face, almost like she was a little shy. She shook her head, looking back up at me as she gripped my chin and pulled my face down. "You're sweet. So, so sweet. Just for that I'll have you know that I thought long and hard about wearing panties under this dress. Rest assured, I'm not naked under here, so if I happen to bend over, no one will get an eyeful. You're welcome." She released my chin and twirled around, her heels clicking against the wood as she made her way to the front door.

I watched the way her dress moved with her, my eyes automatically following the sway of her hips and the perfect silhouette of her ass.

Yeah, I was fucked.

We walked down the pathway I remembered from when we first got here. The red lights illuminating our way with every step we took. Elise led the way with Dani close behind her. I really fucking hated leaving our weapons behind, but she had said we couldn't bring them inside and I would have rather them be safely stored at Beetee's hostel than taken away from me at a demonic club. Not that I actually would have let them.

I heard the sound of laughter and talking, drunken slurs and fumbled footsteps. I could see the area we were headed to, and it was the complete opposite of Beetee's quaint little hostel. The pathway we were on morphed from stone to brick, gray smokey mist and red lights danced and played along the ground. The laughing got louder, and the rhythmic beat of club music thundered into my ears. It wasn't loud enough for me to be bothered by it, but it was there. The sound of breaking glass caused me and Reese to turn our heads, trying to locate where the sound came from.

It smelled like smoke with hints of jasmine in the air. The smells seemed to linger around even with no wind in sight. The smoke would come and go in puffs that burned my lungs, but the jasmine gave this misleading sense of comfort as if tempting you to delve deeper, forget your troubles and just remain.

"Don't mind that. If you acknowledge every fucking sound here, we'll never get anywhere. Just act natural, if that's even possible for you," Elise informed, grabbing both our arms, and pulling us away from where we were frozen in place.

I looked from my left and right, noticing that there were less trees here and more buildings. Each of them were close together and filled with people. Every single building was some version of a bar or tavern. Some were low key, not so flashy with tables littering the front and canopy umbrellas overlooking the tables. Others were much louder, and patrons were tumbling out, hanging off of each other as if it didn't matter whether they had known each other forever or they'd just met.

"Welcome to Devil's Playground." Elise lifted up her arm as if she was putting this place on full display.

"I'm sorry, is that…" Reese pointed to two females making out on the side of a building. They were deep into each other, and their hands had disappeared from our view, more than likely down each other's skirts. When we passed, they didn't pay us any mind, as if nothing else mattered.

Dani laughed. "If you are shocked by that, maybe you should have stayed behind."

"I'm not shocked. I can handle a little public display of affection. I just wasn't aware it was going to be so…public."

Dani and Elise looked at each other with amused expressions but didn't say anything more. Dani looked so in her element, I was a little jealous of this place, seeing as it had her so comfortable. Her shoulders seemed to relax as she walked, that moment with Yuri and the hellhounds felt so far away right now. Even I had to admit, my dark thoughts were simmering, but they were throttled by a different feeling now that we had stepped into Devil's Playground, an overwhelming feeling of unbridled desire.

I really needed to focus. I needed to—

"Watch it." I heard someone say right as my shoulder hit something hard and I had to catch myself from falling backwards. I turned around to face a man about my height, with long dark hair pulled back in a low ponytail. He had a scar down the side of his face and his dark eyes seemed to glow with the way the lighting hit them. He had the temperament of a demon; it was something you just felt and once that feeling hit it didn't go away. He had a cup in his hand that was empty, but then I took in his wet shirt and realized that the contents of his drink was now soaking through, causing the material to stick to him. It smelled like beer. His thick eyebrows turned down when he realized he had caught my attention. "You made me spill my drink. You have something to say, pretty boy?"

I narrowed my eyes, a little thrown off by the hostility. "Not really, since you ran into *me*."

He stepped closer to me, getting in my face. "You made me waste a perfectly good drink, so I suggest you fix it."

"I'm really not comprehending how I'm the problem here."

The guy had a friend with him, a man with cropped dark hair, who stayed behind him, watching this unfold. The man in front of me pushed at my shoulder. "Ah, you don't see a problem? Ha, Rio, pretty boy doesn't see a problem." He turned his head to acknowledge his friend.

His companion cracked his knuckles. "How about we make a problem, then huh."

The one with long hair looked over my shoulder. "What are you staring at?" His tone was forceful.

"If I'm being honest, not much at all." Demons or not, Reese always opened his fucking mouth. "You should be so lucky to be as pretty as he is." I swiveled my head around and glared at him.

"The fuck did you just say?" Rio said, his eyes turning to angry slits.

"Nice move, Blondie," Elise remarked.

I felt my arm being yanked forward, his fingers applying pressure to my skin, harder and harder as if he was trying to break my bones right then and there. "Your friend needs to watch his fucking mouth, or I'll make sure that pretty face isn't so pretty anymore." He used his other hand to clamp his fingers under my jaw, pressing my cheeks into my face.

I used all my strength and pushed forward, shoving him off of me. I readjusted my shirt and looked over my shoulder where Reese had a confused expression on his face. We had been here two minutes and already this was turning into a bad idea.

Reese stood next to me. "Walk away, tough guy. Get yourself a new shirt."

The man laughed a deep, menacing laugh. "How about I shut that mouth of yours, so you never speak again." He barreled over to Reese, but Dani stepped in front of him. "How about you turn around and leave us the fuck alone."

Her voice had a sweet venom in it, like she was trying to have composure, but it was cracking.

The guy looked down at her and chuckled. He wiped down his shirt. "Getting girls to fight your battles? Figures."

Dani gave him a less than pleasant smile, turning around, while Elise gave them both her middle fingers and started walking again. I started to follow them, but our new friends' voices rang out again. This time what he said made my shoulders stiffen.

"You watch yourself next time I see you. You and your two whores." He spit it out and laughed, like he had said the funniest thing in all the realms.

I turned on my heels, ready to throttle him to the ground, when something flew past me and instantly had him by the throat. He gurgled and choked with the grip she had on his neck.

"Such bad manners. We should really fix that." Dani threw him to the ground as she flicked her eyes to me. Her brown irises were gone, her eyes now drowning in black. "It's quite funny that you think whore is a word that would hurt me. So bold of you, yet so stupid." Her black shadows came out of the ground and wrapped themselves around him, holding him in place.

I looked around and noticed there were demons that paid absolutely no attention to what was going on and then there were others who casually leaned up against the buildings to watch. They didn't try to help, nor did they look nervous or uncomfortable in any way. I liked to think that this wasn't an everyday occurrence for them, but I likely would have been wrong. Rio started to head towards Dani to help his friend, but Elise jumped onto his back, wrapping her arm under his chin and pulling upward. He staggered backwards and she pressed her hand on top of his shoulder, pushing herself up and leaped off him, while keeping a hold on his neck. He spun uncontrollably and she watched as he landed not too far from his friend.

"Remember the last time you were a dick to me, Rio? What I said I would do to you if you ever pissed me off again." Her tail manifested from behind her and snaked around, stopping just between his legs. He struggled to try and move away, but she swiped the end of her tail along his legs, creating large gashes.

"Do you think we should interrupt them or…" Reese asked, tilting his head as he tried to take in what we were watching.

I slowly shook my head. "No, I think…I think they'll be fine."

Dani's dagger came together from nothing but shadows as she got down to her victim's level. She grazed her dagger over the side of his face, creating a deep cut. "Now you'll have a scar to match the other one." She brought the dagger down to his stomach and pressed the hooked part to his soaked shirt.

"We were just messing around, Soul Seether." He instantly understood who she was, realizing how fucked he was.

"Oh well in that case—" She plunged the dagger in without hesitation and the man cried out. She reached for his head, pulling at his ponytail as she lifted his face to hers. "You plan to behave?"

He grunted from the strong grip that she had on him. She was likely pulling so hard at his scalp that I'm surprised she hadn't ripped hair out by now. Her stance and the way she looked at him had me remembering how she had been with Markus. How she had demanded he give her answers, how she had handled her weapon using it for so much violence. Thoughts flashed through my mind, but I held myself up, not letting the thoughts run me over. I heard whispers along with the invading thoughts. They were the same whispers from my time with Natalia. They spun around my dark memories and threaded themselves within them as if they were trying to build a bond.

"Dani..." I started.

"*Say it.* You. Will. Behave." Dani demanded of her victim as he yelped from her strain on his hair. She raised her dagger, inches away from stabbing him again.

"Yeah Rio, will you behave?" Elise taunted, replacing her tail with the toe of her boot right at his crotch.

"Dani...*stop,*" I urged, feeling my chest tighten. I felt a whisper of something whip across my neck, like a caress.

"Nick..." Reese said, grabbing my hand and lifting it up. I blinked down at it, my vision a bit unfocused and noticed small bits of light trying to come out. Angelic magic was powerful in its own right. It knew when it was needed even when you weren't aware of it, but I didn't understand why it was happening right now. I closed my hand and yanked my arm away from him.

"Dani, *just stop,*" I demanded, and her head shot up, finally acknowledging me. My brown eyes pleaded with her black ones. I liked her with this fire and fighting for herself, but fuck, I could feel myself going to that place I didn't like to be.

Her eyes started to morph back into their normal state. She huffed out a breath and yanked him up by his hair, the shadows holding him disappearing along with her dagger. Dani dragged him over to me, the wound in his stomach bleeding out. She pushed him forward, so he was staring at me. "Apologize. You ran into him, did you not?"

His lips quivered and he looked like he wanted to fight back, but he didn't. He swallowed hard and looked down at my fisted hands, noticing the light peeking out of them. "I'm not apologizing to a fucking angel...ow! Fuck!" Dani yanked his hair and rammed her fist into his spine.

"Say. It."

He pressed his lips together, muttering a less than genuine *sorry*. Dani smiled. "Wasn't that easy." In one quick motion she had her dagger back and used it to slice his ponytail right off. She grabbed the hair and chucked it at him as she threw his body to the side. "Now get out of my fucking sight."

I heard squealing as we looked over and saw Elise stepping right between Rio's legs and then letting up, before standing to the side. "You should really worry about us being bitches, not whores. Not that your opinion matters much anyway. You piss me off again and I promise you, I will cut your dick off and make you eat it." Rio got help from his friend getting up and they hustled backwards until they were far enough away to not need to look back.

"Umm, okay, well I don't know whether to be surprised or impressed?" Reese admitted.

"We all know you are thoroughly impressed," Elise answered.

Reese rolled his eyes as he looked over to me. "Can we go before you get into any more brawls?" He placed his hand on my arm and shook me lightly. "Are you okay? It's like you went somewhere in your own head again."

I nodded, stretching my neck by rolling my head in a circle. "Yeah, I'm fine. That was just...um, unexpected."

Dani laughed. "Expect the unexpected, Nicholas. Especially in Devil's Playground." She walked past me, wrapping her hand around my fists, causing the whispers to create a low hum. As if she was controlling them in a way, with a power she didn't know she had. "I did tell you that I would take good care of you." She nodded over her shoulder towards what had been our prior destination.

"I knew bringing them would be a bad idea." Elise mumbled. She shoved past us, and Dani followed.

Everyone around us went back to business as usual and I wondered how bad Leviathan really was.

15

NICK

The strobe lights crossed over each other, back and forth as they scattered across the walls of Leviathan. The outside was a tall brick building with large windows on the side. I couldn't see anything on the inside though, telling me that the windows were blacked out, keeping the secrets of the club locked inside. The music that was playing could be heard from a mile away, but visually it hadn't looked like anything special. The building was lined with neon red lights and there was an overhang above the door that had a bright yellowish light beaming down from it.

The inside was wider than I had imagined. There were neon red lights hanging from the ceiling, and they lined the walls in here as well illuminating the club in a deep sensual type of lighting. There was a long bar to my right and a massive dance floor that stood right in front of me and took over more of the left side. There was another bar I could see that was well across the room that looked just as busy as the one closest to us. A group of demon girls holding hands ran into us and headed towards another group of demons on the dance floor. The music was playing from everywhere, but I couldn't find the source, so I assumed that was also some sort of magic.

I noticed a small area of couches near the back where demons caught their breath or just simply mingled. I let my eyes glance over to where there was a wide staircase leading to the second floor, yet I couldn't really make out what exactly was upstairs. I felt people looking at me, but I couldn't really decide what those looks meant. I kept my guard up regardless.

"Let's go," Elise ordered as we weaved around different patrons that were grinding their sweaty bodies against one another. We safely made it to the bar and Reese nearly grabbed onto it for dear life. Dani hadn't been lying about the '*dress code*,' since yes there were different outfits all around us, but for the most part all the women were dressed like Elise and Dani. They definitely played towards whatever asset they wanted on display for all to see.

There was so much confidence in this establishment you could taste it. There was also the smell of sex and temptation. The scent of jasmine was long gone the minute we stepped through the threshold; any signs of its comforting nature was gone. Leviathan had a heady scent of make bad decisions but fuck the consequences. I saw Reese moving his head back and forth, trying to figure out if any of this was real or not. If we thought the two women fondling each other in plain sight was bad, this place was much worse. There was dancing happening on the dance floor, obviously and then...well, there was literal dry humping. If you looked long enough it could have genuinely been perceived as sex happening right before your eyes.

It was difficult to look away from. It was hard to not want to be doing that with—

"I don't see him," I heard Elise tell Dani, leaning in close to her ear over the heavy beat of the music.

"Who are we looking for?" I asked, getting them to remember we were here as well.

Elise pushed her hand into her hair. "The demon we need to talk to."

"I don't know how the hell you plan to find anyone in this clusterfuck," Reese yelled over the music.

Dani ran her teeth over her bottom lip, pushing in between us and leaning over the glass top bar. It was holographic and the small speckles of different colors illuminated as the strobe lights ran over it. The racks behind the bar had four long shelves filled to the brim with various amounts of alcohol. The brick behind the bar was painted all black, causing the red from the lights to pop. A man with a mohawk smiled at her when she approached. He nodded his head in greeting. "Ah, Soul Seether, long time." He didn't say it like they had spent any sort of *time* together, but just like she frequented this place regularly.

"What have I said about being so formal, Ian." She had a flirtatious way about her tone. I got the feeling this place made her a bit different.

He laughed, shaking a drink with both his hands over his shoulder. "What can I do for you—and your friends." He eyed Reese and me, looking back at her.

Dani cleared her throat, getting on her tiptoes to lean further in. "I'm looking for Dimitri."

Ian was pouring his shaken drink into its glass when he stopped. He regained his composure and finished making his drink. Dani tapped her nails against the glass bar, waiting. Ian looked to his right, eyeing a space I hadn't noticed before. It was an open area that almost looked like an alleyway. It was dark and I couldn't see anything beyond the black trimming framing around the entryway. People passed it like it didn't exist or if they knew it existed, they didn't go snooping.

"He's in a meeting."

Elise took her place next to Dani, clearly intrigued. "You know who he's with?"

Ian shook his head. "No clue. He just went in, so he'll be a minute. I'd make myself comfortable." The look on Dani's face was pure frustration but she rallied, scanning the bottles on the shelves behind him. He looked over his shoulder and smirked. "Can I get you a drink?"

"Four shots, please."

"Shots?" Reese and I both said at the same time. Reese moved out of the way as a man walked past him, his eyes lingering a little too long on my best friend.

Elise snorted. "Yes, shots. You two need to loosen up. We're waiting anyway." Ian poured the shots and slid them across the bar. Dani gathered all four in her hands and held them out to us. Elise took hers happily while Reese and I took ours with pure skepticism.

Dani winked at me. "It's just vodka, don't worry. No funny business unless you want a splash of a little something."

I shook my head, pointing at the shot. "No, this is just fine."

We took the shots and the alcohol burned going down. I'd had vodka before, but this was some kind of *only made in the bowels of Hell* type. It was pure fire the way it burned and then it settled into a pleasant warmth in my stomach. "Do you know the demon we're here to talk to?"

Dani looked from the open space where that particular demon was located then back to me. "More or less." She rubbed her lips together almost nervously, but then her eyes seemed to zero in on something behind me.

"The club looks good on you, handsome treat." That voice sounded familiar, but I couldn't pinpoint it.

"For fucks sake." Elise patted the bar, asking for another drink.

I turned around, coming face to face with one of the girls we had met at the hostel. She was closer to me than I expected her to be, like she was drinking me in. I backed up a small bit, giving me some much-needed space.

"We thought you two would never show up." I looked over my shoulder to see her friend come up behind Reese, snaking her hand around his arm.

I kept thinking, racking my brain for their names. Rae and Eva, that was it. The demon in front of me—Rae—flashed her sharp teeth. "An angel in Leviathan just makes this all the more fun. You look even more delicious than I thought."

I heard Elise choke on her drink and there was a tension behind me. Dani had moved to where she could visually be seen by everyone, but her focus was solely on Rae. Her look was calculating and damn near patient.

People scrambled up to the bar, sweaty and out of breath. They would look at Dani and then do a double take. Some of their backs would go rigid and others would immediately whisper to someone next to them. Both women and men alike would give her a once over, a look of skeptical fear in their eyes, but there was desire there as well.

"I guess I should take that as a compliment."

Rae reached out and grabbed my bicep, her long pointed nails lightly digging into my skin. She flicked her eyes to Dani. "Are you two here *together?*"

"He wishes." I heard Reese mutter under his breath.

"So that's a no then," Rae said, licking red lips. "How about me and Eva take you somewhere private. Let you get a *taste* of what Leviathan has to offer." She leaned further into me, her voice getting low and sultry.

"Oh yes, I'm sure you angels need to release your stress somehow." I looked back and saw Eva lean into Reese, snapping her teeth near his ear.

Reese started to laugh nervously, no witty comeback at the tip of his tongue.

"We're alright, I assure you." I hoped my words were heard, but they didn't leave and get the hint.

"You both really don't know when to quit, do you?" Elise questioned, taking another shot and tipping it back.

Rae pouted. "The Soul Seether probably has important things to do here, but that doesn't mean you both deserve to miss out on the excitement.

Demons can be so much fun if you let us." She took her hand off my arm and pointed at my chest. She trailed her finger down, slowly, getting dangerously close to my waistband.

An arm came out and grabbed her wrist, yanking it away from me. Rae was shoved back, nearly landing in the lap of a demon seated behind her. Dani ran her fingers over the ends of her curls, looking as if she had just seen the most amusing thing. "He said they're fine, so I suggest you keep your hands to yourself."

Rae straightened out her dress but stood her ground. She looked a little shaken, but Dani didn't seem to put out her fire. "How about a dance then, hmm." She cocked her head to the side, eyeing Dani. "There is no harm in that."

"No harm? That dancing is foreplay at minimum," Reese pointed towards the swarms of people gyrating on each other as they followed a rhythmic beat. Their eyes were closed like they would rather be nowhere else.

"Personally, I don't mind a little foreplay." Eva said, right before Reese broke away from her grip and leaned into the bar like he wanted it to swallow him up.

Rae started to step up to me again, getting ready to grab my hand, but Dani stepped in front of us, swatting her hand away. "I really don't know if you're just incredibly confident or you're really that stupid, but when I say keep your hands to yourself, I expect you to fucking listen. I respect the rules of this place so you should thank the realms I can't cut off those hands and watch you bleed out. Neither of them are interested," she hissed. Dani exuded so much powerful energy that it was like anyone in the general vicinity could tell the Soul Seether was here and that she wasn't happy. "He doesn't need you to teach him about how fun demons are because I assure you sweetheart, he is very aware of that fact. He's had a taste and he's satisfied." She smiled with all her teeth and propped one of her eyebrows up.

Elise busted out laughing, holding her stomach. "He sure has and he sure is. Nicholas has an affinity for demons."

Rae blinked from me to Dani, but kept her mouth shut.

"As for dancing..." Dani grabbed my shirt in her fist. "I've got that covered."

I looked down at her. "I don't dance."

"Oh, shut up, yes you do," Reese offered, wiggling his brows, but continuing to keep his distance from Eva. I didn't hate dancing; I just wasn't prepared to do it right now. Dancing was more for a night out of fun, not a mission. And if I was being honest, I didn't know if I would survive dancing with Dani.

"I don't," I reassured them.

Dani twirled around, keeping her hold on my shirt. Her face held a smirk, and she couldn't have looked sexier if she tried. "With me you will."

I quickly looked over my shoulder at Reese and Elise. Elise looked from me to my best friend and rolled her eyes. She slapped the bar for yet another drink before waving her hand for us to leave. "I'll make sure Blondie doesn't get assaulted."

I felt myself being dragged past Rae, who Dani nudged to the side as we made our way through the throngs of bodies. It was much hotter on the dance floor, the floor beneath us changed from wood to solid black. The surface was smooth and I could see how someone easily moved along its texture. I felt us stop and she turned around, falling into me. Her smile was playful, and it was hard for me to hide my own. I looked around at the demons lost in themselves or in their partners. "Hmm, you've saved me twice now."

She pushed out her bottom lip. "Oh, Nicholas, are you upset that you got help from a female?" She narrowed her eyes, daring me to say the wrong thing.

I pulled her face up by placing my fingers under her chin. "Not at all. You're quite impressive."

"I'm well aware but thank you." The way she leaned against my chest granted me a good look down at the tops of her breasts. The minute I did I regretted it, because fuck they were perfect. "I think you made your point though; we can head back."

I tried to turn and head back to our friends, but she pulled me back to her. She placed her hands around my neck. "You're dancing with me Mr. Cassial. Whether you like it or not. Or I mean I guess you could go upstairs with Rae."

I placed my hands on her hips and pressed her against me. "No thank you. What's upstairs anyway?"

Dani bit her bottom lip. "Nothing you need to be concerned with at the moment. Just know that this isn't where all the fun is." The beat changed to a more pop sound, but the bass was low and made me want to sway with her and bring her even closer to me, if that was at all possible. Dani reached up and grazed her lips along mine. She rolled her hips and started moving against me. Her nose touched mine and she kept her face there, her breath mingling with my own. Her tongue came out and licked at my lips as she connected with my pelvis again and again. I squeezed her and moved my hips with hers. She smiled to herself as I started to comply.

I fingered the material of her dress as I tried to distract myself from trailing my fingertips further down and sliding them underneath.

"Does this make up for leaving you like I did?" she asked, her voice close to my ear so I could hear her over the music.

"Not even a little bit."

"Oh well then, how about I just let you dance with your number one fan at the bar." She said, her eyes dancing with mischief. "She'd love to sink her pointy teeth into you."

I pulled her forward hard, so that she had to suck in a breath. "You sound like you were a little jealous."

Dani laughed and smiled that smile that I adored in a way that I couldn't quite admit to her. "Jealousy gives off a certain insecurity of not fully knowing if you have something." She moved to the music, never breaking eye contact. "I know I have you, Nicholas. Make no mistake." She leaned in for a swift kiss, but I lightly pushed her away and turned her around, bringing her back so that she was flat against me. Her back to my front.

I moved her hair to the side, burrowing my face in her neck, bringing my lips to her ear. "You think you have me." It wasn't a question; it was just a statement.

I felt her vibrate against me with her laughter. "I don't think, Nicholas." She rubbed her ass against me, feeling how hard my cock was getting. "I'm very, very aware." I groaned, the music filling my veins and the way she fell against me had me gripping her waist with newly found confidence. She lifted her arm and hooked it along the back of my neck, running her fingers into my hair as best she could.

I couldn't help but want to whisk her away and kiss her for hours, to let my fingers explore her skin endlessly. She let out a soft moan when I rubbed myself against her backside as we grinded to the beat of the music. "You're so fucking tempting. You were right, I have had a taste, and I am satisfied, but you—" I bunched her dress a little higher up her thighs and she moved against me, clearly happy with the direction this was going. I said my next words towards her cheek, feeling her start to melt even further into my body. "You make me crave more. All the time."

Her eyes slowly moved to the side at my admission, so she could try to look at me. Her voice sent a shockwave up my spine. "You want to taste me again, so bad, huh." Her body heat was on another level and the number of raging hormones and sexual energy in this place had my head spinning. I didn't overthink it, especially not when her body was rubbing against me in time to the music. That darkness she harbored was almost nonexistent when she was letting go like this, but I knew it was there and somehow, I wanted to keep her closer because of it. Nearly everyone here knew who she was, but out on this dance floor, that didn't matter. It was a little freeing if I actually thought about it.

I slid one of my hands down to the hem of her dress and circled around to the side of her thigh and then the back, "I probably could, right here, right now." I let my fingers follow up the back of her thigh, using my body to attempt to hide what I was doing. I let my teeth nip at her ear. "How wet are you right now, needy one?"

She whimpered while the tips of my fingers trailed along her skin, disappearing underneath the back of her dress. "Why don't you find out." She wiggled her ass against me as she danced, encouraging me to keep going.

I sucked in a breath when my fingers met the heat of her. I felt the material of her panties, discovering how damp they were, and a smirk played on my lips. I started rubbing, gently, sliding my fingers along the fabric between her legs and she backed up into me, her eyes closed and her mouth slightly open. I pushed her panties to the side a bit, to let my fingers explore and touch. I felt her body shiver, as I reached my fingers out further and played with her clit. "So, so wet. Do I do this to you?" I rubbed between her legs, swaying back and forth with her.

She used her hand not holding the back of my neck and reached out behind her, rubbing the front of my pants. That act just made me put pressure on her clit. "Do I do this to *you*?" She was playing with me, but in a way that had me wanting to play alongside her.

I brought my fingers back slightly and rubbed her pussy, sliding the wetness towards her clit again. "I don't think anyone else does what you do to me, Dani." Even in this moment of desire and pure temptation, I couldn't lie about that.

"Now you understand why I'm not fucking jealous." She breathed out through my swipes at her clit. She moved her ass back more, trying to get my fingers where she wanted. I flicked my eyes up and around us. No one was really giving us much of their attention. There were a few, but their expressions showed interest, not disgust by our display. They looked as if they would happily dance with their partners and watch us.

I found myself still relaxed at that thought. I didn't want to stop due to the audience. There was something about the audience that almost encouraged me.

This place was a mind fuck.

I chuckled as she kept winding her hips and mindlessly moving my fingers along with her. "You want me to slide my fingers inside of you, make you come in front of all these people?" I gave her clit one more minute of attention before I guided my index finger down to where she was wet and waiting. I pushed just the tip of my finger in, teasing her.

"Fuck. Yes," she whined, but that whine turned into a moan that sent a vibration from her body into my chest. I continued to probe, not giving her everything she wanted immediately. We still had a reason for being here, there was still someone that needed to be questioned, but none of that mattered to me right now. I still had my head on straight, I knew my priorities.

That didn't mean I couldn't add *getting this girl to come in the middle of a dance floor* as one of them.

I gripped her waist and her head tilted down and a bit to the side as if she was attempting to see what I was doing. I pressed my finger in, inching so slowly I knew on the inside she was getting frustrated with me. I started to curl my finger and push in more when—

"Dani, he's here." Elise appeared in front of us as she shoved away a few of the oblivious dancing patrons.

This was about as bad as when my father ruined the moment in my bathroom with her. This time it was in a public setting, so I really didn't know which was worse. I discreetly pulled my hand out from under her dress and looked at Elise. She was focused on Dani, who was a little flushed, but she wasn't as relaxed as before. Her shoulders were stiffer now and she stepped forward, trying to look through the crowd of people.

I didn't find it difficult to look over the heads of people as I searched for whoever they were talking about, thinking I could tell who they were without a description. As if I would just know when I saw them. A man with short strawberry blonde hair and a shadow of a beard along his jaw walked up to the bar and spoke to Ian, who pointed towards the dance floor. The man turned his head and appeared to be looking right at us. He nodded, unbuttoning his suit jacket and made his way over the lounge area in the corner. A few girls and guys followed after him, settling themselves on his left and right.

"It's now or never," Elise pushed, nodding over to where the man sat.

"Yeah, yeah, I get it," Dani said, agitation filling her voice. She turned around and grabbed my hand. She quickly placed the fingers that I used to touch her in her mouth, swirling her tongue quickly, then popped them out. She lifted up on her toes and pecked my lips. "Don't miss me too much." Before I could even respond, she was off the dance floor and headed towards the mysterious demon.

I eyed Elise who motioned for me to follow her back to the bar. "You aren't going with her to talk to him?"

"Ha, no."

"Can I ask why?"

"Because it's better if she does it alone."

Reese was making conversation with Ian when we approached. He grabbed my arm the minute I settled down next to him. "So, I've officially seen way too many tails, a girl with a third eye, I've been hit on four times and I'm pretty sure I saw a guy with two cocks, so my brain is officially fried."

Elise snorted. "You can't tell me you weren't the least bit tempted to go into the bathroom with the guy that propositioned you."

Ian handed Reese a drink, which he happily took. "Hey, I will give credit where it's due. If you're a good looking male or female, I'll admit it, but I don't want my love story to start with, *we met in a demon club*."

I tapped my fingers on the glass bar, anxiously. I was still thinking about what Elise said. I turned to her, but it looked like she was already waiting for me to open my mouth. "What did you mean by 'it's better if she does it alone?'"

"I meant exactly what I said."

I rolled my eyes to the ceiling. "You know what I meant." I looked over to where Dani now stood in front of where the man sat. She had her hands on her hips and was looking down at him. I couldn't see her face nor his so I couldn't determine how the conversation was going.

Elise leaned her back against the bar, propping her elbows up behind her. "Dimitri would rather talk to her, that's all."

"At the hostel you made it seem like you both knew...Dimitri."

Elise pressed her teeth into her bottom lip and peered up at me, narrowing her eyes as if she was attempting to proceed with caution with her next words. "Well, Nicholas, let's just say I don't know Dimitri as well as your precious Dani does."

"What are you talking—"

Reese cut me off by coughing, slamming down his drink and placing a hand on his chest. When he could catch his breath, he stared at Elise. "Oh shit, are you saying that they fucked?"

My eyes widened and I could feel the back of my ears heating up along with my neck. Elise leaned past me and grabbed Reese's drink, tilting it to her lips and drinking whatever was left in one gulp. "Use your imagination boys."

"So, what she plans to charm him into telling her things?" I asked, my annoyance boiling.

"Perhaps, I mean Dimitri has a grossly lustful affinity for Dani. He likes pretty, powerful things. He's had a thing for her ever since we walked into this place forever ago. He got one look at her and boom, she was being summoned right to that very spot he's at now. You can do things like that when you're the owner," Elise explained, pushing her bangs off her face.

"The owner?"

"Of the club. Dimitri got it handed down to him by his dad. A dad who resides in Hell, hangs out with Lucifer, blah blah blah." She spoke like she was bored. I, on the other hand, was fuming. Elise patted my cheek. "Ah, Nicholas. Your jealousy is showing."

I looked over at Dani again, who was now seated next to Dimitri. They were so close that their legs touched. He had his hand on her knee, his thumb running circles along her skin. He was an attractive enough guy, with tattoos up his neck and on his hands. He looked in our direction as if he knew we were talking about him, but then he looked back at Dani, leaning in as if he was telling her a secret. She laughed and that smile I adored so much made an appearance. I wanted to punch that guy in the fucking face.

"I'm not jealous," I said through gritted teeth.

"Oook, just keep telling yourself that. She knows what she's doing, so just let her do her thing. I'm pretty sure she still wants your dick, so just calm yourself." Elise let out a loud sigh as a dark-skinned female with a completely shaved head passed by. Elise followed her with her eyes and pushed away from the bar. "Well, I'm going to go entertain myself with a snack." She trailed after the female, catching up to her and casually hooking her arm with hers.

"Are you good?" Reese inquired, mild concern in his voice.

"I kind of have to be," I admitted, feeling a tap on my shoulder. I turned my head to see Ian sliding a drink my way.

"Figured you could use it."

I nodded and thanked him, while Reese reached around me and plucked his empty glass from where Elise had been. "Give me another too, since the little psycho put her mouth all over this, please."

Ian chuckled and started making his drink. Reese blew out a breath and nudged my shoulder with his own. "You keep staring and it's going to make it worse."

"I'm not staring."

"Nick, you have to play nonchalant alright. Don't act like it bothers you even if it does."

"I'm cool. I'm completely unbothered." Fuck, I didn't even believe myself. I wasn't jealous, I just didn't like his hands on her, especially now knowing their history.

Reese clucked his tongue, looking down as two demons walked past him giving him a look that I knew for a fact wasn't just friendly. When they were gone, he looked relieved and I kind of felt bad for leaving him at the bar with

Elise while I went and danced with Dani. "You aren't her boyfriend, Nick, so you can't really say much. Just look away and try not to get your virtue stolen by demons in heat."

"You're making way too much sense right now and that's really odd coming from you." The corner of my mouth lifted slightly as I reached for my drink.

Reese took his newly made drink from Ian and tipped it back, his Adam's apple bobbing as he swallowed. "Yeah, I don't know, this place is fucking weird and I, one hundred percent, would not recommend, but for now just let her talk to the guy. You're overthinking the fuck out of this; I can literally hear all the wheels turning in that anxiety ridden brain of yours."

All the desire I'd felt for her on that dance floor was still there, but now it was in competition with my feeling of wanting to win her over. She had forgiven me, and I could say we were in a good enough place but right now that wasn't enough. Dimitri had been with her and now thought he had some claim to feel her skin and be close enough to kiss her. It took everything in me not to go over there and break up whatever the fuck kind of conversation they were having. I oddly wanted to lay a claim on her, and I knew I had no right, but I had a feeling she wanted that too. I took a sip of my drink and tried to focus on my best friend, refocusing my mind until we could get back to the hostel.

"Maybe you can find a nice demon to distract you and make her feel just as lethal as you," he said sarcastically, turning his head to look back at where Dani was.

"You know I don't do that."

"Uh, maybe you should."

I furrowed my brows in confusion, holding my drink to my lips. I turned my head and my whole body went rigid. They were no longer side by side, but Dani had swung her leg over his body and was now settled on his lap. He had his hands on her waist, and I could see the tiniest flex of his fingers as he squeezed. Her dress had ridden up to show more of her thighs and I had never wanted to be another man in my entire life, but I had also never felt so fucking livid in all of my existence.

I felt my fingers tighten around my drink glass and I could almost hear the glass starting to whine under my grip. My hand was empty when I blinked, realizing that Reese had taken my drink from me. He gently placed it on the bar and ran a hand through his hair. "Are you really, *really* sure you want a demon girlfriend?"

I ignored him as I zeroed in on Dani and Dimitri. A demon female was next to me at the bar, and I knew she wanted my attention, but I didn't pay her any mind. I wasn't in the mood, and I never would be. I watched as Dimitri ran his hand through her hair and slid his fingers down her arms. My heart thundered in my chest at the amount of possessiveness I felt. That claim I wanted to have on her started to creep its way back up. She was independent and confident, and I appreciated those things about her. That fire she had was something I never wanted her to lose. I had told her I wanted her to be herself fully, despite whatever path she chose, and I would be there.

She could be independent and also know she was mine. Dimitri could try all he wanted and likely reminisce about their time together—which made me want to vomit just thinking about it, but that didn't change what I already knew about me and her. She had said that she wasn't jealous of Rae or anyone else because she knew she had me. She had been right.

It was time I helped her understand that I had her too.

16

DANI

Earlier

Dimitri watched me as I made my way over to him, that same cocky smirk on his face that I knew all too well. That smirk had been something I'd seen many nights while I rolled around with him in his bed. Those thoughts and his face didn't give me the same feeling of lust and desire as they used to. It's not like I wanted them to, but still it was weird not automatically having that familiar sensation. He had two females next to him, and others were scattered along the other couches probably waiting their turn to breath his fucking air. Dimitri was a demon's wet dream. He had looks, charm and power. Power that anyone would love a piece of even if that meant being a pretty thing on his arm that sucked his dick occasionally.

I had never been one of those. I never fawned over him and gave him attention just because he was seeking it. I gave him my time because he had actually listened to me when I spoke, he'd treated me with respect. Respect I rightfully deserved. Once we were seen together, females stopped flocking to him, afraid that I would drag my dagger through their chest if they spoke to him. I wouldn't have since I never wanted to lay any claim to him; it was just nice having someone of equal stature in my corner or my bed, whichever worked.

I watched as he looked at my dress, drinking me in with his bright green eyes that turned up at the corners. His hair had a wet look and was slicked back a little, but small pieces fell over his forehead. His skin was pale but smooth, not an inch of imperfection to be seen. The top two buttons of his shirt were undone and the tattoos that adorned his chest peeked out. The girls next to him eyed me curiously, their eyes realizing who I was, and I could see the way they shifted in their seats not knowing what to do.

"Dimitri," I smiled at him, wanting to seem pleasant enough.

"You are quite the sight, aren't you?" He responded, always speaking like he was smirking.

"I've been busy."

He looked me up and down, licking his lips. "You sure have. I've heard enough talk, sneaky thing you." His deep voice was smooth and unbothered.

"Rumors, I'm sure."

He wagged his finger at me. "You and I both know we don't do rumors here. It's so boring and you are anything but boring, Soul Seether."

I narrowed my eyes, pushing my tongue behind my front teeth. I placed my hands on my hips. "I need to speak to you."

He had his arms stretched out on the back of the couch, the girls next to him cuddled close. "Is that not what we're doing?"

I rolled my eyes. He said even the simplest things with a charm ridden tongue. "Without bystanders."

He smiled at me. "Wanting all of my attention I see."

I crossed my arms over my chest, waiting. He let out a breath and unhooked his arm from around either girl. He leaned into each of them one at a time and whispered something. The one at his right kissed his cheek and walked off somewhere, while the other one sat in place. She pouted at him. "Ugh, I never get to spend time with you."

I let out a laugh and sauntered over to where she sat. My eyes focused on her, and she drew back a bit at my proximity. "I assure you, you're pretty enough for him to come seek you out, so for now stop whining and get the fuck up." Her mouth popped open, clearly offended. She looked towards Dimitri for comfort I was guessing, but he just looked at me and snickered. I moved back so that she could remove herself from the sitting area, walking away with a sour expression on her face.

"I missed your feisty side." He patted the spot next to him.

I smirked. "I bet." I sat down, making myself comfortable.

"You don't want to introduce me to your friends?" Dimitri asked, nodding over towards where the others were.

I laughed. "Why, so you can charm them with your incredible wit?"

"I recall that you used to highly enjoy my incredible wit." He squinted at me, tilting his head a bit to the side. He moved his hand that was closest to me and placed it on my knee. His skin was warm against mine, his thumb moving in massaging circles.

I looked at his hand for a minute and then cleared my throat. "Hmm, maybe I did. That was a very long time ago."

He shrugged looking out across the room and then back at me, leaning in closer. "I remember you highly enjoying other things as well." He squeezed my knee, and I thought about what those words would have done for me years ago. We probably would have gone upstairs by now if I was being honest.

I ruffled my hair. "I also remember you being able to focus when someone wants to speak to you."

"Touché. Can you blame me though? Look at you. Sexy as ever with that attitude I always adored." He spoke right to my lips, and I thought better of it, flicking my eyes quickly towards the bar. Nicholas didn't look happy, but there wasn't anything I could do about that at the moment. I probably should have been more forthcoming about my prior relationship with our demon of interest, but what's done is done.

"Dimitri, this attitude will become a lot less adoring if you don't listen and answer accordingly," I threatened, making eye contact with him and holding it. He was a worthy opponent when it came to a stare down, his eyes two large intoxicating emeralds.

He smiled at me, squeezing my knee. "Alright, Dani, what is that you want to ask?"

"It's about Lilith."

His eyebrows raised slightly, but not enough for him to look truly shocked. "Is that so?"

"Yes, and you two are still close, I presume."

He tilted his head left and right. "Sort of. Her and my father spoke more, about boring matters and such, but once he bestowed the club to me, we had more conversations, yes."

I mulled this over. "Did you speak at all when I got here?"

He stretched his fingers out and tapped him right below my knee. "Of course we did. Lucifer and my father weren't completely happy with how the demons acted with that whole fight in Oculus and they were increasingly upset with her for not being able to keep her minions in line. Lucifer thought she was punished enough, having a portal lock on her exit out of Purgatory, so he remained out of her way, only coming to see her after she set the anti-aging and procreation curses. Don't ask me why he did that, I've asked and gotten no response." He spoke so casually about past deeds as if he hadn't given anything much thought until he was asked to retrieve the memories and speak them aloud.

He looked at me to make sure I was still with him, and I made a hand motion as if to say *keep going*. Dimitri chuckled. "My father was running this club, but he hated being here, he hated how Lucifer and everyone else essentially babied Lilith and how Purgatory was now this place of wild Enchanters and rogue demons. So, he told me I could have the club. When I started making changes, two demons came to me, told me I was being summoned by the dark queen and I was intrigued so I went. She's something else, your creator."

"So that's when you two became friends?"

"Mm, I wouldn't call us friends. We both just like power, granted we use our power in different ways, but I digress."

I bit the inside of my cheek. "What does this have to do with me?"

He looked over to the bar again for a second and then his emerald eyes were back on me. "Hm, what am *I* getting for telling you all of this?"

"The happiness of helping out an old friend."

He flexed his tattooed hand over my knee. "Oh, Dani, the things I've done to you are far from friendly, so unfortunately, that isn't going to cut it."

"I'm not sleeping with you."

"So presumptuous. As much as I would love that, I just meant we're sitting so formal, and I would like some playfulness between us." He leaned in a little as if he was going to touch my lips with his own, his hand skirting up my thigh just a little. I pushed him back and kicked my leg over his body, straddling him. My hand was still pressed to his chest, driving him into the back of the couch.

"Is this less formal for you?" The position didn't look good, I knew that, but I wasn't going to walk away without new information. He didn't give me that thrill he used to and as much as I knew he would rather us be *not* talking, I actually wanted to hear his answers. If this was the best way to go about it, then so be it. I felt eyes at my back instantly, they felt intense but familiar. *Nicholas.* I could virtually smell his heightened level of testosterone from here.

Well fuck.

"This is much better, if I must say," Dimitri smirked down at my hand and raked his eyes over my body. He repositioned himself a little, so that he was more comfortable, causing his pelvis to thrust up against me. I felt the material of his pants rub against the inside of my thighs.

I tapped his chest. "Start talking."

He let out a sigh and licked his lips. "Lilith had told me she was figuring out something, that she couldn't tell me all the details, but she wanted me in on it. She said that if she was successful in her planning I might have more than just this club. I could make something bigger in other realms."

"Realms like Heaven's Gate?"

He tickled my legs with his fingers. "Yes, exactly like Heaven's Gate. She told me that Oculus would be a good spot, good land for what I could conjure up and from what I've heard about Oculus, well, I couldn't pass up the offer. I simply asked her what she wanted in return, and she said she wanted me to keep an eye on something."

I narrowed my eyes as he continued to speak. "She had brought that pretty unpleasant blonde Enchanter with her to our next meeting and told me that she was calling in her request. She took me to that torture room she has at that castle of hers and I saw you. Just as beautiful as ever." He twirled one of my curls around his finger. I accepted the compliment, but him forming a spiral with my hair felt weird. There was an odd feeling in my stomach that told me I only wanted one person playing with my hair, forming ringlets with their fingers.

"She told me that you would be frequenting the club soon, seeing as you kept the company of Elise. I was told I should take good care of you because you were our key to getting what we wanted." I knew Elise came to Leviathan a lot and I also knew Dimitri knew of her, but there were pieces that didn't sit right.

"So, you monitored me when I came here?"

"If you want to call it that, sure. You didn't seem to mind my monitoring, hmm. You had a smile on your face once I started giving you my attention. Besides, what you told me about all the things you'd had to do, I understood your need for the release, to be with other demons, fill your soul with desire and power."

"You were a distraction," I deadpanned, summing up his words.

"I was happy to do what Lilith wanted, so long as I got my end of the deal. You mystified me a little, Soul Seether. I nearly forgot about the deal entirely." He almost sounded sincere…maybe he was. That didn't matter to me. He placed his hands on my hips, flexing his fingers so my dress rode up a little. Those eyes bore into my back again, like Nicholas wanted me to turn around and look at him but I couldn't, not right now.

"Do you happen to know what Lilith was doing while I was away, anything she confided in you about?" I tried to say innocently, running my hair through his hair. I moved my hips just a bit, so that he could feel the slide of my skin against his pants. If I moved to close, I would be able to feel his cock directly underneath me and that was something I wanted to avoid.

"All she said was that she had big plans for you. That made you more of an interesting pursuit."

I cupped his chin in my hand. "I'm a pursuit, huh."

"I'm not going to lie to you, Dani. And you are asking the questions, so if you don't like the response…"

I released his chin and patted him on the cheek. "Shut up, we both know that doesn't bother me, especially coming from you. Do you know about the demons that Lilith is voiding out?"

Dimitri looked off to the side, thinking. "I never got a chance to see one of her little voided experiments, but I knew everything was a ploy to get into Heaven's Gate. I had wondered where you had disappeared off to since I usually saw you practically every other night. I thought she had ended your life or that she was ending our deal. She told me not to worry, that you were off fulfilling what needed to be done so that she and I would no longer be so limited. She had confidence you would succeed, but she was well aware of how headstrong you were, so she told me she had another plan if you went rogue. She said that sometimes a little taste of the other side could do wonders, but she left it at that.

"I asked her what her Enchanter was for, and she said she needed a way to move through realms since she was locked down here, but that would all change soon enough, one way or another. She had me, her Enchanter and that angel she was using. I can't remember his name, nor do I care, and she said that the angelic realm would be so easily overtaken. She said letting you leave for Heaven's Gate was the easiest plan but obviously here you are and here I am still holding up this place at Devil's Playground. She'll have to move to whatever she's been planning for next."

I hadn't noticed that his hands were rubbing up and down my sides now, applying pressure every so often. "I assure you her angelic puppet is dead." My eyes flared with the thought of Markus's life draining from his eyes when I'd killed him.

"I can't say I'm surprised. The company of angels isn't always the best," he sarcastically, throwing me a knowing grin. I shoved his shoulder and he chuckled. "You can't expect me to not notice your angelic companions as much as they try to hide it, they do make a statement." Nicholas was probably making a huge statement just staring at me, while he got ogled by demonic females. I could smell their pitiful amount of lust from here, but I blocked it out. At least I tried to. Rae had really fucked with my head with her feeble attempt to stake a claim on someone she wouldn't even appreciate. Nicholas was good for a night, but he was so much more than that.

I rolled my eyes. "Have you spoken to Lilith lately?"

"No, but her blonde Enchanter has come in to speak with me on occasion, quite recently actually. She told me how you were back and as strong willed as ever, that Lilith hoped you would be just as vivacious and cutthroat as she left you. She told me to look out for you if you come by. I mean, Dani, you can't honestly believe she isn't watching you, that she isn't in

your head because you have a connection with her whether you like it or not. You may have your own mind, but she's in there even if you choose not to acknowledge it. You are one of the strongest things she's ever created. And yes, she told me about your little hybrid status. Makes you all the more *enticing* if I do say so." He settled his hands on my hips again, using the heels of his hands to push the front hem of my dress up my thighs.

"You couldn't lead with that?" I said, frustratingly. He was telling me things I already knew. What did me being strong and having this connection with her mean for whatever she was doing?

He gave me a one shoulder shrug. "I assumed that bit wasn't important since that didn't work for her while you were in Heaven's Gate. You didn't open the portal for her like she wanted, yet just because you didn't do that doesn't make her stop seeing you as a weapon. She wants to make you into a different type of weapon now. What kind I don't know, so don't ask."

"You and I both know I could go in, darkness at hand, and fight, but she's more calculating than that. I want answers from her, I want her to pay for the things she's done, and the easy kill won't get me that."

Dimitri nodded. "Oh, I'm well aware and frankly so is she. Lilith likes to play games where she changes the rules constantly."

"I'm always the pawn, though."

"The prettiest pawn," he complimented, trailing his hand up my arm and caressing my cheek. "She wants you to come to her, she wants you to choose her over them and everyone else. You are more valuable to her than her Enchanter and probably even me. Her most precious game piece."

"I've never liked her games, and you shouldn't either. Demons aren't innocent by any means, but that doesn't mean they deserve to have their souls taken out for experiments and fun. I did it to the ones who deserved it, I can't say the same for her," I spat out, venom on my tongue.

"Lilith is the kind to try and try again, until something is just right. Like a recipe, Dani. Some of the batches might not be right the first time, but when you find the one that's just right, ah, that's a game changer. She thought her first plan was good and it was but there was still something off and I think it was your freedom of choice. She thought you would seek power over the good will of others. Very bold, not that I'm surprised, coming from you. She couldn't force you to do something when she allowed you a choice, so now she's going to give you no choice" He pulled me closer to him, so that I was pushed further against his pelvis. And just like I suspected his cock was hard, but now I was comparing his size to someone else's, and Dimitri didn't even come close.

"I always have a choice, Dimitri."

"Keep that mindset, pretty girl." He flicked his green eyes over my shoulder as he sat up more, maneuvering me along the way. "You know we've done a lot of talking."

"That was the point."

The vein in the side of his neck pulsed slightly, moving one of his tattoos up and down. "You haven't admitted once that you missed me."

I pressed my tongue into my cheek. "Well, if I say it now, you wouldn't believe me."

Dimitri hummed. "Hmm, true. Is it because you have someone else in your bed?"

I tilted my head to the side. "What would make you think that?" Dimitri moved so that we were chest to chest, his breath was hot near my face.

"You've had an angelic onlooker since the moment we started talking. I'll assume that's the new man that's satisfying you." I said nothing, not giving him the satisfaction. He drew his eyes over my shoulder again, indicating that he knew about Nicholas and how volatile he must be by now. "I don't think he likes this little position you've put yourself in."

I sighed. "No, he probably doesn't. But he doesn't own me."

"He really doesn't like this at all. Angelic possessiveness is a heady scent isn't it." Dimitri, always the instigator, ran a hand through my hair. "Since you aren't claiming one another then he shouldn't mind if you kissed me."

My face screwed up in confusion. "Kissed you?"

Dimitri looked at me as if he was totally serious about his statement. It wasn't surprising coming from him. I would have let that flirtatious forwardness wash over me and thrilled at it. A lot had happened between the last time I kissed him and right now. A certain person had happened. His lips looked plush and soft. I knew they tasted like sin and every single desirable thing you could dream up, but I wanted different lips that tasted equally like sin, but the kind of sin that felt like heaven.

"Nice try, but I'm not kissing you. It's not part of the plan."

Dimitri snickered. "You came over to me, glowing from the dance floor with your angel to ask me questions and you won't even kiss me in return." He lifted his hands up and fell back onto the couch. "I admire you, Soul Seether. It's truly a wonder how you can charm me but still be so far away with another man on your mind, let alone an angel. A lesser man would be insulted."

I nodded over to the women and some men that were huddled hoping to speak to him, or suck his dick, either was a high possibility. "I think you'll survive."

He looked over at where my eyes went, and he laughed. "They will do, I suppose. You come to me though, if your angel isn't enough, which I'm betting he isn't." I nearly looked behind me and whimpered with the thought of him almost fingering me on that dance floor. Oh, he was enough, and he thought *I* was enough. I pushed off his lap, not saying another word as I wiped my hands down my dress and pushed my hair over both my shoulders. I turned to walk away, but he halted me, grabbing my forearm.

"I'll be speaking with Lilith in about a day or so before the club opens. I don't know what she wants, but she is meeting me here. I can help you by letting you in on what she says to me, if you come by the club again," he offered, expectantly. I looked into his eyes for some kind of mischief, some kind of secret agenda. I didn't find anything.

"Fine, day after tomorrow. I'll be back and you'll tell me everything. And don't expect me to kiss you or sit on your lap for the information." I tipped one corner of my mouth upward.

He placed a hand over his heart. Or whatever he had beating in his chest. "You have my word. I can't promise that you won't want to, though." He winked at me before giving his attention to the demons nearly clenching their thighs together just looking at him. The handsome bastard was popular, and demons around here would think I was crazy for not just begging him to kiss me, but I didn't want his kiss. Not anymore.

PRESENT

Before we'd left the club, he didn't really look at me. It was like everything that had transpired on that dance floor had disappeared and now the air was frosty between us. I had to pull Elise away from a pretty dark-skinned girl I'd found her with in a corner of the club and Nick had to take the drink out of his best friend's hand before we left. I tried to tell him we could talk later at the hostel, so that I could explain what happened, but he didn't seem interested. He was almost vibrating with the kind of intensity I'd never seen from him. I had tried to grab his arm, but he yanked it out of my grip. A muffled, *I'm fine*, leaving his lips before he moved away.

The walk back to the hostel was quiet and awkward and I hated it. Elise opened the door for us, and we tried not to be super loud, but that didn't seem to matter when drunk demons were scattered on the couches. I could see a few huddled over the counter in the kitchen, devouring a meal. Beetee was nowhere in sight and after tonight, I don't think I wanted her to be a part of whatever was going to happen here. Elise raised her arms above her head and yawned, "he isn't happy with you. I think he's pouting."

I narrowed my eyes, knowing exactly what she meant. The boys were behind us, and he was looking at me as if he wanted to say something, but he couldn't even fathom speaking two words to me. I knew what happened in the club wasn't something nice to see, but my reasoning was my own and I hadn't given into Dimitri's advances like he probably assumed I did.

"I'm not pouting." His deep voice rang out as he pushed past Reese to close the distance between us.

"Are you sure about that?" Elise pushed.

"It looks like that's exactly what you're doing." I added.

Nick turned his head to me and ran a hand through his hair. "It's not pouting. This is just what it looks like when you aren't told the whole story until it's thrown in your face literally two feet away from you."

"Ugh, I tried to fucking talk to you about it afterwards, but you were too busy ignoring me, so I really don't know what you want from me!"

Reese stepped between us. "Um, okay. As much as I love seeing the two of you bicker, I am far too overwhelmed and overstimulated to try to referee," he said sarcastically. I looked around and noticed we had a small audience discreetly trying to act like they weren't paying attention to us.

"I personally think that you two should just go angry fuck somewhere so you can stop wasting everyone's time. We'll dissect Dimitri's information tomorrow, so fix your shit or go the fuck to bed." Elise rolled her eyes and made her way to the stairs, walking to the second floor.

I let out a sigh and flipped my hair over my shoulder. "Are you going to let me explain and talk to you or do you need more time to get your shit together?"

He looked at me, the anger still in his eyes. "Get my shit together? You were on his lap, Dani. *My* shit is not the concern here."

"Oh, I'm well aware, I was there, thank you for the recap," I said with the fakest smile on my face. I acknowledged Reese, placing my hand on his shoulder. "Have a good night. Tell your friend to come find me when he's ready to have an actual conversation. This back and forth is really fucking boring and I don't do well with being talked *at* rather than talked *to*." I rolled my eyes at Nicholas before I twirled around and made my way up the stairs.

I heard Reese's exasperated pleading voice. "Nick! Nick, fuck!"

Footsteps came behind me, but I didn't look back. I had been pretty much thinking about him the entire time I was with Dimitri, but sure all he saw was me on some other guy's lap. He wasn't in my head; he didn't know my thoughts. If he had been in the loop, the outcome would have been the same, I would have still ended up in that position. I didn't do it for myself, I did it for more knowledge. I was being a team player, maybe not in the way he wanted but we all had our strengths and weaknesses.

I could feel him trailing behind me as I opened the door to my room. I strutted inside with all the sass I could muster. I had to admit that there was a small part of me that liked him when he was this annoyed, this overwhelmed. I tensed a bit when I heard the door slam behind me.

Oh, he was definitely angry.

I hadn't done anything wrong in my opinion. Nicholas and I weren't together in any way and yes, he had gotten on his knees for me, but that was for my trust, not— my heart. He wanted information just like the rest of us and he wasn't happy with the way I had gotten it. He was in my world now, the world I've always known, so he would have to learn to deal with the way things were done.

I had my back to him, but I felt his eyes on me. I could practically taste the anger that he was harboring. It was anger of a possessive nature. I cracked my neck and turned around. He was standing so still and breathing slowly, looking at me as if he was trying to figure me out. His brown eyes were narrowed, scanning my entire body like he was afraid I was going to start spewing curse words at him at any given moment. I crossed my arms over my chest and tilted my head to the side.

"Are you waiting for me to apologize?"

He blinked up to my face. "That's not what I want, Dani. Even if I did, you wouldn't do it anyway."

I shrugged. "You would be correct."

"I want you to explain to me what that was. Is that how you always get information?" He questioned, taking a step towards me.

I planted my feet and squared my shoulders. "Sometimes. It depends clearly. Dimitri is…different."

I noticed the distinct scar under his eye tick at my words. I hit a nerve.

"Different? As in you go about retrieving information differently depending on if you've fucked that person?" If he knew that, then Elise must have opened her mouth and told him.

I stuck my tongue out and traced it under my two front teeth. "You should be thanking me."

He dragged his hand along the back of his neck and took another step. He was getting dangerously close to me, but I didn't mind. I knew he would be mad about what I did at that club. I was prepared for it. I did what I had to do. I didn't rip off Dimitri's clothes and suck his dick, so that was saying something.

"*Thanking you*? I won't thank you for dry humping him."

I leaned forward. "Sex sells, Nicholas, especially down here."

He rolled his eyes in the most annoyed way. "I bet he was so eager to get you on top of him."

I nodded a bit giddy, knowing it would piss him off even more. "Oh yeah, I could feel how hard he was right at my thigh..."

"Fuck, Dani. Stop. Just stop." The tick under his eye was back.

I looked down to where his hands had turned into fists at his sides. I wasn't planning on taking things any further with my former fuck buddy the minute I knew we were going to see him because he was so easy to get information out of, but Dimitri was the type that liked to think he was the center of your attention, he liked to think he could have you at any moment. Maybe there was a small, teeny, tiny part of me that wanted a certain angel to be unleashed by my actions, but I didn't do it on purpose.

"Do you enjoy doing this?" He took another step in my direction.

"Doing what?" I said, innocently.

"Getting under my skin?"

I looked at his face, letting my eyes glaze over his features. "You make it so easy."

He ran an overtly frustrated hand through his hair. "I'm not a fan of your methods."

"For fucks sake, I wasn't going to fuck him right in front of everyone." I scoffed, letting an exasperated laugh leave my lips.

"Try to be a little more subtle next time if that's even possible for you."

"How about next time you don't look." I suggested, rolling my eyes.

He bared his teeth. "God, you are so fucking annoying you know that. It's like you want to help, but at the expense of my sanity."

I laughed at him, again. "Maybe you should keep that crazy in check. I didn't mean for you to feel some type of way about it, but at the end of the day, Nicholas, I can do what I please. I'm not *yours*." I said that last part, looking directly at his lips. I blinked back up to him, noticing the way his eyes were a bit darker, like he was contemplating my words and a whole new emotion was enveloping him now. He was taking in my dress inch by inch, almost like he was committing every piece of it to memory.

I took a step towards him so that we were just inches apart. "We both know that you have a lot of emotions because I left you hard and unsatisfied last time and that wasn't very nice of me. Not to mention you didn't get to feel me come around your fingers on the dance floor." I lifted my hand to reach for his hair, "and then you had to see me grind my tight little body all over another…" My words were cut off by his hand grabbing my wrist, his bicep flexed. My fingers were inches from his dark hair, but I couldn't move any closer. He pulled my hand away from him and looked down at me. Nick pulled me so that I was shoved against his body.

I could feel his breath against my face. My own breathing was becoming a bit more erratic.

"I am upset that you left me like that," he admitted. "I'm also pissed that after that you decided to try to make me jealous by rubbing yourself over a demon you used to share a bed with."

"You should be lucky to know that your jealousy turns me on a little."

"Is that so?" He looked down at my mouth, cocking an eyebrow up.

I nodded, sticking my tongue against my cheek.

I pressed my body further into him, not missing the way his cock, which was growing harder by the second, rammed into pelvis. "You are kind of adorable when you're all dominating and unsettled. I'm free to do what I want and use my body how I want." I licked his lips, loving the way he tasted on my tongue. "Like I said, I'm not *yours*. Nicholas." I let his full name trail out of my mouth, letting the hiss of the 's' settle in the air.

His eyes flared with the kind of fire that had my legs shaking and my thighs clenching together. He took my other hand in his and pushed me back towards the dresser behind me. My back hit the large piece of furniture, sending a stinging jolt up my spine. Nicholas pressed his knee between my legs, kicking them apart. He moved my hands, shoving them both behind me and holding them together behind my back. He pressed his cock against me, letting me feel him and I almost whimpered.

He leaned into my neck, letting his lips ghost over my skin until he finally made contact, kissing, and sucking at my tender flesh. His tongue darted out to lick along my collarbone and up my neck. He moved up to my ear and whispered in a dark voice that nearly made my stomach drop to my ass. "I'm going to make you wish you were mine." He took my earlobe between his teeth and bit down, causing me to let out a small cry.

I leaned towards his face and tried to capture his lips with my own, but he pulled back. I pushed my bottom lip out in a pout. "Do you expect me to beg for your forgiveness, Nicholas?"

He looked down at me and traced one finger between my breasts, towards my stomach and slipped it underneath my dress. He pulled my panties to the side and rubbed his fingers over where I was already wet.

His hand on my wrists tightened as he explored what was between my legs, letting out a deep short laugh. He leveled his gaze at me. "I don't *expect* you to do anything, Dani. I *know* you'll beg." He started to massage my pussy, rubbing his thumb against my clit in the way that I forgot he was so good at. His eyes were on me the entire time he moved his fingers over me, not missing any of my reactions.

"You're a confident one." I mustered through my sharp breaths.

He gave me a lazy one shoulder shrug before dipping one of his fingers inside of me. "I'm confident in knowing that you wanted to get information, but you also liked the idea that I was watching, while I was practically seething over him touching you, so I'll…what?" He curled his finger inside and then pushed a second finger alongside it. I grazed my teeth along my bottom lip, feeling my heart hammering in my chest. "Fuck you till you can't walk straight? Make you forget about all the other guys before me?"

I pressed my lips together and mumbled a low moan as he thrusted his fingers inside of me. A third finger joined his other two and my throat let out an unsettling noise. The sound of how wet I was growing loud with each movement of his hand. He angled the heel of his hand, so he pushed against my clit over and over. Nicholas pushed his fingers up and in so roughly, pulling me closer to him. His breath was hot on my cheek as he gave me a gentle kiss. He was the most delicious contradiction I'd ever faced.

He pulled back and ripped his hand from where I was wet and now so very hollow. He grabbed me from behind my thighs and lifted me onto the dresser, settling between my open legs. Nicholas reached down for the buttons of his pants and before I could even blink twice, he had them past his hips. His cock was incredibly hard and pulsing between us. I reached out to grab it, wanting to feel it but he smacked my hand away. He snaked his hands up my thighs and reached for my panties, taking the fabric in his hands and holding on tightly. He tilted his head down and traced his nose against mine as if he was trying to play sweet Nick. I knew better than that.

His laugh came out sharp and heavy. "You aren't mine, huh? Is that why you're already so wet?" He tugged hard on my panties and the resounding ripping sound that they made was music to my ears. A burning sensation hit me quickly from where the fabric was torn but it subsided within seconds. I liked attentive, patient, slow burning Nick, but this man, this possessive angelic creature in front of me was what I wanted right now.

He threw my discarded panties to the ground and reached around my thighs, pulling me to the edge of the dresser until my ass was hanging right off the end. He closed our distance and brushed his cock against me, sliding easily over my clit. He pushed my dress up my stomach, leaving heat searing touches down my body as he moved his fingers over me. He lifted his shirt a little to decrease the amount of clothing in his way, allowing me to get a view of his abs and the way the lines of his defined muscles were formed. I realized he didn't get to be this Nick often. Maybe with all the other girls he'd been with he could be the Nick from his bedroom that bent me over and took what he wanted but that Nick was different from this one. That Nick had his limits…but this Nick was currently *at* his limit, but I wanted to push it further.

I pressed my hands into the wood of the dresser. "*I'm. Not. Yours.*" Each word came out like a hot, thick challenge.

He continued to slide over me some more, but with one inhale he was pressing inside until he was all the way in. I missed how he felt deep inside of me, I missed how big he was when he was filling me. He leaned down towards me, rocking his hips back and forth, giving me that much needed friction that I craved. "Then I'll have to fuck you like your mine."

He pulled back, almost removing his cock completely from me, and then he slammed back in, clasping his hands onto my thighs, keeping them open.

He didn't go easy.

He didn't go slow.

He absolutely with no remorse, fucked me.

"Oh my god, fuck!" I yelled, tilting my head back and looking at the ceiling. He was menacing with the way he moved his body; he was teaching me a lesson in how he was the only one I should want, fucking me like he wanted my pussy to suffer from the punishment he was giving it.

His voice echoed against my skin. "You're always so fucking tight."

"Did you miss it? You regret spending all that time away from me?" I taunted, before he spread my legs wider and fucked me harder and faster.

"You are such a fucking little demon, you know that." He reached up my dress, letting the pads of his fingers skim over the material and wrapped them around my throat, pulling me to him. He applied pressure, squeezing slightly and I clenched my pussy around him.

I tried not to let my eyes roll back into my head as he kept up his punishing rhythm. "You *fucking* love it."

He shook his head and moved his lips over mine as if he was going to kiss me, but he grabbed my lower lip with his teeth and pulled a tiny bit, biting down. A gasping moan escaped my lips, causing him to push me back using his hand on my throat. He pressed his other hand to the inside of my thigh and looked down, watching as he thoroughly fucked my pussy over and over again. His brows pulled in as if he was concentrating on the visual in front of him. His lips turned into a small smirk as he ran his thumb over my clit, my legs tightening at the touch. "This pussy sure feels like it's mine."

I swiftly took my hand off the dresser and grasped onto his shoulder. "Fuck, right there, keep going." He was an angel with a dirty mouth when he was fuming and proving a point, and I was living for it. I made stubborn, overthinking, spiraling Nicholas Cassial into this punishing, incessant sexual fiend and I loved it. I may be part angel in some retrospect, but right now I was all demon, and I wasn't lying when I had told him once upon a time that he fucked like a one. He fucked me like he could have taken my soul out with just the right number of thrusts. "Oh fuck, fuck, fuck." I repeated, groaning as the burning sensation in my thighs grew. The pressure was building in my stomach and down lower. I would go off like a bomb, I just knew it.

He pulled me back in, his hand on my throat tightening again just the tiniest bit. His fingers pressed on my clit. "Are you sorry for what you did in there?" So, he did want an apology from me.

I didn't say anything, I just pressed my teeth together so hard that my ears started ringing. The dresser started swaying back and forth, not enough for it to start shifting off the ground, but just enough for the drawers themselves to start rattling. He removed his fingers from my clit and moved his hand from my throat to the back of my head, tugging at my hair. He was moving a little slower now, but his cock was still so deep, so fucking perfect that I started to close my eyes.

"*Dani*." he said in a clipped voice, sending my eyes flying open and blazing into his. "Are you sorry for what you did in there? Are you sorry for rubbing your needy little pussy against someone else?" He hovered his hand over my clit, and I tried to move my hips up to get contact, but he wouldn't let me.

I decided right then and there I would beg if he wanted me to. My orgasm was so close, and he knew that. We had only had sex a handful of times, but somehow, he understood when I was right at the edge. He knew how to make sure I teetered back and forth never fully going over.

I looked into his eyes and pursed my lips, nodding.

"Be a good girl and say it," he demanded, unwilling to yield any of the power.

"Yes, I'm sorry." I obeyed, practically panting. The feeling of his skilled fingers on my clit, the way his cock was rubbing me just right had me realizing I was closer to the edge than I had originally thought.

He pulled my hair, tilting my chin up. He kissed along my neck, letting me grind my core against where he pushed inside of me. *"Are. You. Mine?"*

I wrapped my other hand around the back of his neck, feeling the cotton of his shirt at my fingertips and brought him even closer to me. I started grinding myself harder against him. He molded himself against my body, causing me to pull my legs up more so that I was now practically in half on the dresser as he hammered away between my legs. His thrusts were persistent and deep as if he wanted to get further inside of me when he was already balls deep and stretching me in a way that nearly had me crying. Our skin slapping together made the most obscene sound, letting anyone who passed by very aware of what was going on.

He pressed his fingers into my hair and pulled my head towards him so that his forehead could rest on mine. Sweat was covering us both, our breathing so uneven that I was surprised we were even able to speak words at this point. "Dani, you don't answer me, and I'll leave you like you left me. I'll leave you begging for my cock, begging me to make you come."

He was asking me if I was his...*his*. If I answered him the way I wanted to, how would he feel about it? This whole moment between us was all very abrupt, so would he feel the same about it when we were done and spent? I was always one for a risk, so I dove in headfirst.

"Yes." I pressed my fingers harder into his back, looking right into his eyes. My sounds were coming out between short breaths.

He started to rub my clit harder, in circular motions, increasing his thrusting at the same time. "Yes, what? Say it louder."

I caught my breath before he pressed two fingers against my clit and hit the most perfect spot in all of history with his cock buried in me and I gave him what he wanted. "I'm yours, Nick. I'm yours, I'm yours, I'm yours!"

"So fucking good." He kissed me then, lips and teeth clashing as he pounded into me so hard that I'm sure I heard the dresser actually lift off the carpet. And then I felt it, I felt my legs shake and my eyesight begin to blur. My orgasm tore through me violently. I screamed into his mouth as he ground his hips against me through all of it. I felt him tense around me and shudder as he started to come. His cock spasmed inside of me as he let out a grumbled *fucking mine* against my lips and I wrapped my other hand around his neck so that I could pull him against me, deepening the kiss he'd started.

His hair was damp on his forehead as I pulled back. I trailed my fingers into his hair, musing it a little as he looked down at where we were still joined. He blinked a few times as if remembering himself, taking in my spread legs and my dress bunched up at my hips. He looked everywhere but at me, finally pulling out of me slowly, but not moving from in-between my legs.

I squinted, trying to read him. I was trying to get a handle on my breathing when I grabbed his jaw and forced him to look at me. "Nick, don't spiral please."

He raised an eyebrow at me and reached out to caress my face. That dominant side of him was placed back in its cage for now. "I'm not."

"You are."

He sighed, defeated. "Fine, maybe just a little."

"Would you like to actually talk about it? Now that you've released your tension." I offered, circling my legs around the backs of his thighs.

"Not really."

"I think we should."

Nick groaned, bending down to pull his underwear up but stepped out of his pants and shoes. He tucked his hands under my ass and lifted me off the dresser, carrying me over to the bed. He placed me on top of the comforter and crawled over me to settle down next to me. I turned over to face him and placed my head on his chest. He slowly maneuvered his arm so that he could wrap it around me and started to draw lines on my arm and shoulder.

"You do know that I wasn't planning on doing anything with Dimitri, right?"

I felt his chest rise and fall, but at the name of my former fling, his heart stuttered.

"For the most part, yeah."

"But a part of you thought I was about to just pull his dick out right then and there? That's what you think of me?"

He let out an uncomfortable cough. "No, Dani, of course not, but you have to see it from my side. I let you do your thing and the next thing I see is you straddling some other guy. It's just not a fun time."

I pushed my face further into his chest, letting his words sink in and feeling the sincerity in them, "I am sorry and just know that it was never my intention to upset you." I felt his hand around my arm squeeze me. "You are really easy to get a rise out of. Who would have thought you felt so strongly about me?" I teased.

I felt him press his face into my hair and groan. "Don't think too much about it."

"That's difficult when you wanted me to tell you that I was yours."

He tensed a little, but not the type of tense where he was ashamed of his words, but more like he was nervous. "Hmph."

"Was that just for the moment?" I had to ask the question that ran through my head the minute he had wanted me to say it. "I mean it was really fucking hot, but you had to know that I was going to ask."

He was creating circles on my skin with his fingertips. "Can I be honest?"
I nodded.

"I don't know actually. I don't think so."

I let out a huff and pushed up on my elbow, letting my hair cascade to one side as I looked at him. He had one of his arms bent behind his head and the other was starting to trace lines along my back. "What are we doing?"

"What do you mean?"

I rolled my eyes, annoyed. "Nick, I'm used to playing around and not caring when it comes to demons, but you are different, I'll admit that. You clearly don't like the idea of me being with anyone else...," He started to interrupt but I placed my finger to his lips. "And I don't like the idea of *you* being with anyone else, in fact, it makes me kind of murderous. I'm not jealous, but I just don't like seeing it, alright. Those girls can fuck right off." He laughed at this.

"I'm not asking you to define anything right now, but at some point, you're going to have to, and I'll follow your lead. I'm smart enough to know that all of us are under too much pressure for you to have a clear head about this but for now can you just tell me if it was for the moment? Like if this is all pointless and just for fun."

He narrowed his eyes at me, tilting his head a little to get a good look at my face. He moved his hand from my back and caught a piece of hair in his fingers, slipping it behind my ear. "It wasn't for the moment. I liked hearing you say that you were mine." He propped himself up and brought my face to his, kissing me slowly. "It's fun, but it's not pointless, I promise. I don't think I could do anything without there being a point. Especially not with you."

"You called me a little demon, when we both know I have angel powers somewhere in here." I laughed, running my hand down my body.

"I don't care what you have secretly inside of you, you will always be an annoying demon to me." He kissed me again, dragging his lips to my jaw and scattering kisses down my neck causing me to land on his chest in a fit of giggles. "Dani?" His voice was tentative all of a sudden.

My body and mind felt tired, but the kind of tired where I knew I would end up well rested when I woke up. I wrapped one of my legs around his and snuggled closer to him. "Mhmm?"

He cleared his throat as I felt myself drifting a bit. "I do feel things towards you and those are things I can't really put into words yet. I don't want you to think I'm putting anything off or purposely not deciding, I just don't really understand my feelings, but I will. I guess I just don't know what wanting you to be mine means exactly…not yet. But that's what I want." He said this last part like a whisper as if it was just for me and no one else.

I smiled against his chest as I felt sleep takeover. His heart was hammering, so I said one last thing before I let sleep claim me, feeling his fingers start to create spirals with my curls. "When you do figure it out, I better be the first to know."

17

NICK

I hadn't realized I'd gone to sleep, but when I opened my eyes, she was nuzzled into my chest, softly breathing. I'd gently slipped out from underneath her to head to the bathroom. I was a bit shocked at the fact that I'd seemingly slept without waking up in a cold sweat. That was new to me seeing as I'd oddly gotten used to the attacks for quite some time. I would sleep in bed with her forever if it meant no more haunting visuals. That didn't mean that there weren't looming thoughts flailing around in my subconscious. I remembered feeling something curl around my mind while I slept, like a silken snake trying to push its way in, but it was different than the time with Natalia. It felt like there was this weird battle of light and dark fumbling around in my chest and as much as I assumed light would win in my favor, the dark was looming, but it wasn't violently trying to drag me with it. It was forming itself around another darkness, one that was much bigger than it, much more familiar with this overall place we were in.

I shook my head as I turned on the faucet and slapped water on my face, patting it dry with a hand towel. I had this weird connection with the girl sleeping soundly in the other room, but what did that really mean? What did that mean when this was all said and done? I wasn't a fan of the unknown, whatever that may be, but I would try my best to keep it together and figure things out. And I would try my fucking hardest to make sure the Dimitri's of the world never got to touch her skin.

I slowly opened the bathroom, seeing that Dani was no longer sleeping, she was propped up on her knees with her head tilted. The room was dark except for the dim light coming from the bathroom. I shot out some of my light to create another light source once I cut off the bathroom light. She still had her dress on from the night before and the hem rode up her thighs as she readjusted her knees on the comforter.

"My little night light," she mumbled more to herself than to me as she looked at the glowing orb to her left. I sighed, content. I would happily be her night light whenever she needed me.

"I thought you were asleep?" I asked, my voice a little huskier than I would have liked.

She bit her bottom lip, scanning my body from head to toe. I realized I was just in my boxer briefs and t-shirt, but I was never shy about my body, so I just stood there, letting her watch me. Her voice was slow and flirtatious when she spoke, "well, I'm not anymore."

I took a deep breath and steadily walked towards the bed, maintaining eye contact with her. "Did I wake you up?"

She shook her head. "No, I felt around, and you weren't there. Are you okay?"

I nodded, feeling myself wanting to tell her about my sleepless nights and vertigo inducing nightmares. "I'm fine."

"Are you tired?" she asked, tilting her head to the other side, her hair following suit.

I ran my hand along my stomach. "Not really."

"Good." I had to catch my breath when she reached behind her to unzip the back of her dress, sliding her arms through the sleeves before pulling it over her head completely. She was naked in front of me without an ounce of shame on her face. And fuck, she was beautiful. All she did was let out a small giggle. I could see from where I stood that her nipples were peaked, and her breathing was starting to pick up a small pace with anticipation.

She was near the end of the bed, so I stopped right when I was in front of her and leaned down, planting my hands on either side of her legs. My face was level with hers as I skated my nose over hers. "What would you like to do, needy one?"

Dani audibly shuddered at my name for her as she ran her hand down my stomach and over my cock, which jumped at her touch. She stuck her tongue out, licking my lips. Pieces of her hair tickled my face, and I closed my eyes to control myself as she held me tight in her grip, squeezing and rubbing. She kissed me softly as if the kiss never even happened. "I want you to fuck me like I'm yours."

I groaned against her mouth before pulling her in for a deeper kiss, the kind of kiss that left an impression and burned so good you had to go back for more. I pulled away from her and grabbed under her thighs, yanking her around so that she was bent over the end of the bed. I slid my underwear down and reached behind me to pull my shirt off, angling my cock right at her entrance. I grabbed the flesh of her ass in one of my hands and massaged my fingers into her skin. I pulled my hand back just to bring it down on her ass with a smack. I watched her hand grip the comforter and a small moan left her lips.

And then I did what she asked.

I woke up to running shower water and the sound of footsteps outside the door. I scrubbed a hand down my face, not feeling like I got any sleep at all, yet not feeling groggy. I sat up, turning my neck from side to side and hearing it crack. The shower water turned off and I waited, listening carefully to the sound of her feet on the bathroom floor. The door opened and Dani stepped out with a towel wrapped around her body. Her curls were drenched, water droplets falling off the ends of her hair as she walked over to the dresser.

"Hi." I said, causing her to look over her shoulder at me.

"Hi."

"You took a shower by yourself?"

She giggled, turning back around, pulling the top drawer out and rifling through it. "Yes, because if I would have asked you, we would have been in there for an hour."

"Not true," I argued.

She pulled out a few clothing items and placed them on top of the wooden dresser. Dani gave me a knowing look and before I could speak, she dropped her towel. I groaned and brought my knees up burying my head in my hands.

"See." she teased.

"That's not fair." I could literally hear myself whining as I peeked up at her.

She started to get dressed and I, not wanting to miss a thing, watched her. She kept me in her sight by looking at me out of the corner of her eye. She did certain movements slower than others, while at other times she angled herself in a particular way that had me aching to undress her all together and make her come on my tongue…again.

Dani took the towel off the ground and started scrunching the water out of her hair as she looked at me, smirking. As if she didn't just put on the best show I'd ever seen. I shook my head at her, but she knew I was amused. I sighed letting my mind roam to what today would bring. She walked over to the bed, crawling up to where I sat near the headboard.

"You gonna tell me what he said?"

She gave me a confused look. I got more comfortable, pushing the pillows behind me up, so I could prop myself against them. "Dimitri."

"I thought we were talking about all that as a group."

I shrugged. "Yeah, I know, but I didn't know if you wanted to talk about anything right now."

"Hmm…Isabel came to see him when we got here, she told him I was back. So, it makes sense as to why he wasn't all that surprised to see me."

"So, what he's just been waiting for you to show up?"

"I wouldn't doubt it." She picked at invisible dust on the headboard. "Don't get all jealous."

"I'm not." I placed my hand under her chin and turned her face to look at me.

"Remember I ended up in bed with you, having many many orgasms, so be happy and maybe a little smug." She shoved my hand away and kissed me, pushing the covers that were over my lap down and kicked her leg over so that she was straddling me. "Dimitri was a means to an end."

Grabbing her waist, I stretched my fingers up to feel her stomach and ribs. "Did he say anything of merit?"

She pushed her hair back over her shoulder. "He knew about the plan to infiltrate Heaven's Gate, not enough to be involved in the taking over part, but enough to have a stake in the reward if I'd gone through with what she wanted from me."

"And what about now? Does he have any idea what the plan is?"

"I don't think so. She's been busy with her experiments, but everyone including Dimitri just loves to throw my connection with her in my face and how strong I am. Like they are mutually exclusive."

"Maybe it is," I sighed, not wanting to think about falling down into that dark rabbit hole again.

She hummed, stuffing her face into my neck. "Can I be done answering questions for now? Until we have everyone here."

I laughed. "Sure, whatever you want."

She wiggled in my lap. "Whatever I want?"

My cock stirred and I tightened my hold on her waist. "We nccd to go downstairs."

"How about you put that tongue to good use..." She moved her hips over me in the most distracting way possible. "And help me understand why I felt an overwhelming amount of dark energy coming from you in the middle of the night."

I felt my shoulders stiffen as I leaned back away from her. She had a patient expression on her face. "Dark energy?"

She nodded, wrapping her arms around my neck. "It woke me up."

"I...I..." I stuttered, feeling like my throat was clogged.

She started to smooth down my hair in a comforting way. "Hey, it's totally fine, I mean when I woke up you were still very much asleep, but..."

"But, what?"

She chewed on her lower lip. "You were radiating this energy, Nick. I felt like it wanted me to address it in some way, get my darkness to combine with it, but I didn't. It kept pushing and I just kept ignoring it. I waited to see if it wanted to hurt you, but it just simmered and then settled, but it didn't leave you. It just stopped trying to get to me."

I leaned forward, placing the top of my head against her chest and letting out breath after breath. That feeling I felt last night was real. And now Dani could feel it too. It *wanted* her to feel it. She wasn't privy to the things my mind liked to conjure up for me to see when I was in my own head and so deep in the past that sometimes I couldn't find my way out.

"Nick, my own darkness wanted to let it in. It felt like it wanted something to latch onto, but I had to pull myself back. I have a hold on my own shadows, but that dark energy you have is tempting, I can't lie."

I lifted my head up, narrowing my eyes at her. "Tempting?"

She nodded. "There was a part of me that wanted to let it in, but I don't know how connected it is to you, or why it's even there. It was so thick I could taste it and it tasted like..." Her eyes softened and she ran her hand through my hair slowly. "Anger and a lot of sadness."

I nearly opened my mouth and told her everything. It all made sense now, if what she was saying was true, I had all but allowed this darkness inside of me. I was aware of my issues and was getting through it the only way I knew how. It only got this bad once we stepped into Purgatory, so once I was back in Heaven's Gate, then I would focus on how to fix this. How to fix myself.

"Why does it want you?" I asked.

She snorted. "Nick, I feed off that shit, darkness knows darkness. It makes sense that it would try to latch onto something as strong as myself. I can't say that I haven't noticed my shadows wanting to gravitate towards you."

"Maybe it's just because you like me so much." I tried to joke, but I couldn't force myself to laugh.

She shoved my shoulder, but her smile didn't quite meet her eyes. "Maybe, but Nick, what's wrong? Is this place too much? Maybe I should just force you to go back to Heaven's Gate."

I grabbed the side of her face, forcing her to look at me. "Uh, no. I'm fine, okay. I knew this place was going to mess with me, it was going to mess with all of us. I'm a big boy, I got this. I'm not going anywhere."

"Always so stubborn. Like come on, Nick, give me more credit. I know you're a big boy, but I'm not a dumb demon."

I sighed softly. "It's nothing."

"Stop lying," she urged. I could hear the desperation in her voice.

"Maybe it is this place, okay. It's just getting to me. I can handle it. I am an angel if you remember correctly."

She placed her hands on my shoulders and started massaging them. "Things like anger are easy to build off of, but when you add emotions like sadness, a kind of heaviness that weighs on you, then it can amplify it, grow so much stronger than you anticipated. Angel or not, darkness doesn't care. Whatever happened to you when you were speaking to Natalia latched on hard and your light tried to help, but that won't always be the case. You have an engrained darkness fighter already inside of you, but while you're here, the shadows.... they reign free and wild and will tear your light apart if you aren't careful."

I was listening to what she was saying, but I didn't know what she wanted me to do. I couldn't fight off something I couldn't see. I didn't know how to eliminate something when I was awake, let alone when I was asleep. "You underestimate how strong the light can be. I think you're worrying about me too much." It was strong enough to shock her back into remembering herself for the most part, which was something she hadn't brought up oddly enough. I hadn't brought it up either, so I just let it be.

"So, you're allowed to fret over me, but I can't give a shit about you?" She raised an eyebrow at me.

"That's not what I'm saying. I think we're here for a reason and it's not to worry about me. I can handle whatever this is, I promise." I tried to sound sincere even though I had no idea if I could. I had been good at telling myself that for a while now and I always felt like I could in fact *handle* it. Once I thought I was in a good place, something would happen that would set me off and cause me to sweat, feel sick, and I would find myself needing to lean against something just to catch my breath. She didn't need to know about that. Despite whatever darkness she felt coming from me, I slept soundly last night. I was grateful for that if nothing else.

"You don't need to handle things by yourself all the time." She slid her thumb over my pulse point on my neck.

My heart stuttered at her words. I wanted us to be open and honest from now on, but I couldn't do *this*. I couldn't explain myself right now. I grabbed her and flipped us over, so I had her pinned on her back as I hovered over her. "I know that. And I appreciate you caring so much, but like I keep saying I'm fine. I don't know what more you want me to say." I took both her wrists in my hands and pinned them above her head. The dynamic was odd, seeing as she was fully clothed, and I was completely naked.

"I just don't like you having this darkness looming over you or inside of you."

I leaned in towards her face. "Even I can admit that everyone has a small piece of darkness in them, this is no different."

She tried to buck me off of her but to no avail. "This is true, but yours is attaching itself to you because you're letting it. The shadows don't just secure themselves onto nothing, that's no fun."

"Dani, can you not just trust that I have this under control," I placed my face into the crook of her neck and planted a kiss on her skin. Her body tensed when my lips touched that place on her neck that she loved. "You need to focus on not letting Lilith get inside *your* head, okay." I kissed her collarbone that was exposed by the halter top she wore.

Her voice was a bit strained when she spoke. "I know that, you idiot. I just don't want that darkness to burn you out." She wanted me to speak my truth, but I didn't know what exactly speaking my truth sounded like. And I really didn't want to know what it looked like.

I raised my head and released one of her wrists, sliding my hand down her side. "It won't burn out. I have to be your night light, remember?" I kissed her jaw as I guided my hand up her inner thigh, the fabric of her pants tight against her legs.

"Are you trying to seduce me into not talking about this anymore?"

I brought my hand up to the button of her pants and flicked it open, pulling the zipper down. "That depends, is it working?"

She arched her lower body up. "I thought you wanted us to go downstairs."

I tucked my fingers into her pants and under her panties, feeling the heat of her. "Maybe in a few minutes." She giggled for a moment, before she sucked in a breath when my fingers grazed her clit.

"Nick." She moaned against me as I rubbed that sensitive part of her, dipping my hand a bit lower to feel how wet she was getting. My cock started to harden at the thought of being inside of her again, just forgetting about this whole conversation and getting back to something that made us both extremely happy.

I still had one of her wrists pinned but she used her free hand to start to try to pull down her pants, her eagerness almost laughable.

Knock. Knock.

We both stopped, looking over to the door. Our breathing started to match each other's as I slowly took my hand out of her pants. Dani looked at me, pouting as I started to lift myself off of her, sitting back on my heels.

"If you two could finish fucking, so we can get this fucking day started already that would be fantastic. I won't lose time because you're too horny to function," Elise said, giving the door two more good threatening knocks before walking away.

"I'm not afraid of her wrath, so we could still..." Dani wrapped her hand around my cock, sliding it back and forth, flicking her thumb over the tip. I grabbed her wrist and lightly pushed her off, shaking my head with a smirk. I got off the bed and started picking up my clothes from the floor, quickly putting on each piece as I found them.

"You might not be afraid, but I still am, slightly," I admitted, which awarded me a laugh that showed all of her teeth.

She zipped up her pants and hopped off the bed. I tried to walk past her towards the door, but she placed her hand on my chest stopping me. As short as she was, her stare could be so intense it was like she was seven feet tall. "You are quite the distraction, but don't think that neck kisses and skilled fingers can make me forget things, Nicholas. I didn't want you to push me, so I won't push you. You have to know though; you will have to open your fucking mouth sooner rather than later before you let whatever it is consume you." I blinked down at her and nodded. I reached up and tucked a piece of her hair behind her ear, watching as she molded her cheek into my touch. "I'm willing to let you in, so let me in as well."

"So, he has a meeting with Lilith tonight?" Reese asked, turning the dining room chair around and sitting down with his legs on either side of it.

Dani had reiterated her entire interaction with Dimitri, save for the details about his flirtation with her. Dimitri was a social climber even though he was at what already seemed like a high enough tier. He wanted more and Lilith had offered him just that. It was the same with the Enchanters and how they decided to put their trust in her over everything they'd known. She made compelling arguments that hit the spot for whoever it was targeted at.

Dani nodded, having perched herself on top of the table. I'd sat down in the chair next to her, our fingers mindlessly intertwining as she swung her legs back and forth.

"You can't be that stupid. Do you actually trust Dimitri?" Elise barked from across the table. She had already made her case that she had nothing to do with the plan to bombard Heaven's Gate. Lilith had used Elise and Dimitri separately, the only thing they had in common was Dani. Beetee came around the corner carrying a tray of food, her strapless bright orange sundress swishing around her knees.

Dani looked over her shoulder. "I don't. But he is a lot more amicable with her than we are right now."

"Natalia had mentioned most of these obstacles are distractions, even Isabel is a distraction. She's meant to get a rise out of us, watch us, and antagonize the fuck out of us…" I started.

Dani cut in. "She couldn't fulfill one of her purposes which was to try to fix the voided demons, so since we've all come back, she's doing whatever else she's good for, while Lilith lets her experiments run free. She is still strong with all the powers she's consumed so there isn't a point in thinking she isn't useful."

Reese rubbed his fingers between his eyebrows. "And all these voided demons, the hellhounds, just everything has been one big joke?"

Elise hummed. "Not a joke but think like one big shitty present. But the present isn't meant for any of us." She narrowed her eyes at Dani, who didn't look back at her.

"You said Dimitri also knew that Lilith was in your head. She seems to be in your head at every single fight," Reese pointed out.

"I can handle it."

Reese blew out a breath. "Oh yeah, you were handling it alright when you strung Yuri up to that tree, right?"

I flicked my eyes over to my best friend. "Do you *have* to bring up old shit? That doesn't really help us right now."

Reese rolled his eyes and leaned his chest into the back of his chair. "Ugh, fine. But I'm not wrong when I say that her connection with Lilith is only going to get worse. I'm not saying it to be an asshole, I'm saying it because it's the truth. It looks to me like she's just going to sit back and watch you destroy everything around you."

"Well damn. Blondie actually said something useful this time." Elise slapped the table with her palm. Beetee pulled out the chair next to her and sat down. Leah and Garrett bounded down the stairs turning the corner, giving us a small wave before they entered the room.

"I heard you all had an eventful time at Leviathan," Garrett said, crossing his arms over his chest.

I laughed a little. "Uh, yeah, it was eye opening."

"And the son who owns it now, he's exactly what I presume he would be?" The male Enchanter inquired.

Dani side eyed me and leaned back on her hands. I cleared my throat. "I think he was probably everything you assumed he'd to be."

Leah's long dark brown hair was parted down the middle and placed in two braids on the sides of her head. She tucked some stray pieces behind her ear. "Are you any closer to figuring out your next move?"

"Well, that's up to Dani, now isn't it," Reese said, drumming his fingers along the edge of the table. She stuck her tongue in her cheek, clearly annoyed with him.

Beetee rapped her knuckles on the table loudly to get our attention. We all turned to look at her and her cheeks seemed to redden with all the eyes on her. "What Dimitri said to you about the freedom of choice, that does have some merit. She knows this place has a hold on you and every time you fight and draw blood; she is wrapping herself around your soul little by little. What was that line he said to you again?"

Dani sighed, wrapping her fingers around mine. "She couldn't force me to do something when I was allowed the choice, so she's going to give me no choice." But what the fuck does that really mean." She sounded like she was trying to play off her worries. I saw the little lines form on her forehead from thought and concern.

Leah walked over to Dani, placing a hand on her knee. "It means that in the end you will choose her at least from where she stands, that's how she sees things."

"But that's not going to happen," I blurted out.

Dani gave me a small smile. "I mean I don't plan on it."

"It is a possibility," Beetee whispered, trying to remain as quiet as possible with her opinion.

"And here I thought you were all sunshine and rainbow reptiles." Reese wagged his finger at her.

Garrett rubbed his hands together before clasping them together tightly.

"I do think you need to decide on when to infiltrate. I do remember a few doorways to her castle, but we would need to discuss timing and strategy."

"I'm honestly with the big man over here. We go all in, maybe an ambush is just what she needs. I know what we said before, but this is fucking ridiculous. Dimitri did say that Lilith saw you as a weapon and still does, well then be the kind of weapon *you* want to be and let's fuck her up." Elise had this murderous look of intrigue in her eyes.

I had to be the voice of reason in this. "Won't being closer in proximity make their connection even stronger? Fuck with her even more. The woman already wants to pull her deeper in a dark hole, I just don't want to make it worse."

Leah hummed in thought. "This is true, but everyone in this room has taken a risk of some sort one way or another. And waiting longer could also have harsh consequences."

"You're asking her to risk her fucking mind for the sake of an instant kill, a fucking sneak attack," I argued, getting up from my chair.

"It's not like we're asking her to go alone, Nick. We also risked shit to be right here in Purgatory. I'm not going to continue to fight distractions and misdirections," Reese spat back.

Garrett let out a long sigh. "It's all our fight, but it is mainly yours, Soul Seether. Lilith is the reason everything happened near our home that day. I want to play a part in her demise."

Dani sat and listened to us talk around her, but she didn't say anything. She simply nodded and took it all in. She swallowed and removed her hand from mine, running it through her curls. "I want her demise as well, but I want to know my risk is worth it, so that's why I want to know what Lilith speaks to Dimitri about."

"Are you sure you don't just want to spend time with him again?" Reese insinuated.

"Reese, shut up." I gave him a pointed look and he shrugged rolling his eyes.

Dani gave him her middle finger. "No, I would prefer not to, but he wants me to come back and speak with him about it. He wants to let me in on what she has to say, so maybe it will help, maybe it won't, but it'll be information we didn't have. Then I'll decide how we move."

Leah looked at Garrett who placed his hand on her lower back. The male Enchanter looked at Dani with his golden eyes. "We won't wait forever for you to decide but we can give you that. As much as you don't want to right now, Lilith will make a choice for you if you don't."

"Same goes for me," Elise announced, getting a slap on the back of her head from Beetee. "*What?* I want to see that bitch bleed. Or Dani can take care of Lilith and I can have oh so much fun with Isabel. Fun that will last hours and hours and my ears will be filled with her pretty little screams."

"There is something severely wrong with you," Reese acknowledged, raising one of his blonde eyebrows.

I shook my head and focused on Dani. "So, when are we leaving tomorrow?"

She jumped off the table and patted my chest. "I'm leaving pretty late. You are staying here."

"I'm sorry?"

"You heard me." She pushed her hair over her shoulder and moved to walk out of the room.

Leah and Garrett stepped out of her way, while Reese and Elise both followed after me as I was right on her tail. I heard Beetee mutter *oh boy* under her breath.

I caught her arm, twirling her around. "You aren't going by yourself."

"Do you plan to stop me, Nicholas?" I couldn't tell if she was joking or not. Her face was leaning more towards the latter.

"I will if I have to."

Elise busted out laughing. "Good luck with that. You haven't hypnotized her with your dick well enough to get her to do what you say, pretty boy." I gave her a look that said, now was not the time.

"It almost sounds like you *want* to go alone." Reese stuck his hands in his pants pockets.

"Excuse me?" Dani asked, her brown eyes narrowing.

"Last time we saw you with the guy you were all on his lap, so I would be a little concerned too with you wanting to spend alone time with him."

"Reese, just stay out of it," I pleaded, trying to step in front of him so I could just talk to Dani. He knew a good chunk of how I felt about her, so I didn't know why he was pushing. Or maybe knowing my feelings *was* the reason.

"Did he tell you to come alone or something?" I asked, trying to make sense of her decision.

"No, he didn't, but he could sense you last time and I need him focused on explaining everything to me, not to throw digs at you and make himself seem better." Dani answered before looking back at Reese, knocking her shoulder into my bicep. "And I don't *want* to do this, I *have* to. I made that clear."

"And that's all fine and dandy and I can understand letting us stay here—" He pointed between Elise and himself. "But you really plan to keep my best friend in your bed all night and then go running off behind closed doors with one of your special friends?" Reese made air quotes around his last two words.

"Reese, I mean it, fucking stop." I was about to shove him into the other room and shut him up myself, but I could see Dani out of the corner of my eye and it didn't seem like she needed my help with this.

She had smoke tendrils coming off of her hair as she gave him a shove, making him teeter back for a moment. "What I do and who I do in my bed is none of your fucking business, but if you must know, yes, I did have insanely mind-altering sex with your best friend last night and yes, I've also had sex with Dimitri, which now having fucked Nicholas, I know was mediocre at best."

Elise glanced over at me mouthing *good job*. I scrubbed a hand down my face, realizing now that I should have just waited to speak to her in her room.

Dani pointed her finger at Reese's chest, pushing it right into his sternum. "I can do what needs to be done without letting my past get in the way. Dimitri can make all the passes he wants but I know how to say no. The fact that you think I can't do that is insulting and makes me want to slit your fucking throat, but luckily, I'm nice so I won't do that. I don't need to be babysat by either one of you and I'm going whether you like it or not." Reese pushed her finger away, but he definitely noticed the smoke coming from her. Elise shooed Beetee away, silently telling her not to interfere.

"Dani..." I started, but she put her hand up as if shushing me and turned to make her way to the stairs. I let out a sigh as I used my hand to push back my hair, feeling exhaustion wash over me. I gave Reese a hard look which he eventually acknowledged.

"What?" he asked dumbly.

"Seriously? You really don't know what you fucking did."

"I just said what needed to be said."

I shook my head at him, prepared to pull my own hair out. "No, no, you didn't. I wasn't thinking that at all. That's you. I likely could have gotten her to side with me or at least be willing to consider the options, but you had to open your mouth and just speak your mind, when no one fucking asked."

Elise clucked tongue. "Word of advice. If you are trying to get a girl to hear you out, try not to underhandedly call her a whore. Not a good look."

Reese closed his eyes, but there was no real tension in his body, it was like he was deliberating with himself on what to say next. He'd been doing shit like this since we were younger. Opening his mouth and speaking the first thing he thought, but once he really thought about it, he'd regret it. I don't think he ever considered a day when he might not be able to make up for his opinionated tongue. I stepped up closer to him, letting my voice be a whisper.

"You need to go upstairs and talk to her. Everything that will go on after her talk with Dimitri will go to shit if you guys are at different sides. I care about her, alright, more than I think I can comprehend. If you care about me, you'll go up those stairs and you'll fix this. Dimitri is yet another person who basically used her, lied to her and you think she's forgotten that. Give her more fucking credit. I've given you passes over and over again Reese, and I just can't do that anymore." I stepped back and watched as his hazel eyes bore into my brown ones.

I saw the same eyes that I'd seen my entire life. The eyes of someone who cared immensely for me and knew when I wasn't kidding. His eyes softened a bit as he nodded once and ran a hand through his long hair. He was never one to cave so easily but when our friendship was on the line, my faith in him, then he clearly thought twice. I didn't like this divide between my friendship with Reese and whatever this was with Dani. He could keep whatever hostile shit he had going on with Elise, but I didn't want that for him and Dani. They didn't need to be best buddies, but I didn't want to feel any underlying tension between them anymore.

"Both of you have done so much groveling while you're here. I love seeing men admit they're fucking idiots." Elise smiled over to Beetee who just huffed, but she smiled back. Reese gave her fake smile filled with disdain and started to head up the stairs.

"Hey Reese," I said, gaining his attention again. "You say something to insinuate anything like that about her again and we're going to have a serious problem."

He stared at me and muttered, "yeah," before making his way further up the stairs.

I walked over to the arm of the couch and sat down on it. "If she really wants to go by herself, then that's fine. I just don't want her to, I just...." I trailed off, speaking more to myself as if I needed to convince my own brain that it was the truth.

Beetee came over and placed her small hand on my shoulder. "We know, Nicholas. If you thought you were hiding your feelings, well, I'd think again."

18
DANI

I heard pacing outside my door. I waited, hands on my hips and a need to cause pain boiling right at the surface. The shuffling of feet had never annoyed me as much as it did right now. I wanted to remove those feet and string them up on a very, very tall tree. I felt my fingertips buzzing, the shadows blaring and alarming me that something had to be done about the disrespect and simple lack of self-awareness.

Knock, knock.

I tilted my head back to look at the ceiling, willing myself to get my emotions in check. I was in no mood to see his face or hear his voice, but I wasn't totally unreasonable. I walked over to the door and yanked it open, startling the big, mouthed blonde on the other side. I made sure to give him a disinterested expression as he looked down the hall towards the stairs and then back to me.

"I was told I needed to come and talk to you."

I let my mouth drop open in disbelief. "Wow. Should I be honored by your presence or something? Are you going to tell me someone told you to say that you're sorry as well?"

His lack of words told me all that I needed to know. "Yeah, get the fuck away from my door." I went to close it in his face, but he caught the door before it closed completely and shoved it open. I let out a frustrated sigh and turned my back to him. I heard him close the door before I peeked behind me slightly to see him leaning back against it.

"I should have chosen my words better, alright. I shouldn't have made it sound like you were…"

"A demon who spreads her legs for any dick that shows interest in her?" I offered, turning all the way around to look at him.

He groaned. "Yeah that. I know this is going to sound shitty, but you are confusing as hell."

"Me?" I questioned, pointing to myself.

"Yes, you. One minute you're grinding up on Nick, the next you're straddling your demon ex-boyfriend, which he nearly popped a blood vessel over and then you're spending the entire night with Nick like it didn't happen. Now all of sudden you want to go it alone and have one-on-one time with your ex again, I just don't get it." He threw up his hands as if to say he knew I might get upset, but those were his points, and he was sticking by them. When he laid it out the way he did, it didn't sound the greatest, but what I did and how I moved wasn't really his business.

"How I handled the Dimitri situation wasn't perfect, I'll admit it, but Nick and I have already moved past it, so I suggest you do as well. I don't care if you do because, guess what, it doesn't involve you."

He ran his hands through his hair, pulling at some of the pieces. "Not literally, but in some ways it does, because you weren't next to him while he watched you, Dani. I've never seen him look so fucking angry."

I pointed towards the door. "Then go talk to him about that! I'm not trying to hide anything by going to see Dimitri alone, I'm trying to not cause problems by letting you all stay here and be safe. *I'm* not the problem!"

"But you're *his* problem!" Reese shouted, mimicking my movements, and pointing to the door as well. I stood my ground, but I blinked up at him, letting his words sink in. "You think it's cute and probably fiery to see him riled up about you, but from where he stands it's not fucking fun."

"I didn't ask for that."

Reese let out an incredulous laugh. "You didn't have to. Fuck, Dani, Nick will chase you, he will fight, and he will damn near bite his tongue to hold onto you. I need to understand that you deserve even an ounce of that effort from him."

I shook my head, walking over to the dresser and tapping my fingers along the edge. "Why are you so affected by this, by how Nick feels? From where I'm standing it almost sounds like you're in love with him, which wouldn't surprise me since you're practically on his dick all the time."

"Woah, what?"

I leaned against the dresser, crossing my arms over my chest. "I didn't stutter."

"You think because I care about him, that that must mean I'm in love with him?"

"No, Reese. You can care. Of course, you can care. It's the level of caring that's throwing me back. It's the amount of energy you're putting into fighting his battles for him when I'm pretty sure he didn't ask you to."

He pinched the bridge of his nose, taking in one long breath after another. "Nick doesn't have to ask for me to come to his defense. I just will. That doesn't mean I'm in love with him. I love Nick but not like that."

I tilted my head to the side, examining him.

Reese let out a laugh that wasn't meant to have any humor to it. "You know that guy threw me against a wall and got in my face because of something I said about you a few days ago. He didn't know if you two would figure your shit out, but his first instinct was to protect your honor even though I can admit that you don't need someone doing that for you. That's who Nick is. He was on your side, and you weren't even aware."

"So, you think I'm not on Nick's side? You think I'm not team Nick right now?"

"I don't know, maybe!"

"I told him that night that I didn't plan for anything more to happen with Dimitri. He was well aware of that. He was satisfied with the response he got from me, what more is there to say." I raised my eyebrows.

Reese took a few steps towards me. "You want to know why he would cave though, Dani? Why he would make it seem like everything is fine and forgotten?" His hazel eyes looked around my face. "He wants you to be happy, he wants to be in your good graces like fuck, he wants *you*. You can make a million and one mistakes now and guess what? He'll still be there."

"I. Didn't. Ask. Him. To. Do. That." I found myself repeating. My cheeks were turning hot from my temper starting to flare. I wasn't aware that I had to play all my cards, that we needed to feel things at the same time, at the same pace. In the beginning Nick was so fucking closed off and careful about the way he felt and how he moved, how he flirted. Eventually piece by piece, it started to fall away and after the night at this father's house I could sense a small shift. I could feel myself shifting as well and that was scary enough in itself that I didn't know what it would mean when we both found solid ground to meet on, when the cards were no longer near our chests but laid out completely on the table.

"How many times do I have to explain this? You don't have to! I've made so many stupid fucking mistakes growing up with him and somehow, he's still right here, letting me tag along, pulling me out of the dumb situations I get us in and forgiving me when I probably don't deserve it, but that's literally just Nick. His commitment is overwhelming. I don't understand his loyalty to me, let alone his newfound loyalty to you." His hazel eyes looked around my face as if he was searching for some sort of recognition that what he was saying sounded familiar to me. It didn't surprise me when I really thought about it.

I let out a breath, followed by a sigh. I walked over to the bed, sitting down so that my back was propped up against the headboard and I bent one of my legs so I could rest my foot on top of the comforter while my other leg dangled off of the side. "You want to talk about overwhelming, Reese. It's a lot to hear you say that he's so committed to me when we have yet to break real ground on whatever this is between us. I only know so much about Nick, so you have the upper hand when it comes to the way he moves and acts. It's not fair to think that I'll automatically fall in line and swoon so openly just because he has his own way of doing things. I have my own way as well and he and I will figure that out. He's a grown man and if he's making a mistake with me then so be it, lesson learned." I realized he hadn't turned around to face me. His body was still, except for the way his shoulders moved to tell me that he was breathing. He tucked a piece of his hair behind his ear and slowly turned around. Reese walked the few steps it took with his long legs over to the bed and sat down.

He spread his legs a bit and placed his hands on his thighs, staring at the floor. It wasn't an awkward silence, but it was the type of silence where the earlier tension was getting released and now maybe there could be a mutual understanding on the horizon. He gripped the back of his neck, swallowing.

"I guess being in Purgatory and not really needing anyone but yourself makes sense. That's not really how it worked for me, okay. His commitment, loyalty, friendship, all of the above was something I clung to as a fucking kid." He wasn't looking at me yet, he was still staring right at the floor as if it was easier to speak to wooden planks. He took one big deep breath in and then one long exhale. "You remember me telling you that my parents weren't the greatest. That they were very this is how it is and how it will be kind of attitudes toward everything, especially demons and anything not in the Heaven's Gate bubble?"

247

"Yeah."

"I'm self-aware enough to know that some of that stuck with me, but in case you couldn't already put it together they weren't the best people to be around. They uh…they lost someone, a family member in that whole battle in Oculus and they were never the same after that. They were on Jonah's dads' side of the whole thing, and they stuck with him until they got pregnant with me and decided it would be better to live in one of the villages. I almost kind of think that if they hadn't had me, they would have still been by Isaac Zuriel's side, but regardless that's how I crossed paths with Nick and I learned pretty quickly that my parents were not a fan of Maurice Cassial. They called him a traitor behind his back, which I never told Maurice about, but I think he always knew that they gave him a weird cold shoulder." He shook his head, and I remained quiet as I let him continue to speak. "I found myself watching Nick and his dad, their dynamic when they were out, and I wanted that. My parents tried, but it was so fucking forced that it was nauseating. One day out of nowhere Maurice caught me watching them and I guess asked Nick to invite me over to their house, which I had to lie to my parents so I could go, and well let's just say that was the start of everything."

I found myself smiling just a little at their origin story. I felt a small tug in my chest for younger Reese and the lack of affection he got. I could relate, even though Lilith had her ways of showing affection, it was obviously very different from how Maurice was with his son. I had witnessed it myself and I had felt it secondhand with the way his father hugged me. I still didn't understand something though. "Reese, what does this have to do with your obsession with Nick's happiness? Your need to butt in and make your opinions known when they are definitely not warranted."

He finally looked at me with a hardness in his eyes that had my spine straightening. I could tell that whatever he was about to say was meant for me to hear and pay attention to. "Nick has been that one constant in my life. Girls come and go and, fuck, my family is a total mess so I've had him to lean on for longer than I can remember. The first time I ever really spent time with him, his dad made us food, we fought outside, and he even offered to let me sleep over. I actually got him to sneak out of his house and fly around with me in the middle of the night. Which ended up with me getting caught in tree branches and then he also got caught in tree branches trying to help me, which was followed by us both falling and having to walk back with way too many cuts and bruises, but that night I figured hey, this is probably going to be my best friend. He's somehow given me everything I've wanted, a new kind of family, a brother, freedom of choice and a place to fucking breathe…and in exchange, I guess I just silently decided that he deserved the world for making mine better."

I blinked a few times, his eyes never leaving mine. It was as if he was waiting for me to say something to his bomb of emotional vulnerability. "And I just went and curved your plan to keep his life on the up and up."

"You could put it like that, sure."

"I'm not trying to fuck up his life, Reese. I can promise you that. My shit is already fucked up as it is, I wouldn't want to bestow that on anyone else." I snorted.

He nodded, more to himself than to me. "Do I wish that you weren't Purgatory's little hybrid princess, yes, but do I know how he feels about you and want you to feel the same way so that he can be ethereally happy…also yes."

"You do love him, don't you." It wasn't a question; it was just a rhetorical statement that I needed to say out loud for some reason. He didn't respond, but his expression told me all I needed to know. Oddly enough, I understood him wanting Nick to be ethereally happy because I was realizing that I wanted that too. "Do your parents even bother to check on you, I mean I assume you've been staying with Nick the whole time before we met back up."

He scoffed. "Yeah…I went back home once, got grilled like a motherfucker and stormed out. Listen, it's not worth it getting into my issues with them and their issues with the past."

"Case closed," I agreed, squinting up at him. "I don't plan to do anything but talk with Dimitri. Nick's feelings are safe with me."

Reese's eyebrow quirked up. "So, he can go with you?"

I groaned. "Why is that *so* important?"

The blonde angel chuckled. "Importance isn't the issue. I think he knows you can run shit by yourself Dani, I'm pretty sure that's why he likes you, but you don't *have* to. From what you've said Dimitri knows Nick exists, so just let him exist next to you."

That reminded me of what I'd said to my raven-haired angel before we left my room this morning. *I'm willing to let you in, so let me in as well.* I hated admitting it, but I did kind of like the fact that he wanted to be there with me when I spoke to Dimitri, even if I likely wouldn't let him do any talking. I was willing to let him in, I was honest about that and maybe I had to give a little for him to do what I asked. This could be my way of doing just that.

"You're a good friend, Reese," I complimented, gaining a smile in my direction.

"Thanks, let's hope he still thinks so when we go back downstairs."

"I'll make sure he knows." I winked at him, pushing up off the bed.

I heard Reese clear his throat. I turned my head, just to watch his eyes narrow for a moment. "Can I ask you one thing?"

I shrugged and nodded. He stuck his tongue out and licked his lips. "Do you care about him? And I mean really care, Dani."

I pressed my lips together and maintained eye contact with him. I didn't want him to see how nervous I had just gotten. I had told Nick that I cared about him, but that was before we had gotten together again before he had cuddled me against his chest and told me he had feelings before I started to have real feelings too. Bringing him with me to Leviathan, no Reese, no Elise, would be like a calling card that we were together in Dimitri's eyes, and I didn't know how I felt about that; especially since I had played it off like we weren't much to each other. It actually kind of stung my own chest remembering how Dimitri had asked me if he was the person in my bed, and I had acted like it wasn't true. Nick was exactly who I wanted in my bed, and I had him there…and that's where I wanted him to stay. I cared, but now I cared more than before and just like Nick I didn't know how to put that kind of caring, that kind of feeling into words to say to his face.

One corner of my lips tilted up as I answered him. "Yes."

Reese gave me a genuine smile. "Good. Umm, I have a feeling you've noticed that he's been off lately. I haven't wanted to push him because Nick will just retreat further if you do. He says it's not because of you and maybe it's not, but since I have a feeling he'll be sleeping in here more often, can you…watch him?" His eyes glazed over with concern, and I knew that concern well enough. That dark energy Nick played off like he was well aware it was there but didn't mind it. It wasn't like the darkness that had bonded with me, that wrapped around me like we had one soul. It was the kind that infiltrated, hooking its debilitating claws into someone that was susceptible to it. I knew that what happened at The Skies would be hard on them, but maybe I underestimated how much of a mental wound it had left. A wound that was left to fester and now entertain a dark infection.

I couldn't make him talk to me about it, but I could be there for him whenever he was ready. I just hoped it would be sooner rather than later. That kind of energy was way too tempting for even me to resist for long, even if it was a total coward and only slipped in when he was asleep or incapacitated. I didn't want to be the reason he went under completely and couldn't find his way back out.

"Yeah, I can do that," I told Reese, silently promising myself that I would do whatever it took to help.

Reese stuck his hand out towards me, the sleeve of his jacket pulling away from his wrist as he wiggled his fingers. "Then I think this might be the start of a damn good friendship." I took his hand without hesitation and shook it. I held on a little longer and squeezed causing him to contort his face into a look of slight pain. He pulled his hand away, shaking it back and forth.

I giggled. "Yes, yes. Friendship. Be aware though, you insult me again and you'll lose that hand."

Nick looked very, very distraught as both Reese and I came down the stairs. Reese was ahead of me, and he headed straight for his best friend when he made it to the last step. Nick opened his mouth to speak, but Reese laid a hand on his shoulder and leaned in, whispering something in his ear. It took less than a second for Nick to look at Reese and give him a small smile of content and relief. Reese stuck his hand out and Nick willingly grasped it, squeezing and patting him on the shoulder. I didn't know what Reese had said to him, but it was enough to put his tension at ease. Reese collapsed on the couch, winking at me before he got himself completely settled.

"Did Blondie learn his lesson?" Elise asked, pointing her chin over to Reese.

"I think we both learned something," I answered, winking back at him and walking over to Nick.

Elise looked from Reese to me, her face scrunching up into a disgusted look. "Ugh, don't tell me you two are friends now."

"Aw, are you jealous she might like me more than you?" Reese taunted, hanging his arm over the back of the couch to look at her.

She gave him her middle finger. "Not in the slightest. Don't get your hopes up."

I ignored them both and settled myself in front of Nick, nudging his legs apart so I could scooch in between them. I poked my tongue out between my teeth and felt his hands take hold of my waist. "You still want to go with me tomorrow?"

He hesitated for a moment. "If that's what you want."

"That's not what I asked. I asked you if you wanted to go with me tomorrow?" I made my voice stern and obvious that I wanted him to tell me what he wanted rather than just submit whenever he felt like he might push me away.

He squeezed my sides a bit and squinted up at me from where he sat on the arm of the couch. "I would."

I pushed away from him and smiled, nodding towards the stairs. "Follow me."

Nick looked behind him at Reese, who just shook his head and then at Elise who was severely more interested in her nail beds than us. He settled his eyes on me, a bit stunned. "I'm confused, you made it really clear that..."

I let out an obnoxious sigh that interrupted him. "Are you following me or not, Nicholas?" I didn't give him much time to answer before I started walking backwards towards the staircase, eventually turning away from him. He was right on my heels before I could even take another breath. I pushed open my door and walked inside, allowing him to close it the minute he stepped in after me. Once I heard the click, alerting me that the door had closed completely, my pulse started to speed up.

"Dani..." He started to say but was silenced when I turned around and quickly hustled over to him, jumping up into his arms. He caught me easily, wobbling a bit at my surprise attack, but he placed his hands firmly under my ass, holding me to him. I pressed my lips to his in a fierce kiss. He didn't hesitate to reciprocate my aggression and flicked his tongue against my own. He brought his head back, catching his breath.

There were many things I wanted to tell him, but none of it seemed like the right time. I could have convinced myself I was just putting it off, but I didn't want to ponder on that right now. He backed up against the door as I threaded my fingers into his mess of dark hair. "You threw Reese against a wall because of me?"

His brow furrowed for a minute as if he was trying to figure out how I knew that. "He told you?"

"Mmhmm, among other things, but the idea of you willing to fight your best friend just to defend my honor has me a little turned on."

He pulled me against him harder, lifting me up a little and readjusting how he held me. "Just a little."

"You let me do the talking at Leviathan, alright." I kissed his nose, trailing my lips to his cheek and towards his ear.

"And what would you like me to do, hmm?"

"Be there with me and exude that alpha angel energy I know you have," I said with a smile on my face even though he couldn't see it from how I was angled. I let my lips brush the shell of his ear, letting Reese's words run through me. "Exist with me, next to me."

He turned his head, catching my lips with his mouth, a soft groan leaving his throat. He walked us towards my bed, letting go of me so that I fell with a soft thud on the comforter. I took off my shirt as he unbuttoned his pants, getting up on my knees to pull his shirt up and rip it off his body. I reached for my pants and started tugging them down my legs, laughing when he grabbed my thighs, tilting me backwards so that I fell onto my back. He tore them the rest of the way down my legs and threw them on the floor, doing the same thing with my panties. I sprang back up, grabbing his face and kissing him, pulling him down to my level. There was this fire whenever we were together that nearly burned me, it was an inferno. I would happily burn over and over again just to feel like this with him. Lilith and Dimitri and all the problems that plagued us didn't matter; they weren't welcomed here.

I hooked my leg around his body and started to turn him so that he could lay down on the bed. He clung onto my waist, getting me to straddle him in one smooth motion. I fingered the waistband of his underwear, dragging them down towards his knees. I brought my body up so I could hover over him. I felt his breath on me, and his heartbeat was thunderous and pumping with needy anticipation. I kissed him softly, feeling him buck up and slide his cock against where I was wet and ready. I traced my index finger along his jaw as he looked up at me with this adorable expression of pure…something. I didn't know what it was because it felt like so much more than adoration.

I rubbed my nose over his, letting out a breath. "You're mine."

"Territorial, are we?"

I chuckled, snapping my teeth at his jawline. "You're one to talk."

He slid his hand up my thigh and let his thumb rub over my clit, eliciting a moan from my lips. "I never said I didn't like it. I'm all yours."

"Good." I swayed back and forth over his cock, teasing him as I watched his eyes close while he felt me rub myself all over him. He sat up so that we were parallel to each other, and he captured my lips, causing me to wrap my arms around his neck for leverage. He broke our kiss to look down, seeing me grind myself against him, needing that friction. He licked his lips, a deep chuckle coming from his chest, vibrating against my own.

"So, put me inside of you and ride what's yours, needy one."

19

NICK

I hadn't realized I had bitten down on my tongue so hard until I started to taste blood. I had been hanging out near the front door of the hostel, ready to leave when Dani yet again decided to blindside me with a dress that fit her in all the right places. It was as simple as her first dress, but this one was tighter, and the neckline was deeper. It was black with ruched fabric that hugged her body and skinny straps that sat nicely over her collarbones. She played with the frill hem as she made it down the last step, her heels clicking on the wood.

Elise whistled. "Oh shit, Nicholas. Hold onto her for dear life in that dress."

I rolled my eyes, noticing Beetee setting up some items in the little lounge area. "What are you doing over there?"

She snorted. "While you two are gone, I have to make it civil around here since you're leaving me with these two. I have some very friendly card games for us to play. Leah and Garrett agreed to help me entertain." Leah had mentioned to me when she had been glamouring my angelic aura that she had missed Beetee a lot and wanted to spend more time with her. Whether she wanted to have that time split with Reese and Elise was an entirely different story.

"Entertain? Beetee, I am perfectly fine entertaining myself. And that does not involve spending any more time with this one than is required of me." Elise stuck her finger in her mouth and pretended to gag.

Beetee tucked a lock of her hot pink hair behind her ear. "Just indulge me, please, you big grump."

"Yeah, you big grump, indulge your cute reptilian friend," Reese mocked, faking pouting over at Elise.

Elise nearly had steam coming from her nostrils. Axel, who I assume had been dozing off on the couch, jumped up and propped his front paws along the back of the couch, resting his head between his large paws and staring at his owner. "Removing some dead weight from this team is looking so fucking good right now, I swear."

"Just behave, okay." I looked at Reese when he placed his hand on his chest, as if he was offended that I would have even considered him to be an issue.

"Who me? I'm going to be a literal angel." He batted his eyelashes innocently. Reese looked over to Dani, nodding at her as if they both had some kind of friendly understanding. He clapped me on the back. "Go show that Dimitri who has the bigger dick."

"Oh my god. Let's go." Dani grabbed my hand, quickly waved at everyone and dragged me out the door.

We made it past the red lit pathway and a few feet from the club without any mishaps. Without the awareness I had to have with Reese at my side, I could really focus on what was around me. It was the same as before, the taverns, the smell, the creatures, but I now really saw the way there were zero fucks given. There were more people who were dry humping against buildings and louder, wilder laughter inside the taverns with the fully open exterior windows. The smells were more intense this time around and it was heady. I felt almost intoxicated by it, like I could get drunk off of it. There was a weird feeling I got that eyes were on us. Not in Devil's Playground exactly, but outside of this district of Purgatory, where the trees loomed around us in their frozen state.

"Try to keep your angelic magic in check okay. If you're going to have a pissing contest with Dimitri, I guarantee he would rather have a drinking contest than a fight," Dani said, walking slightly ahead of me.

"Don't worry, I'm focused. I don't plan to get distracted. Especially not by him."

"Oh." She turned around, placing her hand on my chest and looking up at me. "So, I'm not a distraction, Nicholas."

I laughed. "That's not fair." She was so much more than just a distraction.

She hummed, squinting her eyes at me playfully, but then continued to walk ahead. "Focus is good, but if you're too focused, you'll end up looking like a fucking bodyguard, like Zane of all people. Great guy, but he needs to get out more. I thought everything that we did last night would have relaxed you, but maybe I shouldn't have gone as easy on you when you said you were tired." She snuck a look over her shoulder and I smirked at her. Tired and relaxed were two feelings I did feel, but not together. I woke up this morning, spooning her, after a night that had my limbs still in agony.

She brought me back to the present as she continued speaking as we got up to the club doors. I started to reach around her so that I could open the door for her, but she stopped me. I looked down at her as she gave me a purposeful look. The lighting above her made her glow even if ideally it wasn't the best lighting generally. "I get it, Dani. Be more relaxed. Don't role-play a bodyguard." Her eyes sparkled with intrigue. "Hmm, I'll keep that whole role-play idea in mind, but I mean it Nick. Relax and let me do the talking."

———✝———

The lights flickered and flashed back and forth, moving between shades of red and dark orange. It was everything I remembered but being here without Reese and Elise let me breathe. I wasn't breathing *too* easily though since I was still here with the only girl who had ever made the oxygen stop running to my brain. She moved through the club in this way that had me watching her every move and wanting to follow her like a damn puppy. There was an entirely different part of me that wanted to take her in front of all these demons and stake a claim that I didn't even know if I deserved, a claim I didn't understand.

I moved around a demon girl with scales down her arms and ran right into Dani's back, not realizing she had stopped walking. She stumbled forward a bit and I reached out to steady her, bringing her back against my body... which was a mistake. My fingers flexed against the fabric of her dress, and I could practically hear myself swallow through the loud bass of the music surrounding us. She swiftly turned around and looked up at me, the lights of the club darting around her face. She stretched up onto her toes and moved to my ear. "I don't see him." The warmth of her breath against my ear could have killed me.

Him? Oh fuck, that's right. The reason that we were here.

Dimitri.

I tore my eyes away from her and looked up towards the second floor of the club. The music changed from a rock beat to a more techno rhythm and I watched as a few demons gathered towards the dance floor and started grinding like no one else was around. I grabbed her hand and guided her towards one of the nearest bars. I made quick eye contact with a demon male who gave me a cheeky smirk before he caught sight of Dani and looked away, quickly, well not before giving her an obvious once over. She sure did make an impression. Ian, the demon bartender from the last time we were here, nodded over to us. He shook his head at Dani. "I'm not sure where he is actually. I know he came in, but I lost track of him about an hour ago." A group of girls at the other end of the bar requested his attention, so he tapped his knuckles against the counter and made his way over to them.

She scrunched her mouth over to one side in thought. "Maybe we should split up," she suggested leaning against the bar. She had to speak up a bit still for me to hear her over the music.

I narrowed my eyes. "Split up?"

She nodded. "Cover more ground and all that. You know what he looks like now, so if you find him, then you find me."

"Yeah, that makes sense..."

"The faster we find him, the faster we can get out of here, which I know is what you want."

I rubbed the back of my neck. "Dani, I never said that. I just don't like the idea of you—," I stopped myself, rethinking my words. "I know you can handle yourself, but with Dimitri, I would just rather that we, together—"

She placed her hand on my chest, her shoulders shaking from her laughter. There was this heat in my chest from seeing her smile, regardless of how it ended up on her face. She tucked a curl behind her ear as she collected herself, grazing her hand up my chest and looking up at me. "Are you worried about what will happen if I'm alone with Dimitri?" She batted her eyelashes at me.

"No, we talked about this. I just don't trust the guy."

She bit her lower lip. "Well don't you trust *me*?"

I let out a shaky breath because fuck she was so close. "Of course, I do." We'd had sex a handful of times now, but every single time with Dani was so different. And it was odd to me that this setting, this club didn't turn me off. If I was being honest, watching demons grind on each other, every single one of them being so sexually aware and free living in this space might have

257

had my head reeling. I wanted her a lot nowadays but, in this very charged vicinity, I wanted her every single time she spoke, took a breath, *fuck*, every time she blinked.

"If I knew any better, I'd say you sound jealous." She pulled back from me and leaned sideways over the bar. Ian was back and giving her his full attention; likely because she pulled her arms in towards her chest, pushing her breasts up. "Can I get two shots of tequila, please and thank you." She winked at him and then gave me her eyes again.

I looked up to the ceiling. "Dani, I told you I'm not jealous. I'm pretty sure I made that really fucking clear." Ian slid the shots over to us and Dani grabbed them, licking her lips. She handed me mine, while staring at my mouth. "Hmm, that you did. Therein lies the question, why are you acting like this now?"

I took the shot from her, tapping my index finger on the glass. "I know you don't need me to defend you and you aren't a damsel in distress, that isn't the issue. The issue is him…"

She paused as she brought the shot to her lips. "Him, what?"

I blew out a breath, severely annoyed. I ignored her question and tipped the shot back, feeling it burn down my throat, but I welcomed it. She watched as I placed the shot glass on the bar and tapped my fingers on the glass countertop. "You told me you didn't want a bodyguard, so everything that wants to come out of my mouth is going to sound like I'm trying to protect you. I'm not jealous, just wary, that's all."

"That's cute. What I meant was you have to act like what you're protecting isn't worth your focus because there was never a doubt in your mind that it could be anything else but yours." Her eyes pierced into mine as she tipped back her own shot, swiping at the corners of her mouth with her tongue. She gently placed her glass next to mine and pressed into me. I instinctively gripped her waist as she grabbed onto my biceps and pushed herself up so she could graze her lips against the shell of my ear. "I'm pretty sure you've gotten me addicted to your cock, so fucking around with Dimitri really doesn't benefit me, now does it. You should really bet on yourself more." She pulled back slightly; her face was close enough so that her breath was mingling with my own.

Her eyes were shadowed in the kind of heated lust I'd learned to quickly recognize, but they were also full of determination, as if she wanted me to understand and believe her. I bent down and kissed her then, tasting the alcohol on her lips. She moaned into my mouth, bringing her hands up to my shoulders as I turned her so that her body was pressed against the bar. She chuckled against my mouth, pushing me back a bit.

"They have rooms here if you want to just go get one already." A golden skinned woman seated on one of the barstools said, rolling her eyes.

I ran a hand through my hair and backed up, giving Dani some room. She stayed against the bar, just examining me. I looked around and noticed a few people glancing our way, but not in the way that told me they were uncomfortable but like they could have watched us fuck if that's how we wanted this to play out. I rolled my shoulders considering the fact that I wouldn't have minded if someone watched. *What in the actual fuck?*

"If you want to split up, then fine, but I would prefer we go together," I said calmly, raising my voice over the music.

Her eyes trailed me from my feet all the way to the top of my head. She cocked her head to the side, squinting at me. After a beat, she shook her head. Her mass of curls bouncing and swaying back and forth. She pushed away from the bar, grabbing my shirt. "We can go together, but not yet. Dimitri always stays until the club shuts down, so we have time. First, I need you to regain that fucking confidence."

"Excuse me?" I questioned, blinking down at her stunned.

A smile played on her lips. She tugged at the material of my shirt, causing me to lean down so I could hear her better. "You heard that girl, there are rooms here, so might as well use one. I want that confident angel with the impressive tongue back." She tilted her face and licked my cheek before moving past me and making her way towards the stairs, various demons making a path for her. I gaped at the space where she once stood, then looked over my shoulder, watching her walk away.

"You should probably follow her," Ian suggested, smirking before clearing our shot glasses from the bar. I internally groaned before racing towards where she went just to find her halfway up the stairs. She snuck a glance over her shoulder and smirked knowing I was following her.

Once we got to the top of the stairs, I pushed past a few people and was able to grab her hand, turning her around to face me. The music was still loud up here but this part of the club didn't have as much bass playing throughout it and the vibration from the music was toned down. The smell of amber and vanilla filled my nostrils. There were so many doors up here with no signs to tell you what was behind any of them. A few demons passed by me that looked disheveled but very, very happy. I remembered Rae mentioning something about taking me and Reese upstairs for fun and now I was finally understanding what she meant. When you listened closely enough, you could hear laughs and moans that were loud enough to fill you in on what was happening behind closed doors. "Dani, you can't be serious."

"I've never been more serious."

"You are doing this because you assume I don't have confidence in myself?"

She moved out of the way for a couple to walk by so lost in each other's personal space that I didn't even think they realized we were standing there. "If the wing fits, huh."

I looked around trying to find any reason to tell her no. "As inviting as this is, we don't have time for...sex." I honestly couldn't believe I was saying that, seeing as that was mostly what we'd been doing for the past few days.

She wagged her finger at me. "Oh, there is always time for sex. Pretty sure it's called a quickie."

"Dani, no." I pressed my mouth into a hard line, crossing my arms over my chest in a way to prove my stance. Her facial expression never changed, but she seemed to somehow look even more mischievous. She looked towards a few of the doors lining the hallway.

Dani shrugged and looked down at her feet, nonchalantly. "Dimitri was super fond of quickies. He always felt the need to show me whenever he *really* wanted me."

She wanted to play *this* game. As much as I knew she was trying to get an obvious reaction, I couldn't help but feel like I wanted to give in to her.

"Dani, no." I repeated, but this time through clenched teeth.

She sauntered over to me, all smooth confidence and sex appeal. "You see the issue with you saying no, is that I'm already turned on by the idea of it, so you either fix the problem with that perfect cock of yours *or* we do what you want and go find Dimitri. He'll likely be so enamored by my scent, he'll want to help fix my problem himself, so..." she trailed off, scrunching her face up as if she was trying to keep her cool.

I wanted to fucking combust, but I didn't move. She was fucking goading me, and I could hear my heartbeat so loudly it was thumping through my ears. Angelic girls I knew didn't play this game and maybe that's why I didn't feel long term sparks with them, maybe I needed someone who pushed my buttons.

She let out a heavy breath. "Fine, have it your way then." She turned on her heel and started walking away but I shot out my hand to grab hold of hers. I pulled her back around, rougher than I had anticipated but all she did was give me a small smile. She started to try to pull away, but I yanked her towards my body, wrapping my other hand around the front of her throat, bringing her face up closer to mine. "You're a needy brat, you know that."

"What are you going to do about it?"

One of the doors opened, revealing what looked like it led to a bathroom.

260

I tilted my head down to let my lips brush hers. "I'm gonna give you exactly what you want." I released her throat and pulled her towards the bathroom. I gently tossed her inside the thankfully empty space before closing the door and locking it.

I watched her let out a small laugh. "There's that confidence I missed so much—"

"Get on your knees," I demanded.

Her brown eyes darted all around my face, as if I surprised her. "What?"

I pressed my tongue to the inside of my cheek, taking the few strides it took to get over to her. I grabbed the back of her head and brought her mouth to mine. She melted into me instantly, her tongue coming out to play with my own. I tugged her back by her hair. "On your knees, needy one."

Her eyes glazed over with this want and desire that made my cock strain against the front of my pants. She licked her lips and started to kneel on the tiled floor. I unbuttoned my pants, pushing them down my hips as my cock jutted out between us. I didn't have to tell her much else before she reached for it and started to stroke, her fingers not fully wrapping around me. I closed my eyes at her touch and nearly bit my tongue. When I opened them, I quickly realized that was a mistake because she was looking up at me, gauging my facial reactions every time her hand glided over the tip of my cock and back to the base of my shaft.

"Fuck. Use your mouth." She leaned her head in and licked the tip of my cock. Her tongue flicked over the head again and again, causing me to let out a groan. This would be fantastic in a different setting—a different moment—but right now. *Fuck*, right now…

I brought my hand to her chin and tilted her head up. "I would love to be sweet with you this time, Dani, but you've made it clear that you want to be a fucking brat so when I say use your mouth, I *mean* use your pretty mouth and suck my cock."

She inhaled a quick breath, and it didn't go unnoticed when she clenched her thighs together. She wrapped her lips around my cock, and I felt my knees buckle. She hollowed her cheeks and sucked, keeping her hand at the base, and making quick strokes, massaging while her mouth and tongue tasted and explored. Her head bobbed back and forth as she found a rhythm she liked, trying to get more of me further into her mouth. She used her hand to stroke the parts of me her mouth wouldn't cover, her fingers not fully meeting as she moved up and down. I pressed my hand to the back of her head, threading my hand through her curls. I started applying pressure to her head, moving her quicker along my cock.

"Fuck, fuck, that's a good girl," I praised as she gagged on me. Her sounds and how her eyes were glassy and almost to the point of watering had me pushing her away, much to her dismay. I kicked off my pants and placed my hands under her arms, lifting her up so that she was standing again. She opened her mouth to say something once she was upright, but her words halted when I wrapped my hands around her thighs, hoisting her up and bringing her over to one of the sinks. I sat her down on the cold porcelain and slid her panties off quickly before I nestled close to her again, letting my cock slide between her legs. She was soaking wet, and I pulled back, bending down and licking a long stripe along her pussy. She awarded me with a long moan and trembling thighs.

I lined myself up at her entrance and slid inside of her. She tilted her head back, hitting the mirror behind her. I brought her legs up, spreading them as I begin to fuck her. I started to pull her against me as our skin slapped together. She gripped the sink for leverage as I started to quicken my pace. "You want *Dimitri* to fuck your," *thrust.* "Pretty," *thrust.* "Little," *thrust.* "Pussy."

Her sounds were meshing with the beat from outside the bathroom. Her chest heaved and her forehead was sweaty. The mirror behind her head rattled from the way I was thrusting her body against it. I leaned in, kissing and licking her skin. "Fuck, fuck, fuck, Nick, no I don't want him. God, fuck don't stop!"

I slammed my hips into her, feeling her clench around me. I looked down at where she took me inside of her. "You weren't lying when you said you were addicted to my cock because I feel the same about your pussy."

She tried to spread her legs wider, tried to take me in further and further. "Please keep going, I'm so close."

"I do like it when you beg." I pulled out of her, clasping my hands around her waist and deftly flipped her over. She gripped the sides of the sink, letting out a loud moan as I put my cock back inside of her. I brought my fingers to her throbbing clit as I continued to fuck her, harder and quicker. Everything was moving so fast, I nearly felt overheated. Her eyes fluttered closed as her breathing came out stuttered.

"*Please* don't stop."

I brought my hand down on her ass and the resounding smack was like music to my ears. She hiccuped at the contact. "Tell me what I like to hear," I commanded.

"Fuck, Nick please." Her voice was strained and pleading.

I pulled my cock out and slid it over her pussy, teasing her. She whimpered as she looked down between us and watched. I grabbed a fistful of her curls and pulled her head back. I gripped her throat with my other hand. "Speak."

Her teeth grazed her bottom lip as she groaned from my cock sliding over her sensitive clit again and again. "It's all yours, Nick. I'm yours—."

I plunged my cock back into her causing her last word to end with a high-pitched moan. I groaned against how tight she felt, her pussy clamping down on me. I could *hear* how wet she was. I started fucking her in short, rapid thrusts. "Are you my good girl?"

Without hesitation, she answered, looking at me through the mirror in front of her. "I'm your good girl, Nick."

"So perfect." I bent down enough to nip and kiss at her exposed neck as she continued to writhe where I had her pelvis pinned to the sink. I pounded into her as she gasped for air with each movement. "You're mine. You want to get fucked like a brat, fine, but good girls get to come. Is that what you want?"

"Yes, oh my god, please. I want to be your good girl, *fuck*." She practically whispered it as if she didn't have the breath to continue.

"Oh no, I want you to let all of them," I nodded my head over to the door, letting my eyes fall back on her as I met her brown eyes in the mirror, "know what's happening to you in here. I want you to go out there so thoroughly fucked that no one will doubt you're mine."

"God, Nick! Yes, okay, please just make me come!" She begged; her tone strained. I let her bend back over right as I brought my palm down on her ass one more time before I grabbed onto her hips, digging my fingertips into her skin and fucked her so hard I was impressed the sink didn't break. I pulled her hips back against me, slamming into her over and over again.

"Be loud for me, baby."

She let out the most intense scream I'd ever heard mixed with my name as she threw her hand forward and slapped it against the glass of the mirror causing it to crack in multiple places and eventually shatter. My own release barreled through me as she was coming down from her own high and I held her to me, letting the aftershock of my orgasm pass.

She swiped her hand over the sink, letting the glass shards fall onto the floor. I leaned down kissing right between her shoulder blades, feeling her exhale. I pulled out of her, helping her turn over so that she could look up at me. She leaned back against the sink as she readjusted her dress. There was a silence between us, and I wanted her to say something, anything that would stop my mind from racing. She rubbed her lips together in thought as she regarded me for a moment.

"You sure know how to show a girl a good time."

I raised one of my eyebrows but watched as her mouth turned up at the corners. I rolled my eyes and kissed her forehead quickly before I picked up my pants, throwing them back on. I plucked her panties from the ground and handed them to her. She took them and immediately went to stuff them in my pocket. "How do you feel, Nicholas? Confidence back in order?"

I ran my fingers along her chin, tipping her face up. "My confidence isn't an issue, I assure you."

"And Dimitri…"

I gripped her chin harder, bringing my face down and brushing my lips along hers. I didn't like the guy, but he didn't intimidate me. I was hardly giving him much thought now. "He isn't worth my thoughts."

"You're sexy when you know what you've got." She winked at me, yanking away from my hold on her. She looked over her shoulder at the damaged mirror, small pieces of glass still hanging onto the frame. "They'll send someone to clean it up."

I chuckled, running a hand through my hair, and feeling less tension with each step I took. Dani unlocked the bathroom door and swung it open as I walked up behind her. The twinge of tension I had thought was gone peeked just above the surface when I saw who was on the other side of the threshold. Two large demons leaned against either side of the doorway, casually waiting for us to exit while Dimitri, with a smug look, stood between them.

"Found you, beautiful."

20

DANI

"Fuck me," I groaned, suddenly regretting dragging Nick up here and having him whisk me away to the bathroom. I felt him tense up behind me, but not in a way that told me he felt threatened but more like he was sizing up the demon in front of him. I snuck a look over at him and he was only looking at Dimitri, not paying the other two large demons any mind.

Dimitri trailed his eyes from my head down to my feet, slowly, making his way back to my face. He flicked his eyes over to Nick, letting out a short chuckle. "Seems like someone already did." I narrowed my eyes at him, but all he did was smile.

He looked around me towards where the broken shards from the mirror littered the floor. "Hmm, it's a good thing I adore you or else I would make you clean that up."

"Yeah, we both know there's not a fat chance in Hell that would ever happen."

He smirked, pointing to the mess and one of the demons beside him nodded and disappeared somewhere. Dimitri clapped his hands in front of him. "Now that you're here, how about we have that talk?"

"*We* now includes all three of us." I reached behind me and pulled Nick forward so that he was standing right next to me. He met Dimitri straight on, seeming to size him up subtly, but I wasn't stupid when I noticed they were both doing it at the same time.

"I think you and I can speak privately just fine," Dimitri pressed, placing his hand on my arm.

"And I think whatever you have to say should be heard by multiple ears, so you know, none of the information gets lost when we relay it to our friends," Nick replied, calmly. He made perfect logical sense. Dimitri ran his index finger over one of his eyebrows, clearly annoyed.

I shrugged his hand off of me. "Can't argue with that. Now lead the way."

Dimitri turned away from us and headed towards the stairs, his demon henchman following him. Nick and I followed behind him but kept a small distance back. We maneuvered around the throngs of demons, giving an acknowledging nod to Ian as we passed. Dimitri headed straight for the darkened pathway that I had caught Nick eyeing the last time we were here. It gave off the feeling that it was an abandoned alleyway. Most—if not all—of the patrons that frequented Leviathan knew that this led to Dimitri's offices. He didn't use any spells or demonic bodyguards to block people from trying to come in.

My legs were sore as we followed them into the darkened corridor. It wasn't as dark once you started walking inside of the narrow space. Once you adjusted to the lack of strobe lights, everything was easy to see. I had a fleeting thought that getting railed out by an angel in the bathroom right before a meeting with my ex-fling might not have been my smartest endeavor. I had looked into Nick's brown eyes and saw that sated expression on his face, and I knew that I'd made the right choice. I liked him confident with his shoulders back and a cocky smirk on his face. I also liked knowing that I got that smirk in private when he somehow got me to submit within minutes of having his hands on me.

The hallway ended with a solid brick wall staring right back at you and two doors were on the left and a plain brick wall was to my right. I knew that one door led to a large meeting area where Dimitri met with different clientele. The other room was his private office, the corridor making it appear like it was probably going to be a small space beyond the door. I knew better. One of the demon henchmen opened his office door and Dimitri walked inside, not looking back at us to make sure we were following him.

I walked into the familiar room and was instantly brought back to every single memory I had ever had here. Most of which had me bent over his desk or pressed against one of his bookshelves, but those memories didn't bring me joy or create a tasteful shiver down my spine. All they did was make me look at the angel next to me and want to do all those things with him and solidify my hypothesis that he would be much better in all ways. Nick unexpectedly winked at me, letting me know that he was cool, calm and collected. I didn't smell any brooding tension in him, nor did I feel that dark energy from before. I wasn't naive enough to think that shit like that just went away, but it simmered, like a predator patiently waiting for its prey to make a wrong move.

The walls were solid stone, completely black and it shined as if he had just had the fucking walls polished. The shelves were lined with books and jars with contents that if you looked close enough, you would see fingers and other remains of those that had crossed him, his friends and probably his father. They passed down the oddest things and had the weirdest traditions in Hell and bringing that to Purgatory had to give you some sort of power when you were waving around severed fingers. Two ruby red tapestries were pulled up and back on the left side wall, revealing a large rectangular frame that displayed an entire overview of the club in real time.

"That's new," I pointed out.

Dimitri walked around his desk and sat down in his chair. He looked over to the frame and shook his head. "No, it's not."

I raised an eyebrow at him. "Yes, it is. I've been here plenty of times, Dimitri. I think I would remember a giant fucking screen."

He laughed softly waving toward the screen. One of the other demons pulled on the tapestries and they instantly draped themselves over the frame, making it look like it wasn't there and just a simple, elegant fabric piece hung in its place. My eyebrows shot up to my hairline. "You were watching us the other night? You knew I was there the entire time, yet you decided to make me wait?"

"The other night? I knew whenever you were in this club from the very beginning. I knew your every move, what drink you ordered and whose attention you'd caught. I not only watched you from a couch, Dani, but I kept an eye on you all the time as I was instructed to do."

"Well, that's not creepy at all."

Dimitri sat back in his chair. "Hm, I do recall you had a liking for being watched."

Nick reached out for the back of one of the chairs in front of us and dug his fingers into the velvet material. I let out a loud, bored sigh and grabbed the other chair and swung it out. I plopped down on the cushion, silently cursing from how comfortable it was. "We didn't come here for you to go down memory lane, Dimitri."

Dimitri waved his hand around. "Of course, of course, no need to make your friend uncomfortable." He nodded for Nick to sit down as well. He hesitated but eventually sat down, leaning back and crossing his arms over his chest.

I eyed the demon henchmen that casually leaned against the walls watching us. They were all so unbothered by my presence, which didn't surprise me since I'm pretty sure most of them were used to me being around their boss.

"So, your meeting with Lilith happened today?" Nick started, bending one of his legs and placing it over his other one, the side of his calf resting right above his knee.

"Yes, it did. And well, she is very eager to have you back, Soul Seether." I rolled my eyes. "So, I've been told by everyone."

"She only wants what's best for you."

Nick let out a small laugh next to me and the look on his face afterwards told me that he hadn't meant for the laugh to be public consumption. Dimitri rested his arms on the glossy wood of his desk. "Something to say?"

Nick placed his other leg back on the ground and scooted closer to the edge of the chair, remaining quiet. I cleared my throat. "Just keep talking, Dimitri. No one here wants to know what happens if I find out I came here for nothing." I crossed my legs, noticing how he watched every one of my movements with hungry eyes.

He knocked his knuckles against his desk. "I am being honest when I say that she does want what's best. She doesn't like that you have this disdain for her, she misses you."

I snorted. "Right. Missing me would mean she has feelings, which we both know she does not."

"Not everyone shows their feelings in the most agreeable way, my dear."

"Oh well, in that case, please elaborate to me how much her cold, cold heart aches to have me in her presence again."

Dimitri hummed, a slight smirk on his lips from my witty remark. "Your sass has been missed." I placed my elbow on the arm of my chair, placing my fingers through my curls. I could feel how calm, but calculated Nick was. I knew at any moment he would be ready to tear Dimitri apart, but he didn't let that overwhelm him. He was enticingly hot when he took my advice.

"And you are still a master of stalling. It's not appealing, so just get to the point."

Dimitri leaned back, sliding his tattooed hands down the arms of his chair. "She knows that Isabel thinks she has this solidified place next to her, but it's meant for you. Yes, she used you, but she wants to make it up by letting you stand by her side when it's all said and done. That's so much power, Dani, and you love the feeling of power even though it looks as if you might be growing a little soft." He tilted his head towards Nick, who kept his lips pressed into a hard line. "She thought things might be easier coming from me than if she sent Isabel to do the talking. She'll let your friends go, live their lives and such, but she wants you here."

"So, you're her errand boy, now?"

Dimitri sighed. "Oh, come on now, you and I are both aware that you are going to try to avoid anything happening to your little posse."

"Lilith is also a notorious liar."

"Perhaps. I, on the other hand, am not. I do feel that she is being sincere."

"Sincerity has no place down here. Sincerity gets used and abused here, left to hang and dry. You think I'm that naive, Dimitri?"

He shook his head. "I would never, but she's willing to give you an option, that's the last time she will do that. She didn't want to seem so harsh with you, so your freedom of choice is restored for now."

"Restored?" I shot him an incredulous look.

"As I said before, you gallivant around here thinking none of this is a big game to her. She would like to cease playing when you decide to cooperate. She stopped experimenting on the demons, she'll let the Enchanters that are still locked away go, so they are no longer held up in her castle. She just wants you to conclude that this is the only correct choice."

I pretended to think this over. "Let me get this straight, so I decide to choose Lilith and she just lets everyone go, full freedom, perfect ending. But, then oh, I do some realm ending bidding of hers and all those people get slaughtered anyway. What does she even want, Dimitri, besides me?!"

"She wants what she's always wanted. For that angel infested realm to pay. I have no quarrel with Heaven's Gate, but I've gotten an idea of what I could have, and I want that. I watch you, relay messages to you, I provide her with whatever she needs from Hell, and I get a piece of whatever she's got in store for the new realm she wants to make, just like I was always owed. She's even willing to let you end Isabel's life yourself once she's fully served her purpose. Poor thing has been trying to work around your High Priestess's wards for some time now."

"And of course, she can't because Isabel is superior garbage. I thought your father wasn't a fan of Lilith, so why would he be providing her anything from Hell."

Dimitri chuckled. "He isn't, but I don't need his permission to bring her the things she wants. Once she succeeds in taking over Heaven's Gate, she'll need the dark magic that Hell caters to. It's all quite simple, we just need you to start playing your part. Choose her, Dani. I mean honestly, sweetheart, you aren't doing them—" He pointed towards Nick. "Any favors by trying to play the side of good and being a hero. It's not your style and quite frankly it's no fun."

"I won't get pushed into a corner."

He held up his hands. "No pushing. Just stating facts. I can taste that dark fire in you waiting to be unleashed and creating havoc like you used too. That's all she wants. It saddens me to know you aren't aiming to reach your full potential."

"It saddens you. Do you hear yourself?" I saw Nick's hands go to the very ends of the arms of his chair and they twisted underneath them. He squeezed, his fingers flexing over and over again.

"I only speak with honesty. She told me that she knows you can't resist the edge the darkness brings; that altercation with that Enchanter child proved that. She wants you to put yourself out of your own misery and head home. That castle that's waiting for you, waiting for you to unleash all that real power. You come to her, and she'll let your friends go, so long as she has you."

"That place isn't my home." He knew about Yuri. How much more was Dimitri aware of?

Dimitri raised his eyebrows. "Oh really? Where then? You think grassy, light filled Heaven's Gate is your home? That is too sweet that you also believe that. It very well could have been, I assume, and without Lilith, you would have been some weak, virtuous creature."

"Are you going to say anything *worth* saying anytime soon?" Nick piped up, tilting his head to the side.

Dimitri rubbed his lips together, clearly annoyed. "She hasn't told me all her details, but she said you would put all her voided demons to shame. You know where to find her, you always have. I will tell you that Isabel warded it a while back so if outsiders tried to storm it and Enchanters who tried to escape, like your little necromancer friend and his family, would be quite literally obliterated if they tried to pass through on either side. So, if you're thinking about ambushing her I wouldn't."

I never wanted to just go into that castle without any sort of plan, but now the options were severely limited. Isabel must have filled him in about Garrett and Leah. Lilith hardly came to Devil's Playground unless she absolutely had to. "There are always ways around things, Dimitri. If Purgatory has taught me anything, it's that there is likely always a loophole. And if not, then you make one."

"Resilience at its finest. And here I thought you couldn't get any more beautiful."

My eyes had never rolled so hard in all of my existence. "I won't choose her."

"Then she will force your hand."

"She can try."

"I told you I would inform you of what we spoke of and that was it."

I got up from my chair, placing my hands on his desk and leaning over. "You always came to Lilith at her castle. She made you come to her; she always likes to make creatures work for her. Why in the hell would she come to you all of a sudden? Meet with you here?"

Dimitri got up as well, mimicking my movements and eventually my exact stance. "Because, pretty girl, despite it seeming like Lilith makes the rules, I am allotted my own demands. Lucifer and my father still and will forever rank much higher than her around here. I don't like to make a fuss, but I am allowed to refuse the queen of darkness every now and again. Sometimes she does come to *me*." He lifted his hand and stroked my face, his thumb caressing my skin. I didn't lean into the touch, nor did I move away. I just stayed still. Dimitri gave me a small smile.

"I'm a pretty simple man to please. Lilith wants what she wants, and I want what I want. I don't want to hurt you Dani, but I can't stop her from doing what she must. Her kindness is fleeting, and your friends won't be able to protect you when the time comes, nor will you be able to protect them." He drew a line from my jaw, up to my mouth and traced my bottom lip. "We would make a powerful team. Everything and *everyone* else are technicalities."

I felt Nick's tall, looming presence before he spoke. He had gotten out of his chair and stood next to me, so close that our bodies almost touched. "I'm pretty sure she said no." He reached his hand out and grabbed Dimitri's wrist, yanking his hand away from me. Dimitri curled his finger back and his eyes flared. His pupils dilated and his irises turned a bright, neon red. I noticed out of the corner of my eye that his men were starting to move in closer. They were surveying their master, making sure they didn't need to intervene.

Dimitri's red eyes bore into Nick's brown ones. "I will refrain from ending your life because I have high respect for this woman who seems to like parading you around, but also understand I could rip those pretty wings

I know your kind has right off your back and throw you into the fiery pits of my home."

Nick held onto the wood of the desk so hard that I heard it start to make a creaking noise. Ugh, men. I slapped my hand down on the desk, grabbing their attention. "Her kindness is not my concern and just like her kindness, my patience is fleeting. It is funny though that you are so forthcoming with all this, almost like she wanted you to relay everything back to me."

Dimitri shrugged. "My meeting with her wasn't a secret and perhaps she did wish for me to explain your options to you. Better it come from me than if she sent more hellhounds to your door and had Isabel do it."

"You damn near acted like you were doing me some kind of favor when all you were doing was her bidding just like everyone else. So please, let's not pretend like you are any more useful to her than Isabel, Markus or even Cullen was."

Dimitri adjusted his suit jacket. "Ah, Cullen. You did quite the number on him." He ran his fingers through his hair, smoothing down a few of the pieces. I let the memories of the Ethereal Bastille run through my mind for a moment and then they were gone. "She underestimated how involved you'd gotten with certain individuals. Clearly your tastes have changed, but that doesn't mean that you can't choose the right side." His still raging red eyes zeroed in on Nick who looked back at him, unnerved and unmoved.

"I can't be charmed into submission, so this meeting was a waste of my time and speaking to you has clearly been a waste of my breath," I said, annoyed that I thought that he would be more useful than he actually was.

He laughed, his eyes glowing a bit as he held his stomach before he collected himself. "It's funny that you think that you aren't already being pushed, inch by inch. Resistance gets you nowhere." He looked over to Nick. "And angels are feeble creatures that will only ever bring you down, case in point." Before I knew it, Dimitri reached out towards Nick's arm, his fingernails extending out to razor sharp black tips. His nails scratched Nick's arm, the sound of ripping skin ringing in my ears. Nick cried out, immediately pulling his arms towards his body as blood leaked out from the gashes. Dimitri brought his nails to his lips and tasted Nick's blood. He let the dark, red liquid settle on his tongue before he swallowed. His red eyes sparkled with intrigue.

"Pathetically weak," Dimitri taunted as Nick held his arm to his chest. "But there is something deliciously dark. You should really consider—" he started but before he could continue Nick grunted and brought his good arm back throwing a stream of light at Dimitri's direction. I hadn't seen angelic magic used that often, unless I counted Jonah and them using it during our fight during the briefing room ambush, but from Nick it was surprising. Without his weapon, he had to result to other things and, as much as he didn't want to rely on his magic, decisions had to be made.

The light was white but had a golden outline that made it look as beautiful as it was potentially deadly. Given the right amount of force and effort, that kind of power could do some real damage. Nick didn't want to cause infinite problems, so I had a feeling he had held back. It was bright enough that Dimitri flinched right as it flew towards him, landing along the side of his face and dispersing off onto his shoulder. When the light dissipated, the entire left side of his face was scorched red and the skin along his jaw was bubbling from the heat damage. The fabric of his jacket had charred off on his shoulder and every time he took a breath, small black remnants fell to the ground.

I was impressed with Nick, but I was also nervous for him because unlike me, he didn't know that Dimitri preferred this form he was in, this body. He was handsome and likable for the most part, but before this, before the club, he presented himself in a different form. It was a form that never scared me but would throw any unsuspecting new arrival off guard. Blood dripped from Nick's hand as he exhaled sharply, looking at me as I leaned away from the desk. Dimitri touched his face delicately and licked his lips. "She doesn't have you on as tight of a leash as I thought. I should really keep you around. Drain you of all that dark energy you keep feeding." He tipped his head towards Nick, who was instantly surrounded by Dimitri's men. They had him down on his knees and pressing their fingers into his wounded arm before I could blink. They had him by his hair, tilting his head back, exposing his neck. Dimitri narrowed his eyes at me, his grin growing bigger, and it was like his old form and this current form started to morph, one would flash in front of me and then the other. "No wonder you keep him around, he must be an utter delight to feed off of, retain all that darkness from him. It has to be a calling to you, pretty girl, it will show Lilith your loyalty. It will show *me* your loyalty. A moment in the Leviathan bathroom with this—" He waved over to Nick, "won't make up for all the years we spent, right? We can do it together, make sure he's wide awake to watch..."

I was grossed out and done. I didn't let him finish, when I lunged over his desk and grabbed the lapel of his jacket. I yanked him down and close to my face. "I will never stand by you." I threaded my fingers into his hair, pulling up and then slamming his face into the desk. I pulled him up and did it again, making sure the burnt part of his skin slid across the wood. I looked behind me noticing one of Dimitri's men was aiming to slit Nick's throat and I manifested my dagger, throwing it in his direction. It lodged into the tall henchman's throat as he staggered back, my daggers shadows wrapping around his head. I felt someone at my back as I willed my weapon back towards me, shifting my stance so that I turned around, continuing to press Dimitri's face into his desk as I plunged my dagger into the demon who was trying to catch me off guard. He fell against the chair, blood coming from the gaping wound in his chest.

Nick shot out light stream after light stream when the demons were occupied. He extended his fist upward, propelling one of them backwards as they hit the wall, slumping against it. He bent down and shot his leg out, tripping one of them and throwing his elbow back, connecting it with the face of another demon before pounding his fist into the demon on the ground in front of him in one fluid motion. I picked Dimitri's face up and his look of pure shock and anger almost made me want to maniacally cackle. I felt my shadows start to brew and rumble inside of me, felt that raging darkness wake up and want to take over my entire being. It wanted to blind me to anything else. He lifted his hand and tried to slice his nails down my face, but I willed my shadows to grab his hand and forced it onto the table, his own magic trying to fight its way out. "Let's not try that shall we."

I summoned my dagger to my side and brought it underneath his chin. "Tell Lilith she can kiss my ass." My vision started to distort, and I knew I was losing my grip on reality. It was happening so much faster this time, so easily.

Dimitri snickered, blood coming from his nose. "Only if I get to as well."

I curled my lips back in disgust, but he wasn't finished. "Poor angel, too fragile to fight off his own demons." I furrowed my brow in confusion when I heard Nick's groan of discomfort. Dimitri was looking directly at him, but Nick couldn't look away and he kept flinching, his eyes squinting, and his ears started to drip with blood. His head tilted to the side as if trying to get whatever was in there to leave. Dimitri's eyes flickered as Nick grabbed his head and yelled. My vision danced between darkness and color as if his pain, Nick's pain, was pulling at that place in my chest and keeping me grounded. His hands glowed, but they weren't as strong, they weren't fighting hard enough.

I yanked Dimitri up further by his hair. "Make it stop!"

"Then put him out of his misery. This place will eat him alive if you don't or Lilith will do it herself. Or you can make the choice to keep him pretty and side with the only home you'll ever know." He answered me through gritted teeth. Nick still wailed behind me, and the last two remaining henchmen hovered over him, smiling at his agony.

"My answer is none of the above. All this proves to me is that I made a solid decision siding with them." I flipped my dagger in my hand and jerked him closer to me so that my lips brushed his ear. "And just so you know, his dick is so much bigger than yours." I brought my dagger down, making a clean slice through his wrist, separating one of his tattooed hands from the rest of him. Blood sprayed out, red and speckles of black. It landed on my arms, my face and I felt an instant thrill at seeing the mess I'd made of my ex-fling. Nick's agonized voice ceased as Dimitri closed his eyes and screamed out.

His henchman pounced on me, but I held my dagger tight and forced it into one of their necks, ripping it out and turning around to throw it right into the eye of the other. He stopped right in his tracks, blood dripping from his eye as he dropped to the floor. I rushed over to Nick, who was slowly picking himself up from the ground. He was shaking and his knuckles were bloody. He blinked and collected himself, all traces of what Dimitri had done was no longer present, at least on the surface.

"You should be so lucky that Lilith wants you alive, that I still know you'll make the right decision. We can work this all out and you'll be mine again, but I will insist that Lilith make slow deaths of every single person you stand with." I heard growling, but I didn't know where it was coming from. There were no windows in here and there was only one door. Dimitri could summon hellhounds whenever he wanted, but where they came from, I wasn't sure. "Get out. Or I will be the least of your worries." The growling got louder and more aggressive, like they were right behind us.

I tugged Nick's arm to get him to move, but he walked forward towards Dimitri's desk. His limp hand sat lifeless, blood slowly coming from the place where it should be attached to the rest of him. I stood next to him, wary of what he was about to do, but then he placed his hand over the removed appendage and light burst out of his palm, bright and white. Golden flecks spewed out and then they were gone. He lifted his hand away and Dimitri's severed hand fell apart in a burnt mess. Ashes piled up and started to scatter along the desk. Dimitri's true form started to appear along his face, the skin on his cheeks and forehead peeling away to reveal gray matter and bones. His eyes started to get more sunken in and his lips curled back, revealing his teeth getting sharper.

"She isn't yours," Nick said, something dark washing over his eyes for a second and then it was gone. He swept the ashes off the desk before turning around, walking over the dead bodies and opening up the door. The growling around us grew louder and I could have stayed and fought but it wasn't worth it.

"Goodbye, Dimitri." I turned on my heels and followed Nick, who was farther ahead of me than I would have liked. I gave Ian a shake of my head, telling him not to interfere if Dimitri came out rampaging. Once we were outside, I reached up and grabbed his shoulder, turning him around to face me.

"Are you okay? That was a lot and he—"

"Dani, I'm fine. Does everything always go from zero to one hundred here?"

"Yes. That's pretty normal."

He rubbed the space between his eyebrows, hissing at the wound on his arm. The lines from Dimitri's nails were embedded deep. His ears had lines of blood coming out of them, but the initial bleeding had ceased. I brushed my fingers around the still bleeding slashes on his arm. "Let's get you back and get this checked out, okay."

He didn't say anything, just nodded. We got looks as we walked back to the hostel. Dimitri had a thing for getting into people's heads. Being one of the sons of one of the pillars of Hell, he could do certain things that every demon thrived for. He had dived into Nick's mind and pulled forward all the darkness that lingered. He filled Nick's head with it, nearly wanting him to go insane over it. I'd seen Dimitri do terrible things with that power, but it had been so easy to do it to Nick. Maybe that darkness he had was worse than I thought, closer to boiling over.

I threaded my fingers through his and a sensation of familiarity ran through my arm, over my shoulders and down my back. This recognizable feeling wasn't something I wanted to smile at. His darkness was greeting me with a more confident stance now. It was touching me and coaxing me. I looked up at the angel next to me as he looked ahead, not knowing what he was letting brew inside of him by letting his feelings stew from within. He looked like his normal handsome self when I simply looked at him, but Nick was so good at making himself seem so put together when he was falling apart piece by angelic piece. Dimitri had given the darkness a thread of power from a true source of Hell and even I knew his angelic light couldn't fight that for long.

My night light would start to dim and dim and eventually it would be unable to create light anymore when it was suffocating in the dark. I wanted to help Nick, but a part of me wanted to pursue this dark takeover that was happening, the side of myself that I had pulled back in hopes of protecting him. Maybe it was that angelic part of myself that made me want to help him. Maybe it was the reason I felt pressure in my chest when he was in pain. Or maybe it was something entirely different that I wasn't ready to admit at the moment. I had already told myself that I wasn't a hero, and I didn't want to be. Nick was so good at playing that part and I would never take that from him.

The hero was broken now, so what exactly did that make me if I might want to save him?

21

DANI

Everything moved quickly once we got back to the hostel. Nick had walked in before me, his arm dripping with dark red blood on the floor. The patrons that were near the small lounge area and the front desk all turned to look at him and gawk. Beetee hustled over, grabbing his arm with enough force to make him wince. She had apologized and flicked her lilac eyes to me as if I would be able to sum up everything that happened in a matter of seconds. I had let my eyes fall to the floor, deciding that I would answer her later. Reese came bounding down the stairs and Elise came from around the corner in the dining room, both of them laser focused on the bleeding angel in front of me.

"What the fuck happened?" Reese asked, panic laced in his voice. I knew his question was directed at me, but he didn't acknowledge me.

"It's nothing, I'm actually fine," Nick insisted, trying to push everyone away from him.

"You bleeding all over the fucking place means you're fine." Reese deadpanned, rolling his eyes.

Elise had walked around the two arguing friends and pulled me away from them. Her face was stern and unmoving to the current situation in front of us. "Is he dead?"

She was wondering about Dimitri and there was a part of me that slightly wished he was dead. "No."

Elise let out a breath. "Good. Killing a Son of Hell would literally cause more problems than we need right now." She looked over her shoulder as Beetee started to usher Nick and Reese towards the recovery room, removing them from my line of sight. "I'm guessing your demon ex-boyfriend gave him that bloody parting gift."

I ran my hands down the front of my dress. "Yeah, and then things got out of hand. None of this was my intention, alright?"

"I'm well aware. But he must've felt a little threatened to have literally dug his claws into Nicholas."

I raised my eyes to the ceiling nearly wanting to rewind and do that entire meeting differently. Maybe I would have had us leave sooner or maybe I would have cut off more than Dimitri's hand. I would never know now though. "Maybe. He dug into more than just his skin, Elise."

She moved us out of the way of clusters of demons making their way to the door. She let out a groan of annoyance and grabbed my wrist, pulling me towards the stairs. She closed the door to her room behind her, letting out a long sigh that sounded like relief. "What do you mean by more than just his skin?"

I ran a hand through my hair and ruffled the curls, not really knowing where to start. "You know what Dimitri can do, so let's just leave it at that." My suggestion fell on deaf ears when she crossed her arms over her chest and waited. She gave me a look that told me she would do the exact opposite of leaving it and would keep me trapped in this room if I didn't open my fucking mouth.

"Ugh, fine. Nick has been having some issues while we've been here. I don't know all the details so don't ask me. There is darkness inside of him and it's not the type that lingers in everybody. It's the kind that's created by the host and taken hold of, enhanced by the not so friendly darkness living here," I explained, turning around, and walking towards her bed.

Elise swiped her tongue along the front of her teeth. "And Dimitri found out about Nick's little issue?"

"Tasted his blood and everything."

"Fucking fuck, fuck. Do we need to send your little boyfriend home? Is he going to last with us being here? You and I both know how fucking eager darkness can be and a pretty angel with a dimming light is a five-star meal."

I shook my head and then stopped. She had a point. Sending Nick home would help him or at least it would get him out of this setting and place him in a more comfortable space to fix whatever was going on with him. That idea didn't last long in my mind when I actually thought about who I was considering sending home. "He wouldn't do it. He's stubborn as fuck and wants to fight this with us. Making him go home, might make things easier for us to not have to worry about him, but he would be fucking miserable knowing that he couldn't contribute."

"And you didn't think telling any of us about his condition might be helpful? I'm pretty sure he's never seen people die before so what happened months ago literally rocked his fucking world."

I raised one of my eyebrows in confusion. "Reese was there too. They both saw death right in front of their innocent little eyes, yet he isn't having these problems. Unless they're both hiding it from each other."

She clucked her tongue. "As much as I hate talking about emotions and stupid feelings, Blondie and Nick are two different angels. They handle things differently, especially shit like that. Or the darkness could just find Nick much more delectable than the blonde one. It really could go either way."

I hummed. "I could ask but I don't think I'll get a straight answer right about now. All I can say is Nick will fight to stay and Reese will follow his lead. No amount of verbal sparring with either of them will change that." I also knew enough about Reese now to be overly confident about that assumption.

Elise plastered her hands to her face and groaned. "Fine, fucking fine. Plan A is out the door then. Plan B is you figure out a way to help him keep his shit together because we really don't need him to get too overwhelmed that he turns around and starts trying to fight *us*." I nodded, silently confirming my understanding. The harsh look in her eyes morphed into a more curious look. "Did you at least leave Dimitri in one piece?"

I tilted my head from side to side. "More or less."

Elise smirked. "Hmph. I never liked the little shit anyway, so I guess I'm a little proud. He gave me small dick energy."

I laughed and bit down on my lower lip, focusing my eyes on the door behind her. She followed my eyesight and snorted. "You can go to your lover boy when we're done. Now sit that ass on the bed and tell me everything that happened. You leave anything out and I'll choke you out myself."

"You act like I'm scared of choking.""You will be if I have to do it. So, sit down, *now*."

Elise had been agitated, but with a disgruntled noise and a whole explanation of prior events later, she let me leave her room. I quickly hustled over to my own room to change, exchanging my tight club dress for comfortable leggings and an off the shoulder black top. That dress reminded me too much of what had happened. If I had been alone, none of it would have occurred. Dimitri would have flirted, and I would have laughed him off, still maintaining my answer at the end of the conversation. I would not be yielding to Lilith, no matter what sort of favor she dangled in my face. The offer to kill Isabel did pique my interest, but I think Elise and I had decided that we would bring her back for Natalia to deal with her instead.

Dimitri didn't like the word no; I honestly didn't think he'd ever been told it before. His words meant nothing to me, but the thing I started to understand was that when Dimitri tried to want something better for me, it was for personal gain and it threatened the lives of so many demons, Enchanters and angels. But when Nick wanted something better for me, it was because he actually wanted me to see another side, venture towards what could have been and explore simply because I hadn't been allowed the opportunity. Nicholas was pretty shit at expressing what he wanted, but he learned from that experience and now we had each other's trust. He was willing to go head-to-head with a Son of Hell for me which was hot all by itself, but not at the expense of his soul.

He could want all the good things for me, but I wanted none of the bad things for him.

I made my way to the recovery room, knocking on the door. The knob turned and the door flung back revealing a stressed looking Reese. He held the door open wide enough for me to see Nick sitting, yet again, on the little bed in the corner, his legs dangling off the side. "How is he?"

"He'll be okay. He told me what happened, well the majority of it. We stopped the bleeding and most of the redness is gone, but it's gonna hurt like a bitch for the next few hours." He tucked a piece of his messy blonde hair over his ear.

"Are you going to turn this into an *it's my fault* thing?" I asked, tapping my sneaker covered foot on the ground.

Reese furrowed his blonde brows. "Uh, no. Nick wanted to go all on his own. This is a *Nick's thing*, but I do have to hand it to you. You cut off the guy's hand?"

I chuckled proudly. "That I did."

"Did I say earlier that we might be friends? I actually want to change that to us being best friends," he joked, but his smile was genuine. We both laughed a little and his face gradually turned into one of concern. His voice was low, a bit like a whisper when he spoke next. "He was off when we brought him in here and I don't know, when I look at him, he just seemed kind of lost."

I noticed the way he wouldn't look at me when he was done speaking as if he hated the fact that he couldn't do anything for his friend. I knew how it felt to be lost in your own head with your crippling thoughts, while someone or something else was pulling the strings. Lilith had been quiet for a minute, and I was happy about it, but the quiet always put me on edge. I was tethered to my darkness, I would have to live with that, but Nicholas didn't have to.

"Lost is a word for it."

"He is in a very *to the point* kind of mood right now, so talking about his emotions isn't really on the agenda. I mean it's hardly ever on the agenda, but you know what I mean." He waved his hand around nonchalantly, but his tone was anything but.

I reached up and punched his shoulder lightly. "I got this. Let me talk to him."

Reese nodded and looked at his best friend who was now looking over at us. Nick's blank expression melted into a small smile in my direction. I gave him one back and then looked back at Reese. "Go get something to drink, like alcohol or something. I'll let you know if there is anything you need to be aware of." His shoulders relaxed as if he knew my words rang true. After our talk, I understood his motivations and his undying support of the raven-haired angel I found myself wanting to be around more and more.

We both wanted this man to be healthy and happy with a clear soul, but his soul wouldn't ever be clear again and Reese would have to come to terms with that. And so would Nicholas. Both of them had tainted souls now, regardless of me or Elise, or anyone. Reese already had this hardened interior from his family and his upbringing that the darkness here likely found him boring, but Nick was different, he was the good boy that had now done some bad things, seen some bad things.

Reese moved past me out of the room, and I entered the space, instantly feeling that wave of tension anytime we were alone in a room together. I walked over to him, wedging myself between his legs as he leaned back to look at me. I gently picked up his wounded arm, peering down at the three scarred lines down his forearm. Before I could really think about it, I brought his arm to my lips and pressed a gentle kiss to the scars. His breathing caught when my mouth touched his skin, but he remained quiet, just watching me.

I placed his arm back down on his thigh and finally looked up at him. He narrowed his brown eyes at me, and they looked just like they always had, but there was something else there. It was like I could feel his tiredness and I ached to fix it, but there were parts of me that wondered if I got too close would I taint him even more.

"Are you *really* okay?" I asked, my tone even.

He sighed like he was annoyed at the question. It was one I knew he had heard way too often. "Yes. I am perfectly fine. All my limbs are accounted for. I have my brain cells and I can even speak in full sentences."

I instinctively smacked the side of his head. "Okay, smartass."

He reached up with his non-wounded arm and rubbed his head. "Sorry."

"You can tell Reese whatever you want, but lying to me isn't something I advise. You've already done it a handful of times since we've been here." I fixed my eyes to stare right into his, almost daring him to look anywhere else.

He blinked. "I don't know what you're talking about."

I rolled my eyes in disbelief. "No one is in a constant state of 'I'm fine' Nick. Like your little spasm while talking to Natalia or when you were quite literally emitting dark energy from your fucking pores right next to me. And let's not forget you sleeping on the bathroom floor because you didn't feel well, that's my personal favorite." My tone was a bit snarky, but I couldn't help it.

"I get it, alright. Do you want me to say I'm sorry? Fine. I'm sorry that I'm allowed to keep shit to myself." His voice was pure agitation.

"Nick, no one said you had to air out all your secrets, but it's honestly not doing you any good keeping it all in. Whatever you're feeling, even Dimitri could sense it, the minute he tasted your blood. It's kind of his thing as fucked up as it is. That's what happened to you in there, he tasted that darkness, and now that it's embedded in your veins, he used it against you." I reached up and placed my hand on the back of his head, bringing his face closer to mine. He molded so willingly to my movements as if despite his irritation with my words, he still wanted to be near me as much as he could. "I know firsthand what an invasion of the mind feels like. It's like she's talking to me here and there, but not enough to fully send me raging, but enough to push me little by little. I almost lost it with Dimitri, but I didn't." I cared more about Nicholas's wellbeing than my own blood thirsty satisfaction and I had never been more content about my decision.

"Dimitri just had an upper hand, but he doesn't scare me. I just need a minute to figure this shit out and I'll be right back at it. You can handle yourself and so can I. I have no choice but to see this through Dani. When

I decided to become a sentry, I had to take an oath to see things through, always find a way to reach the end of the task, the mission, whatever was happening. And if it seemed like there was no way to the end you made a way because that's what you had to do. So, seeing this through is a must," he said sternly as if he was repeating words straight from Ariel's mouth. And I knew he believed every word he said, but those words seemed like such a trap. Like if any little mistake was made then there was this shadow of shame. They had to look in all directions when they fought, but they had to have tunnel vision for their tasks. Then came me and Elise and all the secrets that exploded from Heaven's Gate and it put a wrench in everything they ever knew.

I swallowed. "You told me that I was perfect Nick and while I highly appreciate that, I do have flaws that make my utter perfection just a tiny bit unhinged. And I lean into it. I know that I won't get far thinking that I have no issues. I think you are perfectly imperfect, but I also think that *you* think that you always need to be just fucking flawless."

"I've never once said I'm perfect." He wrapped his arm around my waist and pulled me into him more, seeming to want to gain some power from me.

I yanked his hair causing him to release a hiss, letting him know I still had his attention. "Good little soldiers always think they're perfect because any imperfections could mean death, but in reality, actually accepting those cute little imperfections and following the path where there *is* resistance might be the only thing that will save you. There is no cushy rule book here, so it's about time you stopped thinking your sentry methods work because the darkness doesn't care. You can try to weave around it and find another way as you so stoically put it, but it will always find you because whether you like it or not, you let it. And ignoring it will only fuel it. Why do you think it was so fucking easy for Dimitri to get into your head? I could virtually taste it coming off of you when we were walking back…"

He jumped off the bed, keeping me close to him and I dropped my hand from his hair. "I don't know what you want me to do Dani. I'm not like you where I can somehow communicate with it enough to settle it. It's overwhelming and I need to focus on anything else so I can try not to think about it throughout the entire day." I thought back to his outburst at Ariel. It was out of character and had been a shock to all of us, although it was hot. He wasn't following his higher ups instructions this time; he was following his own and he was the leader of his own mission. The leader was waning now, but he was still trying to make it to the end with as little fuck ups as possible.

"Ignoring. It. Won't. Work," I said each word with purpose, hoping that it would get through that thick head of hair he had and melt into his brain.

He started to walk us backwards towards the counter and I could feel my back hit the cold gray countertop. "If I think about it, it will fester. If I don't think about it, it will also fester. You can see where I don't win on either side. Maybe I could have saved us more issues if I had let you go see Dimitri by yourself, but that wasn't going to happen, so please tell me how to fix my flaws, Dani, since you know all about it." His eyes flickered with that dark *something* that I saw after we had fought Dimitri. It was quick, but it was there. I could feel remnants of his energy slithering towards me, appearing not dark and mysterious but translucent and innocent. It didn't have to show its true colors to me to let me know what it was and what it wanted.

Despite the waves of dark energy, I felt his body heat and could smell his inviting scent. It was warm like after the first shot of whiskey makes its way down your throat and settles. I had never been a fan of the drink, but I could find myself getting used to it. "Speak for yourself, Nicholas. I don't want to fix your flaws you idiot. Dimitri said that you were too fragile to fight off your own demons well, fuck, was he right?"

My throat was enveloped by his hand, not enough pressure to truly hurt me but always enough to gather my attention. "I'm not fragile."

"Then stop ignoring the problem and let someone in," I coaxed, pushing my hips up and out to meet his pelvis. If things didn't get better, I might have to force him back home to his father. Reese would follow and Nick would resent me for making him leave, but maybe that would help him understand that I did care. I wasn't a dumbass who would throw him to the wolves again in his condition, not after Dimitri's mental invasion.

"You sure are bossy when you think you know best. When you think you have all the answers." He leaned down close to my face, letting his breath hit my skin.

I chuckled, not at all impressed by his show of assertiveness. "You sure are the master of deflection these days. Why am I not surprised." His eyes lost the darkness there, but now they were hooded and heavy with a look I knew very, very well.

He tilted his fingers up so that they touched my jaw, and he twisted my head to the side, his lips grazing my ear. "You quiet my head sometimes. I can feel it alright; I know it's there, but I sleep better with you next to me. Even though it's darkness calling to darkness, it doesn't seem so debilitating when you're around and I don't know what any of it means, but I'll figure out whatever you want as long as you're right here."

I brought my face up to meet his lips, kissing him. I put pressure on this kiss, not wanting to come off like I wanted it to be slow and careful. He held onto my throat holding me in place as he kissed me back. His mouth moved over mine, while his tongue came out to play and explore. I took his bottom lip between my teeth and pulled, hearing a low groan come from his throat. I felt his cock against my stomach, getting harder at every second. He let go of my throat, placing his hand next to me on the countertop, caging me in. He kissed along my jaw and down my neck, a wave of shivering warmth shooting down my spine. His lips met that spot he had learned could make me squirm with needy want. He pressed his body into mine, moving his mouth to the other side of my neck.

The sound of footsteps and chatter caught my attention and with his head bent down I could see that I hadn't closed the door all the way. It wasn't wide open, but it was ajar enough that if someone did try to look in here, they would get an eyeful. "Nick, the door." I honestly didn't give a fuck about the door, but I at least wanted to make him aware.

He pulled himself away from my neck and looked over his shoulder. "Huh, what about it?"

"Umm, it's not closed all the way," I pointed out.

His shoulders moved in soft laughter as he turned back to me. Nick leaned down and kissed me again, licking at my bottom lip. "So?" My little exhibitionist.

I heard him wince a little as he trailed his wounded arm down the side of my body, shifting back a bit, so that he could move his hand to the front of my stomach. He grazed his fingers along the top of my leggings, teasing me as he nuzzled my nose.

"Nick, your arm."

"Stop talking."

"We aren't done talking about any of this you know," I reminded, making sure he knew that everything that occurred in the last few hours hadn't been forgotten. His deflection methods were pleasurable in the best ways, but they wouldn't help either of us in the long run.

Nick pushed his fingers inside my leggings and immediately placed them between my legs, rubbing over my panties. I saw the strain in his forearm as he tried to bite back the pain of using his hurt arm. I pressed my top teeth into my lip. "Do you want me to stop?"

I heard the shuffling of feet outside the door and laughter coming from the dining area that was just down the hall. Creatures were still riding the high of Purgatory nightlife despite a bleeding angel coming through the hostel less than an hour ago. He thumbed my panties to the side and ran his fingers over my pussy, not applying much pressure, but letting the pads of his fingers glaze over where I was aching for his touch. His groan of satisfaction almost sent me over the edge. "No." I said in a rushed breath.

"Good because you're so wet that I don't think I could." He circled his fingers over my entrance and brought it up to my clit, rubbing. I didn't have much to hold onto in my current position, so I reached up and grasped the back of his neck. I let out a soft moan as he applied more pressure to my clit, his bicep flexing from his movements. He trailed his fingers back to my pussy and pressed two of his fingers inside, extending them upwards, massaging and rubbing that spot that made my eyes flutter closed.

"*Fuck*, Nick..." I started, but I was cut off when he flicked his wrist up in a steady motion, rhythmically fucking me with his hand and his fingers felt good and right. The sound of my wetness echoed into the room, but I didn't care, it was the last thing on my mind. I let out whimpers and a loud moan that was entrapped by his lips on mine. He kissed me so fervently that I was almost worried I wasn't giving enough back to him.

He shushed me. "We don't need someone to come in here and watch how well you take my fingers, have them watch when you come all over my hand, do we, needy one?" He raised a sneaky eyebrow at me and kept pumping his fingers into my pussy over and over again. He thumbed my clit, making rapid circles, almost mimicking his punishing fingers.

I shot my eyes to his, my voice was breathy and low when I spoke again, "something tells me you might get off on someone watching you make me come." I pulled his face down more and licked his earlobe. His whole body shuddered, and his hand started moving more forcefully. There were no voices in my head during this, no darkness brewing, no need to see blood or force someone's hand. I wanted this feeling to remain forever, but I knew it couldn't so I would ride it out for as long as I had it. And riding it out while also riding the hand of my stubborn emotionally withholding angel was probably the perfect way to do it.

I heard heels click outside the door and someone running past, but I didn't care. All I wanted to do was scream from the way Nick's fingers stretched me and curled over just the right places. His hand moved faster, pumped harder as his chest rose and fell. He didn't look like he felt that pain in his arm anymore, like he distracted himself from it. He was distracting himself from a lot it seemed. "Nick, fuck, I'm so, *fuck*, close." I dug my nails into his neck as he rammed his fingers into me, rougher and filled with so much need that it was almost—*almost*—too much.

"You want everyone to hear you come, baby? Or do you want it to be just for me?" His thumb pressed on my clit, sliding back and forth from how wet I was. His cock was straining against his pants, rubbing up against me, practically begging to be let out.

I opened my mouth to speak, but every little sensation caused me to have to close it and try again. There was a tingle settling low in my belly and it churned, bubbling up.

"Just for you." It felt like I was saying a lot without saying much at all. It had a sexual undertone obviously, but when he looked at me, there was so much more to it. Lilith wasn't in my head, at least not for the moment and it was a nice feeling not to be judged and looked at like the Soul Seether. His darkness wasn't something I could sense right now even though I knew it was present and waiting for another chance to strike. If this is what he needed to feel like he was in control and that everything was alright in his mind, then I would let him have this.

He brushed his lips over mine. "That's my girl, come for me. Just for me."

My stomach was in knots as I closed my eyes, his fingers curling one last time and I saw stars. My sounds didn't have time to release because his mouth was there, stealing them from the rest of the hostel, the rest of the realms. I brought my other hand up and placed both my hands on either side of his face, keeping him near me as he pulled back. I gave him one more peck and looked down, feeling his fingers pull out of me, but he drew lazy lines along my throbbing pussy.

I giggled a little. "You should add master of deflection to your angelic resume."

He kissed my nose. "It's not deflection."

"What would you call it when we are discussing something important that you would like to avoid? A cease in the conversation where you finger me into some sort of hushed compliance?" I questioned, raising my eyebrows at him. His facial expression told me he wasn't getting away with anything and he knew it. I reached down and pulled his hand from inside my leggings, being gentle when I turned his hand towards him and placed his fingers in his mouth. His eyes never left me the entire time he tasted me on his skin and my knees nearly buckled watching him. He pulled his arm from my grasp and wrapped them around me, taking full advantage of palming my ass.

He let out a heavy sigh, one that took up his whole chest. "I'll talk about it, I promise."

"Oh promises, I pride myself on taking those seriously." He leaned down and kissed me again. I tasted myself on his lips and that warm scent of his wrapped around me. His darkness wanted to connect with me, but I felt like so did his light.

"I promise. Please, trust me."

"I do trust you. I'm just..." I rubbed my lips together trying to find the words. "Worried about you."

He smiled at me and none of that nonchalant dull sadness was there. I wondered how long this would last before the darkness put him in pain again. I wondered how long it would be before Dimitri gave Lilith my message and she rained pure tyrannical hellfire on us all. They wanted to storm her castle, so maybe I should let them. Maybe I should quit playing her cat and mouse game. Nick would never last in there like this, she would have the dark engulfing him in minutes.

"I know baby, I know. I'm not the priority here though. As much as you don't like me saying it for my own sake, this mission is the priority."

"Ugh, Nick..."

A knock at the door shocked us both and we looked towards the semi-open door. Reese poked his head in, a mischievous grin on his face. "What are you guys doing?"

"Nothing. What do you want?" Nick answered.

"The little psycho is getting agitated in the living room and would like to have our group discussion. I'm only here because apparently Beetee made desserts and I'm nice enough to let you guys know so that you get some before they're gone," Reese explained.

"We'll be there in a minute."

Reese looked over both of us and rolled his eyes. "Also, uh, Rae and Eva, the sharp tooth twins, are also in the living room, so just a heads up. I feel like I never have enough clothes on with them two."

Nick scrubbed a hand down his face, and I let out a laugh because Rae and Eva didn't bother me. I may not always enjoy the Soul Seether label most times, but in this case, I would enjoy the fuck out of it if they came near what was mine again. Nick gave Reese a look and the blonde angel nodded and lifted his hand up. "Okay, okay, I'm going. Hurry up though, do *NOT* leave me out there for too long with all of them." He backed up and closed the door as he went.

I pushed away from the countertop and walked past Nick as he eyed me carefully. "Don't worry, the sharp toothed twins don't bother me. Not when I'm the one who gets to sit on your face later."

"Is that right?"

"That's right."

That light warmth curled around me, and I swore I could feel it coming from myself as much as it was coming from him. He chuckled and kissed my forehead, letting me walk ahead of him to the door. I swiveled around, halting him from going any further. He looked startled at my sudden movement, but he waited for me to speak. "You're fighting something unknown to you Nick,

I'm fighting something familiar. Our fights are the same in some aspects, but they have wild differences. I know you think that you have to keep it together, be that good soldier, consider all authority and think of yourself last, but maybe it's time you stopped and let yourself be selfish. I've had to be selfish my entire existence just to be at the top and survive, now so do you," He looked down at the floor, but I placed my fingers under his chin to force him to look at me. "Stop and let yourself fall apart while you still have people surrounding you who care."

"Dani…" I shook my head, silencing him. I didn't want a response, I just wanted him to listen.

"The darkness will take that choice from you. Here the darkness and Lilith are one so you might as well be letting Lilith own you just as much as she claims she owns me. Neither of us wants that." I got on the tips of my toes and ran a hand through his hair, kissing the scar underneath his eye. "You quiet my mind sometimes too, you know."

22

DANI

I heard him softly snoring next to me, that same vibrating dark energy rolling off of him in waves. Earlier, without me asking, he had summoned a ball of light that floated in a corner of the room, casting a small amount of illumination. My considerate night light. One of his hands was above his head while the other was wrapped around my side of the bed. I had woken up to voices in my head, but they weren't loud and obnoxious. They were soft, almost featherlike in my subconscious. It was nothing like the alarming cry that I heard when we were fighting the hellhounds, but I knew it was Lilith's voice trying to coax me into submitting, into being hers again. It was enough to wake me up, not in a panic, but just enough that I couldn't get back to sleep. I had awoken to a strong arm around the back of my neck and a chest underneath my cheek.

Lilith must have been furious when Dimitri told her I had refused. I wasn't a petulant child that made enormous rash decisions like that, but this was all getting to be too much, and it was hurting the people I cared about.

Elise wanted to just go in, shadows blazing, but even she knew that it wasn't worth it if we lasted all of five minutes. We were strong together, but as much as Lilith sat back and watched, she had her strength, and it was fucking scary when she put it on display. As much as I didn't think Nicholas and I had all that much in common, I was a creature who did enjoy the facts just as much as I enjoyed the thrill of going in blind. This mission needed both. The facts were so much easier when Heaven's Gate was the surrounding and the angels were the only ones to truly be concerned with. Now there was so much more to think about, so many questions. Some questions were answered while others would likely not be acquired until I was right in front of Lilith herself. Everyone we had spoken to seemed to have small facts, small pieces of conversations that matched up and made sense, but they never told the whole story; Lilith always left things out for only herself to ever know.

She couldn't force you to do something when she allowed you a choice, so now she's going to give you no choice.

Play her game and everyone wins. I would never.

I propped myself up on my elbow, looking down at the angel next to me. He looked gentle and serene as he slept. It was amazing how things looked on the outside. Demons rampaged inside his head and yet, he looked just as handsome as the day I met him. I watched the waves of dark energy dance around his body as if they were smoke fumes from a boiling pot. They slithered over to me, disappearing as they touched my skin. It would be so easy for me to let his darkness in, let it become one with me and just seek out the rest of his vulnerability. I could make his soul so dark while we were down here and then pull it out with so much ease, he wouldn't feel a thing. A part of me wanted that. I wouldn't deny that and pretend like I hadn't been manipulating darkness and seething souls for my entire existence, but I couldn't push myself to do it. I wasn't eager, it was just a habit of circumstance.

I brushed a piece of his hair away from his forehead and dragged my finger lightly down the side of his face, tapping the scar under his eye. I kept forgetting to ask him about it. I ran my thumb over the scar, watching as his eyes rolled under his eyelids. I wondered what he was dreaming about, I wondered if I really did make things better for him when he slept next to me like he said. I let out a breath and pushed the covers off my naked body, swinging my legs over the side. I found his shirt on the floor and tugged it over my head. I got up and felt a bit shaky standing up, my legs wobbling. I had told him that I would be sitting on his face later and I did like to maintain the things I said. I wanted to give his hurt arm a break and it was only fair that I provided him with the kind of care only I could give. He didn't complain. Eating me out was like a remedy for him.

I felt myself smile as I padded over to the bathroom, closing the door softly. I ran my hand through small tangles in my hair as I used the bathroom. When I was in front of the mirror I took a long look at myself. It was starting to feel like his overthinking was rubbing off on me and I fucking hated that. He could rub off on me in any other way, but he could take that overthinking bullshit back and lock it away. I was about to riot in my mind when I felt the ground shake under my feet. I looked down and it happened again. A growl rippled through the walls, and I knew that growl.

It was late enough to where the noise enchantment would be in effect, so when I opened the door, I didn't hear any footfalls and no screaming. Another loud growl, barreled through and *fuck*, it made my ears throb. Nick had a startled look on his face as he shot up out of the bed, quickly finding his underwear and pants. "What the fuck is that?"

I stepped outside of the bathroom, absentmindedly finding the rest of my clothes. I removed his shirt, throwing it at him, while I tugged on my loose crop top from earlier. "I don't..."

In a matter of seconds, every single sound entered my ears. Running, screaming, crying. It was like someone had lifted the enchantment to alarm everyone. Shuffling thundered from outside the door and Nick grabbed my hand, swinging it open. It was pure chaos in the hallway. Before we could take a step beyond the threshold, bodies were plowing past us. When it was safe to walk, we spotted Reese holding both his weapon and Nick's.

"Thought you might need this." He tossed the sword over to Nick, who caught it effortlessly.

Nick nodded at him and looked down towards where we could see the top of the stairs. "What's going on?"

"No fucking idea. It sounds like Axel isn't happy," Reese explained right as the ground shifted again. "I think..." He was cut off by a male voice, yelling from the outside. The voice was loud enough that every word could be heard, every piece of his tone accounted for.

"*Soul Seether*, come out and play! Bring your angels with you, huh." It didn't sound instantly familiar, but it did sound like someone pleading for a death wish since they seemingly decided that tonight was the night to piss me off.

"Friends of yours?" Reese said sarcastically. I pushed past both of them and a bunch of other patrons, taking the stairs two at a time and nearly jumping from the last two. Enchanters were huddled in the lounge and dining area, some of them hugging their children to their chests. I ripped the door open, stepping outside to not just one male demon threatening me, but a hoard of demons. I spotted Elise and Beetee, trying to hold different sections of them back. Beetee looked at me, one of her eyes was that pretty lilac and the other the diamond pupil of her snake form. She was trying to hold it in, but issues like this meant it was time to let that go.

Axel settled next to Elise, drool dripping from his mouth and his red eyes boring into the demons as he snapped his teeth at them. Reese and Nick walked up next to me surveying their surroundings. The plethora of demons were on all sides. I took a second, noticing that they were coming from the pathway that led to Devil's Playground.

"Finally! We just want to talk, Soul Seether." The voice from earlier said, walking past the crowd and stepping in front of them. It was the piece of shit from our first trip to Leviathan, the one who wanted to cause a fight for no reason, other than to just have a fight.

"I highly doubt that." I answered, keeping my eyes on each individual but always coming back to him. His hair was uneven from where I'd cut it, and it almost made me smirk thinking about our last encounter.

He snickered, the other demons taking a small step forward. "You really shouldn't go around making a fucking mess and not expect others to come looking for retribution."

I heard the door swing open and saw Leah and Garrett, taking in the sight. They looked alarmed, but they squared their shoulders and remained in place. "I'm sorry I don't even know your fucking name. What the hell are you talking about?" His friend, Rio, came up next to him, his hands cast in dark shadows as if he was readying himself for whatever tonight may bring.

He brought his hands up, shrugging. "How rude, I'm Erick. Dimitri wasn't so happy with your decision and of course he couldn't come here himself, busy man and all that, so he's letting us have some fun. Granted us permission to tear you and your little friends apart. Ready to have some fun, Soul Seether?" He looked behind him and cocked his head towards us. "Leave the demon princess for me."

Before I could blink, they were charging towards us. Dust kicked up around us when a large tail dropped to the ground. The iridescent scales shimmering as the tail rattled and swung. Beetee's large snake form descended upon the group while they tried to climb on her lengthy body, but she shook them off, slithering through the crowd as she went, causing demons to run and jump over her to get to us, to me. I could feel Nick moving next to me and Reese was following suit, readying his bow. He launched glowing arrow, after glowing arrow. They started falling but others would just take their place. Dimitri had a lot of sway when it came to demons, he was much more likable than Lilith and seeing as he was much, much closer to Lucifer, demons seemed to love that power high he was always wafting.

Erick swung his fist out, but I caught it, bringing my hand up and shoving it into his face as shadows propelled from my palm and encapsulated his head. I pushed him back, watching as he stumbled backwards onto his ass. Elise jumped up onto Axel's back and rode him through the crowd of demons, shooting bright red fire shadows at them. They clawed at Axel's paws and legs, but he opened his mouth removing their presence with his fire. Leah made the flames bigger, pushing out her magic to illuminate the flames even more, making them burn even hotter.

Everyone in the surrounding buildings and houses stayed where they were. They didn't think of taking a chance stepping outside into this mess. There were so many groans and grunts around me, so much yelling and the sound of slaughtering bodies bled into my ears. It was music if I was being honest, but I had to pay attention and make sure that it was the sound of the elimination of the other side I was hearing and not my friends. I felt a rope wrap around my waist and I was pulled backwards, the heels of my shoes skidding across the dirt. I hit a body that smelt of sweat and pure pathetic disappointment. "None of this would have to happen if you would just do as you're told," Erick breathed in my ear before taking the back of my head and throwing me forward. My face hit the ground harder than I anticipated and I felt his hands wrap around my ankles, but I twisted around and kicked my leg into his stomach, then further up so I kicked his face as well before springing up and grabbing his throat to yank him close to me. "Aw, does Daddy Dimitri tell you that you're a good boy when you do his bidding? What's your prize? Does he let you suck his dick cause you look like you have a great mouth for it." I gripped his throat harder and with all the strength I had threw him away from me towards the exterior of the hostel. I watched his body fly and then dust exploded around where he had been, followed by the sound of cracking wood.

Nicholas was doing well for someone who had every reason to want to sit this fight out. His sword was lit up, every single slice and movement was precise, and he glided through the footwork like he was born to wield a weapon and slay his enemies. He definitely didn't fight like a man who just got so severely scratched by a Son of Hell and now had a very large helping of darkness in his veins. Perhaps that was the sentry angel in him, pulling through and making shit work until it didn't work anymore. He dodged and weaved, using his blade to block most of their shadows, but it was odd that they seemed to be coming at him in waves...

They could sense it too. Darkness had a kinship with all of them and whatever Nick had was a four-course meal and the fact that it came from an angel was even worse or better depending on who you were. Garrett plowed through the demons, removing Nick from the circle that they had created around him and told him something I couldn't quite hear before he started fighting them himself, his own magic propelling out of his hands in various colors. My very stubborn angel had pushed out his wings and ascended to the sky, followed by Reese as they fought side by side, their glowing weapons making the dark sky not so dark anymore.

"I told you what would happen if you pissed me off again, Rio." Elise jumped off Axel as he continued to trudge through the throngs of demons, stepping on them and ripping them apart with his large teeth. She grabbed Rio by the back of the head before he could turn around and see her. Her tail slithered up his thigh and right between his legs. He thrashed in her grip, as other demons lunged for her, but she whipped her tail around in a complete circle, bringing each of them to the ground, writhing in pain. "And I make good on the things I say." She flung her tail back around and sliced him right between the legs, the blood immediately flowing down his legs and his wailing was loud, but also soothing. I knew it was to Elise as well when her face came into view as she then broke his neck, and the most satisfied look presented itself on her face when she dropped him to the ground. Axel came back around picking her up in one easy movement.

The few demons that had wings were in the sky as Nicholas struck them down one by one and Reese used his now aerial view to shoot his arrows, never missing his targets. He dipped down low and glided in smooth circles as he cast his arrows downward, creating beams of light as he shot them off his bow. Beetee took out all the ones she could, ripping them apart with her fangs, scooping them up with her hot pink forked tongue. I let my eyes go black, my soul dimming more than normal when I shot a wave of ripping darkness over the ones headed for me, knowing they had no intention of killing me, per Dimitri's wish to keep me alive, but I wouldn't just go with them because they felt like they threatened me, scared me. I had never scared easily, if at all. I ran my arm into the throat of one of my attackers and tripped the other one, placing my foot on his neck as he lay on the ground. I put pressure on my foot, hearing the crack of bones and the rush of blood.

"Mommy! Mommy!" A small cry fluttered into my ears and my heart thudded. A thundering heartbeat came from behind me. I whipped my head around to see Leah's little girl, Jasmine, standing outside the door of the hostel, eagerly searching for her mother. I saw startled faces from the doorway, hands reaching out trying to extract her from the situation she walked in on.

"Oh, look at this! How sweet!" I heard Erick say next to me as he cracked his neck. Leah turned her head around to her daughter and started to run towards her, but demons grabbed her and spun her around so that she knocked her head hard against the exterior of the hostel and passed out.

"Leave her alone!" Garrett shouted running towards Erick who stopped Garretts magic with his own shadows, gaining more power from what I would assume was Garrett's nervousness for his daughter, his angst. Erick shoved his arm out, throwing Garrett in the other direction.

I could feel myself wanting to know that innocent soul, have it and distort it. I wanted to see what it looked like and how much she would cry when it happened.

Soul Seether.

Fuck. No. No. No.

Do it. Do it.

Erick ran over to Jasmine, who had a frightened look on her face. She had nearly seen her own brother get torn to pieces. I tried to push the voice, Lilith's voice, away. It was so welcoming, so familiar. And then another voice came that was also those things, but it made my heart warm.

"Dani!" It was deep and assertive, causing me to blink and focus myself. There was something about Nick's voice that made me want to stop, rethink, and reevaluate my efforts. The darkness still enjoyed what I was about to do, but it hated that it couldn't do what it wanted, feed off the small girl in front of me. I charged over to where Erick was about to pick up Jasmine and elbowed him right in the face. He stumbled back and I punched up under his jaw, sending him flying backwards. I grabbed Jasmine's shaking body, her eyes wide and scared. I probably wasn't the best face to look at, but there was a part of me that wanted her safe. "Go back inside now!" Her lower lip trembled but she did as she was told, huddling into the body of an Enchanter that grabbed her as the door opened.

"That's how you want to play, Soul Seether, then by all means let's play your way," Erick threatened. His eyes turned into black whirls of nothing, just like mine were. "We tried to be nice."

Beetee slithered around, but Erick caught her tail. She hissed as he gripped it tightly and swung it in Reese's direction. Her tail hit his stomach, sending him backwards and landing on the roof of the hostel. The last arrow he shot was caught by a demon who managed to climb onto Axel and plunged the still glowing arrow into Elise's side. They pulled the arrow out and slammed it into her side again. Axel used his tail to jerk the demon off of him, throwing him into a pile of others before spewing fire at them all. "*Fucking* arrows. Fuck." Elise slumped forward a bit as she held her side.

Erick still held Beetee's tail, black flames appearing around her iridescent scales, and she started to wiggle and thrash, wanting to get rid of the pain as it began to travel up her body. Reese slid down from the roof, grabbing onto the ledge for dear life. Axel made quick work to swing back around to the hostel and grab Reese before he completely let go of the ledge, the back of his shirt was shredded, and blood was coming out of the scrapes and open wounds.

I manifested my dagger and went to swing at him, but he caught my wrist, twisting it. He enveloped his hand in darkness and punched me in the stomach. All the wind came out of me, and I hunched over. He let me go and came around so that he was behind me before kicking me down, so I landed on my stomach. He yanked me by my ankles towards him and crouched down, lifting me up by my throat. I shifted so that one of my arms gained freedom and without really looking I stabbed him in the shoulder with my dagger. He made a grunting sound and grabbed my hair, pressing my face into the ground before lifting me up again. "I can't really hurt you, which is fortunate for you. But now you've really pissed me off, which means it's time for the grand finale."

He turned my head to look at Nicholas fighting demons off, next to Elise who was still managing to fight even though she was wobbling and holding her side. Reese used Axel's height to continue to shoot his arrows as best he could, but he was weak. Erick chuckled, "I can smell it from here you know, his weakness. Dimitri did say this would be worth it."

I didn't know what he was talking about until I heard it. I heard the grunt of pain, the groan of mental strain. Nicholas held his sword out to swing, but the glow of it started to stutter. It sparked and faded, over and over again. He looked down at his weapon as his face contorted into one of pure pain. Erick came down to my ear, his breath unwelcomed. "Dimitri didn't say your little angel would make it so easy."

I heard his weapon drop as demons were still fighting but others were so focused on him, pushing everything they had to make him stumble and eventually he fell to his knees. Elise and Reese tried to rally, but were overpowered, too hurt and damaged from this fight to try as much as I knew they wanted to. Nicholas grabbed the sides of his head and his whole body began to shake. Even from where I was and how dark the night sky was, the dark waves that were so soft while he slept, twisted, and lashed out at him now as if they were realizing they were winning, they had the upper hand.

"Eventually he'll be nothing but an empty shell, forever lost in his own pathetic fragility. Poor boy, so many nightmares, so much hidden sadness."

Nicholas pulled at his hair and tried to get up, but it was like a weight was on his shoulders, forcing him down. "Make it stop! Make it stop! Make it stop!" he screamed over, over, over again.

There was fire in places surrounding us and it brought to light everything I didn't want to see. A frail Beetee hovered over a still unconscious Garrett, her legs reddened and scarred from the dark flames. Elise and Reese were on their knees near Nicholas, forced to watch him fall apart while they each took labored breaths from their own wounds they'd sustained. Their faces were dirt covered and sweaty, Elise's tail disappeared, not much use when its user was out of commission and Reese hissed at the way they pulled his hair forcing him to look. Leah remained out cold near the outside of the hostel and Axel had been forced down by so many demons, a dark rope around his thick throat, pulsing dark shocks into him. Even a beast as large as him knew his limits. Flames licked at the ground around us making everything so much more dramatic and daunting.

I ran my fingers into the ground, hating this, hating all of it. I wasn't the type of demon who sat down, was forced down, and did nothing. Erick had gained so much power from those around him and likely from Dimitri himself, but I was still who I always had been and creatures like Erick didn't have the right to think me weak. I forced my shadows to work with me because while I was in control, they didn't tell me what to do. I wouldn't get my fill of rage from young things like Jasmine, I would get it from halfwits like Erick. I placed my hands flat on the ground feeling it shake under my palms. Smoke started to rise from the dirt and gravel, translucent, but it was menacing. It belonged to me, it did what I said. Dark smoke filled the air, shadow silhouettes presented themselves around us. I felt Erick slowly let go of me as he took in what was happening.

The silhouettes grabbed each and every demon around the neck and twisted. They twisted until the angle was odd and a resounding snapping sound was made. They then shoved through their bodies, creating ghastly holes right in their stomachs as they all fell to the ground. I pushed back and shoved my elbow into Erick's face as I flipped around. As he stumbled back, I hooked my leg around his foot and plucked his leg from the ground causing him to topple backwards. I was on him in minutes, his face shining with that perfect scar I left from before. I took my dagger and ran it over the wound again, opening up his scar as blood spilled from his face. "Fortunately, you won't have to tell Dimitri you failed." I willed my shadowy silhouettes to pull his arms behind his back, breaking his wrists. I quickly went behind him, tilting his head back. I held my dagger to his throat, the hooked tip just piercing the skin. "Did Lilith tell Dimitri to send you?"

His eyes bugged out with his will to try and not answer me, but the resistance was futile. "Yes," he got out in one breath. I let thick ropes of dark magic thread out of my fingers and around his neck, squeezing. His face started to turn a different color and I yanked his head back further, making him to look at me.

"Fucking with me twice was your mistake. Dimitri did you dirty." I started to press the dagger into his neck, but he caught me with his final words. Words that he had to get out between breaths from how hard I was gripping his throat.

"Do yourself a favor and submit, Soul Seether. Lilith plans to see you soon, you have too much to lose if you don't." He started laughing as best as someone could when their esophagus was being deflated. I looked over his head at Nick who was beside himself on the ground, his hands over his face. He was in the fetal position and my brow furrowed, narrowing my eyes down at the demon at my feet. I had nothing to say to him. I bared my teeth, dark smoke coming from my hair and wrapping around my body and hands. Instead of cutting my dagger across his neck, I shoved it into his throat, hooked end up. I walked around to his front as he gurgled on his own blood. Grabbing the hilt of my weapon, I tilted my dagger up and pulled down, hearing ripping sounds from the inside of his throat. I removed my dagger from his neck and watched as he slumped over, his eyes rolling back and then my dark silhouettes descended on him, doing whatever they did to rid me of my problems.

I'd never called on them or anything like that before. It was new to me, but it wasn't something I could dwell on at this moment. I willed my dagger away and ran over to where Nick was on the ground. Elise limped over, pressing her hand to her side, blood coming out from between her fingers. I knelt down and placed my hand on his shoulder. He flinched away from me before looking up and seeing my face. His breathing was labored, and his face was so distraught, like the pain and agony he felt prior to this moment wasn't gone. I kept my hand on his shoulder and started rubbing it. "Hey, it's me. I'm right here."

I heard a groan from my right side and noticed Leah finally waking up. As big as Garrett was, Beetee seemed to have no problems carrying him against herself as she slowly came over to us, sitting him down next to his wife. Reese leaned against Axel who softly licked his face, but the giant hellhound also crowded over Nick, seeming to shield him as much as he could. Nick blinked a few times as if he was seeing everything normally for the first time. My stomach boiled with renewed disgust for Dimitri and Lilith, for what they put him through. He was so close to breaking and I almost hadn't been able to stop it.

I brushed his hair from his forehead as I helped him sit up. He looked so scared, so much younger than I knew he was. I didn't know what the darkness showed him, I didn't know what it manifested in his mind, but he was shaking, and it looked as if he wanted to cry but he didn't let tears fall. Maybe he needed to. I placed my hand gently over his heart, it was beating so loudly that I was surprised it didn't explode from his chest. He blew out an unsteady breath and closed his eyes, immediately opening them, probably afraid of what he would see when left in the dark.

I spoke softly and didn't pay any attention to those around me. Nothing mattered right now, but this angel and his pain. "I'm going to take care of you."

23

NICK

Everything felt like a blur. It felt like the room was spinning, but unlike all the other times, I didn't feel sick. My head throbbed and I felt so confined, like I couldn't get enough air or that my mind didn't have room to expand and let loose. I felt trapped in my own head and where I was—where my head was at—was dark and manipulative. It was the type of mental prison that made your thoughts worse or manipulated something good into something ugly. I felt like a thousand rocks were on my chest and every intake of breath was rough and felt like my throat was being rubbed raw. I had never been afraid of the dark, not as a child, but now, it was the scariest thing I knew.

I felt myself being picked up and watched as bodies I recognized, friends of mine walked around me. I knew Reese anywhere, could feel him place my weight into him as he held me up. I smelt the familiar scent of cinnamon and a calm rushed over me in a way nothing else could. It didn't change how my insides felt at the moment, as much as I wished it did. Dani might quiet my head at times, but she couldn't quiet the rest of me. They were talking around me and some of it was too fast, but at other times I could hear them perfectly.

"What happened to him?" Reese pressed.

"What I was afraid would happen to him," Dani explained, the nervousness in her tone hard to miss.

I felt myself being pulled in one direction and then turned in another. "He isn't going into that recovery room. That's close to too many people right now. We'll take him to my room." Dani's voice was stern.

"Are you sure?" Beetee's high pitched voice had a delicate softness to it right now.

"Let Dani and Blondie take him upstairs and we can see about everyone else down here. We'll reconvene later…" Elise trailed off, the sound of her footsteps fading away from my ears.

I heard running around me, tiny feet stomping. Their voices were small and the sound of them crying for their parents was vibrating around me.

We were walking again, up the stairs, one foot after the other. I felt the plush softness of a pillow under my cheek. My feet were lifted and placed on the bed as well and I wanted to relax, close my eyes, but I couldn't. I didn't know what that would mean for me, for my mind. My body started to shake from the chills I felt, even though from what I could see neither Reese nor Dani looked cold at all.

"You can go. I got him." I heard Dani say.

"I'm not going to leave him alone like this." Reese's words sounded scared and fearful.

I watched Dani step up to him and squeeze his shoulder. "I got this. Please just let me do this." I blinked and saw Reese's shoulders lift up and then down as he submitted to her plea and nodded. He looked over at me and took a few steps in my direction, leaning down so his head was hovering over mine. He smelled like sweat. "We got you." He took my hand and squeezed it, the pressure of it sending a wave through my arm, letting me know I was here. This was real, I was okay.

He walked out, closing the door behind him. Dani sat on the bed, the small weight of her not even causing it to dip a little. Her breathing was soft and careful. She shifted so that she could bend her knee and stretch it out so that it was angled onto the bed, her other leg dangling off the side. She was looking down at me, her mass of curls shadowing the sides of her face like a curtain. I saw blood on her neck and near her hands and arms. I wondered if it was hers, or theirs. So much blood, so much blood that I spilled. There was an orb of light in the corner of the room that I remembered creating, giving the light I knew some sort of tether, but the tether was weak and fragile.

Did that make me fragile and weak as well?

"Nick."

I stared off into the distance, hearing her voice but not knowing how to answer her.

"Nick," she repeated. I peeked over at her. "Nick, how do you feel?"

I looked away from her immediately. "Fine."

"Answer me."

"I just did."

She huffed out a breath. "No, you didn't. You gave the same answer you always do."

"Dani, just stop," I pleaded, stuffing my cheek into the pillow more. It was so soft and inviting that I could have just stayed here forever. Maybe I could try to hide from what was chasing me, what had my mind spinning in circles.

"No. I won't. I'm done coddling you. You need to tell me what you're feeling or what's happening is only going to get worse."

I placed my hand on the side of my head and nearly bit down on my tongue, needing the pressure of my thoughts to go away. It hit me all at once now. That light I created seemed so far away. Jonah. All those sentries that died. So many secrets. The darkness closed in as if it was a dance. A dance fated to ruin me and revolt against anything other than the pain I felt.

I did this. You did this. I did this.

You weren't good enough. You did this. No hero.

My body started shaking over and over again. The darkness hissed from the interruption. I was turned around onto my back. Her body leaned over mine, her eyes were wide and alarmed. "Nick! You can't let it take over. You have to talk to me!"

My mouth was dry, and my throat felt like it was shrinking. "Nick! You have to fight it and just stop holding it in. Talk. To. Me." She gave me one last hard shake and I felt it as my body hit the bed again. I removed her hands from my arms and lifted myself up and back so that my back hit the headboard. Her brown eyes waited for me to speak, they looked desperate to hear my response.

"I don't know what to tell you Dani. I'm sorry I'm not strong enough to push back, just leave me alone and just fucking let it happen."

"You need to say this shit out loud, Nick. If and why you're sad, scared, angry, nervous…all of it! You need to do what I've been pleading for you to do. You've let something else in and it's tearing you apart because of your own self-deprecating behavior and now you need to let someone else in to help you find your way out."

I pressed the heels of my hands into my eyes. It wouldn't shut up. It felt like it was right in my ear. Blinking started to be something I couldn't do when flashes of Jonah's dead body ran across my mind.

I did this. You did this. I did this.

You weren't good enough.

"I can't."

"You can."

I lifted my head towards the ceiling. So, so tired. "I can't."

"Nick..."

"I CAN'T! I CAN'T! I CAN'T!" I screamed, pushing off the bed, my whole body was vibrating that it made it difficult to stand still. I wanted to pull my fucking hair out, I wanted to punch something. I wanted too—

I didn't want to not feel like this anymore.

Dani tentatively got off the bed, taking small steps towards me. I towered over her but at this moment I felt small and useless. It was like every single bone in my body wanted to break and there was nothing I could do to repair it, so I was forced to watch it crumble into something no self-respecting angel could live with. She didn't touch me. She simply stood by me and steadied her breathing, probably hoping I would try to match it. "Nick." She said my name in this voice that had me wanting to release the tension from my shoulders. "Maybe not all at once, but piece by piece. Can you do that?" Her words were slow and easier to follow than the rapid things going on in my head.

I swallowed the lump that had settled in my throat. And I tried to push the negative thoughts down enough, just enough to give her a fraction of what she wanted. I nodded, every dip of my head feeling like too much weight at one time. "Jonah died."

Her eyelashes fluttered as she blinked a few times. "I know."

"In my arms."

"Yes."

I raised my palms up and I could see Jonah lying there as I sat on the ground, taking his last breath. I could see the dark waves starting to waft off of my skin. It was the first time their presence had made themselves known to me. "H-he was right here. R-right in my a-arms," I stuttered, closing my eyes tightly and peeling them open again, hoping that the visual would be gone, but it was only much more vivid now. I shook my head, frantic to remove it.

I did this. You did this. I did this.

"I can't do this. I'm s-sorry," I apologized, backing away from her.

She took the same number of steps forward. "No, no, Nick. Keep going. It will keep pressuring you to stop, but don't stop. Tell me more."

I let out a shaky breath, licking my lips. "I thought so badly about him. I thought the worst and it wasn't him. He wasn't the bad guy. He died always thinking the best of me and I had a small moment of thinking the worst of him." She nodded, telling me to keep going.

I ran both my hands through my hair, keeping them there. "I shouldn't have let him die. I watched him die. He died. His blood was on my hands. All of it. All of their blood. Fuck. *Fuck*." I remembered slashing through angels I'd gone to school with, angels that at the moment I didn't remember their names but if I had been given time it likely would have come to my mind. "I killed so many of them. They're all dead. Dead. Because of me. I didn't even give it a second thought; I just killed them. They're dead." I repeated my thoughts. Every moment, every feeling I recollected came back stronger and started to rip at my chest. It burned and pulsed. Sharp breath after sharp breath left my lungs.

"All their blood is on my hands, Dani." I lifted up my palms to show her what I could see as bloody, dripping with the dark red liquid, but her eyes fluttered from one hand to the other as if she didn't see anything. She didn't look at me like I was insane though, she looked at me like she understood. "I wasn't enough. I'm a monster for it. I didn't think, I didn't *try* to think. Jonah died thinking I could make things better, but I can't. My father thinks that I can make things better, but I fucking can't. I'm not the one who makes things better! I let them all fucking die!"

She took another step towards me, but I backed up again. I turned around to face the wall. "So many secrets. Jonah, my mother, parts of my head are fucked up and it's all so much. It's one thing after another and I have to push through to be better than what I did, what I let happen."

"Nick, the circumstances for what happened with Jonah was out of our hands..."

I whirled around, my chest heaving. "So many families had to know that their children weren't coming home because of something we did, something *I* did!" I pushed my index finger into my chest. "That's on *me*. And I've tried my best to move on. Be this sentry angel Jonah, my father, and everyone else wanted me to be. I've moved on to the next thing, spent my time mourning the loss and compartmentalized. I just keep seeing their faces...their blood..." I trailed off, wobbling a little on my feet. The burning in my chest continued and the darkness danced around my skin and scorched my veins. "They won't leave me alone. I was too weak to stop Markus, too weak to help Jonah, too weak that someone was able to go inside my fucking head at some point and mess with it." My voice was shaking, and I backed up against the wall, the wood hitting my back that was starting to sweat.

Dani crowded me against the wall. "Jonah didn't want you to save him."

"I shouldn't have let him make that choice. I should have saved him. That would have made me good, that would have made me everything he thought I was. He would still be here. Markus would be dead, but Jonah wouldn't be."

"Markus did this. Lilith did this. Fucking Isabel did this Nick, not you."

I punched the wall from behind me with my fist. "What did I do to stop it!? I fought and wasn't good enough. I bled on the lawn and for what? I did all that just to be stuck with this." I waved my hand over myself. My voice cracked at the end, my throat felt constricted, but not from the weight of the darkness, but from my own emotions. My eyes burned; they burned so fucking much. "It's like trudging through life day after day. Every time I feel like I get closer to feeling better, I get sucked down to feel like shit. I'm weak and it knows it. I proved it to myself that day and it's been apparent every single fucking day since." I placed my hand at the back of my neck, lifting my head to the ceiling again. The darkness was screaming at me.

Shut up. Shut up. You did this.

You weren't good enough.

I blew out breath after breath, the view in front of me slightly blurring. I didn't know what was happening. "I'm not a hero, Dani. I hate Markus for what he did. Isabel, Lilith, everyone involved. I do, I really do, but I—I hate…" I wanted to hyperventilate over the rapid-fire images that were happening through my blurry vision, but the blur was making them less noticeable. They were there, but they weren't so threatening. "I hate myself. I'll go back to Heaven's Gate if that's what you want. I just want to stop seeing their faces, I just want to stop seeing it all…" My cheeks felt wet as I felt myself being pulled forward and into her arms.

Dani held onto me as the wetness on my cheeks grew and I closed my eyes. We were both dirty and bloody, but I still wrapped my arms around her lower back and squeezed, holding on like my entire existence depended on it. Like my sanity depended on it. Maybe it did. My shoulders shook and I buried my face into her shoulder as she stood on the balls of her feet. I felt her shirt getting wet under my face, but she didn't pull away. My voice was muffled, and my words felt like they came out choked. "I'm so sorry. I'm sorry that I'm not strong enough, I'm not good enough. I want to tell Jonah I'm sorry, but I can't. I can't do that, Dani. I won't ever be able to do that because I wasn't enough. You deserve someone who isn't fucking broken and holding you back. I'm sorry, I'm sorry, I'm fucking sorry."

She reached up and rubbed my back. "It's okay, baby. It's okay. I may not understand it all, but I know pain and I can feel yours. It knows you're accepting things, and it isn't happy, but let me ease it." It was a strange feeling as the darkness started to remove itself from me. It was its own entity, slow moving and wispy. It tumbled within itself as it flowed into her body. She took it with ease, as if it knew exactly where to go even though it didn't enjoy the fact that it was being pushed out. It wasn't completely gone from me, it probably never would be, but there was a lightness to my body now and the tears flowed harder at the relief. I felt my hands heat from the light generating itself back into my system, no longer diminished by so much venomous darkness.

Dani ran her hands through as much of my hair as she could. "You are always enough, Nicholas Cassial. Broken and in pieces, you are enough. Heroes are allowed to be broken; it doesn't make them any less of a hero." I shook against her, thinking that I was holding her too hard, that I would break her along with how much I realized I needed her. "We'll figure everything out, the secrets, your dad, and whatever else there is, I'll be right here."

"I'm so fucking tired of trying," I said between the tears flowing down my cheeks.

She kissed my cheek again and again. "Then stop for a minute. Breathe. Just be here and think of nothing else. Just exist. Exist with me."

I couldn't stand on my feet anymore so she fell with me onto the floor, holding onto me the entire time. She held me like she couldn't imagine herself anywhere else but wrapped up in me. For the first time in months, I sobbed and sobbed and sobbed.

My body felt numb when I woke up. I had a moment of panic thinking I was back in one of my nightmares. When I tried to stretch out my arm it told me that the numbness was from sore limbs, likely from the fight or possibly from being so wound up for a long while and finally letting it go. Or at least speaking it out loud so that it wasn't trapped inside my own mind any longer. My arms had dirt on them and cuts and bruises in various places, most of them turning into scabs already. I felt a body underneath me and I peeked up from where I was laying, noticing that I was resting my head in Dani's lap. I could feel the hard wooden floor beneath us, telling me we hadn't moved since I'd broken down. Her eyes were open when I looked at her and she was just staring off into the distance, as if she was lost in her own thoughts. Her hand was absentmindedly petting my hair. I moved my body a little more, letting her know I was awake.

She blinked down at me and gave me a small smile that didn't quite meet her eyes. "Hi."

"Hi." I didn't know what to say to her. I was mildly embarrassed at what had happened, but also grateful that it had. It was overwhelmingly painful to speak the truth, but in the end, it was worth it, like she kept trying to get me to understand. "How long have I been out?"

She shrugged. "Around two hours maybe."

"And you've just been awake this whole time?"

She brushed a piece of her hair behind her ear. "A lot just happened alright. I wasn't going to just take my eye off you, just in case."

"Your verdict?"

She slid one of her fingers down my cheek. "I'm proud of you."

For some reason, that tugged at that beating organ in my chest. "I might be a little proud of myself." I pushed my body off the ground, feeling the undeniable knot in my neck from the position I slept in and mimicked her position against the wall. She watched my movements skillfully as if anything and everything could trigger something. Nothing happened though, I just leaned down and kissed her. One soft, quick peck on the lips. "Thank you."

She waved me off, giving me another kiss. "Angels are allowed to make mistakes, Nick. You are allowed to fight and draw blood when necessary. You will watch people die. I just don't understand why you didn't talk to your father or Reese. Maurice Cassial doesn't seem like the type to spread toxic masculinity."

I let out a short humorless laugh. "He isn't. And Reese tried to get me to talk, I mean they all did, but I just thought I could handle it. I thought I *was* handling it. Things weren't as bad back home, but here, it just got elevated. I was overwhelmed and by this time it was just too late to try to explain it all."

Dani hummed. "I think Reese feels sad over everything, but I do think he has more anger over what happened. He thinks more straight ahead, a blatant disregard for anyone in his way. I also think he's kind of obsessed with your well-being. The darkness loves the angry and resentful, but it thrives on the sad and regretful, and the untapped pain that an entity harbors just so they can exploit it for themselves."

"I should have listened to you. I know."

She narrowed her eyes at me playfully, but there was a hint of worry in her eyes. "I can understand wanting to fix things yourself, needing things to maintain order or you'll lose all control, but sometimes while you're trying to ignore the issue, you end up not seeing that control is being lost anyway. You are allowed to do things on your own time, but not at the expense of your sanity." She placed her hand on my chest, turning her body and pulling her legs up so that she was cuddled into my side. She was scolding me in the gentlest way. "I don't know much about grief, Nick. I don't mourn the loss of souls or cry when Lilith rips people to shreds, even if I knew them. I've never attached myself to someone so fucking much that my chest ached over them."

I brought my legs up so that they were parallel to my chest. "It's an exhausting feeling."

"What I'm trying to say is my chest does ache over you. Seeing you hurt, seeing you cry, I don't like it, it was necessary, but I wish it hadn't been." I'd had a feeling that resembled that perfectly when I saw her bleeding out during her death when Lilith took her away. I remember thinking I was happy she was the one holding me and telling me that my emotions were valid while I sobbed into her shoulder. I felt like there was something I should say here, but I couldn't get my mouth to form the words, and neither could she with the way she was looking at me.

"You and I both. I wish I didn't make you worry about me."

"It's only fair", she cleared her throat. "How are you feeling?"

I looked down at my body as if I could see some sign of how I felt before. "I know something is there, but I don't feel suffocated by it. I don't feel like if I close my eyes, I won't open them again." I looked over at the glowing light from earlier and I felt closer to it again. I opened my hand, palm facing up and bits of light danced and pulsed along my fingertips. I had told her that everyone had a bit of darkness in them regardless and I was no exception, it would always be there, but it wasn't in charge. My soul would probably always be a bit tainted, but it wouldn't take over my entire being.

"And you'll let me know if you feel like that again? You'll let *someone* know, Nicholas."

I closed my eyes, taking in air through my nose and letting it out from my mouth. "Yes."

She leaned her head on my shoulder, her hair tickling my jaw. "You *should* talk to Reese. As much as I adore being the one you seek comfort in, I think he would like to know you can still rely on him as well." I liked that they were getting along in some way, that I didn't have to keep watch over them and their interactions with one another.

I nodded knowingly. I hadn't necessarily pushed my best friend away, but I hadn't been forthcoming either. Despite his faults he's always just wanted the best for me. So did my father and oddly so did Jonah. I remembered something and started to thread my fingers through hers as they both rested on the ground between us. "Are *you* okay?"

"What do you mean?"

"Well, I happen to remember you taking some of the darkness from me. Wasn't that something you were trying to avoid?" I raised one of my eyebrows.

She nuzzled her face onto my shoulder, kissing it. "Yes and no. It's different when it's offering itself and wants me to help it break you down. I willingly took it because *you* were actively pushing it out as painful as it was. I would rather harbor it myself than have it try to dig its claws into someone else here."

"That sounds dangerous. For you I mean," I said hesitantly.

"I can handle darkness, Nick. Being dangerous is kind of the point. Despite the angelic part, I am a whole lot of darkness and adding a little more won't change that. I won't say sorry for wanting to fuck people up for the sake of a successful ending. I have to maintain this to be able to face Dimitri's wrath after what happened and the fact that I might give Elise and Garrett the ambush they wanted. There isn't much more holding us or me back. We've already severely angered a Son of Hell, so why not just dive right into the clusterfuck of a mess we've made. Screams Purgatory, doesn't it?"

I laughed softly nodding. I squeezed her hand in understanding. "Just like you didn't want it for me, don't let it overtake you as well. Remember who you are, Dani."

"And who's that? A monster?" She asked it like that was the obvious answer. She had meant it like a joke, but I knew that deep down that was probably what she thought, what her head was telling her. Unlike what she did for me, I had no idea how to fix her connection with Lilith, how to fix an eternity of Lilith's words. She had the most innocent face, but she had seen and done terrible things. She was this powerful being that I still wanted to protect just as much as she wanted to protect me.

I could feel something warm humming underneath her skin, her body, and her soul. It was grasping at threads, but I felt it. I just hoped maybe one day she would be able to embrace it enough to feel all it had to offer. I reached my hand around and gently grabbed her face, tilting her chin up. I placed my forehead against hers. Bloody and deadly, she was still so, so beautiful. "Someone good. Someone worth saving."

A smile graced her face, and she pressed her forehead harder into mine. "Remember who you are too, Nicholas."

"Hmm?" I responded, letting my nose rub against hers.

"A hero."

24

DANI

I watched as Nick and Reese grabbed some food the next morning and headed back upstairs to talk. We had gotten so many looks when we'd come downstairs and I didn't mind them staring, I was pretty used to it by now, but Nick was different. It looked as if he wasn't letting it get to him, but I could tell that he hadn't been in the mood to answer anyone's questions unless they came from his best friend. When I'd buried myself under my covers, after tucking him into the bed, he had pulled me into his body and held me there. I listened to the beats of his heart and felt his warm chest against my cheek. We didn't clean ourselves up or even try to remove our clothes, we just fell asleep together in all the blood and dirt of what had happened. He fell asleep so easily when he was in my arms, and I watched him rest peacefully for a good half hour until I finally dozed off myself. We'd woken up and gone our separate ways to change clothes and clean up before making our way downstairs together.

Nick gave me one last look and probably the sexiest wink in the history of Hell before disappearing. Beetee had her legs propped up on the couch, the redness and swelling still there but not as significant as I thought it would be. She had her arm thrown over her face while Elise prattled on about something while lazily sitting in one of the armchairs.

"Nice of you to finally join us," Elise said as a way of greeting. She had on a sports bra and a large bandage was attached to her side. I took my coffee off the countertop in the small kitchen and walked over to them, shifting past some demons who hustled past me like I wasn't one of the creatures that saved them from the demons that likely would have burnt this whole place down.

I plopped down in the chair opposite her and rolled my eyes. "I was busy."

"Ah, yes. Having very loud, very obnoxious sex with your boyfriend," she teased.

I took a long sip of my coffee and then placed it on the coffee table. "No. Far from it." I scratched the top of my head, getting pieces of my hair tangled in my fingers. "And we aren't that loud."

Beetee snorted from her place on the couch. She moved her arm from over her eyes and her golden-brown skin started to redden with a blush. "I wouldn't say you guys try to be quiet." She tilted her head to look over at Elise who shrugged at how right she was. Beetee flinched a little as she tried to sit up. Her lilac eyes focused on me. "How is he?"

I tilted my head from side to side. "Um, he's okay. As best as he can get right about now. It was a long night."

"Did he decide he wanted to go home?" Elise asked, arching one of her dark brows.

I shook my head. "Nope. He has no desire to go home. I mean he mentioned it, but he thought that's what I wanted I guess."

Beetee ran one of her hands over the shaved part of her head. "Do you think he should go home?"

I slumped back in my chair. "I think I can't make decisions for him."

"I think he values your opinion more than most," Beetee looked down and patted her chest. Axel, who I hadn't known was on the floor, jumped up and landed with an odd amount of grace on her chest. He snuggled against her body and immediately started to fall asleep. There was a scarring ring around his neck from where the demons had tried to restrain him. It didn't seem to stop him though.

"What even happened back there?" Elise inquired, leaning forward. Her face showed a small sign of discomfort, but it was gone faster than it had been there. I stared down at my feet, not really knowing where to start. I explained it the best I could to them, gave them the details that mattered and left the personal things for Nick to explain when and if he desired. They were owed some sort of explanation for what happened, especially Beetee. Once I was finished, they both looked at each other as if they were waiting for the other one to speak first.

Elise waved her hand in the air. "So, Dimitri elevated Nick's darkness?"

I nodded. She tilted her head to the side as if considering that this made sense to what ultimately happened later on that night. She didn't stop there. "You're telling me that we now have Dimitri, Lilith and Isabel to deal with at the same time?"

"And no one seems to know why she wants you to just surrender yourself over?" Beetee added.

"Yes and yes," I answered, reaching for my coffee cup. Before I could reach it, Elise had gotten up from her chair and raced over to sit at the edge of the coffee table, nearly spilling my drink over. She reached for her side, tapping her fingers along the wound dressing. I leaned back startled, readjusting my sitting position. "I mean per Dimitri's words she's "trying to be nice and give me a choice", even though she's made it clear, also per Dimitri's words, that "she'll make it so I have no choice", it's all a mindfuck, which tracks pretty well, seeing as it's Lilith."

"Are you reconsidering the ambush plan now? Dimitri said he wouldn't suggest it, which is honestly all the more reason to do it. Piss the little dick off."

Beetee smoothed her hand down Axel's back. "Dimitri has the backing of his father and, likely Lucifer, so I don't see this as some easy mission, Ellie." Axel's ears twitched.

Elise scoffed. "I am by no means afraid of Dimitri, his father, and especially not of fucking *Lucifer*." Axel's ears twitched again, and he raised his head, looking at Elise. He barked once and she whirled her head around squinting at him. "Oh hush. We both know you would love to go to Hell but that's not in the cards buddy." The hellhound gave a rough, annoyed huff and curled back into Beetee's chest.

"I have been doing some thinking on it," I admitted, tentatively reaching for my cup of coffee.

"And?" Elise pressed.

"I..." Little footsteps running down the stairs caught my attention. I slung my arm over the chair as I turned around and watched Jasmine and Yuri race after each other. Leah and Garrett followed after them, small cuts and bruises on their faces and arms. Garrett had a slight limp to his walk, but they looked good.

"What are we speaking about?" Garrett asked, curiously.

Elise crossed her arms over her chest. "Dani was just about to give us what we both want."

I let out a sigh as he raised both his eyebrows at me. His braids were flowing over his shoulders. "And what may that be?"

"Raiding the castle. You have to face it head on Dani, or this is never going to end. This trip will have been totally pointless if she just keeps using all her stupid little puppets to antagonize us."

"I get it alright, fuck."

Leah sat on the arm of the couch Beetee laid on and looked at her husband, her dark hair in waves down her back. Her tattoos were on full display, thanks to her tank top, and they were intricate and beautiful. They must mean something, when it came to Enchanters, and I didn't know if I would ever have time to really ask. "You saved our child. We are in this with you and can provide you with as much as we know about, or remember, about Lilith's castle. There are more ins and outs to that place than you can imagine."

"We're in your debt for what you did last night," Garrett offered. "We may not be on the best of terms since what happened with Yuri, but I was told you fought against it this time, you worked to save my child. As much as I can't forget what you did before, I can't just forget this either."

"I don't want a debt, Garrett, I just want to know that when push comes to shove, we are on the same side with the same enemy in mind." I peered up at him from where he stood, and he gave me one solid nod. His golden eyes were sincere and true.

He let out one solid chuckle. "Jasmine isn't afraid of you, you know. She's shocked at what she saw but she's a resilient little girl. You might be her hero." I looked away from him and took up interest in the blank wall.

That word again. That word was reserved for beings like my angel upstairs, not for me. I didn't save Nicholas, he saved himself, I just pushed him along. I didn't save the creatures in this hostel; I just took out the trash that, for some reason, did Dimitri's bidding.

"What's the verdict, Dani?" Elise asked, her gray eyes sparkling with this blood thirsty lust for revenge.

"We can do it." We had enough minds to build a solid plan, one that Nicholas would be proud of, and Lilith wouldn't be able to think less of any of us. I would make her beg for my forgiveness before I made sure she could never speak again.

"I think I know some others that can help," Beetee piped up.

We all looked at her, waiting. Her hot pink hair was even more vibrant against the blush on her face and her freckles. "My parents."

I knitted my eyebrows together. "Your parents?"

"They were with Lilith way before Garrett and Leah ever got caught up in this mess, so I don't think it would hurt. They know that castle just as well."

"They were pretty close with Lilith?" I questioned.

The freckle faced demon pressed her lips together. "They don't talk about it much. Never wanted to subject me to all that, but yeah, they were close enough. They kept me as far away from her as possible and once all the Enchanters came, she wasn't really bothered by them or anyone else. And then you came, and the rest is history."

"Your parents hardly come out of their bubble as it is," Elise pointed out.

Beetee scratched behind Axel's ear. "I'll go and bring them here myself. They won't help you fight physically but they will help to stop her in any way they can. They're good people."

"To raise you they must be," Leah complimented, causing Beetee to give her a smile in return.

"Well, I'm going with you, to your parents I mean." Elise didn't say it like a suggestion.

Beetee snorted. "Sure. Just try to emphasize that you aren't working for Lilith anymore. They're already a little scared of you as it is."

Elise rolled her eyes but agreed. "We'll head out this afternoon then."

"That's perfect. I want to make sure the boys are in their most perfect shape for this. Some time to get their bearings together would be good. Once we have everyone together, we'll finish this." I said the last words like they were final, like it would happen just like that, no fuck ups. I noticed the small looks I got as I sat in my chair, there were ones of simple uncaring, ones of admiration that I'd seen before, but then there were the ones that boiled my blood. They looked at me as if I had brought those demons here and put them in danger, as if it was all an act that I'd put together to keep them in their fear.

Leah followed my gaze and cleared her throat. "Don't worry about them. You should know demons can be fickle with their emotions and loyalty."

"So can Enchanters," Elise spat back, reminding Leah of how she and Garrett got here in the first place.

Leah nodded and opened her mouth to continue but was cut off by a voice I really didn't want to hear at the moment. "True, but we are well aware when ties need to be severed and sacrifices need to be made," Rae, one of the sharp toothed twins commented, rounding the front desk and sauntering over to us. "We are just wondering when you'll figure that out for yourself."

Axel snarled as he jumped from Beetee's chest to the coffee table. Elise narrowed her eyes at her but remained quiet to my surprise. She side-eyed me, telling me that I needed to respond.

"Excuse me?" I answered.

Rae shook her head. "I would like Lilith gone just as much as the next demon, but if handing yourself over will stop her from terrorizing us then just fucking do it. Hasn't your little angel rubbed off on you so that you can make some good decisions."

"I would back off, now," I warned.

"You've given yourself so many enemies. Lilith doesn't even have to be near you, yet you've already caused some much havoc. Don't get me wrong I love messy and chaotic, but not when it's coming from some girl practically getting everyone killed while trying to get mommy's attention."

I instinctively grabbed her by her throat, my eyes turning their inky black and chucked her against the nearest wall. She landed with a heavy thud and all the eyes that originally weren't paying any attention to us now had us in their sights. Rae bared her teeth and growled. She jumped up from the ground and barreled towards me. I was about to have my dagger ready, wanting to create so many stab wounds in her skin it would be hard to count them in the end, but Elise got between us. She flung her tail right into Rae's face, halting her. The inky venom dripped from the tip.

"As much as I would fucking love to let this fight proceed, I'm going to have to be the boring one here and say not today ladies."

Rae huffed. "I'm late for something anyway." She nodded over to me. "The more you resist the worse it gets for everyone else. Be a good little monster and run home to your master." She pushed around us and towards the front door. I closed my eyes and counted to three before opening them again.

There was that other word again.

Monster. Monster. Monster.

I saw Yuri and Jasmine looking at me, startled expressions on their little faces. I couldn't look like much of a hero now. Their parents were following me into this unknown abyss without any guarantee that the outcome would be positive. Just because we all wished for the same ending didn't mean we would all be alive to see it. And when that happened, if that happened, who would they blame?

Lilith? Well, yeah. But they would blame me. They followed me. They believed in me.

Doing the wrong thing, people got hurt. Doing what I thought was the right thing, people got hurt. Pain would come one way or another and I couldn't help that. My buttons got pushed so I pushed back. I didn't ask for anyone to follow my lead and stand beside me. I would have been fine on my own. I didn't need them, but they wanted to be here, so what the fuck did everyone want me to do? Lilith wanted me, but with having me came facing all the people who wanted to have my back. They always had the option to back down, go back home, and they didn't.

The onlookers gazed at me, their shoulders stiff and their expressions less than thoughtful. My head was a mess, and it would probably be more of a mess when we got to Lilith's castle and the catastrophic dilemma ensued. That's why we were here though, so why did I think that I was causing this mess. Lilith damn near created it.

You will ruin them, you know. Ariel had said that to me, and I was starting to believe him.

I had watched Yuri and Jasmine play with Axel for a few hours before Beetee and Elise took him away to head to her parents. She'd said that they would do nearly anything for her, but they would take some mild convincing, so they would be back before the red sun was up. Maybe it was the lack of the Heaven's Gate sunlight that was making me moody. I waved to them alongside Leah and Garrett who had ushered their kids back inside the hostel.

Elise assured me that if they ran into Isabel that she would kill her on sight and she would apologize to Natalia later. I had chuckled and told her that I wouldn't have it any other way. I retreated to my room for the rest of the day to gather my thoughts and if I was being honest, that only made things worse. I brought my dagger out and my name glittered in the soft glowing angelic light that Nicholas had yet to snuff out from yesterday. I didn't want to snuff it out myself because that felt like a weird metaphor. I felt like it was mocking me, like even when it was forgotten, and placed in a corner, it was always there just waiting to be noticed. Here I was noticing it, and it made a humming sound as I stared right at it. A low hum that sent a chill through me.

Maybe I was nervous to know what it meant to hold onto both. The dark and the light. I was so good at being one thing so what was the point of trying to be anything else? I remembered what I told Nick about not having to be the angel he thought he needed to be. Maybe I didn't need to be the demon I always thought I was. A low hum vibrated through my body again and I glanced at the light. I tilted my head to the side and mentally tried to will it over to me, trying baby steps to see if I had some kind of remote connection to it.

It stayed where it was, just bobbing back and forth in its corner, and creating light everywhere but inside of me. I pushed my fingers into my hair as I dug my heels into the bed. There should really be a class on how to speak with your angelic light 101. My raven-haired angel could be the teacher and that light would be very, very traumatized by the things I would do to him when class was over. I felt dumb for making myself laugh, but I was going crazy in my own head. Ridiculous thoughts were better than the ones I could be having. I could have been thinking about the darkness I took from Nick and how I'd never done that before, but it was in the moment and I felt like I could do it, so I did. I had told him it was fine, but I didn't actually know what that meant. I didn't feel any different.

Knock. Knock.

I kicked my feet off the bed and quickly shuffled over to the door, swinging it open with way too much excitement than I should have at seeing who was on the other side. Nick gave me a smile before walking into the room as I closed the door behind him.

"You took your time," I pointed out, noting that he and Reese had been together for pretty much the entire day.

"There was a lot to be said, Dani." He ran his fingers over his healing forearm scars and turned to look at me. "Plus, we might have fallen asleep."

"Aw, that's cute. Together? Like you cuddled and spooned?"

He rolled his eyes. "No, separate beds. But we talked and then just kind of passed out."

"Good sleep?"

He shrugged. "It was okay, no nightmares." He took a few steps towards me, touching the tips of his fingers to my own. "Nothing compared to when I sleep next to you though."

I turned my nose up at him. "Thank you for clarifying. I thought I was going to have to rage with jealousy." He laughed in a way that I hadn't heard in a while. The kind of laugh that made him hold his stomach and mildly catch his breath.

When he was done, he spoke again. "You sound like you missed me."

I reached up and touched my thumb to the scar under his eye. "Maybe."

Nick cleared his throat. "Leah told me Elise and Beetee left hours ago."

I nodded, stepping away from him and aimlessly walking towards the bed. "Yeah, to go see Beetee's parents. Hopefully to bring them here to plan for invasion. Garrett and Leah are all for it and Elise has been waiting for this moment so why not."

"We're completely ready whenever you are," he offered.

"Reese is completely ready to fight the Queen of Darkness?" I deadpanned, raising an eyebrow.

Nick tilted his head from side to side. "Okay, maybe he's not super excited about it, but it's what we've been waiting for. And I know what you and everyone else are thinking and I'm okay, truly, I'm fine."

I chewed on my thumbnail. "I don't doubt you. I just…"

"You just what?"

I sat on the edge of my bed and placed my face in the palms of my hands. "I just don't want to keep being the cause of all this shit. And do *not* tell me I'm in no way, shape, or form *not* the cause, Nicholas." My words came out muffled.

He opened his mouth, but wisely closed it, thinking about his next words. "Dani, it's not like we came here blindly."

"Yes, yes, dutiful angels do missions well, I get it. Let's not forget that you underhandedly came here because you're kind of infatuated with me." I peeked up at him and saw his expression filled with nothing less than adoration.

He rubbed the back of his neck. "That's one word for it."

I placed my hands on my knees and gave him a patient look. "What are some other words?"

Nick forced his mouth into a hard line and shook his head. "There are probably way too many for me to appropriately list."

"Oh well now I feel special." I fluttered my eyelashes and delicately placed my hand to my chest. He chuckled and walked over to me, squatting so that he could be close enough to my eye level. He placed his hands on my exposed thighs and ghosted his fingers over my skin.

"I am in a much better place now Dani, thanks to you, and I'll take care of you just like you did for me." His dark hair fell over his forehead in a naturally messy way. "We both know you don't need me too but let me pretend, okay?"

I ran my hand through his hair and I sighed. "Okay."

He gave me a smile and stood up, taking a step back when I got off the bed. I grabbed his hands and slid my own up his forearms, his biceps, over his shoulders and down to his chest. I let my palms rest near his beating heart, the organ drumming into my ears. It was like I could feel the forever lingering darkness, a hissing viper of mental destruction. It was just the remnants of a time that changed someone forever. The darkness that I'd taken from him pulsed inside of me wanting to get out, jump back into him and try again, but I wouldn't let it.

It was fine living inside of me, but darkness was volatile and fitful like a child with a tantrum. I wouldn't let it win, I couldn't for his sake and my own. He leaned down and kissed my forehead. His lips were warm on my skin, soft and thoughtful. I felt his hand on the back of my head, threading into my hair as he kept us like that for a moment.

I pulled back and looked up at him. I fisted his shirt and yanked him down to my level. His eyes were casting this gaze that told me he only saw me. He didn't see anything else but what I was right in front of him. His eyes were gentle, a bit tired, but they gave off a feeling of genuine affection and caring. I wasn't afraid of who I was, what I could do, and I knew my past would always follow me and practically haunt me, but he would be there to help me fight it off if it got to be too much. "A lot can happen once we go and enter her playing field. I just don't want to think about that right now. I don't want to strategize or give her any more of my time tonight."

"Okay," he agreed, his voice quiet.

"I just want to be with you." The request came out in a rushed breath, like I was actually shy about what I was asking. He smirked, but not in a cocky way. He did it in a manner that told me he wanted the exact same thing. "I want you to be inside of me and to keep looking at me like that."

His eyebrows pulled together. "How am I looking at you?"

I took a shaky breath that had been lumped in my throat. "Like I'm something good."

"You are." I didn't get a chance to answer when he jerked me against him and kissed me. My body melted against his as he moved his mouth over mine. I dragged my hands down his chest and clutched at the hem of his shirt. I tugged it up and removed it, throwing it on the floor. I reached for his belt, but he halted my movements, a shake of his head causing my expression to morph into confusion.

"Slow down, needy one." He tucked a piece of my hair behind my ear and leaned down, kissing the place on my neck just below my ear. "Let me take my time with you." He continued to kiss my neck as he slowly unbuttoned my shorts, letting them slide down my legs. I stepped out of them as he nudged me towards the bed. I laid back, lifting my hair off of my neck and letting it fan out around my head. Nick got onto the bed after me, pushing my legs apart and bringing one of them up to his face and kissing my ankle. Each press of his lips sent a pleasurable fire through my body. He kissed down my leg, bending so that he could get to the inside of my thighs. He skipped to my other thigh and traveled down my leg towards my other ankle, making sure every inch was accounted for.

I was squirming at his incessant teasing. He moved slowly and tastefully like it was an art form and as much as I was in awe of it, I was—as he'd always said—needy. He dropped my leg and placed his face between my legs, getting dangerously close to my panties. I dropped my eyes to watch him as he slid one of his hands up my inner thigh and traced one of his fingers down the lace of my panties. He stuck his tongue out and mimicked his finger and I bucked up against him. He chuckled and did it again. There was so much deja vu in this moment between us, him showing me what it was like to take his time, yet I didn't have to be quiet with him now. He pulled my panties down my legs and threw them to the floor settling between my legs again.

His focused eyes flicked to me as he spread me open with one of his hands and used the other to rub my clit. I bit my lip and whimpered, feeling so overly sensitive and he hadn't even been doing all that much yet. I felt his breath against me as he moved his tongue over my throbbing clit, circling it and then sucking it into his mouth. He flattened his tongue and swiped it over my center entirely and then focused back on my clit. I cried out, moving my hand into his hair, pulling him closer. He slipped one of his fingers inside of me in an achingly slow movement. In and out. In and out. He added another finger, keeping my clit in his mouth and gracefully sucking and swiveling his tongue to find what I liked, paying attention to when my body nearly screamed for more of it. His fingers curled and the scent of heavy arousal was so poignant in the air that I was happily suffocated by it.

"Fuck, Nick, don't stop. That feels so good."

His eyebrows lifted, catching my eyes as he licked me. "I know." His wrist arched as he kept fingering me. "I know how to treat you and your pussy, Dani."

I was pulling at my curls when he pressed his fingers into that spot inside of me that had me seeing a light behind my eyes. My back arched off the bed as my orgasm pulsed. "Yes, yes, right there."

He kept going until my breathing evened out. He pushed himself up, so that he was sitting on his knees and scrubbed a hand down his face, wiping his mouth. I could see the outline of him through his pants, he was so hard. I rose from my position on the bed as he let me remove his pants and underwear. He hovered over me as his cock jutted out between us. Nick pulled my shirt off my body, and I dipped down to lick at the tip of his cock. I wrapped as much of my hand around it as I could and took him into my mouth. His smooth texture ran across my fingers as I jerked his length, bobbing my head along the rest of him.

"Fuck, that's good. So good," he praised, letting me set my pace and gently worked his hand into my hair. I was just getting into it when he had me stop. He leaned down and brought his mouth down to mine. He reached down to grab my sides, flipping us over so that I was straddling him. I slid my wet pussy over his cock, and he squeezed my waist. My eyes never left his when I reached between us and placed his cock at my entrance, working my way down slowly until he was all the way inside. We both let out a shuddering moan at the feeling.

"It's just you and me," he whispered as I started to move my hips. He was so big and perfect, I wanted to be wild with him and I knew he would enjoy it all the same, but he wanted to take his time—he wanted us to take our time. I didn't know what tomorrow would bring. I didn't know if this was the last time that we would ever be this, be us. Just me and him. He tipped his head back as he groaned at the way I rode him. I grinded my body and every so often would lift myself up and come back down, giving us both the kind of friction that we craved. He played with my breasts, toying with my nipples. I splayed my hands out on his chest and continued to move, noticing that he had gone back to looking at me as his hands never stopped touching me.

He lifted himself up but didn't remove me. He simply pressed my body to his as he sat up and helped me grind into him more. Our breathing was matched, and time just didn't seem to matter right now. He caressed my face, his thumb moving over my cheek. "So imperfectly perfect." He had heeded my words, taken them to heart. I wanted no harm to come to this man and his way too good heart. A heart that was beating against my chest, looking right at my own heart. I saw his Adam's apple bob as he swallowed. A groan left his throat when I started to dig my pelvis harder against his, his eyes glancing down at where we were joined. His brown eyes looked back at mine and there was something about the way his pupils dilated and how he held me that told me all I needed to know about the next words out of his mouth.

"Dani...I..."

I immediately pressed my hand to his mouth, silencing him. His eyebrows pulled together in confusion. I leaned into him, pressing my forehead against his and removing my hand. "Don't."

He groaned again, sliding his hand down to my ass and pulling me harder into him, but my movements were still slow, still savoring every second our bodies were in contact. "Don't what?"

"Say whatever you were about to say."

"You have no idea what I was about to say."

I nudged his nose with my own. "I think I do. And I can't—we can't—not now."

He squeezed my ass harder, sweat starting to populate on his skin. His eyes shined with understanding and maybe a tiny bit of embarrassment from his feelings being called out so blatantly. He knew exactly what he wanted to say. "When?"

A moaning laugh came out of my mouth as I wrapped my arms around his neck as he tucked his head into my neck and kissed my skin. I thought about how I wanted to explain this to him, but nothing of substance came to mind, so I just told him the truth. "I've never had someone say *that* to me before," I started, noticing how he stopped applying kisses to my throat and slowly looked at me. "I don't want it to happen because it sounds like something that *needs* to be said. I don't want an impending face off to take the magic out of those words." I kissed him. Once, twice, three times.

He held me close to him and rolled us over so that he was on top of me, still inside of me, but he was more in control. I lifted my legs up higher, so he felt deeper as he slowly thrusted into me. "*When?*" He repeated. It almost sounded like a plea.

I took his face in my hands, forcing him to look nowhere but at me. "I don't know when, but not now. Just wait. Say anything else, but just don't say that- *fuck* -not now." The words came out a bit choked and there was a lump in my throat that I'd never felt before. He moved in and out of me, taking my arms and holding them above my head. He made sure I felt every inch of him, every inch of his slow, tortuous frustration at what I wasn't letting him say. He respected my wishes and didn't say it, as much as I knew it burned him to keep it to himself. His hand tightened around my wrists as he licked at my collarbones and across my chest, up my neck to my jaw and lightly kissed my cheek. "I want you, Dani."

My voice vibrated with his thrusts. "Nick, I know." The noise of our skin rhythmically slapping together echoed within the quiet room, mingling with our heavy breaths as he shook his head.

"No, Dani, no. You won't let me say it, so I'll say this. I want *you*. Every second of every minute, of every hour, of every single day. I want it all. Your darkness, your light, and everything in between. Whatever a life after Lilith looks like, I want that with you." Each word came out solid and true. My heart pulled from my chest, and I wrapped my ankles together around his back. I broke my hands out of his grip and grabbed his face. Our mouths crashed together as I ground myself up against him, feeling him groan into my mouth. "It's all yours," he said against my lips.

"What is?" I could feel the orgasm building and my stomach clenching as I let every single thing he'd said wash over me.

"My heart."

I gripped his hair from behind his head and everything felt so strong as I closed my eyes and let my climax consume me. "Yes, yes, yes." My voice cracked.

I should have told him not to say anything at all because I wasn't the swooning kind, but those words made me swoon just a bit. Nick pressed into me over and over until I felt his body tense and shudder, a soft *fuck* leaving his lips as he came. We stayed like that for a moment, just the feeling of each other's presence enough to fill the silence. I rubbed my hands down his back before he settled in front of my face and kissed me. The kiss was quick, but deep, our tongues meeting. He shifted off of me and shuffled under the covers, holding them up for me to go under as well.

We faced each other, our legs touching. I didn't know how to reply to his admission. I wasn't sure if a response was something he wanted. I reached up and traced the scar under his eye. "How did you get this?"

He grabbed my arm and kissed the inside of the wrist. "Two best friends having the most mature of fights. I then ended up in a fight with a piece of furniture and lost. At the time it looked pretty bad, but now I hardly notice it anymore."

"I like it. We can exist together with all our scars. Imperfectly perfect."

He nodded as he traced the side of my face with his finger. The light that glowed from that one fingertip warmed my skin and something inside of me practically purred. There was something dark that raged inside as well, but his light made whatever kind of light that was inside of me feel comforted. I turned over on my side and I felt him at my back, wanting me as close as possible and I didn't resist.

I sighed, pressing my cheek into the pillow. "I can't tell you what to expect when we head to her castle, Nick. I've pushed back every chance I got and yet she still wants me for some reason, I'm still her plan, through and through. I enjoy the unknown, but this is too much of a mystery even for me."

"We aren't going to let her just have you, Dani."

I smiled to myself, watching his glowing light orb bob back and forth. "So noble. This is still mainly my issue."

"We'll make it *our* issue then." He was frustratingly pushy sometimes. His heart was actually way too good for me, but he would never believe that.

"Sacrifices have to be made. And I'm fine being just that." I didn't try to look over my shoulder at him, but he didn't mind. His lips met my shoulder blade as he hummed.

"If sacrifices have to be made, then we'll figure it out as a team, as a last resort. Mess or not, we're here to help you pick up the pieces and fight the bad guys." He kissed my shoulder again and then my temple. "You aren't the villain in this story, remember that."

I cuddled back into him and wanted his words to mold against me. I wanted them to soothe me as much as his words usually did. I fell asleep realizing none of that happened. I still felt like a mess and whatever steps I took with them in my stead—only a mess would follow.

25

DANI

The sky was dark and foggy when I opened my eyes. The fog was so thick it created a cloud in my vision that no matter how many times I blinked it would seem to just get thicker. My feet moved easily as I made my way through, but I kept looking behind me as if I was being followed, as if there were eyes on me that I couldn't shake. I heard the subtle sounds of breathing, but I didn't move any faster nor did I stop to rethink my direction. I just kept walking as if subconsciously I knew where I was going.

The breathing became a bit louder, telling me I was getting closer and closer. My skin started to feel hot, and my muscles became agitated with tension as I stepped forward. I heard the sound of water under my feet with my last step. I blinked down to where my foot was submerged in liquid, realizing that whatever I'd stepped in was in more places than just under my shoe. I bent down and slid my finger into whatever it was, realizing that the residue was stickier than water and much thicker. I brought my index finger to eye level and a dark red color was staring back at me.

Blood. It dripped from the pad of my finger back onto the floor. My heart started to panic in my chest as I looked around, searching for wherever the fuck I was. The smell of blood filled my nostrils as if my senses were just now realizing what was around me. As if someone just now wanted me to smell the pain and agony.

The fog started to disappear, slowly, meticulously. I pushed up from the floor and watched as the thick clouds that once impaired my vision revealed a sight that had me shuddering. My breath caught in my throat when I saw my perfectly loyal, over caring, too kind for his own good, angel kneeling on the ground. Blood leaked from his stomach, shoulders and around his neck.

I screamed for my feet to move but they felt like bricks with every step I took, but I tried my best to run towards him. I was exhausted the moment I had my hands on him, even though he had likely been two feet away. He was alive but barely, his breathing sounded like the small shallow breaths I'd heard moments ago. I lifted his head up to look at me and his once bright, curious brown eyes looked lost, pained, and just tired. There was blood coming from everywhere as if whoever did this wanted to make it hurt. I placed my hand on his cheek, my eyes burning from holding back tears I didn't think I could muster.

"Nick." My voice came out like a choked plea.

His lips quivered as if he wanted to speak but couldn't. His hands held onto the deep wound in his stomach, and I knew I couldn't save him. I knew I couldn't do anything but watch. I was meant to watch him suffer.

"Who did this to you?" I growled, as if I expected him to be able to answer. I heard a sharp laugh. One I'd heard before, one I wouldn't forget. I felt a hand on the back of my head, stroking my curls.

"You sound so angry." Lilith said, almost in a soothing voice. "Isn't this what you expected?"

"I didn't want this." I looked at Nick's perfect face and into his eyes that were opening and closing as if he didn't have the strength to decide what he wanted to do with them.

"Oh, Dani, you and I both know things will never work out in your favor." She removed her hand from my hair and stepped around me. Her long, almost white, blonde hair hung over her thin shoulders. Her eyes were dark and lined with black that tipped up when it met the edge of her eyelids. She stopped when she was behind Nick, placing her hands on his shoulders. He flinched. "Not when you keep aligning yourself with others that are less than you."

I wanted her hands off of him. I wanted her dead. I wanted her begging me for her death. My hands were too weak right now though, my thoughts too preoccupied. "You're doing this to punish me."

Lilith sighed, ruffling my angel's hair. "No, no. I am simply letting you see what's to come if you keep making the wrong choices. I don't want to see you upset, my love, but I can only be patient with you for so long. Whatever happens after you make your decisions is on you."

"You really think killing him—*threatening* to kill him— is going to make me want to be at your side?" I cocked my head to the side, genuinely wanting to know her answer.

Lilith shook her head and smiled, clearly amused by me. "I know you'll never like it. You'll never like the things I've done, but you will soon understand that he will never truly be what you need. He can try, pretty thing that he is, but he won't win. He wants to fight for you my Soul Seether, and you should know that I know how to fight for what I want as well."

I looked at Nick with his easy on the eyes face, I remembered that smirk that somehow made me want to kiss him even more and I cut my eyes to his chest. The chest that held a heart that was too big and too hopeful. I had no business wanting a piece of it and he had no business trying to keep giving me chunks. Look where it got him.

"Him and his little friend and everyone who is willing to follow you and fight beside you are following a dangerous path. I must admit I do enjoy your little journey but it's time you said your goodbyes and took your place where you belong."

"He doesn't want to change me, you know."

Lilith brushed my hair back from my shoulder and I moved out of her reach, slapping her hand to the side. She gave me a skeptical look. "And you think I do? You may not know your own power yet, but I made you what you are, and I've loved you ever since." She walked over to me and my feet were like bricks again, unable to move. Lilith tucked her finger under my chin and tilted my head up. "I never want to hurt you, my love, but you will give me no choice and I can guarantee you will not be happy with my methods of getting my way."

She squeezed my chin, hard. I clenched my teeth as I spoke. "You don't scare me. You never have."

Lilith stuck out her tongue and licked at her red stained lips. "And that's why you were always my favorite. So ferocious. So brave. Bravery is an admirable trait, but sometimes..." she looked back at Nick who had seemed to stop breathing. I made a move to rush over to him, but she stopped me. "Sometimes bad things happen to the bravest people. No matter the intent, you will be to blame."

I used all my strength and shoved her back. "No! It will be *your* fault!

You did this!"

She didn't look mad or upset. She looked content and that was even worse. "I've never claimed to be anything I'm not, that's on you. It's quite comical watching you play hero when you've brought them to their deaths all because they followed your lead. I tried to give you a way to save them, yet you chose to turn away from my generous offering. So, whose fault is it Dani?" I watched the clouds swirl around us and Nick's limp body began to disappear before my eyes.

Of course, this was all an illusion. A dream state, a mind trap. I had always thought she was in my head before, but this was different. She was really done playing with me, this was her last straw. "You won't touch him. You won't touch any of them!"

Lilith stroked her long-manicured fingernail over her chin, unfazed. "I won't ruin them, my love, you will." She gave me a wide mouth smile that showed all her teeth. I felt something in my palm, something familiar. I looked down and saw my hand wrapped tightly around the hilt of my dagger. Thick pulses of blood dripped off the hooked tip. I blinked and backed up, noticing blood was covering the floor around me, caked on my legs and my hands were slippery with the warm substance.

"What is this!" I screamed.

Lilith pressed her lips together. "Dimitri did warn you and to think, it didn't have to be this way." The room seemed to pulse, and my head was pounding. I kept walking backwards as Lilith's form kept distorting and then piecing back together. I tripped over something and landed backwards on my back. The clattering of the dagger rang through my ears, and I pushed myself off the ground.

"I loved this chat of ours. I'm sure I'll be seeing you again." Lilith waved her hand as if to shoo me off before she completely disappeared. There was a dark dust of shadows that surrounded her and colorful magic that looked like Enchanter magic. I was about to yell something back at her when I noticed a pair of feet in my peripheral vision. I let my eyes roam up the body and scurried back as quickly as I could when I realized it was Elise. Blood leaked out of her neck, from the large slice right through it. I moved back further and hit another body. I gasped when I saw Reese, lifeless and covered in blood and I felt the tears, the hurt, the hate for myself because maybe Lilith was right. My back hit a wall that I didn't even know was there, as I tried to move away even faster, and tried to grab it for leverage as I hyperventilated and rose from the ground.

Bodies manifested and scattered at my feet, each and every time I blinked. It was harrowing but my inner shadow raged and reveled in it. I was sick from seeing it, but I wanted more. I didn't understand, I couldn't understand. That's when I noticed Nick in the same position I'd found him in earlier. His head hung down between his shoulders and blood still leaked from his wounds.

Had I done this?

I let out a shrill sound as my dagger manifested itself back in my hand. Fresh blood on the blade as if it was always meant to be that way. I shook my hand to try to get it off, to let it go, but it was glued to me. I violently shook my head and I felt myself crying harder and harder. The air grew still and silent then. It was a deafening silence that I didn't like. I peered over at Nick's sullen form and all at once, his head tilted back, and his eyes opened wide. His mouth opened and a silent scream erupted.

I shot up from bed, screaming and thrashing. I kept my eyes shut tight, swinging my arms around, wanting to remove the mental image from my mind, but it was replaying over and over. My dagger felt like a weight in my hand, pulling me down into darkness I knew, but maybe it was one I didn't want so deeply anymore. My throat was dry, but I kept screaming, I kept begging for a way out.

Hands wrapped around my arms and tried to hold me still while I flailed around needing to find a way out. "Dani! Dani! Stop! It's me." The voice was familiar and did something to my insides. It halted the toxic waves rumbling through my body. I started slapping at the hard chest in front of me, blinking my eyes open. I pushed and tried to get away, but the hands held me in place. I felt my body start to shake.

"Dani! Stop! Wake up!"

"No! No!" They were shaking me. My eyes fully opened, and the pieces started forming, the picture started to come together. Nick's face became my primary view and my fists pounding at his chest moved slower and then eventually stopped. He was breathing heavily, and his eyes looked crazily around my face. There was so much worry coming from him. He was right here. He was fine. "Nick." I had to make sure he was fine, he was real. I patted his chest, his shoulders, and traveled my hands up his neck to his face, making sure that every single feature was as it should be.

He released his tense hold on my arms and slid his hands up to my face, holding me there so he could inspect. "Yes. I'm right here."

Elise and I were different in how we displayed our feelings and emotions. She liked to pretend like she didn't have any and I simply showed mine in parts. Throughout whatever this was between Nicholas and me, he was slowly collecting those parts. It wasn't my favorite thing, knowing someone was rummaging delicately inside my emotions, making themselves at home, but I couldn't say I didn't like not feeling so alone. He had done the same and ultimately given me his heart, so I felt like it was my place to make sure no harm came to it. I always made sure no harm came to the things that were mine. That's exactly what Nicholas Cassial was.

He was mine.

Tears fell down my face as I spoke. "She got into my head. You. Everyone. Bleeding and dead because of me. I should have listened to her, I can't…Nick…I can't." I could barely make out sentences. My head started to ache just from trying to formulate a response. I was choking on my own words, and I hiccupped trying not to flood this entire room with my tears that were of no use to anyone. His thumbs brushed under my eyes, and he pulled me into his chest, wrapping his arms around me.

"I'm fine, okay. I'm right here, I'm fine. Everything is okay, baby," He whispered, reassuring me as he smoothed down my curls and kissed the top of my head.

"I'm the problem, Nick." I said, my voice muffled against his chest.

"You are not the problem. Stop believing her and start listening to me," he pleaded. "We are with you. I'm with you, existing with all the scars. You're not a monster." His heart was beating loudly against my ear.

He wanted to believe so much about me that I wished I could join him in his ideals. I was very capable of the things she made me see, I was capable of doing so much more damage. I absolutely didn't hate being a demon, but sometimes I *did* hate the way it made me feel when I wasn't on a high from torturing or manipulation. When I was alone without Elise's sass or another demon's body pressed against mine to dull the pain.

I lifted my head up and saw the concern etched on his face. His eyebrows pulled together as he tried to assess what to do next. I nearly climbed him to get to his face and kiss him. He didn't pull back, but he was surprised. His lips weren't as open for a moment, wondering if he should give into what was happening. I moaned against his mouth and used all my strength to push him back onto his pillow and swing my leg over his body, straddling him.

His hand touched my shoulders and pushed me up. "Dani, what are you doing?"

I leaned down and let our foreheads touch. "No more questions. No more thought-provoking words." I reached between us and grabbed his cock, it wasn't rock hard like it usually was, but it was hard enough to give me what I wanted. I slid him over my entrance, and I heard him stifle a moan.

"Dani, we don't have to talk, but we also don't have to do this." I kept moving the tip over my pussy, back and forth. He flicked his eyes to where I held him. "This is what you need?"

I nodded. "Please."

He held onto my hips, flexing his fingers so they dug into my sides. "Okay. Take what you need." I sighed in relief when I lined him up and slid down. He watched me like he knew this was for me and only for me. He would have been happy to have a long conversation, discussing all the details of what happened. I didn't want something where I had to bring up that miserable nightmare, I just wanted something that didn't require much thought at all.

I took hold of his shoulder and started to grind against him. He fit me so perfectly that I could have cried from that sheer thought alone. His hands were on me, but he wasn't trying to make this about him or create a rhythm that he wanted. He dragged his eyes down my body and then back up at my face, watching me as I took what I needed from him, as I chased my own pleasure using his body.

"Fuck," I gasped, squeezing his shoulder as I started to rotate my hips back and forth. He was breathing heavier as he surveyed my movements, groaning at how good it felt but not wanting to take control. I closed my eyes, needing to block out every minuscule thought that could choose to invade this moment.

His fingers ghosted over my cheek. "Look at me. Eyes on me, baby."

I whimpered at his words but did as he said. I looked at him and his eyes narrowed as he took me in. I slid my hands down his chest towards his abs and I wanted to jump into his skin and stay there forever. His hands found their way to my ass and helped me move, guiding me forward and backwards. I cried out, letting out every feeling I had in this dim room, where it was just the two of us. "Touch me," I begged.

He complied quickly, moving one of his hands to my front, circling my clit, continuing to watch me. I could feel it all building, faster and faster. My body vibrated with its need to explode. I moved faster and harder against him, leaning over and burying my face into his neck as I bucked my hips again and again. "Fuck, fuck, yes."

My orgasm had weight to it as it tumbled out of me. My breath was caught in my throat as I tried to breathe through it. Nick held onto me, not letting me go anywhere, helping me ride it out. "That's it. That's it, baby. You're okay. Shh, you're okay." I shuddered at his comfort, my shoulders relaxing, and my legs suddenly felt wobbly like if I tried to stand, I would just topple over. I felt his lips kiss my hair, inhaling my scent like his life depended on it. I touched my own lips to his shoulder and moved so I was back on my side of the bed.

I bit my lip as I trailed my hand down his abs and started to reach for his cock that was still wet from me. He snatched my hand up and brought my palm to his mouth, kissing it. "I'm good."

"Nick…" I knew I'd told him I needed what had just happened, but now I just felt bad for taking and not giving back.

"No. Relax and go to sleep. Your happiness is just as good as an orgasm."

I chuckled and gave him a smile I knew didn't quite reach my eyes. I snuggled under the covers, and he pulled me towards him so that my head was on his chest. This was probably one of my favorite places to be and I had to fight back my own overly emotional tears thinking about how this would be the last time I'd get to be here.

I buttoned my pants, quietly, tiptoeing around the room. I had slipped out of bed and gotten dressed, not wanting to wake my sleeping angel and explain myself to him. He wouldn't like what I was doing and maybe he might even hate me for it, but this was my decision, and I was pretty sure I'd made it right after I'd woken up from that nightmare Lilith had bestowed upon me. I'd debated with myself over and over again in the bathroom mirror, but I always ended up in the same spot with the same decision. And I ultimately ended up making the same choice.

I stood over the bed and bent my knees before I leaned down to hover over Nick's sleeping face. He looked so innocently serene that I nearly had to look away. I couldn't think about what his face would look like when he realized the decision I'd made. I softly played with the messy pieces of hair that fell on his forehead and I so desperately wanted to snuggle back into his arms, but that kind of ending was never in the cards. Helping me, saving me was futile and letting me handle this on my own was what needed to happen. They were all technicalities, casualties to her. Dimitri had tantrums and caused chaos because his ego was bruised, Isabel sought out chaos for the love of seeking Lilith's approval, wanting to seem useful, but Lilith… she wanted her chaos to cut deep, personal. She wanted others to provide the mess, when all of a sudden they realized they never wanted it in the first place, but now they were too deep to remove themselves from the shit storm they'd tied themselves to.

I pressed my lips softly to his forehead, silently saying goodbye.

Whatever a life after Lilith looks like, I want that with you. Fuck, why did he have to go and say stupid shit like that. Sweet, stupid shit.

I reached for his arm, extending it out ever so slightly. My dagger shadowed into my hand and as quickly as I could with the hooked end, sliced his finger. He groaned and I held my breath, waiting as he settled back into his sleep. The cut wasn't deep, but blood started to bubble to the surface, and I swiped my finger across, collecting some. I dragged his blood along my dagger and placed my hand over the metal. When I removed my hand, his blood was gone, now drawn into the dagger itself. My weapon was always mine, even though Lilith had given it to me, she had no connection to it like I did.

Back in Heaven's Gate I'd felt comfortable knowing it was in Nick's hands even though I was very, very aware I could have taken it at any point. The dagger would have found me if I wanted it too, but I had let him keep hold of it. Now he had a connection with it also, nothing like mine, but enough so that if I needed a safe place for it to go, it had one. I wasn't putting him in any harm, and I was still its primary master, but if I did learn anything from Lilith it was to have a contingency plan. He wouldn't understand it, but hopefully he would understand what I wanted, why I did what I did. I placed his finger in my mouth and his head turned to me, his eyes sleepy and barely even open.

"Go back to sleep, Nick. Everything is okay." He blinked a few times and sleepily nodded. I sighed in relief as I moved my mouth to his ear and whispered something I knew he wanted to hear, hoping that maybe he'd remember it when he woke up. I stood up and pulled on my black jacket, carefully opening the door to the bedroom without looking back. I walked down the hall, hearing the mess of chatter downstairs, not paying them any attention. I looked around before I opened the door catching Garrett's golden eyes as he sat in the dining area, a steaming cup of what I had to assume was tea in front of him.

He narrowed his eyes in confusion as he looked at me. I pressed my lips together and said nothing. He started to get up from the table, but I pulled open the door and stepped outside. The dry air hit me instantly and I took a few deep breaths. I looked up and over the trees towards Lilith's ominous castle and clenched my fists tightly at my sides. I manifested my wings, the leathery black appendages feeling like they'd been tucked away for so long. I pushed off the ground and flapped my wings until I was above the tree line and headed towards my destination.

I didn't know if she'd be waiting for me or not, but something in my gut told me she was. That's what she'd been doing this whole time.

Waiting for me.

26

NICK

Earlier

"So, you want to tell me what happened?" Reese asked, balling up his napkin and tossing it in the waste bin in the corner. I slowly chewed the pastry that was in my mouth, considering my words. Dani had told me that I should talk to him, and she was right, but I didn't really think about how difficult that would be. We weren't really the type of friends who shared their feelings like that, not that I felt like I couldn't, but we had never done it before. Even when it came to his parents, he would say small things here and there, but never enough to bring up any sort of emotional back and forth. Maybe it was time that changed.

I swallowed my food and started to fold my napkin in my lap. "I really don't know where to start."

Reese scratched his jaw, small bits of stubble clinging to his skin. "Maybe try the beginning."

I continued to fold the napkin into tiny pieces. "That's probably more than you would like to hear."

"At this point Nick, the beginning is the only place I would like to start. I won't believe you're fully okay until I know everything," he explained, leaning back on his hands as he sat on his bed.

I sighed, not wanting this conversation to set me back after I had released everything to Dani the night before. If I could get how I felt out once, then I could probably do it again. I had that thought in mind when I opened my mouth and started from the beginning. I dragged him through every detail I had, from the moment the nightmares started to the day it almost took me out. Reese hardly blinked as words flew out of my mouth. I didn't know if I was speaking slowly or too fast, but he never stopped me. He never interrupted. I wasn't even sure if his face changed expressions as I prattled on. I knew he was listening though; every minute detail was accounted for, and he was just soaking it all in.

I blew out a breath when I was done, suddenly feeling very thirsty after talking for what felt like hours. I licked my lips and rubbed the back of my neck, nervousness creeping its way up my spine as I waited for his reply. His chest rose and fell as he stared at me. He started to nod slowly as if everything I'd said was starting to make sense. Everything that had happened after Jonah's death was starting to populate in his mind and all the weirdness I'd displayed, all my reasons for being so cagey at times were now making perfect sense. He ran a hand through his waves of blonde hair and clucked his tongue. "Well."

"Well?" I asked, confused. "Well, what?"

"I don't know, I kind of feel like shit now." He wasn't saying it to make things about him, I knew that much. He looked down at his feet, rubbing the tips of his shoe against the wood floor.

"You feel like shit? Reese what the hell are you talking about?"

He grumbled under his breath. "Ugh! Because I knew something fucking weird was going on with you and yes, I thought it was just because you were having a rough time with Jonah's death and everything else that came with that, but I didn't think it was this bad. I didn't ask because come on Nick, your father is the most understanding person in the whole realm, and you wouldn't even speak to him, so I never really stood a chance." Reese shook his head, more to himself than to me. "I should have asked though. I should have tried more. I literally thought for half a second that your issues had to do with Dani, like the fuck is wrong with me."

"I probably wouldn't have been so open even if you had tried more. It's no one's fault but my own. Lilith and Markus and everyone else may have birthed the problem, but I held my feelings in, that was all me." I tried to reassure him.

He waved me off. "Yeah, well maybe you wouldn't have felt like you needed to stuff it inside, bottle that shit up, if I had pestered you. I didn't want you to push me away and then bad shit happened, but bad shit happened anyway. We all almost lost you to whatever succubus darkness is in this place and all I would have thought was 'I could have fixed things if I would have just pushed him more, told him it was okay to tell me what was going on.'"

I opened my mouth to speak, but he was right. I probably would have pushed him away if he had kept trying to get me to open up. Dani had tried and maybe I hadn't pushed her away, but she didn't get any closer to what I was feeling until she had to force it out of me. "I hate causing problems, let alone being a problem. You and I have always skimmed over the details on things, probably thinking it's better to keep the friendship lighter and not get into the deep stuff."

"Fuck, I know. And I get it, okay. I should have made you talk the minute I found your ass on the bathroom floor; I should have sat you down and just waited it out until you opened your mouth. Maybe we both would have just started talking until neither of us shut up and cleared the air completely. Every inch of emotion and trauma unloaded." He let out a humorless chuckle.

"I wasn't really ready to talk then and who knows, forcing me too early could have made it worse. I've always known you cared; I just don't think it mattered because I wasn't really ready to see it for myself."

He nodded solemnly as if he still felt semi-responsible. Reese had latched onto me when we were kids, and he never had any intentions of letting go. Sometimes his loyalty to me could be a bit much, it could be overwhelming and suffocating, but I remembered when all I had was my dad. As fun as Maurice Cassial could be, it just wasn't the same. I was a popular kid, but there had never been someone I felt comfortable enough with. Then a very rambunctious kid, with a mop of blonde hair, barreled into my life courtesy of my father's need for me to make a connection that wasn't him and I never looked back. I gained more broken bones, a concussion, and several very aggressive verbal punishments with our friendship but I also gained a best friend I wouldn't have traded the realms for.

"And you're okay now?" He asked in the smallest voice I didn't even know he was capable of having.

I tilted my head back and forth. "I'm not, not, okay. I just have a better understanding now. I'm still sad and angry, but it's not taking over my mind anymore. I think I'm slowly starting to forgive myself in pieces."

He coughed and let out a loud sigh. "Good. I want to know if anything else happens though. Any negative thought enters your little brain, you tell me. You feel even a sliver of self-deprecation, you fucking talk to me."

I tried to screw my mouth up so that my smile wasn't so apparent. "You got it."

"I honestly cannot believe the demon princess got us both to open up. It didn't feel like compulsion, but it fucking could have been."

I raised one of my eyebrows. "What?"

Reese rubbed the space between his blonde eyebrows. "Yeah...she got you to talk about your deep dark feelings and somehow I ended up telling her some of my feelings about my parents and enough about my past that we ended up being weird friends I guess." His eyes glazed over a bit as if he was remembering the entire conversation.

"Wow, I mean you keep the parent stuff close to your chest, so like wow. I guess I never wanted to push you on that either. My dad actually told me to leave it alone when I tried to discreetly ask if he knew anything. So, I just let you tell me as much as you wanted, but whenever it's really bothering you, you tell me alright?"

Reese pressed his lips together and pushed himself even further up his bed. "Alright, but this conversation is not about me, it's about you. Let's just agree that you will never do scary shit like that to me again and we'll both open our fucking mouths and talk to each other about the deep stuff."

I leaned back on my bed as well, feeling the soft pillow hit the back of my head. "I promise to never scare you like that again."

"And if we cry, we cry," he added, saying it as if it was some kind of royal decree.

I placed my arm around the back of my neck, so I was laying on it. I repeated his words back to him. "If we cry, we cry."

"I was wrong about her you know," Reese started, his Adam's apple bobbing as he swallowed. "Someone who stuck with you through that, helped you out during all of it, she's a keeper in my book."

"I think so too."

Reese hummed, clearly not done. "While we remain on the topic of speaking up, you should really tell her how you feel." I looked over at him and saw that he was looking at me with two raised eyebrows as if the answer was as clear as day. "I think we *both* know what I mean."

PRESENT

I heard voices outside the room, shuffling feet moving and casual conversation. I placed my arm over my eyes and yawned. I wasn't tired enough to go back to sleep, but I could feel that my body was tired from the night's events. I had never seen Dani so shaken up, so terrified before. I actually had never seen her cry, but all that had happened in a single night, and I honestly wasn't sure how to handle it. I would have to try for her, especially with how this day was planning to go. I would let my girl take the reins and all of us would be at her side, just like we planned. As much as she would like to pretend like a one demon show was what she wanted, what she preferred, I knew she liked knowing she had us to fall back on. I know I certainly did.

I wouldn't have been totally opposed to cuddling in bed with her some more though. Maybe do something that would release all the tension from both of us. Once that was done, perhaps I could convince her to let me say what I wanted to say last night. The three words that had been sitting on my heart. I turned over, extending my arm out hoping to feel her skin, but all I felt were cold sheets. I patted around her side a few more times as if she would magically appear. I shot up from the bed, my heart racing a little.

"Dani?" I said to no one. She wasn't in the bathroom, and I just didn't think she would just abandon me in this room without saying something. "Dani?" She would have given me any indication of where she was going. I ran a hand through my hair, pulling at the strands. I hustled to put my clothes on, feeling a sense of panic creep up my spine. I swung open the door and darted into the hallway, clearly not looking where I was going and ran straight into Leah and Garrett's children. They stumbled back a bit but looked to be just fine.

I bent down, matching their eye level as best I could. "Have you guys seen Dani?"

They both looked at each other and shook their heads at me. Yuri tilted his head to the side, his dark silky curls flopping over. "Is she okay?" He seemed genuinely curious given the fact that she did almost kill him days ago. That glamour Leah used on him must be made of the toughest magic because he didn't even flinch when I spoke about her.

"I'm not sure," I answered honestly.

"Nick?" I heard Reese say behind me. I straightened and turned to face him. His expression was slightly confused as he looked from me to the kids. "You good?"

I scratched the back of my head. "Um, have you seen Dani?"

"No, I assumed she would be with you."

"Yeah, I woke up and she wasn't there."

Reese moved to the side as the kids ran past him. "Why don't we go downstairs. I'm pretty sure she didn't go far." He nodded towards the stairs, and I followed him, my shoulders tense from how on edge I was. We both looked around the first floor, no sign of her anywhere.

"She wouldn't just up and leave without telling you where she was going, right? Without telling any of us." I nodded absentmindedly, not really knowing the answer to that. I wasn't so sure anymore.

"Hey, now, slow down," Leah scolded, pointing a finger at her children as she walked around the countertop in the small kitchen. "What's wrong?"

I looked over her shoulder as if all this panic would have been a mistake and Dani would come waltzing around the corner. "It's Dani, she's gone."

"Gone?"

"Yeah, you haven't seen her, have you?"

Leah shook her head, her dark waves set in a messy bun on top of her head. "Garrett, honey."

Garrett, who was on the couch in the lounge area, jumped up and came over to us. One of his dark eyebrows was raised in question. Leah licked her lips and cautiously looked at both of us before opening her mouth again. "Have you seen Dani?"

Garrett sucked in a breath as if what she said triggered something in him. I narrowed my eyes at him, waiting for his response when the front door opened. We all turned simultaneously to see Elise strolling in as if everything was fine. She was picking at her black polish covered nails before she noticed us staring at her.

"The fuck are you guys looking at?"

There was a silence among us that clearly irritated her when she rolled her eyes. She waved her hands around. "Beetee is getting Axel settled and helping her parents. Interesting people, I mean I've met them before but there was always something off about them." She looked around us, searching for something, or someone. "Where's Dani?"

"We were wondering the same thing," Reese said, nudging me.

"I woke up this morning and she was gone."

Elise's eyes expanded, the gray of her irises more prominent now. "What the fuck do you mean gone?"

I shrugged. "Like no one knows where she is."

Elise pressed her fingers to her forehead and started to rub it. "Did she say anything to you last night? You know before you went to sleep, but obviously after all the fucking you did."

I ignored her statement. "She had a nightmare last night, involving Lilith and all of us. It actually really bothered her; I'd never seen her that distraught. She kept talking about how she didn't want to cause any more of a mess. I kept trying to reassure her and I don't know, she seemed okay when she went to sleep."

Elise raised a hand up to my face. "Wait, she told you that she had a nightmare about Lilith? Like Lilith was in it and talking to her?"

I nodded slowly. She ran her hand over her mouth and let out a laugh of utter disbelief. "Fuck. She really got in her head. Like quite literally fucking got in her head." Before I could answer, she was coming towards me with her finger pointed at my chest. I had enough height on her, but she was intimidatingly unnerving when she had that crazed look in her eye. I started to back up right as her finger touched my shirt. "You knew Lilith had really gotten to her and didn't think to come and alert one of us of it."

"Alert you? Lilith has gotten into her head before."

Elise scoffed. "That's different. Lilith in her head to bother her, annoy her is one thing. Lilith in her actual dreams, making her see things, force her hand, that's another. That's cause for getting everyone out of bed and addressing it." She dug her finger into my skin. "And what did you do, huh? You tried to comfort her with your angelic voice and life altering cock and thought you fixed the problem." Her voice was louder now and much more demanding. There was a small hint of concern in her features, but I wasn't about to point that out now.

"No! I was trying to help her because I fucking care, but I didn't think she would just up and disappear because of it. If I had known she was going to leave, obviously I would have made different decisions."

"I saw her leave last night," Garrett announced over our voices, his own booming throughout the room. Elise swiveled her head towards him. Reese stepped forward getting closer to him. "You saw her? Do you know where she went?" Garrett shook his head, his braids slowly flinging back and forth.

"Hey guys, I want you to meet some people," Beetee said as she opened the door to the hostel, two women coming in behind her. One of them had pale skin and short red hair, cropped into a pixie cut. The other one had brown skin and white hair that fell into ringlets around her shoulders. Circular framed glasses hung around her neck. They both looked about the same age as Leah and they took Reese and I in as if we were just another set of bodies in the room. They had the looks of two innocent demons having fled from Lilith's grasp, but there was something about them that instantly made me think there was more to them then they let on.

I wasn't always the inquisitive type, but after learning about Dani, I figured some things couldn't always be as they seemed. Beetee's face fell as she took in the room. She wiped her hands down her bright green dress and ushered her parents to the lounge area. She said something to them in a hushed tone and walked back over to us. "What's going on? They already feel weird as it is."

"Dani's missing. No thanks to the angel boy here."

"Excuse me? It's not like I pushed her to leave. If I know Dani at all, I really don't think there was anything we could have said that would have changed this outcome." My chest puffed out and I felt light-headed from how much energy I was giving this conversation.

"She had..." Garrett started, placing his hands on his hips. "She had this look in her eyes, like determination. I tried to get up and follow her, but by the time I was out the front door she was gone. I'm pretty sure she flew."

"Flew where?" Reese asked.

"Lilith," I answered under my breath.

"Yes, Lilith, Nicholas. She went all by her fucking self because somewhere in that very dense but clearly vulnerable mind of hers she thought she had to," Elise pointed out. She was clearly upset, but I didn't know if it was entirely aimed at myself. There was something that told me that she was also outraged at Dani, but not in the way of wanting to ring her neck but upset because Dani did this without her. "What exactly does Dani expect us to do now?"

"If I were her, I'd probably want everyone to go home since the *burden* is gone." Reese put air quotes as he said burden and shrugged. "Listen I like the girl, I don't think she's a burden, not that much at least, but that's what I'm thinking. And we can all agree that everything that's gone on could put a toll on someone who doesn't want anyone else involved in their issues."

Elise crossed her arms over her chest. "Oh yeah, well fuck that. If she really thinks she's just going to do this fight all on her own, then she's a fucking idiot. We all came here knowing that we were putting Lilith shaped targets on our backs, so suck it the fuck up."

Leah huddled next to Garrett. "So, what now?"

"We go on with the plan as usual," she looked over at Beetee who had broken away from the group to go be with her parents. "Get your parents ready for a little meeting of the minds. With or without Dani, we are getting to Lilith and then when we find Dani, I'll kill her myself for freaking me—us—out." She cleared her throat and looked anywhere but my face as I tried to catch her eye and acknowledge her slip up. As much as she was angry, she was also worried—that made two of us. I looked over to where Beetee had settled down next to her moms, determination in her eyes. Leah and Garrett followed her as they listened to what she had to say.

I was about to head over there when Reese bumped my shoulder with his own, gaining my attention. "She didn't say anything to you before she left? Leave a note? Nothing?"

"No, she..." I cut myself off when the ghost of a whisper came through my mind. Her breath caressed my ear as her voice flooded my thoughts. The last words that she'd wanted me to hear. Just for me.

I want every second of every minute, of every hour, of every single day with you too. I'm sorry.

I felt her kiss on my skin and then the memory was gone. Her voice was nothing but the still air around me and I blinked seeing my best friend waiting for my response. I cleared my throat and shook my head, lifting my shoulders. "No, no she didn't."

27

DANI

I plunged my dagger into one demon and then another. Blood was dripping over my eyes, and I could hardly see, but I didn't need to see when I was this full of rage. One of the shadows twisted around my ankles, pulling me down and I kicked forward trying to get it to remove me from its clutches. I was being dragged and the jagged edges of broken stone clawed at my back. I used my dark magic to shadow a hole in the floor and dug my dagger into it, ripping the floor of the castle as I went. I used the hilt of my weapon to slow the shadow down and it whipped its head around and looked at me, stunned, when I lifted up and sliced across its wispy body. It disappeared altogether, but the hisses didn't stop, the pounding of footsteps and so much powerful energy didn't stop. I wiped my hand down my face, blood coating my hand. It was black and dark red, sticky and warm.

It shouldn't have been a surprise to me that getting inside Lilith's domain would have been easy. She knew I was coming; she was just biding her time until I did. The doors opened wide when I stepped foot on the premises and I noticed the demons circling above, I could feel their eyes on me. I heard my own footsteps when I walked through, a wave of memories flooding me, as I scanned every wall and passed every open door. Nothing came at me, there was no instant fight. There was just silence as I held tension in my shoulders. The Skies and Lilith's castle had similarities in its structure and its need to pretend like it was so much better than everything else. I had never been on this floor for long, but I did remember the thick stone doors that lined the walls on either side of me and the broken lanterns that still seemed to hold just a small bit of flame.

There had been a large staircase that greeted me, one that had a tattered carpet running along it as if it should have been replaced decades ago. I knew the second floor was where Lilith had her chambers and whatever the fuck else was up there. It had smelt like fire and pain when I really took in my current surroundings. I had followed that smell past the large staircase which had led me to an opening with a curved top and a darker staircase within. I felt a pull to whatever was in—down—there and I tilted my head from side to side, cracking my neck. I wasn't afraid of it because I knew what was there for the most part, I'd lived down there. I'd tortured the fuck out of people down there. When I'd come back from Leviathan all those times, I knew what would likely be waiting for me when I got back.

I had thought about Nick for one more minute and then I'd descended the stairs into so much darkness that my eyes had to adjust. Fire lit sconces suddenly lined the walls of the decrypted looking hallway that I remembered so well and then I felt a hand around the back of my neck and my body being shoved into the stone wall. Demons had sprung from everywhere and my first and only instinct was to fight back. That's what I'd been doing for what felt like hours. Fighting demons and shadows, wanting to beg for a moment of reprieve but I couldn't do that. If this was her way of making me feel small, punishing me for taking so long, then I would accept the punishment...like I'd always done.

I elbowed a demon behind me and kicked my foot out, knocking one back with a shove to the stomach. I whirled around and sliced one through the chest with my dagger and then I heard a laugh. It was littered with malice and a bit of crazy. Scratch that—a lot of crazy. It suddenly felt like wind was rushing past my ears and then like a body moving too fast in front of my eyes. They were on either side of me, so I swung to the left then to the right. They were in front of me, so I swung upward, but then I felt a whooshing behind me, so I spun around and struck there. Another miss, again and again.

That cackling, maniacal laughter was back. It was close to me, so close I could feel their breath. And then there was a buzzing in my head, like something had turned my brain up in frequency. I felt more demons circling around me and I lifted my arm to fight, but whatever was fucking with my head stole my focus. My vision started to blur; it was like I was drunk. Or better yet, like I was being fucked with by magic.

Heels clicked on the stone floor as my knees landed on the ground with a cracking pain I didn't even register. "Does that hurt, Soul Seether?"

I willed my dagger away and forced my head up to look at Isabel. Her blonde hair swished near her ears and her earrings shined in the firelight. Her icy blue eyes were stuck on mine as she grabbed my face and kept me in place. I flinched as she forced her magic further into my head, letting it seep into my veins. "I would think you enjoy a little pain, seeing as you sure do you love dishing it out? Or are you too good for a little torture nowadays?" She looked over her shoulder and nodded towards me to whoever she had acknowledged.

In a matter of seconds, I felt a hand on the back of my neck and restraints made of shadows around my wrists. The hand against my neck applied pressure, so much pressure that my airway was getting smaller and smaller. Their nails, which were pointed and sharp, dug into my skin. Isabel moved out of the way so that I could be pushed forward, landing on my face. I sucked in a harsh breath, catching remnants of gravel into my mouth.

"Get her up," Isabel commanded. I felt shadowy hands around me pulling me up and facing Isabel again. Whoever had pressed their nails into my skin was gone. They hadn't been a shadow demon, so who the hell were they?

My hair was matted in my face, and I could taste blood in my mouth. "Where is she?" I demanded, gritting my teeth through the pain. Isabel was a pain in my ass, but she wasn't who I wanted. I wanted vengeance on Lilith for my own benefit, but I found that I also wanted it to keep her away from everyone else.

Isabel tilted her head and smirked. "She's around. She said I could play with you first before she got to see you. Your time of waltzing in here with some sort of celebration waiting for you has long passed. You made her wait and damn near beg, so you are going to feel a little pain before I even consider letting you near her. I have to see if your little friends have made you weak." She extended her arm out and flexed her fingers toward me.

There was a burning in my throat, and it was like all my dark magic was suffocated by an electric current. Colorful crackles exploded from her fingertips, and they mimicked what was happening with her eyes. My vision blurred again, but I couldn't fall forward as I was being held upward by other demons. "So noble coming here all by yourself. Like you really had a fucking choice." She clenched her fingers and I started to scream from the pain. "It was so much fun getting inside your pathetic little head, watching Lilith work you over so easily, seeing you panic from seeing all your dead friends. It will be such a special moment when you get to see it actually happen, huh. I can't wait to watch you gut them one by one, and the best thing is that you'll enjoy it."

"That's never going to happen!"

"Oh, you're in for a treat." She stepped forward and placed her finger on my forehead and it was like a kaleidoscope of colors, but each was so much more painful than the last. "It's pathetic that you…" I started, but I was thrown against the wall, my entire body vibrating with pain. I grunted out, pushing it down. "It's pathetic that you think she'll always keep you around. You'll be nothing to her once your usefulness dries up." I rolled onto the stone floor, fixing my position so I could look at her again.

Her blue eyes bore into mine, rage bleeding into them. She hustled over to me, her heels clacking against the stone. She grabbed me by my hair so hard that my scalp twinged in pain. "I can't wait to see you tear your little boyfriend apart. Let him see what a monster you really are." She dug inside my mind and caused me to see everything from my nightmare. Every color was more vibrant, every wound I had inflicted much more brutal. She glamoured my vision so that every time I blinked things were enlarged and screams of agony were loud and brutal.

"Isabel, I think that's enough."

It was a voice I knew so well that it almost soothed me in a weird, fucked up way. It was a woman and she tsked at Isabel. "Get her up." Isabel huffed but did as she was told. I felt unbalanced on my feet and Isabel didn't make it any better as she yanked me up. I looked down at her wrapped hand, remembering when I stabbed my dagger through it.

"How's your hand, you bitch," I taunted. She sent a shock through me, causing me to groan out in pain. I felt a tingle of magic around my wrists, but I couldn't get a good look at whatever Isabel had done. The mystery woman stepped out of the shadows, and my heart sped up. My fingers flexed from behind my back and my blood boiled.

Lilith looked me up and down, her white, blonde hair was bone straight and parted down the middle, the ends meeting right below her breasts. The black dress she wore was long and fell off her shoulders. It was covered by red lace, and it shimmered in the light of the fire around us. "Still so feisty."

I remained silent, not wanting to give her the satisfaction of my words. Not yet anyway.

"Oh, you aren't speaking to me. Well then, you can be upset all you want, but I warned you this would happen, did I not?" She reached out and caressed my face. Isabel made it so I couldn't pull away, that I had to endure her touch. "I told you that you would make the right choice and here you are. As stubborn as you are, you always end up doing as you're told."

Black, wispy tendrils came from her fingers and slid over my face, gliding along my skin. They were comforting to that part of me that they knew so well. I could feel myself wanting to move towards her, be with her. This was where I belonged.

Remember who you are, Dani.

I thought back to Natalia's words. The same words Nick gave me as well. That was so hard to do when everything was so tempting around her. I shook my head, violently. I would rather die than openly submit to her. Her magic was snuffed out by her hand waving it away. "I have missed you. I can be a patient person, Dani, but not when it comes to what's already mine. I plan to make sure you don't ever forget that." She brought up her finger to tap my nose before turning away from me.

I mustered up all the strength I had and jerked my shoulder up as hard as I could, landing it right in Isabel's face as she teetered backwards. I worked to get my hands out of their confinement, but nothing happened. My own magic would be strong enough to get out of any of those demons' shitty restraints. I was brought to my knees by debilitating pain when sparks of colorful magic shot up my arms and down my chest.

"Did you really think I was going to leave you to your own devices? We need to keep you in check, don't we, Soul Seether?" Isabel knelt down next to me as her eyes flashed over with different colors. She'd used her magic to handcuff me with her dampening powers.

"You leave them alone and we can fight just you and me," I offered, narrowing my eyes at Lilith's back.

She looked over her shoulder and her red-stained lips turned into a terrifying smile. "You think I want to fight you?"

"*She* sure wants to fight you," Isabel said.

Lilith's dark eyes became a little soft, but that could have been a trick of the light if I was honest. "I have never wanted a fight with you, my love." She sighed, shaking her head towards the ground. "But when I'm done with you, I will be the only person you trust. The only person you won't want to fight. As it always should have been."

I was brought into one of the smaller torture rooms. It had less rows of seating and it didn't give off the feeling of wanting a big show to happen.

It wasn't intimate by any means, but with the lack of patrons and just me, Lilith, and Isabel present it felt like the smallest room in the world. The dust around my feet kicked up as I struggled to remove myself from the chair I was tied to. Not only were Isabel's nifty magic dampening ropes annoying, but so was the way Lilith looked at me, like she was still deciding what she wanted to do and how she wanted to go about her next move.

Isabel leaned up against the wall to my right, staring at me with her blue eyes that basically said she would instantly kill me if Lilith gave her the okay. Like the good pet she was. "I bet Markus is so proud of you. He isn't far from here you know, since he's probably getting ridiculed relentlessly in Hell," I gave her the fakest smile as she clenched her fists at her sides. "Are you sure your mother would be happy with what you've done?" I added, hearing Isabel audibly hiss at me as she started to take a step towards me.

"Not now, Isabel." Lilith waved her hand at her, motioning for Isabel to go back to her spot against the wall. She rubbed her hands together, smiling at me. "You really came here to try to battle it out with me, didn't you? I would never want to hurt you intentionally."

I snorted, pulling at the restraints. "You could have fooled me."

"It's called tough love. And you deserved so much more of it. I went easy on you."

"Easy?"

"I didn't throw anything at you that you couldn't handle. And well…" She laughed a little. "If you couldn't then I knew you weren't as strong as I assumed you were. Simple enough."

I tilted my head back, readjusting myself in the seat. "You're just a coward who hides behind all her puppets and pets."

Lilith placed her hand on her chest delicately. "A coward? On the contrary, I'm a strategist. I wouldn't go into something without a chance that I would win. You are quite a change in plans though." She tapped her index finger along her chin in thought. "I honestly didn't see that angels could be as tempting as they were. Especially the handsome one you're so fond of."

I bared my teeth as she spoke about Nick, hating that she knew anything about him.

"Heaven's Gate did quite a number on him. And to think the two of you could have been so happy here together, side by side, darkness to darkness. I could use muscles like his, but it seems like you went and fixed that as well, for now, because you and I both know once something like that leaks into your mind it never truly leaves." She circled around the chair, one step at a time. Her finger traced over my shoulders, over the back of the chair and glided over my other shoulder.

I scoffed. "You did this to yourself, you know. You put yourself in this prison when you killed that baby and caused that huge war. You have no one else to blame!" I clawed at the arms of the chair, its wooden texture waning under my hold. I looked over to Isabel. "Your mother died because of her. She told Dimitri that I could be the one to kill you if I chose her. She doesn't care about you. She doesn't care about anyone!" I felt the chair rattle underneath me as my body shook with anger.

Lilith settled in front of me again. She brought her fingers to her mouth and gave me a thoughtful look. "Ah, that baby. I knew letting everyone mingle like it was normal was a bad thing, but Lucifer didn't think anything of it, so he let it happen. Hybrid children weren't unheard of, but they weren't something you aspired to have, but of course, when entities love each other, they just have to show it in a physical way and out pops a baby that should have never been born." She raised her head to the ceiling, her long hair cascading down her back. "I took matters into my own hands, like a good leader does and I got rid of it before it could get rid of me and tried to take over everything. People were over the realms for that silly baby, but you really think that Isaac Zuriel was thrilled to know that it could one day destroy him, his son and everyone else."

"It was just a baby!" I yelled.

"You cut things off at the root, Dani. You don't wait until it becomes a threat, because then it's too late. You no longer have the upper hand." She closed her eyes and smoothed her hands down the side of her dress. "I didn't expect everyone to lose their fucking minds over it, but it was quite a sight to see. Angels acting less angelic than usual, Enchanters harboring their powers and losing faith in their leader. Chaos that I didn't actually mean to cause but they did it all to themselves. It just goes to show that everything isn't always what it seems, and it just takes one small shift for blood and fury to take precedence. I'm learning that's the way to make anything happen nowadays."

I rubbed my lips together, realizing how dry and chapped they were. "Your plan for Heaven's Gate and a way out of here didn't work, so what is it that you want with me now? Why am I still so important to you?"

"You are going to be what you've always been. One of the most feared creatures they've ever known."

"You have your voided demons for that. Your toxic hellhounds. What am I compared to them?" I flashed the darkness in my eyes at her.

"Oh, my love, you are so much more. You should really learn to stop making so many friends, Dani. That traitorous necromancer and his wife, that cute little pink haired demon and oh, that adorable hellhound. You are only making this harder on yourself."

"I asked you to leave them out of this."

She pointed her finger at me. "And I asked you to come to me days ago and you chose to disobey me and fight me at every turn, so I'm done giving you and your companions a chance. Luckily for you, I won't be the one to make them suffer." Her eyes glittered with maniacal wonder. She couldn't be serious.

"And we all get a front row seat to the show." I turned my head over my shoulder to see Dimitri sitting in one of the pews. He had come in so quietly that I didn't even know when he had gotten into the room in the first place. He unbuttoned his suit jacket and turned his face, so I could see the burn mark that Nick's light magic had left. "Isn't that right, hmm?" He said to the woman at his side. One of the sharp toothed twins, Rae, smiled at him, tucking a piece of her dark hair behind her ear. I took note of her nails, they were filed down to sharp points. My neck tensed at the memory of her digging them into my skin.

"You said you wanted Lilith gone just as much as the next demon," I said, confused as to what she was doing here.

"I did, but she wants to get out of Purgatory, go roam and take over a new space, infiltrate Heaven's Gate or some other realm. You are her ticket to doing that, so the quicker she has you and you submit, the faster she explores someplace new. Dimitri can have an even better Leviathan." She traced her knuckles down his cheek, and he winked at her. "You clearly came here for the good of your friends, so just bow down like a good little bitch."

I flung my head away from her, nearly biting down on my own tongue. "No."

"Summon your dagger." Lilith commanded.

I furrowed my eyebrows and shook my head. Isabel huffed. "Do it!"

"Fuck you!" I yelled.

Lilith came up to me and leaned down, placing her hands on the chair's armrests. "Summon. Your. Dagger." Each word was announced on its own, one by one. Her eyes flashed a menacing red and I felt a pain in my head, like she was digging into it. It felt like Elise's venom, but instead of paralyzing me, it made me compliant. It was like her voice was the only thing I heard, echoing into my mind. I tried to say no, no, no over again and then it was there.

My dagger, with my name etched in the center, was at my feet.

Lilith gave me a smile that showed all her teeth. "Still such a good girl, aren't you?"

I nearly vomited since that kind of endearment made me think of being happily naked with my angel. Now she'd done what she was good at and tainted something. She bent down to grab it, but I moved on instinct and kicked it away from her. I sent it flying towards the wall behind her as I grasped onto that connection I had with it, giving it instructions.

Find him and don't come back to me.

It vanished, like the good obeying weapon it was. Lilith watched as smoke puffed from nowhere and took the dagger with it. I watched her body tense as she faced away from me. She slowly turned toward me. "Get it back."

"No. I would say get it yourself, but we both know you can't."

She narrowed her eyes, the dark irises flaming red for only a moment.

"Where did it go?" Dimitri asked, curiously.

I didn't answer him, but it seemed that I didn't need to. Lilith chuckled as she continued to stare at me. "Oh, Dani. Of course, you would." She said it like everything clicked into place, like all the answers to the realms had come to her at this very moment.

"What are you talking about?" Rae asked, sounding dumbfounded, which didn't surprise me in the slightest.

Lilith smoothed down her hair and took a few steps back over to me. "You think just because I gave you that dagger as a gift, that I bestowed it upon you and no one else, that I don't know what you did with it. Just because I can't summon it myself doesn't mean I'm so naive." She wrapped her fingers around my chin. "You trust that boy too much."

Isabel let out a short laugh. "You sent it to that stupid boy. I'll kill him myself."

Dimitri, who was now next to me, brought his hand up to stop her. "Oh no, I would rather enjoy doing that."

Rae grazed her hand along Dimitri's shoulder as she came up behind him. "I would love to play with him a little, watch him squirm before you do."

I wanted to throttle her. I wanted to kill every single one of them. "Just leave him out of it. None of this makes fucking sense anyway! Jonah is dead, there isn't a high executive's magic to take to do whatever the fuck you wanted to do with me. I have no more of a handle on that angelic side of myself than I did before, so that's not much of a plan either. You. Make. No. Fucking. Sense."

Lilith made her fingertips touch, creating a sort of triangle and brought her hands up to her face. "You see Dani, when I originally had my plan, I thought I needed all sides to see it through. I didn't mind that my partners had their own agendas, so long as it didn't take away from what I wanted to do. Markus, poor thing, he did everything I asked, but he was so enraged towards Jonah that it blinded him. Angels do not make good company, no matter what side they're on." She clucked her tongue, wagging her finger at me. "I learned that while it would be fun to nurture both your sides and watch you make a mess and give me all the things I wanted, that maybe I was going the easy route. Angelic magic is powerful, especially matched with demonic magic in one body, it would have been a sight." She lifted one of her shoulders. "But Dani, you've been such a good demon, so good at making sure that light gets shadowed by the dark that I should really let it flourish, shouldn't I?"

I blinked at her, not fully understanding.

"Your dagger would have just been the perfect artistic touch, especially when I make you murder all your friends." She smiled at me proudly, her lips pressed together. "But I can work without it, I mean it's not like that boy can use it. It's not like you really need it for what I have planned for you."

"You can't make me do that, *I won't*. You can show me fucked up shit all you want, but I'll go down *with* you before I let you manipulate me." I struggled against the restraints, feeling a burning sensation as Isabel forced her magic into me again.

Lilith sighed as if she was bored. She delicately rubbed at her arched blonde eyebrow. "Oh, my love, it's quite hilarious that you think you have choices. You came to me because you thought this was your only option left. I made it clear—Dimitri made it clear— to you that my generosity was waning, and you chose to ignore it. So now you have no more choices. That independent nature of yours, that confidence that I graced you with, will not be kept all to yourself anymore."

She was closer to me now and I could smell the power radiating off of her, I could sense her need to do whatever she was planning. It put me on edge, and it was the kind of antsy feeling that I hated because I didn't know what the other person was planning. I didn't have any indication of what may be coming next. Her breath was hot against my face as she leaned down near my ear. "I've always accepted you for who you are. Always pushed you to be the best you could be, and you think that you're going to have some cute little happily ever after with that pretty angel. You think that they're going to accept you with open arms over there, just forget about everything you've done and give you a clean slate? You think they didn't second guess you when you almost killed that child, when I kept getting in your head, did you think they weren't giving you sideways glances hoping you wouldn't use your weapon against them?" She pulled back and almost gave me a look that could have been assumed as loving, but I knew better than that. "It's never fair to limit yourself, Dani."

"Be the monster, Soul Seether. It's really all you're good for, huh," Isabel snarked, taking a few steps towards me. They had me surrounded but there was a calmness to the air, like they were waiting for some big finale.

"I'm not a monster, you traitorous little shit." I spat, turning my head to burn my eyes into hers.

Lilith grabbed my face, forcing me to look at her again. She squeezed my cheeks as she spoke. "She's right, Dani. You *are* my pretty monster, but I think you've forgotten what that means." She traced her finger down my neck and tapped my chest. She tilted her eyes up to look at Dimitri. "And your father is okay with this? Even though I shouldn't need permission."

Dimitri adjusted his jacket. "Lucifer and my father don't want much destruction to Purgatory, and they *don't* want it bleeding into Hell, but they don't care about much else. Do what you must and make sure I get what's mine in the end."

Lilith dug her nails into my chest, cutting me. I flinched from the initial pain, biting my tongue through the rest. "I know you've been wondering about my little experiments, my little voids, and it was just killing me trying to figure out what I was missing, but then it hit me. I need a connection; I need something with strength and resilience, preferably one that can survive with or without a soul to guide them because they'll have me. Their darkness calls to the same darkness that they were bred from. They would feed off of it, I'd be their guide into the world of so much power. Power and darkness strong enough to push past any force of magic."

"Your boys have enough angelic magic for me to siphon and use, so don't worry about them not being useful before you kill them," Isabel added with a bitchy smirk.

"You'd be a parasite and I'm not going to be your host," I answered, pushing back.

"Ugh, again with the choices," Rae mumbled under her breath.

Lilith dug her nails in further, sliding them down to open her cuts up more. Blood was starting to run from the open wound. I continued, "You can't take out the angelic side of me. You'd have to kill me, and we both know that's obviously not what you want."

The dark queen let out an open-mouthed laugh as if I had just said the funniest thing. "Oh, my love, there are ways to kill you that are much worse than pure death itself."

"I did once tell you that you were her strongest creation, did I not?" Dimitri said, wrapping one of his fingers around one of my curls and letting it go. It was only then did I notice his missing hand. I knew I had been the one to cut it off, but it was strangely satisfying seeing it again.

"You will learn that I am the only family that matters to you. Or maybe that's because I'll be the only one you'll have when this is all over. I'll give you everything, Dani, make it so you are the strongest you've ever been. The things I'll make you do." There was a stinging pain in my chest as she plunged her nails further into my skin and ripped them into my chest. There was blood and then it was like her hand had gone right through as if I was hollow. I had never been on this side of things before and it hurt, *fuck* did it hurt. My chest felt tight, and my vision kept flashing from black to gray to red and back to black. Lilith's eyes were a bright red as she dug around inside of me. I could hear myself screaming but it sounded like everything was underwater. The air was dry and humid, I felt dehydrated. It felt like there was a massive stone on my chest causing the air in my lungs to come less frequently, eventually threatening to stop altogether.

"There you are." Lilith yanked her hand from my chest, and I let out a sound that made it seem like all the air had been pulled out of me. I looked over at the ball of translucent matter. It danced along her palm as she held it.

"What are you going to do about that pesky little angelic light, hmm?" Isabel asked, watching me take in breath after breath. It felt like something was missing, but I couldn't reach it. I didn't know which way was up and my mind was foggy and confused.

"See I can't just destroy it like all the others, no you are special, my love." Lilith motioned for my soul to go over to Dimitri, who grabbed it and created a ball with it in his hands. His eyes flashed red and then went black. Dimitri had the power of Hell on his side and despite my hatred for him, he unnerved me even more than Lilith. The soul hissed and pulsed in his grasp, but the once translucent matter turned a deep gray and then solid black. Dimitri's eyes went back to normal, and he gave my soul back to Lilith. "I told you Dani, there are fates much worse than a traditional death. I'll poison you from the inside and every single thing you do, every single one of your friends you slaughter, every single angel and Enchanter that you watch bleed to fulfill my wishes will make it worse. You will darken yourself over and over again and it won't stop until I decide when your death will come." She held my dark, bleeding soul in her hand and slowly closed her palm. There was a rush to my chest as she crushed it. I cried out from the pain; it was nothing I'd ever felt before. She opened up her hand to small bits of my soul bobbing up and down.

Lilith gathered them into one hand and then settled in front of me. "I have the perfect first thing for you to do since I'm so generous, but you still need to learn your lesson. I won't make you kill your friends." Without warning she slammed her fist into my chest, and I cried out a blood curdling scream as she extended her hand and let the pieces of my toxic soul find its way into every crevice of my insides. "I'm going to have you make *him* do it." She removed her hand and leaned back a bit to look at me.

I felt an electric sting around my body, knowing it was Isabel using her magic on me like she'd done with all the other demons Lilith experimented with. I felt like she was cocooning me within myself, making it so I had nowhere to go but wherever Lilith told me, wherever she could ensue the most chaos. My body started to flood with this wave of poisonous venom that was darkness incarnate. That part of my soul was screaming for joy, drinking it in. There was this tiny, tiny part that was crying, damn near begging me to notice it. It was a glint of light that I saw. I tried to swim towards it, trying not to drown and gag on the darkness that was clouding everything. I reached out my hand to grab it, but I was pulled back, ripped away from the one thing connecting me to the other good thing that had come into my life. I slumped over in my chair, exhaustion taking over.

Slowly, so slowly, the light was smothered and suffocated as my eyes closed fully. That glinting light, that warmth was now nonexistent. It was being molded into something else, something I didn't recognize, as if the darkness was enveloping it in a prison of my own making, silencing it. I couldn't see it anymore. I couldn't feel it anymore. All I felt was nothing, just like she wanted. She made it so the only person who could guide me through was her.

You are my pretty monster, but I think you've forgotten what that means.

My eyes were closed but I felt Lilith behind me, it was like I could feel her everywhere. She leaned down to my ear and whispered something.

So, now you have no more choices.

My eyes flashed open and all I saw was nothing but a void, but I'd heard what she'd said. I may not have had any choice left, but I didn't want one. I knew what I wanted to do and *who* I wanted to make do it.

28

NICK

We sat around the dining room table while Elise had her arms crossed over her chest, staring daggers at me. I tried to ignore her, but it was hard to do when her eye contact cut so deep you felt it in your bones. One of Beetee's moms sat at the head of the table and the other was on her left. The red head with the pixie cut was Louise and the one with white hair was named Willa. Beetee sat next to Elise while Reese leaned back in his chair to my right. Garrett leaned against the wall, holding Leah to his front with her back facing him. I tapped my fingers on the table, feeling the uncomfortable silence nearly swallow the room whole. I bounced my eyes from Reese, to Beetee, to the wall behind Elise's head and then back to Elise herself. Her gray eyes were still burning into me.

"Can you stop staring at me?" I asked, raising one of my eyebrows.

Elise tilted her head to the side, tapping her finger on her chin in thought. "How about no."

"It's not like I made her leave and do this shit on her own." I couldn't believe this was an argument I was having.

"This could have been prevented if you would have just thought for one second that you may not be what she needs all the fucking time. Maybe she would still be right here if you would have woken me up since I'm literally the only person who would understand that little nightmare she had, I might have known what to say to her to perhaps dissuade her from gallivanting off like some sacrificial idiot..."

Reese cleared his throat, causing her to meticulously move her eyes towards him. Her head followed suit. "Something to say?"

My best friend shrugged. "Sounds a lot like you give more than a few shits about her. It kind of sounds like you're worried."

Elise growled at him. "How about you keep your opinions to yourself. I would hate to have to castrate you in front of them." She nodded her head towards Beetee's parents. "And we both know I'm not afraid to separate you from your most precious appendage."

Beetee's golden brown skin turned a bright shade of red as she rubbed behind her neck. "Ellie!" Reese shifted uncomfortably in his seat, while I heard Garrett and Leah snickering over to the side. Elise rolled her eyes and waved her hand towards the older demons at the table. "I'm sorry or whatever." They didn't acknowledge her half-assed apology, but just continued to survey their surroundings, looking nervous.

Beetee reached for Louise's hand and squeezed it. She nodded, encouragingly. "Go ahead, mom." Louise looked over at her wife and took in an unsteady breath. "Willa and I used to work with Lilith ages ago, well I guess I should really say we worked *for* Lilith because at the end of the day there is no sharing with her."

We all started to lean in as if she hadn't been saying much but her voice was haunting enough to draw us in. In a matter of seconds, she had our attention even though you could tell she would rather be anywhere else but at the center of our little situation. Louise pulled her bottom lip into her mouth and mulled over her thoughts before she spoke again. "In our younger years we would bring her souls from the human world, ones to torture or ones to discard and leave for Lucifer. She trusted us and held us close, well, as close as someone like Lilith can. That went on for quite some time and we started getting older and it was just starting to wane on us."

Willa rubbed her wife's shoulder, adding, "We had paid our dues, so we wanted to reap the benefits of that. There were so many demons worthy of what we had been doing. We knew all the secret ways in and out of that castle and we were willing to pass down all that knowledge if we could just continue on our way in peace."

Louise scoffed. "By time Lilith had Cullen following her every whim and this one," she pointed to Elise who just narrowed her eyes at the older woman. "We just didn't understand why she was holding onto us, and we couldn't just leave her. As bad as things are now, everything wasn't as high stakes back then."

Willa finger-combed her all white hair. I wondered if it had always been that color, or did it gradually become that way courtesy of the life they'd lived—pre-anti-aging curse. "We were going to tell her we wanted to leave and that if she didn't take it well, then we would leave out the underground passageways. It comes out right at the edge of the woods, towards one of the more docile parts of Purgatory. We, of course, didn't know when we had initially discovered the pathway but the more on edge Lilith became the more demons wanted out. They wanted to do their own thing, seek their own pleasures in life instead of catering to hers.

"There are multiple ways to enter the passageway if you know what you're looking for, and if you want to take her on, I suggest using it. Flying there, especially with your angel wings on display so openly would get you killed in an instant. You wouldn't even know what hit you." She wagged her finger at Reese and me. We both nodded obediently.

"You can take Axel to whichever spot you deem fit and then follow it from there. I'll glamour it over so no one tries to follow you through it," Leah offered.

Beetee smiled. "That's perfect." She looked over to Garrett. "Are you staying behind or fighting?"

Garrett rolled his shoulders and smirked at her. "I'm fighting. I was always going to fight."

Leah lightly punched his stomach. "We both are."

Willa placed her tiny elbows on the table. "The path is quite easy to follow, so no detours along the way. You'll know when you're close and when you're there. It leads to an empty spider infested room on the bottom floor. I'd keep my wits about yourselves while you're there, it may seem empty and unassuming, but she'll likely know you're coming since that Soul Seether is there. Hell only knows what's happening to her now that she's back in Lilith's hands."

I nearly flinched at that thought, but I shook my head, continuing to try to picture the moments before she made this monumental decision to try to go at it alone. Maybe if she had just let me say what I wanted to say, then she would have had something else holding her here. Something that would have allowed her to stay right next to me in bed and not have me waking up without her.

Reese cleared his throat. "So, we are legitimately sneak attacking the

Queen of Darkness. I'm actually pretty in love with this idea, I'm not gonna lie."

Beetee giggled, still holding onto her mom's hand. I hummed. "Um, how did that conversation with Lilith go? You said you wanted to talk to her about leaving and well, from what Beetee told us you both clearly don't want to be found by anyone except your daughter, so I assume the talk didn't go well all those years ago." It was a legitimate question to a part of their story they never concluded.

Louise quickly looked over at Willa in a way that told me she didn't know how to answer the question. I wasn't trying to make things awkward for them, but my thoughts were valid. Willa furrowed her brow at her wife, and I felt a wave of deja vu wash over me as I watched them. The look they exchanged was one I'd seen before. My father had that same look in his eyes whenever I asked him a question he never answered, or if he did answer, it always seemed incomplete or skewed. They were hiding something.

"Mom?" Beetee said, making me blink and bring myself back into the moment.

Louise ran her hand through her short hair and rubbed her lips together, as if she was trying to keep the words in. Her wife pulled her glasses off, folded them and placed them on the table. "She said she had something to do and needed us to wait for her in her chambers and that she would be back. Only then would we be free to leave without issue."

I nodded slowly, the visuals casually playing out in my head. She continued, "Around this time there had been a lot of chatter about one of her own demons and an angel creating a baby. Everyone knew all the stories about those kinds of hybrid children, so even though there was no strict law about fornicating with another entity, you just made sure not to procreate with one."

"Yet…it happened." Elise pointed out, placing her palm facing up as if to say *so what*.

Louise licked her lips, hesitating. Willa nodded to her wife. "We need to, Louie. We don't do it now; you know we'll never do it." Louise placed her free hand, that wasn't currently being held hostage by her daughter, against her chest. "Well, Lilith eventually came back for us, but she didn't come back alone. She came back with a baby."

Reese, who had been tapping his foot along the floor, stopped moving. We all could feel the room shift into something much more intriguing, like a dam was about to be broken and everything would be flooding out. "A baby?" I asked.

They both nodded. "She came back with it and damn near tossed it at us. She told us that our last task would be to dispose of it. We could go live whatever lives we wanted but get rid of the child first and foremost. She had that look on her face like she was hatching a plan, but it wasn't all the way formed yet." Willa practically shivered.

"How does one rid themselves of a baby?" Reese questioned.

"Oh, come on Blondie. Get creative. You can't sit there and not think that there are plenty of ways to dispose of something or someone." Elise taunted, sticking her tongue out at him.

Willa fidgeted with the ends of her jacket sleeves. "We had the baby in tow, and we were all set to get rid of the problem. Start our lives away from Lilith and her grip on us..." She trailed off, placing her hand over her mouth.

"So, you killed that baby..." Reese started to say, but I patted his arm, letting him know to stop talking and let me speak. I rubbed my index finger above one of my eyebrows thoughtfully.

"Your moms never told you any of this?" I looked over to Beetee who seemed a little taken aback by my question.

She shook her head. "No. I mean they didn't take me in until after all that mess with Heaven's Gate and Oculus. I guess it's something they didn't want to think about anymore, something they didn't want to bring up." She placed her other hand over her mom's, a gesture that said she was with her parents, despite whatever they'd done for Lilith. Louise gave her daughter a half smile, but it was filled with sadness. The wheels in my head were moving as if someone had thrown oil in the cogs and they were starting to move at their normal pace again.

"After? Like as a teenager? An adult?" I understood that these women weren't her parents, but there was something that didn't make any fucking sense. I couldn't have been the only person to see it. I eyed Garrett and Leah who were looking at Louise and Willa with the same stare as my own. Beetee tilted her head to the side, her lilac eyes concerned. "No, Nicholas. I grew up with them. They are parents in every way except biological."

I opened my mouth to say something, but Reese cut me off. "Grew up?"

Elise looked from side to side, her mouth opened slightly as if she was trying to do math in her head but somehow the answer kept ending up wrong. "Right after the whole dead baby thing, Lilith put that whole anti-aging, anti-procreation decree on Purgatory, all those born here and in Hell along with all those created by her..." I'd never seen Elise lost for her words, but this was something I was too invested in to really capture the moment like I should have.

"It took her years to find Dani and create a hybrid of her own. And you're knowledgeable about when Dani came around?" I focused on Beetee.

She looked a little out of sorts.

"Um, yes. Like I told Dani, I never went to Lilith's castle, never really got close. But I knew the Soul Seether existed, there was so much talk about her. Especially when I got old enough to check out Leviathan, the one and only time I went. I learned a lot about her from Elise, but most of my childhood and beyond was getting this anchoring tattoo in check."

Willa let out a small chuckle. "Ah, that tattoo was something I was not prepared for. Those things don't fully develop until around the pre-teen stage and oof, I didn't think I would ever have to wrangle a reptile in my lifetime."

I slammed my hand on the table sensing a headache creeping up on me. "Do you hear yourselves? Pre-teen stage? How the hell did you even get that far? You came to them *after* the war in Oculus and grew up with them as your moms." I waved my hand in Beetee's direction, motioning towards her entire body. "This doesn't make sense. She would still be a baby if that timeline had any merit."

"She wouldn't...oh shit, she would." Reese's hazel eyes widened taking in my words.

Garrett stepped around his wife and moved closer to the table. He closed his eyes and then opened them, taking in a solid breath and then letting that same breath out. "Louise, Willa, what happened to that baby?" He asked like he already knew the answer, like he knew they had one true thing in common. They were both parents to children they loved deeply.

I could see Louise vibrating with nerves. Her voice was shaky when she spoke. "We couldn't do it. We had done some terrible things in our time, murder being one of them, but we couldn't gather the strength to do that. We'd heard and read things about hybrid children, but Willa is also one to read the fine print and everyone should know that those children don't have to turn into raging dictators, they don't have to be rulers and destroy worlds. They can live perfectly semi-normal lives, deciding how they want to be without any manipulation." She sounded like she was trying to sell us on that point, she was trying to defend what they had chosen not to do and ultimately explained why they didn't come out often.

"What?" Beetee said in a small voice, her breath barely coming out.

Elise made a tiny choking sound as if she had just had an epiphany. "Woah, woah! You keep aging because you were neither born down here nor created by Lilith. Please nod if I'm correct." Elise looked towards Beetee's moms. They gave her two short nods, the solemn look they both displayed made me a little sad for them. "Right. So, you guys rekidnapped a baby that Lilith had previously kidnapped and then raised it as your own." She wasn't really talking to anyone now; she was just putting the puzzle together.

I helped give her pieces to that puzzle, "you're that baby. You're Daya's niece. She thinks you're dead. They all think you're dead. That whole catastrophe in Oculus happened because of some underhanded blaming and finger pointing because everyone wanted to believe that everyone else murdered…you." I couldn't actually believe the words I was saying. I looked at Beetee, really looked at her. There were pieces of her that reminded me of Daya and how I suppose her cousin would have been. She had this forward way about her, but it was wrapped up in this loving nature that truly seemed like it was written into her personality so that she would remain like that forever.

Beetee shook her head and then shook it again. "Anti-aging? What the hell are you guys talking about?"

It looked like each of us was about to explain, but Elise gave us all a stark look that screamed *shut the fuck up*. She faced her friend and plastered on that tough love expression she wore so well. "Beetee, Lilith put an entire curse on this realm after that war. She didn't want anyone producing anything she couldn't control, and she didn't want the people she found to stand beside her to go out of commission due to old age until she was ready for them to leave. You said that you've been with them from the start and you've fucking aged like you're untouched by any of this." Elise leaned in. "Because you aren't *from* any of this. That tattoo you have, that's from your dad and that weird, annoying go-lucky nature you have that's from your mom. I just thought your parents raised you all funny for you to want to have this place and actually help people, but now I guess it all makes sense." She shrugged, leaning back into her chair.

I watched as Beetee looked down at the hand she had over her mom's. She stared at it for so long I swore she zoned out. My stomach dropped when she slowly removed her hand from Louise's grasp. Her mom let her, but not without flinching a bit at the loss of contact. Beetee wrapped her hand into a fist at the table and her whole body was tense as if she didn't know what to do with all this information, all these sudden emotions.

Reese sucked in a breath. "So, you—you and Dani—you guys are…"

"They're the same," I finished.

Beetee violently shook her head. "No, no! Dani was supposed to be an angel, Lilith created her. She made her a demon. I…I mean, I…."

Leah walked around the table and gingerly placed her hand on Beetee's shoulder. The pink haired demon peeked up at her from where she sat. "Dani was made, Beetee. You were born, to an angel and demon. You're both hybrids respectively, but by two different means."

"So, you've been lying to me." Beetee whipped her head to her mom's.

"We did it for your own good," Willa explained. "We had no way to Heaven's Gate ourselves to put you back and even if we had a way, placing you back with your parents would have been a huge risk. So, we took a different kind of risk and raised you ourselves away from everything and everyone for a while. When you didn't show any signs of stunted growth, we just hoped no one would notice and with everything that was happening and eventually Dani coming into the picture no one ever did."

Louise tried to grab her daughter's hand again, but Beetee pulled away, standing up. "Honey, eventually you grew up and we couldn't shelter you. We raised you so that you didn't want to hurt people which if that's the kind of demon you wanted to be, we would have accepted it, but you only wanted that side of you to appear when necessary. All you ever wanted to do was be happy and take in strays as friends." Louise nodded over to Elise who scoffed but didn't argue. "You never wanted to be like how they wrote your kind in history because we gave you other options."

"But I'm not *just* a demon, mom!" Beetee yelled, gaining all of our attention and by the look she gave us back she had stunned herself. I could see her eyes starting to form into those diamond pupils and then they flashed back.

"Beetee if Lilith would have found you, she would have killed you herself. They were just trying to protect you," I said, thinking about my father and all his secrets. I wasn't anywhere near ready to just let things go, but this right here, had me seeing things from his side a bit. I wondered if whatever he was hiding was exactly like this, something done with the best intentions but the matters leading up to them weren't flattering.

She looked at me with sympathetic eyes, like she knew I was right, but I understood her feeling of betrayal and deception. "I know, I just…I can't deal with this right now. We need to solidify the plan and go find Dani. Dani is what's important." After all she'd just learned, Dani was still a priority. Deflection wasn't just *my* strong suit; it was also hers. Beetee's freckles were more pronounced along her face as her face reddened. "I need to go lie down, please don't follow me." She said that last part to Willa and Louise, turning her back towards them and walking towards where I knew the recovery room was.

Louise covered her face with her hands, and I heard a muffled cry coming from her. Willa rubbed her back, holding her close. I felt bad, but I didn't have any words of comfort. "Why didn't you just tell her? She seems like one of the most levelheaded, understanding individuals I know."

Willa gave me a stiff smile. "Because knowing something like that, you might fight harder for one over the other and we raised her to not put herself in a box. We wanted her to sway to whatever side felt right for her, be her true self. *We* wanted to follow Lilith, find souls and watch her work. *We* made those choices. Whether Beatrice became the most feared demon like your Dani, or the owner of a hostel for the lost and broken. It would be her choice."

"And what if she asked about Lilith? Wanted to work with her?" Elise interrogated, pushing her chair back and standing up. She placed her hands on the table and leaned forward.

"When you two met I thought that would be the case, but no, she still didn't want that. And we would have told her, I swear. We only…we only wanted the best for her. We won't apologize for our past and we won't apologize for wanting only good things for our child's life."

I started to continue the conversation, but Garrett put his hand up, silencing pretty much all of us. When it came to the best for his children, Garrett would forever be an advocate for that kind of motivation. He reminded me so much of my father that my heart hurt just a little. "How about we get you both settled in the room Beetee set up for you. We'll figure this all out in a little bit." He looked at me over his shoulder. "We'll get Dani, I promise."

He ushered the woman upstairs, Leah following close behind. The three of us were left at the table to think. "You had no idea about any of this?" I asked Elise, who gave me an incredulous look.

"Fuck, no. I don't think there is any way in Hell I could have kept the secret of both these very annoying women being hybrids to myself. I love drama, but this shit is wild."

"That is way more information than I bargained for," Reese admitted, leaning back in his chair.

"And to think, Jonah's father and everyone else started that whole war over a child that has been alive this whole time. All that blood for nothing. Such a fucking waste." Elise shook her head. "Make sure to tell Natalia about this little fun fact."

I officially had so many reasons to want to make it out of Purgatory. I wanted to see my father again, I wanted to know what a life with Dani was like without something trying to tear us apart at every turn and now I wanted to go home to tell Daya that she was wrong, that a piece of that family member she lost was still around.

Lilith didn't always have to win.

I needed to keep that mindset if I had any hope of getting my girl back.

Elise had gone to find Beetee, not saying a word when she'd left us both in the dining area. Reese had opted to stay right downstairs and down a beer or two before we all reconvened again to move along with the plan. I'd taken myself upstairs and back to my room, planning to run all the options through my brain again and again. Beetee's moms had thrown a giant wrench in the mix and the fact that Dani wasn't here to learn that she wasn't alone in her hybrid nature was something I hated. Beetee and Dani were completely different beings and it seemed like they had nothing in common whatsoever, but maybe this could be their common ground that made them even stronger than they actually were.

I bent my legs up so that my knees were parallel to my chest as I shifted back towards the bed's headboard. I let out a sigh and peered down at my arm where the remnants of Dimitri's nails remained. The slashes weren't red and swollen anymore, but the scars were present, and I didn't know how long they'd be there. The wounds from Elise's tail had all but disappeared but maybe these were different based on who gave them to me. Elise's had been an accident, technicalities of a fight, but Dimitri's had been personal and purposeful. The guy still boiled my blood every single time I thought about the way he spoke to her and every time little images of what they would have been like together infiltrated my mind.

I felt a whisper of magic near me, the sound was like a *whoosh* right near my ear. I looked down to my right and my heart stuttered as a finely crafted dagger sat next to me. Its hooked end glinted, and her name was on perfect display, my eyes flying right to the place the letters were etched into it. I just stared at it for a moment, my body unmoving and my mind ran through so many reasons why it was here and not with her.

Was she hurt? Was she trying to tell me something?

Why was it here with me? That was the question. Why me?

I want every second of every minute, of every hour, of every single day with you too. I'm sorry.

I tentatively reached my hand out and took hold of the hilt. It was smooth and had weight to it. I brought it up to my face and for some reason, assumed something would happen, but nothing did. The room was still silent, and I was still alone, without her. There was a humming in my veins that warmed my blood after a few seconds. That warmth locked itself within me, but I wasn't scared or thought I should place my guard up for it. It was like the dagger was happy to have found me as much as I was apprehensive to have it in the first place. Having it just told me that I needed to get it back to her, which amplified my need to get the ball rolling again.

I held it tight in my grip and jumped off the bed. I had made it a few steps from the door when the room started to shake, I didn't know if it was real or if I was just feeling things like a hallucination. I didn't feel the raging guilt or sadness I had felt for so long, so what the fuck was trying to mess with me now? I placed my hand on the wall steadying myself and looked down at the ground. Dark smoke was coming from the wood and started to wrap itself around my legs. I tried to pick my feet up, get to the door to alert the others, but my mouth wouldn't move and when I felt like I was close to the door, it moved further back. My vision was spotting and I started blinking rapidly, seeing only certain colors over and over again.

I backed up into the wall, my breathing starting to become erratic. My hold on the dagger loosened and eventually it clattered against the floor. I watched as it enveloped itself in smoke and retreated away from me. Whatever this was…it was pushing into my head, but it wasn't like the kind of darkness that I was used to, if darkness could have a texture this one was smooth and silky. It moved like it wanted to comfort me—like it knew me.

I could feel it in every crevice of my body, my ears were ringing, and the tips of my fingers started tingling. I saw my hands start to light up and then stop. Start, stop, start, stop. It was strong, so much stronger than the darkness from before. I tried to pull my strength together, work against whatever this was, but then it pulled at my heart, it wrapped itself around my chest. I already felt connected to it in some way.

Nicholas.

Nicholas.

The voice said over and over again like it was a song. It was familiar. So, so familiar. I would know Dani with my hands tied and my eyes closed, but this wasn't her.

I felt myself being dragged down, my fighting subdued, and it was like I was retreating further into myself. I was getting smaller and smaller, while whatever was trapping me was gaining more control. I was screaming out to myself, my body, to let me out, but nothing happened. There was nothing to get me out, nothing to pull me from within myself when something this strong was in charge.

I felt small caresses from a familiar presence, but the familiarity was off. It wasn't the same.

I watched from the hollows of my being as I clenched and unclenched my hands, walking over to my side of the room and grabbed my sword.

Now, Nicholas, you are going to do everything that I say.

29

REESE

The first beer was what I needed, the second, well that one was probably unnecessary, but who really fucking cares at this point. I leaned against the small kitchen counter, the bottle of alcohol staring back at me. Usually when I was stressed out, I would have downed about six of those things, but right now, I was drinking slower than usual and even then, it still wasn't helping. Hybrids were popping up out of nowhere. When I found out about the last one, I was in close proximity to my home, but now I was stuck in this world of demons and hellhounds. When I was stressed out, I talked to Nick, but that was a no go since he was off in, *I'm in love with a demon, but I probably haven't told her and now she's gone and decided to say fuck you guys, I'm doing this shit alone* land. I picked up the beer and took a drink, letting it run down my throat. I smacked my lips together, thankful that it tasted decent enough given where we were.

Elise hadn't come out from where she went to find Beetee, thank the fucking realms. She cared about Dani even though her cold, shriveled bitchy heart would have everyone think otherwise. I wasn't as dumb as she clearly thought I was. As much as I couldn't stand any moment she breathed near me, I knew she was worried and bit on edge with everything that had just transpired. I didn't have the kind of connection either of them had with Dani, but I could admit I had *something* with her. We both truly cared about Nick, and I could honestly admit that I believed her when she'd told me that she did care about him. Nothing about her admittance sounded fake and I had let out a breath of relief knowing that he wasn't in this for some kind of one-sided attraction, that I probably wouldn't be able to talk him out of.

I swirled the contents of the bottle in my hand and downed the rest of it. I was never scared by much, nothing really ever shook me to my core, but when I actually really thought about it, thought about what Dani had done...I considered things differently at times. Maybe she didn't do it to spite us, to give us a giant middle finger. Perhaps she did it because of us, because in her own head she formulated it as her battle to fight. Not ours. I was pissed she tried to relieve us from fighting, but then there was this other feeling that if we fought Lilith and somehow made things right then I could take that heroism to my parents. I could use what I'd done as some sort of olive branch—if they even wanted that.

I looked up, hearing some commotion upstairs. I was immediately on alert, but then it stopped. There were demons and Enchanters sitting around the lounge area, who hardly took notice of me or the noise that I had just heard. I wasn't surprised though, since for the last few days I'd heard bits and pieces of Dani and Nick fucking and that was something I was mentally never going to recover from, so random noises weren't something to be so alarmed over. I heard footsteps on the stairs, letting out a relieved breath when I saw Nick coming down.

He hadn't noticed me yet as he faced straight ahead, descending the stairs in an almost stoic kind of motion. It was odd but given the circumstances I wasn't about to call out anyone's moody behavior.

"Nick," I called out, waving my hand in his direction.

He turned his head to look at me and something about the way he rotated his body, the way his eyes flicked to mine made me eerily uncomfortable. I was looking at the same person I'd always known, but then again, I wasn't. He started making his way over to me and that's when I noticed his sword. The hilt was in his grip, his knuckles were white, like he was holding on for dear life. He didn't respond to my greeting, he just kept coming towards me and I found myself backing up.

"Nick, are you okay?"

He stopped when he was a few inches near me, his breathing was calculated and even. He flinched a little, his face flickering with some kind of pain. He closed and opened his eyes and looked at me again, his brown eyes more muted to me now. Devoid of emotions. "I'm fine." His voice was monotone and lifeless.

I opened my mouth to protest against his response, but then he lifted his sword and swung at me. I jumped back, nearly hitting a wall as I stumbled backwards. I tried to catch my hands on something so that I wouldn't fall. "Woah, Nick, what the fuck!"

He didn't respond, he just tried to strike me down again, moving closer and closer. The demons having their casual conversations before were now looking at the situation in front of them. Some of them retreated upstairs, probably already having dealt with so many catastrophic issues in their life, they didn't want to deal with anything else that could come close to that. Others started running over to us and tried to get Nick under control.

They grabbed at his arms, but he just threw them back as if he didn't have a care in the world. He brought his sword down towards me and nicked my arm. I grabbed the area he had struck, blood appearing on my fingers. Some of the demons tried to create dark magic to subdue him, take him down, but he just shook it off. It was like it didn't matter to him. He yanked one by the arm and threw them against the wall. He threw his elbow back, hitting another in the face and swung his sword around, nearly slicing them right along their neck.

I couldn't get around him, so I made my way to the dining room, noticing he was stalking after me. He had so much determination in his eyes. My bow was upstairs, but even if I had it, I wouldn't want to fight my best friend. I mean, we'd fought before but this was different. I was fearing for my life at this point, I was in crisis mode, and I didn't know how to navigate the waters of my best friend trying to kill me when I'd literally done nothing wrong. I felt my magic brewing inside my body, so I let that out instead. Light flashed from my palm and towards his chest. It dissipated when it landed on his body and he stumbled back, but he remained upright. I did it again and again, but he wouldn't budge. He just kept taking the hits, but never submitting to them.

He took one big swing at me, and I reached for a chair, holding it up and blocking him. He struck blow after blow as pieces of wood flew around my head. He swung his leg out, and I was sent backwards to the ground once he yanked my feet out from under me. The chair clattered to the ground, and I tilted my head up, rubbing the back of my skull from where it landed on the floor. He smirked down at me and held his sword in front of him.

A door slammed open and feet shuffled into the room.

"What the fuck are you two absolute dickheads doing!" Elise screamed,

Beetee settling behind her. Her lilac eyes were wide as they bounced from me to Nick. When neither of us answered her, she spoke again. "I asked a fucking question. Nick put the sword down, what the hell."

Nick slowly turned his face to her. If his neck could have made a creaking noise while it happened, that was the sound that would have played during that moment. Elise looked at him and then her eyebrows raised up behind her bangs. Her eyes fluttered closed as she took one long exhaustive breath. "Nick. Put. The. Sword. Down."

One side of his mouth ticked up as he ignored her and held the sword with both his hands, lifting it up and bringing it down with every intention of killing me. A long shadowy tail wrapped around his wrists and turned him away from me, yanking him forward. The sword flew from his hands, and he fell onto his face. Nick recovered quickly, barreling towards Elise and using his whole body to take her down. They both ended up on the floor, tangled up together until he broke free, grabbing onto her shoulders and started banging her head against the floor. Beetee grabbed him by his hair and yanked his head back. She opened her mouth, displaying what looked like snake fangs and bit down into his skin.

He cried out and eventually let go of Elise. Frantic footsteps came from the stairs as Leah and Garrett came into view, startled with what they were seeing. Nick grabbed Beetee from behind him and easily lifted her and threw her over his shoulder. He reached for his sword, getting up. I kicked my leg out, tripping him, while his head nearly missed the dining room table as he fell backwards. I jumped up to get on top of him, forming a fist with my hand and punching him right in the face. I didn't know if I thought that would knock some sense into him, but maybe it might. "What's going on?!"

He didn't answer me, he just struggled to remove himself from under me. I punched him again and again, but then he caught my wrists, shoving them back and swiftly moving to my throat. He maneuvered his legs so that he rolled us over so he could slam my head into the ground as he choked me. He removed one of his hands and grabbed his sword, placing it near my neck. His eyes were these whirls of anger, but they weren't his own. He wasn't himself and it was like a tiny piece of me could feel him trying to stop, trying to talk some sense into himself.

He made no move to slit my throat. His eyes flickered all around my face, all around the room. He brought the hand that had been around my throat to his eyes as if he was trying to wipe a visual away that only he could see. I turned my head and saw Leah, her fingers sparkling with a purple hue. She was glamouring his vision.

I shoved away from him and brought my leg up to kick him in the chest, but right before he could stagger backwards to the ground, Elise swiftly wrapped her tail around his neck and started squeezing. "I told you to drop the sword, Nicholas."

He clawed at her tail, the black, inky venom, dripping out slowly, but not touching him quite yet. He started making choking sounds as she yanked him back and off of me. Beetee came around them and ripped the sword from his hand, nearly shaking as her eyes flashed from diamond pupils to their lilac coloring. Garrett ran over and helped me up as Leah stayed in place, keeping the glamour she had on him up. Elise brought him to her chest as he shook his head, whipping it left and right as if he was in a whole other world inside his own head.

"Let me out," he said more to himself than to us. "Let me out, let me out, let me out!" He kept shaking his body, thrashing back and forth in her grip. He forcibly moved to the left, grabbing the blade of his sword from Beetee. Blood started to instantly drip from the wounds he caused himself and he shoved her back with his strength. He lifted up his other hand, bringing it up slowly as if he was trying to stop himself, but couldn't. He opened his palm toward Leah who was sent sailing back by an invisible force, but when she hit the floor with a thud, black smoke dissipated around her.

What the hell was going on?

Nick's eyes cleared and he readjusted his grip on his sword, and swung down low, cutting Elise right at her calf. She unwound her tail, hissing as he swiveled around and sliced at her other one. Garrett ran up to him, but Nick took his sword and slammed it into Garrett's shoulder, ripping it out and shoving him to the side. Nick looked stunned at the empty space where I should have been, his hand gripping his sword more tightly.

His head swung around right as I got behind him and struck him hard with the leg of the broken chair from earlier. His face looked like he was back to himself again, but then as quick as that came it was gone, so I reared back and hit him again. The wood snapped in half, and he fell to the ground. Elise pushed past me and grabbed his face, opening his mouth. Her tail slithered around her, the end dangling over his mouth. Three drops of her black venom fell on his lips and dripped into his mouth. His body started convulsing slightly and his eyes opened, showing just black emptiness, but then he slumped over and retreated within himself, falling silent and still.

"Did you kill him?" I asked, concerned.

Elise rolled her eyes. "*Did I kill him?* This coming from the guy who nearly bludgeoned him with a piece of wood." She wiped the still open wound on her calves and shook her head. "No, Blondie, he isn't dead. He's just out, but whatever took over him got a piece of my mind just now."

"Took over him?"

"Possessed him," Beetee explained, rolling her shoulder with a wince.

I kicked his sword away from his hand and looked down at him. "Who would do that?"

Leah let Garrett lean on her as blood leaked from his shoulder. "Lilith most likely." Garrett nodded in agreement with his wife.

Elise clucked her tongue. "You're wrong."

Beetee looked from me to Elise and took a deep breath. She stepped over to Garrett and Leah. "Let me get you guys some help and then I'll go check on my parents." She gave Nick's unmoving body one last look before she hustled the Enchanters towards the recovery room.

"What do you mean wrong?" I said, wiping the sweat from my forehead.

"Wrong as in not correct."

I bent down to press my fingers to my best friend's neck, feeling his pulse. "Please don't be a fucking smartass right now."

She bent down as well and narrowed her gray eyes at me. "I could feel it, the darkness that was harboring in him and it felt familiar. I would know if it was Lilith's doing. I've spent most of my life with that woman. This darkness felt like it knew him too much, the way it settled behind his eyes. You may not be able to see a possession easily, Blondie, but I can."

I scratched my eyebrow a little confused. "So, if Lilith didn't do this you think Dani did? It's Nick, she wouldn't. I mean she has compulsion sure but isn't possession like an entirely different evil on its own."

Elise placed her hand on her cheek, looking at me like I was the most ridiculous creature. "Surprisingly enough, you are right about that. You need a shit ton of dark magic to be able to pull off a possession. Compulsion can morph into possession if given the right motivation, the right push from the right host if the powers were just bestowed on you. It happens a lot in Hell, but Lilith has been the only one I've seen be able to do it with ease here. Possessions are so much easier when you have an attachment to the entity you're pursuing." Her eyes looked a little far away as she finished.

I turned Nick's head, noticing the blood coming from the side of his face where I'd hit him. "But why? Why would she even do this? Especially if Lilith could just do it herself."

"Dani wouldn't want to if she had any control on what she was doing." She grabbed Nick's arm and started to hoist him up. I helped her by draping his other arm over my shoulder. "What's the point of her doing it herself, when she could…" Elise groaned as we started to move Nick past the front desk and towards the stairs. "I think I might know what's going on and with that, I'll have you know I'm never nervous about anything nor am I ever scared but this shit right here…might change that."

The little psycho was nervous and even though I didn't like her, at all, I found myself on edge again. During the entire time I'd known her, I never heard anything Elise said, but maybe this is time I would start listening.

30

DANI

I felt the pain in my chest as it flooded into my veins, it was strong. I felt my connection with him simmer and then shrivel up and die. That shit was awful, the venom leaving a bad taste in my mouth. I knew Elise was strong, but I didn't know she could do that. The more I learned about her the more I realized how little I still knew and how much she had kept from me because maybe I wasn't worth telling those things to. My body pulsed with negative thoughts, so much anger and self-loathing running rampant within myself. I took a deep breath remembering what it tasted like, conjuring up his darkness again, letting it wrap itself around him and forcing him to submit to me. I tasted his fear again, his sadness, his guilt and it was so heady knowing I had so much of it. I couldn't quite remember why I had it in the first place, but that wasn't important.

I felt a hand at my back. "You did so well, my love." Lilith praised, holding my elbow and helping me up off the ground. I looked around as Isabel, Rae, and Dimitri were watching me, their faces a bit stunned at what

I'd just displayed.

"Let me guess, no one is dead because she clearly can't follow simple instructions?" Isabel scoffed.

I cut my eyes to her, and a flat thick black rope circled around her neck and cinched. Gagging sounds were coming from her as her airway was constricted. I watched as her blue eyes looked over my shoulder to Lilith who simply let out an exhaustive breath. "Dani, stop now."

I immediately let Isabel go as she coughed viciously. She grabbed at her throat, sucking in air.

"I would like to see their deaths in person, so maybe this was for the best. That boy will be coming to find you and I sincerely cannot wait for when he does." Lilith waved over to where the others sat. "You did as I asked with such vigor, so you can kill someone tonight." She leaned into me, whispering in my ear, before turning around and sauntering out of the room.

My mind formulated what she had said and I smirked with the intent to make this one hurt. I willed my shadow silhouettes to appear as they shifted and swayed near me. I didn't need to say anything for them to understand what I wanted.

Dimitri moved out of the way as they circled around Rae, grabbing her arms as she struggled to release herself. She started spewing obscenities at me and I would have silenced her if I didn't want to hear her scream so much. I let my shadows twist her arms back in the most unnatural way possible.

This would be torture for her. And it would be torture for everyone else, I would make sure of it.

31

NICK

I woke up in my bed, staring at the wall. My eyes hurt as if an intense amount of pressure had been behind them for a long time and I was just now feeling it. I felt myself wanting to go back to sleep, but then I started to remember where I was, what had happened with Dani, what we learned about Beetee. I must have fallen asleep instead of going downstairs like I thought I'd planned to. I started to turn over, but the side of my head started throbbing and I reached up to touch where I could feel the pain but all I felt was some type of gel liquid, kind of reminding me of the stuff Dani had put on my wounds when I got struck with Elise's tail. Why the hell would I have this near my face…again?

I actually took in my surroundings, noticing Reese and Elise huddled around me. They didn't make a sound, but they just watched me as if any of my movements could be something to account for. I dropped my hand and started to shuffle back and up so that I was parallel to the headboard. Reese leaned over and propped the pillow up so that my back was supported. My jaw felt like it had been hit and my stomach was screaming like it had taken a foot right to it. I wanted one of them to start talking, say anything, so I didn't feel so completely out of sorts right about…

Reese connected his fist to my shoulder in one solid punch. I winced, clasping my hand around my shoulder, until the pain subsided. He pointed his finger at me. "That's for trying to kill me."

My eyes widened in confusion. "I tried to do what?"

"Kill me! End my life. Remove me from the realms. Take your pick, Nick the Dick."

"No, I didn't, I wouldn't do that."

Elise laughed. "Yeah, *you* wouldn't. Very annoying, lovestruck, pretty Nick wouldn't. But then again, you weren't…*you*."

I raised one of my eyebrows. "So, you're saying that I went around and tried to kill you without really knowing it." I pointed a shaky finger at my best friend trying to pull together any recollection of what they were speaking of.

"You tried to kill all of us, Nicholas." Elise backed up and plopped down onto Reese's bed.

"You stabbed Garrett. You cut up the little psycho's legs, you tried to stab and strangle me, none of it was pretty. I eventually had to knock you out, hence the…" Reese motioned towards the side of my face.

"I stabbed someone. Is he okay? Also, is there any reason why my mouth tastes like smoke?" I tried to process his words as I stuck my tongue out and smacked my lips.

Elise tapped her chest. "He has a hole in his shoulder, but you know he is just fine. And it's the venom I dropped into your mouth. It doesn't taste good going down, but it's great at severing unwanted bonds, seizing them, and making them retreat."

"First you have a tail and now said tail produces venom that can do more than just paralytics." Reese sounded astonished.

Elise ruffled her bangs and leaned back on the bed resting on her hands. "There's a lot you don't know about me, Blondie. And probably some things you'll never know." She winked and looked back at me. "Nicholas, before Dani left, did you guys make any kind of connection? Like besides your incredibly vomit worthy love connection."

I scratched the side of my head, thinking. "Not that I'm aware of."

"Are you sure? Like I know your head is a little fucked, but nothing happened between you guys that might give her a tiny hint of leverage towards you."

"Elise, I don't…why the hell are you even asking?"

She swiped her tongue across her front teeth. "Because Nicholas, your little girlfriend is the one who possessed you. Hence why the last thing you remember is what, being in this room? The talk with Beetee's parents?"

I opened my mouth, but then closed it because she was right. Everything else beyond those times were a blur. I felt the allure of magic, just a whisper, and my eyes cut to the end table next to my bed. Reese followed my gaze and walked over to it, opening the tiny drawer and reaching inside. He hesitantly pulled out Dani's dagger, examining it, as he closed the drawer back. The dagger shook and then disappeared from his grasp. It reappeared in my lap and we all made no moves towards it.

"Where did you get that?" They both said in unison.

A small memory of it appearing next to me before everything went dark flashed across my mind and I slid my fingertips along where her name was etched into the steel. "It just appeared."

"What the fuck do you mean it just appeared?" Elise shot up from the bed and stalked over to me.

"Exactly what I said. I remember sitting right here and it just appeared. Out of nowhere. But I feel like I'm connected to it in some way, like it was trying to find me."

"Dani just gave you her dagger without even telling you." Reese tucked a piece of his blonde hair behind his ear and angled his eyebrows inward.

Elise placed her face in her hands. "Fuck, fuck, fuck!" She sat on the edge of my bed and wrapped some of my shirt in her fists pulling me up close to her face. "Think fucking hard Nicholas. Did you make any other connection with her? Anything at all, even if it was the smallest thing."

I did what she asked, and I thought back, searching my mind for anything that could be useful when...

"S-she took some of it."

"Some of what?" Reese asked.

"All the darkness that was harboring inside of me, she took some of it. Not in a bad way or anything like that, but she wanted to help ease it out, so she took it into herself. She was fine afterwards; I mean she told me it was fine."

Elise released my shirt and let me fall back against the pillows. "It probably *was* fine, but now it's fucking not. Dani sent you her dagger for a purpose because with Lilith around, her having it is likely the opposite of good. I don't love saying this, but Blondie did make a point when you were knocked out. Dani wouldn't hurt you purposely, I don't think she would hurt any of us if she had a choice."

"You think her taking that darkness from Nick made it easier for her to take him over?" Reese questioned.

"Yes, idiot, that's pretty much what I'm saying."

I stuck my tongue in my cheek. "But...why?"

Elise let out a long sigh. "Possession takes a lot of dark power and even though Dani is one of the best, she doesn't have enough to pull something like that off. Not unless she's being told what to do, manipulated. Enough power is being filtered into her to perform this kind of possession and her taking some of that darkness from you, that closeness that you two have, just made it that much easier."

I felt a small pain in my chest thinking about it. "And let me guess, Lilith is feeding her more darkness and more power."

Elise nodded and looked down at the dagger. "Exactly. And the only way Dani would ever let that happen is if she wasn't herself, if she'd lost herself entirely, and wasn't able to fight back. I felt it, okay. I know Lilith and Dani's particular flavors of darkness all too well and I felt them both when you were in rage mode. I also felt hellfire, like the darkness had been molded with the pure essence of Hell itself. Lilith's doing what she's always doing. She's being a puppeteer and she's added Dimitri to the mix if Hell is involved, that's for sure.

"I may not call us the best of friends, but I know Dani well enough. She absolutely hated complete darkness and that's what you have to embody when you choose to possess someone, compulsion is so simple compared to it."

Reese sat on the bed and brought his legs up, crossing them over one another, and tucking his feet under his thighs. "Well, what about when she went all rogue, almost killing Yuri and all that."

Elise shrugged. "She's always going to be connected to this place and sometimes the darkness can take over, but there was always a part of her that pushed back, always *someone* to help do the pushing." She snuck a glance in my direction. "She doesn't have that anymore. I think Lilith has made her the kind of voided demon she's been wanting."

I looked down at the comforter, sliding my hands along the soft material. "Garrett and Leah did say the other demons weren't strong enough to hold their own, they listened to her but never enough. She needed something with...connection, something with enough power to match her own."

"And what better connection than with the one who made you." Reese mumbled more to himself than to us.

I picked up the dagger and flipped it over in my palm. "Dani went against Lilith so many times. She told her Dani could kill Isabel if she went with her, Dani refused. She said she would let us go, Dani still refused, but after that nightmare, I guess Lilith got too close..."

"And she doesn't take kindly to creatures making her ask multiple times for their loyalty. We're all casualties now, Nicholas. And you, lover boy, were the easiest first target, get you to do all the dirty work upfront. Dani is a strong one and she didn't have any weaknesses until now. *You* are her new weakness, and she knows it."

"We can get her back though, right?" I asked, trying to sound more optimistic than I felt.

Elise raised her eyes to the ceiling. "She won't be the same person; her light is smothered in darkness and Lilith's manipulation. I felt malice and brutality when I came close enough to sense that darkness on you. So, I can't tell you I know what saving her will look like."

"But you do want to save her, right?" Reese pressed, giving her a skeptical look.

"Of course, I do. She's my fr–" She caught herself then cleared her throat. "Nice try Blondie." Reese laughed quietly, shaking his head. He placed his hands on his knees and glanced over at me before he spoke. "My only thought is I just don't know how putting her completely in the dark will help with destroying Heaven's Gate, Oculus, the portals, any of it."

I placed my hand on my chest feeling the portal key Natalia had given to me. I reached into my shirt and pulled it out, examining it. "Neither do I, but I think I know someone who might."

I smoothed down the front of my pants as I got comfortable in bed. I held the portal key firmly in my hand and looked around at everyone. Axel sat comfortably on Reese's lap and Elise shook her head as she took a seat at the very end of my bed. Beetee sat on the other side, nervously biting at her lower lip. She hadn't told us if she'd spoken anymore to her parents besides when she went to check on them, but I had a feeling pushing her to speak wouldn't get us anywhere. She seemed adamant on saving the issue for later and kept insisting that she wasn't the priority.

Leah and Garrett said that they would set up the foundation of the plan with Willa and Louise downstairs, but to come get them if they could be of any help during my outer body talk with Natalia. I hated thinking that this talk with her could potentially get us nowhere or that she would end up telling me something I didn't want to hear. If I was being honest, I didn't know which one I really preferred, but I was blatantly aware that Natalia would tell me the truth whichever way it went.

"You tell her everything and leave nothing out. If she doesn't know the answers, then I would be very certain that we're fucked." Elise shrugged, dangling her feet off the side of the bed.

"And that's the reason we won't let you do pep talks anymore," Reese said, rolling his eyes and petting Axel's head. "Get what you need so we can finally do this thing."

I nodded and felt Beetee's hand as she grabbed my own and squeezed it. We were an odd team, but we were a team nonetheless and I found myself not wanting it any other way. I gripped the portal key tighter and closed my eyes. I felt myself drifting as I had before and then I was back in that forest. I was back in that silent place with moving trees and the smell of cedar wafting in my nose. I stood still waiting for her to appear, preparing myself for if she decided to pop up out of...

"Nicholas." I jumped at the sound of her voice. I turned around and watched as she came from a cloud of fog that dissipated with every step she took. Her dark hair was down, parted in the middle and a glittering crown was on her head, while pieces of her hair were weaved throughout it. Her dark skin glittered with colorful sparkles along her cheeks and arms. There was a bangle on both her arms and various amounts of rings adorned each of her fingers.

She picked up her long, velvet, red dress as she stepped through some leaves and finally stopped in front of me. "Is this another checkup?" She looked me over, focusing on my face, her hand reaching up to gently run her thumb over my head wound. Her honey-colored eyes roamed around my body and then stopped at the slashes on my arms. "What happened?"

I shook my head. "None of this is important. Or maybe it is, it's just... I'm not the point right now. Dani is."

The High Priestess tilted her head to the side. "Dani?"

I ran my hand through my hair, fidgeting. "Yeah. She left the other night to go see Lilith. I don't really know what she was thinking, but it's bad Natalia. We had every plan to go after her, but now..."

She gripped my forearm, causing me to look into her eyes. "Tell me everything and maybe we can figure something out together."

Everything came out in rambles. I probably spoke too fast and there was a definite chance that I said some of the same things over again, but throughout the entire story, she listened. Natalia stood there with her eyes on me, and her hands clasped in front of her, as I prattled on. She never interrupted me, and she never seemed to act like something else would be a better use of her time. She almost had me believing that she could have spent all her time just listening to me and not like she wasn't an actual queen with people to rule over. I hesitated when I got to the information about Beetee, I didn't know if it was my place to let her in on that new fact and frankly it was a shocker, but it wasn't the most important piece of information right now.

Natalia pressed her lips together in thought once I'd finished. "So, Lilith has turned Dani into a voided demon, just like the ones from the ambush, but stronger." I nodded, catching my breath after finishing.

She hummed. "And Dani is the one who possessed you and not Lilith, almost like a punishment to Dani herself, but also in a way to hurt you." Yet again, I nodded.

"I just don't know how putting her completely in the dark will help with whatever plan she's pursuing," I said, feeling a slight breeze.

Natalia placed her hands behind her back and started pacing around me. "Well, the first way she tried, getting Dani to take in Jonah's magic was obviously a logical first attempt." She stuck her finger up as if halting her own thoughts. "But it's not the only way. If I were putting it lightly, she did things the "nice" way before, now she's choosing the route with the most destruction. The most impact."

"What she did before wasn't the most destructive?"

Natalia shook her head. "Not quite, Nicholas. There were always going to be casualties and loss, but with what she's doing now, I don't know how Heaven's Gate is going to survive that. Dani is already a feared creature, she's already strong, Nicholas. You stop her from holding back, give her no limits, take away her conscience, and give her no way to connect with the other half of herself, you will have a mess on your hands. Lilith is now the voice in her head, the source of her increasing strength." Natalia pressed her index finger to her lips. "There are stories that a dark enough power can break anything, ideally a strong enough light power could do the same. You said she has a Son of Hell on her side, which just increases her wealth of power. She has Dimitri and Dani, along with Isabel who has a large sum of magic that unfortunately will start to challenge my own.

"With enough dark power she won't need executive type light magic, she probably won't need any light magic around, but that doesn't mean she won't want to keep you as some kind of angelic plaything. Especially if you were under their control, using your magic when they say and never getting a say so." Her eyes widened as if a thought popped into her head. "You do have that key, which can take you home, who's to say she doesn't want you alive to use you in that way. She could use your key to get Dani in and then completely demolish everything as she goes. There are so many possibilities, Nicholas, but without Dani at her absolute worst none of it will happen, so she has succeeded in step one. She wanted Dani to have you hurt others, which in return would hurt her even if she didn't know it. If you would have gone through with it, killed all of them and woken up, you would have had all their blood on your hands and…" She lifted her arm up and threaded her fingers into my hair in a comforting way. "I don't think you would have survived that."

I gave her a small smile of understanding. I hadn't told her everything about what happened between Dani and I after that fight outside the hostel, but I told her enough so that she was aware that I was okay, that what she felt around me before we even left for Purgatory wasn't wrong. She hadn't wanted to push me, but she had always known something was off as she usually did. "How do we stop it? I can fight demons and nearly most of the things I've seen down there, but how do I fight…her?"

Natalia gave me a sympathetic look. "First off, Dani isn't your villain, remember that. But what Lilith has turned her into is something that involves the work of Hell magic and soul loss."

"Dani still has her angelic magic, her angelic soul. That can't be gone unless she's dead." I sounded like I was arguing with her.

Natalia snapped her fingers. "Correct. Hell magic can make it so it's invisible. That darkness she's in will take over and suffocate her light, so much so that it wishes it didn't exist. The only way to cure that is with strong enough light magic to bring it out."

"I don't know if I'm strong enough to do that, even with Reese's help."

The High Priestess pulled her bottom lip into her mouth, carefully thinking over her next words. "That's not the only issue. Just because you may cure the light doesn't mean you've dealt with the dark. If she is possessing you with such ease, I think it's safe to say she is trapped in the dark and it isn't letting her go, not without a fight. You'll need to fight for the light and fight against the dark simultaneously."

"Okay, how do we do that? We'll do anything. Just tell us how we win."

Natalia's face fell a little as if she didn't want to tell me something that would put me even more on edge. She tucked a piece of her hair behind her ear and took a deep breath. "Winning is so subjective, Nicholas. It truly depends on how you look at it." The glitter on her face shimmered and moved. "You have her dagger, yes?"

I hesitantly nodded at her. "What about it?"

"A weapon made of pure dark magic, forged in darkness. And you said you felt a strange connection with it when you touched it. *You* have pure light. I don't know how far gone she is, how deep into the void she is with Lilith, that is for you to decide, but you will have to destroy that darkness from the inside, where it only grows stronger and festers."

"From the inside?"

"You'll need to mold your magic with the dagger, making it a simultaneous dark and light weapon and then you'll have to make that choice. You'll have to make it quick, and you'll have to use every ounce of your angelic magic to do it because her dagger won't hold back once you've started."

I rubbed my palm against the back of my neck. "What choice? Natalia, what do you mean from the inside? Her dagger has nothing to...." I trailed off, looking into her eyes as she watched me take in her meanings. A lump formed in my throat when I tried to swallow it down, and I felt like I was choking. "You want me to use her own dagger on her? I don't have soul seething powers, Natalia."

"You don't have to, Nicholas. I'm not telling you to be a soul seether, I'm telling you that the only way for you to release her from the dark is to eradicate it from the inside. Inside of her."

I held my mouth open and just stared at her. "You're telling me to kill her."

Natalia vigorously shook her head. "No. I would never tell you to do that. You can try to find some other way to fix this but I'm only telling you what I know. The dagger will be a catalyst for your magic, threading itself within the darkness it already holds. It will do the seething all by itself, you're essentially turning it on its master...it knows what to do all on its own. I know that if the host is strong enough the impact from the dagger will hurt, but it won't be the end, but if the darkness is too strong...Nicholas that's why I said it will be your choice.

"Her angelic light is vulnerable, so it could take a hit, or it could not. It just depends on how hard the dark is willing to hold onto her and fight. That, I just don't know. I'm only telling you how you can end it, but it just may not be the ending you want."

I gave her a noncommittal nod and looked off to the side. She huffed out a breath. "These are things I've read in books and knowledge I've gained over time, and it could be outdated and wrong. You know her better than most, you have a connection with her that I will never understand, so you could surprise all of us in the end, just know that this is the advice that I'm giving you. I don't want her gone from this world, same as you, but she had to have known sacrificing herself doesn't always lead to the happiest of outcomes."

I blinked a few times, letting my own emotions settle before looking back over at her. "I don't think you would ever give me bad advice. I guess I just didn't think you'd tell me that."

"Well, Nicholas, let's just hope your girl is strong enough to fight to get back to you, to get back to herself." She gave me an encouraging smile and looked over her shoulder. "Just so you know, Ariel hasn't made any progress on figuring out where Jonah's magic went, and I think he might be attempting to just take Jonah's place, tradition be damned. Your father is by no means happy about it, but they do miss you and you coming to me now at least gives me the opportunity to tell them you're okay."

"Thanks, I'll be sure to make it back home." I just hoped I wasn't coming back home without the one person I wanted by my side.

"Hmm, I will highly enjoy seeing Ariel's face when you come back successful. And Nicholas, please know I would not have told you this if there were another way, another path I could steer you towards."

I took her hand gently in mine and then placed my other hand over it. "I know. She called me a hero you know. I just don't know what that means if I do this."

"It means you are doing what you have to do to save people, to save her. Even if it's from herself." I thought back to when I had Dani in my arms and how shaken she was after the nightmare, how that must have been the last straw in her decision making. Dani could be alright, and a little shaken, if I stabbed her with her own dagger flooded with my angelic light or she could succumb to the wound, and I could lose her. I already had so many scars from this mission and I knew that would leave the biggest one.

If anyone was going to help her remember who she was, it was me. I would be her light.

32

NICK

"What the fuck did you just say?"

I knew the conversation with the others wouldn't go over well. I was still trying to process things myself. I had understood what Natalia said, but that didn't mean I had to like it or go through with it, even if I knew she wouldn't tell me something just for the hell of it. I knew I'd stuttered through my explanation of what happened and by the looks Elise had given me, I'd taken too long to get to the point but when I'd finally finished, all I'd gotten back was a few blank stares and some confused expressions.

I blinked over to Elise who stepped away from the wall in my room and stood in front of me. "I don't know how else you want me to put it."

She rolled her eyes. "Any way but that. You can't honestly have me believe that Natalia told you to do any of that."

I stood up from the bed and squared my shoulders. "Well, she did and that's what we have to work with. I don't like it any more than you do."

Garrett cleared his throat. "From what I heard it sounded like she said that it was a possibility. We don't really know how far gone your Soul Seether is, so he might not have to go that route at all."

I pointed over to Garrett, grateful that someone heard anything other than *stab her with her own dagger*. Elise scoffed, not paying him any mind. "Lilith wouldn't make it so that Dani has a way out of this. That's too easy if you're just able to sweet talk her out of being this vicious little devil. The minute I realized that she was possessing you herself, I knew that was it."

"That can't be the only thing that has you set on this idea."

Elise wagged her finger at me. "I think you highly underestimate her feelings for you, pretty boy. She would have fought hard to not do that, to for some reason keep you unharmed, but that didn't happen. What happened downstairs told me all I needed to know." She pushed her finger into my chest. "And now you're telling me that killing her is the only way to solve this."

"That's not at all what I said."

"He said killing her is a potential outcome. It's an outcome none of us want to see but there is a fifty-fifty chance," Reese explained, getting a cold look from Elise as she crossed his arms over near the dresser. "My main question is, can you even do it?"

"The guy holds a sword; I think he can handle a fucking dagger." Elise gave him a dumb look.

Reese presented her with his middle finger and continued. "No, I mean if worse comes to worst can you do what needs to be done. I don't need you wandering back to that dark lonely shell of yours all because you had to make the decision to possibly kill the girl you lo—"

"I'll be okay." I cut him off quickly. I didn't want those words out in the open unless I was the first one saying them. It seemed like everyone could see my own feelings but me, but that wasn't new in any regard. I gave him the most honest answer I had. "Worse comes to worse, I'll make the decision that I have to make, but I won't know what that means until that moment comes."

Leah and Beetee came through the door, anxious looks on each of their faces. Beetee nodded towards the door behind her. "My parents think it's probably the best time for us to leave, unless you aren't up for it, you know after everything." She gestured towards me.

I shook my head, walking over to where I'd left the dagger sitting on the bedside table. "No, I'm ready. I just want to make sure everyone else is ready as well."

"Of course we are," Leah said at the same time as Beetee, who said. "One hundred percent."

"Woah, woah, I'm sorry but you're not going." Elise swung her head around to Beetee. Her short dark hair swinging near her earlobes. I could feel us all go slightly on edge, thinking that Elise would give her an earful, but Beetee just smiled the most tender smile anyone could imagine and walked over to her friend. "Ellie, you are very sweet, but let's not pretend like you intimidate me in any way. I'm going."

"And your moms are alright with that?" Reese said.

Beetee placed her hands in the pockets of her hot pink overalls, running her top teeth over her bottom lip. "I don't think they have much say in what I do at the moment." She said it with such finality that no one moved to say anything more. "Besides like I said before, this is about Dani. I can go on believing that my life is super freaking normal until this is over and then I can spiral into a million and one thoughts."

"Oh, you and lover boy here will have so much in common. He loves to spiral," Elise laughed, turning on her heels away from us. "I'll go get Axel ready."

Leah stepped up to me, watching, as I slowly placed the dagger in my waistband at the back of my pants. "Garrett and I thought it would be best if I stayed here with the kids. I was what Lilith taunted him with for so many years and I don't want to give her reason to do it all over again." She looked like she was about to cry, but she held back her tears. She eyed the portal key around my neck and then looked up at me. "How is the High Priestess?"

"Good, doing way more than her job description specifies but that's just how she is."

Leah nodded in understanding as she dug in her back pocket for something. She brought out two bracelets, each one had intricate weaving with different colored thread and small opal orbs within each braiding. "I picked up glamouring quite well while I was in Oculus, but with glamouring can come a knack for shielding as well. It's, of course, a stronger glamour meant to keep things out and protect. Creating large mental battle shields takes a lot out of me and I've hardly ever touched that power of mine in forever, but there are minuscule ways to keep it alive. Like this." She held the bracelet up to me and I tilted my head to get a better look at it. "The bracelet itself is a shield. Or at least it has the power I've given it to provide that for you."

"What's it shielding me from exactly?"

"Enchanter magic," Garrett explained. "She used to make them for us while we were in Lilith's castle. It wouldn't stop us from using our own magic, but while we were around, Enchanters in that castle were very unpredictable, especially when everything was so fresh and new. I don't know how many Enchanters are truly left in that place, but better safe than sorry." He gave me an encouraging smile which I offered him back. Mine probably seemed a bit forced, but it was all I could give him at the moment.

Leah held the bracelet out for me. "There isn't much I can do about dark magic, but I can help with this. You can make Dani your main priority in this fight, no need to worry about Isabel and her magic…at least, I hope. I truly don't know how strong she is now, but even if they help a tiny amount, I at least know I did something."

"You've done a lot already. Don't worry about that." I let her place the bracelet around my wrist. I felt a tiny spark as it touched my skin, and she placed a hand over where the accessory rested along my wrist. Garrett took the other one from her hand and tossed it at Reese. He drew his wife back so we could make our way out of the room, but I noticed she was staring at me. Not in a way that made me uncomfortable, but her mouth was slightly open, and she looked like she wanted to speak but no words came out. It felt like wheels were turning in her head over something. Garrett looked down at his wife as Reese nudged my shoulder to get us moving. "Honey, are you alright?"

Leah blinked and shook her head. "Yes, yeah, of course. I just um…" She looked at me again and took a deep breath. "Just good luck I suppose." It was like she wanted to say more but either the right words weren't there, or she just wasn't prepared to speak on whatever it was at all. Either way it would have to wait.

Reese and I walked over to where our weapons sat and adjusted them onto our bodies. I fiddled with the bracelet on my wrist as we took the stairs two at a time. We walked through the hostel and met Beetee and her parents at the backdoor of the building. Elise was propped up against the wall and I could feel Leah and Garrett at our backs. I didn't want to show it, but beyond Beetee's moms, I was the only one with a small piece of doubt embedded in my mind. There wasn't a doubt I could fight or that I had probably the world's oddest but most loyal team on my side, but there was a doubt that *I* could do this…

I had to put my feelings aside and forget that I…that I might *love* her. *Dani isn't your villain.*

I was afraid I would have to fight her as if she were.

Purgatory was always an eerie place but right now it felt like all the things I'd been told in stories. I felt overheated and like a million and one eyes were watching me. Beetee hadn't said a word to her mom's before we left, at least not out loud, but she'd hugged each one of them before opening the back door and letting us out alongside her. Her parents had told Axel the location which somehow he could understand and waited for us to climb onto his back before he began walking. Beetee had decided to walk alongside us rather than ride Axel herself, not giving much of an explanation except for the decision itself. Garrett had offered to walk with her, which she accepted even though she vehemently told him that he didn't have to.

The whole ride was quiet and the sound of Axel's large footsteps padding through the leaves echoed around me. I felt like everyone was having the same feelings as me, but no one wanted to speak on it. If we spoke whatever was on our minds into existence, the entire reality of what we were going to do, how we were going to behave would be real and it was better if we just let things happen naturally without trying to overanalyze. Maybe that last part was just me, but I liked to think I wasn't alone in that aspect. Axel made turns and ducked underneath trees before he made a wide turn near a shallow swamp area. You could see the outskirts of buildings and it looked like Lilith's castle had gotten closer if you looked the right way through the trees.

The hellhound bowed his head and then laid the rest of the way down on the ground, letting each of us slide off of his back. His eyes were pools of black and his tongue was pushed out to the side. Those large, hooked bottom teeth dipped just above his upper lip, giving him a dopey-like snarling look. I patted the big creature on the head and turned around, beginning to look for the secret entrance we'd been told about. All of us broke apart and searched various parts of the spot Axel had stopped, but we found nothing. They'd told us what to look for, but we weren't seeing it, unless every single one of us were just completely oblivious.

"What did your parents say again?" Reese asked, kicking up some leaves as he walked.

Beetee was crouched down near two large tree trunks. "They said it was a tree stump that was split in half. It's blocked by other trees so it would be hard to see, but we would know it if we saw it. It's also marked with a carving they drew in it."

"This would be a lot easier if it wasn't just a tiny shade of dark as fuck out here," my best friend huffed.

"It's not that dark Blondie. I haven't heard you run into anything so be grateful," Elise scolded.

"Hey guys, is this it?" I said, standing over a low tree stump with a vertical split down the middle. I bent my knees and squatted down so I could check around it for a marking of any sort. I noticed that a number of trees were in closer proximity to it, so I ran my hand along the sides, stopping when I felt the indent of markings. I felt bodies around me as the others were starting to huddle around.

Garrett reached down and brushed some leaves off the top of the broken trunk. "The carvings?"

"Right here," I answered, running my fingers along the chipped wood. It felt like letters. I followed the carvings, making out a W and then an L. "Your parents carved their initials into it?"

Beetee looked down at me with her hands on her hips. "Not surprised. They have been pretty in love with each other since the beginning of time." She sounded sad at the statement as if she liked knowing these facts about her parents. She looked as if she thought she knew everything there was to know about them but apparently, she hardly knew a thing. Especially about herself.

I stood up and stretched my back, grasping her shoulder. "We'll figure it all out, okay. It's up to you how you want this to play out." She gave me a small smile and nodded her head.

Reese started to sit on the edge of the tree stump. "Okay, we found the big stump. What do we do…" Right as he sat on the edge it started to push away from the rest of the wood. It was like the tree stump had a lid, so he jumped off of it and we both slowly pushed it away from the rest of the stump. We stared down at a gaping black hole as Reese flicked a small ball of light into it, seeing how far it traveled. It was snuffed out pretty quickly, telling me that the bottom wasn't too far down. I turned around and nodded to the others.

"Remember what they said," Leah instructed. "No detours, just take the path as it comes."

"You couldn't pay me enough celestial coins to make a detour in this place," Reese said, peering down into the spot we were about to head into. I watched as Elise headed over to Axel, petting his head and placing her forehead against his nose. She gripped his hooked teeth and bared her own. It was like they were having some kind of silent conversation only they could understand. Axel came up and nuzzled Reese's entire body, nearly pushing him over and did the same to me.

"He'll take you back to the hostel," Elise said to Leah, who nodded in understanding. Garrett gave his wife a kiss goodbye, which we all turned around for, wanting to give them some sort of privacy.

"You really don't have to come." I looked at Garrett who gave me a thoughtful expression. His confident voice made me feel like I was surer about this than I originally planned. "I'm coming with you Nicholas. Worse comes to worse, my children should know their father was doing the right thing."

I admired him and left it at that. Leah nudged us over to the tree stump, while Axel remained behind her watching us. I almost thought I heard a whimpering whine coming from him as Elise gave him a pointed look as if to say, *for the love of Hell be a good boy*. Leah confirmed that she'd glamour the stump to look like a normal everyday tree in Purgatory and would be nervously waiting for us to come back. I felt her grab my arm where my bracelet sat, and I turned around to face her.

"Nicholas, I..." She looked down as she ran her thumb along the accessory she'd given me. She seemed confused as to how to get her words out, like something had put her at a loss. It was the same kind of confusion that I'd seen back at the hostel. I looked down at the bracelet as well and waited patiently for her response. She shook her head, almost laughing to herself about whatever it was she was thinking. "It's nothing, I think I'm just nervous that's all."

"You and me both," I admitted. I felt around behind me to my waistband, feeling Dani's dagger burning a hole in my skin.

"Ready?" Reese asked, leaning over the tree stump. I gave him a thumbs up and without warning he jumped into the dark hole. I heard feet hitting the ground and then a light loomed from within. Reese's blonde hair glowed as the light created a dim flood around the otherwise dark underground passageway. I gave Leah one last smile before I jumped in after him, followed by Elise, Garrett and Beetee. I heard when Leah moved the top of the stump back in place and then there was pure silence again.

"Let's go." The pathway was pretty straight forward as long as you didn't let the weird smells, the tiny scratching sounds and scurrying distract you. I had to take the lead when Reese got startled at every single sound that seemed to whisper down the path at us. With every step closer we got the heavier everything seemed. My thoughts weighed heavily on me as well, more than I'd like to admit. It was crazy that even now, knowing that she wasn't herself, I still knew I would be in awe of the things she could do, even if they were life threatening.

I had it bad for that girl and I couldn't even lie to myself about it anymore.

We were all planning a fight with Lilith, not Dani, but maybe this was the end goal all along. Lilith played the long game and used everyone and anyone to do it. We all had Isabel as an enemy and I hadn't made things easier getting on Dimitri's bad side even if he was a dick, but none of it mattered. Maybe it was always going to end up this way with me holding this very big, very emotionally jarring decision in the palm of my hand. The passageway smelt wet and moldy as we trudged our way through it. Some of the dirt we walked through turned thick and muddy, while at other times dust would kick up and we would all collectively cough from it getting into our lungs. Reese used his light as a guide the whole way through while managing to stay next to me pretty consistently on our journey.

It felt like we had been walking forever when something in the air shifted. It felt like a lead weight had been pressed over top of us and I heard us all collectively catch our breaths. Everyone except Elise, who as usual, looked just as unbothered as she normally did. She eyed each of us, watching as we all took long inhales and exhales. "We're definitely here," she pointed out, walking ahead of us and towards the dead end. She leaned her body against the right wall, pressing her fingers into the dirt. She moved to the other wall, her neck tattoo pulsing with tension. "Aha!" She pushed her whole body into the wall and just like that, a section disintegrated and turned to dust on the ground. We all peeked into the open space in front of her and dirt stairs were staring back at us.

"If I wasn't so fucking on edge right now, I would be thoroughly impressed." Reese's hazel eyes took in the newly open space.

"Let's just openly admit you are thoroughly impressed by me daily."

Reese rolled his eyes. "I would let Lilith eat me alive before I would ever admit that."

"Do you guys ever stop?" Beetee asked, her lilac eyes bouncing between both of them.

"Unless one of us dies, no." Elise said, starting to walk up the stairs. I saw Garrett shake his head, letting out a low chuckle as we all followed behind her. The air grew a bit thinner as we climbed. I could feel my light happily settling within my body, but there was dark scratching at my skin. It felt like tiny bugs nipping and biting at small pieces of my flesh wanting to get just a taste of me. I wasn't the only one either.

Reese rubbed each of his arms and the back of his neck as if he had a rash. "The fuck is this?"

"It's just the darkness that lives here. If you think this is bad, you've haven't felt anything like being in *her* presence," Elise answered, continuing to climb the stairs.

I looked back and noticed that Beetee was fine, you could tell she felt something was off, but it wasn't anything like what Reese and I felt. Garrett kept close to her, his golden eyes everywhere. "Is that it?" He nodded ahead, causing me to turn back around and see a square steel door. It looked like a trapped door of some kind, with its singular metal handle and bolted sidings.

395

There was thick, brown mud along the edges, and it looked like no one had used it in years.

Elise took hold of the handle and yanked it down. There was a small creaking noise, but I didn't really notice it when the overwhelming feeling of every single nightmare I'd ever had washed over me. It didn't embed itself within my skin and veins like before, but it curled around me like it was testing me out, testing each of us out. I could taste it in my mouth, and it was like it clouded my eyesight for a moment. I nearly thought I heard it whisper my name but then it was gone. All I was left with was the eerie feeling again, like I was headed into something dangerous, but it was too late to turn back now.

"Ditch the light Blondie," Elise said, pointing at the looming angelic light near us. Reese reached for it, removing it. Elise popped her head cautiously into the opening of the door and then tugged herself up. We each followed behind her as Garrett reached down, closing the steel door. Willa and Louise weren't lying when they said it was a spider infested room. The bugs were crawling along the walls and floor. Cobwebs hung from the corners and pounds of dust were clumped in the corners. Stone lined the walls, the smell of brimstone settled around us and I could just ever so slightly feel the weight of power somewhere in this castle. I didn't know whether that dark power was coming from Dani or Lilith but either way it wasn't good.

"Where are we even?" Beetee asked.

"The lowest floor. They're here though, I can feel them," Elise replied, pressing her lips together into a hard line.

"Yeah, I can feel it too," I agreed, looking around and seeing everyone else feeling the same way. Elise walked over to the door in the far corner and turned the rusted knob, slowly, poking her head around the door. She looked back at us, her bangs hitting right near her eyebrows. "All clear, let's go." She snuck out the door and each one of us followed, taking in our surroundings as we went. It was quiet in this castle, which was something I was surprised by but then again maybe not. I would have every right to assume shit went downhill once she manipulated the Enchanters here and then creatures started wanting out one by one. I knew The Skies was an entirely different way of life, but I was used to the hustle of what went on there, the constant chatter and incessant high energy that was always on display.

None of that was here. The stones we stepped on didn't make too much noise. It just felt drab and like the only way to feel alive or to gain any happiness was to increase the pain in another person. I would think that if you always felt like that constantly then at some point another's pain would somehow mask your own. It made me understand why Dani and Elise left for Leviathan so often, maybe even why Dani sought out comfort and attention in Dimitri. That thought made me want to vomit so I banished it, hopefully forever, from my mind.

Elise stopped and seemed to listen for a moment, waiting to see what our next move should be. There were sconces lined along the wall, small firelight in them, casting an ambiance that I wasn't interested in embracing. The whispering voice caressed my ear and touched my cheek like a kiss. I nearly slapped myself, but it was gone before I got the chance.

"I honestly don't miss this place," Garrett muttered, more to himself than to us.

Elise looked up, completely ignoring us. She immediately turned down a hallway that we hadn't even known was there and headed for another door.

"Do you actually know where you're going?" I asked, catching her arm. She snatched it back, practically growling at me. "Yes, Nicholas. I've spent the majority of my prime demon years here. I think I have an idea." She swung open the door and started up the stone steps that greeted us. The air on this floor was even worse, but it felt like we were closer than before. It felt like something was here, right in front of us, but we couldn't see it.

"Do you guys feel that too?" Beetee asked, nervously biting her lip.

"Does anyone else feel hot?" Reese said right after her, swiping his hand across his forehead, moving his long hair out of the way. Once I paid attention, the temperature had risen, but I had a bad feeling that was strictly for our benefit.

A high-pitched scream flooded my ears, and I had no idea where it was coming from. Whoever it was sounded like they were in pure agony. The screams kept coming and coming and it was like they were pounded against my skull. I pressed my hand to the side of my head to release some of the tension, but it wasn't helping. The screams were coming from the walls and floor, they were vibrating off other screams and becoming louder and making my chest tighten.

I saw something run past me, but it was like a shadow. The remnants of its mist were left behind and then it disappeared. I felt something behind me as well as I turned and saw Reese reach for his bow. I did the same motion, taking hold of the hilt of my sword. Garrett's fingertips illuminated with colorful magic while Beetee's eyes flashed back and forth between their regular color and her diamond yellow pupils. Elise was the only one who seemed to not have the screams affecting her in any way, like she was used to this. Reese shot an arrow out when a shadow figure ran full force towards him and then was gone, the arrow moving right through them.

Another shadow figure barreled between Beetee and Garrett causing both of them to stumble to opposite sides. Then another one came, and another, moving past us as if they were there to taunt us, collect us, or even prepare us for what was to come. I got my sword out and started slashing left and right, missing them as they moved past me. They were the same kinds of shadows that Dani had summoned during the fight outside of the hostel. I had been pretty out of my mind during that, but I had been aware enough to notice what she had done. It was something I didn't even know she could do, but she was angry then. She didn't like seeing me in pain, so she channeled all that rage and frustration into manifestations that fucked people up.

The shadows hit Reese in the shoulder making him shuffle to one side and then another came, making him move to the other side this time. He was getting turned around while one of them ran right into Beetee, sending her flying against the wall. Garrett and Elise started to rush over to her, but one of the shadows knocked Garrett clear in the face and sent him backwards. Elise dodged another and whipped her tail out, seeming to catch one with it and fling it across the room, running over to help Beetee off the ground. I felt a hit to my face, and I was getting more and more agitated with this. I saw one of them out of the corner of my eye and pushed my angelic magic into my hand and watched as my hand glowed before I caught the shadow by the throat. It halted immediately, thrashing in my grip. I squeezed hard and the light filtered through its wispy dark form and sparks of black and white with gold flecks splattered around.

Reese nodded over to me, and he started to use his own magic to take the shadows out. I continued my efforts over and over again, one after the other. It was working and what was left over, Garrett electrified with his own magic while Beetee and Elise took down another side of the room. The shadows started coming less and less, which should have put me at ease, but it only made my stomach drop thinking that this was just the beginning. I had impaled a shadow demon with my sword on the ground, infusing light magic into it as it writhed when I felt a touch against the back of my neck.

A maniacal laugh came from the walls and then it was almost like the voice was right against my ear. I pulled back, doing a full turn around and nobody was there. The laugh was feminine, but familiar. "Valiant effort, Nicholas. All of you really." *Isabel.*

I felt something swing along my legs and I was tossed backwards, hitting the floor. It wasn't Enchanter magic this time though, this was power that I had felt before when it started clawing into my head. I tried to focus, keep it out. I heard a body hit a wall and then Isabel chuckled. "Long time no see Garrett. She'll be so delighted that you came back, though, it's such a shame it's under these circumstances."

Reese was thrown forward, digging his nails into his head. "What the hell is this?" The words were pushed out through his gritted teeth. Elise lunged at Isabel, wrapping her whole body around her as they tumbled to the ground. Through my fumbled vision I could see Elise on top of her, her tail curling out and nearly wrapping around her throat, until the shadow demons came back and pulled her hair and yanked on her exposed tail, distracting her enough for Isabel to gain the power back and kick Elise off of her. She slapped her in the face, hard enough to make her head turn and send her to the ground.

Isabel stopped Beetee from going full snake, seeing that her eyes were fully diamond pupils now and her skin had started to shed. She grasped the side of her face and stopped the transformation, the colorful currents coming from her hand seeming to stun the pink-haired demon. If Beetee knew enough about both sides of herself maybe she could hone it somehow and be more powerful than all of us, like all the books and stories foretold, but that wasn't happening right now. She was the kind of creature that never really wanted to fight unless it was completely necessary.

"It's quite funny, Nicholas. That you think that you can beat me, beat her, because you can keep my magic out. You don't really interest me all that much anyway, but you are quite the prize to someone else." She was speaking towards Beetee's face but talking to me. Elise was coming too, picking herself up from the floor, while Garrett shook his head from his place slumped against the wall.

I knew exactly where I'd felt this pain before. The darkness screeched and screamed for me to let it back in, but I refused. A pair of feet stopped on either side of my head and a face I wished I could throttle came into view. The burn that I'd given him on his face was still present and brought me so much fucking joy I could have smiled if he wasn't assaulting my mind. One of his jacket sleeves bunched a bit at where his hand should have been, while the tattooed hand still attached to him sat on his hip.

Dimitri tilted his head to the side, his perfectly fixed strawberry blonde hair slicked back. "I can't wait to watch what she does to you. Then, you can watch all the things I plan to do to *her*."

33

NICK

"Fuck you."

I reached for his leg, but he moved backwards away from my grasp. I tried to reach for my sword, but the shadow demons plucked it from the ground before I could get to it. I bared my teeth as I pushed back against Dimitri's horrendous clawing into my mind. He wasn't going to win, but fuck was he trying. My head was burning, like he was injecting hellfire right into my skull. I splayed out my fingers and let my light release from my fingers, fusing with my sword. The shadow demon holding it convulsed violently and eventually dropped my weapon before exploding into tiny, wispy particles.

"Leave them the fuck alone, Dimitri. It really is pathetic that you hold a grudge over a girl for this long. You reek of pettiness and I'm not surprised." Elise ran a hand over her cheek where Isabel had slapped her and Dimitri casually turned as if he just noticed she was there.

"Oh, aren't you a sight for sore eyes." His tone was normal, not at all like someone in the middle of a fight. Elise flung her tail sideways and wrapped it around Isabel's waist. The Enchanter sucked in a breath and tried to turn around, only to be squeezed tighter in Elise's grip. Elise hurled her towards the ceiling and then over towards the other side of the room.

Dimitri just laughed at the display, unaware that Garrett had thrown a magical blast at him, sending yellow currents through his body. They didn't debilitate him like it would most, but Garrett didn't care. He shot out current after current; Dimitri was less focused on me, and I was free of his mental torture for the moment. I used my foot to bring my sword closer to me before swiping it from the ground and helping Reese up from the floor. Garrett used his entire body to slam into Dimitri, sending them into the stone wall in a puff of dust, smothering them both in gray matter.

"Get out of here," Beetee warned us, her body shaking as her skin began to flake off. Her legs looked like they were melting as they started to morph together; she was letting us go ahead of her while she fought them.

"Beetee, stop." Elise tried to get her to stay in her normal form, but Beetee just shook her head and pointed away from her. Reese looked behind us to find Garrett still fighting Dimitri, the Enchanter nodding over to us— he and Beetee could try to handle it as best they could. I gripped my sword tighter and grabbed Elise by the arm. "Where would she be?" She gave me a confused expression before she realized I was talking about Dani, Lilith, and anything else likely waiting for us.

Elise didn't answer immediately and we heard Isabel groan as she started to come to. Garrett yelled as Dimitri dragged his nails down his arm, blood oozing from the wounds, but the Enchanter didn't stop fighting. I could make out shadow demons from the corner of my eye, it was almost like they were multiplying.

"Any day now tiny psycho," Reese pressed.

Elise let out a groan and ran past the chaos without looking back. We followed her, the grunting and sounds of pain behind us, as we sprinted down a hallway of red stones. I kept looking behind us, making sure we weren't being followed, but in all honesty, I knew we were. I felt dark eyes on us, keeping track of our movements but letting us continue until we were in the right place. Without warning, a hiss vibrated around us, and Elise's shoulders tensed as we realized it was Beetee.

She halted in front of a large door with snakes for handles and craned her neck to look it over. She glanced over at us and gripped the handle, pulling it open quickly as if there was an ambush on the other side and she wanted to go in with all the confidence in the realms. The inside had red stones decorated everywhere. There were pews set up in a circle, as if made for an audience.

The room was dim but empty, and I could feel my face morphing into confusion. Elise took a few quick steps into the room before she tripped over something, and we followed closely behind her, stopping as she caught her footing. Reese and I held our breath as we peered down at Rae's mangled body. One of her arms was twisted in the opposite direction, bones were sticking out of her legs and her throat was slit. Her head was lying in a pool of blood, flowing towards our feet. We moved to either side of the current of blood, too focused on the dead body to notice the doors closing behind us.

The doors slammed shut, and we simultaneously gave it our full attention. Reese hustled over to the door, reaching for the serpent handles and shaking them. A slow clap came from the other side of the room— I should have known that once we stepped foot in this place, we were never truly alone. I heard Elise growl at the tall figure in the corner of the room. Her hair was straight and platinum blonde, which made her pale complexion even more haunting. A smirk appeared on her red-stained lips; her eyes were so dark that they practically pulled me in. "Well, done. You are quite a resilient little group, aren't you?"

I remembered Lilith vividly now from my time in the past seeing Dani. Her voice was inviting as if she was hypnotizing you without even trying. She walked towards us, her heels clicking on the stone as she eyed me flexing my fingers around my sword. A girlish giggle left her mouth as she watched me. "Oh my. Do you plan to fight me with your big, tough sword?" She placed her hand over her chest in fake fear. "I doubt it will get you far, handsome. Besides, there is someone much more eager to see you than me. You are quite the recurring presence in my little monster's thoughts."

"She's not a monster," I choked out. The air was thinning, a haze cast over the room, starting at the ceiling and trickling its way down. Lilith raised her thin eyebrow with intrigue at my statement, but before she could speak Elise lunged for her, her tail curling behind her. Before she could get within an inch of Lilith, thick dark black ropes captured her, flinging her towards one of the walls. Reese spun around, and I followed his eyes, trying to find the source of the darkness.

Lilith looked over to where Elise was slumped against the wall, and she sighed, as if disappointed. "Nicholas, right?" She caught my attention, tilting her chin up. "Fighting me is futile. I'm not your concern." Her tongue stuck out between her teeth, and her lips turned up, as if holding in a secret.

"Fuck," I heard Reese say as shadows slashed along his legs, forcing him to the ground and then tying themselves around his feet. He was dragged across the room, his bow scraping along the floor. He tried to hold onto the stones, his fingers scrambling to grasp at something, but he couldn't quite get a good grip.

"Let them go." I readied my sword in front of me, prepared to fight.

Lilith didn't make a move towards me; she just casually stood there, her arms at her sides. "You think *I'm* doing this? It's quite comical."

"Where is she?" I demanded, taking a step toward her. I felt my hands burning with the need to throw all the light I had in her direction.

Her eyes seemed to light up then. "Dani? Ah, of course, she's right here. She's been here the whole time." Her smile showed all her teeth, and it was anything but friendly. The room was suddenly void of sound, as if everything moved in slow motion. I felt a presence behind me, but it didn't seem large and overbearing. Rather, it felt discreet, like it wanted you to think it was nothing until you let your guard down.

I slowly turned around, but not before seeing Elise's eyes open as she rubbed the back of her head. My heart stopped when I came face to face with the presence—lost and in the dark, I felt like I knew her all the same. I looked down at her beautiful brown eyes, that same brown skin, same mass of curls, more disheveled than usual. My breath caught in my throat as she placed her palm flat against my chest, running her hand over my collarbones, using her knuckles to stroke the skin along my throat.

I shuddered at her touch, at the feeling of maybe thinking she was okay. The moment felt too good, too perfect. Her small smile turned flat when her eyes shifted from warm brown to black. I didn't have a chance to step back when her hand claimed my throat, her fingers pressing into my skin. I choked, wrapping my hand around her wrists to try and ease her hold on me. She wouldn't budge as smoke escaped from her hand, skating over my shoulders and tracing along my fingers. I desperately held onto my sword, not willing to let it go.

"You see, Nicholas, you will never be what she needs…" Lilith started, but she was knocked to the side, her dress bunched around her knees as she skidded across the floor. Her blonde hair fell around her shoulders as she huffed out a laugh. Dani shifted her focus to what was behind me as she threw me across the room, discarding me like weightless trash. I shook my head as I placed my hands along the ground, watching her stalk over to Elise. She stretched her hand out, creating shadow silhouettes that grabbed Elise by the hair and yanked her back. When Dani got close, Elise jumped up, extending her leg to kick Dani square in the stomach.

I pushed up from the ground, only to see Reese notch his bow and point it straight at Dani. I ran to him right as he released his arrow. It sailed across the room, aimed directly for her, but she turned around at the last moment, catching it in her hands as it disintegrated into black dust. Reese let another arrow loose, but she caught it as well. Elise wrapped her tail around the legs of a demon and spun around, releasing them into the other one. Red shadow-like flames bloomed in her hands, but Reese sent another arrow flying by her head, the glowing weapon eliminating the demons immediately.

Lilith was right next to Elise now, looming near her ear. "Getting boys to fight your battles, huh?"

Elise thrashed her arms out, but Lilith was gone. She turned back around just to face Lilith again, but the dark queen raised her hand and smacked her across the face before grabbing her by the chin, raising her up as if she weighed nothing. "You were such a wild card when I took you in." She tilted Elise's face right to left, inspecting her.

Dani let shadow demons loose and I ran through them, shredding them with my sword one after the other until they puffed up in black smoke or shook violently and disappeared. Reese shot into the sky to reach the high ground, releasing his angelic arrows at any demon he could. Dani followed suit and let her wings out, pursuing him as I fought my way to Lilith, dipping my sword down and aiming for her side or her stomach.

Right as my sword slashed at her body, I heard Elise's strained voice. "It's a shame you can't kill me, right?" My blade cut into Lilith, and she immediately dropped Elise, who caught herself before she completely fell to the floor. Lilith clamped hand to her side and hissed at me. I was about to run my blade into her again, but I heard wings behind me, felt hands grip my shirt. I was yanked from the ground and flown high toward the ceiling; I looked up to find Dani staring back at me with pitch black eyes, her expression uncaring and unmoved.

An arrow whizzed by her head and she ducked, snarling over at where Reese had another arrow ready, blazing with his angelic magic as he aimed right for us. Right for *her*. He let the arrow fly and she smiled in return, but she also let me go. I sailed to the ground faster than I thought, but I manifested my wings out, catching myself right before I hit the ground. The tips of my wings glazed over the stones as I soared upward.

Elise shot out red shadow flames, causing the shadow demons to run rampant, running into each other and making the flames grow higher. Dani flew up behind Reese and lassoed a dark rope around his throat, throttling him forward then back. He dropped his bow, and she held him against her, tightening the rope. He brought his elbow back towards her face, causing her to pull back and growl. She readjusted her hand on the rope and pulled again as he twisted his arm around, collecting light in his hand and pressing it against her face as best he could. I could hear her scream as she let go of the rope and used more shadows to cinch his wings together, harder and harder. She tugged so hard, parts of his wings tore and fell to the ground.

I flapped my wings harder, shaking off the shadow demons that had jumped onto me, trying to pull me down. I flipped my sword in my hand and hit Dani with the hilt before she realized what was happening. She fumbled back and I cut the rope with my weapon, severing her connection to Reese. He yelled in agony as he flew towards the ground, and I quickly followed, trying to catch him, only to end up falling over once he was in my arms.

Elise had her tail aimed at Lilith when the doors slammed open. Dimitri pushed Garrett's scarred, bloody body into the room, while two shadow demons dumped Beetee's naked, bruised one next to him. They were both breathing, but just barely. "Haven't seen a demon with an anchoring tattoo in some time now." Dimitri fixed the sleeves of his jacket, the material ripped in places, his shirt untucked and covered in dirt and blood. Blood gathered near his lips, but he stuck his tongue out to lick it away.

Isabel sent rainbow-hued magic towards Elise, tying her hands behind her back, sparks flying from her wrists. Lilith watched on with interest but then looked over at Beetee. "Anchoring tattoo? Hmm…we'll have to keep that one then, won't we? And Garrett, it's about time you returned to me."

"Your fight is with us, not with them!" I yelled, gaining her attention. She gave me a knowing look, pushing her foot against Beetee's arm as the pinked haired demon groaned.

"Anyone who threatens what I want is a problem. I wish you would understand that." The doors closed behind Isabel and Dimitri as they looked down at the friends we'd made with disgust. Reese tried to get to his feet, but Dimitri pinned him down with a look, his eyes turning red. I knew every angry feeling Reese ever had was coming back to haunt him when he screamed out, holding a shaky hand to his head. Isabel released another stream of colorful magic at Elise, taking hold of her throat. Every time her tail tried to remove them, it snapped back, singed from the electric current.

I felt my hands burning with angelic light and I shot it at Isabel who raised her hands towards her face, trying to shield herself from it. Unfortunately for her, angelic magic could be hot, close to the temperature of the sun if you really felt like it. Her arms were red and bleeding as the skin melted off, and she screamed as she held her arms out from her face, seeing the disfiguration I'd caused.

"You little fucking shit!" she cursed while Dimitri stood nearby snickering. Lilith put her hand up, using her magic to shut Isabel's mouth, silencing her for the time being.

"Finish this, my love," Lilith ordered, not talking to either of the creatures in front of me, but to the demon who shifted towards me the moment Lilith commanded. "I'm eager to see Heaven's Gate fall to the one who saved them, the Soul Seether who wouldn't yield. Look at her now: everything they knew she'd be." Dani gripped the front of my shirt, slamming me into the wall, putting pressure on my chest.

"I do love when she puts on a show," I heard Dimitri say as he leaned against the wall.

Lilith admired Dani from a distance. "Start with the handsome one first." She said it like she knew that if Dani was herself, it would hurt her to hurt me. The dagger in my waistband dug into my skin, reminding me it was there.

The room rumbled as shadow demons erupted from the floor, and alongside them, vines of silvery black thread snaked from the cracks. Dani's magic overtook Isabel's, wrapping around Elise's tail and then around the psycho demon herself. Elise thrashed and fought, trying to use her own reddish shadows to deter Dani's, but it was no use. Dani was stronger, and she lifted her up, not looking away from me, and pressed her against the wall. Elise was trapped like a spider as the shadows covered her mouth, stopping her from speaking as they moved into her eyes, cutting off her sight.

Reese was pushed back down by shadows, a misty foot slamming down on his back, pressing into his broken wings. The silvery black threads grew from the ground, and one of them formed itself into an arrow, aiming for his calf. He let out a loud cry of pain as it made contact, and blood gushed from his leg. Incredibly, the arrow was still there, as if holding him in place.

I tried to fight Dani, wanting to use my sword in some way against her, but she used her shadows to trap one of my wrists against the wall, her hand grasping the one holding my sword. I hadn't realized how strong she actually was, how much effort she wasn't putting into keeping me pinned. She slammed my hand against the stone over and over until the vibration sent my sword flying to the ground.

She brought her other hand up and cupped her fingers, as if she was squeezing something and I felt the shadows tighten around my wrists. She did it again and again before she flicked her wrist, and I heard a snap. I swore and bit my tongue when I heard my wrist snap. The sharp pain pushed through me, but I couldn't dwell on it, not right now. Her shadows were like pin pricks on my skin and her black eyes bore into my soul. I knew she was right in front of me; I could feel her skin and even smell that familiar cinnamon scent, everything else, though...none of it was the same.

"Dani, stop." Her shadows wrapped around my legs and around my chest, pushing down, making it hard to breathe. She reached up and gripped my hair pulling my head back. "Please, remember who you are," I pleaded, feeling the sting at my scalp. Shadows wrapped around my throat, burning my skin as they pulled at pieces of my soul.

I felt her laughter vibrate through me, dark and hollow. "Poor Nicholas— so lost, so pathetic thinking you can save anybody." Her voice was the same, but it was missing the tone that made her...*her*. Shadows swirled near us, and they started to tear apart and morph into something else, but she kept her eyes on me. I heard Reese's cries of pain as he flexed his fingers and tried to reach for his bow, mere centimeters from his fingertips.

"You only have yourself to blame. So weak, such a sorry excuse for an angel." I looked to my right, stunned to see Jonah's face, I looked to my left and again, Jonah's face. I tried to blink it away, but they only got closer. She tugged my hair harder, tightening the shadow around my neck. Her nails forced themselves against the fabric of my shirt, and I could feel my skin starting to break from the pressure. She'd taken some of my pain, some of my hurt, and now she was relaying it back to me. Whatever she was now, she was using it against me in the worst way.

You are always enough, Nicholas Cassial. Broken and in pieces, you are enough.

Her words ran through me, and I held onto them, knowing they were said by the real Dani. That was how she really thought about me, not this. This wasn't her at all. "Dani, you have to stop." I took a breath as I watched Lilith assessing the scene. She looked proud of Dani. She'd turned her into the monster she always thought she'd be, the monster I told her she never was. "It's me, Dani, you have to know that. This isn't you."

She smirked as she pressed harder, and I could feel my heart race as I felt her shadows plunging into my veins. She wanted me to hurt, and she wasn't even hesitating. She didn't have to harm me in any way that left a physical bruise because what I was seeing, what I was feeling was hurtful enough.

Heroes are allowed to be broken; it doesn't make them any less of a hero.

I closed my eyes, telling myself Jonah would forgive me and maybe one day I would be able to forgive myself. Darkness or not, I was okay, even when I wasn't. The shadows that mimicked Jonah's face were so vivid and life-like that they almost made me cave, but I couldn't, I wouldn't give them the satisfaction. I could accept my pain, but it didn't own me.

"I can't wait to see you submit," she smirked as I yelled out from the pain of her fingers digging into me.

"You're good, Dani, you're something good," I said, hoping there was some glimmer of light in her black eyes. Then she blinked, and it was like I had hit a nerve. Just as quickly as it came, it disappeared, and she raised an eyebrow as she continued to block my airways. My vision was starting to get hazy, and that darkness was starting to burn my insides, binding themselves to my entire being.

"Nick!" I heard Reese shout from the ground. "Do it!" He had managed to grab his bow, and even collapsed on the floor, he held it like the best marksman I knew. His magic enveloped the bow, and he pulled back, releasing it. It hit Dani in the shoulder, causing her to stumble forward a bit. Her brows turned inward, and she whipped her head around, aiming her focus on him. She eased her tension on my wrist, while my broken one remained in her shadowy hold. Dani brought her hand back and ripped the arrow from her shoulder, throwing it to the ground.

Reese sucked in a sharp breath. "Nick, fucking do it!"

I looked up at the ceiling, counting to five as fast as I could before reaching behind me with my free hand and untucking the dagger from my waistband. Dani snarled at Reese, and just as quickly as she turned back to me, I brought the dagger to my front, holding the hilt as tight as I could before I thrusted it into her stomach. The moment was so quick, I wouldn't have realized it happened if I wasn't the one doing it. My knuckles were white from where I was gripping the leather hilt as tight as I could, and I did what Natalia said: my angelic magic flooded down my arm and through my hand, trailing around the dagger and fusing its power with my own. My hand felt like it was on fire, the hilt scorching hot as I kept holding on, pulsing my own light into her.

She looked down at where the dagger pressed into her stomach. The light kept moving into the dagger, emanating through her chest and her arms. Her hair flashed with golden light as the dark tried to fight for dominance. She looked up at me as if it didn't hurt, as if it didn't work.

"What the hell are you doing?" Lilith raged. "Do you really think your weapons will work, you stupid boy?" Dani started to move towards me, trying to come after me, but then, suddenly, she stopped. Her eyes flashed from black to brown, back and forth as if she couldn't make up her mind. She brought her hands to where her weapon sat, lodged inside of her, and she took a few steps back, her hand shaking as she touched the hilt. The shadows had stopped pulling on my neck and I took a moment to try to breathe. When she looked at me again, her eyes were their beautiful solid brown.

"Nick." One word. She said one word and I knew she was my Dani again. She said my name and all the pain she'd inflicted on me was instantly forgiven.

The shadows surrounding my face and my neck disappeared and I reached for my throat, pressing my hand against my skin, feeling an indent from where it held me. All the shadow demons around us dispersed, removing themselves, as if they never existed in the first place.

"What the hell is going on?" I heard Dimitri shout, his irritation showcased in his tone.

I hardly felt my broken wrist as I raced over to Dani, wanting to tell her that everything would be okay, that we fixed this. She started to give me a small smile, but it faltered as she teetered on her feet. "Dani?" She started to cough and then her knees buckled as she pulled the dagger from her stomach. Black blood covered the blade and more of it pulsed out and onto her shirt. I almost didn't catch her when she fell to the ground, landing on her knees.

The shadows released Elise from their hold, and she tumbled to the ground with a loud thud. Reese shifted his leg up slowly and pushed himself up from the floor, his legs covered in thick, red blood. Lilith fumed with dark red and auburn smoke.

"What have you done?" She started to race towards me, her hands out like she could strangle me, but Elise wound her tail around her wrist, twirling her around. She slashed her tail along one side of the dark queen's face and then the other.

Lilith threw out her own magic at Elise, who met her with the same force. Their magic met in the middle battling it out, almost as if they were equal. Isabel shook her head and nearly screeched, "We should have just killed them from the very start, like I said! I would rather see them fucking dead!" She started to send her magic towards a helpless Beetee still struggling on the ground, finally starting to come to. Elise's magic looked so much thicker than Lilith's, I didn't know if that made it stronger, but it looked that way oddly enough. Lilith jerked her hands forward, propelling her magic at Elise which sent the demon toppling over in a huff. She moved her bangs out of her face and stood back up, her tail swinging behind her. Lilith looked at Elise, then at Dani who appeared as if she wanted to throw up. She opened her mouth and copious amounts of black smoke streamed out, flooding onto the floor before becoming translucent.

Reese cleared his throat. "Not today." He pulled his arrow back and launched it in her direction, burying itself into her chest, and she ran into Dimitri as she tried to regain her footing.

"Do something!" Isabel shouted, reaching up to pull the arrow from her shoulder, but Reese shot another one, making sure she remained in pain. Lilith ignored her and stared at Beetee on the ground, then Garrett.

"You seem so much into friendship these days. I would hate to see that be for nothing, but it looks like it already was, you insolent little demon. A conscience is a dangerous thing to have, my dear." Lilith waved her hand towards Dani as Elise raged, creating thick, red orbs of dark magic.

"You said this would go smoothly," Dimitri complained, shaking his head. "My father will have a field day with this. They all will." He looked over to Dani, taking shallow breaths on the floor. The look he gave her was one of longing and I wish I could have wiped it from his fucking face. Lilith scoffed, keeping up the facade of nonchalance.

"She'll remain here like she was always meant to." Elise rushed over to her, but she was gone in a dark flash, leaving only smoke in her wake. Dimitri adjusted the lapels of his jacket before he waggled his fingers in my direction, taunting me as followed Lilith's lead, just barely avoiding one of Reese's arrows.

Dani fell further to the side, and I caught her, careful not to put too much pressure on or make too much movement with my broken wrist. Still, I fought through the pain. Her head rested on my thigh as she placed one of her hands over her bleeding wound. A light pulsed there, flashing over and over.

"Oh no, where do you think you're going?" Elise tsked, racing over to Isabel and pulling her by the back of her neck. "We know someone who is *very* interested in seeing you again." Isabel started to fuel herself with her own magic, ready to fight again, but Elise readjusted her hold and thrusted Isabel into the wall, making sure her head connected with it until the Enchanter was truly out cold. Reese and Elise knelt down next to Garrett and Beetee, gently rolling each of them over and examining them.

Dani drew in a breath that sounded like it hurt, and I used my good hand to stroke her face and move her hair from her eyes. She looked up at me, taking another deep breath in. "Hi."

"Hi." I watched as that light near her stomach kept pulsing, but it was faint. "You're going to be okay."

She closed her eyes and tried to readjust herself so she could cuddle closer as she made a noise of pain. "Mmhmm, this definitely feels okay."

"We'll get you back. You'll be okay. Everything will be okay." I said the words, but they felt more like false reassurance. She knew it too, and she simply shook her head as best she could. She looked down at her wound as she lifted her hands, her palms were covered in the black blood, and I felt her shudder with a kind of nervous understanding that what she would say next was probably something I didn't want to hear.

"Nick…" she started, and I shook my head as she pressed her lips together at my stubbornness. "Nick."

I bit the inside of my cheek to stop myself from being overwhelmed, from letting my emotions take over and wreck this moment. "No. No! You'll be okay. You have to be."

I heard Reese's voice over all the noise in my head for just a moment. "Nick, we have to go." I knew he was speaking, but everything sounded like he was underwater. It was like his mouth was moving but no sound was coming out. I didn't need to be anywhere but right here.

I cradled her head closer to me. "I'm sorry, baby. I'm so sorry." I felt one, two, three tears slip down my face, and I couldn't hold the rest of it in. I had caused this, and I didn't know a way to fix it. "We're going to get you back. Natalia is going to make sure you're safe and good. I'm going to take care of you. Is that okay?"

She nodded carefully. Her eyes looked tired, and her breathing was shallow, slow, like it was taking all her strength to make out one or two words. "Nick, stop. You did…everything…you could have. I don't…blame…you." As if she was mirroring me, small tears appeared at the corners of her eyes. She reached her hand up and stroked my face with her thumb.

I leaned into her touch, hearing Garrett and Beetee in front of us. I could be aware of our surroundings and still not care to acknowledge them right now. Even though my wrist hurt, so fucking much, I delicately brought it up to place my hand over hers, moving my thumb against her skin. "It's my fault. I could have figured something else out. I did this. I did this. I did this." I repeated. It reminded me of the things that voice would tell me in my head when I was so lost in the dark, I almost couldn't find my way out.

You weren't good enough. You did this.

As if she knew where my mind had gone, she pinched my jaw with as much force as her fingers would let her. "You are good, Nicholas Cassial. You are still very much the hero I've always thought you were." She sucked in a deep breath, and I noticed the light was even dimmer. It pulsed slower and every second it took too long, my heart would fumble. I closed my eyes, not wanting more tears to escape. She shushed me, soothing my heart rampaging in my chest. "It's kind of funny, you know? You spent so much time trying to get me to accept my light—I wanted to try, I swear—but it all seems so silly now, when you were right here. You're all the light I needed." She laughed to herself which came out so much less happy than it originally would have.

I smiled down at her, taking in her words, feeling my face get hot and my shoulders aching to slump. I shook away those thoughts, needing to be strong for her when she was so weak. "I'll be your night light whenever you need me. I can't do that if you don't come back with us. You have to come back with me." I felt the portal key under my shirt.

Reese limped over to us. "Nick, she isn't going to make that trip and you know it."

"Shut up," I told him.

"Nick," Reese started again. I knew he wasn't trying to be a dick. He was being realistic. I didn't care about being realistic; I just wanted her.

"Reese, shut up! Shut up!" My words came out choked and strained. My cheeks were wet, and I felt her run her fingers under my eyes as she removed the tears. "I'm not leaving you. I can't do that, Dani. I *won't* do that. It's you and me, existing together, remember? I c-can't do t-that w-without you."

Her tears trailed down her face and over her cheeks, disappearing past into hair. She gave me a closed-mouth smile as if my words hit her right where they were supposed to, but that didn't mean they didn't cause some sort of pain knowing they were true. "You have to." She tugged on my shirt causing me to lean down closer to her. I caught Elise out of the corner of my eye, slowly moving over to us but not saying a word. Dani rubbed her nose against mine and that only made me cry harder.

She kissed me with as much passion as she could muster, all the tears and pain wrapped up into something I couldn't have explained to anyone else. "I should have said it sooner," I said against her lips. "I shouldn't have listened to you."

She kissed me again, and this time it was short and sweet. "I know. It's the only mistake I ever made—telling you to wait." She closed her eyes and reopened them, closed, opened, closed, opened.

I tugged her closer, hating every minute of this. "Dani, no, no, you can't do this. Not to me." I leaned down further, pressing my lips to her temple. "I'm sorry I didn't say it sooner. I'm sorry I never told you I loved you… because I do. I love you, dark or light, riddled with scars." My voice was no more than a whisper when I was done, but I felt lighter after those words left my lips, like they were holding me back from something completely.

I noticed she wasn't moving, her body so still, it was scary. Her eyes were closed, her eyelashes fanned out across the tops of her cheeks. I heard a rattling sound and realized it was her dagger, the blood-soaked weapon ricocheting off the stone as it rapidly fell apart, becoming nothing but dust and memories. It was like it had never existed and the light that was so faint, so weak inside of her, blew out. It no longer pulsed, no longer gave me the small notion that she was okay enough for me to fake it for both of us.

Natalia had warned me this could happen. She had let herself be consumed by the dark, and she couldn't fight it like she wanted. Dani was strong and I would bet her way anytime in a fight, but she wasn't prepared for the two sides of herself to fight for dominance. That darkness had taken her so far down that, when it could possibly seem like the light had won, I don't think she could find a way to it. Maybe I could have helped her, if that was at all possible, maybe I could have done something other than take her away from me.

I felt a hand on my shoulder and a familiar body hovering over me. "Nick, I'm sorry." Reese's voice was so low I hardly heard him. Beetee pulled herself up from the ground as Elise ran over to her. She watched me, sadness in her lilac eyes. Garrett was on his side; I could see his shoulders move slightly, but he wasn't as coherent as the rest of us. "It's not fair," I muttered to myself as I said fuck it to the pain in my wrist and wrapped both my arms around her.

"It's not fucking fair. She was…" Elise caught herself as if showing any emotion close to mine was something she couldn't fathom. "She was annoying, but she didn't deserve this. Blondie is right though, Nicholas. We do have to go."

I narrowed my eyes at her. "I'm not leaving her here."

"Beetee needs help, Garrett can hardly keep his fucking eyes open, and your best friend has a seriously gnarly wound in his calf. It's a difficult choice, but it's one we have to make," Elise argued, "you need to use your stupid key and take us back."

"I…I can't."

Reese let out a sigh. "Nick, you bring her back to, what? Ariel will never let her be buried anywhere near other angels; despite everything we know about her. You'll just put more strain on her body taking her through a portal anyway." He knelt down, but I didn't look over at him. "I don't like saying it, but you have two very alive people who need help right now. As much as you want to help her, you can't anymore." I refused to acknowledge him, but I knew somewhere inside of myself, that he was right, and it was a choice I knew she would want me to make.

I grabbed my key from around my neck and yanked it down, breaking the clasp. I handed it to him, feeling his fingers graze my own as if he was hesitating. I found Elise looking at me again, but she immediately looked away. If I had known any better, she'd swiped her hand under her eyes— gray eyes that looked glassy from where I sat.

Reese pushed off from the ground and began to start maneuvering Garrett so that they could help him through the portal. They would need me in a minute, but I couldn't move. My sadness was evident from my tears and heavy chest, but I was also angry that yet again this happened to me. Someone I cared about so immensely had died in my arms. At least, with Dani, I'd never doubted her throughout this journey. I had lost another person. There was another hole in my existence that would never be filled again, because this beautiful creature had made such an impact on it. It wasn't fucking fair. My heart was beating so roughly, I almost felt like I could pass out if I didn't control myself.

I just wanted her back. I wanted to tell her so many things, I wanted to tell her that I loved her over and over again until she couldn't stand it. I wanted everything I'd said that night in bed. I wanted a life with her outside of Lilith, regardless of how those circumstances had changed. I wanted to continue to fight Lilith with her and take on anything else that threatened the things we wanted, the life we could create together. I know the ins and outs of how any of that would play out, but I was seething with so much untapped rage that I ached to rewind time to that night, the night she'd left to do things on her own. I couldn't do that; I wouldn't get a chance to do that, and…. fuck, fuck, fuck!

There was a hollow feeling in my chest—she had my heart, and I didn't want it back.

I wanted *her* back.

I wanted her back.

I wanted her back, because I loved her, and she was mine.

I held her tighter, my eyes closing as I felt no tears, only the need to speak what I wanted into existence. "I want you back," I whispered to her, not actually caring if anyone else saw or heard.

My eyes were closed but I could see a slight glow from behind my eyelids. I cracked my eyes open to watch small light blossom at her wound, tracing around it. As I watched, it gained more power, more movement, as it spread along her body, moving over every inch.

"Nick…" Reese said, trailing off as he stopped what he was doing.

I tentatively reached out to touch the light and it glowed brighter, encapsulating my hand, but it didn't hurt. It felt like it was a part of me— like it came from me. It wasn't white with hues of gold like angelic light— instead, it was a mix of a dark red and neon green, the tips black, the colors seemed to dance with one another.

What was this?

"Nicholas, what the fuck is going on?" Elise stood back, watching with confusion written, plain and simple across her face. I looked at Garrett and Beetee who mirrored our expressions, but Garrett flicked his golden eyes from Dani's body to me, his eyes widening. The light stretched out around her, and then in a flash it pulled together in one bright burst before dissipating. Our breathing filled the silent air as we all stared at her, waiting.

"What the hell was that?" Reese asked, running a hand through his hair, my portal key dangling from his fingers.

I opened my mouth to explain that I didn't have an explanation when I heard a tiny intake of breath, then another. It almost sounded like a hiccup, but my shoulders jumped at the noise. I looked down at her and, ever so slightly, I could see her chest rise. I was about to say her name when she opened her eyes, wide and startled. She sucked in breath after breath, trying to move her arms around and awkwardly bending her knees as if she had no idea where she was or what had happened.

"Holy fuck," I heard someone say, but I didn't turn around. I only looked at her, and in a matter of seconds, she looked back at me. I peered into those same brown eyes I knew so well, but right now, they looked at me for answers. I didn't have them, but I knew one thing for certain.

She was alive.

34

DANI

I didn't completely hate the dark—I just hated it when darkness was the only thing available. If I knew there was a light somewhere or that the darkness wouldn't last forever, I was alright. I could keep moving from day to day, doing my tasks like a good little demon.

That light Nicholas had pressed me to consider understanding had fought so hard to assist me, but it was no use. I was so used to the taste of dark magic, so susceptible to its pull, no amount of angelic alone time with my angel would help. I hadn't known that was what she wanted to do; Lilith had only ever used me, and she'd done it again.

Death was something I knew came for everyone. I wasn't afraid of it, especially since I'd seen it ten times over. I'd inflicted it among others, and I had shrugged it off in the process. I hadn't considered that when I died, that I would truly miss anyone. I didn't think anyone would miss me. I hadn't actually realized that dying was a darkness far worse than the one I'd been inhabited by. It felt like I was torturing myself with how slow it was. I was sad to say that as much as I enjoyed Nick's face, I could really stand to see it more. Without a second thought, I knew he would turn back time and delete this moment from history if he could have.

The darkness of death was lonely, and I accepted my fate. Like Lilith had wanted, I would remain with her now, but at least I wouldn't be a burden to anyone or wreck the havoc she wanted from me.

I felt myself falling into a never-ending abyss that made time move slowly but made you look your loneliness in the face. Then the loneliness turned into something else, something too bright, too much like a heartbeat. It sounded like mine. It was faint and weak, but then it pumped harder, blood moving at a rapid pace. My body felt like it was being pulled in a different direction. My very being was being threaded back together by something…

I didn't have much time to think when I opened my eyes. Everything was far too bright even though I knew Purgatory was never bright enough for anyone. The smell of brimstone and blood filled my nostrils. My senses were overwhelmed; it almost felt like I was being born for the first time. Every normal function was difficult for me. I swallowed dryly, desperately wanting some water.

What the fuck?

I felt a warm body as I maneuvered my own and looked up. My heart thrummed when our eyes met. He was in shock, rightfully so, but his fingers flexed around my body, almost like his way of pinching me to make sure I wasn't some sort of manifestation of his imagination. His eyes were red from crying, but he was still the most handsome creature I'd ever seen. I swallowed again, feeling a scratchiness in my throat.

"Hi."

His mouth twitched, as if he was trying to form words but couldn't, like no sentence could match what he was feeling. He said the only thing he could, "Hi."

He pulled back, keeping me close to him as he brought me up with him. He winced when I took hold of his wrist, and I slightly remembered harming him in some way, but it was all fuzzy. My legs wobbled, but he held me still, still looking at me as if I would just burst into a cloud of smoke like nothing happened.

"An explanation?" Elise pressed, scanning her eyes down my body in disbelief.

He started his sentence three times before he just gave up and shook his head. Beetee was resting against Reese's side, her smile the brightest thing in the room, but then I saw her bruises and cuts. *What had happened?*

I patted Nick's arms, silently telling him I was okay. He delicately let me find my own balance and I took a deep breath, trying to stand up straight.

Garrett grunted behind me, reaching his hand out for Elise to take as she helped him all the way up. "We need to talk to Natalia. Now."

"I was thinking…" Nick started, but then he stopped talking. He took a few steps backwards and then to the side. It looked almost like he was drunk with the way he teetered on his feet. He shook his head as if remembering himself and started again. "I was…" He stopped, swaying a little before blinking once, twice, and then placing his good hand on his head.

He tilted to one side more and more until he tumbled over, and then he was out cold.

35

NICK

I felt exactly like I did when I woke up caught by Markus and Isabel. My head throbbed, and my arms and legs had an odd, tingling sensation, as if something was still vibrating through me. I felt the plushness of a pillow under my head, and my fingers splayed out revealing cool sheets against my skin. I slowly blinked my eyes open, instantly realizing that this wasn't Lilith's castle. No, this wasn't the recovery room at the hostel, but the infirmary at The Skies. The white walls were such a stark difference to the muted tones of Beetee's hostel.

I heard voices speaking in hushed tones and I turned my head in their direction. The movement caused me to let out a groan, making me just a little nauseous. The figures all turned around to look at me, and I made out Natalia, the Enchanter I'd met in the apothecary—Xander—and my father.

My father clamped his hand over his mouth as his eyes started to well up with tears, but he closed his eyes and took in a breath before he rushed over to me, propping himself on the edge of the bed. He ran a hand gently through my hair and then over the side of my face. His eyes roamed over me, inspecting. "How are you feeling? Do you want something to drink? More pillows?"

I shook my head, regretting it immediately. He was fussing over me, but I let him. "Dad, I'm fine."

He looked as if he didn't believe me, and he looked over his shoulder at Natalia and Xander. "Look him over again." The Enchanters did as he asked and came over to me, giving every inch of me a once over. Xander's teal-colored eyes were friendly, and I focused on his gold earrings as he ran a hand over my wrist. I winced as he applied pressure to it. I looked down to see it was bandaged, and it was like I could nearly feel the bone being put back together.

"He's alright, Maurice. No internal bleeding and no broken bones besides the obvious. I'll give him something for the cuts and bleeding." His accent sounded musical as he gave my father a confident nod. His hair had grown out a little since the last time I saw him; he still had a buzz cut, but his hair wasn't so closely shaved. He wore a vest with no sleeves and no shirt, which showed off the various tattoos that decorated his chest. He almost rivaled Zane with his level of tattoos. Xander circled around the bed, patting Natalia's arm.

The High Priestess clasped her hands in front of her body. "We are so glad you're back, safely." She worried her bottom lip as if she didn't know what to say to me, but I helped her out as best I could.

"We're all safe. That's what matters."

My father ran his hand through my hair, his face finally calming. "What the hell happened? Daya and I are getting ready to eat dinner one minute, and the next, you all come barreling into my living room. The addition of three more people than you left with was a shock."

"I don't know. I must have blacked out. I remember giving Reese the key so that he could take us home when I…" I trailed off, running that moment in my head. Dani's death, my need to want her back, and then her reanimation.

"You were completely out when we got to you. We rushed you and everyone else here. You haven't woken up once until right now."

Natalia nodded in agreement. "He should know, he's been here the whole time." I pushed myself up and grabbed my dad's shoulder. He understood what I wanted, letting me wrap my arms around him in a hug. There was so much tension in his shoulders that released the minute we made contact, and I wondered how often he was stressed while I was gone, how many nights he went without sleep because of his worrying.

He pulled back when Xander came back around and rubbed some

ointment onto the side of my head, then over places where gashes were open or scabs were starting to develop. Natalia peeked down at my arm, noticing the three scars Dimitri left me. "What's that?"

"A present from a Son of Hell."

My father's eyes widened, as did everyone else's. "Son of Hell?"

I gave a dutiful nod. "Yup."

"You got into it with a literal spawn of Hell. You are way cooler than I thought you were," Xander said, shrugging innocently when Natalia shushed him. "I'll go check on your blonde friend. Let me know if you need anything, hero boy." He winked at me, his last words inflecting with his accent as he walked out of the room.

"You should rest, Nicholas. I'll get Daya and Alex from the house so you can see them."

I licked my lips. needing to ask the question that was currently at the forefront of my mind. "Ariel?"

Natalia and my father gave each other a knowing glance, and Natalia slid her hands down her golden dress. "Ariel is taking matters into his own hands, claiming his place since the previous executive's magic has yet to reveal his successor."

"He can't do that."

My father sighed. "He can, actually. There is a ceremony that can be done, and it has only happened once in the history of this realm, but it *can* be done. Unfortunately, there isn't much any of us can do about it."

I groaned in frustration. "That's just perfect."

Natalia giggled. "You have made quite an impression though, coming back in one piece. He was a bit stunned. You've gained much attention due to this mission. I don't know if that's what you were aiming for, but well, you've got it now."

I huffed, my head reeling from waking up, but I was happy to be back home. I thought about what my father had said. "Garrett and Beetee, how are they?"

Natalia answered me quickly. "They are both okay, still very much alive. I gave the pink haired one a little sleeping tonic so that her broken ribs would set. The other one, the Enchanter, well…" She looked down at the floor.

"What?" I pressed, sitting up even straighter.

"Like I said, he's okay, but one of his arms is pretty mangled. It's from the inside though, like they burned him. His entire left arm is charred on the inside. We are trying to figure out how to fix it if we can."

"Fucking Dimitri." I muttered under my breath. My father filled a glass with water and walked it back over to me. I happily took it, downing the entire thing. "Elise?"

My father answered this time. "She's a little beaten up, but still the same little sour puss. She was running back and forth between Dani and...uh... what's her name? Beetee? We told her to rest, but I'm pretty sure she gave us the middle finger."

Natalia rolled her eyes, as if she was remembering that exact moment. A small smile played at her lips, but it was gone as she looked at me again. "Elise brought Isabel back."

My eyes widened. "Where is she?"

"Somewhere you don't need to worry about, you have my word." Her face told me a million different things, mainly that she was trying to be regal when all she was thinking about was making Isabel know pain.

I cleared my throat, gaining my father's undivided attention. "Where is *she*?"

One side of his mouth tipped up. "She's two doors down." I had never moved so fast in my entire life, and I regretted it almost instantly when I wobbled a bit on my feet. My father raced around the bed and caught me, his tone scolding. "Nicholas, lie back down."

"I'll lie back down *after* I see her."

He started to say something, but he caught himself, knowing that arguing with me was futile. He brought his fingers to my chin and tilted my head up. "As long as you're fine. Be honest."

"I'm obviously not one hundred percent, but I'm okay." He looked satisfied enough with my answer and stepped back, allowing me to walk past him. To my father's surprise, I turned around and hugged him.

"I love you, son," he said into my hair, before he shooed me away. Zane was right outside the room, as if he had nothing better to do than to keep watch. I guess when it came to Natalia, all he ever wanted to do was to protect her. I nodded at him and he mirrored the action back, giving me a pat on the back as I passed him. I walked past a room with the door ajar and looked inside. I saw Beetee asleep, her hot pink hair fanned out behind her. In the corner of the room, Elise sat in a chair, staring at her nails. She looked content just sitting there. The Beetee situation would need to be handled, and whenever my father brought Daya and Alex here, the story would have to come out.

I popped my head inside when I found a completely open door and saw her. She had both her hands flat on the bed as she leaned into it with her head down. Her curls created a wall that hid her face, but I knew it was her. I always would. I knocked on the wall inside the room, causing her to jump. She faced me, curling her fingers toward her body as she extended her arm, motioning for me to come inside. I only made it about two feet in front of her before I stopped. I wasn't totally sure what she wanted from me after everything. I didn't know where we stood, but I didn't want to push her.

She fidgeted with her fingers, as if she was a little nervous. "Nick."

"Yes?" I was prepared to talk. I was also ready to not talk and just sit in silence, soaking up the fact that we could both be alive in the same room together again.

She didn't want either one of those things.

"Can you please kiss me?" She gave me one of those shy smiles I didn't see very often, but the words were said with a confidence I knew all too well. It took me only a second before I had her pulled into me, my mouth on hers. It was like every single good thing that had ever happened to me was all wrapped up in this one kiss. She arched her back but took my head with her as she braced her hand along the back of my neck. She tasted sweet, but a little like fire. I broke the kiss, and she pouted.

"I came here to see you, to see if you were alright," I said, unwrapping her arms from me.

"Don't I look alright?" she pointed out, trailing her hands down her body.

I rubbed the back of my neck. "Yes, you do, but Dani, you...you were..."

"Dead."

That word made me cringe as I remembered her dead body lying in my lap. "Yeah, that. Now...you're not."

She turned her body as she leaned back against the bed. "Looks that way, huh?" I rubbed my hand across my mouth, trying to find the words to describe how I felt in those moments.

"Nick, what happened?"

"I don't know. I just know that I wanted you back. I hated that, yet again, someone I cared about was leaving me. I felt like I failed you, but it also wasn't fair that I had to move on...without you." I exhaled a long breath, avoiding her eye contact.

"Then all of a sudden I'm alive again?" She questioned.

I shrugged, conceding.

"So, you resurrected me." It wasn't a question. No, it was simply a statement.

My mouth formed an O at her bluntness. "Well, I mean, I wouldn't say..."

She lifted herself up onto the bed, dangling her feet off the side. "I would...because that's what happened. The real question is not why it happened, but how."

I walked to where she sat and cocked my hip out to lean against the bed.

"How indeed."

She walked her fingers along my shoulder. "Have you been holding out on me, Mr. Cassial?"

I laughed a little. "I swear, if I knew something like that from me was possible..." I let the words fall away as I reached over and trailed my knuckles over her stomach. "I'm sorry."

"Nick, stop. Just stop being sorry because, frankly, it's rather annoying and weird, since nothing is your fault."

"I fucking stabbed you."

"I was trying to kill you. Saving a shit ton of people while only losing one, to me, is worth it in the grand scheme of things."

I wrapped my hand around her knee, squeezing. "Not when it comes to you."

She tucked a piece of her hair behind her ear. "It was scary, dying. I didn't actually think I'd ever be scared, but I think leaving you was something I found myself hating the most. Don't let that go to your pretty head, though."

"I didn't like you leaving me either, which probably triggered something, whatever pulled you out of death."

"They think I'm dead, you know. Lilith and Dimitri. What's going to happen when they find out I'm not? Lilith has lost twice now, Nick. She isn't just upset or angry—she's fucking fuming." Dani kicked her legs out, one after the other.

"I'm not afraid of her or fucking Dimitri."

"I'm well aware." She sighed and gave me an incredulous look. "Nicholas, you used the power of an Enchanter. I think you, of all people, know who to ask." She raised an eyebrow at me.

I chuckled. "I probably have some other things to talk to her about anyway." Dani just hummed, watching me. "I can stay with you if you want. I can get you something, anything you need."

"Nicholas, you are very, very sweet, but I just want to rest for now. Something feels weirdly off, but calm yourself, I'm fine. Just probably the aftereffects of previously being dead." She tried to sum it up as if that was the logical answer, but something about her tone told me she was a little concerned.

I hesitated, but started to turn around when she called my name again. I faced her, only to be met with mischief. "Is there anything else you want to talk about?"

I shook my head. "Not that I can recall."

"Are you sure? Nothing you want to get off your chest, since I'm telling you it's totally okay to say it right now?" She wiggled her eyebrows as she tilted her head to the side, resting it on her shoulder as she leaned back further onto the bed.

I coughed, remembering how distraught I'd been. I had wanted to say those words to her for a while, but no time had seemed right, and I was so emotionally fucked up that I just didn't know how to explain myself. "No idea what you're talking about."

"Ah, so I guess you *didn't* mean what you said. It was just a chunk of hefty bullshit."

I fast-walked over to her. "I fucking meant it, alright? I, ugh, I really wanted this to happen in a normal, romantic moment."

"I really don't think we'll ever have one of those. Maybe I prefer it that way." She winked at me as I gazed at her. I was completely lost in how close we were, but I steeled myself for what I was about to say.

I cupped her face in my hand and moved the pad of my thumb along the soft skin of her cheek. "I do love you, Dani."

She sighed, but this sigh had the essence of swooning, something I would keep with me for the rest of my life. "You want to know something?"

"Hmm?"

"I just might happen to love you too, Nicholas Cassial."

I smiled before I kissed her. It wasn't a rough kiss. It was slow and I could feel all the softness her lips provided. Whatever I'd done allowed me to do this again—be in her space, kiss her just because, and maybe, eventually, just be so irrevocably happy. I wanted to remain in this love filled bliss forever, but I knew I couldn't. She was here with me now, feeling the same way I did, and I had time to explore that with her. I had made it happen so that she had more time with me, so we had more time to exist together. A tiny spark of warmth shocked me as she took my hand in hers. It was a spark that I recognized in myself, but it wasn't coming from me.

I pulled back and looked at her as she gave me a cute and confused look back. I dropped my eyes down to her hands, only to find nothing was different. Maybe I had imagined it. She pulled me back in, giving me one last peck on the lips before pushing me away. "Go talk to her. Get your answers. I'll be here when you get back."

I did as she said, that warm spark replaying in my head. Right before I walked out the door, I looked over my shoulder. "I love you."

She tried to hide the smile pushing its way to her face. "You too, you handsome night light."

I heard a hiss as I passed by a door on my way to find Natalia. I heard the sound of my best friend on the other side, whining about the pain. I knocked, but then remembered he hardly knocked on any of *my* doors, so I just walked in. Reese was lying face down on the bed, while Xander placed a thick gray cream on his wound as Natalia watched.

"It's fucking cold."

"You didn't complain this much when I was looking at your wings, you big baby. You sound about as bad as your vicious little demon friend," Xander laughed, continuing his work.

"Don't ever compare me to her, for the love of all that is ethereal."

I caught myself laughing. Reese finally noticed I was in the room and shot his head up. "You finally woke up."

"Like thirty minutes ago, yeah. Wings in one piece?" I knew he wouldn't be able to extend them for a while until they healed.

"From what this guy says, yes, but I'll see for myself in a few days." He side eyed Xander with a skeptical look.

Xander patted around Reese's leg, letting him sit up and gingerly scoot his way to the edge of the bed. The Enchanter rolled his eyes as he turned away from Reese to go wash his hands.

"Feeling any better, Nicholas?" Natalia asked.

I looked at each of them, running my finger along the bandage at my wrist. "I need to speak with you about something."

Her dark eyebrows raised in curiosity. "I'm all ears."

I glanced over at Xander, not really knowing if what I was about to divulge was something he could hear. She followed my gaze and shook her head. "He pledged his loyalty to me a long time ago. If that loyalty is mistreated in any way, there are consequences." It was always ominous the way she spoke, but I let her leave it at that.

"I took the advice you gave me. I put my power into the dagger and I…" Bringing up what happened made my mind numb and I couldn't finish.

She nodded in understanding. "And she was no longer of this realm."

"Yes, um, she was gone. Right in my arms and then she wasn't."

"What do you mean, she wasn't?"

I scrubbed a hand down my face. "As in she wasn't strong enough to fight things off herself, so she died, Natalia. She died right in front of me, and then she…she…"

"She came back to life. That shit was fucking insane," Reese interjected.

Xander wiped his hands on a towel. "You resurrected her?"

I pressed my lips together. "I mean, I didn't say that—"

"But you were going to."

Natalia waved him off. "Xander, hush. Did you do that, Nicholas?"

I bit my lower lip, tasting blood from where I had pulled at a piece of skin too hard. "I think so."

Her honey-colored eyes went to the side, as if she was in deep thought. "Strange. As an angel, you have the power of an Enchanter, and your parents are both angels."

I nodded. "I may not know a lot about my mother, but I know she was an angel. I'm pretty certain Enchanter doesn't run through my veins. It's not in my DNA."

"Could someone in your family maybe be some sort of Enchanter hybrid, skipping generations until you," Reese offered, making my brain work overtime with his theories.

Xander cut in. "Most necromancers or resurrectors, whatever they want to be called, never really fucked around outside of their own kind. That kind of power was coveted so much that they wanted to keep it purely among Enchanters, well I mean, at least that's what I thought."

"I did as well. Hmm, there is another way it *could* happen. Not many people do it, but it does exist." The High Priestess looked at me, squinting as if she almost couldn't believe what she was about to say. "How much do you know about transference, Nicholas?"

"Nothing," I admitted. Xander came up next to Natalia, crossing his arms over his broad chest.

"It's exactly how it sounds. It's the transferring of power. Any power can be willingly moved to another host. It's not the most pleasant experience and most definitely something you wouldn't forget," she explained, watching me to make sure I was still with her.

"Why would that matter in Nick's case?" Reese asked, hopping from one foot to the other, relieving the pressure from his wounded leg.

"She thinks that's what's going on. That would probably be the only explanation," Xander answered, getting a look from Natalia to, in the politest way, shut up.

I thought this over. "You just said it's not a fun experience and that I would likely remember it if it happened. How does that make any sense then?"

Natalia's eyes widened, as if she was having an epiphany, and then she shut her eyes in the same moment, let out a short breath, shaking her head. "It's so obvious now." She was speaking more to herself than to us. I brought my hands to her arms, bringing her attention back to the people in the room.

"What's obvious?"

She tapped a gold painted fingernail against my skull. "Your missing pieces."

"Wait, is she talking about when you basically time traveled, and she found a gaping hole in your mind?" Reese had an odd way of summing up the things I said to him, and I found that I wanted to laugh, but my mind was elsewhere in this conversation.

Natalia gave him a soft smile. "Yes, that's one way to put it. I could be wrong, but if transference is the culprit, then I don't think it happened in your adulthood. Your friend Garrett is almost the last of his kind and there is maybe only one I know of in Oculus currently, so there wouldn't have been one around to make it happen. Plus, just because you have a power you want to give away doesn't mean you have the power to make it happen.

"The act of transference has to be done by someone skilled enough to make sure both parties aren't harmed and that it sticks. It's painful. It's essentially someone placing a foreign entity into your very being."

Reese hopped over to the bed, resting against it. "Well, if not in the last few years, then when?"

"Childhood," Xander said, his voice low so as not to upset Natalia with his interruption. She just nodded over to him and then looked back at me.

"Exactly. You see, children are more susceptible to it. It is, of course, not a pleasant feeling still, but it could happen more easily. Your body would mold with it as you aged, and if you did find yourself using it, it would grow with you."

I looked at her confused. "I didn't, though. I didn't know anything about this until now."

"Precisely. I think someone transferred those powers into you, but then took away the memory of you ever having it transferred in the first place... along with other things. There were too many missing pieces for that to be the only one." Natalia looked a little sad as she explained things to me, as if she was telling me about myself, knowing full well I had been in the dark this whole time. "It was likely dormant, never having been used, and then with Dani's death, you manifested it without really trying. It also explains the passing out seeing as necromancy is a whole-body kind of power. You put everything you have onto repairing a soul, finding the pieces and linking them together to create an entire person again."

Garrett had mentioned something like that when we'd first met, how it took so much out of him to perform with his powers. I flashed back to his face when it was happening, how he had looked like he recognized the colors of the light, the way the power moved through her body. That had to be why he was adamant about speaking to Natalia before I'd blacked out.

"Why would someone do this? Why me?" I asked.

"I hate to butt in yet again, but I don't think we're the best people to be asking," Xander shrugged. Natalia didn't scold him this time. Instead, she continued to look at me like she was gauging my reactions.

"Well, you're Enchanters. This is an Enchanter power, so wouldn't that kind of make you the best ones to ask?" I said, looking between the both of them.

Natalia shifted on her feet. "We weren't there for that time in your life. I wouldn't know the people you surrounded yourself with. The only thing I can do now is figure out who transferred it and maybe help you find the missing pieces to your mental puzzle."

"The only person I would think to ask would be..." I stopped myself and swallowed the developing lump in my throat. I snuck a glance at Reese, who raised a blonde eyebrow at me, and I ran a hand through my hair, giving my head one good shake. "I have to go. I'll be back to check up on you." I nodded over to Reese and gave Natalia and Xander a quick wave goodbye.

I needed to find my father and I needed to find him *now*.

I heard voices as I entered my room at the infirmary. Daya and Alex noticed me and headed in my direction, both of them giving me a big hug. I embraced them, but my eyes were set on the man I was slowly realizing I knew so little about. Maybe he didn't know anything about this transference nonsense at all, but something in my gut told me he did.

"You are a badass, you know that?" Alex complimented me, her blue streaked hair tied up in two large buns on either side of her head.

Daya kissed my cheek and rubbed her hands down my arms. "You look good, Nicholas. We were all worried out of our minds, but we never once doubted you would come back."

"We also heard Lilith is still on the loose. This shit is about to get wilder," Alex giggled, earning a swat on the back of the head from her mother. "What? You can't tell me Lilith is just going to stand down, all because they made a show of coming to Purgatory. Brave, but you've put a pretty gnarly target on your back."

Daya sighed, her nose ring twinkling as she turned to her daughter. "Honey, please stop talking." She shook her head. "Zane portaled us in. He didn't want to make your father fly us all the way here."

I nodded in understanding. "Can we have a minute?" I pointed to my father, who raised both his eyebrows, as if he wasn't expecting to have a one-on-one conversation with me.

Daya waved nonchalantly at me. "Yes, yes, of course. We'll be right outside." She gave me a warm smile, and I almost wanted to blurt out that

Beetee was right down the hall if she wanted to see her, but then that would involve me telling the whole story and I wasn't quite prepared to dive headfirst into that can of worms. Beetee deserved some grace, so we would all give her that. Daya ushered her daughter out of the room, before leaving after her and closing the door.

"What's up, son?"

I reached up and scratched my jaw, not knowing where to start, so I just dived in. "Umm, Dani died in Purgatory, Dad. Just like Jonah, right in my arms and it was a little debilitating after what happened to Jonah. I've been struggling with that for a while and I'm okay now, so don't freak out, but obviously she's not dead anymore." I blew out a breath, letting that first part soak in.

He leaned against the counter. "Okay. Natalia told me that Garrett fellow is a necromancer. Did he bring her back?"

"No, Dad, he didn't. I did."

His brown eyes widened at my admission. "You?"

"Listen, it's a fucking shock to me. She was dead, Dad. She wasn't fucking breathing and then I wanted her back with everything I had, and there she was, as if nothing had happened."

My father opened and closed his mouth as if he were a fish. No words came out, but his eyes told me he was blown away by the news. I kept going, kept talking. "Natalia told me that it was likely transferred to me when I was a kid. If that's true, that means you are the most likely person to know who I got it from, or anything close to that."

"Nicholas…"

I pointed my index finger at him. "No, no! You promised me that when I got back you would tell me everything. This is part of that somehow and I'm tired of being in the fucking dark about it. Be honest with me—full honesty, not the half truths you think will hold me over."

His shoulders sagged as he slowly walked over to the bed. He perched himself at the end and buried his face in his hands. I tentatively walked over to him, not knowing if I had hit a nerve or not. He threaded his fingers through his dark hair and sighed as if he was defeated. Defeated and a little tired.

"I was going to tell you when you turned ten, but then you met Reese and life was good for you. Then, I was going to tell you when you turned sixteen, but you were so invested in preparing yourself for The Skies and all their tests that I didn't want to interfere. I decided to tell you when you turned twenty, but you were so content, so confidently yourself, and I wasn't going to ruin that. I selfishly thought, oh, well maybe you didn't have to know. Maybe I could just leave it and let your life run its course. You were happy, and as your father, that's... that's all I wanted."

I remained silent. I couldn't move. I was transfixed by his speech as if everything I'd been wanting to hear was about to be put on blast, at full volume, and I didn't know if I was prepared to hear any of it. "I had everything planned out how I was going to tell you, from start to finish, but nothing ever seemed right. It always felt like I was telling someone else's story, and in a way, I would have been." He ran a hand over his mustache and down his mouth. "She made me promise that I wouldn't tell you. She didn't want you seeking vengeance, stifling all the good you could do, so I told her I would keep it to myself. I would let you grow up with an open mind and an open heart. I would bring you up in the best way possible and you'd be okay." His eyes started to get glassy, and I noticed goosebumps gracing my arms.

"Dad, I don't understand."

He nodded to no one but himself and patted the spot beside him. I sat down, placing my hands on my knees. "I told you I would tell you everything."

"You did."

He let out a shaky breath; I'd never seen Maurice Cassial this nervous in my entire life. "This is the only promise to her I've ever broken, but I think it's time this story was told." He shifted and turned his body slightly, so he was looking at me. A tear slid down his cheek, and he placed one of his hands over mine. My heart was beating rapidly in my chest, hardly prepared for all the things I should have known years ago. "Nicholas, I think it's time we talked about your mother."

EPILOGUE
ELISE

She screamed over and over again—music to my ears. It was my favorite song, and I wished that it would never have to end. This kind of music was my favorite, but the fact that this was coming from a blonde bitch who thought she could get away with her shit was even better. Isabel was bleeding from her mouth, nose, and from where each of her fingers were supposed to be before they'd been removed. She had been spewing hateful words the entire hour and half we'd been here, and I was nauseated by it. When Natalia asked for my assistance, I happily obliged. The High Priestess didn't let her hurtful words dent her regality; perhaps her pain was on the inside. I wouldn't know much about that since feelings were the most overrated thing in the fucking realms.

I'd honed Dani's torture skills, so why not a High Priestess? She was doing well on her own as I leaned back against the wall, watching as Isabel writhed on the ground, pain shooting through her body as Natalia sent her own dash of poison into her system. Her veins protruded from her arms, and I nearly thought they were going to pop out when she stopped. Natalia turned around, her long dress flowing around her ankles. There were specks of blood on the fabric, but she hardly noticed. I could hear Isabel's shallow breaths from where I stood, and she gathered her strength and picked herself up only to fall again. She coughed towards the ground, blood splattering against the floor of wherever the fuck we were.

Zane had brought me here and the circumstances were too good to try and ask questions. "You are quite a natural at this," I complimented. "I would say cut her up a bit more, but hey, this is your show."

Natalia raised an arched eyebrow at me. "You can take over if you'd like. I don't know if I can stomach this any longer."

"She fucked you over, therefore, she deserves an immense amount of pain. I don't make the rules, nor do I follow them, but you get the point." I glanced over at Zane, who was still fucking here. If he wasn't her bodyguard, I would think he was a stalker, with the way he nearly hovered over her in the weirdest fucking way possible.

Natalia laughed, nodding her head. "Well put, but it's been quite a while. I don't know how much more of this to throw at her."

I gave her an emotionless expression. "You do it until she's dead."

"I would think living with the pain of what she did and all the physical scars I've given her would be enough." Natalia looked over her shoulder as Isabel wiped blood from her nose.

I snorted. "Right. She isn't remorseful, so let's get that through your big brain. She would snap your neck if you let her get close."

Natalia hummed. "She deserves the worst kind of treatment, but she also didn't have the best role models to help her choose a different path. Markus, Lilith, they both set the plans for her."

I barked out a laugh. "Fucking hell, please don't tell me you plan to let her go to some Enchanter rehabilitation classes or something. Different path, my ass. It's death or nothing. She's an attention seeking little twat who had some bad parenting, but that doesn't mean anything. Dani was subjected to Lilith's version of love, and so was I—we both turned out just fine."

I heard Zane scoff but ignored it. The fact that he was showing any sort of personality was a little intriguing. I wanted Natalia to get on with this shit so I could get back to Beetee and make sure she was still okay. This whole caring for another person nonsense was exhausting, and I would rather go back to the days of me, myself and I.

"I guess you are right. We don't have to end up on the paths of our caregivers." I let a fleeting memory pass my mind but didn't give it any time or effort. I wouldn't be going down that road anytime soon. No fucking thank you.

I groaned. "Ugh, fine. Give her one more good throttle and then I'll end this for you."

Natalia gave me a dutiful nod and sauntered over to Isabel, who swiped at her with her right hand, one that only had two fingers left on it. It was comical to watch. Natalia sent an electric blue cord of magic around Isabel's neck, yanking it down and sending her flying to her knees.

"All this torture will do nothing for your pathetic little conscience. We both know you can't muster up the strength to just kill me," Isabel taunted, blood pouring from her mouth. Natalia brought one of Isabel's arms up and started to bend it backwards at an unnatural angle, until a few of her bones started protruding. Natalia held onto the rope of magic, yanking Isabel's head back so she could watch.

Natalia let go of her arm, but not before grabbing one of the bones and ripping it out. Isabel screamed so loudly; I swore my ears could have been bleeding. "You have a very bad habit of thinking little of me." Natalia plunged the bone into Isabel's side, making sure it was nice and snug into her skin. The High Priestess swayed a little as she hustled over to me. "You'll handle it?"

I rolled my eyes but nodded. Natalia gave me an appreciative smile and walked past me, taking my place against the wall. Zane eyed both of us but remained at his post. I licked my lips as I made my way over to Isabel, her weak body shaking from all that she'd endured. She caught sight of me and spit in my direction, the blood-soaked liquid landing right near my shoe. "Lilith will come for you, and so will Dimitri since your little monster bitch ruined his plans. Your useless angels will watch this entire place rot!"

I bent my knees, squatting so I could be in front of her. "It's such a shame Lilith would never come for you. You want to know why, you traitorous shit?"

She stared back at me with her blue eyes, waiting. "It's because she never cared about you. If Dani was such a pawn, so were you. Now you can go and tell your dead mom about all the shitty things you've done. Oh wait, probably not since you'll be going straight to Hell, so I guess in that case, say hi to Markus for us." I uncurled my tail, floating it toward her face so I could shove it down her throat, choking her with the venom. It would come out of her eyes and ears, and I would silently wish I could capture the moment forever.

I stopped mid-kill when she said words I didn't think would come from her mouth. "He misses you." I reared back and opened my mouth, but no sound came out. I looked over my shoulder to where Natalia watched, her honey-colored eyes were focused on us, but I knew she couldn't hear anything. I was a bit stunned, but I shook my head. I knew she wasn't talking about Markus or Dimitri, and I knew she wasn't just spewing nonsense to try to get under my skin. The way she looked at me told me she knew so much more than I anticipated.

I didn't care. It didn't fucking matter.

"The feeling isn't mutual." Instead of giving her a fast death full of venom, I'd make this slow and bleed her out. I kicked my foot up, knocking her right in the center of her face. She was thrown backwards and I scrambled on top of her, grazing my hand over the bone sticking out of her side. I wrapped my hand around it and yanked it out. I crawled up her body and placed the bone in her mouth. I loved the screams, but I needed to concentrate. "Watch and learn, your highness!" I shouted at Natalia, not looking at her. I tilted my head down at Isabel whose teeth were clamped around her own bone. "Now, where should we start?"

My husband. You are my rock, my favorite (most annoying) person in the entire realms and I wouldn't change you for the world. Thank you for pushing me to continue writing this story and for not letting me stop every time I really, really wanted too. You are my light in the darkest tunnel, David. I love you.

To my mom, the best mom there ever was and there ever will be. End of story.

To my besties from day one of this writing journey. Britt, Kaylah & Amanda. There are no better human beings I would fly to see than you. Thank you for keeping me in check even when my insecurity got the best of me.

To my writing wifey, AJ Nicole. I will tell you guys that this book wouldn't have happened as fast as it did if not for this chaotic person. Our nights writing until 4 in the morning and our scene exchanges in the sprinting chat will forever be engrained in my psyche. I can't wait to continue this wild writing lifestyle with you. All the ups, downs and squishy peens, bestie!

To my arc readers, street team and everyone in my readers group, you all are the best. I may have written these characters, but you give them life. Thank you forever and ever for that.

Lastly, thank you to all the readers who loved Living Legend enough to continue on. You motivate me every single day. The power of a reader is amazing, and the simple fact that I get to mentally teleport you to places of my own design blows my ever-loving mind. I hope this book makes you scream, laugh, cry, and emotionally voided until book 3. Sorry not sorry, love ya!

Allie Shante was born and raised in Georgia and graduated from Georgia State University with a biology degree. While science was fun, books have always been a part of her heart and writing right up there with it. After writing and never finishing any of the books she started, she buckled down years later to finish a novel she never actually expected to write, let alone finish.

When she's not reading and writing confident females and stubborn men, she enjoys being an overprotective dog mom and crushing escape rooms with her husband.

Check her out at:
www.authorallieshante.com

Follow Allie on Instagram:
@allieshantewrites

Follow Allie on Tik Tok:
@allieshanteauthor

Made in the USA
Middletown, DE
02 July 2024

56693459R00267